THE COTTAGE GIRL.

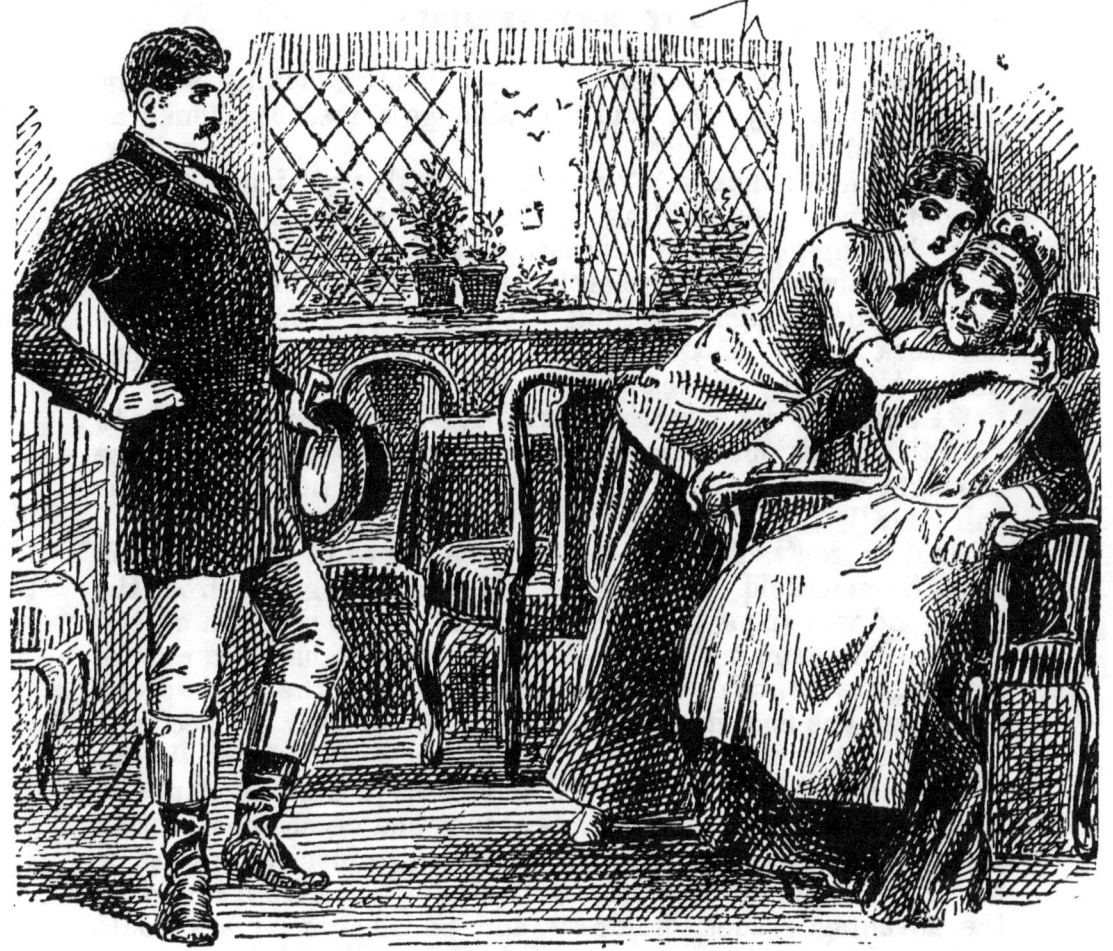

RUTH'S FIRST INTERVIEW WITH THE SQUIRE'S SON.

CHAPTER I.

" Seek not to know, ah ! sweetest maid,
  That which would blight thy opening youth
But let it, let it rest in shade,
  And joy thou in thy own bright truth.
That smiling look would altered grow,
  Thy step no more would lightsome be,
Thy gentle heart would burst with woe,
  Knew'st thou what I could tell to thee."—ANON.

SATURDAY evening was drawing in ; the labours of the week
were at an end.   Wearied, but still alert, the Cottage Girl
prepared for her father's return from the field where he had
been toiling since daybreak.   The implements of industry were
laid aside ; the younger children dispatched to bed ; the supper-
cloth spread ; the fire supplied with sweet-smelling fuel freshly
gathered from a neighbouring copse ; and the iron pot, containing the frugal materials for the evening meal, hung on the
crook amid the blaze.

A pleasant and very cheerful picture did the interior of the
rustic dwelling then present, but its cheerfulness penetrated not to

the heart of the cottager's wife—a delicate-looking woman, whose melancholy eye, and irritable gestures, betokened an unsettled mind.

"How much longer?" she impatiently exclaimed to her daughter, who was braiding up her long amber hair before a small looking-glass that reflected a countenance of exquisite loveliness and captivating simplicity, "how much longer, Ruth? Will you be all night dressing up that hair? Don't you know our clock is slow, and that your father will expect his supper on the table, and you ready to receive him?"

"I have just done, mother," said Ruth, quietly, hastening to bind the obnoxious tresses. "It is scarce ten minutes since the eight o'clock bell chimed, and father will not be here this half hour."

As if to contradict her, a foot was heard at the threshold. Mrs. Summerfield hastened to lift the boiling pot from the hook, and was about to transfer its contents to the dish on the table, when, catching a view of the person who had entered the cottage, she let it fall with a loud scream, and the soup spread itself over the floor in a copious flood. Fortunately the accident did no more mischief than Ruth, in a few minutes, was able to efface; and while thus engaged she stole a curious glance at the individual whose sudden appearance had occasioned it. She thought his aspect the last in the world to inspire distrust or terror. To the natural elegance of his figure were added all the advantages superior dress and polished manners could bestow; his countenance was dark and intellectual; his eyes too vivid to be gazed upon by the bashful Cottage Girl, who ventured not to encounter their burning glances a second time.

Ruth had seen him before more than once, though always at a distance, and she knew him to be her father's young landlord, the representative of a family which had once figured in the brightest annals of England's aristocracy.

When first he addressed her mother on the present evening she thought his voice the most pleasing she had ever heard, but the tenor of his speech was such as at once to dissipate her girlish admiration, and fill her with anxiety for her parents. After a few polite inquiries respecting the health of Mrs. Summerfield, and the present avocations of her husband, he stated that the object of his call was to remind the cottager of six pounds arrears of rent expected from him on Monday.

"We cannot pay it, Mr. Clifton," said Mrs. Summerfield, shortly.

"I must hope otherwise," said the gentleman. "From

quarter to quarter, my agent tells me he has been put off, and he is now resolute to distrain unless the money is paid. You are aware I leave all my pecuniary affairs in his hands, and never interfere with his management, as for me to do so would be to violate the terms on which he undertakes my business."

At the word distrain Mrs. Summerfield dropped into her chair.

"Why, Mr. Clifton," she said, "you would not have the heart to take from us the little we have?"

"I should be sorry if my agent is put to that necessity," he indirectly rejoined.

Ruth drew close to her mother, and passed her arm around her neck, wholly unconscious of the sudden look of admiration with which Mr. Clifton regarded her. Mrs. Summerfield put her back, unaware of the motion, and without looking at him to whom her words were addressed, asked if her husband and his family were to be driven out of the cottage which had been their home so long.

"That is a question Mrs. Summerfield, which, for the reason I have given, must be answered by my agent," said Mr. Clifton.

"And if your agent acts ever so cruelly, you have no power over him?"

"I have no reason to believe that he is a man disposed to be unjust, otherwise I should not entrust him with my affairs. He certainly has not behaved harshly to you. I was not aware until a day or two since that you were at all in arrears—and I assure you I was much displeased that he had been so indulgent."

"Oh! sir," cried Mrs. Summerfield, "I beg you at least not to suffer him to turn us out of the cottage! Let him take all, but leave us here! I should expire before I could quit this place!"

Alarmed by her wild and pallid look, Ruth listened eagerly for her father's approach.

In another instant, a heavier and sadder step than Percy Clifton's was heard, and Roger Summerfield entered, bearing his scythe on his shoulder. He was not past his prime, but thoughts and cares of no light nature had left their deep prints on his embrowned face.

"Good evening to your honour," he said, doffing his hat to his young landlord, with a perceptible, but not awkward embarrassment. "You have come about the rent, I suppose?"

"I have; and I regret to hear you are not prepared. My agent tells me you are much in arrears, and is bent on extreme measures."

"That must be as you and God please," said the cottager

wiping the dew of fatigue from his manly brow; "I have had a hard two years of it. The bad harvests have lowered my wages—and at the highest they were low enough, Heaven knows—farm labourers have much ado to live in the best seasons; then my wife has had long bouts of illness; our cow died of distemper; and last ploughing time I caught a rheumatic fever and was two months earning nothing. We must have perished had not He who fed Elijah by the hand of ravens sent us aid." The cottager looked reverently upwards as he spoke these words, and there was a momentary silence. "However," resumed Summerfield, "your agent has been lenient with us hitherto, and I must not complain if he now ceases to be so. I cannot ask for more time; one way or the other the rent shall be paid."

"Enough," said Clifton, and not receiving from the cottager any encouragement to prolong his visit, he courteously withdrew

Summerfield remained some time standing in one posture, then depositing his scythe in its place, and flinging his hat on the floor, seated himself, and covered his face with his hand. The sight of Percy had been as unpleasing to him as to his wife, though he had more dignity of mind, more firmness of nerve, to sustain it; and the mental disturbances of both chiefly originated in a source hidden from all but themselves. While he sat buried in troubled thought, a cry from Ruth brought him to the side of her mother, who had fainted. Summerfield was not surprised.

"Make no alarm," he said to Ruth. "I know the cause of this too well. Help me to carry her to bed—she will soon recover."

"Is it not her trouble about the rent, father, makes her so ill?" asked Ruth, struck by the mystery implied in his words, and the manner in which they were pronounced.

"The rent, child? No," answered Summerfield, "it was the sight of young Clifton, it was the dread of leaving the cottage."

"But cannot we live as well elsewhere, father?"

"Elsewhere, child? no—God forbid! To leave this place would be fatal to us."

He spoke in a whisper, and Mrs. Summerfield then reviving, the strong impression his words made on his daughter was heightened by her mother's terrified inquiry if he thought there was any hope of their being allowed to remain in the cottage.

"Yes, yes," answered Summerfield; "be calm; when the agent has the money, or part of it, we shall not be disturbed."

"Take all to raise it!" exclaimed the agitated woman. "Take

this bed—my children's bed—anything—everything—only save us from the horrid danger we shall incur if this cottage is tenanted by others; oh! save us from that, Roger, and never mind if we have only bare bricks to sleep on!—never mind, though all but roof and walls be gone!"

Trembling, and looking from one to the other, Ruth asked of what danger her mother spoke?

"Be more guarded in your speech, wife," said Summerfield, sternly, "if you would not by your imprudence bring on that which you dread. Then, turning to his daughter, and enforcing his speech by authoritative look and accent. "Ruth," said he, "I have told you before, and now I tell you again, that, as you value our lives, you must be both deaf and dumb respecting the secret which exists between your mother and I. On your prudence our safety depends."

These words shot a deadly chill through the heart of Ruth. The "safety," the "lives," of her beloved parents! What could the secret be which endangered these? She had heard of crimes done by ruffians, and expiated by fearful punishments, but to connect the names of her parents with a deed of guilt was a sacrilege too shocking to be endured for a moment!

Her father guessed what was passing though her mind, and said, with austerity—

"Do not wrong us with evil suspicions, Ruth. God knows the past, and in his sight we are justified, though our short-sighted fellow creatures might judge us harshly."

"Oh! father," ejaculated Ruth, falling upon his neck, and for a moment she could articulate no more.

"We have alarmed you, dear child," said Summerfield, kissing her cheek. "I am sorry for it. Had your mother been less weak, no whisper of this would have reached you. Already it has shaken the intellect, and ruined the health of one, and to see yours destroyed by it too will be dreadful."

"You shall not see that, father," said Ruth, erecting her slight figure, and speaking with vivacity—"what you can bear, I can bear. Only trust me with this secret, and you shall judge whether I prove myself a strong woman or no. Do not deny me! I will be careful of every word I speak! No one shall guess anything from me!—and I will not even mention it when we are alone, except you wish."

"You don't know what you ask, my dear," said her mother. "At night you would not sleep for terror—by day, to see any stranger come to the cottage would throw you in an ague; the sight of a Clifton would be as a spectre—and

your flesh would turn to stone when your foot trod the soil of the cow-shed !"

Perceiving that his wife was growing more excited, Summerfield directed his daughter to retire into the outer room, which was that commonly used by the family, and adjoined the little chamber occupied by himself and his wife. These two rooms, with the addition of a dairy, or wash-house, and a loft in which the younger children slept, comprised the whole of the interior of the cot. Ruth's nightly accommodation was in the common apartment called " the house," and her couch

> ' Contrived a double debt to pay—
> A bed by night, a chest of drawers by day."

Having lowered this piece of furniture, she was sitting thoughtfully on its edge, when her father rejoined her.

"Your mother," he said, "spoke something wildly about the cow-shed—surely I need not bid you give no heed to such nonsense? There is nothing there more than you have seen a hundred times."

"But I have often thought it strange, father," remarked Ruth, "that she never would go inside it. I have heard her declare she would drop dead if she did."

"She is a weak fool!" exclaimed Summerfield, with an angry energy that made his daughter start, adding more composedly, —"There was never any just reason for her horror of that place —it is complete delusion! Her conscience is as void of guilt as yours, Ruth."

"I could never doubt it, father."

"Hold to that faith!" said Summerfield, his manner conveying an impression that something might ultimately transpire to shake her from it. Her spirits were again damped, and, eager to penetrate the mystery, she threw out an observation relative to Mr. Clifton's call that evening, wondering that neither he, nor his sister Miss Amy, had been at the cottage before.

"They have," said her father, " though you did not see them. They called together, but their stay was as brief as your mother and I could wish. We have never courted their favour in any shape, nor will! and the rent I owe would not sting me half so much if it was due to any but a Clifton."

Utterly at a loss to understand this deeply-rooted antipathy to a gentleman so handsome as Percy, and a young lady so free from pride, and so charitable as Miss Amy, Ruth inquired if they had ever injured her parents in any way unknown to her.

"No," replied her father; "the only fault I find with them is one they are not accountable for; it is that they are Cliftons."

Ruth thought this very unjust, but dared not say so.

Summerfield went on, speaking at intervals, as he walked backwards and forwards across the room.

"Their characters I don't like. Since their mother died, and left them to their own guidance, they have kept the old house yonder full of gay company. Up the town there is not an assembly, ball, concert or play, but Amy and Percy Clifton are there in the midst of it."

"And how else could they dispose of their time?" inquired Ruth, very simply—"gentlefolks have nothing else to do. But if I had not heard to the contrary, I should have thought they must be rich to support such a life."

"They are poor, compared with what the family used to be," said Summerfield. "Nevertheless, they find little want of money, I dare say."

"Their father was a great spender, was he not?" said Ruth, and Summerfield groaned as he rejoined—

"Yes, yes, he scattered his thousands—little good they brought him."

"Do you remember him, father?"

"I wish I did not," replied the latter, "I should be a happier man."

More disturbed with this theme than Ruth had ever before seen him, Summerfield, as he spoke, would have retired into his chamber, but she renewed her entreaties that she might be entrusted with the secret.

"It is not from any doubt of your prudence that I do not," said her father, "but for your own sake. Your peace must not be ruined by such a story as we could tell thee."

"If you study me, father, you will trust me," said Ruth eagerly.

"No, no, child, it is impossible."

But Ruth was not easily to be beaten from her point. Tears came to the aid of words, and she found an abundance of argument calculated, as she thought, to shake the resolution of her father. But it was immoveable.

"Never shall you learn it, Ruth," was his inflexible answer, "unless—" The monosyllable was pronounced with awful emphasis, accompanied with an upward look.

"Unless what, father?" was Ruth's pressing inquiry.

"Unless that come to pass which is your mother's dread, and which even I dare not think of."

"What is it you mean, father? Do tell me!"

"I can give it no name to thee. Be at peace, Ruth, and trust that God will shield us from it."

Left alone Ruth trusted as he desired, but it was because she trusted still more in the guiltlessness of her parents. And what should the guiltless fear? To them all must be well. Such was the Cottage Girl's simple philosophy;—the antidote to her fears, her light amid the gloom in which her youth was enveloped.

Before closing her heavy eyes in sleep, and having waited until she supposed her parents soundly at rest, Ruth stole softly into the wash-house, unfastened a door opening into a garden which supplied the cottagers with herbs and vegetables, and, screening the candle from the wind, with her apron, moved timidly towards the cowshed, which stood at the end of the garden, thatched with straw, and roomy enough to shelter two cows. Here the cottagers had kept one, before their evil days came on, and the ground within was still covered with straw and manure, which Summerfield would not have disturbed, though Ruth had often suggested to him, when they were hard pressed for food, that they might sell the manure for a few shillings to any of the farmers round, and clear out the shed at the same time.

His obstinacy in this respect did not even now strike Ruth as anything extraordinary, but, with a beating heart and eager curiosity, she scrutinised the rafters, hayrack, and every other part within her reach, for some clue to the mystery which, since she could remember, had shed its gloomy shadow over her home. No clue was there, and she was turning to quit the shed, when her foot stumbled over the litter which strewed the ground, the candle flew out of her hand, and she was in total darkness. At that moment, as her heart leaped to her throat with terror, something stirred by her feet,—she saw a pale gleaming light,— heard what she imagined to be a human groan, and shrieking, she rushed from the shed, and across the garden, with the speed of an arrow, closed the wash-house door with a loud clap, turned the key, and reaching her quiet bed, sank down breathless.

In the morning she was glad to find that she had not disturbed her parents, and by a kind of fascination, at the first favourable opportunity, her steps were again irresistibly drawn to the spot where she had received so severe a fright. Opening the shed door a large cat bounded forth, and, clambering up a tree that grew in a corner of the garden, disappeared over the wall.

"Oh, oh," thought Ruth, her cheek dimpling with a humorous smile, "that was the spectre, was it? It was puss's great yellow eyes that I saw shining through the dark. What a

coward I was! And to have mistaken her purring for a groan!
I shall be wiser another time."

Much relieved, she entered the shed, and happening accidentally to fix her eyes on a corner of the thatch, immediately above
a rafter where the fowls and pigeons sometimes made their lodg-
ment, she perceived, in a hole they had formed by plucking away
the straw with their bills, some glittering metallic substance of
the size of a half-crown. With the help of a small ladder kept
in the shed, she was able to look closer at this substance, and to
touch it. It was smooth and yellow, and in her surprise she
could not refrain from audibly exclaiming—" It is gold!"

PERCY GALLOPED FLEETLY BY.

" And suppose it is ?" said an angry voice behind her.
She turned her head, and, with the shame of one detected in
a guilty act, beheld her father. His countenance was inflamed,
his eye angry, and bitterly he asked if she was searching for evidence to destroy her parents. Ruth only answered by a flood

of tears, on which the cottager smoothed his brow, bade her come down from the steps, go into the house, and keep silence.

She obeyed him, and next day the shed was securely pad-locked, so that she could enter it no more. Still the circumstance of the concealed gold, connected with her mother's systematic avoidance of the shed, and her extraordinary words that "if Ruth knew the secret, her flesh would turn to stone when her foot stepped within it:" these circumstances, together with her parents' antipathy to the Cliftons, her father's solemn warnings to her to be secret, and her mother's half-insane terrors of some terrible catastrophe yet shrouded in futurity, these would not easily be banished from the thoughts of Ruth.

But the rent now absorbed all anxieties.

"How do you mean to pay it, father?" asked Ruth; "for I heard you promise Mr. Clifton."

"How can I pay it," he rejoined, "but by giving up the goods? Here is enough to satisfy him for the whole, and let us hope that better harvests will bring me better wages to replace in time what is taken away. You and Sally, too, must go to service to help us."

Summerfield was now firm and tranquil. It was not in his nature to be overwhelmed by any peril or misfortune, by any trial, perplexity or sorrow. Undauntedly and steadily he could breast the full tide of afflictions, upborne by a sturdy spirit of endurance, and by what appeared a high consciousness of integrity, and a firm religious faith. He was industrious, kind, though not fond, to his family, and, in general, even-tempered. In general, we say, for beneath Roger's calm exterior was concealed a fiery volcano, whose eruptions, happily occurring at rare intervals, spread terror through the little household.

While such was Summerfield's temper, that of his wife resembled the lowering clouds of November, through whose dense medium few rays of cheerfulness could find their way. Tender of constitution, weak of mind, neither sustained by philosophy or religion, she was wholly incapable of supporting the weight of any real affliction, and in their absence would certainly have invented imaginary ones. Not a petty domestic transaction but her unhappy temper could extract trouble from it; not a difficulty could occur but her feeble capacity deemed it insurmountable, and by her helplessness she assisted to make it so. Despondency, complaint, and fear, were her favourite elements, and with these she tormented grievously the beings she best loved. Still the cottager's wife was dear to her family, since, notwithstanding her deplorable weakness, she was an affectionate

and well-intentioned woman; nor did she ever fail to find indulgence and support in the superior nature of her husband. Their union had taken place early in life, with love for its basis and cement. Roger was the oak round which she grew, the firm pillar that propped her shattered being, and often had she been heard to say that deprived of him she must at once cease to exist.

Ruth was the eldest surviving child of the cottage pair, their chief comfort, pride, and assistance. Not only was she housekeeper, nurse, and servant, to the family, but filled up every spare moment in the weaving of pillow-lace, at which she was remarkably expert, and so eked out their scanty subsistence. Never was seen a prettier, more active, more promising girl than Ruth Summerfield in her seventeenth year, which was her age at the period of the opening of this narrative. Of her intellectual acquisitions we cannot boast; all the learning she had received was from the parish free-school, and barely enabled her to spell over the contents of her Bible, and to write her name. She had never been beyond her native village; never visited any places of public resort but the church, the market, and the annual village feast; and the highest pleasures she knew in life were the discharge of her duty, and the approbation of her parents. But Ruth Summerfield, in this contracted sphere, was still a lovely and useful character. Pure, loving, guileless—a modest, exquisite lily of the valley.

To transplant this lily to his house and to his bosom, had for some time been the secret wish of a near neighbour of the cottagers. Henry Maynard, the Miller of Rosedale, was a saving, industrious man, who, in the space of twenty years, (for he was near forty), had accumulated, it was suspected, no inconsiderable sum of money for one of his class. So high an influence did the reputation of Maynard's thrifty hoard give him, that it was believed he might have taken his choice among the fairest unmarried belles in that rustic vicinage. But Henry kept the even tenor of his way—a bachelor. His affection for Ruth he studiously concealed even from Summerfield, who often, in his necessities, experienced Maynard's kindness; and if in the mind of the Cottage Girl herself the thought that she had a lover in the miller had sometimes obtruded, it was too disagreeable not to be immediately banished.

After many scruples, and much delay, Henry Maynard at last made up his mind to declare himself, and terminate the tormenting fears with which he was harrassed, that some more youthful rival might steal away the prize at which he aimed.

On the Monday when Mr. Clifton's agent or attorney called

for Summerfield's arrears of rent, and immediately after he had departed, the miller was seen coming up the lane which led to the cottage. "whistling aloud to keep his courage up." The sight which greeted his entrance beneath the lowly roof, transfixed him with surprise. The poor but neat furniture of the dwelling was all in confusion—a broker was making out an inventory and valuing the articles, which two ill-looking fellows waited to carry away. Leaning her elbow on the window-sill, and weeping, stood Ruth. Mrs. Summerfield's sobbings were heard from her chamber; and the cottager stood with folded arms overlooking the operations of those who were desolating his little home.

After one glance round, Maynard whispered to Ruth Summerfield to know the cause of this distressing scene.

"We owe a year's rent," she replied, "and the goods are to be sold to pay it. The broker rates them so unreasonably low," she added more passionately, "we shall lose everything, —and then what will become of us!"

"And have I been so poor a friend to your father that he could not have applied to me?" said Maynard, reproachfully— "or had you, Ruth, so little kindness for me, that you could not yourself have come to the mill to make me acquainted with what was going forward?"

How relieved was Ruth at that moment! She thought not of what might be expected from herself as the price of Maynard's generosity, but, transported with the prospect of rescuing the few familiar articles of furniture her parents possessed from the hands of the broker, smiled brightly through her tears on the friend of their adversity.

"I did think of you," she softly said, "only six pounds seemed so much to borrow, and you had helped us so often. But if you will indeed help father this time, and let it stand over a few months, I hope myself to be able to pay back the money, for I am going to service, and the first year I shall spend little for clothes."

"You are the best girl living, Ruth!" exclaimed the miller, in a suppressed but fervid tone, and turning to the broker, and demanding the bill of the rent, he produced from his pocket a leathern purse, weighty with silver and gold, and told down the required sum.

"Hold!" cried the astonished Summerfield, pushing back the money to his friend with the firm principle for which he always seemed remarkable, "I cannot have it so, neighbour Maynard—I have no prospect of returning it."

"Between me and you, Summerfield," said Maynard, "you

can pay me a hundred times over before sunset this day, if you are willing."

The cottager regarded him with inquiring looks, to which he answered by a significant glance towards Ruth. A moment, the father hesitated—the broker and his men then received their dismissal.

As soon as the cot was cleared of the unwelcome strangers, the cottager grasped his friend's hand.

"Maynard," said he, "you have preserved me and mine from more than you can guess. I can't thank you—but when I forget this piece of service may heaven forget me."

"Nonsense, man, nonsense," cried the miller; "I will do more for you yet when Ruth is mistress of the mill. But where is Sally? Here, my lively, run to the Three Crowns and bring us a gallon of their best brewing, and mind the change out of the pound."

Sally was Summerfield's second child—a merry, giddy, high-spirited girl, just entering on her thirteenth year. Quickly she executed her commission, and having received a shilling for her trouble, a greater sum than she had ever possessed before, occupied her stool by the fire, listening with ecstacy to every word that had reference to the good fortune intended for her sister. Ruth, meantime, had stolen out of sight; and Mrs. Summerfield, called from her chamber by the joyful voice of her husband, poured out her thanks to Maynard so warmly and profusely that the miller was abashed by his own praises.

"Enough of this, wife," said Summerfield, coming to his relief. "Henry courts other thanks than words—what say you to bestowing Ruth on him?"

"Ruth is very young," she answered, with hesitation.

"A fault every day will mend," argued the miller; "and if you insist on it, I don't mind waiting a couple of years, so that we understood one another."

"I think you would be kind to her," faltered the timid mother.

"My deeds shall show," was Maynard's unvarnished response. "You know me well; what I have been, and what I am, and that is your best security for my kindness to your daughter. Trust me she shall never have to complain of Henry Maynard."

"I do not think she will," said Summerfield.

"Then speak decidedly," said the miller, "is it a bargain?"

"It is," said the cottager; and his wife, by her silence, acquiesced.

Maynard then filled and presented the glasses, with an overflowing heart.

"Drink prosperity to this union!" he said. "And you, dame, be happy! from this time forth you shall never want. If your son-in-law, unfortunately, has more years than beauty, he will make amends for that by his deeds. The morning of my marriage-day with Ruth, shall see you, Roger, in a more thriving way, or it shall go hard. And Sally, here, shall live with her sister at the mill."

Sally was almost too happy at this announcement, and, unable to keep longer silence, was about to remind her mother that little Billy could run her errands, and assist a good deal in cleaning the house, when she was bade to call in Ruth.

She found her sister gathering potatoes in the rustic vegetable garden behind the house, and called out in a tumult of delight,

"It is all settled, Ruth! it is all settled! And I am to live with you. Won't you be a rich woman! and shan't I be happy!"

"Your giddy pate is always running away with you, Sally," said Ruth, the blood receding from her cheek and lip. "How shall I be rich, you foolish thing?"

"Why, by marrying Mr. Maynard, to be sure," replied the child gleefully. "Mother said you was too young, and Mr. Maynard said every day would alter that, so it is all agreed, and you are to come in directly!" and away she flew back to the house.

"I marry the miller!" said Ruth to herself; "no, no, not me. He is nearly as old as my father—I would rather die."

The light canter of a well-trained horse just then was heard along a narrow bye-road, from which she was divided by a range of low bushes skirting one side of the cottage garden. The rider was a lady aged about twenty, in no-wise distinguished by beauty of form or feature, but fascinating in the eyes of some for her inexhaustible gaiety and enthusiasm. Smiling and nodding as Ruth dropped her lowly curtsy, Miss Clifton reined her beautiful grey steed close to the bushes, and beckoning the Cottage Girl nearer, inquired what her father had done about the rent. Ruth replied that Maynard, the miller, had lent the money.

"It gratifies me exceedingly that your father has found so good a friend," said Miss Clifton. "Something else I was going to mention—it was this—if, while your parents are so distressed, you have intention of resorting to service, which I should certainly advise, there is a vacancy at Rosedale House. My own maid is leaving me."

Ruth gladly replied that she was looking out for a situation, and, if the lady thought her capable, she should like the one now proposed above all others.

"Well, you can think of it," said Miss Clifton, and cantered off.

Scarcely had she gone ere Percy dashed into the road, leaping his high-mettled courser over a high-barred gate, and galloping fleetly by in a style that rivetted the admiring gaze of the simple cottage maid. But swiftly as he rode, he managed, at the moment that he passed her, to detach a flower from his breast and fling it at her feet. It was a trivial action, and Ruth could not tell whether it was by accident or design that the rosebud exactly reached her. But her heart palpitated unusually as she gazed down upon it; and as she lifted it in her hand, it communicated a tremulous sensation to her frame, and brought a lively colour into her chcek that boded ill for Henry Maynard.

CHAPTER II.

"Little he said, but his wistful eye
On the maid of his love was turned,
And well might be known, by his struggling sigh,
The grief in his bosom that burned."—BALLAD.

SLOWLY and reluctantly, after a second call from Sally, Ruth re-entered the house, where, elated by the success his straightforward suit had met from her parents, the miller sprang forward to meet her.

"My pretty Ruth!" he said, "your father and mother have given their consent for you to be my wife. Tell me that I have yours, and you'll make me the happiest man that ever trod on earth!"

Ruth shrank coldly from him, but he went on.

"I have a thousand pounds in good hard cash at the town bank, Ruth, and you shall live well and dress well—no wife in Rosedale better, that Henry Maynard pledges his word to. Your father and I will set up in a farm, and Sally, if she behaves well, shall live with you."

"Why don't you answer, Ruth?" demanded Summerfield. "Do you forget the misery from which Maynard has just preserved us?"

"Oh! no," replied the trembling girl, "and I hope to be able to repay him myself, by degrees, when I am in a situation."

How did these cold words quench the glowing hopes of Maynard! His countenance fell; and the acute anguish of disap-

pointed love paralysed for a moment both speech and frame. The tempest cloud lowered darkly over Summerfield's brow.

"Could the wages you would get in a situation," he asked, "repay the hundred obligations before this that we have received from our best friend? The only way to repay him is by giving him your hand, and that I, as your father, require you to do."

"You are too hasty," said the mother, drawing Ruth near to her. "She is but a child yet."

"The younger she is," said Summerfield, "the more reason is there she should be guided by those who know what is best for her, and have her welfare at heart."

"If when I was young I had been altogether guided by those who thought they knew best," said his wife, "my name would not now be Summerfield."

This well-timed allusion to the days of his courtship mollified the cottager; but, deeply grieved at his daughter's tacit refusal of the miller, he required her reasons, and asked if she had formed any other attachment. As she still stood pale and silent, he assured her that if this singular conduct was the fruit of idle fantastic caprice, he would not yield to it, since he knew she would hereafter see cause to rue her folly.

"Take courage, my dear," said her mother, "and let us know what your true feelings are."

"I have no liking for any one else," faltered Ruth, "and I have nothing to say against Mr. Maynard."

"Then why do you refuse me, Ruth?" asked the miller.

"I have no wish to marry until I am older," she tremulously answered.

"If that is all," said Maynard, brightening again, as he espied a forlorn hope, "all may yet be as I wish, for I will wait any time in reason, so that I have only a likelihood to succeed at last."

"Yes, yes, give her time," said Mrs. Summerfield, glad to pacify her husband. "Ruth will see clearer what is for her good when a couple more years have passed over her head. Henry knows it is not our fault that he has to wait."

"I am quite satisfied on that score, and thank you heartily," said Maynard. "And Ruth, I hope, will love me yet."

"Tell him that you will, my dear," whispered Mrs. Summerfield to her daughter, "for he takes your coldness much to heart, and so does your father."

But not to gratify either could Ruth compromise truth; yet, the words, "I will try," came faintly from her pretty lips, while a deep blush spread over her beautiful face.

THE COTTAGE GIRL.

RUTH HAD RETREATED BEFORE THE TERRIFIC ASPECT OF HER FATHER.

WITH this concession, the miller, who had seen his hopes nearly foundered, and was glad to avail himself of any means of redeeming them from destruction, satisfied himself as he could.

Evening in the cottage passed away with but a flitting and variable cheerfulness. Plum-cake, cream, and fresh fruit on the tea-table; but none of the little party who partook of the feast was happy, excepting Ruth's sister, who chattered incessantly and unrebuked, inasmuch as her volubility covered the silence of the rest.

Ruth's thoughts were far away from the little family party; but none knew how much her heart was troubled. She was thinking of the rosebud and Miss Clifton's proposal, wondering if her parents would allow her to go to live at Rose-

dale. House, and hoping they might, while her fancy anticipated
—half timid, half eager—the novelty of the life she should lead
there.

Mrs. Summerfield's reflections for some time were solely occupied by the conquest her daughter had so unexpectedly made of
the moneyed miller, and a ray of long-smothered vanity danced in
her eye, while comparing Ruth's ivory skin, vermilion cheek and
lip, large brown eye, soft sunny curls, and gracefully proportioned
figure, to her own in former days. In her youth she herself had
been the pride of Rosedale, and many lovers contended for her
hand. Her early triumphs, and early joys, rolled back their
bright waves on the memory of the cottager's wife, who heaved
a pleasurable sigh as she recalled them. Amid these flattering
reminiscences, why did a spasm of anguish shoot over her
colourless face?—why shuddered she?—and why grew her eye
wild and insane? Was it that the triumphs of her beauty in
former days had led to the nameless secret, which for fourteen
years had lain buried in her husband's breast and her own?
And was it from this cause that the growing loveliness of her
daughter, of which most mothers would have been proud, in
general affected her only with pain and anxiety? It was so;
and thus she reflected as her eye rested on Ruth :—

"Beauty has been my curse, and who knows but that in some
other way it may prove her's? Had I my wish, she should be
the plainest girl in Rosedale, instead of the fairest. Then I
should see no such foolish refusal as that of to-day, but she would
be glad to take the first offer, and make herself happy with it.
Beauty puts ambition into girls' minds, and ambition too often
has sad endings. God keep my girl from any such—let her
grave rather be dug before the passing of another week. Yet
it was not ambition led to my troubles. Roger was more to
me than a king could have been. And it is a sad thing to
reflect on, that without a fault in him or me, we have been
made wretched for life !"

Maynard was taciturn, and cast down, but his good-nature
was frequently breaking through the cloud his disappointment
had cast over him. No morbid pride envenomed the wound
Ruth's coldness had inflicted. He felt as a man, but not as a selfish
one, not as one in whom the passions triumph ever the more
amiable feelings. Fearing, by the stern looks of Summerfield,
lest the good understanding between the father and daughter
had been disturbed by Ruth's conduct on this occasion, he frequently, when she could not hear, sought to suggest palliatives
for her, some of them depreciatory of himself.

"We must be considerate, friend Roger," he said, "we must be considerate in this case. I have too many years on my head to be a very acceptable wooer to so young a lass—my face and figure, too, to speak the truth, are none of the likeliest to please the eye of one who, every time she looks in her glass, sees features pretty enough to win a duke. We must be considerate."

"Neighbour," said Summerfield, "you are as God made you, and she is no more. And if I thought it was in her nature to presume on the perishable beauties He has given her, so as wantonly to grieve a worthy man who does her the grace to choose her for his wife, I would disown her! Beauty is as beauty does, friend Maynard; that is what I have always striven to learn my Ruth. You have the qualities to make a wife happy; and it is for this, and not because you have a thousand pounds, that her refusal grieves me. Mind you understand that, Henry. I give you my solemn word, that not ten thousand pounds, nor ten times ten thousand, with youth and beauty into the bargain, would have bought my consent, without good qualities of heart and life. I had rather see her picking oakum in a workhouse, or begging from door to door, than the wife of a profligate. And if you, Henry Maynard, were at this moment as poor as I, I would still say to my daughter, 'Ruth, if you will please me, you will marry him.'"

"Many thanks, Roger, for your goodwill," said the miller—"I shall live in hopes, since you and dame here are my friends. Ruth is a good daughter, and has a high respect for your judgment. I say I shall hope to persuade her yet, and perhaps in less a time than two years."

"I hope you may, my satisfaction will be greater than I can tell," said Summerfield.

"And mine," echoed his wife; "but, Henry, if you will take my advice, don't be too pressing. See her as often as you will, but give her plenty of time to know her own mind."

Maynard promised to be guided by the mother's counsel, and, as it was late, arose to take leave. Opening the cottage door, the harvest moon appeared in majestic loveliness above the groves that intervened between his mill and Summerfield's dwelling. But no pleasure did that beauteous sight afford the miller—the light of his life he was leaving behind; and hopeful as he had striven to appear, a sad foreboding voice whispered him that that sweet light would never shine for him!

At parting he received from the youthful object of his generous affection no word or look of encouragement, no kind inquiry as to when he would come again; but coldly she shrank

from his proffered embrace; and deeply sighing, and regretting that he had ever known her, or ever loved, the miller wended his lonely way over the silent fields.

As the picturesque mill rose high and massive before him, its sails motionless in the pale beams of the moon, that threw its glancing sheen on a stream of water by which the machinery of the building was worked, the miller sickened at heart, and a despairing tear stood in his eye.

"I was in hopes," he said, half aloud, "to have seen her settled there—but now I doubt it will never be. No! Harry Maynard must sit by a lonely fireside till the day of his death, and leave the money he has scraped together so hardly to persons who care not a straw for him. Yet why care for that? When I am gone what will it matter to me who has it? And what should I desire for my lifetime more than I have? My business is one I have all my life delighted in—Kitty, my housekeeper, knows all my ways, and would rather serve me than the vicar— and it is no slight thing to have money in reserve for anything may strike one's fancy. Surely I ought to be satisfied. And I am a fool to fret myself because I cannot win the fantastic affections of a young girl. Tut, tut—I will grieve about it no more."

As he came to this resolution, he crossed the slight plank thrown over the mill-stream, and ascended a few steps to a door above the basement of the building containing the machine-works. His watch-dog met him as he entered, and courted his caress in vain. Kitty, his housekeeper, plied him with a dozen unanswered inquiries as to where he had stayed so late, and threw out, unheeded, as many innuendoes respecting Summerfield's daughter—for Kitty had cherished some hopes of being mistress of the mill herself. Maynard got rid of her as soon as possible, and leaning comfortably back in his seat, with a glass of ale by his side, began to feel his spirits revive.

"Ruth may be mine yet," he said; "she promised to try to love me, and I will spare no pains to win her."

The next and each successive day, while Ruth remained at home, found Maynard at the cottage. Keeping in mind Mrs. Summerfield's advice, he rarely spoke of love or marriage to her, but contented himself with bringing her presents, and showing her every quiet attention. But while the miller thus assiduously strove, though with no subtle, no flattering art (unless pure love itself teach such), to win the affections which he found so necessary to his peace, Ruth already repented that she had suffered him to be deluded by a hope which she well knew could never be realised, and it was chiefly to avoid him

that she took an early opportunity of naming Miss Clifton's proposal to her parents, and entreating their consent that she might live at Rosedale House.

Rather contrary to her expectation, they, after much private talk between themselves, granted their permission The truth was, had they forbad her wish, they must again have manifested to her their extreme antipathy to the Cliftons, and this, Summerfield convinced his wife it was important should fade out of her mind as quickly as possible. He was sleeplessly anxious to lay to rest in his daughter's mind those dismal suspicions which he could not but fear had recently been called into play. The discovery she had made in the shed filled him with apprehension, for what could she think but that the article she had seen there had been obtained by dishonest means? After consulting his wife, the cottager spoke with Ruth, when none but himself and her were in the house—Mrs. Summerfield being at market, the boy at school, and Sally seeking for a place.

"Did we not tell you, Ruth, it was only for your own sake we kept our secret from you?"

"Yes, father," replied the abashed girl.

"And did you think we spoke falsely?"

"No, father."

"Then why were you prying about the shed on Monday morning?"

Ruth was silent, and hung her head.

"Eve's passion misled you, I suppose," said Summerfield; "it was lucky you had not to suffer Eve's punishment for it—it is lucky you have not forfeited for yourself and us, by your disobedient curiosity, this little paradise here, and brought on us ruin and death. Well, it is done—you have found in that shed what we desired to keep from your sight—in that gold watch lies all our secret."

"I did not know that gold was a watch," said Ruth; "I saw it shining in the thatch, and went up to look at it, just as you, father——"

"Came and caught you. Well, and now what are you the better for having seen it?"

"None at all, father," answered Ruth, "unless I could know how it came there, and who it belongs to."

"It came there through the villany of one who would have blasted the character of your mother," replied Summerfield, in a tremendous voice, "and it was to him it belonged."

Ruth had retreated before the terrific aspect of her father, and laid her hand on the latch of the door. Her strong desire,

however, to know the mystery, overcame her fears so far that she asked where the person of whom he spoke now was.

Summerfield, then striding to and fro the apartment, stopped with an instant and remarkable change of gesture. Stern exultation diffused a dreadful light over his features, which seemed to Ruth to change their natural size and shape. His stature reared itself like a tall column under the influence of the mighty passions which swelled within, and it was in a deep tone, as changed as his appearance, that he answered.

"He is in a foreign land, Ruth, and thence he shall never—never return. His crimes have met their due, and he will trouble neither me nor mine more."

"May I not know his name, father?"

"To whisper it would be the death of us all," Summerfield replied. "When I and your mother are under the turf, not before, my children and the world shall know all, and judge betwixt me and my enemy. In the meantime that watch is the pledge of our safety—while that is secure, we are secure; but if it once sees the light, we shall fall victims to a train of circumstances, originating entirely in the treachery of the villain I have just spoken of—circumstances which Heaven knows we have not had it in our power to control."

"I am sure if I was questioned ever so much, no one should know from me there was such a thing as a watch about the cottage," said Ruth.

"I have told you how much hangs on it, and I feel tolerably easy in trusting our safeties to your prudence. But you must not only keep silence respecting the watch, but mind never to breathe a word of anything uncommon being known to your mother and I. And your thoughts, Ruth, must be guarded, too. Make your faith in the uprightness of your parents a part of your religion—pray to have it confirmed and increased, that if a time of darkness should approach, and the law array its terrors against us, your confidence may not waver, but be our comfort and our stay."

The last words were pronounced with deep gravity and pathos, and Ruth, melting into tears, assured him, with all youth's trustingness of soul, she would never believe her mother and he had done anything wrong, unless she had it from their own lips.

"But I should like to know, father," she said, "what the law could bring against you, and why you could not clear yourself by telling the truth?"

"A time will come," Summerfield rejoined, "when all shall be made plain to you, Ruth. But that time I have often said

will not be while your mother and I live—unless we are called to a public bar."

"Why not, father?" urged Ruth. "What danger can follow from my knowing all more than from what I know already?"

"None, perhaps—yet it is my will, and that is enough. But you wondered why my telling the truth in a court of justice could not clear me, I being innocent of any crime. This is the reason—I have no witnesses to prove my story true; and, that being the case, I should have left England, and gone some thousands of miles over the ocean, if I had had the means. But I have striven for them to no purpose, and here we are—only protected by a merciful Providence."

The decisiveness with which he finally declared his innexible will that she should remain in ignorance of the nature of his peril, compelled Ruth to give up the hope of moving him, nor durst she again hazard his displeasure by attempting it.

"Our honesty," said Summerfield, "you cannot at any time doubt, for if I had chosen to be dishonest, we need not have placed ourselves under obligation to Maynard. There is about that watch, gold and precious stones enough to have paid our year's rent twenty times over. But what is not mine, Ruth, I would rather perish that touch."

"I am sure you would!" exclaimed Ruth, and their conversation was broken off by Sally, who had hired herself to a farmer's wife near.

Soon after came Mrs. Summerfield, saying she had met the miller, and told him of Ruth's intention to engage with Miss Clifton, on which Maynard had observed—"Ruth would do better to be her own mistress;" and Mrs. Summerfield responded—"Yes, indeed; but let her have her own way—she will soon be tired of service, and then be glad to have you."

"I am vexed you said that, mother," said Ruth, piqued almost to tears; "I shall never be glad to have Mr. Maynard, for I can never love him."

"Then you cannot love worth," said her father.

"Indeed I can," replied Ruth; "and I should like Mr. Maynard very much—if he would not want me to marry him." She stopped,—then added, "If ever I have a husband, he shall be one I can love better than all the world beside, as mother does you."

Summerfield smiled.

"You have it all your own way," he said, "but don't think you have convinced me of the wisdom of refusing poor Maynard."

"Wisdom!" cried Mrs. Summerfield, "it is sheer obstinacy. She may go farther and fare worse, that I can tell her."

"I will go farther then, mother," said Ruth; "and if I must fare worse, I can't help it."

Lightly she spoke, little imagining the sorrows that lay before her; and hastening to put on her Sunday gown and bonnet, set out for Rosedale House, to learn from Miss Clifton the terms and duties of the proposed situation, and the time when she should enter upon it.

Mrs. Summerfield, from the cottage entrance, observed the bounding step with which Ruth passed down the lane.

"Poor Henry!" she thought within herself, "there is little hope for you! Why, there," she exclaimed, "if he is not coming over the stile and meeting her! He talks to her—he is trying to persuade her not to go—and she impatiently turns from him. Ah! silly, silly girl!—you must think life is paved with gold, and strewed with roses, or you would never fling away so good a chance. Would anybody believe that a girl in her senses could choose service instead of a comfortable home of her own, a thousand pounds in the town bank, and the satisfaction of seeing her father and mother provided for?—Would anybody believe a girl could be so blinded? They are going to cross the fields together, I see, but her gait tells me well enough she would rather the miller was a hundred miles off. Silly girl—silly girl. Not but I could excuse her if she loved another, for I would not have given up my Roger for the best man in England—but, as it is, such foolish obstinacy is enough to vex one to death."

CHAPTER III.

"Dea\ England! how thy beauteous vales I love;
  Thy vales of sweetest flowers, and time-worn trees,
Of warblers that in spring-tide hither rove;
  Of rippling streams stirred by the autumn breeze;
Of grassy hillocks shadowing o'er the dead,
  By crumbling ruins half in ivy hid;
Of village, hoary church, and churchyard dread,
  And their long hedge-rows sweet-briars bloom amid."—M. B.

ROSEDALE HOUSE was two miles from the cottage, and it would be difficult to find in the same space, even in England's verdant vales, a walk of more attraction to a lover of quiet nature. On the one hand, the lark hovering in the gilded clouds, looked down on a succession of fields clothed in the richest garb of cultivation, whose varying tints of green the hand of autumn had lightly blended with her favourite yellow, and whose combined surfaces, divided by neat hedge-rows, and besprinkled here and there with cottages and farms, swelled beautifully upward in wide-extended perspective, to form the southern boundary of Rosedale.

When the eye had wearied itself of that gratifying prospect—gratifying alike to the simple husbandman and the individual of more polished taste—bold, sterile, stony hills, bounding the dale on the north, presented a picture by contrast approaching the sublime. There the sportsman sought the game which shun the abodes of man. There the only dwellings to be seen were a few huts, miserably small and comfortless, where the poor Irish that worked on the quarries found for their squalid families partial refuge from the inclemencies of our damp and variable climate. There mineral springs, issuing from deep caves, poured themselves into reservoirs prepared for their reception, and proved their healing efficacy on many of the wealthier classes who had the courage to spend part of the hot season in a watering-place yet unrecognized by fashion. There the air was keen and bracing, the paths narrow and precipitious, and every turn presented to the wanderer among those heights some bold and striking features.

The small town of Rosedale lay at the foot of these wild hills, and a road, bordered with noble trees, ran from hence to a secluded park in the bosom of the vale. The park was not extensive, but comprised many objects of interest. It was tenanted by several species of deer, browsing beneath oaks whose majestic

forms seem to bid defiance to decay. The splendid pheasant made its habitation in the deep-hidden coverts, and the peaceful dove fluttered from lofty bough to bough. There had been a time when sounds other than the quiet ones of bird and breeze had awakened the now slumbering echoes of Rosedale Park. Here had armed knight pealed his soul-stirring trumpet-blast; here had thundering cannon discharged its flaming combustibles on hostile ranks; here had many a gallant horse and his rider fallen in the fierce shock of war. In the days of the Commonwealth, Cromwell had here found a vigorous and able supporter of his views, for the good of Britain, in the person of Arthur Clifton, then master of Rosedale Park, and the house was fortified, and manned with his determined adherents. Besieged by the Cavaliers, these adherents made a desperate defence, and during a sally led by Arthur Clifton, he was taken prisoner, and his head struck off on a felled tree opposite a tower from whose roof his distracted wife waved him her parting adieus. No sooner had the barbarous stroke been given by which she was rendered a widow, than, with a dreadful shriek, she precipitated herself to the ground, and expired almost at the same moment with him she loved. The spot on which Arthur suffered was commemorated in after times by a statue from the hand of an Italian sculptor of eminence, and that part of the building from which his wife hurled herself was afterwards designated the "Lady's Tower."

The Lady's Tower was now in disuse, like many other parts of the old mansion which history and tradition had hallowed. The crumbling battlements no more were thronged by steel-clad men—the oak-carved hall was deserted—the gothic stables received no more barbed steeds—the worm-eaten staircases seldom felt the pressure of a footstep—indeed, when the father of the present young proprietor came into possession, in the latter part of the reign of George II., Rosedale House was a mere ruin; but he made many repairs, and spent a considerable sum of money in adding a set of modern apartments to the west wing, fitted up with luxuriant taste for the reception of his bride. Seven years after his marriage Mr. Clifton disappeared, and all search after him proved ineffectual; and at a latter period, when her children, Percy and Amy, had attained the ages of eighteen and nineteen, Mrs. Clifton was borne to the tomb.

A little time passed, and the birds that inhabited the leaf-clad walls found their solitude often disturbed by the gay visitors of the brother and the sister; the cobwebs were swept from many an antique lattice; over the inlaid floors glanced the light fan-

tastic steps of dancers ; and the hollow roofs returned, instead of dreary echoes, the laughter of light hearts.

But it was when all was hushed in the deep repose natural to the place that the contemplative visitor found most abundant material of interesting observation and reflection in and about Rosedale House. When the moon poured her delicious beams on the dark and crumbling relics of the Lady's Tower, or when the starlight just enabled the gothic outlines of the exterior of the house to be defined through the midnight gloom—then to look round, to recall the dark and stirring events which were enacted there in the olden time, to reflect how many generations have been swept into eternity since the date of those traditions on which the fancy loves to rest, and what mighty changes the world has seen that the gallant spirits of former times never so much as conceived—this was the truest enjoyment of that romantic place.

Others, however, loved best by cheerful day to ramble over the hundred passages that led to nothing—the crooked stair-cases—the dark closets—and to hear their voices dying along the walls in sepulchral cadences, while fear and awe mingled with delighted curiosity.

The young squire was proud of the antiquities of his house, and when the mood came upon him, none could be more deeply moved by the reflections they were calculated to call forth, But, in general, he disliked the melancholy, which, he said. " hung like a mildew over the whole estate ; he felt it in the very air ; it infected every sound ; and wherever he trod within fifty yards of the mansion, he fancied himself treading on the bones of his ancestors."

The melancholy of which he complained chiefly existed, how-ever, in himself—in his unemployed faculties—in the want of a direct pursuit—in the lassitude generated in an ardent mind by indolence and luxury. He was conscious that he required a more active life, but could not decide what course to pursue. From the army he was deterred by his affection for his sister; the bar required too much laborious application ; and no other pro-fession suited his taste. Contenting himself, therefore, with resolving ultimately to enter on some honourable public career, he continued to make pleasure his sole business. In the sport-ing season, his time moved with a less flagging wing than at other periods. Then with his gun he might be seen traversing the bleak hills, or winding along the dale by stream and meadow.

It was in one of these rural rambles that he had been first struck by the loveliness of Ruth, who passed him accidentally

with her mother; and the real motive of his call at the cottage the Saturday before Summerfield's arrears of rent were to be demanded by the agent, was chiefly to obtain a nearer view of the rustic beauty.

CHAPTER IV.

"O, fresh is the rose in the gay dewy morning,
    And sweet is the lily at evening close;
But in the fair presence o' lovely young Jessie,
    Unseen is the lily, unheeded the rose.
Love sits in her smile, a wizard ensnaring;
    Enthron'd in her een he delivers his law;
And still to her charms she alone is a stranger,
    Her modest demeanour's the jewel of a'."—BURNS.

ON the evening when Ruth came to Rosedale House to engage herself there as a domestic servant, Miss Clifton sat negligently by a French window, her imagination wholly steeped in the magic pages of a romance which rested on her knee. The elegant room within—the costly plants, whose sweetness and brilliant hues invited her regard—the beauty of the landscape before her—all was forgotten; and the sands of Palestine, the rush of meeting warriors, and the grace and pomp of chivalry, moved and lived about her. Amy was in another clime and age—the expression of her face was elevated and abstracted—and when she lifted up her eyes, they swam in ecstatic tears. Suddenly the book was taken from her hold, and Percy stood beside her.

"You are everlastingly poring over those romances, Amy," he said. "Come, throw them aside, and look more like a being of earth. I have had excellent shooting to-day on the peak."

"Every one to their taste, Percy," said his sister—"you to mangling poor birds, I to reading romances. Which is the most rational, think you?"

"Which you will. I have just met Walters, and he gave me a most affecting description of the Summerfields at the time he was levying the distress. He has a heart of iron, or he could not have endured it."

"And why did you suffer him to proceed to those extremities, Percy?"

"Because I considered there had been sufficient indulgence granted, and that to have postponed the payment longer would

have been tantamount to losing it altogether, for how was Summerfield to meet an old debt, if, as was the case, his earnings were not sufficient for his current expenses?"

"And how was he to live when his goods were taken?"

"That was his own affair. And yet, between ourselves, I intended, if the miller had not forestalled me, to have stepped in and relieved them in their need."

"Your charitable intentions were too tardy," said Amy; "mine, I hope, will be more effectual, for you must know that I too have had my plans for their benefit, and proposed to take their eldest daughter into Rosedale House."

Clifton could ill disguise the pleasure this intelligence gave him, but, counterfeiting reluctance to the measure, urged some feeble objections, which his sister, as he intended, soon overcame.

"Ruth is an exceedingly pretty girl," observed Miss Clifton; "do you not think so?"

Percy did think so, and the question rather confused him; but carelessly he replied—

"Rather pretty—for a homely cottage girl."

"She is more than rather pretty, Percy; her hair one might fancy composed of fine threads of gold; her features and head have a Grecian contour, delicate and small; and I can imagine nothing more perfect than her fairy-figure."

"Is that conned out of your romance?" said Clifton—and before Amy could reply, a servant apprised her of the arrival of the very individual whose personal merits they were discussing.

"Let her be shown in here," said Miss Clifton; and then turning to her brother, she bade him observe Ruth well, and see with his own eyes the beauties she had described. Percy smiled to himself as he promised that he would.

Unconscious of her own attractions, with an air of bashful simplicity, Ruth made her appearance. The walk, and the flutter of her spirits at finding herself for the first time in a place which seemed to her so unspeakably grand, together with the pleasing, dreadful thought that she was about to launch her little bark on the great world, brought to her cheeks a double dye of the rose, which spread itself over her forehead and throat, as her eye, for a single moment, encountered that of Percy—and the rosebud rushed to her recollection.

Amy darted a triumphant glance at her brother, whose gaze remained rivetted on the lovely girl.

"Well, Ruth," Miss Clifton then said, addressing her, "have you reflected on the proposal I made to you?"

"Yes, ma'am," answered the downcast maiden; "and, if

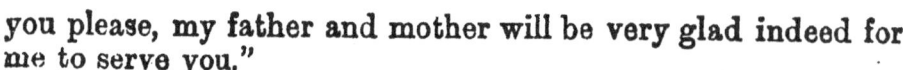

you please, my father and mother will be very glad indeed for me to serve you."

"If that is the case," said Miss Clifton, "you may come and take up your residence as soon as you will."

Ruth made a grateful curtsey, and her countenance was radiant with joy.

"And if you please, ma'am, what shall I have to do?" she timidly inquired.

"Nothing very difficult or laborious. If you are only attentive and well-behaved, you cannot fail to please me."

"One so pretty could not be otherwise than well-behaved, were she to make the attempt," interrupted Percy; and Ruth felt her heart beat strangely at the compliment, while Amy smiled, gratified that she had won her brother to her own opinion respecting the Cottage Girl's beauty.

The salary Ruth was to receive was then named, and its liberality proved a new joy to her, being intended by Miss Clifton to assist the family, as well as to provide for herself.

After this, Ruth made her parting obeisance and withdrew; but, by the suggestion of Percy, she was conducted into the kitchen, and refreshments set before her, which had scarcely been done, when the young squire looked in, on the pretence of giving some trifling direction to his servant, who was there, and passing close to her, took a rosebud out of a jar of flowers in the window, with a significant look at our innocent heroine, who then blushed deeper than ever, certain that the flower Mr. Clifton had flung from his hand when he rode past the cottage garden, had been intended for her.

She left the house, and was rejoined by the miller, who had waited for her at the margin of the park. Never had his presence been so unwelcome. She would fain have loitered on her way homewards alone, pondering every word that had been spoken to her, recalling each object she had seen, and more than all, the dazzling looks with which the young squire had regarded her, and the compliment he had passed. But there was Maynard to interrupt this pleasing train of meditation, and to tease her with remonstrances against her going to service. To his inquiry as to the result of her errand, she answered briefly and pettishly that she had engaged herself, on which, with a grieved heart, Maynard rejoined—

"It is useless for me longer to try to dissuade you, Ruth. Go—since nothing else will serve you; and I hope you will be as happy there as you can wish, and that no thought of Henry Maynard's sorrow may give you a pang. I should be grieved if

it did, for I wish you nothing but good, whether you are my wife or no."

Ruth spoke so as to soothe his wounded feelings without encouraging his hopes, and then they finished the walk in silence.

Reaching the cottage, Ruth, in delighted terms, communicated the pleasing reception she had met from Miss Clifton, and the large wages she was to receive, but Mrs. Summerfield was now in one of her unhappy fits of irritability, and reproached her daughter bitterly for choosing service in preference to a good husband, to whom they were so much indebted.

Summerfield promptly interfered, and imperatively enjoined silence on the fretful complainings of his wife.

"You forget," he said, "that Ruth, if she marries, marries for herself, not for us. We have but a right to advise her for her good; if she does not see with us, the consequences must rest with herself."

"You are right, friend Roger," said Maynard; "her will must guide her; and it is guiding her not for the best, I am afraid—but time will show. Enough of that. You must all spend one half day with me at the mill before Ruth leaves home. Say we name Thursday next, that will give Kitty time to prepare."

No objection was raised, and the friendly invitation was accepted.

Meantime, Clifton, when Ruth left the park, observed from a window that she was joined by some one whom his heart told him, by its unpleasant sensations, could be no other than a lover. To ascertain who this lover was, and the degree of favour shown him, became a burning impulse, and it was to no purpose that he argued with himself on the absurdity of employing his thoughts on such a matter.

"What can it concern me," he said, "who this simple lass chooses for her swain?—he is some clod-hopping ploughman, I doubt not."

But Mr. Clifton found himself mistaken in this conjecture. A servant, to whom he purposely remarked, in a jesting manner, that the pretty Ruth had brought a sweetheart with her to the park, told him that it was the miller of Rosedale.

"Aye!" exclaimed the squire, in no small astonishment, "so rich a bachelor in her train already! I should have thought the miller, after waiting so long for a wife, would have chosen better."

"They say, down in the town, that he doats on her," said the domestic.

"And no wonder," muttered Clifton between his teeth, as he rejoined his sister in her favourite sitting-room.

"What say you now, Percy," she cried, "is not Ruth more than rather pretty ?"

"I have something else to think about," said Percy, disguising his real feelings, "if you have not. Our father—the mystery in which his fate is enveloped, disturbs me more than you can imagine. My anxiety to penetrate it grows with my growth, and strengthens with my strength."

"You remember him ?" said Amy.

"But slightly," replied her brother. "His frequent altercations with my mother are more clearly impressed on my mind."

"And I can find in my memory no trace of either," said Amy. "How strange, Percy, if, after all these years, he were actually to reappear, a living man !"

"Living or dead," exclaimed Percy, "I would give a thousand pounds this moment to trace the cause of his disappearance."

"Neither money nor wishes, I fear, will accomplish that end," said Amy.

"So I suspect," responded Percy; "and the rather that his character and associates seem to lead irresistibly to the conclusion that he has met with foul play."

"A dreadful conclusion !" exclaimed Amy, and shivered at the thought. "Yet it is one, I confess, that appears but too inevitable. My ill-fated father ! It is fearful to conjecture what his end may have been ! Murdered—and his assassins, for aught we know, moving about us unsuspected and secure !"

"It is useless, and worse than useless, to suffer our imaginations to launch out on this dark sea of doubt," said Percy. "All is fathomless darkness, which we seek in vain to penetrate. If I thought any good could be anticipated from now resuming the distressing inquiry, I would resume it though my last guinea were spent in the pursuit ! But there can be none. We must despair of ever knowing our father's end."

"And will you permit your sister to whisper a warning word to you, Percy ?" said Miss Clifton.

"To what intent ? How can I need warning ?"

"Oh, you know what I mean," she said, playfully. "You would flutter about gay life like a moth about a candle— until you had singed your wings. You are too apt to court the smiles of fair ladies, and to sit long at the wine, of the peril of which the wise king of Israel assureth you. Oh ! my dear Percy," she said, with graver earnestness, "let your father's mysterious fate be as a lighthouse to guide you from the rocks on which his life was wrecked and lost."

THE COTTAGE GIRL.

"DO YOU," HE SAID, HIS VOICE TREMBLING WITH PASSION.

PERCY made no reply.

His sister watched him carefully, waiting to receive an answer. At length getting impatient, she said, "Percy, have you no reply to my words? Will you not be warned in time?"

"You are extremely thoughtful for me, but what of yourself, Amy? Have you nothing to fear? Is there nothing to be apprehended from your romantic visions?"

" I would not exchange them for any thing earth could offer!" said Amy. "But look out!—What a magnificent starlight night! Oh, that I were a star!"

"If I were one," said Percy, laughing aloud, "I should entreat for a place where I might look down on something more agreeable than this confounded old house and park. But I will not disturb you longer—I perceive you are eager to return to your romance,"

" Thank you, for I should like to finish this work to-night, it is so very interesting," said Miss Clifton, casting herself on a damask couch, by the side of which burnt a lamp, whose soft shaded light fell stilly on the pages which she began rapidly to turn over, while her hand supported her head, and her elbow rested on a sloping pile of cushions. Percy stood a few minutes looking over her, while his thoughts in reality were straying to the miller and Ruth Summerfield. He then caught up his hat, and strolled into the park.

CHAPTER V.

" Were mine the spell
    To call fate's joys, or blunt his dart,
    There should not be one hand or heart,
But served or wished thee well."—HALLECK.

ENTERING on service for the first time is an important epoch in the history of a maiden of lowly life. She is going to test her abilities and moral strength among strangers. She is going from the freedom and indulgence of home to contend, perhaps, with severe and difficult tempers, where all that she does and says must be squared according to rules, the utility of many of which she cannot comprehend.

If she has been tenderly brought up the hardship is greater, and more time has to elapse before her feelings are blunted to the necessities of her condition. But it is not until the change is actually experienced, and cold looks and harsh or haughty speeches come chillingly upon the young and sensitive heart, and the familiar faces of parents and relatives are no longer visible, and ease and gay delights are changed for thankless labour and con-

straint—it is not until then that the poor girl feels the full force of the contrast between "sweet home," however humble, and a residence among strangers. Previously the passion of curiosity engrosses her mind, and paints all the prospect fair because it is new. Eagerly she looks forward to the hour which is to usher her to the scenes she anticipates.

And now the heart of Ruth was as blithe as if it would never be sad more. Light and active as a bird, she darted to and fro the cottage, making her preparations for the coming change in her lot, and every now and then uplifting her clear voice in some rustic ditty, imitated by her favorite bullfinch, that hung in a cage by the window. But Mrs. Summerfield snappishly repressed these overflowings of innocent delight.

"It is well you can be so cheerful!" she cried—"I wish I could be so. I wish I had no more care on my head than you. And yet if you have no trouble of your own, you might remember that your father and I have."

"Why, mother," said Ruth, "it is as much for your sakes I am happy as my own. You have often said how it would please you if I was in some good situation—and now I am not only going to one, but shall be able to help you."

Mrs. Summerfield murmured inaudibly—

"Yes, going to the place in all the world I detest most." Then aloud she said—"You might have helped us better by living at the mill."

Ruth burst into tears.

"It is unkind of you, mother, to keep upbraiding me with that. One can't like who they will. I am sure I would do what you wish if I could."

"Well, well," said the mother, kissing her, "I was wrong to say any more about it. You mean well I am sure. Dry your eyes, and don't let your father see there has been any thing amiss."

The bullfinch while they spoke fluttered in the cage, pecked at the wires, and uttered a few short, shrill notes, to attract the attention of Ruth, whom it knew perfectly. She spoke fondly to it, and it piped its loudest strains, challenging her to a competition.

"No," said she, "I must not sing though you may. But come you shall pay a visit to the fields once more before I leave you," —and opening the cage door, she suffered it to fly out, and it alighted now on her hand, now on her shoulder and head, and then circled round her with an ecstatic motion. Presently Ruth set wide the casement, and away it flew far as the eye could see. Mrs. Summerfield angrily exclaimed the bird was lost, but Ruth

had often permitted it a temporary freedom before and was confident of its return. · Its absence was now prolonged so as to
give her some uneasiness, but after two hours it darted in at the
same casement whence it had issued, and flew direct to the bosom of the Cottage Girl. She caressed it, and replaced it in its
prison, which the wondrous force of habit had rendered more
agreeable to the bird than its natural haunts.

The day arrived on which the cottagers were to be entertained
at the mill; and Henry Maynard coming to escort the object of
his regard thither was disappointed to learn that Mrs. Summerfield did not consider herself sufficiently well to go out, an excuse
Ruth privately attributed to a reluctance to leave the cottage
with no one to watch it. In this notion she was confirmed by
overhearing her father whisper to her mother—" We have no
right to fear any thing from shutting up the place a few hours.
You alarm yourself without occasion, and by your odd behaviour
will be drawing on us suspicious eyes, if you do not mind."

To which her mother replied—

" I shan't have a single minutes peace if the cottage is left
alone. I cannot, and will not go

Summerfield then whispered more authoritatively to her, and
quitting the chamber in which they were, stopped on the threshhold to bid her hasten and dress for the party.

As soon as he had left her, Mrs. Summerfield fell into a long
weeping paroxysm, during which Ruth knew not how to console
her. In the midst of this the chamber door re-opened, and Ruth
was summoned by her father to accompany Maynard to the mill.
Ruth hesitated to leave her mother in such a condition, but Mrs.
Summerfield peevishly desired her to " go along, and not mind
her; she must bear her load of misery as she could. Her existence could not last very long, that was one comfort, and she
cared not how soon it ended, for no peace of mind could she
ever have more."

Summerfield called his daughter again, and Ruth, bending to
her mother, softly whispered to her to—

" Trust in God;" adding, "father loves you, and knows what
is best; do as he wishes, dear mother; and don't fret if you
have anything on your mind that you could not help."

Then in a simple white gown, and coarse straw bonnet, Ruth
joined her generous but unsuccessful lover. His appearance he
had been at no small pains to improve, as he thought, by means of
a light fashionable suit of clothes, instead of his ordinary formal
garb, and a white starched neckcloth with broad ruffles below.
Alas! to what absurdities will love reduce its votaries. Henry

Maynard in his customary guise was a sensible respectable countryman, but in this he looked neither sensible nor respectable, but as if he had found his way by mistake into the habiliments of a linendraper's shopman, and felt uneasy in the transformation. Ruth's quick sense of the ridiculous, almost induced her to laugh outright, and Summerfield, whose lofty character was galled to the quick by the sight of his worthy neighbour's amiable folly, bit his lip, and raised his eyebrow in vexed astonishment, at the same time reproving his daughter apart for the risibility that his penetrating eye readily perceived she was tempted to indulge in.

"Dare you," said he " laugh at a man whose weakness comes from a desire of pleasing you? Respect the feeling, if you can't the manner, in which he shows it."

" But that little coat, father, and those large ruffles!" exclaimed Ruth, tittering the more as she endeavoured to restrain herself.

"Silence!" said her father, sternly.

But every one has felt that a laughing mood is not at all times to be controlled, and the next glance her eye took of the miller set her off in a burst of mirth highly displeasing to Summerfield, and he turned from her with a frown that speedily recalled her capacity of self command.

"What is it that so much pleases you, Ruth?" Maynard inquired.

"The cut of your clothes," replied Summerfield, determined not to spare her. "My daughter, Henry, as you may have discovered, thinks little of people's merit or demerit, compared with the shape of their gown or coat."

"Well now," said the miller, surveying himself with a disappointed air, "I thought I had just hit the fashion. I employed young squire Clifton's tailor; and, thought I, if he cannot make a gentleman of me there is no one can. I daresay I shall have a fine long bill for these things—double the charge, or nearly, that old Hoskins would have made."

"And what is fashion to you or I, friend Maynard?" said Summerfield, "or why should we run after gentility? 'An honest man's aboon it a'.'"

"Deuce take it, but you are right," said the miller; "and I shall not feel like myself while I have these foppish things about me. But it was all for Ruth, and there she stands laughing at me for my pains."

And involuntarily, though with some awkwardness, the good-natured miller joined her in a second ebullition of merriment.

"I am sure I meant no harm," she said, as soon as it had subsided, stealing an apologetic look to her father, not a muscle of whose rigid features had relaxed.

"Is it no harm to hurt the feelings of a good man?" he said.

"Nonsense," said Maynard, "my feelings are not hurt. Ruth meant it innocently. And now let us be jogging. You, friend Roger, can come after with the young ones and your wife, if she can be persuaded, as I hope she will. Tell her it is only a mile and a half to the mill, and the walk will do her good instead of harm,—she stays in the house too much."

"She shall come," said Summerfield.

And now the reader must imagine the miller and Ruth tracing the footpaths over the smiling meadows, the mill with its sails in active motion on a gentle acclivity before them. There is not in rural scenery a more picturesque object than a corn mill. In Maynard's eyes, in especial, nothing on earth could be more pleasing except it was the sweet girl now by his side.

"Ah! Ruth," he said, pressing her arm, "what a happy man should I be if yon house of mine was from this day to be shared with you!—if I was now taking you there not as my visitor but as my wife! Tell me, Ruth, don't you think if it were so you could be happy? Ask yourself the question once more, and think of all I would do for your relations, and how comfortable I could make you. Kitty should go or stay, just as you liked—you should have twenty pounds to buy your wedding clothes—and any thing else that would give you pleasure if you only said the word it should be yours."

Ruth was a young girl, and a poor girl, and it was not to be supposed that she could be entirely insensible to offers so tempting. For a minute the prospect of ruling Kitty (who hated her as a rival), and of dressing in fine clothes, and carrying a full purse in her pocket, and being able to boast a thousand pounds in the bank, and placing her father and mother above the reach of want for the rest of their lifetimes, staggered her resolution; but, as if fate strove against the miller, her eye lighted at that critical moment on a wild-rose and its buds blooming in a hedge, and—(on such trifles do important events sometimes hinge)—that single glance was fatal to Maynard. Why it was we cannot say, unless the first mysterious promptings of the "master passion" on behalf of Clifton had begun to make themselves felt in the breast of the incautious girl, and linked themselves to the form of a rosebud by those fine threads of association with which life interweaves the different passions of the soul. Certain it was, that the noble form of the young squire, his polished manners, and eye of fire, rose somewhat too vividly on her recollection at the moment when she saw that wild-flower; and the contrast between the image of her fancy and that of poor Maynard brought back all her aversion to the latter.

She was some time silent, unable to find words that would correspond with her sentiments without wounding him, but, pressed for an answer to his unaffected pleadings, resorted to her former excuse "that she was too young, and did not wish to marry yet."

"It must be so then," said Maynard, sighing. "And yet—Oh! Ruth"—His heart at that moment heaved almost to bursting.

Ruth felt the strong arm tremble that her hand rested upon, and as she raised her eyes to his face she saw a tear trickling there. Much she compassionated the pain she was giving as far as she could understand, but as yet Ruth was ignorant of that bitterest anguish, unrequited love, and was as much inclined to wonder at its manifestations as to sympathise with its pangs.

They arrived at the mill. Perhaps Maynard nourished some idea, that the sight of its comforts might work a favourable impression on his companion; and so they did, but not enough to conquer her strong repugnance to a matrimonial engagement with him. Kitty received our young heroine with manners determinedly framed to assure her that, as, yet the individual to whom she spoke was second in authority in the mill, and would make good her position as long as that was possible. Leading Ruth to her own white and comfortable bedroom, and waiting while the latter removed the bonnet from her sunny curls, replied to a remark on the extreme neatness of every thing, in her own elegant phraseology—

"Why yes, Mr. Maynard, I thinks, will hardly mend himself in that respect howsomdever he may in any other."

And then sailed out of the room in her silk gown, coral necklace, and huge flaunting cap, like a moving mountain, Ruth following in her shadow with a raised complexion.

It is extremely painful to ingenuous youth to be the object of dislike, and Ruth felt that causelessly she was with Kitty. Every word that vulgar woman addressed to her, and every turn of her countenance, though artfully concealed from the dull perception of Maynard, was calculated to inform Ruth how deep, how inveterate was her jealous malice. Instinctively Ruth shrank from her as from some loathsome creature whose fangs were wetted for her destruction; and her pure mind revolted from the disgusting servility and corrupt blandishments with which this woman sought to inveigle the affections of her master.

Maynard liked Kitty from having been long habituated to her society, and because she studied all his domestic likings; and if he ever suspected that she aspired to a higher place in his home and heart than he had allotted to her, he only smiled at her

vanity, deeming it worth no farther notice.   Perhaps at the same time, unknown to himself, the solitary bachelor was soothed by the thought one woman in the world could entertain an attachment for him, though that one, unhappily, was not her on whom he had set his heart.   He would have been little soothed, however, could he have understood the truth, namely—that Kitty's attachment was not to her master's person, but to his money.   This he did not see.

"Poor Kitty," he said to Ruth, after the latter returned to the sitting room, "gives herself lofty airs, and dresses something too smartly for her station—but she is a good woman in the main, and would rather serve me than the vicar.   I don't know what I should do without Kitty."

What could Ruth answer?   She saw he was completely in a delusion respecting his housekeeper's character, but it would not be becoming in her to endeavour to withdraw the scales from his eyes, and walking to the window, as a relief from the topic, her gaze fell on the park of Rosedale, whose dense and grateful foliage at the distance of half a mile from the mill more than half concealed the ruinous battlements of the house.   From the park a zig-zag lane, deep cut between lofty banks of earth overgrown with bushes, conducted past the mill, and where the town road merged in the lane Ruth beheld her parents and brother and sister approaching,   Maynard went out to meet them, ordering Kitty, as he went, to bring up dinner.

At the first entrance of Mrs. Summerfield, Ruth too well understood, by the death-like hue of her fascinating features and the wandering of her eye, what it had cost her to leave the cottage with her secrets unguarded, and she could not refrain from saying to her father, anxiously—

"I am afraid mother was hardly well enough to come."

"She would have been worse to stay," said Summerfield, with significance, adding for Ruth's ear alone, "Who was to remain with her?—you know she would be terrified to be left alone."

"I would," said Ruth, "as Sally and Billy were so eager to come.   I would not have minded it at all."

"But I should," said Summerfield.   "No, Maynard has received too many denials from us lately, and in this trifling matter I was determined he should be pleased."

"Come, friend Roger—come, dame," cried the miller, cordially- "here is a prime goose, and one of Kitty's best pear pies, and a gallon of her home-brewed, as clear and strong as any you could get at the Three Crowns.   Mrs. Summerfield, take the head of the table here and carve for us."

I am no carver," said Mrs. Summerfield, languidly; and, to save further debate, Kitty, nothing loth, took the post of honour herself, and maintained it with an affection of considerable stateliness.

The pleasures of a good dinner are not confined to the gourmand or the epicure; the poor who fare hardly have more keen enjoyment in an abundant and savoury meal than can be imagined by those whose envied lot it is to fare every day sumptuously. We shall not say how the children revelled in the pie—how even the solemn dignity of Summerfield relaxed under the influence of Sir John Barleycorn—or how his wife became gradually inspirited by the sight of her children's glee. Jokes went round, but they would sound dull in the repetition notwithstanding the mirth they excited. Each heart was cheered; and the smiles that wreathed themselves over the housekeeper's coarse but not unhandsome features were less false than usual. The cloth having been removed, a dessert of strawberries and cream, nuts, apples, and blackberry-jam, and mince pies, bestrewed the table, and Maynard, drawing his chair closer to that of Ruth, rested his arm affectionately on the back, while he whispered in her ear.

That action called forth all the malevolence of Kitty's nature, and being invited by her master to drink of the sparkling ale, she filled a glass slowly, and as she raised it to her lips, said—

"My duty to you, Mr. Maynard, and I hopes your intended may meet all the happiness I wish her;" subjoining, in her secret mind, "and that will be little enough."

The miller was elated with the toast.

"I wish, Kitty," he said, "that this dear girl here would give me leave to thank you in her name. But she detests me. So hateful am I to her, that rather than she will have me she will be a servant to others. Don't you think that hard for me to bear?"

"Oh, Miss Ruth knows how to make a bargain, I dares to say," replied the eloquent housekeeper, still more aggravated at finding that our heroine could reject what she, with all her cunning arts, had not been able to gain.

Maynard was not so dull but that he could understand the spirit of this remark, and would have resented it, had not a loud and rapid knock at the parlour door arrested his attention. Mrs. Summerfield started, and grasped the arm of her husband, who himself changed countenance at the unexpected appearance of the young Squire of Rosedale.

CHAPTER VI.

"His graceful form was middle size;
For feat of strength, or exercise,
    Shaped in proportion fair;
And hazel was his eagle eye,
And auburn of the darkest dye
    His short curled beard and hair.
Light was his footstep in the dance,
And, oh! he had that merry glance
    That seldom lady's heart resists.
Lightly from fair to fair he flew,
And loved to plead, lament, and sue;
Suit lightly won, and short-lived pain;
For seldem did he sigh in vain."—SCOTT.

ALL arose at the appearance of the squire, except Mrs. Summerfield and her husband, the former being incapable from internal agitation, and the latter unwilling from pride, or some other feeling nearly akin to it. The pleasure Ruth felt was painted on her cheek and in her eye beyond the possibility of concealment; yet she cast her eyes on the floor—a symptom Clifton did not construe unfavourably.

"Keep your seats, I pray," he frankly and familiarly said, waving his hand. "Maynard, I thought to have found you alone, and looked in to have a social glass with you, and to conclude the debate that was broken off somewhat abruptly when we last met. Our worthy miller, Summerfield, is a strong politician, on the democratic side, and I am anxious to convert him to sounder principles, lest, when I solicit his suffrage for my admission into Parliament, I should find Henry Maynard wanting from my list of friends; a circumstance I should regret."

"So you do think of standing for this borough, one day, squire?" said the miller, drily.

Clifton, with a low courteous bow, dropped easily into a chair Kitty placed for him.

"One day, yes," he answered. "But I am afraid I have broken in on your merriment."

"Not at all," said the miller; "we should be proud of your company. Kitty, hand the squire the fruit and ale. Our pretty Ruth here is going to live under Miss Clifton, and this is a little merry-making in her honour."

"Miss Clifton will be much gratified in so lovely an addition

to her establishment," said the squire, his glances expressing that he should be as gratified as Miss Clifton.

"My daughter is not used to compliment, sir," said Summerfield, in a strong accent, that warned the squire to be careful how he betrayed the admiration he felt.

His desire was to render himself agreeable to the present company, until he had fully ascertained the nature of the engagement actually subsisting between the miller and Ruth, and how far the affections of the latter were concerned in it; and none knew better than he how to adapt himself to high or low, or how exactly to regulate his demeanour with the latter so as, without relinquishing the general polish of an educated gentleman, to place them perfectly at ease. He readily partook of what was presented to him and, entering into the spirit of the meeting, drew forth a cigar to accompany the steaming pipes of Maynard and Summerfield, inquiring—

"What was the amusement going forward, and if there had been no songs or forfeits? Come," said he, "let me be the proposer of something entertaining. Mrs. Summerfield, your daughters can sing, I doubt not?"

"More than I wish sometimes, sir," she replied.

"Then to encourage them to gratify us," said Clifton, "Maynard or myself will make a commencement."

"Well thought of, squire," cried the miller, merrily—"and I care not which of us, for my part."

"Then do you begin," said Clifton; whereupon the miller, laying down his pipe, taking a long drink, and giving a loud "hem" to clear his throat, set the example required; and it cannot be denied that

> "If unmelodious was the song,
> It was a hearty note and strong."

Sally followed with a tolerable specimen of her vocal powers.

Ruth declined, not as some, to enhance the value of compliance, but because, for some inscrutable reason, she felt it would be impossible for her to sing in the presence of the squire.

The latter, then flinging the relics of his expended cigar into the grate, gave the fine Scottish melody of "Roy's Wife," with a bold pathos that searched every heart. At the couplet

> "How happy I if she were mine,
> Or I were Roy of Aldivalloch,"

he threw into his manner an expression which Ruth might justly have applied to herself. Whether she did or no the song moved her exceedingly, and, as he ceased, the tremulous exclamation "how beautiful!" escaped unconsciously from her lips.

Clifton's fine voice and musical taste had been often praised by the gay and fair, but never had flattering encomium given him the pleasure that he now received from this simple and heartfelt exclamation of the humble maiden before him. Again and again he sang, all his soul breathing through the matchless melodies he selected. At one moment, his voice swelled to the loftiest pitch the confined limits of the room rendered agreeable, at another suspended the listener's breathing by the tender sentiment its soft and lingering tones conveyed.

"There," he said, as he came to a final pause, and lit his second cigar. "I have zealously acquitted myself, as I trust you will acknowledge."

"We are much obliged to you, squire," said the miller. "What d'ye say, Ruth, we don't hear singing like that every day."

"Oh! no," ejaculated Ruth; and the miller was hurt by the fervency of the response, and internally muttered—

"I never heard her praise so warmly any thing that ever I did, though some of my actions have been worth a million such songs."

Ruth saw he was discomposed.

"Let us hear you again," she gently said.

"No, no, Ruth," said poor Maynard, his face deeply crimsoned, "soft words and fine singing I shall never excel in, and I leave them to others more fortunate."

"Your bride-elect must not escape so," said Clifton.

"How has it reached your ears, squire, that I have been thinking of a bride?" asked the miller.

"Common report," replied the squire.

"Common report must have swift wings, then. Yet why should I deny the truth? Yes, squire, after living so long a sensible man I have turned fool at last."

"You have a fair excuse at least," said Clifton, glancing more ardently on Ruth than Maynard liked.

"It was not only because Ruth was fair that I loved her," the latter said, "but because she was a good and dutiful girl to her parents, and for another reason that I have never yet told."

"Let us know it by all means," said Clifton.

The cottager and his wife expressed curiosity; Kitty, occupied at a cupboard behind, loitered to listen; only Ruth was indifferent.

"It is twenty years (a long time to look back)," began the miller, replenishing his pipe with tobacco, "since Roger Summerfield and I first came acquainted. At that time you, dame, lived with your mother on Thornwood side, and a livelier, prettier lass, the sun never shone on. You have not forgotten how many

admirers you had, but perhaps this is the first time of your learning that Harry Maynard was among the number."

"You!" exclaimed Mrs. Summerfield, excessively surprised, and her husband repeated the monosyllable. "Why you were only a boy!"

"I was eighteen, and you sixteen," said Maynard.

"But I hardly recollect our exchanging a word" said Mrs. Summerfield.

"Perhaps not; you were too much taken up with my friend Roger. I was shy and awkward, and never told my love—he was bold, forward and clever. So he carried off the prize, and I turned for consolation to business. That is one half of my story. Well, for ten or twelve years, I never crossed your threshold, and only saw you now and then at church, field, or market. Ruth after that came often to the mill for meal and malt, and I took delight in the young creature; and as she shot up into the pretty girl that now sits beside me, I loved her both for her mother's sake and her own —I might add, for her father's too, since Roger in his young days was a brother to me."

"And I have since found you more than a brother to me!" exclaimed Summerfield, much affected. "But my daughter shall recompence you for all."

Clifton closely observed Ruth at this moment; she was speechless, and he detected in her looks fear and aversion to the proposed match. This discovery delighted him without any just reason. Nevertheless, from the little history the miller had given of the origin of his love, Clifton learnt how firmly Maynard's mind was fixed on Ruth, and his natural rectitude told him how dishonorable it would be to seek to cross him in his hopes. But while sensible of this, a flame of passion for the beautiful cottager, to which obstacles only served as fuel, began to be lighted in his heart.

"So this lovely creature," he thought, "is to be sacrificed to an unsuccessful lover of her mother—a man who, by his own confession, is older than one of her parents, and I am convinced not much younger than the other. Preposterous!"

He abruptly left his seat, and took his hat from the peg on which Kitty had hung it. The miller had no desire to detain him, and Summerfield and his wife longed to be relieved of his presence. Not so Ruth. To her his departure was like the extinguishing of the sun, and his voice lingered on her ear like the strains of an archangel.

As Clifton was bidding good evening a thought occurred to him.

"Summerfield," he said, "you and your wife, and Maynard here,

were living in Rosedale at the period when a certain mysterious and painful event took place, in which I am deeply interested, and I have never yet personally inquired of you relative to your remembrance of it, though it has been long in my mind to do so."

"You allude to your father's disappearance?" said Maynard.

"I do. And if the least clue could be obtained, at any cost, by which his fate might be ascertained, and his assassins brought to justice, it would be both to me and Miss Clifton a great relief."

The miller shook his head.

"The squire was a desperately bad character," he said—"no offence to you, Mr. Clifton—and it is impossible to guess how or where he may have perished. Perhaps by the hand of some who have since graced a gallows, or been transported to the other side of the world. His companions were the worst of both sexes."

"But is it not remarkable that literally no trace of his fate should be left? There was on his person at the time of his being missed a valuable gold watch and—"

"A gold watch" echoed Ruth, (inaudibly, as it fortunately happened). And who can imagine her sensations of astonishment, suspicion, and horror, as she received the conviction that the watch concealed by her parents in the cottage shed had belonged to the missing Squire Clifton!

The powerful eye of her father was, however, upon her, and seemed to say—"Now has the trying moment come of which I warned you—now is your firmness tested—and our lives depend upon your self-command!"

And she did command herself, although a cold tremor ran through all her veins. And Clifton was going on to say that there had been about his father at his disappearance, in addition to the watch, a diamond ring and several bank notes, and that he had been last seen crossing at night a meadow called the "barley close," which was situated very near Summerfield's cottage, when Mrs. Summerfield was suddenly taken ill, and sank gasping into her husband's arms. She was removed into a chamber, and laid on a bed, and all were busied in her recovery excepting Clifton, who presently found an opportunity to say to Maynard, apart—

"Can you understand what is the cause of this poor woman's melancholy state of health?"

"No more than you, squire," replied Maynard. "She was once as different a being as you can imagine. It was three or four years after her marriage, as near as I can remember, when I heard that she had fallen into a nervous fever that confined her to her bed twelve months, since that time she has been subject to

fits, faintings, and odd delusions, and takes unaccountable dislikes, not only to persons, but to things and places. I have seldom seen her so melancholy and wild looking though as during this afternoon.

"It occurs to me that I am one of the persons to whom she entertains an antipathy, and that her husband shares in it," said Clifton.

"Perhaps," said the miller, "in the matter of the rent they think you were too sharp upon them—I own that I do."

"Too sharp!—I am surprised! Unless I had given them the cottage rent free I could hardly have been less so. The indulgence they received was such as few landlords would have granted, and they would have been ejected long ere this. The fact is, Mr. Maynard, I should have insisted on their rent being paid by the week, instead of allowing it to accumulate to a sum which the nature of their occupation rendered it impossible they could liquidate. This has been my error, but it shall be remedied in future."

"Squire," said Maynard, "if Summerfield could have occupied a house of yours without any reasonable prospect of paying for it, I should despise him; but the man is of a very different stamp, as you might have known. One more strictly honest, aye, to the very heart's core, you never met with. A host of troubles beset him during the last two years, or you would have had your rent without making a second application for it. He has lived very long in that cottage of yours, and was never complained of before for tardiness of payment—at least that ever I heard of."

"You are right," said Clifton; "but why should I lose six pounds because he had made payments before?"

"No one wished it; but I will speak my mind openly and fearlessly like a true-born Briton, and tell you, Squire Clifton, that if he had been my tenant as long as he has been yours, and I knew it was through misfortune only his rent was unpaid, I would rather have lost the six pounds than have sent to drag the poor man's goods from him."

"Possibly you might," said Clifton, coldly. "And I assure you, whatever you or the Summerfields may think of my severity, it gave me no more pleasure than yourself. Nevertheless, it was perfectly plain that a summary process was the only mode by which the payment could be enforced, and that prolonged delay could be productive of no good to the cottagers."

"You would think otherwise if you had ever known what it was to be left in a bare house with a sickly wife and family," muttered the miller, as Mrs. Summerfield, leaning on her hus-

band's arm, re-entered the parlour, still marble pale, but sufficiently restored to walk home. Summerfield, now almost fondly attentive to her, shook hands cordially with Maynard, excusing himself for taking leave.

"It was necessary his wife should be at home," he said, "but Ruth and her sister would finish the evening at the mill, and Henry would have the kindness to see them safe over the fields." He then "wished his honour the squire a good day ;" but when Clifton, simply as a test of the cottager's feelings toward him, familiarly stretched out his hand, Summerfield passed as if he had not observed the motion.

The aristocratic blood in the squire's veins boiled over.

"I have done the fellow too much honour !" he exclaimed— "but he shall not refuse my courtesy a second time,"

Maynard had gone out with his elder guests before these indignant words were pronounced, but Ruth heard them, and felt them not undeserved, for she considered that her parents were singularly unjust to Mr. Clifton. The wrath of the squire subsided as he beheld her near him alone.

"Do you," he said, his voice trembling between passion and pride, "share in your parent's aversion to me ?"

"No, indeed."

"Then why—" began Clifton, about to add—" why did your father refuse——? " but the insolence of that act from a mere field-labourer like Summerfield was too much for words. "Believe me," he said, "not to you or your LOVER" (the word was scornfully pronounced) " would I condescend to vindicate what I have done, or to make known what my full intentions were. But to you I will say that my design was, when it had been clearly proved that your father could not obtain the money without the sacrifice of his goods, to have forbade the distraint."

"Oh !" she exclaimed, "I knew others could be generous as well as the miller."

"The miller's generosity ! " repeated Clifton, "the miller's generosity ! What was his generosity but self-interest ? "

Maynard's generosity had before lost its lustre in Ruth's eyes, by a view of the price she was expected to pay for it. Still she was visited by some compunctious feelings on his behalf.

"He has often assisted us," she said.

"And who that had it in his own power would not render such assistance a hundred times over to gain you ? " said Clifton.

THE BIRD FLEW DIRECT TO THE BOSOM OF THE COTTAGE GIRL.

THE COTTAGE GIRL.

"I WISH TO LEARN THE CAUSE OF THESE TEARS," EXCLAIMED MISS CLIFTON.

RUTH deeply blushed; and Maynard returning, the young squire found just time to say to her:

"Do not let them detain you from Rosedale House;" and then with more distant manners than he had entered, quitted the mill. But he loitered near at hand, to obtain another glimpse of Ruth. Night came on dark and cloudy. Every minute the mill grew more black and ponderous, and the wind crept by in September's withering leaves with the voice of decay and mourning. It was cold, too, and Clifton shivered, buttoned his coat closer, and walked more sharply to and fro. At length three figures descended the external steps of the mill, crossed the mill-stream, passed without perceiving him, and a creaking gate admitted them into the fields. Clifton, in the dark, remained with his face turned on that gate some minutes after they had disappeared.

"Extraordinary fascination!" he mused, at broken intervals, "How is it that I am thus enslaved by a simple uncultivated girl? I hardly exist where she is not. My soul strains after her as though it would burst its prison. Wherever I go, her beaming face—her sweet simplicity—her delicate shape—her gossamer step—her chaste yet loving eye—haunt me unremittingly! I can think of nothing—hear of nothing—dream of nothing but Ruth! What is to be the end of this?—'aye, there's the rub.' Why do I wish her at Rosedale House? What good is to come of that to myself or her?"

Clifton started forward along the park-road toward his home without finding himself able to elucidate these problems of conscience.

CHAPTER VII.

" Wildly he roamed, as mountain blast
Worthless as leaves before it cast
   The follies he pursued ;
But fiercest whirlwinds sink to rest,
And pure affection in the breast
   Can sway the wildest mood.

" Her lot, to love, to laugh, to dream,
At ease to float down life's gay stream
   In the bright morning ray ;
She little recks what storms will rise,
Nor fears the stream, which sparkling lies,
   Can glisten to betray."—BALDWIN.

PERCY CLIFTON, when his father so strangely disappeared fourteen years before, was at the age of six. By that time the groundwork of character is generally laid, and never were more pains taken to form a worse one than in that of the boy Percy. Between his parents there had been unceasing war, and his possessing the love of one was sufficient to procure him the dislike of the other. He was indeed the idol of his father, who never allowed his dominating spirit to be curbed in the least degree, and knew no better enjoyment than to see the handsome child transported with fury at some trifling contradiction—flinging about glass and china—kicking the servants—and imitating, in half-formed accents, the squire's customary oaths. Percy was not to be educated in any vulgar mode, but in a bold and novel manner, after his father's own heart. He was to be the hater and derider of his mother—the scorner of all things commonly held sacred—a renouncer of study and moral restraint—and to live chiefly for the turf and the wine-cup.

This admirable scheme had hardly commenced when the squire was missing. Percy was thenceforth to be subjugated to treatment very different. He was sent to a high class academy, and might have got on very well but that the superior and he differed in one particular—Percy would govern himself, the master insisted on governing him; when the contest arrived at a certain pitch, the young heir of Rosedale House was expelled.

Percy was next entrusted to the management of a reverend gentleman in Wales, whose orders were, to " break his spirit by strict coercion." But the clergyman was wiser, and by firm and gentle treatment during four years, succeeded in eradicating some of the poisonous shoots which the profligate and ignorant squire, and the unskilful academician, had implanted in the boy.

In his twelfth year, Percy was unfortunately deprived, by death, of this first judicious friend of his youth, and returned home, after a long absence, expecting the plaudits of his mother for his progress in learning and manners—expecting the fond reception due to an only son. He was sadly disappointed. Mrs. Clifton was unwilling to believe any good of one whose every look and feature reminded her of the tyrant she had lost. Toward Percy, her affections were cold as December's snow.

The boy felt his mother's dislike the more acutely, because to his sister she was extravagantly partial, and his full heart, denied its natural outlet, soon overflowed in irregular channels.

"See," Mrs. Clifton would exclaim to her pitying friends, as the youth advanced towards manhood, " what an unfortunate woman am I! Percy is treading in his father's steps—he behaves to me with insolence—he is never happy but when revelling with libertine companions!"

It seemed, indeed, but too probable that the profligate courses of the elder Clifton would be emulated by the younger; though had the mother of Percy been competent to judge her own conduct, she would have been aware that she herself had chiefly been the means of precipitating her son upon them. Her sudden

death, when he was at the age of nineteen, acted, however, as a
check upon his growing licentiousness. In the hour of dissolution she called him to her bedside, and bade him a moderately-
affectionate farewell; and even then, it was chiefly her anxiety
for Amy that softened her heart toward him.

"My daughter," she said, " has been my sole comfort; with
your father I knew not one day's peace; of yourself I will say
nothing. But I forgive all the trouble you have occasioned me,
on the condition that you promise to be a tender brother to my
orphan girl. She will have none but you to protect her—
none but you to love her."

"Make yourself easy," said Percy; " my sister shall always
find me affectionate to her while her conduct merits it."

He then urgently inquired if she had left anything undone
which she could imagine it was possible might lead to the discovery of his father's fate. Her reply was decisively in the negative. Greatly as she detested her husband's memory, she had
been indefatigable in pursuing the inquiry after him, and nothing
remained to be attempted that presented the least mark of likelihood.

Mrs. Clifton died, and the two orphans, in the prime of youth,
were left sole occupants of Rosedale Park. Prior to this, there
had been little interchange of affection between them; on the
contrary, their mother's partiality had nearly made them hate
each other; but now they all at once became dear friends. Percy
was pleased by the docility with which his sister yielded to all
his wishes, (for he had not yet learned to brook contradiction);
loved her for her warm heart; admired her refined and poetic
mind; and felt grateful for the indulgence she extended to his
errors.

On Amy's part, it was a surprise to find that her brother could
really love her, and little else was required to attach her to him.
She was of an easy, happy, indolent turn of mind—very gay, and
very visionary. The education of Miss Clifton had been conducted by a governess of a highly romantic but shallow intellect,
who, instead of wisely directing the vivid imagination of her
pupil, and instructing her judgment to regulate it, indulged her
without restraint in fiction and poetry, and left her at nineteen
with a heart wholly unprepared against the delusions of fancy and
the world, and with notions of human nature as opposite as possible to the reality. Hence Miss Clifton, pure and intellectual as
she was, was liable to make perilous mistakes in love and friendship.

At the period, then, of this narrative's commencement, the

high energies, and enterprising and courageous spirit of Percy, which in the military or civil service of his country, would have raised him to eminence, were expended on the idle pursuit of pheasants, woodcocks, and grouse. He had a passion for the country—but it was only as a place to shoot birds in. The effervescence of his ardent nature overflowed in mirthful company, but a regard for his sister)s delicacy restrained those indulgencies within the nicest bounds of decorum. He professed to make honour his guide, but we shall presently see how it deserted him in temptation.

The habits of Amy were irregular. She was seldom out of her dressing-room before mid-day; and invariably spent some part of those hours when the rest of the world were asleep in the perusal of her favourite authors, or in strolling alone over the old house. Her harp or guitar might be heard when all other sounds were at rest. And if her health suffered, she had not strength to resist the luxuries so dear to her. In dress she was alternately negligent and magnificent—grave and gay,—just as the sentiment of the moment prompted.

The balance between her reason and imagination was most unequal. Her companions were chosen with no caution or knowledge of life, and her soul was given up to them as if their's were all that earth or heaven could wish, instead of being actuated by a hundred meannesses, jealousies, envyings, and so on, all through the sad catalogue of human nature's frailties.

Aptly the motto at the head of this chapter applies to Amy, whose sole occupation and delight was—

> ———" To love, to laugh, to dream,
> At ease to float down life's gay stream
> In the bright morning ray."

Her want of worldly foresight too is aptly expressed—

> " She little recks what storms will rise,
> Nor fears the stream, which sparkling lies,
> Can glisten to betray."

It will have to be seen to what painful events her mistakes led and how momentously they wrought on the destiny of our cottage heroine.

CHAPTER VIII.

"Alas! from the day that we met.
    What hope of an end to my woes?
When I cannot endure to forget
    The glance that undid my repose."

THE forenoon was one of September's loveliest, when Ruth parted from her mother to take up her abode at Rosedale House. Her father was harvesting in a field through which she had to pass on her way. Maynard, in his miller's frock, stood at the door with a disquieted brow, and gave a brief "good bye" to her as she tripped away with her bandbox and bundle. Mrs. Summerfield shut herself in her chamber after Ruth had gone, to grieve alone over the loss of her daughter's society, and the choice she had made of living under the Cliftons. Even Sally looked sad, and ejaculated with a sigh—

" How dull we shall be without Ruth!" while the miller sat silently down by the cottage fire, and in a solacing pipe of tobacco strove to forget the aching of his heart.

In the barley field Summerfield saw his daughter approaching. and, drawing on his coat and joining her, walked by his side to the park gate. Not a word of the hidden watch or the missing Squire Clifton escaped him ; and Ruth, feeling his silence designed, durst not introduce the mysterious subject, though it was uppermost in her mind. He gave her much advice respecting her conduct, and, as she turned into a carriage way winding through a plantation by which the house was approached, uttered these emphatic words :—

" You are as the apple of mine eye, Ruth ! but rather than see you in any way act unworthy of me I would bury you this day !"

" Why should you doubt me, father ?" Ruth asked. " Have you not taught me to love all that is good, and shun all that is evil ?"

" I have striven to do so, my child," said Summerfield, " and God forbid I should have a doubt of thy forsaking the way in which I have led thee. Yet I could wish it was to some other house you were going. I may have done foolishly in giving my consent ; it may be a dangerous step on many accounts. I am not easy about it."

Strong misgivings shook the frame of Summerfield, and after all, Ruth feared her wishes would be prohibited. Her sprightly look was changed directly to one of disappointment; but the word of her father, once given, was never recalled, and after a minute of dubious reflection, he said—

"It is too late now for me to draw back. You like this situation—I have consented—there is no more to be said."

But Ruth instantly desired to show him that she could conquer her inclinations.

"If you don't like me to live under Miss Clifton, I will not," said she. "You shall take my box, father, and wait here while I go and excuse myself to her."

"Good girl!" said Summerfield, with paternal pride and pleasure; and Ruth tasted a more exquisite gratification in his approval than any selfish pleasure could have given her, and the rather because he seldom praised and never without just occasion. Nor was the cottager one to take advantage of the filial affection of the daughter. Her ready and cheerful concession having partially soothed his doubts and relieved his anxiety, he hastened to reward it by a renewed permission for her to go whither her wishes prompted.

Ruth was then dismissed with a smile and a benediction from the lips she reverenced most on earth.

Approaching the house, she beheld Miss Clifton in a loose white morning wrapper, at the front of the glass door of a conservatory, feeding a tame fawn.

"Good morning," cried the young lady, with a smile and a lively indication of the head. "You are very welcome. Thomas," taking from the footman's hand the silver salver out of which she had been regaling the petted animal, "conduct Ruth Summerfield to the housekeeper's room—Mrs. Wilson has my directions respecting her."

Ruth was charmed with all she beheld. The numerous, intricate, and highly-decorated stairs, passages, and lobbies; the various costly lamps with which they were besprinkled; the plate-glass windows; the paintings, busts, and rich furniture; the self-important looks of the well-dressed domestics, and the lady-like appearance of the housekeeper, all wore to her an air of delightfully awful novelty, and she could hardly believe that the master of such splendour, and so many servants, had condescended the day before to sit down in the mill familiarly, and amuse her parents, Maynard and herself, with beautiful songs.

A few days sobered these exaggerated impressions, and Ruth at times was not sure but she would have preferred her home.

Her sleeping closet communicated with Miss Clifton's dressing-room, and though it was a pleasant room, and looked on spreading trees, green hillocks, flowering hollows, and browsing deer, she was not easily reconciled to it. She missed, at the dawn of day, her own bulfinch, which had been used to waken her in the cottage—missed the kind and merry sister who had shared her pillow—and a depressing sense of loneliness, to which hitherto she had been a stranger, stole over her youthful spirit. The initiation into her duties was formidable, too. She had to learn from the girl whom she was to replace how she was to attend the toilette of her young lady, and perform its mysteries with a ready and rapid hand, and a tasteful eye. Ruth was sensitive and timid, though quick of apprehension, and when her attempts happened to fail, she was presently in tears and longing for home.

A fortnight, however, again changed the complexion of her feelings. She could now dress the hair, dispose the jewels, methodise the wardrobe, and perform all the other et ceteras of her avocation with ease. She had familiarised herself with the house —made friends among the servants—given satisfaction to Miss Clifton—and began to be very happy. Only one cloud—the mystery—was in her horizon; and though that was dark indeed, habit had withdrawn it to a seeming distance, and sanguine hope had over it cast its sunlike hues.

November set in—the black and gloomy November—and Ruth was still happy, so she said, though her eye was often looking on the empty air with a soft, intense, mournful expression, and a slight trembling sigh often escaped her rosy lips; her smile was less animated, less spontaneous; her step had lost much of its buoyancy.

One rainy foggy evening, as she sat with her needlework in Miss Clifton's sitting-room, while that young lady sung with her harp the melody of "Roy's Wife," Ruth dropped her head on her bosom, and her face was suddenly drenched in tears. Miss Clifton remarked her emotion with deep concern, and pushing the harp aside, sat down beside her and took her hand.

"Ruth," she said, "tell me why is this?"

"It is nothing, ma'am," faltered Ruth; "I ask your pardon —I was overcome—you sung so sweetly I could not help it" —and again the tears gushed forth like rain.

"Sit still, Ruth," said Miss Clifton, kindly. "I must know what ails you. I have observed you much these last few weeks, and feel assured there is some other cause for this than you have told me."

"Forgive me," repeated Ruth, half mechanically—"indeed—I could not help it!"

"Help what?"

"Interrupting you."

"Nonsense; I wish to learn the cause of these tears—this changing colour—this sighing breath."

"Indeed, ma'am, there is no cause—that I know of," said poor Ruth, her colour changing still more rapidly.

"Just look at the girl!" exclaimed Miss Clifton, laughing, "she stands trembling as if I were judging her for life or death! What are you afraid of? Speak to me as a friend—confide in me. You must have seen by this time that I would do any thing within the scope of my ability to promote your happiness. Silent still? Well, then, I will guess at your malady—you are in love. What a start was there! Ye gods, that shaft hit home. But what now, Ruth, have I touched you so deeply?"

Deeply, indeed, the light words of Miss Clifton had penetrated to the heart of Ruth, and, covering her face with her hands, she averted her head. The next moment, as Percy opened one door, our heroine fled from his presence by another, leaving Miss Clifton astonished at the scene which had taken place.

At first, neither brother or sister spoke. A thought, a singular thought, occupied the mind of Amy. Percy appeared entirely engaged with a valuable pointer that had entered in spite of interdict. Finding, however, that his sister continued silent, he asked her, as indifferently as might be—

"Whom his entrance had scared away?"

"Ruth," laconically answered Miss Clifton, and again Percy had to endure a pause of suspense. He walked to the window, humming an air.

"What tune is that?" Miss Clifton inquired.

"Why do you ask?" he said, turning quickly round.

"For a particular reason."

"I heard you practising the same not half an hour ago," said Percy.

"Exactly!" ejaculated Amy, with the look of one who has made a great discovery, or of one who witnesses some highly-wrought scene in a thrilling drama. "Yes—my idea is correct!"

"And why that oracular 'exactly,' my dear Amy? With what new crotchet are you possessed?"

"A very extraordinary one," said Amy; "and if you will close the doors against listeners, I will communicate it."

As Clifton jestingly did so, his dark but clear complexion was richly crimsoned, and he was only able to conceal the intensity of his expectation from his sister by again turning to the window.

" Why don't you come near me and listen ?" she said.   " Perhaps you little dream that what I have to say concerns you."

" Proceed," he said, without altering his position—" I daresay it is something very foolish."

" Since you think so I will not impart it," said Amy, rising and resuming at the harp the song by which Ruth had been so extraordinarily affected.

Percy was extremely provoked.   He was burning with desire to know what had passed between Ruth and his sister, for that something uncommon had, he felt assured, by the hasty flight of the one, and the looks and language of the other.   He stood meditating in the shade of the window drapery, his toe beating an impatient measure on the carpet, his elbow resting on a gilded ornament, and his hand pressed to his heated temples.   Once he attempted to request his sister to make the communication she had announced, but his tongue faltered with a secret consciousness of feelings which, for the world, he would not have had her fathom. He left the room, but soon returned again, as the inconstant Amy, wearied of her harp, was painting in her album from a bouquet of natural flowers before her.

" Amy," he said, " you would soon paint well were you not indolent—that rose is well imitated—the tints are beautiful."

" Not so beautiful as a certain cottage rose we wot of," observed Amy, and Percy congratulated himself that her eye was on her painting brush instead of his kindling cheek at that moment.

So disconcerted was he by this remark, meant to imply he knew not how much, that, although in a fever of suspense, he again turned on his heel.   At the door, however, he vacillated.

" I must know what has passed between them," he muttered; and raising his voice with sudden decision, " Come," said he, " are you disposed to make this disclosure ?"

" No," replied Amy, " I have thought better of it.   You are too much a scorner to be entrusted with it.   You are one of those who lay themselves out to allure, and then despise the beings they have entrammelled.   Get you gone.   You will know nothing from me.   I was in the vein ten minutes ago—now I am not."

" But my dear Amy," said her brother, approaching her persuasively.

" I am deaf.   You would not attend while you might—now the opportunity has passed."

" Tell me. at least, why Ruth fled from me ? and why she was in tears?—as I had just time to perceive when I surprised you both."

" You supplicate in vain."

" Then just say," continued Percy, affectionately pressing the shoulder - of his sister as she leaned laughingly back in her chair, " what connexion the tune of ' Roy's Wife ' had with the matter of your thoughts ?"

" I remembered you enumerating it to me among your performances at the mill on the day when you played the part of Apollo there in the presence of the Summerfields and their host '

" You have an excellent memory, upon my word—it is a month ago since we talked of it."

" A little occurrence to-day brought it into my mind."

" While you were practising the same melody ?"

" Yes."

" In the presence of Ruth ?"

" Yes."

" And did she recollect hearing it from me in the mill ?"

" I am not sufficiently acquainted with her mind to answer that. She was greatly disturbed, however. And, if you must have it, Percy, I entertain a sort of distant suspicion, I hope unfounded, that her regard for her master is of too tender a character."

" Take care—take care what you say," cried Percy, breathlessly, his eye glowing with the splendour of vehement joy, which the quivering tones of his voice confirmed, but his studied words denied. " Remember what the girl is—meanly born—meanly connected—uncultivated—poor !"

" Aye, Percy," said his sister, " but, allow me to say, there have been times when you have appeared to forget it."

Percy laughed, but not without some confusion, assuming that the few trifling familiarities he had shown her were merely natural tributes to her sex and beauty, and involved no serious meaning."

" I am glad to have this explanation," said Amy, " for, I tell you plainly, there have been times when I have not known what to make of your attentions to her. And let me put the question to your conscience, whether this poor girl's affections may not have been deluded by them ?"

" Psha! she is not so foolish as to dream of impossibilities," said Clifton, speaking sharply, to disguise the towering elation of his spirit. " She is not steeped heart and soul in romance, if you are."

" Neither has she been accustomed to flattering familiarities from gentlemen of rank and attainments like yourself, Percy."

" No more of this," said Clifton, hastily—" those familiarities are not worth your remembrance : nor is a chance fit of tears from Ruth a theme important enough to engage my attention. And you must be wary how you suffer such extravagant notions as you have now named to me, to enter your mind, or you may work more mischief than you are aware of. To tell silly girls they are in love is to make them so."

Here, whistling to his pointer, he withdrew to vent his real feelings in privacy, in a room where he was accustomed to spend many of his leisure hours, and entertain his sporting companions, free from the restraints and formalities of the dining and drawing-room. There was a bright fire. The pointer found two companions of its race comfortably sleeping on the hearth-rug. The stately antlers of a stag projected over the wide-spread fireplace. Guns and other implements for destroying game, and some for ensnaring them, hung about the walls; and over the leathern seats of chairs of carved black oak, and on the table of American walnut-wood, newspapers, sporting chronicles, prints of animals, and books, were strewed disorderly. At the farther end of the room hung a large and clever oil-painting of a steeple-chase, whose foremost figure, nearly as large as life, represented the lost Squire Clifton, Percy's father, clearing a ditch on a horse which had once been famous for its high qualities, but now, like its master, slept unseen in dust.

In this room no domestic intruded, on any pretence, without the especial direction of Percy. Hence the dust which clouded the polished surfaces of the tables—hence the cobwebs which stretched their netted fibres at the corners of the vaulted ceiling—hence the darkened windows, and the littered floor. Miss Clifton herself was excluded.

Here, then, Percy was entirely alone—alone with his warring passions;—vehement love—vehement pride—rapturous joy in the conviction that his love was returned—and conscience, that uttered its warning denunciations against the course he was pursuing with clear and impressive tones, but uttered them in vain. The mask of policy which he had deemed it necessary to wear in his conference with his sister was flung off. He breathed heavily—drew loud sighs—indulged in short reveries, from which starting as if struck by electricity, he paced the room, muttering many contradictory expressions in a variety of tones. At length, stopping before the fire, fixing his eyes on the flames, and folding his arms, Clifton suffered his distracted thoughts to shape themselves into one desperate resolve.

"Marriage is impossible! I cannot stoop to it. Yet I must have her! Some may call me a villain; my dear, amiable, blinded sister, may despise and hate me; Ruth's friends will curse me;

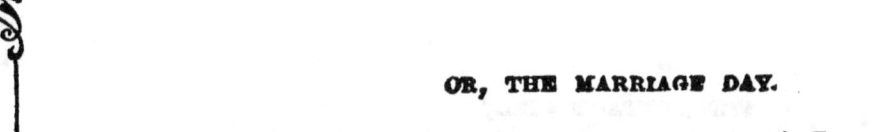

I shall curse myself. But I must have her! I am floating on a swift, and irresistible current, and let it bear me whither it may, onward I go!"

As he spoke he rang for his valet—a sly, insinuating Frenchman, aged about twenty-five, who, for sordid interest, was ready to place all the heart and soul he had—and that was not much—at any one's command, for any purpose. In all the world there was not a wretch more basely devoted to selfish interest than Jean Andre. Yet he was an accomplished servant, understood his business well, readily took a hint, knew when to talk and when to be silent, was quick and wary in all his movements, and could lie and flatter himself into the confidence of his superiors with excellent address. It was rather to be wondered at that, with so many advantages, Jean had not been able to retain, for any length of time, the situations on which he had embarked during his seven years' residence in England.

The summons of his master, on the present occasion, Jean answered with fawning servility in his attitude, promptness in his speech, and sharp sagacity in his small ferret eyes. His first glance of Clifton's countenance conveyed to his ready discernment an intimation of some secret service required; and, carefully closing the door behind him, he waited patiently and quietly until it should be unfolded.

"Jean " said the young squire, " hand out the claret."

The valet crossed the room to a cupboard, produced a bottle, uncorked and decanted it, placed a single glass, stirred the fire, snuffed the candles, and again stood in a waiting posture.

" Is Ruth in attendance on Miss Clifton ?" asked the squire, and Jean answered in easy English—

" I believe so, sir."

Percy drew a small gold snuff-box from his waistcoat pocket, and a half-sovereign rolled over the carpet.

" Keep it," said the latter, as Jean hastened to pick up and present the stray coin.

" Shall I send Ruth here, sir ?" inquired the valet.

" Why, yes—if you see an opportunity."

Jean Andre understood, and glided away.

Half an hour at least had passed, when a slow and hesitating step, so light as to be inaudible to any but the listening ear of Clifton, approached along the narrow carpeted gallery without. Opening the door, he drew the faultering, blushing Ruth into the room.

" Jean bade me come, sir," she said, not daring to look in his face, and laving one hand tenaciously on the door handle. " He

said you had to give me something for Miss Clifton."

"Perhaps I have. But why is Ruth so fearful of me? Look up. Eyes so bright were not made to be veiled beneath lids however fair. I am afraid you hate me."

"Hate you, sir!"

"Yes; or why did you fly my presence to day?—and why do you now stand trembling as if I were something hideous?"

"Oh! sir, give me my orders for Miss Clifton, if you please, and let me go!" exclaimed Ruth.

"You must tell me first why you hate me."

"Oh, sir, if you please, don't detain me. My poor father!— my poor father!"

"Why that pitiful exclamation?"

Ruth could not answer.

"Why do you think of your father at this moment? I have not injured him, and would do much for him for your sake."

Clifton, while speaking, gently detached the hand of our heroine from the door handle, and pressed it within his own.

"Ruth," he said, incoherently, and in a voice full of passion, "sweet Ruth! I love you. My soul lives on you! No woman on earth is half so dear to me or ever shall be. Do you believe me?—tell me if you believe me."

Ruth raised her face, now pale as death, and as she sharply disengaged her hand, angrily exclaimed—

"Mr. Clifton, how can you talk of love to one so poor and ignorant as I am? I will leave this house to-morrow. I—"

"And if you do," interrupted Percy, "you will not escape me. But can love only be found where circumstances are equal? I know at this moment, unkindly as you look and speak, that your heart responds to mine. You love me, little tormentor—I have seen it often—I see it now."

Overborne by this charge, which her truth and simplicity alike prevented her from denying, Ruth wept in painful confusion and distress, and suffered herself to be drawn to a seat by Percy's encircling arm. By degrees he re-assured her, though her downy eyelashes still continued to veil their pure and liquid orbs, from which a sparkling tear at times descended over the celestial red and white of her softly rounded cheeks.

"You have made me suffer a thousand fiery torments!" he said. "Never shall I forget the day when first your beauty impressed itself on my heart, and decided its happiness or misery for life. You had not a glance for me, or one of no more than mere momentary interest, while I could have worshipped you! At a distance I followed your steps; and your shape and movements, as

well as your face, lived from that hour in my thoughts as those of an angel! Daily I watched, after that, for opportunities of beholding again those incomparable charms by which I had been so fascinated. When I visited your parents' cottage, the lovely tenderness and patience you manifested toward your unhappy and irritable mother enchanted me with the conviction that Ruth Summerfield possessed a heart as beautiful as her person. But who was to possess this rare person? Maynard of the Mill? Could he appreciate her? Ruth, when I heard you intended to marry him, I was delirious with jealous suffering. I had no rest until I had ascertained, to my infinite relief, that your affections were not in his keeping, and that with a spirit and determination marking your natural superiority of mind, you had refused him—thousand pounds and all."

"Mr. Maynard is a kind man," said Ruth, faintly; and she could not refrain from an involuntary sigh of regret that she had not been able to recompense his kindness; perhaps, also, she felt a cold foreboding fear lest the happiness resulting from her present attachment, though it might be more exquisite, might prove more transitory also, than that which an alliance with the steady unselfish miller had promised, could she have reconciled herself to it.

"I can afford to do his good qualities justice now I am assured they will not prevail on you to become his wife," said Clifton. "Yes, I grant the miller is a kindly man, ready to serve a friend in need, upright in his dealings, independent, and jovial. I have shared many a friendly glass with him, and hope to share many more. In his sphere he is all he should be; but you, my lovely Ruth! are entitled, by the advantages with which nature has endowed you, to look up to a higher! How I should delight to see these charming proportions fitted with apparel more worthy of them—this hair wreathed with pearls—these hands glistening with rubies. And it shall not be very long before all these things, and more, shall be at your command, if you will only love me."

"My father always taught me to despise gay dress," said Ruth, timorously, though a smile of ineffable joy began to mingle over her face.

"Your father, Ruth, is a man of tillage, not of taste," said Clifton; "you must rise above his narrow prejudices and adapt your ideas to higher modes of life than he has been accustomed to. I repeat it, you shall be a lady if you will love me."

"I do—I always shall!" she said, in a low, but distinct voice, her face again covered with blushes, each intenser than the last.

Clifton was transported with her modest, yet frank, avowal

but its very directness awed and subdued the boldness of his passion. He felt himself in the presence of perfect, unsuspecting, heavenly chastity, and its influence revived the better impulses of his soul, so that for his life he could not offer her the smallest rudeness. Swept away by this new current, he all at once resolved to abandon his iniquitous purposes, and to immolate pride at the shrine of pure love. Why not? Others had done so whom history had recorded in the annals of noble families. She would not be the first who had been elevated from a lowly condition.

Visions of virtuous happiness with the spotless being whom he now pressed in his arms, swam before his mental eye in colours bright as heaven. No—he could not deceive her, and inly he swore that he never would. Reviving sincerity unlocked the deepest fountains of his spirit, which poured themselves out to her in eloquent vows of eternal devotion, and rapturous and elevated homage. He spoke to her of the educational preparations he wished her to make for the station to which he designed to raise her; sportively he made her exhibit to him her present proficiency in common attainments, and promised her, as soon as they should be married, instructors in all the branches of polite education.

Ruth literally believed every word the squire said to her— literally trusted to every protestation he made, and to every promise for the future.

She could not dream of peril, because she had no knowledge of vice.

That Clifton could vow one hour and repent the next, she could not understand, because her own affection was even and constant as the light of day. And that in one who looked so true, and spoke so fair, there could be any evil, she was too young, inexperienced, and untaught to comprehend. And if it seemed marvellous that he, high-born, a scholar, the companion of the great, the wealthy, and the fair, the master of Rosedale House, could stoop to a marriage with her, she satisfied herself with the argument of a fond woman, that if he were poor and she rich, it would have been her greatest joy to prove her love by sharing all with him.

She told him this.

"I believe it, for your sex are more capable of sacrifices for love than ours. But man has much to uphold in this world, And I, Ruth, though I now waste my hours in love, shall not rest until I am great in fortune, great in influence, great in reputation, and have gained your love, dear Ruth."

"BREATHLESS, RUTH SUFFERED PERCY TO SUPPORT HER."

THE COTTAGE GIRL.

SINKING HIS FACE ON THE BACK OF HIS CHAIR, HE WAVED HIS HAND FOR HER
TO LEAVE HIM.

"I SHOULD not have thought there had been anything in the world you could have wished for more than you have."
"Excepting you, you should have added," said Clifton, with increased animation and warmth, pressing his lips to her cheek; "and were you once my wife, I might, perhaps, live on without desiring, at least without seeking, more. I might, perhaps, renounce the restless wishes after unattainable objects with which

manhood has cursed me   I might be content to wile away my
time to the end in fireside joys, and woodland sports.   I wish the
experiment were tried !   If it could be, I would have us married
this very hour.   There is danger in delay."

"What danger ?" doubtfully inquired Ruth, looking tenderly
in his face.   A fierce light was gli tering there, but in a moment
it vanished.

"By Heaven ! I will do thee no wrong," he exclaimed, straining her more tightly in his arms, and then putting her from him.
"My wife, and nothing else, you shall be !"

"And what else could I be, sir ?" demanded Ruth, stepping
back from him in instinctive alarm.

"Nothing but what is pure and exquisite !" ardently exclaimed
Clifton, again drawing her, in spite of resistance, upon his knee—
"nothing but what, under any name, I must love for ever !"

" Mr. Clifton !—sir !—let me go, or I will call for help !" exclaimed Ruth, alarmed by his fiery caresses, and the wild glittering of his eye.

He immediately loosed her, and sinking his face on the back
of the chair waved his hand for her to leave him.

"You are right," he said, "I am not be trusted with you.   My
sister will have missed you—retire."

Trembling from head to foot, wondering, doubtful, astonished,
angry, yet, most of all, fearful of having given him offence, the
poor girl turned to the door, where she lingered a moment under
these contending feelings.

The supreme happiness which, a few minutes before, seemed
so certain, now appeared dubious.   She questioned whether all
that had passed was not an unsubstantial dream.   Yet it was not
so.   She had, in one little hour, passed the greatest epoch in
woman's existence—she had received and reciprocated a confession of love ! In one little hour she had lived an age.   She had
entered that room ignorant of the nature of her feelings—she was
leaving it with an overwhelming consciousness of their depth and
importance.   An interview had taken place never to be forgotten.   Words had been pronounced which, in weal or woe, as
long as her being lasted, must haunt her ear as the sweetest tones
that time could yield.   Looks had been exchanged, at the remembrance of which her heart must palpitate until its beatings
were stopped by death.   She had found an ardent lover in one
whose most careless attentions would have been received as an
honour by every girl of her acquaintance.   Had this been all.
But something else had happened —a nameless, suspicious fear of
that high-born lover had been suddenly infused into her mind-

and who can paint the agony of such a suspicion in a breast so tender and confiding? And then the future, which just now Mr. Clifton had painted to her so glowingly! Was she, indeed, to consider herself as engaged to him?—and if so why had he evaded (as he had) her solicitous request that Miss Clifton and her father might be acquainted with his intentions? Why, if he loved her so much, should he care though the whole world knew them?

As these thoughts presented themselves, not, however, in the order in which we have placed them, but confused and indistinct, Clifton rose up, and taking in his hand a glass of claret, which had stood filled on the table during their conversation, came with it to Ruth.

"Drink this, and forgive me," he said, in a low voice; but breathing quick with terror, Ruth flung open the door, and would have darted through it, but he prevented her.

"You must first promise to meet me here at this time to-morrow," he said. "If I have made you fear me, I regret it; but you must not think so much of a slight offence."

"It was not slight," said Ruth, her bosom heaving with resentment and wounded modesty, "and I will not come to this room alone any more, let Jean invent what falsehoods he will."

"You are angry," said Clifton, soothingly; "but believe my word of honour, sweetest girl, I will not displease you as I have done to-night if you will oblige me by meeting me here to-morrow. Come, now, cease to frown, and convince me of your love by trusting my word. You will come?"

Ruth again uttered a negative, and taking pleasure in probing her character, and proving its texture, Clifton assumed the tone of a master, and endeavoured to overawe her into compliance. But the attempt only elicited more spirited resistance.

"I will not come, either for your command or entreaty," she said.

"Bold and saucy girl!" exclaimed Percy, "is this my reward for loving you? What now, Jean?" he asked, as the valet rapped the door.

"Miss Clifton, sir, has been inquiring for Ruth."

"Very well."

The valet retired.

"Will you promise to come?" Clifton inquired in persuasive and importunate accents—"I will not let you go until you do."

"Indeed, sir, I will not," replied Ruth, "unless you will acquaint Miss Clifton and my father with what you have told me."

"To that," said Clifton, "I should have the greatest objections.

I should not choose to have my sister's fifty dear friends canvassing the merits of my intended alliance; nor should I care to have all the township of Rosedale ringing with the news that Squire Clifton intended to marry Ruth Summerfield."

Clifton might have added as another and the most potent reason, that he had no certain confidence in the stability of his own intentions—that his mind was unsettled—that he shrank from openly committing himself to any decided course.

"However," he said, thinking by that means to secure her consent to the appointment he wished, "to-morrow evening we will discourse more of this, and it is possible you may persuade me to yield my own wishes to yours. Miss Clifton, all the latter part of the day, will be engaged with the friends she expects from London."

"And with whom will Mr. Clifton be engaged?" said Amy, suddenly suprising them. "Not with Ruth, I can give him my assurance."

Ruth had been three quarters of an hour with her young master when Miss Clifton first missed her. The latter felt surprised that in that space of time her hand-maiden had not been seen by any of the servants, and her surprise was accompanied with uneasiness when she was told that Ruth had been last observed in a gallery which separated the squire's private parlour from the rest of the house.

"She could have no proper errand there," observed Amy. "If my brother required attendance, he had his own valet; and no other apartment opens from the gallery, nor does it form a means of access to any but Percy's room."

Miss Clifton then questioned Jean Andre as to where his master was and how occupied. If Jean had any passion beside base covetousness it was a love of mischief, purely for its own sake.

"The squire has been shut up in his sporting-room this hour past," he said. "I fancied I heard some one with him; I might be mistaken."

Then as Miss Clifton hastily sought her brother, and he returned to the kitchen, he whispered, with a distorted grimace on his meagre visage, to the footman—

"They will be nicely caught! Sacre! what is that to me? I have made a half-guinea by it."

"You don't mean to say master is courting Ruth?" asked the astonished footman, with rounded eyes, and a broad grin.

"Hold your tongue, you fool!" whispered Jean. "Sacre! what is it to any but themselves?"

Passive in her disposition as Miss Clifton usually was, and

erroneous as were her views of life, the fate and character of her
father had quickened her to a vigilant watch over her brother's
conduct; and though she had overlooked much that was wrong
in him, she now experienced a sentiment of warm moral indignation at his double-dealing with the innocent and amiable girl
she had taken into her service. We have intimated that Miss
Clifton was rather plain than beautiful, in respect to shape, features, and complexion, but that in expression—that highest beauty
—many thought her hardly to be surpassed. Expression certainly made her seem beautiful, almost majestic, when she suddenly burst upon her brother and the credulous girl whom she
believed his dupe. A lofty severity sat on her animated features,
which at first chained the tongue of Percy, and made Ruth to
hang her head in giddy confusion like a guilty thing.

"Ruth," said Miss Clifton, "go to my dressing-room;" and
Ruth was stealing away in agony inconceivable, when Clifton,
starting from the momentary thraldom of his sister's accusing
glance, bade her remain.

"Sister," he haughtily asked, "what has brought you here to-
night?"

"I came in search of Ruth," she answered; "and, brother, I
must tell you that I feel equally grieved and astonished at your
renewing the freedoms of which I so recently complained, after
the communication I made to you; and it is really not honourable
in you to continue to foster in Ruth false and dangerous hopes."

"But if I do not intend them to be false, how then, Miss
Clifton?" exclaimed Percy, unable to endure the shame-stricken
looks of Ruth, and the unusual assumption of superiority in his
ordinarily indulgent sister.

"Not false, Percy? How, in the name of patience, can they be
otherwise?"

"That is my affair," said Percy, with a haughty frown. "One
word only I have to say to you, Miss Clifton—let nothing be
spoken to Ruth which can distress her regarding what has now
chanced, or you will make your brother your enemy."

"I must speak to her the truth," said Amy, warmly, "be you
ever so angry, or let it pain Ruth ever so much—and it shall be
pronounced here before you both. Take notice, Ruth, whatever
Mr. Clifton may have said to you, he has said before to others. It
is a mere matter of course to him to make love; and after the
words have been spoken he thinks no more of them. There is
not the slightest dependence to be placed on his tender professions, as some of my acquaintance, ladies, rich and accomplished,
could attest. As you dread your father's displeasure, Ruth—as

you value your mother's peace—as you would escape being miserable for life—pay no attention to his flatteries."

Clifton laughed. He felt his sister read him truly on the whole, and was rather surprised to find her so penetrating. Still, in the present instance, he was conscious of a superior, more profound, and irresistible passion, than any he had experienced before. Though too much of wild fire was blended with it, the celestial flame was there. He loved Ruth sincerely, but it was not the less the love of a libertine, and therefore pernicious and perilous.

Like most libertines, he had a disinclination to the marriage "fetter," and regarded it as a mere institution of priestcraft and conventional convenience. He was loath to put his "free unhoused condition into circumscription and confine," and often he had promised himself that if ever he did, it should only be to raise the depressed house of Clifton by connexion with a title, and wealth, and power. Thus pride, interest, and licentious habits of thought, arrayed themselves in mighty force against the dictates of honorable affection, and made him restless, undecided, and wretched. At the moment of his sister's appearance, at the sight of Ruth's painful confusion, he felt prompted to a straightforward and manly avowal, but the good impulse was evanescent, and a laugh was all his reply to his sister's warning to Ruth.

The latter was less depressed by that warning than animated by Clifton's guarantee to his sister; as she understood him that her hopes should not prove false, and remembering how he had so lately looked and spoke, she could not doubt him. Miss Clifton's angry caution she persuaded herself was unnecessary and unmerited, and chiefly to be attributed to a fear of Percy's uniting himself to one so lowly as herself.

Ruth hardly noticed the peculiar manner in which his sister's charge of lightness and inconstancy was received by him, and as she silently obeyed a second bidding from her young mistress, and moved away, there was nearly as much pleasure as pain in her heart. But a new trial awaited her, the most galling she had ever known. She had to endure the whispered taunts, the malignant scandal, the prim disdain, of her fellow servants.

Turning from Clifton's private gallery to ascend the stairs to Amy's dressing-room, she heard a smothered tittering, and the housemaid and cook, who had followed Miss Clifton as near to the squire's room as they durst, in hopes of hearing a fracas, fled past her from their hiding-place, one exclaiming to the other, just loud enough for Ruth to hear—

"Kitty at the mill told me that she was, and now I believe her

At the dressing-room, Ruth encountered the good house-keeper, who looked on her with coldness and regret.

"I thought better things of you, Ruth," she said, and turned away, shaking her head.

The cheek of our young heroine tingled with a blush of fire.

"What have I done amiss?" she inquired of herself, as she stood alone, before the dazzling toilet of her mistress. "Do I deserve to be scorned, and renounced, and hated, because I love Mr. Clifton and Mr. Clifton loves me? Why did those women laugh, and look so impudently at me? and what could Kitty of the mill have said to my disparagement? Mrs. Wilson spoke as if I had disgraced myself in some way. But have I? I have not! and let them behave to me as they will, I shall not trouble myself."

Hastily she banished the indignant tear-drop from her eye, and sitting down with her work by the fire, determined to be calm.

Miss Clifton presently joined her, and Ruth, though inwardly trembling for the admonition she expected, summoned up a look significant of her ability to maintain her own cause.

"Ruth," said Miss Clifton, "what think you your father would say if he knew the encouragement you have given to my foolish brother's advances?"

"He might be very stern, ma'am," said Ruth, "until he knew all."

"And what is that all on which you lay so much stress?"

"I am afraid to tell it to you, ma'am, you will think me so presumptuous and bold. And yet if the squire had not flung me a rosebud when he rode past our cottage, I might never have known my present feelings. It is here, ma'am," she said, drawing a fold of paper from her bosom in which the withered leaves reposed, "and my heart must be as dead as them when it ceases to love Mr. Clifton."

This was an incident just calculated to touch the romantic soul of Amy; and as Percy had vindicated Ruth from the in-discretion of voluntarily seeking his room, and had taken on himself the sole blame of detaining her there, asserting that in a mood of idle frolic he had refused to let her go, Miss Clifton was now more inclined to be easy and sympathetic with her handmaiden than severe. To Amy pity was at all times more natural than censure. Never had she been so chafed as on the present evening; but her anger had subsided already; and now that fond love was the excuse urged, Amy found herself quietly listening with open heart to the plea.

With little difficulty she drew from the earnest girl a recapitu-lation of all that Percy had said to her, but of the boldness which

alarmed her, Ruth said nothing—perhaps she wished to annihilate the remembrance of it in her own mind—perhaps a delicate sense of shame withheld her—perhaps she judged that to impart his fault to another after he had entreated her forgiveness would be unworthy her attachment.

"And so he actually promised you marriage?" ejaculated Miss Clifton, in astonishment. "Inconsistent Percy! But of course you have no reliance on his promises?"

"Would Mr. Clifton speak what is not true?" Ruth ventured to ask.

"That is a difficult question," said Amy; "but it is written that Jove laughs at lovers' perjuries, and I am sorry to say that is my brother's creed. I see you droop, but the fact must be clearly understood. It is not because you are poor and my servant, that I discourage you; many standing in my position would cast you from their house, and load you with opprobrium; but in me you have a friend as safe and kind as if you were on my own level. If Percy will assure me that he really loves you, and will fulfil the intentions he has expressed to you, I will offer no opposition. But if he will not be so explicit, you cannot blame me if I require you to hide your love within your own breast, and abstain from private meetings with him."

Ruth had nothing to object, and her gratitude for Miss Clifton's unexpected friendship was expressed in every pleasing way. Each trivial duty that fell to her lot was performed with a heart-felt willingness, a quick attention, a sweet grace, which made her absolutely beloved by her young nd enthusiastic mistress.

Clifton said nothing more explicit to his sister respecting Ruth, but for some time affected a singular coldness towards both. Amy believed him offended with her for interfering, and Ruth, in secret, wondered and wept. The truth was, he thought it advisable to let his sister's watchfulness abate, and wished to practise upon the feelings of Ruth awhile, that he might, by and bye, mould her with less difficulty to his will, when he had vanquished the troublesome scruples of honour by which he was disturbed. With these views he restrained his passion carefully, spoke to her as seldom as he could, and then with a mask of reserve that he was far from feeling. So well he played his part that Ruth at times was tempted to relieve that her memory deceived her, and that no such interview had taken place as that which it recorded. A still more effectual means of testing the extent of his power over her, occurred to Clifton.

CHAPTER IX.

" If I do prove her haggard,
Though that her jesses were my dear heart-strings,
I'd whistle her off, and let her down to the wind,
To prey at fortune !"—SHAKSPERE.

CHRISTMAS eve arrived. The park of Rosedale had changed its emerald robe for one of sparkling snow. The vegetation which clothed the walls of the house was bedropped with icicles. The thick moss on the dismantled battlements of the Lady's Tower was hard as rock beneath the foot of the shivering and solitary marten, that now and then, with a cry of hunger and distress, was seen to perch upon it. Almost impassable were the deep narrow lanes and roads of the vale; while the denuded forms of elm, and oak, and sycamore, displayed their stately symmetry and harmonious combination of multitudinous branches, whence many a pellucid gem of frozen dew or rain flashed back the rays of the sun.

The evening was without moon or cloud. Lofty, vast, obscure, the starry universe lay all unfolded to the gaze, and seemed to challenge the highest efforts of human science and imagination to explore its depths.

Through the small town or village the north wind blew down from the hills in sharp intermittent gusts; but the fierce invader was jealously, and for the most part securely, excluded by close-barred doors and shutters, through whose chinks shot forth on the snow many a ruddy gleam of firelight. Sounds of social and convivial mirth also often greeted the ear of the solitary female who was picking her way over the slippery pavement.

It was Kitty of the mill, well defended from the sharp air by the folds of an ample cloak. She was on her way to the Three Crowns, her ostensible errand being to bear to Maynard, who was supping there, a great coat and extra kerchief for his throat, which she thought the extreme coldness of the night required. But Kitty had other motives. She had that evening received a visit from the cook of Rosedale Park, and heard, for the first time, the slanders current among the servants at the great house, respecting her beautiful rival. Nothing could exceed her wicked exultation at receiving such news, except her eagerness to spread

them. That Maynard had left his great coat at home, furnished her with a ready excuse to follow him to the Three Crowns, and spread there the defamatory tidings, while it offered her another advantage in the opportunity of impressing Maynard with her anxious thoughtfulness for his comfort. Such apparently slight attentions were, she knew well enough, among the most powerful incitements to affection, and it was part of her cunning to omit no opportunity of availing herself of them.

At times a slight laugh escaped her, and a few indistinct sentences: "A fine pass! after living four years and a quarter in the mill, to give up my place to her. I should think not! The proud baggage, to have the assurance to refuse him, too! That vexes me more than all. But now or never is my time, that is as plain to be seen as this here lantern I carry in my hand."

A fierce gust of wind broke her musings, and she heard the harsh creaking of the Three Crowns, which two tall posts upheld in front of an old-fashioned stone porch. The house seen by day had a pebbly front, high sloping roof, and small windows of stone surrounded by the Saxon zig-zag ornament, showing through how many ages they had opposed themselves to the defacing elements.

The jocund sounds of a violin issued from the interior, and looking through an opening in a shutter, Kitty espied the miller smoking with Summerfield and a stranger at a table, while the young people of the house, with a few friends, were performing a homely country-dance. No candles were lighted, but the intense glare of the huge fire that sent its flames roaring up the wide chimney to meet the descending blast, filled every corner of the spacious room with glowing light.

Kitty jealously scanned each face. Excepting the stranger all were known to her, and none was there whose influence over Maynard she could have cause to apprehend. But who was the stranger? His age was about thirty; his dress fashionable; his figure slight but elegant; his physiognomy melancholy, penetrating, and impressive. The exposed parts of his complexion were deeply tinged with brown, and Kitty concluded he was either a foreigner, or had travelled in foreign parts, which last was the fact. To a less illiterate observer might have been suggested, when he smiled, the beautiful simile of Moore—

> "As a beam o'er the face of the waters may glow,
> While the tide runs in darkness and coldness below;
> So the cheek may be tinged with a warm sunny smile,
> Though the cold heart to ruin runs darkly the while,"

for the momentary cheerfulness or his lip was contracted by the sarcastic coldness of his eye.

Strangers of his appearance were not seen every day at Rosedale, and Kitty, after scrutinising him very attentively, hastened to inquire, within the house, who and what he was. She only learned that he had arrived that morning on the stage-coach from London, and engaged a bedroom (not the best) in the Three Crowns.

Kitty then delivered to her master his great coat, and though he laughed, he was not ungratified at her attention.

"There was no need for your taking this trouble," he said, "the cold was nothing to me, for the short distance I had to go."

"Ah! Mr. Maynard," cried Kitty, "you are too venturesome, that you are. I don't know what would become of you if you had not some one to watch over your comforts, for little thought of them do you take yourself."

"And I am likely to take less in future," said Maynard, with a hasty sigh. "But now you are here, sit down, and make yourself comfortable an hour. I suppose no customer has called at the mill since I left?"

This was the opening Kitty desired.

"No customer," she said; "but the cook from Rosedale House looked in."

"And how gets Ruth on?" asked Maynard, "for her father thinks her not quite so happy in her situation as she expected, and when I saw her a month ago she looked but poorly."

"There are reasons for all things," observed Kitty, pursing up her mouth.

Maynard turned a quick and dubious glance on her. The stranger was intently occupied in peeling an orange. Summerfield had his hand to his furrowed brow, and his eye bent on the table, nor seemed to attend to anything passing around him. The dancers were too hilariously engaged to mark the motions of the group by the chimney; and the confused noise occasioned by the rapid stamping of feet, the loud strings of the violin, the shoutings of the fiddler of "hands across!—down the middle!" and so forth, the boisterous laughter of youths, and mingled voices of the girls, nearly drowned every other sound.

Kitty managed, however, to impart the cookmaid's story to Maynard, and we may be sure it flowed "mended from her tongue."

Had a dagger pierced the miller's heart, he could not have experienced an acuter pang. He did not doubt the truth of the report, for it harmonised with a secret suspicion that he had en-

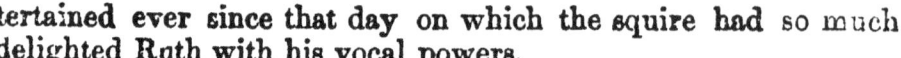

tertained ever since that day on which the squire had so much delighted Ruth with his vocal powers.

"No wonder," he said, with bitterness, "that she despised my poor efforts to please her! I courted her with plain sincerity, but plain sincerity would not do for Ruth. Her metal must be gilded. Well, Harry Maynard's hopes are over!"

He paused, for his heart was full. But the magnanimity of his nature prevailed even in that most trying moment.

"God bless her!" he exclaimed; "I will never blame her for discarding me, though she has left me with a sore heart. I know too well that our affections are not in our own power. If she ever needs a friend, she shall always find one in me."

"Ah, poor thoughtless young creature!" sighed Kitty, "it is quite unpossible that the squire should abase himself to her in the way of matrimony."

"Is it though!" exclaimed Maynard, his cheek and colour rising. "If Mr. Clifton does not, after he has been trifling with her feelings, and injuring her name, he will deserve all the curses of hell, as a deep-dyed and shameless villain! and, for my part, I will assist her father to see her righted, as far as law can do it, as long as I have a shilling left in Rosedale Bank."

"Her father thanks you, Henry," said Summerfield in a deep, composed, emphatic voice, "but in such a cause he will never ask or require your aid. If my daughter can have forgot the lessons of her youth so far as this woman says, she has no longer a father—I cast her off for ever! Whether Mr. Clifton marries her or not, she is no longer my child, nor will I ever see or own her more!"

"No, no, that will not do," said Maynard; "the poor girl must not be made desperate by harsh treatment—I would never see that."

"Hear me again, Henry," said Summerfield, with the same profound emphasis—"if Ruth has abandoned virtue—if she has lent an ear to folly, and stooped to shame—if she has brought dishonour on my yet unspotted name, and given an infamous example to her sister and her brother—if she has done this, I renounce her, so Heaven bear me witness! But she has not done this! If she could deceive my confidence, why, then there is no such thing as purity in the world. But she has not deceived it. I stake my life on my daughter's integrity! Temptation she may have had—but as for her being sullied by it, I credit not a word of the story. It is a foul calumny—an odious lie!"

The blood left his lip; the look was terrible that he threw on the tale-bearer, and her mean malignant soul quivered and quailed beneath it.

It has been said that Roger Summerfield, though in general possessed of an unfaltering self-government, was capable of tremendous gusts of wrath. On these occasions his aspect was fearful, his language elevated and powerful to a degree which we could not hope to convey. Othello in his deadly mood of blood could not be more awful. It was a tempest of the tropics sweeping all before it. At the present moment, nothing kept down his swelling fury at the slanders poured on his child but the presence of strangers, and this was evident enough in the ashy hue of his cheek and the darkness that gathered in his eye.

"Mean, detestable woman!" he muttered, clenching the hand that rested on the table, "you have proclaimed this falsehood here to disgrace my child, for some bad motive which Heaven will judge! But to-morrow I will know the whole truth, and that from Miss Clifton."

At the moment he spoke there was a pause in the dance, a bustle at the lower end of the room, a sudden suspension of the strains of the violin, and the tall, symmetrical, aristocratic figure of Percy Clifton made its appearance. Summerfield at once started up, and seizing his hat, and griping hard the hand of the miller, rushed from the house. Maynard, too, made haste to retire with Kitty.

"A merry Christmas to you, miller!" cried Percy, as soon as he distinguished him among the crowd.

Maynard lost command of himself at that moment.

"I would return you the wish, squire," he said, "but they who spread misery have no right to be merry. If I spend a merry Christmas, it shall be at the expense of no one's happiness—that is more than some can say."

All in the room hearing this, no small astonishment was excited.

"Make haste and draw your cloak about you, Kitty," said the miller, "and let us be moving."

A momentary blush of confusion passed over the face of Percy. He had caught a glimpse of Summerfield's hasty retreat, and the bold speech of Maynard assisted him to interpret that action. How either had been able to attain to any knowledge of his designs toward Ruth, he was at a loss to conceive; but that, more or less, they had attained to such knowledge, and that from this cause he had incurred their enmity, he felt well assured. It was an annoying discovery, and its consequences he feared might be such as permanently to wrest from him the object of his wild passion.

"But come what will," he inwardly resolved, "that shall never

If I am pushed to extremity, I must adopt extreme measures.   None but myself shall have her, I swear!"

These reflections occupied but a moment, when, assuming as much sang froid as the rapid play of emotions excited within him would permit, he adroitly turned the ideas of the auditors from the real grievance in question.

" It is to be regretted, Mr. Maynard," he said, " that you will judge so illiberally of my dealings with your friend.   Far from a desire to diffuse misery, I earnestly wish for, and will ever study to promote, the prosperity of my tenants."

And that there might be no reply to this, Clifton called to the landlady for wine, and retired to a private room, where a fire less large than that he had left, but not less bright, was burning.   The landlady having obeyed his orders, and placed two candles on the table, was retiring, when Clifton inquired who the stranger was seated by the chimney in the other apartment, and learning all concerning him that she knew, requested her to invite the gentle-man, in Mr. Clifton's name, to join him in drinking the good liquor she had provided.

The stranger, with pleasure, complied; and we shall leave the two pleasantly engaged while we follow to his home the stern moralist, the high-minded father, whose child Clifton was study-ing to destroy.

Summerfield's experience of the corruptions of the world had been, in some particular instances, so painful as to leave on his mind the gloomiest impressions of the race to which he belonged. His confidence and regard was extended to none but Maynard and his own family.   Nor could it ever more pass those limits. But in proportion to the narrowness of the stream was its depth. Where such natures as his plant their affections the roots strike deep and are not easily removed.   In Ruth he had unconsciously garnered up his dearest hopes.   She was his glory and his joy. In her beauty he saw the youth of her mother renewed; in her opening mind he traced the likeness of his own.   That the breath of defamation should pollute her, " his favourite and his flower," was insufferable torture! Still more excruciating was the incipient doubt which, despite his strong trust, would rend his mind, that she had really given cause for defamation.

According to the tale told by Kitty, Ruth had spent one whole evening with the squire alone in his room, while her fellow ser-vants were looking for her in every direction.   Miss Clifton had found her with him, and threatened to send her home immediately, but she begged to be allowed to remain.

"Could they invent this?" Summerfield gloomily considered. "I fear I have been too confident—to-morrow, however, shall

determine; and if I find she has really disgraced me, my heart will be broken quite, and day and night my supplication will be that the gates of death may be opened to me!"

"What did you mean by the expressions you used in your prayer to-night when you named Ruth?" inquired Mrs. Summerfield of her husband, as they retired to rest.

"You had better not inquire," said the cottager.

"Ah!" gasped the unhappy woman, ever ready to catch at some new alarm, "why should I not inquire? What has happened to her? Speak, Summerfield! Tell me, oh! tell me quick, what has happened to my Ruth!"

"I will tell you nothing if you will not be calm," he rejoined, supporting her shivering frame in his arms. "A mysterious Providence affects us, Hannah, with its visitations. but we must submit with patience and firmness, since it is the will of One who knows what is best for us. Yes, dear wife, the hand of affliction is to press still more heavily on you and I, but one consolation remains—that we have each other's love. For this let us be thankful."

"I am, God knows I am!" murmured Mrs. Summerfield, raising her streaming eyes upward, and clasping her hands together. "You, my love! my husband! are all that holds me to life. Not even for my children's sake could I sustain my load of misery unsupported by you! But what of Ruth?"

"Why, I have heard something to her disparagement to-night at the Three Crowns. The cook at Rosedale House, according to the report of Maynard's housekeeper, says she is too friendly with the young squire."

"With Clifton!" shrieked Mrs. Summerfield. "My God! I felt a presentiment of this last summer. Oh! his father's spirit is alive in him to torment my child in revenge for—"

"Hush!" interrupted the cottager—at that moment a gust of wind shook the cottage, as though it would have levelled it with the ground.

"He is there!—he is there!" screamed Mrs. Summerfield, clinging franticly to her husband's neck. "It is he who is driving the wind against the walls to bury us beneath them! I hear his horrid voice menacing us as on that dreadful night! But let him threaten—I never will submit!"

"My Hannah—my poor wife—you rave," said Summerfield, soothingly, caressing and comforting her. "The Clifton you are thinking of can trouble us no more. It his son, Percy Clifton, I was speaking of."

"I remember—I remember—" said the unfortunate woman,

passing her hand over her forehead—" yes—the squire I know lies in his undiscovered grave. But is it not fearful, Roger, to think whose hand laid him there ?"—a convulsive tremor seized her, and an icy coldness, as of death.

" Not fearful at all, Hannah, if viewed rightly. My conscience is without a blot in that matter, and, therefore, if I knew that to-morrow I must publicly answer for the deed, I should wait the moment with a calm, unanxious breast."

" And I," said his wife, " should not live to see that morrow's light. The bare thought of such a possibility as that you allude to is present death. Never mention it if you would keep me alive. You spoke of Percy Clifton and Ruth. Surely my sad history is not to be repeated in my child ! He has not offered her insult, has he ?"

" I can tell you no particulars to-night," replied Summerfield, " for I have heard none that I rely on ; but to-morrow I shall go to Rosedale House, and know the rights of the whole."

" Ruth is coming to spend the Christmas day with us."

" I know that ; but I shall not be satisfied until I see Miss Clifton."

Accordingly, the next morning, after a frugal breakfast, the cottager, dressed as neatly as he could, and went to the Park.

CHAPTER X.

" She loved him for his soul. His converse high,
  Recounting strange adventures in far lands,
  Where nature's fairest and sublimest works
  Are stored ; his talents bright, which circumstance
  Opposing only hid from deathless fame ;
  For these, and for the constant mournfulness
  That gave a charm of sentiment to all
  His looks and tones—she loved him ; nor had guessed
  A moral canker marred the stately flower."—OLD PLAY.

THE beautiful old custom of ushering in the morn of the Saviour's nativity with minstrel harmonies was not forgotten in Rosedale, and three, at least, in the house of the Cliftons were awake to hear them. The inquietude of love had banished slumber from the pillow of Ruth—Percy was up and dressed in his room with fire and lamp, racked with passion, indecision, and guilty projects ;

"THERE SHE COMES!" CRIED KITTY, WHO IS THE CAUSE OF ALL THIS."

THE COTTAGE GIRL.

"MR. CLIFTON, WILL NOT YOU PROTECT ME?"

AMY, on her lofty couch of silk, lay rapturously listening to those glad notes breaking the solemn silence of the dead winter night.

Broken images of fanciful delight occupied her waking and dreaming faculties after that early hour, until the reluctant, feeble clouded sun was high above the landscape, and sent its warmest beams through the closed silk window drapery.

She awoke, and touched the bell-rope for her attendant, as the watch suspended above her pillows announced the hour of twelve. But the luxurious indolence of the young lady was at once dissipated by a sight of the unusual gait and look of her favourite (for such had Ruth decidedly become), and hastily she asked what had so whitened her cheek?

Ruth replied that her father waited in the housekeeper's room, soliciting leave to speak with Miss Clifton respecting his daughter.

"I had not dared to see him," she added, "for I am afraid he has heard something unpleasing of me. I would not increase the ill-will of the servants by telling you before, but, dear ma'am, they have spread cruel falsehoods of me, and if you are not kind enough to defend me to my father, I shall never venture to go home more, for I would sooner fling myself destitute on the wide world than meet his anger."

"My dear Ruth," said Miss Clifton, rising and dressing with alacrity, "I will vindicate you with all the pleasure in the world: and if I find any one in this house has been spreading libellous reports concerning you and my brother, they shall not remain another day."

Ruth then entreated Miss Clifton to say nothing of any attachment existing on her part, or of any proposal having been made to her by the squire, as by his subsequent silence, Mr. Clifton, she thought, repented what he had promised, and she desired it to be forgotten for ever, except in her own heart, where the recollection of it could never—never pass away. And it was not possible her father could understand how her love had arisen—she could not understand it herself—and he would think it inexcusable in her low station, and be very angry, and remove her at once from Rosedale House, where her pleasure in serving Miss Clifton was too great to yield it without pain. Her father was severe in his notions of what was right, and she besought Miss Clifton with language the most moving, to shield her from his displeasure. Miss Clifton promised that she would, for Percy's inconsistent conduct to Ruth had warmly engaged her sympathies, and the simple fervency of our heroine's humble attachment to Clifton met a ready excuse in one who herself almost idolised him. The whole circumstance reminded the fanciful young lady of events which had often drawn tears from her eyes as related by the romancist, and the novelty of finding the poetry of love, in defiance of insurmountable obstacles, actually existing in real life, gave her a delight to which Ruth was not a little indebted for her friendship.

Descending to the housekeeper's room, where Summerfield's mind had already been disabused of a great part of the story which Kitty had retailed, Miss Clifton persuaded him the rest was

not worth remembrance. Her brother's statement was that to which she confined herself, namely, that it was merely in an idle frolic that he had detained Ruth in his room during the hour she had been missed.

The father's heart was lightened of a heavy load ; at the same time he made it his request, that if any thing of the kind occurred again, whether by the fault of the squire or his daughter, Ruth might be at once discharged. Miss Clifton hoped that her brother would know better than to attempt any such folly more, and rejoined Ruth with the comforting assurance that her father was completely propitiated, and that those of the household who had made free with the names of Mr. Clifton and Ruth would presently receive their discharge from the housekeeper. Forgetting then the evil they had attempted to do her, Ruth became their intercessor, and, by succeeding, bound to herself in bonds of enduring kindness one of those by whom she had been calumniated. The other, the cook, a woman of coarser mind, and the intimate acquaintance of Kitty of the mill, became her inveterate enemy. So true is it the bad often hate those who have benefited them— so true is it that returning good for evil, though effectual in disarming animosity in natures whose stamina is good, will often produce a different effect in the mean and corrupt.

Ruth accompanied her father home, where she was received by her mother with painful reproach.

"Nay, wife," said Summerfield, "Ruth has done nothing that deserves any great blame; on the whole, I have received an explanation that satisfies me."

"You have!" hastily ejaculated the mother—"then Heaven be praised!" Rapidly the tear flowed down her cheeks as she embraced her daughter. "Oh! Ruth," she cried, "I have been more miserable than you can think since I heard what was given out against you. Your father had more trust in you than I had, I am ashamed to say."

"Don't stop talking," cried Sally, who was placing on the table a dinner of mutton and turnips, "the meat has been waiting an hour for you."

To this plain wholesome fare the family sat down in renewed concord. The heart of Ruth overflowed in joy at finding herself again established in their love and confidence. Summerfield encouraged her by exhibiting as much cheerfulness as comported with his character; and Mrs. Summerfield had not been as lively in spirits for many a day. Not another unpleasant word was spoken. The discourse ran chiefly on Ruth's experience at the great house, respecting which Sally in particular exhibited an inexhaustible fund of curiosity.

The latter, during the last few weeks, had been employed part of each day at the solitary dwelling of an elderly maiden lady, residing at the foot of one of the bare hills overlooking Rosedale. With this old lady dwelt her niece, the intimate and beloved friend of Miss Clifton. Respecting Miss Charlotte Monckton, Sally had a good deal to say. She was the daughter of an East Indian officer, and both her parents died abroad, leaving her in a French convent, to which they had sent her to be educated at the time of their leaving England.

Miss Charlotte Monckton's aunt, her father's sister, had some interest in the convent to which she was sent, had herself been taught in it, and though she had not bound herself by any vow, always wore the dress of the order.

Charlotte had been only a year in the convent when she eloped with some unknown gentleman. Her aunt traced them from place to place, found them living together at a village in the Pyrenees, where they had been married in secret, and remained with them some months. But the strangest part of the story was to come, as Sally had heard it from an old French servant of Miss Monckton the elder. After the aunt had lived with the young pair some time, she used her influence with the French-Catholic authorities to have the marriage set aside, on the grounds of Charlotte's youth, the heresy of the gentleman, the non-consent of the young lady's guardians, (she herself being one), and other reasons which Sally had forgot.

Charlotte assisted her aunt to take the necessary steps to accomplish her wishes, and appeared as anxious to be divided from her husband as before she had been for his society.

The marriage was declared not valid; Charlotte resumed her maiden name, and returned with her father's sister to the convent. There they did not remain long. Three years before Ruth entered Miss Clifton's service, the aunt and niece came to England, and sought a retirement in Rosedale.

To Sally's narrative we may add, that when Amy Clifton first heard of the arrival of these persons, and the reports current respecting the nun-like habits and costume of the elder lady, and the lofty beauty and foreign appearance of the younger, her imagination was highly stimulated. She determined to make their acquaintance, and in one of her morning visiting rounds left her card. The next time she called, Miss Charlotte Monckton received her with that easy vivacity, that indescribable fascination, which belongs exclusively to French women, or to those who, like Charlotte Monckton, had been bred among them.

Amy Clifton was dazzled by her appearance and manners, enchanted by the high-toned sentiment which flowed from her

tongue, and gave her ready credit for every imaginable goodness. Henceforward, Charlotte Monckton was the depositary of her most secret feelings, her dearest friend, her adopted sister!

Ruth, of course, had often seen this lady at Rosedale House, and her quicker insight into character had often led her secretly to question whether Miss Clifton was really beloved by Charlotte Monckton. She had often beheld a smile of contempt curling the proud features of the latter when Amy indulged in the flights of romance to which she was prone; sly touches of satire, too, on the weak points of her dear friend, would ever and anon escape her, though she never proffered to Amy any direct counsel by which she might have been improved, but at all times echoed her sentiments, however exaggerated, with as much readiness as if they were the wisest in the world.

Having noted all this, Ruth was not surprised to hear from Sally that Charlotte Monckton, in the presence of a lady who sometimes visited at the Hermitage, (as the solitary dwelling was named) had stigmatised her fond friend as a " foolish sentimental child."

" Come, come," interrupted Summerfield, " enough of this. What you happen to hear your employers say when they are private, must not be repeated abroad. Let there be no talking on matters that do not concern you. Ruth has just suffered from a tale-bearer; take care to guard your own speech, that no one may suffer from you."

Sally then began to talk of Ruth's dress, which was much superior to what she had been accustomed to wear.

" I wish Miss Monckton would give me as many fine clothes as you get from Miss Clifton," she said.

" Wish for no such thing," said her father; " wish for a fair remuneration for your labour and no more. Never be mean enough to covet what is not lawfully yours."

" Miss Clifton is certainly very liberal to me," said Ruth, " and through her kindness I am able to offer you this in part payment of the money Mr. Maynard lent you for the squire's agent."

She placed thirty shillings on the table, a proud sum for her to tender.

" So you are determined to requite him in no other way ?" said her father. " Well, I say no more—this day must not be saddened by harsh reflections."

" I am afraid, Ruth, you will need this money before your next quarter comes due," said Mrs. Summerfield.

" If I do, Miss Clifton will assist me," rejoined Ruth; " but I have had so much given me that I am very well off."

"Aye, yours is a wonderful good place—if only it was not under the Cliftons," sighed Mrs. Summerfield.

"I had rather live with them than the king and queen," said Ruth warmly.

"That is because you know nothing of the stock they spring from," said her mother.

Impressed by the remark, Ruth longed to say—"Mother, you allude to Mr. Percy Clifton's father; I know you have property of his secreted here, tell me what has become of him;" but it was the mysterious will of him whom she was bound to obey that on this topic her lips should be sealed—sealed, therefore, they remained.

Summerfield saw his daughter's countenance overcast, and the remains of the dinner having been put away, he bade her draw her chair nearer to the fire and would have her sing an old Christmas carol, whose quaint burden provoked much laughter from the younger members of the group. Then followed some of the incomparable songs of Robert Burns, to which the cottager was extremely partial, though he never read a line of any other poetry.

"We want Maynard here to give us ' Auld Lang Syne,'" said Mrs. Summerfield, "no one can sing it like him."

"True," said her husband; "and without him my family hardly seems complete. But he was obliged to spend the day with one of his rich customers. I know he could not have excused himself without giving offence."

Hardly had he spoken when Maynard arrived. His anxiety for Ruth had prevailed over his prudent reluctance to offend a customer; and having despatched Kitty with an excuse to the parties with whom he should have spent the day, he hurried off to the place where his heart was lodged. Perceiving the family circle so much happier than usual, the miller looked astonished; and when Summerfield had given him the account of his visit of inquiry to Rosedale House, the sadness and anxiety of Maynard's breast was not wholly dispelled.

"Yes, yes," he said, "I see very plain what the squire is after, and Ruth must be removed."

"I have told her and Miss Clifton," said Summerfield, "that if the young squire takes any more such frolics into his head, Ruth shall instantly return home."

"She must not go back," said the miller, much excited. "I know Percy Clifton well. He has not done sowing his wild oats yet. He thinks any villany excusable where a pretty girl is concerned. I say she must not go back, Summerfield; and if the loss of her situation is to be weighed, and her heart is still hard

to me, I undertake to find another situation as good, or nearly, within one month from the present time."

"Henry," said the cottager, "your wishes are mine. But Ruth has found a kind mistress in the young lady of Rosedale House, and Miss Clifton has my word not to remove her without some strong necessity."

"What stronger necessity can there be?" said Maynard, still more warmly.

"My view of the matter is this," said the cottager—"if Ruth is inclined to evil, all my authority could not restrain her from it; but if, as I firmly believe, she loves virtue, she will be virtuous let her live where she may. She is now old enough to judge and act for herself, and to choose between the broad and the narrow way. I have no distrust of her choice."

The miller shook his head impatiently.

"Her choice was not the point at issue. But he would argue no farther, her parents ought to know best." Here he broke off with a sigh.

The vermillion lip of Ruth pouted with resentment as he placed himself by her side. His endeavour to increase her father's prejudice against Percy vexed her in the extreme, and sharply she plucked her hand from his caress.

Maynard then abandoned himself to a melancholy silence, only broken by occasional monosyllables. The mirth of the children failed to move him to a smile. His characteristic heartiness and joviality had departed; and altogether he looked forlorn and harassed.

Grieved by his depression, the cottager strove to remove it, and Mrs. Summerfield seemed disposed to second his argument for Ruth's returning no more to Rosedale House. On this point, however, her husband had made up his mind, and when this was the case nothing could shake him.

After tea he presented to Maynard Ruth's thirty shillings, as his first instalment on his debt for the rent, but by no means could the miller be induced to take it.

At ten Ruth returned to Rosedale House, accompanied as far as the Park by Maynard, who several times, in the way, strove vainly to give voice to his swelling feelings and apprehensions for her sake. At last, when they separated, a few broken words of caution escaped him. They were standing then within the Park gate, surrounded by trees yet undespoiled of their leaves, though laden with frost. The night was calm, and the cold was less intense than in the early part of the day. Ruth paid little respect to her companion's cautions, they were the result of

jealousy on his part, the thought, and over suspiciousness. Yet formally she thanked him for his consideration, " knew he meant her nothing but kindness, only was sorry he should have spoken so ill of the squire to her father. Mr. Percy Clifton was not the character he had described, but an honourable gentleman."

" Honourable !—yes, that is the word," echoed Maynard, with ironical expression. " The worst libertine of them all calls himself honourable, and would shoot or horsewhip the man who dared to deny his right to the title. Honourable !—Faugh ! "

" And why should you deny that Mr. Percy Clifton is honourable ?" asked Ruth with quickness, the angry colour mounting into her cheek.

" First answer me a question," said Maynard—" has he given you to understand that he admires you? I ask not by what means ; if he has he is dishonourable, for his admiration can lead to no good result."

" It can lead to no bad one, Mr. Maynard ; and I will not let you speak to me in this way any more. My father trusts me, and why should not you ?"

" The wisest err sometimes," said Maynard ; and with these words of sad augury, he left her.

Ruth hastened along the carriage-road through the Park plantation, her thoughts reverting to the first time she had trodden it four months before, and to the novel hopes and fears which she had since experienced. Years, not months, seemed to have passed while she had resided at Rosedale House. Her mind in that interval had remarkably expanded. The dazzling probability that had at one time presented itself that her young master might make her his wife had created in her an ardent thirst after improvement, and in the frequent opportunites of leisure which had been permitted her, she had contrived to read many of the works which supplied the teeming fancy of Miss Clifton. The refinements of manner, speech, and pronounciation of her superiors, she also had begun closely to observe and eagerly to imitate, though not with affectation or servility. The simplicity and originality of her own character remained, and were likely to remain, unimpaired, for all her improvements were distilled through an alembic of native good sense.

She was in the midst of the grove, which extended close to one side of the house, and through which the carriage-road took a sinuous course, with many paths diverging from it, when, from a turning on her right, proceeded the sounds of loud laughter, shouting, and singing, and, as she was hurrying forward, Clifton, with several of his boon companions, burst into the road.

"Tallyho! Tallyho!" vociferated one of the boisterous band as he caught a glimpse of the retreating girl, and started in pursuit after her. "A stray doe! Give chase!—give chase!"

"Yoick!—yoick!—hark-forward!" echoed his companions; and, to her infinite terror, Ruth found herself in a minute surrounded by the whole party of riotous bacchanalians. One immediately plucked off her bonnet that he might the better see her face, and, with a tremendous oath, declared she was a perfect houri of paradise. Another demanded a kiss; and a third declared she should pay the same forfeit all round before she should go.

"Gentlemen!" exclaimed Ruth, stamping her little foot on the ground while she writhed in the grasp of her captors, "I am Miss Clifton's waiting-maid, and if you molest me, you will have to answer it to her. Mr. Clifton—Mr. Clifton, will not you protect me?"

Percy, like the rest, was inflamed with wine. Violently he answered her appeal by pushing aside his companions, and vehemently exclaimed, that the first who laid a hand on his sister's favourite domestic should give him satisfaction ere twenty-four hours passed! Loud peals of laughter followed, and many free jokes at Percy's expense, at which he took great umbrage, so that a quarrel became inevitable.

Ruth, as she fled, like a greyhound from the slips, left them at high words, but, before she arrived at the house, the voice of Percy, who had disengaged himself from his party with angry menaces, came from behind, entreating her to stop. She did so, and breathless, and trembling in every limb, suffered him to approach and support her. The bonnet that had been snatched from her head she had caught up from the road as she made her escape, and now held it crushed and shapeless in her hand. Percy insisted on himself restoring it to form and tying it on.

"The fools have spoilt it," he said, slipping his purse into her hand, "you must replace it by a new one. Nonsense," he said, as she rejected the money, "all I have shall one day be yours; do not then hesitate at this trifle."

And he proceeded to repeat all his former protestations, as he gently impelled her steps down an obscure alley of drooping birch trees.

Ruth wept as she told him how she had thought, by his long and cold silence, that he repented his former promises, and pathetically she entreated that, if his mind was undetermined, he would not mislead her. Clifton vindicated the strangeness of his conduct since their former important conversation, on the ground of her having sedulously shunned all opportunities of private conference

with him, which he attributed to his sister's influence; but he considered if Ruth loved him she should submit to be guided by him. He started when informed that she had imparted to the ear of Amy all that had passed between them; and ridiculed the compact the latter had made with Ruth.

"So I am either to unfold my intentions to her, or lose you!" he said. "The first I assuredly shall not submit to, and the last depends on yourself. Not even to father or mother would I be compelled to make any such disclosure. To the woman of my heart alone shall my purposes toward her be displayed, and from her I expect implicit, undivided reliance. Tell me, Ruth, whether or not I shall have it?"

"Always," emphatically answered Ruth, with a gush of emotion. "Let Miss Clifton blame—the servants taunt—my mother reproach—I will rely on you, and you only, and meet you when and where you will. Only, dear Mr. Clifton!" she said, looking confidingly in his face, "spare me as much as you can—it is terrible to bear calumny and reproach—and oh! more terrible even than that would it be to meet my father's wrath."

She shuddered, sobbed, and hid her face. Again Percy's better feelings combated with the darker projects he had entertained. Could he bring on a being so guileless the misery her words depicted? Honour answered, No!—but sophistical passion argued that, perhaps, he exaggerated the misery she would suffer, and that if he removed her to ease and luxury in some place of complete seclusion she would forget all but his love, and the charms by which she would be surrounded. Hurried away by the idea, he hastily propounded it to her in most glowing terms.

Ruth listened under the impression that the beautiful bower he described was to be her marriage residence; and though her pride of feeling was something touched by his anxiety to envelope their union in secrecy, she persuaded herself that, sooner or later, the time must come when the disguise so foreign to her frank temper should be laid aside, and she should step forth in society as the acknowledged wife of Clifton.

Embarrassed by her utter unsuspectingness, Percy had not the courage to undeceive her, and presently it occurred to him how her delusion might be made to effect his object by separating her from her friends, and placing her in his power, after which he trusted to find no great difficulty in reconciling her to his society, unshackled by church forms and irrevocable pledges.

To this bad scheme he now bent all his soul, and Ruth, believing that in a few short weeks they were to be united by the most sacred of ties, gave up her heart to him without reserve, and, after

the present Christmas evening, often met him by secret appointment in the groves and solitary places of Rosedale. As these meetings were conducted by Percy with the utmost precaution and circumspection, they remained utterly unsuspected.

At this period the mind of Amy was much absorbed by a new acquaintance, who, in a short interval, had made rapid inroads on her affections. He was the stranger whom Percy had first met at the Three Crowns on Christmas eve, and whom, on the following day, he had introduced to his sister as Mr. Charles Tracy, the youngest son of a family of high lineage, but reduced circumstances, in Kent, a distinguished artist, who had studied in Italy, France, Spain, and Portugal, and was now making a tour of England, for the purpose of taking sketches of local scenery. Mr. Tracy was recommended to Miss Clifton, by her brother, as one conversant with every spot in or about Rosedale boasting a trace of beauty, acquainted with every point of view whence a pleasing prospect was to be had. Miss Clifton, moreover, had a passion for things of past times, and would show him the old trees in the Park, the old tapestries and oak carving of the house, and other curiosities of the Clifton property. She was herself a dabbler in water-colours, and would be glad, Percy doubted not, to take a few lessons from Mr. Tracy while he remained in the neighbouroood, and look over his splendid copies from foreign masters. If the stay of Mr. Tracy at Rosedale could be sufficiently protracted without inconvenience, Percy would be glad of oil paintings of himself and sister from his hand, and a sketch of the old house, for the specimens Mr. Tracy had exhibited to him had given him a high opinion of his abilities.

Thus favorably introduced, the accomplished artist became an established guest at Rosedale House. To him, hacknied in life, the freshness of heart and of fancy—the uncalculating gaiety— the daring enthusiasm—the transparent heart of Amy Clifton, were peculiarly delightful, and their influence stole on his parched and desolated bosom like sweet refreshing dew. His love was not a passion, but a sentiment. Passion's electric flame had once smitten him with blighting effect—but could do so no more. Once it had plunged him in sin and ruin—but its influence had passed, the tempest had rolled by. There was an aching void, however, left in his heart, which nothing but love could fill; and, as he grew intimate with Miss Clifton, he became conscious that the ove of such a woman would more than compensate for all his wrongs and sufferings past.

There were reasons, however—fatal reasons—why he ought not to attempt to win her, even were his circumstance on a level with

her own instead of being absolutely dependent on a precarious profession. It was no wonder, then, that the shade of sadness which disappointment and ill-usage, and error, had shed over his pale and contemplative features, deepened while he lingered in Amy's society.

Since she had known him she had been accustomed to rise earlier in the mornings, that before dinner she might sit to him for her portrait. It was in her boudoir that these sittings took place, a small room filled to overflowing with all that was light and tasteful in household decoration. Sometimes these periods, instead of being employed in their legitimate occupation, were wholly given to conversation. Tracy could not weary Miss Clifton with his anecdotes of foreign life and manners, and his descriptions of foreign scenery, which were graphically aided by the bold sketches with which his portfolio was filled. Literature, too, was a boundless field for them, and here their minds exactly assimilated. Not all his painful experience had weaned Tracy from a certain soft idealism which floated through all the manifestations of his character; and this was the magnet which drew the love of Amy. Like her, he had hitherto dreamed and sighed alone without meeting the kindred spirit he desired; and now, as their thoughts wandered in unison over the magic creations of poesy, it was with a woful pang he inly exclaimed—

" Had we but met before !"

" You are very desponding," Amy once said to him—" entrust me with the cause. Believe me, I can estimate the confidence of a noble mind."

" Who could doubt it ?" said Tracy. " And all my sorrow may be compressed into one word—loneliness. I have neither relations or friend, and am doomed to solitariness for ever."

" You have a friend," said Amy, her countenance replete with pure and glowing feeling. " I will be your friend. You shall be lonely no more. Not as the world giveth, give I my friendship—but, such as it is, it is your's."

She frankly extended her hand. Tracy accepted it with profound homage.

" You offer a rich treasure, Miss Clifton," he said, with a mournful smile, " to one so bankrupt in affection as I am; and the only return I can make is the assurance that I will ever regard it as a sacred deposit, the most precious and dear that an iron destiny has left me !"

CHAPTER XI.

"Lives there in human form, that bears a heart,
  A wretch, a villain, lost to love and truth,
That can with studied, sly, ensnaring art
  Betray sweet Jenny's unsuspecting youth?"—BURNS.

SIX miles from Rosedale stood a small villa, in the midst of a spacious garden planted with fruit trees. This Clifton purchased through the medium of his agent ostensibly for the use of a friend who expected shortly to bring a bride from the continent, but in reality for the reception of his intended victim.

Percy then took a journey to London, and, at the best warehouses, ordered furniture to fit up three rooms in a most luxurious manner, in addition to the ordinary requirements for servants' accommodation.

On his return to Rosedale, he dispatched Jean Andre to the villa to receive the goods from London. The ready-witted, adroit, knavish fellow, then found two suitable women-servants to bring all into order, and take the domestic management. Jean never asked for whom or for why all this was done ; a mere hint—half a hint—sufficed to secure his prompt and efficient service, if accompanied by a gift of money, and the larger the gift the more active and complete were his performances.

Spring was blooming over the land ; Ruth was one night retiring to rest, when there came a low tap on her door, and as she softly unclosed it, a note was slipped into her hand.

"All is ready, my dearest !" Clifton said, in his hurried billet—"only attend to my directions with carefulness, and you may leave Rosedale without exciting the smallest suspicion—which is what I particularly desire. To morrow we shall not be able to meet, except before witnesses ; but let Jean convey to me though but in a single word, verbally or otherwise, the day on which I may expect you to seal my happiness—and it must be within this week. Disturb yourself with no thought of your family, or of my sister—all must eventually reconcile themselves to what they will not have it in their power so alter. And if not, what then ? I will make you amends for all you may sacrifice for me, if eternal love

can do it. Be courageous and collected—think of me and of none else; let not your gentle heart sink, as it seemed to do to-day. My love and constancy shall never fail you.—P. C."

Ruth sat down on her bed; the letter dropped on her knee. A tumultous happiness quickened her pulse, but it was held in check by the fearfulness of her youth and sex, longing for a mother's breast on which to repose for sympathy and encouragement at so agitating a crisis, longing for the hallowing sanction of a father's approbation. Why, oh! why did Percy deny her these? Was it kind—was it considerate of him? She checked such thoughts, but others, more unsatisfactory, arose in their place. She re-read the letter. There was not a word of when or where the marriage ceremony was to be performed, That was strange! —very strange! It must have been an unintentional omission— and yet how he came to omit that, she could not conceive.

While dubiously reflecting, she heard her name pronounced in a whisper at the door. Jean was there to receive her answer to the note.

"Mr. Clifton wishes to know if Wednesday will do—that is, the third day from this?'

"Oh! no," said Ruth, hurriedly, "that is too soon—much too soon."

"Thursday, then?"

"No—no."

"Friday?"

"Not this week."

"Mr. Clifton directed me to say that Saturday would be the latest. By that time all will be prepared."

"All, Jean?—are you sure he said all?"

"I shall procure the licence to-morrow," said the lying knave.

"Then say Saturday—if it must be so," said Ruth, turning her face from his view.

The valet bowed, and, with velvet pace, glided away.

Ruth no longer had a doubt. Andre was to procure the licence to-morrow. The ceremony, then, was to be performed after she had bade adieu to Rosedale House. The manner of Jean had been calculated to impress her with a living sense of the reality of the great change she anticipated; it had been as deferential as if she were already the sharer of his master's name and fortune. Her young untainted heart was fraught with an overwhelming tide of bliss, that had no alloy but concealment.

"And that will not last long!" she persuaded herself; "and then, dear father, dear mother, what joy shall I not bring to you both!"

It is true, there were some moments of dark and painful doubt in the interval that elapsed before the important day on which so much was staked—the thought of her intended bridegroom's father stalked like a grisly spectre between her and peace—the mystery of his disappearance was still brooding over the cottage of her parents, and what it portended she dared not trust herself to conjecture. Percy's conduct, too, had still something singular about it, which inspired uneasiness. In fact, as the decisive day approached, he shunned all occasions for their being alone, because he dreaded her questionings—her very looks. He kept as little at home as possible, and communicated with her only through his valet and by letter. Then the deceptive pretence on which she was to leave Rosedale House, jarred on her perception of the sacredness of the occasion. By Percy's direction she had solicited and obtained leave from Miss Clifton to spend the Saturday and Sunday with her parents. It was the first time in her life she had ever given utterance to a deliberate falsehood; and had Miss Clifton's eye been fully upon her, her disordered manner must have betrayed her.

On Saturday morning, before any of the other servants were astir, Ruth quitted the house. Percy, two days before, had departed with his valet on a distant excursion, as his sister and the household believed. She tripped rapidly along over the dewy ground, until a variety of paths crossing and intersecting each other through the plantation, brought her to a wooden bridge, thrown over a stream of the purest water, in which every streaked pebble over which the rippling current flowed, and every little fish that darted along might be distinctly seen.

This bridge had often been the trysting-place of the master of Rosedale and the Cottage Girl. Here Ruth now found herself joined by her lover. They exchanged few words. Jean was in waiting a few yards off with a post-chaise. Ruth was handed into it—Andre himself served as postilion—and a swift drive of half an hour brought the pair before a small private door in a lofty wall, that might have served to guard a nunnery or a prison. Without a moment's delay, the valet, flinging himself from the horse, and taking a key from his pocket, opened the door, and the agitated Ruth, supported from the chaise by Clifton, entered a garden, where perfumes loaded the air, and where a thousand warblers were singing. The walks—the parterres—the terraces of stone and of earth—were all laid out to produce a striking effect, and in every suitable situation the umbrageous foliage was seen to overshadow some graceful vase or urn, or some beautiful production of statuary. When the rural villa itself was disclosed,

framed octangularly of wood, after a continental model, the lower of its two storeys projecting, so as to require the support of a colonnade of slender pillars admirably formed of tree trunks, with the bark remaining, and twisted with honeysuckles and roses, that attracted a crowd of bees—the ensemble was such as to take Ruth by surprise.

At the same moment a richly-plaintive burst of melody issued from one of the woodbined casements, and died off in the distance as if struck by a seraph's hand from some instruments inimitable by mortal art. Tears of ecstasy rushed to the eyes of Ruth as she turned them on her lover. Again that wild strain came—deeper, fuller, it swelled on her enchanted ear. All heaven was in the sound! Even the guilty Percy was hushed in transport until the last low quivering note had expired.

"Would not one think," he said, "that a spirit resided in the wind which touches those wires with such a masterhand!"

He showed her the magic Æolian, from whence the sounds she had heard proceeded, and then conducted her into the house, the doors of which stood open. The rooms into which Percy led her, surpassed anything at Rosedale. They were three in number, and opened into each other on the same storey. In the first, a costly dejeune was already served up on the finest plate and china. She saw no servant, at which she rather wondered; but these having been chosen with a single eye to expediency, had readily obeyed the instructions given to them to take care to be invisible until Mr. Clifton required their attendance.

They sat down side by side, and assiduously and tenderly he pressed her to partake of the delicacies before her. As she attempted to do so, she momently expected to hear him speak of the ceremony which was to be performed. But as his impassioned discourse conveyed no allusion whatever to this primary topic, she modestly inquired where and at what hour the marriage ritual was to be read.

"Nay, sweetest girl," he said, persuasively, "what care we if it is not read at all? For my own part, I consider such forms utterly valueless—useless where love exists, mischievous where it does not. They are chains forged for priestly profit. How, for instance, can they make us one jot the more constant to each other? The omission of the mummery of a prayer-book could in no shape affect love like ours!"

Ruth's colour changed rapidly. She arose from the blue satin couch on which Clifton and herself had rested, but his arm was thrown around her, to prevent her from retreating.

NOTICE.—With this Number is Given Away a Coloured Picture for binding with the Work. Another will be given with the Next Number. Order early.

'A SOFT HAND IS LAID UPON HIS, AND AMY SINKS ON HIS NECK.'

THE COTTAGE GIRL.

RUTH THREATENS PERCY CLIFTON.

"WHY did you bring me here, Mr. Clifton," she demanded, "if it was not to be married?"

"We are married—in heart."

"There again!" exclaimed Ruth, turning her full brown eyes upon him with bewildered apprehension—"that look!—that laugh!—those strange words!—Oh! Mr. Clifton, tell me truly what is it you do intend? Are you deceiving me?"

"Deceiving you, my beautiful girl?"

"For pity's sake—for my honest parent's sake, Mr. Clifton, do not trifle with me! You have some purpose in your mind that you have not discovered!—at this moment I read it in your face."

"Silly trembler! is it not enough for you to know that I adore you, and will share all I have with you ?"

"Shall I share it as your wife ?"

"Yes—the wife of my soul."

"The wife of your name ?"

Clifton answered by seizing her in his arms, and endeavoured to overwhelm her by a torrent of fierce caresses.

But he had erroneously calculated his power over her. Much as the simple girl loved him, she loved virtue better. The moment the full extent of her peril burst on her, she gave no parley to her own affections, but, with the prompt determination that could alone have saved her, resisted his treacherous attempt.

"I will never forgive this," she panted, as with set teeth, she struggled in his grasp. "False, wicked man! from this hour I will detest you: let me go! or I will tear the hair from your head, ant the flesh from your cheeks!"

Determined as she was, however, his superior strength at first prevailed; but catching up a knife that lay on the breakfast table, she threatened to stab either herself or him unless he resigned her.

Loath to believe she was in earnest, he strove to detach the dangerous implement from her grasp, and received so severe a cut in the hand as to compel him to relax his hold on the affrighted girl. The next moment she had fled to the farthest of the three rooms, which was the bedchamber, and fastened the door. Clifton, exhausted at the moment by the violence of his own passions, and satisfied that she could not escape him, threw himself on a couch, twisting his handkerchief round his bleeding hand. After a little time, hearing no sound from the chamber, he approached it on tiptoe. All was perfectly silent. He looked through the keyhole. The window was open—and his captive had escaped! Maddened with rage, he searched the garden in every part without result. Through half the day he continued to look for her, believing that there was no possible way of her obtaining egress through the garden wall, as the only door was locked, and no key within reach. The women servants assisted in the search, and were even more astonished than their master at the suddenness with which she had vanished. The villa was examined throughout. No place was left unscrutinised in or about it, excepting a pond which lay at the bottom of the garden. At the mention of that pond Clifton stood aghast.

"It is impossible she can have done anything so rash!" he muttered, with blanched lips. "And yet never saw I desperation like that with which she resisted me!"

The dreadful thought had hardly been conceived when the cries of the women announced to him that a scarf was floating on the surface of the pond. He rushed to the spot. It was the one he had seen but a few hours before shading the fairest neck in the world. In wild distraction he leaped, without a moment's deliberation, into the centre of the pond, and dived to the bottom. He rose—he dived again—and clambered up the bank without having found the body.

An hour of torturing suspense had to pass before he could get the proper implements brought to the spot for dragging the pond. In that interval he never ceased to pace the brink with wild disordered steps, holding the wet scarf in his clenched hand, his apparel dripping from the effects of the immersion, his complexion stony pale, and his features terrible to look upon with remorseful horror.

At last he was relieved from the worst of his apprehensions—the pond was dragged and no corpse was there! Infidel as he was Clifton could have dropped on his knees to bless God for that tidings. He shed tears as he turned away, and promised himself that he would never forget the lesson of that day.

"If I find her again unharmed," he said, "she shall be mine lawfully. So excellent a creature deserves the highest good that earth can offer, and I abhor myself for my attempt to wrong her!"

Thus repentent, he at night returned on horseback to Rosedale House, trusting that by some means unknown the garden door of the villa had been opened to her, and anxious to know if any news of her had reached his sister, or those who had been Ruth's fellow-domestics.

Satisfied in the negative, his restless steps next bore him to the cottage of her parents, and could perceive, at a glance, that some extraordinary occurrence had happened there. Lights were rapidly moving to and fro across each of the small lattices. The house door was opening and shutting frequently, and many voices sounded from within. Drawing close to one of the casements he heard Mrs. Summerfield's piteous exclamation:—

"My child!—my child! She is dying!—my fairest and my best is dying!"

"Peace, wife!" her husband said; "your lamentations can do no good. Be still, and trouble not her parting moments."

"She shall not die!" franticly cried her mother; "she is the prop of our life. Oh! Ruth, my dear, my lovely child! don't you hear your poor mother's voice? Answer her, if it be but a word, and tell her that you will will live!"

In the silence that followed, Clifton listened in vain for the answering voice of the poor girl whom he had so bitterly disappointed. A noble impulse prompted him to enter the cottage, openly avow his offence, and pledge himself, if she survived, to compensate her by honourable marriage. Unhappily—most unhappily for all parties—he recollected how Summerfield, in the mill, had refused his proffered hand, and that was an insult his pride could not overlook even for Ruth's sake. No, not in the presence of the stern cottager or his wife would he humble himself, but to Ruth individually he would make any apology, any concession. During most of the night he wandered about the humble dwelling, avoiding the sight of any one, yet burning with sickening anxiety to know the particulars and the progress of Ruth's disorder. At length, after midnight, he beheld the parish doctor entering the cottage, and watching for his departure, accosted him in the middle of the lane.

"A fine night, Mr. Walcot; one of Summerfield's daughters lies dangerously ill, I am told. He is a worthy tenant of mine, and I am sorry he is so repeatedly marked by misfortune."

"Dangerously ill, sir!" echoed the doctor, a lean, ghastly-looking personage, whose chief distinctive characteristic was a profound sense of his own professional importance. "Sir, the family owe their daughter's salvation from the grave this night to me. She must have gone, sir—there was no remedy—all the materia medica could not have saved her, Mr. Clifton, without the skill of Anthony Walcot. I had not my diploma for nothing, sir. My practice is well known. I cure where others would kill. Sir, of that I could give you a hundred curious instances if time served."

"I nothing doubt it, Mr. Walcot," said Clifton. "But do I understand you that all danger is past?"

"Yes, sir, I have destroyed the most formidable features of her attack."

Clifton drew a sigh of relief.

As the two walked on together along a narrow road, the loquacious conceit of the doctor led him to dilate on the event of the night, insomuch that his companion, without the awkward necessity of interrogations, which might have betrayed his deep interest in the sick girl, obtained nearly all the information he desired.

Summerfield and his wife were out, and his youngest daughter and little son weeding in the garden, at the time when Ruth arrived at the cottage. Sally first saw her sister, who was then sitting before the fire with her feet resting on the fender, her face buried in her hands and her whole figure huddled together as with extreme cold. She said she had leave of Miss Clifton for that evening and the next day, and that she felt herself ill. As she shivered very much Sally made her some warm tea, but she was unable to drink it, and grew so rapidly worse, that, on her mother's return, Ruth was unable to speak to her. Billy was then dispatched for his father from the farm, and Summerfield found his best-loved child momently expected to expire in fits of spasmodic convulsions. He sent off without the loss of a moment for Walcot, who, though enjoying indifferent patronage, really had professional capacities something above the average, and displayed a humane heart toward the poor, whom he attended as solicitously as if they were able to reward him with guinea fees. That sagacious professor at once hit upon the true source of Ruth's malady—the mind; but he did not consider, as some would have done, that therefore his aid was useless, but strove to rally the vital powers by his pharmacy to cope with and resist the fatal encroachments of the mental foe.

After three visits in the course of a few hours, he succeeded to his own perfect satisfaction, and he knew not whether most to rejoice in having rescued the pride of Rosedale from an early grave, and her parents from the agony of losing her, or in having added another laurel to his self-decorated brow.

When Clifton had gathered all the information he could from the parish doctor, he parted from him, and returned to Rosedale House, where, wearied as he was, he spent the rest of the time ordinarily allotted to sleep in writing to the poor girl for whom he had prepared so cruel a disappointment. His genuine feelings breathed forth in these glowing pages, unclouded by the artificial reasonings which depraved society and a vicious mode of education had created. He humbled himself before her for his late trangression, entreated her pardon, and a continuance of her love. He was highly grateful for her concealment of the painful transaction of the past day from her parents, and prayed her still to conceal it, not only from them but from all. He earnestly requested to see her, if by any means she could gratify him. In conclusion, he trusted she would recover quickly, and return to his sister, in whom he would then confide, and their marriage he promised should take place immediately, in Miss Clifton's presence.

Before this letter was sent away, Sally Summerfield came to Rosedale House to acquaint Miss Clifton with Ruth's singular illness, and as the child was leaving the park, Clifton followed her, and easily prevailed on her to be the bearer of his epistle to her sister.   Proud of the confidence reposed in her, and transported with the thought that Ruth was to be a lady after all, Sally hastened home with a more rapid step than usual, and the first moment when she was left alone with Ruth, she slipped the letter in her hand.

Ruth had been lying motionless with closed eyelids, from which now and then a tear slowly descended over her delicate features, but at the touch of the letter she opened wide her eyes, and, glancing at the direction, flung it with energy to the furthest end of the room.

"Burn it !—burn it, Sally !" she exclaimed.

"That will offend the squire," said Sally, "for it was he who gave it me."

"Let it offend—the letter shall be burnt."

"Indeed it shall not," said Sally; "if you won't read it, I will take it back to him and say so."

"Do what you will with it," said Ruth,   only keep it from me.   I will read no more of his letters," she ejaculated to herself—"I will read no more of his deceitful words."

It was then Sunday evening, and thinking Ruth sufficiently recovered to be left, Summerfield and his wife attended divine service at the town church.   Clifton, as it began to be dark, was again moving about the cottage, and having seen the elder people go out, he lifted the latch of the door, and entered.   The room was in partial darkness; there was a small clear fire burning in the grate, and within the circle of its radiance appeared a neat bed, lowered from an upright frame.   He glided toward it, and paused.   On her side, with her face turned to the fire, and her bare arm negligently supporting her head, he beheld the object of his restless passion.   Her neck was half uncovered, and her brown hair strayed over it in graceful disorder.

His heart beat with distracting admiration.   The unrivalled fairness of her skin—the bright flush which emotion had kindled on her cheeks—the large expressive brown eye floating in tears —the sight of these had well nigh brought again the tempter to his soul.   He sprung forward, dropped on his knee by her side, and covered her hand with kisses. Shrieking aloud, Ruth drew the coverlid about her neck, and hung fearfully back.

"Ruth, my dearest Ruth !" he imploringly exclaimed, " why this extreme terror?   You are in no danger. ● Here comes your sister to bear me witness that I have sought you with no intention but that of kindness and conciliation."

"Oh ! Sally," exclaimed Ruth, "are you too assisting to betray me ?"

"Your sister talks wildly, my good girl," said Clifton, rising to his feet. "I have affronted her, and she is angry with me —but we shall soon be reconciled, and Ruth will be my wife. You therefore must not attend to any hasty expressions she may utter, but do your best to assist us, and unite us, and it shall hereafter be to your profit."

"Do not heed him, Sally!" cried Ruth; "his tongue is smooth, but false: he don't mean me to be his wife—we never shall be reconciled. And if you bring any more of his letters or messages I will make them known to my father."

"Your sister perceives that you are out of temper with me," said Clifton; "but she is a sharp girl, and will not be deceived by your heat into a betrayal of our correspondence with your parents, for she comprehends that by doing so she will blast your future prospects."

"I have no future prospects," said Ruth: "yesterday morning I had—but they are gone, they are gone, they are gone!" and, burying her face in the bed-clothes, she wept bitterly.

"Think not of what is past," said Clifton; "for that the future shall requite you."

"How may I know that?" demanded Ruth, raising her face.

"I give you my word."

"Your word was given to me before, and you shamefully broke it."

"Trust it once again."

"No, I will not—never, never. As soon as I am better, Mr. Maynard shall know how you have deceived me, and if then he is willing to marry me, he shall."

"Shall he!" cried Clifton, pale with jealousy and the fear of losing her—"he had better not attempt it. Maynard the miller!—no, no! If I yield to a rival, it shall not be to an inferior. But it was a foolish unmeaning threat, and as such I pass it over."

"I assure you, Mr. Clifton, it was not unmeaning. I repent very much having behaved so coldly to Mr. Maynard. He is a good man, and would never deceive me or any other woman, I am sure of that. I can depend on his word. In him there is no falsehood—no hard-hearted trifling—no wicked arts. I respect him as much as I despise you! and I will endeavour to love him as much as I now hate you!"

Words, words, Ruth!" cried Clifton—"you can neither hate me nor love him."

"I can—I will—do both!" said Ruth. "He is a worthy man, I tell you, and you are a—"

" What ?"

" A dishonourable villain! as Maynard said you were."

" As he said! Did he presume to apply those words to me?
If so I must instruct Mr. Maynard, by rather unpleasant means,
how to amend his language towards his superiors, in future."

" Yes, he said you would shoot or horsewhip the man who
called you dishonourable."

" And, by Heaven, he is right !"

" But you will neither shoot nor horsewhip him, Mr. Clifton !" cried Ruth, afraid she had gone too far.

" Be not too sure of that," said Clifton. " Hark! I hear a
step on the gravel without—your parents cannot have returned already."

" It is Maynard !" said Sally, in a fright. " Run out by the
back way, Mr. Clifton, if you please—through that door."

Clifton stood a moment hesitating whether he should at once
confront the miller, but cooler judgment came to his aid; and
with a few words of warning to Ruth how she ventured to fulfil
the threat she had made, he darted through the washhouse and
garden, and leaped the low hedge of bushes into the road.

As he dsappeared, Maynard who had only heard of Ruth's
illness a few hours before on the same day, knocked at the
door anxious to be allowed to speak a few words with her.

Ruth excused herself, as not being sufficiently well, but
hoped she would be better on the morrow, and then she had
something particular to say to Mr. Maynard.

On the morrow he came. She was dressed and sitting up,
but looking ill and unhappy.

" Would you have any objection, my dear mother, to leave
us alone a little time?" said Ruth. " I have something important to say to Mr. Maynard."

Mrs. Summerfield gladly complied with her wish, hoping
some change had been effected in her daughter's mind favourable to his suit. This hope was not disappointed.

" Mr. Maynard," said Ruth, as soon as her mother closed
the door upon them, " I am going to confide to you a secret,
and you must promise me not to divulge it to my parents neither at this present nor at any future time."

" My pretty Ruth !" said Maynard, " what secret can so
young a lass entertain that her parents should not share? It
is wrong for young women to have secrets. They should be
frank with their friends, as you have always been until lately."

" You speak well," said Ruth, " but unless you promise to
keep my secret I shall not reveal it."

"Well, well, I promise. It shall be as sacred with me as you can desire."

Ruth's bosom rose and fell—the color faded from her cheek.

"Mr. Maynard," she tremulously began—"since I have first known you I have seen many good actions you have performed, and never one bad one—I have received many kind works from you, and I am sure not an insincere one—you have borne with my childishness, my coolness, my injustice, never ceasing to be the same good friend you were before I refused your generous offer."

Earnestly she spoke, and the miller's heart dilated with new-born happiness.

"Yes, Mr. Maynard," she said, "the obligations I owe you are more than I can number; and if you can forgive the pain and uneasiness I have occasioned you—there is my hand—I will be your wife."

"This is almost too joyful to be true!" returned Maynard, distrusting his ears, which drank in the unexpected sounds. "Forgive!—I forgive! My dear Ruth, I could not help doing so if I were ever so much inclined. Your father will be so delighted—so will your mother! Bless you for your acceptance of me!—bless you for the kind way you have spoken of me—bless you for making the rest of my days happy! I can hardly contain myself, this has so taken me by surprise."

"But you have not heard my secret," said Ruth, gently, as he continued to pour out his thankfulness and joy.

"True, I had forgot the secret that I am not to whisper even to your parents. What can it be? Speak it out, my girl, and let me know the nature of it without more ado."

"Perhaps when you do you will reject the hand I have just offered you."

"It must be a weighty secret to make me do that," said Maynard, laughing. But come, out with it."

"Mr. Maynard," said Ruth, with a quick stifled sigh, "since I first refused you, I have loved—deeply, and most unwisely."

"Ah! I suspected it—Mr. Clifton?"

"Yes. He—"

"Go on."

"He misled me. He persuaded that he purposed marriage, and Saturday last was to have been the day. You look astonished—but don't interrupt me. That morning I left Rosedale House with him, but in a few hours I discovered—ask me not how—that he had no honourable intentions."

"I knew it, and warned you."

"You did; but I loved him, and therefore trusted him. The house to which he conducted me was miles from Rosedale. There I presently escaped from him and hid myself behind a projectio of a high wall that entirely surrounded the garden. As soon as Mr. Clifton and his people began to search for me they opened the door in the wall, that had till then been locked. I watched my moment, darted through it, and reached home in the condition of health you heard."

"Execrable villain! he deserves to be hunted through the world with firebrands!"

"I will not tell you what the disappointment cost me," said Ruth," but I am resolved not to give way to grief. Clifton has since striven to reconcile me, but I never will be deceived by him more. I see my folly. His station is too far above me ever to reach it by proper steps, and I will tread no other. So now, Mr. Maynard, I have told you my secret, and I wait your answer whether, after what has happened, you will venture to take me for your wife?"

"Will I not!" cried Maynard. "My dear girl, I almost feel thankful to the villainy which has been the means of opening your eyes to see on what a precipice you were standing! I had given up all hope of you. I believed that my years and want of gentility, made you despise my offer; and I was afraid you would rather choose a gay and splendid infamy with the Squire than share my sober lot. Fancy, then, my, joy at finding you have been put to the proof, and have come off victorious! It surprises me it should have been so, for all that is tempting to woman has, I know, been employed to tempt you. Clifton was too good a judge to make the trial by halves, and as you loved him, it is wonderful how you escaped. But you ask if, after what has happened, I will venture to marry you? Yes—more willi gly, if that be possible, than if nothing extraordinary had occurred, for now I know your virtue is not a thing of accident, nor such as trial could overcome, but a safe foundation for a husband's honor to be built upon. But the treachery of the squire must not sink to silence; it deserves to be published wherever his name is known."

"Leave him to his conscience," said Ruth. "I am very sure it must upbraid him grievously. Remember, you have promised silence."

"I have, and it may be for the best; for although, without questioning you closer, I am satisfied, and more than satisfied, with your part in the transaction, there are some ill-natured persons who might cast a slur on you. Summerfield, too, would

most likely be betrayed into violence against Clifton, and it is unequal warfare between a poor and a rich man. And so, considering all things, we will agree to confine the secret to ourselves; only I will find an opportunity to speak my mind to the squire. To that you will have no objection."

"I had rather you would not. When he knows I have accepted you, he will be desperate, and, at the first opportunity, will seek to retaliate on you. But be on your guard, and on no account enter into strife with him; but let him know that your wish and mine is to have nothing more to say or do with him except in the way of needful civility."

Ruth was right in the hypothesis of the state of mind into which Clifton would be thrown by her intended bridal with the miller. Desperate, indeed, he was when he found his ascendancy over the heart of Ruth was broken—when he found that the result of his falsehood had been to make even his truth disbelieved—when he found that, with a firmness on which he had never calculated, she refused to hear from or speak with him, and was about to place herself under the protection of a husband whom he considered his inferior in all respects except, (important exception!) uprightness and steadiness of purpose. His raging pangs could not be appeased. He had little hope of any abatement of her resentment, since he keenly felt that it was just, and since each action of her's proclaimed its abiding character. That she still carefully preserved the secret of the wrong he had attempted, was the only token he could perceive of his having any influence of a gentle character left in her bosom. Sometimes he was inclined to found expectations on it of her ultimately relenting; but mostly he despaired, and that despair, in some of his stormy hours, was the handmaid to thoughts of deep design, more rash and wicked even than those in the execution of which he had been so signally foiled.

The situation Ruth had held under Miss Clifton had been resigned as soon as her marriage with the miller was arranged, and it was not long before the bans were published in Rosedale church.

On the Sunday of the first asking, Clifton, to the surprise of many, entered the church, which he had not visited ten times before in his life, and took his seat in the curtained pew which his deceased mother had been accustomed to occupy. But he came not there to pray. Through the opening of the curtains, himself screened from view, he saw the miller, with Ruth leaning on his arm, walk up the aisle, followed by Summerfield and his youngest daughter. The four seated them-

selves in a pew near his own, and throughout the service he was engaged in watching their every look and action. After all, he could come to no satisfactory conclusion respecting Ruth's state of mind. At one moment he triumphed in the conviction that she looked depressed—at another he was compelled to acknowledge that her countenance revealed a sort of pensive contentment. Now he plumed himself on discovering some slight token of her aversion to the miller—but another minute he had a different impression.

The engaged pair read from the same prayer-book, and at the moment when the clergyman pronounced their names with others shortly to be joined together in the holy estate of matrimony, Clifton perceived the hand of Maynard enclose that of his intended bride, who replied by an expressive look of confidence, almost of affection. His feelings at that moment, it will readily be conceived, were not very enviable.

The service over, and the hearers dispersed, Clifton followed at a distance his successful rival and the Summerfields, until he beheld the miller separate from them, and cross a stile into a field then rich with ripening wheat, when he hastened to overtake him.

"Mr. Maynard," he said, speaking rapidly, and with excitement, "it has been some time a purpose of mine to call you to account for certain expressions you have thought fit to apply to me. I understand that you have presumed to stigmatise me as a dishonourable villain, with other phrases of like import. I ask you now if you are prepared to apologise to me for those offensive epithets?"

"Mr. Clifton," said Maynard, with perfect command of temper, "what I may have said I am not inclined to retract. Neither am I inclined to come to any open difference with you, for you have been, and are, a liberal customer of mine, and we have shared some pleasant convivial hours. Pass on therefore, squire, if you please, or stand out of my path. We cannot be friendly together more, and your conscience will furnish you with the cause. Nevertheless, it will be your fault if your discreditable doing are spread abroad. Good day!"

"Presuming upstart!" cried Clifton, in uncontrollable rage, "do you talk to me of conscience?—to me? You forget the distance that divides us! I have honoured you too much by my notice."

"We differ in opinion respecting the honor of your notice," said Maynard, coolly. "To be sure, you have a few hundreds a-year for life, but it was neither your industry nor talent that

acquired that income; while the thousand pounds I have in the bank was every penny hardly and honestly earned by the sweat of my brow. Your ancestors, you may say, were great folk in their time, but how do I know that I should not find mine had been greater if I had records of them? Then you can keep your liveried lackies; but I don't envy that privilege, for if I had thousands per annum no bedizened slave should degrade the name of man by wearing livery of mine. As to your feasts and costly furniture, what are they all worth if they do not content you? If it was necessary to your happiness to ruin a simple girl, what was the good of all your possessions and hereditary honours? There is nothing of any worth but what conduces to happiness; and if Harry Maynard, with his plain fireside, homely table, and daily toil, is a happier man, and can boast a more independent and peaceful mind than gay Squire Clifton, why, I should like to know, am I to consider his notice as so vast an honour?"

A deep blush of angry shame stained the cheek of Clifton, as, from the allusion to Ruth in this speech, it was apparent to him that she had entrusted to the miller the whole story of her disappointment—another evidence, most galling, of the confidential understanding existing between them. But he consoled himself with the thought that the more perfectly Maynard was acquainted with what had taken place, the less difficult it would be for him to give utterance to a certain proposition with which his mind was labouring.

Divided between the embarrassment of conscious guilt and precipitate resolution, after a pause of a minute, in which Maynard passed by him, and proceeded some yards along the path between the tall ranks of wheat, Clifton followed his rival, and, touching him on the shoulder, said—

" Maynard, you observed, I think, that you were not disposed to come to an open rupture with me; neither, in truth am I with you. If we can mutually serve, instead of injuring each other, it would be more desirable. Grant me your careful attention, and I will point out how this may be."

" I am attentive," said Maynard, carelessly.

" First then, let me remind you of the power in my hands for putting you to trouble. Uour lease is about to expire. In a few months I may eject you from the mill; and as there is no other unoccupied within ten miles, you would be much inconvenienced, and lose your trade."

"To inconvenience I certainly should be put, since the renewal of my lease being nearly completed, and no hint having been

given me until this moment of any intention to withdraw it, I never once contemplated such a dilemma. But it does not alarm me, squire, for in such a case I should employ the money I have saved in building another, as near to yours as I could purchase ground."

"To the injury of the occupiers of each. But confess you would be loath to desert the old place."

"So I should."

"Would you gladly convert it into your own property?"

"Why, yes, if you take the sum I offered some time ago, there is a difference, I believe, between us, of a hundred pounds, and that is considerable."

"Maynard," said Clifton, taking him by the hand, and continuing to press it hard as he spoke, "the whole shall be yours, a clear gift made over to you by bond, for the term of your natural life, if you will only yield Ruth. Do not be in haste to spurn my proposal. Consider your disparity of years—consider seriously the fact that she does not entertain for you those sentiments which can alone ensure fidelity and tranquillity in the marriage relation—consider that for me, whose passion for her has reached a height at which it ceases to be under the control of the judgment, or even, I am sorry to say, of the moral principle—consider, I say Maynard, that for me she does entertain those sentiments which toward you are wanting, and judge whether it will not be wise on your part to renounce a band which would not have been yours had not I erred, and enter into a compact with me, to be kept inviolate, by which Ruth may be prevailed upon to return to my protection, and you become possessed of a valuable freehold."

"If I understand you," said Maynard, his round face as red as a harvest moon, "you mean to infer that the girl you could not seduce while single, you hope to when she is married. I am much obliged to your honour for the notion; at the same time I can assure you, that if my wife did not know how to guard herself, I should know how to guard her. As to the sentiments you boast Ruth feels for you, she has candidly told me she did love you, but she also tells me, and I believe her, that your vile usage of her has turned that misplaced love to detestation, and shown her the danger and the folly of having ever listened to you. And you talk of your love for Ruth, but I should be sorry to match mine with it. I can be satisfied with nothing less than her happiness—you with nothing less than her misery. Upon my honest word, if I thought her happiness was to be ensured by no other means than giving her to you, I would resign her, that would I, Mr. Clifton. I thank God I am not selfish in my wishes."

"Resign, her then—for, unquestionable, her happiness must be found with me, or not at all."

"You are very positive on that head, squire. Excuse me if I am not. Your protection, I am afraid, would supply but a sorry sort of happiness for her. If you had said, 'Give her up to me, and I will take her openly by the hand, and present her to my connexions as Mrs. Percy Clifton,' your words would have had a better sound, though I should not have thought them a whit more worth listening to."

Percy's reluctance to an obscure alliance was not yet overcome. But to regain possession of the lovely girl he had lost, was an object to be attained at any price.

"Resign her," Maynard," he said, "and by the heaven above us, the protection I will give her shall be a legal one, and the freehold shall be yours just the same."

"It shall never be said that I stood in the way of Ruth's happiness," said Maynard. "Walk on to the cottage of the Summerfields, make your offer like a man, and promise, as I do, to abide by the desision of Ruth and her parents. You look dubious—undecided—I think I have put your sincerity to the test. You flinch."

"You shall see otherwise—lead on."

They went accordingly. The cottagers had just sat down to dinner, and were surprised at seeing Maynard, after he had so recently parted from them, especially as he had guests at the mill that day. Still more were they surprised when the young and handsome squire's tall figure darkened the doorway. Mrs. Summerfield dropped her knife and fork and uttered a half shriek of terror. Her husband whispered to her with hasty anxiety, and then rising, demanded to what cause they were indebted for the presence of Squire Clifton.

"A very particular one," said Maynard. "Shall you or I state it, squire?"

"Permit me," said Percy.

"Stay, Ruth," said Maynard, as she was attempting hastily to pass out; "you must not quit the room—what the squire has to say concerns you."

"Me!" echoed Ruth, gasping for breath, "what can Mr. Clifton have to say that concerns me?"

"I will address myself to your father," said Percy, aristocratical pride predominating in the first part of his speech, and persuasive energy in the latter. "Mr. Summerfield, I have been holding with your friend here a conversation relative to Ruth. I have been exhibiting to him a variety of motives for resigning his present engagement with her; and I am not without an impression that the momentousness of some of these is as evident to him as to myself. Forbear to interrupt me, sir—I shall comprise what I came to say in a few syllables. The benefits that will accrue to Mr. Maynard personally from a renunciation of his claim on my behalf, chiefly concerns himself—while to you, Mr. Summerfield, and your family, it must be superfluous to point out the improvements in your circumstances which must naturally flow from a connection with me. In brief, then, I am here to lay all I have, and all I am, at the feet of Ruth, who, within any given time you please to name, shall receive my plighted faith at the altar."

"Father," said Ruth, with decision, "I have given my promise to Mr. Maynard, and mean to fulfil it!"

"If your promise is not mine with the free consent of your heart and will, I renounce it," said Maynard, with emphasis. "Here stand Mr. Clifton and myself—choose between us, and choose freely."

"Where my word has been given it shall not be revoked," said Ruth.

Summerfield then addressed Clifton.

"We are sensible of the honor of the unexpected proposal," he said, "but you hear my daughter's decision, squire; and I must say it gives me high satisfaction, for were a prince to propose to Ruth, I should prefer Maynard before him. You will not think this refusal personally disparaging, therefore, and in declining it, we give you our humble thanks."

Here Mrs. Summerfield twitched her husband's sleeve, and he withdrew for a moment apart with her.

"If the squire was Ruth's husband," she eagerly whispered, "we should be safe—don't you think so?"

"Safe!—how?"

"If that should be brought to light, he would never prosecute his wife's parents!"

"But the authorities of justice would."

"Still Roger, it would be a good deal in our favour to have him befriending us. Or, while all is safe, you might get from him money to carry us over sea, away from this dreadful place and this horrible life of fear."

"And you would sacrifice our friend the miller?"

"Ah! no—he shall have Ruth—she shall be his wife, whatever may betide her fate."

PERCY FLUNG HER ARM ON HIM WITH A JERK

THE COTTAGE GIRL.

PERCY CLIFTON INTERCEPTS RUTH ON THE BRIDGE.

"MAYNARD himself," said Summerfield, "may perhaps assist us to emigrate, when he is united to Ruth. He promised to do something liberal for us; and I intend to propose that he advances us money to leave the country, instead of establishing us in a farm. There is an emigration society would send us out to Australia for no great sum—I shall see about it next week. It is no great matter whither we go, provided we can have but a resonable chance of getting a livelihood."

"It is strange to me that Ruth should have had no expectation of this offer from the squire," said Mrs. Summerfield.

"It is stranger to me that she should so readily refuse it," said the cottager. "Something more has occurred than we are aware of. However, it is as well she has been so decided, for as she had sufficient time to know her own mind, and liberty to exercise it, not by my consent should the promise she gave the miller have been broken."

In the few minutes occupied by this private colloquy between the husband and wife, Clifton made a second strenuous and ineffectual attempt to alter the decision of Ruth.

"Enough of this, squire," said Maynard, interfering. "We agreed to abide by her determination. If it had been unfavourable to me I should have submitted, and as it is unfavourable to you, you must submit. You will grant she has been quite uninfluenced?"

"O quite," said Clifton, bitterly.

"You will grant," continued Maynard, "that I have forborn to urge anything on my own behalf, or to your prejudice?"

"You have been wonderfully disinterested."

"So I have; for, as I told you, I am not a selfish man! and if I thought the banns we heard this morning were contrary to Ruth's inclination I would silence them before another sabbath."

"Questionless!" ejaculated Clifton, sarcastically, making proud efforts to conceal his poignant mortification at having failed to secure to himself a more favourable arbitrement, notwithstanding all his advantages of fortune, birth, and appearance — notwithstanding the influence he had boasted with Ruth—notwithstanding his condescension to her father.

"And now Ruth's free choice of me has been put beyond dispute," said the miller, "I will not hide from her what has passed between you and I, Mr. Clifton, just before this general meeting here. The squire, my pretty one, would have persuaded me that it was necessary for your happiness to return to his protection, such as you experienced it before. What think you of that?"

Clifton waited not to hear the rejoinder.

"I have yet another offer to make to Ruth," he said, in accents almost inarticulate with jealous agony, and a sense of disgrace. "It is one which she shall not have it in her power to spurn as she has done this of to-day; and I postpone it only for a few days." Thus ambiguously speaking, as Summerfield and his wife re-appeared, Clifton bowed haughtily to them, and left the dwelling with a swift, uneven step.

"I never knew anything so extraordinary in my life!" exclaimed Mrs. Summerfield. "Ruth, my dear, are you sure you had no idea of the squire coming to make this proposal?"

"Not the least, mother," she said, with perfect sincerity.

"Where did you meet Mr. Clifton, Henry," asked Mrs. Summerfield, "and how came he to open his mind to you?"

Ruth cast an imploring look on Maynard, to induce him to say nothing that might impeach the rectitude of Clifton to her parents, and, though unwillingly, he complied.

"I met him near where we separated," the miller said; "and I suppose his inducement for opening his mind to me was the hope of persuading me to give up my intended wife."

"Such arrogance," observed Summerfield, "richly merited the reception it met from my daughter. But I wonder you endured it so tamely, friend Maynard."

"I felt anything but tame," said the miller, with a sparkling eye; "but how knew I that when Ruth came to learn the squire's willingness to wed her, she would not repent having bound herself to a homely fellow like me? That was a hazard I cared not to encounter. I had no wish to decoy her to my bosom by hiding from her the glittering prospects she was relinquishing. No. If to shine in the drawing-room of Rosedale House, (and shine she would there or any where else,) would give her more lasting delight than to sit a quiet housewife in my mill, why to Rosedale House, and to its master, let her go. I would not detain her. I am her friend as well as her lover, and wish that which will give her most permanent peace."

"She will find it with you, Henry, or not on earth," said Mrs. Summerfield.

"I intend she shall," said Maynard, taking one of Ruth's fair taper hands in his right, and stroking it with his left. "I don't forget her tender years, and shall make great allowances for her, and expect no more from her than candour, kindness, and a willingness to abandon herself to my guidance. By and bye, as months roll on, she may learn to prize me better than I dare look for at present. In the meantime there is no deception between us, and our wedlock will be based on a true and hearty friendship—a better groundwork for married peace than many couples commence with."

CHAPTER XII.

"Black was the night, the watch-dog howled,
   The fierce blast shook the tower,
Restless the dark Betrayer prowled
   About the maiden's bower.

"The damned spirit of the dead
   Shrieked nigh in airy space,
A deed of cruelty and dread
   Was done in that lone place."—OLD BALLAD.

PERCY Clifton had in vain tried to corrupt our heroine by dazzling her senses, bewildering her judgment, and inflaming her
love—after having, in the extremity of his passion and despair,
propounded to the miller that infamous compound for rendering
back Ruth to his protection—after having been maddened by finding this last precious demonstation productive only of a failure
more complete, and of a stain on his honour more deep and inde-
lible, than any preceding—and after having submitted to solicit
the hand of Ruth in marriage, and suffered a refusal, stinging to
his pride, and bitter to his feelings, he became impressed with the
full unmitigated conviction that without resorting to means more
desperate than any he had yet grappled with, Ruth was utterly,
irretrievably lost to him; on which, thirsting for retaliation, and
fiercely resolved at any hazard to prevent Ruth's being appropriated by another, Clifton determined on a plan at once barbarous
and subtle, and as it is said the devil never withholds fit instruments of evil from those who wish them, Jean Andre was at hand
for a co-operator, and the period chosen for the unhallowed
scheme was during the absence of Amy Clifton on a visit for
a few days to the Hermitage, the residence of her friend Miss
Monckton.

   Amy's kind heart had been gratified at discovering that Ruth
had overcome her misplaced attachment to Percy, even whilst her
romantic fancy was shocked at discovering that to be perishable
which had seemed framed to outlive life, change, and death. Several times before leaving home she sent for Ruth, and presented
her with a variety of presents suitable for her bridal, and having

as little moderation in her liberality as in any thing else that leaned to the side of virtue, proceeded to procure for the fair young bride's appearance at the altar a complete dress of expensive and elegant materials, above what was consistent with the station in life of any of the parties concerned. Miss Clifton also volunteered to honour with her presence the marriage dinner at the mill, which was to be prepared at an added expense, to do credit to her condescension.

It wanted but a week to the important day—the second MARRIAGE-DAY to which Ruth had looked forward within the space of twelve months—and she had been from noon to evening with her father and a number of young people in a harvest field belonging to the farmer by whom Summerfield was employed, when, at the ringing of the curfew, (which old custom had been retained unaltered in Rosedale since the days of feudal slavery), she separated from her mirthful companions to keep an appointment she had made with Maynard. and, from some sentiment not to be too closely analysed, went out of her way a quarter of a mile to cross that rustic bridge where she had been used to hold her stolen interview with the young squire. It was a spot just such as nature might have formed expressly for lovers' meetings. The brook babbled below; the shady boughs rustled above; and so still the scene that not a step pressed the hollow-sounding planks of the bridge but startled from its momentary rest on twig or spray some sylvan songster, whose quivering pinions defied the quick glance to follow them as they plunged into the thickets, or vanished aloft in a towering wilderness of innumerable branches. The brook which flowed beneath the bridge issued from the plantation, precipitating itself from the top of a high bank of verdurous earth to form a mimic waterfall, and plashing along an irregular channel interrupted by stones and gravel, and here and there by the encroachments of vegetation, which, in a hundred beautiful shapes, bent over and studded its sparkling waters. And all around there was a gentle drowsy hum of summer insects, and blended sounds of rural life softened by distance into soothing harmony.

To this familiar spot Ruth approached, her eyes cast down in sad regretful rumination, her step listless and slow, and supporting on her arm a sheaf of corn she had gleaned; and she was upon the centre of the bridge ere she perceived that Clifton leant against the rail. Her first thought was escape. but as that was impracticable, she rallied her courage and her resolution to listen to his vehement reproaches and importunate appeals.

Hard it was for her to endure the first, difficult to resist the latter. But the invigorating example and counsels of her father

had blessed her with the force of virtuous purpose and self-denying will more than at her age many could boast possessed of superior education, according to the ordinary notions entertained of education.   There was no confusion in her m.nd as to what it was right for her to do, no infirmity of reso ution as regarded its performance.   Her inexperience of evil had been painfully corrected; the trustingness inseparable from a woman's first attachment had been outraged in her bosom and converted into suspicion and fear; and the bewildering ascendancy Clifton's rank, education, and authority, as master, had given him over her, was annihilated.   The sunny veil had been rudely torn away from her young vision; she saw clearly the temptations which menaced her.   She was not the girl to flutter passively about the flame until consumed by it.   "She who deliberates 's lost," one has observed who knew human nature well, and whether Ruth abstractedly knew this or not, she followed, without looking to the right or left, the proper course, and steeled her ear and heart to all that Clifton could say.   With brevity, quietness, and simplicity, she replied to him that she had promised Mr. Maynard her hand, and would not disappoint him.

"And why did you promise him, unkind girl?" Percy exclaimed.   "If to revenge yourself on me—if to put me to the torture—you have succeeded well; but beware what you do.   The misery you have devised for me may recoil on yourself."

"There were good reasons for my pledging myself to Mr. Maynard," said Ruth, "and I don't believe I shall ever repent having done so."

"And you are positively inexorable to my entreaties?   You will bestow yourself on the miller, and leave me to endure your loss without giving me so much as a sigh of pity, which the veriest wretch on earth might claim from gentleness and goodness?   You frown on my penitence, Ruth—you refuse to pardon my error—you are deaf to my prayers that I may be allowed to recompense you for the past by my hand, my heart, my fortune!"

"I do forgive you, Mr. Clifton, though you have made me suffer much.   But I am not your equal in condition, and I would never more think of uniting myself to you even if I was not engaged to Mr. Maynard.   I am ashamed I was ever persuaded to such vain dreams."

"Why vain, if I am willing to realise them?"

"Yes, IF—but, Mr. Clifton, you know that you are not willing, and that there is no dependence to be placed on what you say. You have treated me as a weak, foolish girl, whom you could prevail on to believe what you chose, and whom it was a light fault in you to

deceive. I know I have been both weak and foolish, but I will be so no longer. I wish you all happiness, Mr. Clifton, with a lady of your own degree; and I beg of you to forget me, except as another's wife, and I shall make it my study and prayer that I may forget all the wrong you have said and done me, and that God may forgive you, and that you may learn a better way of employing your thoughts, and better deeds to grace your station."

An oath half issued from the lips of the chafed Percy, whilst his fingers so nervously pressed her wrist that she uttered a cry of pain. Gnashing his teeth, he then flung her arm from him with a jerk, and telling her she would repent her obduracy, strode away.

Next day the cook from Rosedale House brought to the cottage the marriage dress Miss Clifton had purchased for Ruth, and desired her, in her young lady's name, to hasten to Rosedale House, where Miss Clifton wished to detain her if she could spare the time, until the following evening. Ruth asked if the woman knew for what purpose Miss Clifton sought her attendance, and was answered there were more presents for her, to which the speaker added in no very pleasant tone—"It is well for you to be so befriended. Some people might be married a dozen times and never meet such luck."

"True," Ruth responded with sweet humility, "and I hope I shall know how to be thankful to Providence and my friends. And when you, Betty, find a husband to your mind, I hope you will be as fortunate."

With this, Ruth pressed on the ill-natured maid a pair of gold ear-rings, which had been given to her by Miss Clifton before her marriage had been seriously thought of. Some touch of compunction must then have been felt by this woman, who was the same that had been confederated with Maynard's housekeeper to take away the good name of the inoffensive girl to whose destruction she was again lending herself, her present embassage being performed for her master instead of Miss Clifton, the latter having the same forenoon left home for the residence of her friend; and Betty was aware, by the nature and falsity of the message, and by the bribe she had received for delivering it, that something wrong was going on.

Miss Clifton had left directions for her rich present of the wedding apparel to be conveyed to the cottage during the day, and this facilitated the plans of Percy by giving an air of reality to Betty's false errand thither; who was further instructed by him, to let drop, as by accident, that he was from home, and not expected to return for some days.

By such means Ruth was completely beguiled, and made all haste to obey the summons she had received without a single throb of foreboding or doubt.   As she left the cottage she smilingly said to her mother—

"I shall call at the mill, and Maynard and I will be here together by dusk to-morrow evening."

Alas! many morrows had to pass before she again entered her beloved home, and when she did, it was under what altered feelings! what changed circumstances.

Preparations for the approaching marriage had thrown the interior of the mill into temporary confusion, but another and more direful cause of disorder also prevailed.   The housekeeper of Maynard, a woman under resentment and disappointment absolutely ferocious, exasperated by the expectation of her master's endowing Ruth instead of herself with all his wordly goods, on receiving notice of dismissal, in a moment of frenzy attempted to poison Maynard; and being detected in the act of dropping the arsenic from a paper into his ale, she swallowed, ere she could be prevented, a quantity of the undiluted powder, and was, apparently, on the brink of death when Ruth came to acquaint the miller that Miss Clifton had sent for her.

In a few hurried words Maynard imparted the dreadful event to the horror-stricken girl, who, entering the sitting room, beheld the wretched woman supported on a seat by an old decrepid creature, her mother, whom she had for years maintained with a filial kindness, anomalous in her character.   Many other persons were gathered around, and Dr. Walcot had been sent for, but had not yet arrived.

At the entrance of our heroine, Kitty raised her almost gigantic stature from the chair, and exclaimed to those who stood by—

"There she comes who was the cause of all this.   The sight of her is worse than arsenic!   To look at her painted face makes me sick, and plunges me in hell before my time!   Keep her off, for God's sake!"

"Don'na talk so, Kitty," said the old mother, in a strong northern patois, "the lassie has done ye na harm."

"No harm!   Why, what have I been driving at all these years do you think?—to keep drudging in service, or to marry respectably?   Was it my intentions to live always toiling and moiling at another's beck and pleasure, or to be my own mistress?   Why have I looked after all Mr. Maynard's little comforts, and put up with all his whims and nonsense, if I did not expect it was his intentions to make me his wife?"

"You had no right to expect anything of the sort, Kitty," said

Maynard. "I never gave you any encouragement, and never would."

Kitty here fell heavily on the floor, and Ruth, dismayed and shocked as she was, sprang to her help, and was the first to raise her head, and to entreat Maynard to send again for the doctor. It was, however, fearfully evident that life was departing.

"It is dreadful to think of her dying in such a frame of mind," said Ruth, shuddering. "Oh, Kitty, if you think you have been ill-used, forgive, that you may be forgiven. Do not die in enmity with us."

Kitty only answered by turning her protruding eyeballs on her poor old mother.

"You will not be destitute," she said, in the intervals of her agony, and with gasping breath. "In my box are twenty sovereigns—and—clothes—bury me cheap—do the best you can with what is left—I am going."

With the words a film came over her sight, and she was gone to her account.

An inquest being held next day on the body, it was hastily and privately interred by night, followed by one solitary mourner, the miserable old woman whom this tragical event had left entirely desolate, and who died of grief and old age shortly after, in the parish poor house.

Two hours after the dreadful catastrophe at the mill, when Ruth had in some measure recovered the shock it had occasioned her, she proceeded to Rosedale House, contrary to the dissuasive advice of Maynard, who was justly apprehensive of the designs of Clifton; but as Ruth had been told that the latter was not at home, she saw no reason for apprehension, and therefore retained her purpose.

It was dark ere she reached the house, when the cook was looking out for her, and the tale of terror Ruth had to tell as a reason for her tardy arrival was already known.

"Heaven be merciful to us!" exclaimed the woman, "it was only last Sunday Kitty and I were together, and though she looked wildish, she talked pleasantly enough. Lord! Lord!—to see what a world this is! One does not what they may come to. I was going to drink tea with her to-morrow, and if she had only have waited until then, I think I could have told her news would have prevented this."

"What news do you mean?" Ruth inquired, but to this interrogative the woman was deaf, and spoke instead of Miss Clifton, who she supposed would be married shortly to Mr. Tracy, then her daily companion.

Ruth wished to know where she should find Miss Clifton, and was told, as she had come so late, the latter could not see her to-night, but she was to sleep with the cook, and go to the young lady's chamber as soon as she rose in the morning.

The cook's room, to which Ruth was directly conducted, was not the same as the former had occupied when our heroine was an inmate of the house, but, rather to her wonder, one situated in an isolated, and by traditionary supposition, haunted, part of the building, that had not been used for domestic purposes during many, very many years.

"What could have induced you to lodge yourself here?" Ruth asked, unnerved by the scene she had witnessed at the mill, and hence peculiarly alive to the superstitious tremors which assailed her on finding herself the tenant for a night of a room in which supernatural lights were reported to have been seen, and unusual noises heard, which was cut off from the apartments of the other persons in the house by a long flight of corkscrew steps that seemed to her only formed for ghosts to tread, and by several rambling passages, where the wind, that now began to rise high, stirring the old tapestry, made a sound suggestive, in a very high degree, of dreary thoughts.

"I like to be here as little as you," the cook replied to her; "but I had no choice, for yesterday and to-day Miss Clifton has had a large batch of visitors, and my room is given up to them, and Mr. Clifton's, likewise, as well as Mrs. Wilson's, who went to Bath by this morning's stage to see her married daughter there. But although I have consented for this night," she added, "they won't find me stay here a second."

"If Miss Clifton has so many visitors, I should not have thought the housekeeper could have left," observed Ruth.

"O dear, yes. When our lady heard that Mrs. Wilson's daughter was lying at death's door, or thereabout, she sent her off directly."

Pained to hear that affliction had lighted on the excellent old gentlewoman of whom they were speaking, Ruth expressed an earnest hope that she would return happier than she went; while the cook stirred into a bright blaze, before which the dusky shadows of the wide chamber vanished, a fire that had been kindled, to dissipate the damp that clung to the walls, notwithstanding the heat of the weather during the few past weeks; and having spread a supper of more than ordinary delicacy, and placed before Ruth a small glass of hot negus, and compounded another for herself, to "scare away the blue devils from the old place," she remarked to her companion "that they were not so uncomfortable, after all."

After both had finished supper, and sat talking a little time of the tragical occurrence at the mill, the cook coolly observing that she would be wanted in the kitchen, but would soon return, left Ruth alone, and as she went out, locked the door behind her. Rising to ascertain what this could mean, the latter found herself strangely affected with dizziness, sickness, and stupor, insomuch that, in attempting to cross the room, she sank down powerlessly on an antiquated bedstead, which, raised horizontally but a little above the polished oaken floor, reared its carved posts to the ceiling, like four tall monsters, garmented in gloomy hangings of quaint device.

Here, while the loud blast every few minutes shook the tower to its foundation, she reclined in dubious wonder at the sensations she experienced, straining her ear for the cook's return, and her mind still running on Kitty's murderous attempt on the life of Maynard, and her subsequent suicide, until the fearful suggestion arose, whether, by some means unknown, the malicious woman had not contrived to administer arsenic to her, against whom she bore most rancour. Rallying her utmost powers under this ghastly impression, to resist the stupefaction then fast reducing her to a state resembling death, and steadying herself by grasping at such pieces of furniture as came within her reach, Ruth succeeded in placing her hand on the ponderous door-lock, and shook the door with the violence of mortal fear; but she was unheard, or if heard, unanswered; and tottering back to the bed, the betrayed girl sank across it perfectly insensible.

Turn we now to Clifton, who, in the dark, was walking to and fro his sporting room in a high state of mental excitement, his stock cast aside, his shirt collar unbuttoned, and his uncovered neck exposed to the wind which blew through the open window from the park. One of his dogs came fawning about his feet—but a kick sent the affectionate creature howling to the other side of the room.

"I am a barbarous wretch," he muttered, drinking off a large glass of undiluted brandy. "But what may not be expected from a seducer—a ravisher! Perdition seize me, but I shall never get through with it! She shall go back—by all that is precious, she shall! Oh, Andre, here you are at last."

"Yes, sir, and the chaise is drawn up close to the house under the trees, and as the night is dark, it will not be seen."

"You are a precious villain, Andre!"

"Sir!"

"Have you no belief in hell, Jean?"

"Me, sir?—no, sir."

"Has there occurred no moment when the thought has pressed home upon you that there might be?"

"Not that I can recollect sir."

"Then you think there will be no retribution for a sordid villain who assists to decoy from a peaceful home a pure and lovely creature, and plunges her deep in vice, infamy and misery?"

"Really, sir," ejaculated the valet, quite at a loss to understnd this new turn his master's mind had taken, "I don't know what you wish me to say sir."

"The truth, if you know what truth is. I ask if you have ever felt that you have a soul, and if you nourish ao apprehension that it will be endangered by this night's work?"

The ready-witted valet replied, that as he had found Mr. Clifton so good a master in this world, he would be content to share his lot in the next. Clifton laughed, and after a brief silence—

"I think, Andre," he said, "we will proceed no farther in this."

"As you please, sir," said the valet, with a dash of ridicule in his accent; "but I should think the narcotic by this time must have taken effect; if so, she will be incapable of leaving the house without assistance, and her parents and intended bridegroom may wish to know how she came in that state."

The words were on his lips, when the cook appeared to report the success of her part of the black plot.

"Fate will have it so," Clifton muttered, and giving five guineas to each of his agents, and whispering to Andre, who answered briefly, "I will be there, sir," he moved with stealthy strides toward the lonely chamber where his helpless captive was confined.

Louder and louder swelled the wind that night; over the gleaming stars the clouds heaved and rolled like billows of the sea; many of the finest park trees were dismantled of their branches; and a stately oak in front of the Lady's Tower, which had resisted the storms of five centuries, fell with a crash of thunder to the earth. The whirlwind was at its height about four o'clock in the morning, at which hour a chaise drew up to a small door in the Lady's Tower, and received Clifton and his lovely victim, who lay passive as a corpse in his arms drove furiously away. In this perfectly inanimate state Ruth was placed a second time in the luxurious villa her betrayer had prepared for her.

CHAPTER XIII.

"Ours was no passion frail and fleet,
  No idle fancy of the heart,
We knew but one delight—to meet!
  We felt but one regret—to part!"

OCCUPIED so intensely and so long with his own unhappy passion, Percy had neglected the precious charge his mother had consigned to his affectionate safe keeping—we mean his sister—and had ceased to concern himself about her peace just at a time when it was most seriously menaced; though of course it had not escaped his observation that she had formed an intimacy of no light nature with the artist introduced to her by himself. Both, that is, Clifton and Amy, had latterly discontinued their habits of gay society; their lively entertainments had become rarities; and the one divided his time chiefly between his gun and Ruth, the other between her books, Charlotte Monckton, and Tracy. Clifton had been well pleased that her attention was diverted from his movements, and Amy was equally well content at being left unmolested to ramble away her forenoon with the travelled artist, in order to select natural scenes and objects from her native vale and hills for his gifted pencil, or in her boudoir to listen to his inexhaustible flow of conversational eloquence, garnished with anecdote, description, poetical allusion, and a kind of pensive wit peculiar to himself.

What happened was a natural result in so enthusiastic and imaginative a being as Amy; under the mask of platonic friendship, she cherished a love that had wound itself intimately with the springs of life, to whose dominion she unresistingly surrendered herself.

Yet of his past life she knew little more than that he had travelled and studied. What his moral conduct had been, or what connexions he might have formed, she was ignorant, nor cared to be enlightened, content with an implicit belief they must have been all that was desirable. His brilliant talents, and the fascination of his manners, completely blinded her vision, so that she could discern none of the spots that lay concealed amid the glorious brightness of the sun of her idolatry.

> " She loved—her soul did nature frame
> For love, and fancy nursed the flame.
> Silent she loved; in every gaze
> Was passion—friendship in her phrase."

She often found the unbidden tear springing to her eye—the unbidden sigh to her lips. Whatever in the books she read touched on the master passion, affected her as it had never done before she met with Tracy; and to hear a melody of tender expression was almost more than she could sustain. When he was not with her, her favourite enjoyment was to steal unnoticed to some retired nook, and there to lose herself in tender and imaginative reveries.

> " Such was her wont; and there her dream
> Soared on some wild fantastic theme
> Of faithful love, or ceaseless spring,
> Till contemplation's wearied wing
> The enthusiast could no more sustain,
> And sad she sunk to earth again."

Miss Monckton rallying her on these habits of solitary abstraction and the enjoyment she seemed to take in them, told her she would make an excellent votaress of the cloister, subjoining " for there you might have solitude to your heart's content, and dreams enough, Heaven knows."

" It is just what I should prefer of all things," said the enthusiast; " and if there was only such a thing as a Protestant convent in Rosedale, you would see how soon I should rank myself among its members."

" You would do no such thing if they adhered to the monastic law of celibacy."

" Why should you say so ?" asked Amy, bending her face that her hair might shade her kindling cheek from view.

" Only because you maintain so extraordinary and determined a silence respecting the gentleman who engrosses so large a portion of your time, that I conclude your heart is trammelled to a degree that you are backward to confess."

" I shall not attempt to deny that Mr. Tracy is dear to me," said Amy, in much painful confusion—" he is so; and when the hours arrive, as arrive they must, in which I shall see him no more," (her voice faltered,) " then shall I be able to say with truth I have lived to suffer."

" But why must the hour arrive in which you will see him

no more ? What is there to prevent your union ? You have none to oppose your inclination."

"My dear Charlotte," said Amy, casting herself on her friend's neck, " cannot you divine why it is I cannot marry Tracy ?"

" No, indeed."

"Then I am sorry to have to say," said Amy, weeping hysterically, " that I fear—I fear it is only because—he has not asked me," and the weeping hysterical fit was instantaneously converted into one of laughter.

"You are a strange girl," said Miss Monckton, also laughing. "But pray am I never to be introduced to this lord of your affections ? I shall certainly begin to think that you are afraid of finding a rival in me.'

Amy was instantly grave.

"You know, my dearest Charlotte," she said, "that I never intentionally hide a thought from you, though it tend to my own disparagement. What will you say to my weakness when I confess that I do dread your meeting with Tracy, for to see you is to love you. In your presence your poor friend would be soon overlooked. Do you doubt it ? Survey us both in that mirror, and mark the contrast. I can easily conceive your form, mind, and features being copied for a statue of the majestic Juno, or the sublime Siddons; while you have the finest brunette complexion —the richest raven hair—the most resplendent dark eye—that it was ever my fortunate lot to look upon. I, alas! on the contrary, have nothing to distinguish me from the vulgar herd. In figure only have I the smallest pretension to notice. My cheek is neither pale nor red—my eye neither bright or dull—and, in brief, all about my unfortunate person is mere commonplace, or below it."

Miss Monckton raised the resplendent eye of which her friend had spoken, to the large mirror before them, and an expression of self-gratulation added to its lustre. She, however, affirmed that Amy's opinion of her own attractions was too mean, and all she required to charm was a greater attention to dress, and more propriety of manner. Even thus much correction of her friend's foibles was a novelty in Charlotte Monckton and dropped from her unawares, for it was no part of her policy (and she was politic) to render Amy's character more perfect, or its defects less conspicuous to the common eye.

Miss Monckton, we may as well inform the reader at once, was a lady perfectly incapable of returning the enthusiastic, single-hearted attachment of Amy Clifton, being essentially cold in heart and fancy, and cherishing the bad wish of seeing Amy shortly separated from her brother, and disappointed in her pecu-

niary expectations from him, which were considerable, while he remained unmarried. Charlotte's motive may easily be conjectured. As a handsome young bachelor of mark and likelihood, possessed of no inconsiderable fortune, and highly connected—as one whose wife might claim admission to the most brilliant circles of ton—Percy possessed considerable attractions in her eye; and there having passed much occasional flirtation between them, and knowing that he admired her fine person, and that he was not insensible to the stately polish of her manners, and the effective precision of her superb costume, Miss Monckton was already preparing herself to enact the part of mistress of Rosedale, and had no intention of allowing her sister-in-law, however unassuming, to share with her the dominion and the display which would then be hers, or to suffer the property of Percy to be lessened by acts of generosity to his orphan sister.

There were yet other views warring against the friendship which Amy Clifton imagined Charlotte entertained for her. These arose out of envy; for it happened that, notwithstanding the personal inferiority of Amy to Miss Monckton, and the great anxiety of the latter to attract admirers, Charlotte inspired far less liking, and obtained much less ascendancy than her companion, owing, perhaps, to those flashes of lovely and unaffected feminine feeling, and intellect in Amy, the magic of which, unknown to its possessor, was felt more or less keenly by all who approached her.

Soon after the conversation between the two friends just recounted, Tracy and Miss Clifton found themselves, towards the close of a mild summer day, gently following the windings of the wild uplands to the spot which had become a favourite with both. It was the summit of an elevated rock, whence the view of the surrounding country was beautiful in the extreme.

Here they paused to rest, and Tracy, addressing his companion in those deep tones of penetrating sadness to which Amy's heart had learnt to respond but too intensely, said, as he drew from his pocket a miniature resemblance of himself—

"To-morrow, dear Miss Clifton, I must bid you farewell; and I would fain flatter myself that, when at a distance from you, this may recall sometimes the recollection of one whose happiest hours have been spent in your society—I would fain persuade myself that over this memento of our friendship you will sometimes, when we are sundered, breathe a sigh for the unfortunate wanderer it portrays."

"To-morrow! Did you say to-morrow?" Amy faintly articulated, looking timidly up to Tracy's face. "Must it be so?"

THE COTTAGE GIRL.

MAYNARD AND SUMMERFIELD'S VISIT TO MISS CLIFTON.

"EVEN so. But, believe me, that in heart I shall never leave you."

Control over her feelings was the last lesson experience could teach Amy.

Her bursting tears told the secret of her soul; and though it was not on the present occasion that Tracy descried it first, he was excessively moved.

"Let us return to the house," she said, rising, after a protracted and agitating silence, "the night grows chilly."

They moved forward, along a narrow path that wound down the rugged face of the hill, between high banks of a bare quarry, where the clink of the labourer's hammer, or the screams of the large wild fowl that bred on these bleak heights, were the only sounds that broke the deep stillness of the evening hour; and coming in sight of the Hermitage, a house to which immovable iron window-blinds, and a cross elevated above the door-way, imparted much of a romantic appearance, Amy falteringly said—

"That is the dwelling of Miss Monckton, of whom you have heard me speak so highly. Let us enter—she is anxious to be acquainted with you before you leave."

Tracy's aspect changed so remarkably as she spoke, that, observing him with astonishment, Amy inquired whether he had not previously been acquainted with Charlotte Monckton, as, whenever she had happened to speak of her friend in his hearing, he had always been more or less disturbed, and she fancied also he had purposely avoided her.

"Yes, I have met Miss Monckton, before, in France," replied Tracy, his voice as altered as his look, "and I have no desire to renew the acquaintance."

"Indeed!" ejaculated Amy, with no small uneasiness, "and pray will it be impertinent in me to inquire how long you were known to each other, and what circumstances have rendered Mr. Tracy unwilling to renew his acquaintance with Miss Monckton?"

"My dear Miss Clifton, those brief circumstances do not merit repetition; but I will not withhold from you that they have imprinted on my mind, an impression of your friend unfavourable in some respects, and I think it to be regretted that you have formed so close an intimacy with her."

"You amaze me! and it fills me with no less wonder that Charlotte has not recognised your name, so often as I have spoken it in her presence."

"Possibly I have passed from her memory," said Tracy. "But let not these precious—these melancholy—these fast fleeting moments, be expended on useless discourse."

And leading Amy in an opposite direction from the Hermitage, along the brink of a stream, under the shade of a row of ash trees, Tracy continued, frequently breaking off in his speech, as if overcome with strong emotion—

"This is the last time, in all probability, that we shall tread these paths together. Could it be otherwise, how should I rejoice!

But stern necessity demands our separation. We must—we must part. Honour—even the love I bear you, my tender, my sweet Amy, prevents our lot from being united. Nay, hear me calmly, —do not weep—you make me bewail the destiny, which, not wearied with inflicting on me twenty years of varied sorrow, sent me to destroy the peace of the gentlest and purest of God's creation. I know my conduct seems incomprehensible—I ought not to have remained so long in this neighbourhood, but the sweet charms of your society have been too powerful for me."

"O, that which is lightly won is lightly prized," faltered Miss Clifton. "I have betrayed to you feelings for which you despise me—for which I despise myself. Go and forget me—it is the best kindness you can now accord to—" She paused, overwhelmed with emotion.

"You agonise me by this language!" exclaimed Tracy, "and I can no longer restrain myself. Miss Clifton, from this hour I am devoted to you utterly. Command me as you will—I scatter all scruples to the winds.

Amy wished to be entrusted with the nature of these scruples.

"Ask me not now," said Tracy, "of one thing be assured, they relate wholly to myself;" and then yielding to the soft tenderness so accordant with his graceful character, as they crossed the darkening valley to the park by the most unfrequented paths, he proceeded to give utterance to the most unmeasured professions of attachment, couched in language sweet as the honey of Hyblas, and smoothly flowing as a pastoral stream, whose surface is enriched with many a perfumed flower.

The moon had commenced her brief and gentle reign ere they entered the house, where Percy, to whose frequent absence at all hours his sister had of late become accustomed, not being visible the lovers seated themselves by the drawing room window, lighted only by the celestial luminary, which revealed to each the face best loved on earth, touched with a spiritualising radiance in admirable accordance with the fine toned feelings of both on this deeply-interesting occasion.

Tracy remained in the neighbourhood of Rosedale some months after this important evening, still pertinaciously and sedulously avoiding a meeting with the friend of his betrothed, being no more explicit than heretofore on the subject of his melancholy or on the circumstances which militated against the serious engagement he had now entered into with Miss Clifton. He surrendered himself entirely to the entrancing interchange of affection, avoiding remembrances of the past, or considerations of the future. Occasionally the familiar cloud of sadness would return, and steal the sunshine from his face, but these moments became more and more rare, while the buoyancy of successful love was also experienced by Amy, who scarcely existed out of his presence, and whose happiness was little obscured by anxiety, since so long as Tracy loved her, she could anticipate nothing amiss.

In this stage of their intimacy, Charlotte Monckton prevailed on Amy to spend a few days at the Hermitage, and the morning previous to her leaving home, the latter was in her boudoir, waiting with expectant eagerness the daily visit of Tracy, when in his stead came the following note:—

"It is with regret, my dearest Amy, that I am compelled to resign your beloved society for a few days—few in number, but many they will seem to me. By the time you are returned from visiting your friend, that is, next Monday, I shall be again in Rosedale—until when, forget not yours, while life lasts—

"CHARLES TRACY."

Even this brief separation Amy felt to be painful, and she proceeded to her friend's residence in languid spirits, counting the hours of her lover's absence. It was on the second evening after her arrival at the Hermitage, as she sat at supper, with Charlotte and her venerable old aunt, listening with no small pleasure to the many interesting anecdotes told by the latter of the French sisterhood at Tours, to which she had belonged, when a loud and peremptory knock, repeated twice, ere any one could have time to reach the door, startled the little group, and a moment after, the voice of Maynard of the mill, more rough and loud than ordinary, was heard inquiring for Miss Clifton.

The elderly lady, who, in all her habits strictly adhered to the rules of the convent, retired hastily, as Maynard broke unceremoniously into the room, followed by Summerfield.

In the looks of the former, it were difficult to say whether frenzy or grief most predominated; he stammered in his speech; his eyes were red and full of tears; and his brawny chest heaved like one gasping in death, while rudely demanding intelligence from Miss Clifton, whither her brother had conveyed Ruth.

Summerfield, whose appearance no less betokened extraordinary agitation, though his mind was strong and dignified under his present trial, as under all others that he had experienced, advanced and addressed the young lady more respectfully.

"We ask your pardon for intruding ourselves here," he said: "but my child has been carried off by Mr. Clifton, and we must know to what place he has conveyed her."

"If my brother has so degraded himself," said Amy, "I assure you I knew nothing of it until this moment, and it fills me with

pain and indignation more than I can express. As to where he is I am as ignorant as you."

Being then informed of the false message by which Ruth had been trepanned to Rosedale House the preceding evening, and that when late in the afternoon of the present day the miller called for her according to appointment, he found that she had eloped with the young squire, Amy immediately, late though it was, returned to her home, and examined the servants in the presence of the father and affianced husband of the missing girl. Sullenly the cook confessed, "that she had carried the message of Mr. Clifton to the cottage—if it was a false one that was his sin, not hers."

Highly incensed at the woman's unblushing effrontery, Miss Clifton commanded her to quit the house on the morrow, and desired to be informed how long Ruth had been there on the previous night, and by whom she had been seen.

"By none but myself and master," the cook rejoined. "He was with her until four o'clock in the morning, and then they rode away together in a chaise."

"She left it by force, then!" exclaimed Summerfield.

"There is Jean," said the woman, sulkily, "you have heard what he says."

"Say what he will," exclaimed the cottager, " if my daughter remained any time alone with Mr. Clifton, or left this house with him, it was by force!"

"The chaise was brought up by myself," said Andre, "and if Ruth uttered a word or cry when Mr. Clifton handed her into it, may I never touch a guinea more!"

"I am compelled to believe, Mr. Summerfield," said Amy, as soon as the servants had withdrawn, "that although Ruth was ensnared hither last night by deception, she departed with my brother of her own free will. The evidence is but too conclusive, and I the rather incline to this because some time ago she confessed to me her love for Percy. Yet I own I can hardly credit that which seems indisputable, when I think of the cruel wrong this step has inflicted on you, Mr. Maynard, and how little such injurious treatment harmonises with Ruth's natural disposition."

"And if your brother has succeeded in seducing the affection of my child, Miss Clifton," said Summerfield, "what is to be the remedy?"

"Marriage certainly," replied Amy, firmly. "Though poor, she is beautiful, amiable, and clever, and you may rely on my endeavours to promote the justice which she has a right to expect."

"Would to God, young lady," exclaimed Summerfield,

"others of your name had resembled you! Ruth's cause I leave in your hands; and from this hour," he added, with a deep-drawn breath of stern determination, "I have one child the less."

"I am sorry you should say so, Mr. Summerfield," said Amy, "for it appears to me that all the blame of this sad affair attaches to my brother, all the pity to Ruth."

"You never spoke more truly, Miss Clifton," said Maynard; "and I will tell you what convinces me more than any thing else of Ruth's blamelessness. I promised to keep the matter secret, but I consider what has happened this day acquits me from that promise. When Ruth left Miss Clifton's service it was, as she supposed, to be married to the squire, but she was no sooner in his power in a lone house, than she found herself deceived, and in peril so great that it was almost a miracle she escaped. To me, during the illness that disappointment and alarm brought on her, she told the whole story of the snare she had fallen into, and repented that she had been so easily persuaded to credit the squire's professions. Now, it is plain to me, as that two sacks of flour are not one, that the girl who on that occasion could resist all the splendours that had been prepared for her sole gratification, all the persuasions that Mr. Clifton employed, ought not to be suspected of acting unworthily, however appearances be against her."

"She acted then just as I should have expected of her," said Summerfield; "but now, I see, with Miss Clifton, the stamp of guilt upon her."

"I won't believe it!" impatiently exclaimed Maynard. "But what are we waiting for? Can no means be pointed out for discovering whither she has been conveyed? The squire's sly-looking valet knows, I would wager all the corn in my mill. I have heard of racks used in old days for extracting the truth; it would give me great pleasure to see that lanky Frenchman stretched on one."

"If you choose," said Miss Clifton, "you can go the kitchen and interrogate him more particularly."

When Maynard had done so without eliciting the desired information, he returned with a desponding countenance.

"To-night there remains no more to be done," said Miss Clifton, "but in the morning I will make more extended exertions to ascertain the place of Ruth's concealment, and the moment I receive the slightest clue, you may depend on my transmitting the intelligence to you."

"Thank you, young lady," said Summerfield, his voice slightly broken—"and it would give me satisfaction if the place she had been taken to was the grave."

The father and lover proceeded in heaviness of heart to the mill, where they remained up together all night, and at dawn of day returned to the cottage, where a scene of anguish took place that baffles all description. Could Percy Clifton have looked in upon it, how would the gross selfishness of the conduct that created all this misery glared upon him!

The unhappy mother weeping on the breast of her husband—that husband speechless in his own strong agony—Maynard groaning and raging over the destruction of the long-cherished hopes that had been just on the eve of fulfilment—and the children wailing because their mother did so;—all this formed a picture that Percy could not have viewed unmoved.

It may easily be conceived, as the day wore away, with what intense anxiety the family and Maynard expected the promised intelligence from Miss Clifton, and the evening sitting in without their suspense having been relieved, Maynard, unable longer to control his impatience, snatched his hat from the table, and pursued his way with all haste to Rosedale House. Miss Clifton had had no success—not a trace of the retreat of Clifton and his companion had she been able to discover. Her kindness to the miller was such as in some slight measure to alleviate the poignancy of this announcement; she made him take wine and refreshments, sympathised with his distress, and with delicate tact proposed arguments of a consolatory nature.

"Assure Mr. and Mrs. Summerfield," she finally said, with the most earnest sincerity, "that I partake of that anxiety, while I would prevail upon them to hope that our fugitives are married, and that the only serious evil to be lamented is the breach of Ruth's engagement with you, Mr. Maynard, a flagrant piece of injustice certainly, which both Percy and Ruth must hereafter repent."

Very, very loth was poor Maynard to believe that his fair young bride was really lost to him; but as day after day passed over without bringing tidings of her, the certainty of the fact became too well established to be questioned. He neglected his business wholly during this period of doubt and sorrow, and the trial was not rendered less burdensome by the loss of Kitty, and of all the comforts her assiduity had provided. His mill, so recently the paradise of his hopes, was now hateful to him; the sight of the new furniture he had purchased for the accommodation of his bride, and the chilling loneliness which reigned when

he had expected joy and love, smote him with bitter pangs, from which he uniformly fled to the cottage of the Summerfields or the Three Crowns.

The manners of Summerfield under his misfortune, after the first day or two, evinced more quietude than had been expected, from his lofty virtue and powerful character. He went through his daily drudgery in the field with wonted diligence, and with the exception of the austere lines on his brow being something deepened, concealed successfully from the common eye the ravages of the scorpion grief that preyed within him.

Not so his wife. Her eyes were turned to fountains of tears, and she ceased not day nor night to bewail "her beautiful—her darling!—her lost—her lovely Ruth!"

At Rosedale House, Tracy, had recommenced his visits before anything was heard of Clifton. He found Amy plunged in anxious uncertainty respecting her brother, and occasionally disposed to yield to depression at the neglect with which he treated her. At length a letter arrived by the post to the following effect :—

"Has my dear sister been very much alarmed at my disappearance? Has she begun to apprehend that my adverse stars have assigned me a doom as mysterious as that of our father, and that she would hear no more of me? If so these hasty lines will re-assure her. It may be yet some weeks ere I return to Rosedale —the cause whereof must be too notorious. I have committed myself terribly, my dear Amy, in that quarter, and shall never endure it again as long as I live. Would the past could be recalled! The rest of my life shall be of a different tenor. She has left me, and I suppose to return to her home. May a repentant prodigal solicit from his sister a few lines, addressed to the White Hart, Stainford, informing him whether you have seen Ruth, and how she is received by her father and the rest? Had the foolish girl remained with me, it was my full intention to repair the error I have committed by an honourable alliance. I can scarcely presume to take Miss Monckton's name on my lips, loaded as I am with obloquy, or I would beg some interest in her remembrance. Tracy, when I see him next, will, I expect, have his declaration ready cut and dried—it has been sufficiently long on the stocks."

When Amy came to this concluding sentence she handed the letter to Tracy, who, after meditating over the mention made of him in it, caught up, as by a sudden impulse, a guitar which rested on the table beside him, and fixing his pleading eyes on Miss Clifton, as she bent over a vase of beautiful flowers, sang in

a subdued voice, a few stanzas in the beautiful language of Italy
—a language perfectly well known to her to whom his melody
addressed—

> Canst thou forsake thy stately hall
>   To share my lowly lot;
> To dwell where distant torrents fall;
>   Beside the mountain cot?
>
> Canst thou forsake the giddy throng
>   That sport round fortune's shrine,
> To list the peaceful shepherd's song
>   Beneath our cottage vine?
>
> Canst thou, while wealthier lovers press
>   To court thy smiles, my fair,
> Go hence my humble home to bless,
>   My simple joys to share?
>
> And wilt thou never wish unsaid
>   The vow that made thee mine,
> When waves above thy lovely head
>   Our pleasant cottage vine?
>
> Thy answering eye is filled with tears
>   That sparkle as they fall
> They chide thy lover's doubting fears
>   And all his trust recall.
>
> Yes, blest and blessing wilt thou go,
>   Contented to be mine,
> Where the fresh mountain breezes blow—
>   Where blooms our cottage vine.

"It is to no mountain cottage that I wish to beguile the steps
of Miss Clifton," said Tracy. replacing the instrument on the table,
"but the sacrifices I am compelled to solicit from her affection are
very large—so large that 1 shrink from the task of giving them
utterance, oppressed by the fear that to name them will be to lose
her."

"Why, I thought you considered my affection superior to that
of every other mortal," said Amy, sportively; "yet now you talk
of my shrinking from the very mention of sacrifices, as if my love
was like the bee, only stirring in sunshine. Come, what are these
weighty sacrifices?"

"Ah! Miss Clifton, it is perilous for me to name them—and
yet this opportunity afforded by your brother's lengthened absence
must not be suffered to pass unimproved. There are reasons—
urgent reasons—for my settling during the rest of my life in Calcutta. Can you make up your mind to accompany me thither?
Still further, can you consent to leave England with me unat-

tended, in privacy, and without whispering a word of the voyage to your brother or your friend? I have put the ordeal in the plainest and strongest language, for I would not have you act from blindness, but from love. If you are not equal to it, our final parting is near and inevitable. If you are, the plan I propose is this—I shall immediately repair to Liverpool to secure a passage in some trusty vessel, while you make your preparations. On my return, my dear Amy shall condescend to a private ceremonial which shall give us everlastingly to each other. We will then await, in a hotel at Liverpool, the vessel's weighing anchor, and from thence transmit to your brother our letters of parting and of explanation, though it will be imperative that he does not receive these until after we have set sail."

"And I should see him no more!" exclaimed Amy—"nor Charlotte—nor this dear old house! Oh! no, Tracy, you have well judged—I am not equal to sacrifice such as these. I cannot so suddenly—entirely—tear myself from all I have loved to go into a land of strangers."

"Your reply is what I foresaw," said Tracy, mournfully. "I did not deceive myself. That you could forsake your home, your friends, your country for me—that for me you would renounce the splendid alliances which your charming natural gifts, your accomplishments, and your high descent, must place at your disposal—that you would follow he fortunes of a poor unfriended man to a foreign clime, and to do this with the cheerful fortitude which could alone render the offering worthy acceptance, this I have not suffered myself for a moment to anticipate. I do not blame you for refusing; few would have done otherwise."

"I would rather be amongst the noble few than the ignoble many," said Amy, as the formi able measures he propounded became more familiar. "You have indeed applied a sharp test to my love, but you will find it capable, in the main, of enduring the application. Convince me only of the necessity of your plan—remove the veil of your secret counsels—unfold the circumstances which call you to Calcutta, and in what manner your professional views, (on which, I presume, your prosperity will depend), may be promoted there—and then—and then—oh! dear Tracy—"

He caught her to his breast, as with a flood of tears, she pronounced the yielding words, and, uttering a thousand expressions of encouragement, gratitude, and joy, he seated her beside him, and supporting her with his arm while her head drooped on his shoulder, proceeded—

"A near relation, to whose generosity I was in early life in debted for an education and tastes to which my pecuniary expectations were ill adapted, has been for some years resident at Calcutta, and holds there no inconsiderable office for the English government. He is rich, aged, without family, and much attached I believe to myself. I have received a letter from him, where he pledges himself to advance my fortunes. In his house I have reason to believe you will find a comfortable home until our resources and arrangements shall be fully settled. I shall despatch immediate letters to prepare him and his wife to receive us; entertain no doubt of a cheering welcome, and of our ultimate prosperity."

"But this only shows the desirableness, not the necessity, of our going," said Amy.

"As to that," Tracy hurriedly rejoined, "you must trust my asseveration. I assure you there is a necessity, both pressing and important."

"Why withhold the nature of it from me?"

"For reasons sufficiently powerful; how else could I bear to limit my confidence in one so dear? Truly difficult and painful do I find it to be reserved with you, and my gratitude is inexpressible for the patience with which you receive my half disclosures, and for the faith you repose in me."

"I am not patient," said Amy, pettishly, "but on the contrary exceedingly impatient. How can you dream of my making the terrible plunge you require until my mind is prepared for it? You remind me of a reckless old woman at Cheltenham, who, when I was a child, and taken thither by my mother, would not permit me to descend into the dreadful sea-bath by the gradual steps I preferred, but would insist on my sudden and violent immersion, for which, to this hour, I detest her remembrance."

"I trust," said Tracy, "you will never detest mine for inducing you to consent to my plan. Your present plunge, I fervently hope may be as fortunate as that of an individual recorded in Irish tradition, who, beneath the chilling flood, found a region of unfading beauty and delight. If all my future life, devoted to repay the confidence you repose in me, can make you blest, you shall be so."

The voice of Charlotte Monckton in the lobby without, interrupted their conference, and immediately on hearing it, Tracy exhibited the same remarkable change of aspect which Amy had before observed when her friend happened to be near or suddenly named. With clenched hand and bended brow he arose from his seat, as if to confront the lady, but as she opened the door, and he caught a view of her features, his resolution failed; he struck his forehead with his hand, and precipitately retreated through a door opening on the lawn.

"I am infinitely obliged to your cavalier for so nimble an exit," said Charlotte. "I came hither this morning to take you by surprise, knowing that he was with you, and anxious to convince myself whether my conjecture was not correct that it was not to you but himself I owed remaining a stranger to my friend's lover. Pray, knows he anything to my disparagement? or what are his reasons for shunning me so determinedly?"

"I believe he had some acquaintance with you abroad," stammered my.

"I remember nothing of his name," rejoined Charlotte, "nor of his person either, if I may credit the glimpse I had of him just how. Tracy—Tracy—no, that name certainly belongs not to any continental acquaintance of mine. "But," here the speaker's voice lost a little—a very little of its customary firmness, "why should he shun me because he knew of me abroad? Some would suppose that to be rather a motive for seeking me."

At this moment a footman placed in the hands of Miss Clifton a slip of paper, on which Tracy had written in pencil—

"My unconquerable aversion to the lady now with you has impelled me on an act of rudeness for which I entreat your forgiveness. Nevertheless, to her I desire no apology on my behalf, but I wish her to know that her conduct to her HUSBAND—from whom she has been divided contrary to the laws of God and of nature, is regarded by me, to whom she is well known, as deservedly excluding Charlotte Monckton from the ordinary forms of respect, and as rendering her utterly unworthy the friendship of one so estimable as yourself. Let her read this. TRACY."

Below was appended:

"I rely securely on your inviolable faithfulness to me in preserving from the knowledge of every other individual beside yourself whatever of consequence may have transpired between us."

"Her husband!" ejaculated Amy, in uncontrolled amazement, "Charlotte Monckton's husband!"

"What have you there?" demanded Charlotte, rather snatching than taking the paper from Amy's hand, and reading it several times over, while her mouth was drawn into an expression of affected scorn and indifference; then tossing it over the table, she exclaimed:

"This Tracy must be a consummate blockhead to talk of the laws of God being opposed to a separation which the infallible church decreed."

"Then you have a husband?" exclaimed Amy.

"I acknowlege none," rejoined Miss Monckton, vehemently, losing her artificial elegance in the energy of her passion at a discovery which she had taken the greatest pains to avert. "The church of Rome—my church—dissolved the connexion."

"You surprise me, Charlotte," said Amy, seriously. "With your strong sense, you must very well know, that no church could properly have the power to do so, except on extraordinary grounds."

"O, don't sentimentalise about it," said Charlotte, scornfully. "All that may be dispensed with extremely well. Depend on it, I knew perfectly what I was about."

Amy, though deeply wounded by the insulting air that accompanied these words, was unwilling to believe that her friend could really mean unkindly, and, therefore, quelling all personal feelings, she implored to know the particulars of Charlotte's unfortunate marriage. The name of the husband was Merton; he was an Englishman, aged five-and-twenty, devoted to the fine arts, and when Charlotte first saw him, had been painting in the Louvre, in the French Metropolis, to which she had resorted for a brief space, as the companion of a fellow boarder of the convent of Tours, whose relations moved in the gayest and richest circles of Parisian life. on Charlotte's return to Tours, Merton followed her, and they held frequent interviews by stealth in the aisles and purlieus of the convent church. Merton represented himself as in possession of five hundred pounds a year, beside the profit accruing from professional avocations, and in this belief Miss Monckton, early one morning, aided by the Parisian boarder, eloped with him, and they were united.

"But," said the narrator, "from that day I repented what I had done, and would have given much to recal it. I found him averse to all my wishes, contradictory and obstinate, cynical and solitary; indeed, our natural tastes would have carried us as wide apart as an isolated ocean-pearl buried in the shell of an oyster, and one of a cluster on the neck of a court beauty seen by a hundred eyes amid the blaze of festal magnificence. Nothing but the life of a hermit, or something akin to it, would suit Merton, while I expected a dashing establishment, the hope of which, to speak truly, had chiefly drawn me from Tours. En passant, I have often thought how well you two would have accorded had the lottery-bag of life jostled you in each other's way. How you would have scrambled up and down the wild places of the Pyrenees, how regaled yourself in the desert on goat's milk and romances, sour wine and poetical lucubrations, olives and sublimated ideas! Holy Mary!"

Again Amy was hurt by a certain tone and air of scornful ridicule, but she refrained from interrupting the course of the narrative.

"Merton and I quarrelled frequently," continued Charlotte, "during the short period that elapsed between my elopement and the arrival of my aunt to our retreat in the Pyrenees. She remained with me during the birth and decease of an infant, when, finding that Merton's income was but in perspective, and by some law process, likely to revert to another, and that his professional emoluments were inadequate to the maintenance of a family on the scale of respectability which would alone suit me, I deemed it only just to myself, (considering also the incompatibility of our tempers and habits of life) to support my aunt in an endeavour to obtain a revocation of the marriage. This was accomplished, I being a ward under age at the time of contracting the tie, and legally bound, as heiress to my aunt not to ally myself out of the pale of the Catholic church, or without her express consent. Thus Merton and I separated."

"And was he willing to part with you?" Amy asked.

"Far from it. He would have made any concession to dissuade me, but I was unshaken. We had some sharp contests towards the last; they terminated in my return to the convent, and then to England. I believe my aunt selected Rosedale for our place of residence chiefly because it was near the seat of the Catholic bishop you have seen at the Hermitage, with whom these thirty years, she has kept up a correspondence. My narrative is wound up, unless this Tracy, who is so zealous for his friend, choose to append malicious additions of his own or Merton's invention."

"Mr. Tracy may have been too severe upon you," said Amy, "but he is incapable of being the vehicle of malice."

"It is indifferent to me whether he is or not," returned Charlotte, disdainfully.

Amy made no other observation at the time, but her friend's recital had been to her unpleasing and painful, and while Charlotte endeavoured, though coldly and stiffly, to turn the conversation to less exciting topics, she was reflecting on the trivial motives which had been assigned for the extraordinary conduct der which the friend of Tracy had suffered. When, on the evening of the same day, Tracy rejoined her, she drew from him a summary of the occurrences in question, and found them substantially the same as in Charlotte's account, except that her heartlessness, vanity and ambition, aqpeard in stronger colours.

Amy's perception of right and wrong, being extremely delicate

in all that concerned the affections, she was shocked at the part her friend had acted, and shortly took occasion to express her censure of it to Charlotte, declaring she must ever think of Merton as possessing the right to her society, unless he forfieted it by actions less defensible than any that had been named. Accustomed to Amy's yielding temper, of which she had taken unlimited advantages, Charlotte was unprepared for so decided and independent an attack, and expressed herself in terms which betrayed her genuine feelings towards Miss Clifton, who then, for the first time perceived that there had never been the slightest congeniality between them, and that while she had been investing her friend with all the imaginary virtues, that friend had been secretly ridiculing and despising her. The fate of most rash, ill-assorted intimacies followed—the two were alienated, and on one a wound was inflicted whose scar could not be effaced till the heart that bore it crumbled to dust. Thus one of the strongest ties which attached Amy to England was rudely sundered to unite no more, while her voyage to Calcutta was yet under consideration. This heavy disappointment led her first to reflect on that disagreeable subject, the corruptions pervading the human character, and to turn a discriminating eye on the lights and shadows of those she loved. She endeavoured to analyse the character of Charlotte Monckton, untinctured by partiality on the one hand, or irritation on the other, and the result was, astonishment at the extent of her own blindness. The chief attribute of Charlotte was a strong worldly sagacity, which supplied the place of all the higher qualities; she was wholly devoid of enthusiasm, ready at any time to sacrifice the pleasures and interests of others to her own, cold of heart, venal and uncharitable, a devotee to fashion, thirsting for drawing-room supremacy, and even the witcheries of her manner artificial, and imbued with the most glaring affectations.

While thus dissecting the friend who had been so dear, the knife seemed to enter her own heart, and she turned sickening from the task to the recollection of the unfortunate Cottage Girl, concerning whom she wrote, in reply to the letter of Percy, acquainting him that nothing had been seen or heard of Ruth at Rosedale, and entreating him not to expose the poor girl to a meeting with her stern father until he himself could be near as a legal protector to shield her from Summerfield's wrath. She described to him the wretchedness of Maynard, and the austere sorrow of the cottager, and assured him taht, if, in her sisterly love, she was inclined to forgive her brother's errors, it could only be on condition that he repaired them immediately as far as it was in his ability.

This letter Percy received at the village to which he had requested it to be directed. He was greatly at a loss what step to pursue respecting Ruth. Though deeply anxious for her sake, he was not prepared to comply with his sister's entreaties that he would return to Rosedale with her as her husband.

The ardour of his passion had cooled; and having fallen in with some political friends, who strongly urged him to present himself at a forthcoming election to the small agricultural constituency of the borough of Rosedale as a candidate for a seat in the House of Commons, the smothered flame of ambition burst out in its energy, and his thoughts became as entirely occupied with questions of government and state policy, and with schemes of practical aggrandisement, as if he had never loved—as if he had not exposed to the horrors of shame and infamy an innocent girl —as if he had not vowed in the strongest language to restore her to an honourable position in social life. At this time active measures were put in operation for nominating Percy Clifton as a candidate for his native borough.

It was a period of great excitement, when the whole nation was deeply stirred by the mighty question then in agitation, and in such times the latent talents of individuals are frequently called into sudden action.

While awaiting a reply to a letter he had sent his sister, Percy entered with all the natural vehemence of his temper into the excitement of London political life, made many valuable acquaintances, exerted himself in defence of his party with uncommon vigour and ability, and three weeks after the discharge of his first pamphlet, sent a second thundering through the political hemisphere. The day after its appearance his health was drunk at a Westminster dinner with loud applause, and he returned thanks in a speech of startling brilliance.

But while yet the deafening acclamations which followed were resounding through the illuminated saloon, while the glow of gratified pride was on his handsome face, a footman touched him on the shoulder and informed him that a stranger in the lobby urgently requested to see him.

———

NOTICE.—With this Number is Given Away a Coloured Picture for binding with the Work. Another will be given with the next Number. Order early.

"HE SEATED HER BESIDE HIM, AND SUPPORTED HER WITH HIS ARMS."

THE COTTAGE GIRL.

THE TWO THEN PLACED THEMSELVES IN POSITION.

PERCY, on entering the lobby, found that the visitor, who was impatiently pacing the apartment, was none other than his agent from Rosedale, and the news he communicated well-nigh curdled the blood of the young squire, and for the moment deprived him of the power of movement or of language.

With a torrent of words, and almost breathless energy, the

agent informed him that Miss Clifton had left Rosedale House in a carriage, accompanied by Mr. Tracy, some fourteen days before, and that now the mansion was in the sole occupation of the servants. Miss Clifton, he said, had gone over every part of the house and grounds a few hours before her departure, and had been seen to weep bitterly. She had also hung the picture of herself, which Mr. Tracy had painted, over the chimney of her brother's sporting room, remarking, with bitter sobs, that he would probably never again see the original. The servants, he continued, after Miss Clifton had been a week absent, were very uneasy respecting her, and Mrs. Wilson, the housekeeper, becoming seriously alarmed at the continued absence of her mistress, applied to him, and requested him immediately to journey to London, and inform the squire of all the circumstances of his sister's departure.

On receiving this distracting intelligence, Percy made his hurried excuses to the hilarious party, sent for his horse from the livery stables, and that same night rode with speed toward Rosedale, to investigate more particularly the circumstances which excited his alarm. The night was pitchy dark, and he became bewildered in the cross roads, in a district extremely uncultivated and bleak. But his impetuosity urged him onward until his panting horse could hold out no longer. He was then fain to knock up the inmates of a small house by the road-side and request their hospitality until daybreak. This being accorded, and his horse lodged in a rude shed, he learnt, to his extreme vexation, that he had ridden miles out of his way. He continued to chafe at the delay until dawn, when he again set forth, but halted at the first inn to give his horse another brief rest, and supply him with provender.

Entering the bar, the first person on whom his eye rested was Tracy, seated in conversation with a seaman-like personage beside the fire. Without hesitation Clifton walked up to him, and placing his hand on his collar, with a fierce expression of countenance, pointed to the door. Tracy was very pale at the moment, but instantly recovering himself, said—

"Remove your hand, Mr. Clifton—I am ready to attend you to a spot where we may speak unobserved."

Clifton led the way to a small green hollow at a little distance from the inn.

"Here," said he, "we are alone; and here I demand from you, Mr. Charles Tracy, an explanation as to the clandestine manner in which you have removed my sister from her home, and the protection of her natural guardian."

CHAPTER XIV.

"Cursed be my tribe if I forgive him!"

"Mr. Clifton," said Tracy, with steady composure, "at present I have but one explanation to give, which you may think far from satisfactory, but it is all that you must expect until a few days have passed, then all shall be made clear to you."

"All shall now be made clear to me, sir!" said Clifton. "But proceed."

"Miss Clifton has done me the honour to confide herself to my tenderness and care, and—"

"Is she your wife?" hastily interrupted Clifton.

"Not as yet."

Clifton repeated the words with an outburst of indignation.

"Not as yet, sir!—your cool audacity surpasses thought. Damnation, sir, my sister has been a fortnight in your society!"

"And is pure as angels are!" exclaimed Tracy, emphatically.

"Where have you concealed her?" demanded Clifton, almost suffocated with rage.

"I shall not answer that," said Tracy, quietly.

"Is she in yonder inn?"

"She is not, nor near it. But you will in vain attempt to trace her, until I am willing; and I advise you to restrain your choler, and not to wonder if others steer by the example which you yourself have set up."

"Ha!" exclaimed Clifton, conscience-stricken. "But there is some difference between the honour of my house and that of the girl you allude to."

"That girl," said Tracy, "has parents, has connexions, who feel her dishonour as acutely as you can feel your sister's."

"Your retort may be just," Clifton returned with vehemence, "but it is beside the purpose. Once more I demand where you have concealed my sister."

"I believe," said Tracy, "that the afflicted parents of Ruth Summerfield had to remain in ignorance of the place to which their daughter was conveyed."

Clifton turned from the speaker, and the rising accent died in confusion on his tongue.

"Restore the blasted fame of Ruth Summerfield before you let your angry passions loose on me," said Tracy, pursuing the advantage he had gained. "Suppose your worse conceptions of my treatment of Miss Clifton correct, with what face can you, who have been equally guilty, accuse me? The poverty of your victim renders your case the worst of the two, since it is the perfection of inhumanity to burden with the sorrows of an abused attachment a poor child of labour, who, unless she resorts to the worst extremes, must not only bear the world's contumely, but the pangs of hunger—not only laceration of heart, but the dreariness of poverty."

"You are ill-informed, sir," said Clifton, violently, "on the matter of which you presume to speak so positively! Ruth has not been abandoned by me to any such alternatives as those you name. I have expressed my willingness to provide for her during her life."

"Will money, Mr. Clifton, repair the breach you say is made in the honour of your family? Would not the mention of pecuniary compensation from me be an aggravation of the injury of which you complain?"

"So much so, that were we two capable of ten thousand deaths you should die them all or inflict them on me, before twelve hours had winged their flight after that in which you had dared to pronounce such a proposal!"

"I guessed as much; yet I see not why the same vice should not show equally black in you as in me. But so it is; the evils we abhor in others, we are able to gloze over in ourselves."

"There has been something too much of this," said Percy. "I attempt no defence of my past actions; but if I am responsible for them, it is not to you; whereas, for your dishonourable conduct to Miss Clifton, and your abuse of the hospitality I afforded you, I feel well entitled to demand personal satisfaction. This spot is favourable to the purpose—we have but to obtain weapons and seconds.

"Hold a moment!" exclaimed Tracy; "I have ever entertained the strongest repugnance to these unnatural rencontres—not, I flatter myself, from cowardice, but from the impossibility of reconciling them to rational principles. Let us think also of your sister—whichever of us two falls in this engagement will be equally lamented, nor can the survivor expect ever more to be pleasing in her eyes, while his hand is red with the blood of her brother or her husband."

" An instant ago I was told you were not yet married."

" To-morrow morning was to have dawned on our union."

" And why was it to take place under a cloud? why was I not apprised of it?—and why was not my consent solicited, and the whole affair concluded in a straightforward and respectable manner? Had I been opposed to my sister's forming such a connexion, she would not have been allowed to spend so much time in your society. I have even hinted to Amy that I wondered at your delay in expressing your sentiments; and hence the conduct of both is without excuse, and highly disparaging to the delicacy of the one, and the honour of the other. Nevertheless, so dearly do I love my sister, that I will forgive much of what I blame, provided there is now an end of these underhand dealings."

" Believe me, Mr. Clifton," said Tracy, " I feel more regret than you will give me credit for at being compelled, by circumstances the most extraordinary, to withhold from you the confidence you so justly require, until a week hence."

" During which time I presume Miss Clifton is to remain your companion?"

" It must be so."

" And who are to be the witnesses to your marriage?"

" The clergyman, his clerk, and a servant girl."

" Add to these myself, and I will endeavour, for Amy's sake, to rest content respecting your motives for these clandestine operations until the expiration of the period you mention."

" No, Mr. Clifton, you can neither be present at this marriage, nor, to speak in decided terms, can you have any interview. however brief, with Amy, until the week is at an end."

" Then, sir, you are a false, juggling scoundrel! and I place no reliance whatever on your representations, but believe you and your motives to be foul as foulness itself! I palter no more with you! Follow me to the inn! the host probably will consent to act on my side, the seaman I surprised you with on yours, as witnesses to the fairness of our encounter, and between them we may be provided with pistols, unless you choose other weapons."

Tracy laconically replied in the negative, and observed it was indifferent to him who were selected as seconds, and that he should await Mr. Clifton's return to the spot.

" For the bravest that live," he mournfully observed, " if uninfluenced as I am by angry passions, would desire some few minutes' solitary preparation ere bidding farewell to life."

" I will not suppose you so utterly contemptible as to attempt escape," said Percy.

"Fear me not," returned Tracy; "when you are ready, if I am not in sight, call aloud and you will presently see me."

The young men separated, but met again after the lapse of an hour, when Clifton returned, accompanied by the innkeeper, a facetious personage, of uncommon size and height, with a red face, red hair, and a carbuncled nose. There was also the seaman, with a weather-hardened visage, and an unprepossessing exterior; and a surgeon from the nearest village, all sworn to secresy on the promise of a considerable fee. The group, of course, wore their gravest looks, and made their endeavours to reconcile the antagonists, but in vain.

Tracy, when the paces were measured, drew from his pocket a small sealed packet, and presenting it to the seaman—

"Tom," he said, "if I fall, convey this to Miss Clifton, and assist the squire to leave the coast until the affair has blown over."

"Oh, aye," ejaculated Tom, "blow high, blow low, I'll get him off if he trusts to me."

Tracy turned to Clifton and presented his hand, which was proudly rejected. The two then placed themselves in the proper position—the lookers on retreated—the signal was given—and Tracy dropped on the grass, the pistol still loaded as when it had been placed in his hand.

CHAPTER XV.

"That breathless agonised suspense,
  From whose hot throb, whose deadly aching,
  The heart hath no relief but breaking."—MOORE.

"IT's a very bad business this," observed the innkeeper to the surgeon, who was examining the wound of Tracy. "I think the other gentleman had best lose no time in getting off the coast."

"I agree with you," said the surgeon, proceeding to extract the bullet on the spot; "the injury, it is my painful duty to inform all concerned, is likely to be attended with melancholy consequences; what I can do I will, but I have small hopes of success."

Clifton knelt on one knee by his prostrate antagonist, insensible to his own danger, until thus reminded of it, he then started up,

and seeing the seaman, who was to be the guide of his flight, ready mounted on a rough-coated galloway belonging to the innkeeper, and holding his own horse by the bridle, bent again to Tracy to inquire from him where his sister was, and to exchange with him a parting forgiveness. But Tracy was incapable of speech, and could only return the strong pressure of his antagonist's hand.

"I hope you do not conceive me to have taken any unfair advantage in the firing of my piece," said Clifton. "The signal was certainly given before I drew the trigger."

After several fruitless attempts Tracy was able to pronounce a brief reply, in which he said that "all had been conducted with perfect fairness, and the reason of his own pistol being undischarged was his having previously resolved not to fire."

Clifton then drew forth his purse and liberally rewarding the surgeon and innkeeper, earnestly recommended Tracy to their care, and requested them to forward an account of his state the next morning to a fishing hamlet close to which the seaman's little trading vessel lay moored. With this understanding he sprang to his saddle, and, followed by the galloway and its rider, galloped over the open downs in the direction the seaman had pointed out.

Drearier every mile grew the prospect; the heavens were one sullen mass of leaden cloud, and the distant horizon showed the singular phenomenon of falling rain that had not yet reached our travellers. It came on, however, forming another disagreeable concomitant to that melancholy ride. The country now changed its character of monotonous dreariness for one more picturesque, but not less barren of inhabitants. Narrow glens and thick wooded hills opened on either side a road which was one of the few left in England untouched by the hand of modern improvement.

Clifton had become heartily tired of its rugged undulations by the time the roaring sea made itself seen and heard, the surge of the in-flowing tide foaming high over the sands, and the waves hurling themselves against a rampart of mountainous rocks. Leading their horses, Clifton and his guide descended to a level of the briny flood by means of a track formed in an angle of two precipices. At the foot the brazen-lunged seaman hailed "his craft," a much larger vessel than Clifton had been prepared to see, which lay beating about the waves at a short distance, and when the summons had been twice repeated, an answer was distinguished above the din of the vexed waves; a boat was put forth, and after some colloquy, Clifton was

received on board, while the seaman who had been his conductor turned back to leave the squire's horse for the present, with the innkeeper's galloway, at an appoined place, whence the host, who had played the part of second at the rencontre, was to send for them on the following morning.

Clifton, though inheriting the courage which had formely distinguished his ancestors, was not a little affected with unpleasant sensations on finding himself in the midst of a crew of sailors the most ferocious in personal features he had ever looked upon, and as night fell murkily over the heaving bosom of the billowy element, obscuring the outlines of the shore, and permitting the ill-looking men moving about him on deck to be visible only occasionally by the lantern-lights they carried, while their movements and equivocal language led to a conviction that they were engaged in nefarious traffic, he experienced a degree of terror to which, until then, he had been a stranger. He had about him a large sum of money, beside a valuable watch and chain, and a diamond ring whose value was great. On the ring he had seen one of these suspicious mariners gazing with an eye of alarming admiration, and subsequently he observed this man whispering with a comrade whose eyes were turned on him with a kind of ferocious greediness.

While uneasy thoughts were passing through his mind concerning what might be the result of his sojourn among these strange men, he was gruffly informed that he must go down to his cabin. He did so, rejoicing internally that he had secured about his person the undischarged pistol which Tracy had held at the moment of receiving his antagonist' shot.

The cabin was but a few feet square, and contained a single hammock, a stool, and a small table. The door was the first object of Clifton's scrutiny; it was without fastening, to obviate which deficiency he placed the table against it, and on that contriving to recline, his senses were soon lapsed in forgetfulness, notwithstanding the heavy tramping of the mariners above, and the hoarse swell of the winds and waves. In this welcome oblivion he lost for some hours the unpleasant sense of the position in which his rashness had placed him, the dismal expectation of the news of Tracy's death on the morrow, and the consideration of the anguish that event must cause his sister. The lamp he had left burning was low in the socket when his sleep was broken abruptly by some one endeavouring to force back the cabin door.

Inquiring who was there he was answered there was news for him.

"Speak it, then. where you are," said Clifton.

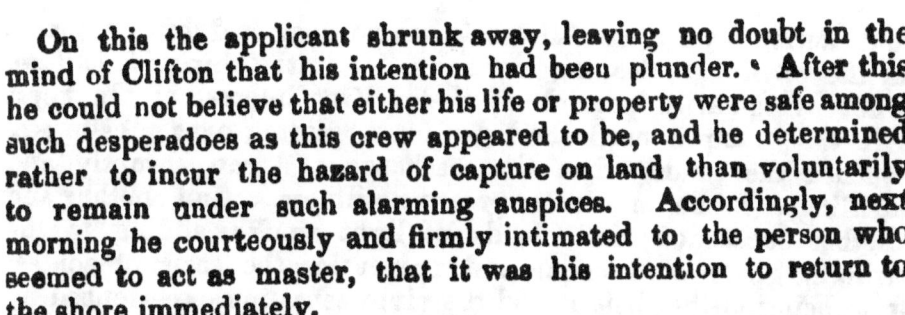

On this the applicant shrunk away, leaving no doubt in the mind of Clifton that his intention had been plunder. After this he could not believe that either his life or property were safe among such desperadoes as this crew appeared to be, and he determined rather to incur the hazard of capture on land than voluntarily to remain under such alarming auspices. Accordingly, next morning he courteously and firmly intimated to the person who seemed to act as master, that it was his intention to return to the shore immediately.

"That can't be nohow," said the captain, "for you see you came on board for your convenience, and now you must stay for ours. We run inland a cargo of rum and brandy to-night, and the Custom-house sharks are all on the look-out. If you were to leave us now, you might do us harm, but as soon as this job is over you shall be free as air. Meantime we'll have a jolly carouse! —you never tasted better rum than we brought from Jamaica on our last trip."

Clifton being in the power of this man, submitted in silence, and presently he beheld his guide of the previous day, who had just rowed from shore with the intelligence that Tracy still survived, and that Miss Clifton had received his packet and joined him at the solitary roadside inn near which the duel had taken place. This man had on the previous day refused to name to her brother the place whither he should convey the packet for Amy; but now conceiving that all secresy was at an end, he surprised Clifton by the information that she had been the inmate of a merchant vessel lying in harbour a few miles further up the coast, and expected to sail in three days for India.

Tracy, at the period when Clifton fell in with him, had absented himself from the lady for the purpose of concerting measures for their hasty and secret union, and to meet the seaman, with whom he had private business to transact. This last intimation was darkly given, and although the fact of Tracy's honourable intentions to his sister being thus confirmed, aggravated at first the regret Clifton felt for the sad consequences of the duel, that regret was materially mitigated when he reflected but for that consequence his sister's hand would have been given to a man in mysterious connection with smugglers, and that she would have been removed clandestinely, and perhaps for ever, from the sight and protection of her friends.

The desperate business of the landing of the contraband goods with which the smuggler's brig was stored, did not commence until nightfall, by which time the whole crew were on the alert, armed with cutlasses and pistols, and the casks being lowered into the boats, they sprang after, and began to row with silence

and caution toward a small creek, where they had hiding places in the precipices, leaving but one sailor in the ship with Clifton, who involuntarily partook of the exciting interest of the hour. All was tranquil until the laden boats, gliding over a calm sea, touched the sands, when the discharge of a gun abruptly and thrillingly broke on the impressive stillness. And another and another succeeded; and clouds of light smoke, adding to the twilight gloom of the hour, and preventing the scene of contest from being visible, heightened the vivid sensation experienced by the beholders on the ship and crags. Red torch lights whirled in front of the precipices—the human voice, which, in periods of silence or peril, comes on the ear with impressive effect, uplifted its wildest tones of defiance—Clifton even thought he could distinguish the clash of the cutlasses. After what there was every reason to believe had been a fierce skirmish, the dropping shots receded gradually in the distance, and seeing no boat return-ing, the sailor on the brig threw himself into the tranquil sea, and, under cover of the twilight, swam near the creek to ascertain the result of the adventure. Clifton, who excelled in all manly exercises, and was anxious to be free of his present company, hesitated not to follow his example, but bent his course to a spot lower down the beach. He rose unobserved to a firm footing among rocks strewed with shells and sea-weed, and making his way along a narrow strip of sand between the sea and the cliffs, came to a poor fishing hamlet in a small bay, where, engaging a room in an obscure tavern, he determined to abide until he should hear something conclusive of the fate of Tracy. The smugglers and their cargo, as he supposed, had been captured, and next day their vessel was taken. Three lives had been lost; and when Clifton reflected how much bravery had been expended on this and similar occasions, which, in a nobler warfare, might have done the State good service, he was led to consider deeply the policy of raising a revenue by interdicting the free interchange of com-modities with other nations, a policy that, in the natural course of things, must unavoidably create an illicit traffic most demo-ralising to all concerned.

Turn we now to a room in the inn where Tracy lies. The window looks on swelling pastures covered with peaceful kine and sheep, and irregularly enclosed by the remains of an ancient forest, whose shattered trees exhibit at once all the majesty of antiquity, and all the bright tints of the autumnal season. Stretched on a couch, his eye dwells on that prospect with a melancholy rapture, until a soft hand is laid on his, and Amy sinks on his neck. Long—long she weeps there, nor does he attempt to stay the flood.

"You know all now, Amy," he said, after a long and affecting silence.

She answered faintly in the affirmative.

"Yes," he said, "I am that unfortunate Merton whom your friend so basely forsook. Can you forgive me that I had not fortitude enough to relinquish your love, and that I cherished the hope of being happy with you in a country where my connexion with Charlotte would be unknown?"

"It is not you, but myself, that I blame," said Amy.

"In that you are wrong," rejoined Tracy, gently; "mine was the error in remaining so long near you, but my excuse must be that I was slow to believe in the actual possibility of having inspired love in one surrounded by more brilliant admirers. And when I did believe this, I found it impossible to tear myself away. In the packet you have received are detailed all the principal events of my life—is there aught left that seems obscure?"

"Nothing—nothing."

"And may I hope that I shall not bear with me to the grave either your contempt or your hate?"

"To the grave!" echoed Amy, wildly; "oh! talk not of the grave."

"My love," said Tracy, encouragingly, "what better lot could you wish for me than to die, thus separated from you? If I recover, it must be known how I am related to your friend; and can you dream that your brother or his friends would countenance your alliance with one so singularly and unhappily situated?"

"Alas!" ejaculated Amy, "our parting is indeed inevitable! for he whom, in my conscience, I consider as still the husband of Charlotte Monckton, can never be mine."

"It is a determination consistent with the fine sense of propriety which, in spite of Miss Clifton's enthusiasm, and even her faults, is possessed by no lady in a more exquisite degree. I am not at present able to offer arguments to change that determination. If, however, I had carried out my plan—if we had left behind us all whose displeasure could have wounded, or whose taunts have irritated you—if you had known me as no other than Tracy until we had been established at Calcutta, I feel confident that you would not have deserted me."

"I do not believe I should," said Amy, frankly. "But, oh! Tracy, how must you have despised your wife who could have been led so blindly! While I live shall I never forget the lessons I have learned from my past weakness. In future I will know the histories and weigh the qualities of persons before attaching myself to them in the sacred bonds of friendship. But, alas!

how am I talking! as if, after being alienated from Charlotte, and divided from you, I could ever dispose of my affections to others!"

"I trust you will," said Merton, "and that you will find serenity, if not happiness, among them."

At this moment a carriage with four horses, covered in dust, and occupied in the interior by a stout gentleman of advanced years, was driven up to the door of the inn.

"Have you one Mr. Tracy, or Merton, staying here?" inquired the old gentleman, thrusting his bald head through the carriage window.

The innkeeper hesitated in his reply, but the voice of the traveller had reached the object of his enquiry, who, with an exclamation of astonishment and delight, and forgetting his wound, rose to the window, and made a movement of recognition with his hand.

"My dearest Amy!" exclaimed Tracy, "this is the very relative of whom I spoke as residing in Calcutta. What has brought him to England, or how he has contrived to trace me, is more than I can understand."

"Aha, Charley Merton!" exclaimed the traveller, throwing open the door, "I have ferreted you out at last, then."

"My dear Salscroft!" exclaimed Merton, "you are the last person in the world I should have expected to see here. When did you arrive in England? I hope no unpleasant business has been the occasion of your voyage."

"My poor dame is gone," said the old gentleman, dolorously; "and as I made money enough, and began to get the worse for wear, I threw up my office, converted my property into cash, and came to old England to lay my bones in a certain churchyard in Kent, where my father and mother were laid before me."

"And how did you discover where I was?"

"I can hardly tell you—a roundabout chase I have had of it. This young lady," (bowing to Miss Clifton), "is, I suppose, Mrs. Merton?"

"No, sir," Merton replied, in embarrassment, introducing them to each other.

"And what ails you?" inquired Salscroft, observing the extreme paleness of his countenance, and the weakness with which he seemed affected.

"I have been so foolish as to engage in a duel," Merton replied, "and am at present suffering under the consequence."

"A duel, sir!" exclaimed Salscroft, snappishly—"no wise man has any thing to do with duels."

"I know it, sir,',

"Indeed, sir, and if you know it, sir, how came you to engage in so murderous—so irrational—so unchristianly—ahem!—I may say, so absurd an act?"

"A gentleman challenged me from a supposition that I had injured him, and I gratified him by receiving his shot."

"You did a foolish thing, sir," said Salscroft, with good-humoured irritability; "and if you no not forswear duelling for the rest of your life, I will rather adopt a match-seller for my heir than you."

"In that," said Merton, smilingly, "you must be guided by your pleasure. I assure you I am chiefly anxious that you should live long to enjoy your wealth, and I hope whoever inherits it will put it to as good a use as you have done."

"Aye, aye, that may be smoothly said," cried Salscroft. "But, do you hear, Charley, I must have no more duelling. 1 have come to make you rich. You were always my favourite. When you was no more than a foot high, I used to tell you I would one day make a nabob of you, Do you mind it?"

"I mind your kindness, sir," said Merton, affected, "which has followed me invariably through a long series of years and under many trying events. To you, when the spiritless passiveness of my father to the dominating will of an artful woman, would have suffered me to spend my youth in ignorance, I owe a superior education—to you, when that step-mother sought to enrich her son at my expense by her insulting conduct drove me an exile from my natural home, I was indebted for the means of prosecuting my favourite studied in the scenes most calculated to promote their advancement—to you——"

"Her son!" cried Salscroft, suddenly falling into a study; "that was Harry—an undoubted rascal. Is he gibbetted yet?"

"Not quite so bad. He died scarce a year ago, among the daring smugglers whom he associated with during life. One of the least hardened of his intimates sought me out with tidings of the event, and assured me that the captain was much disturbed in his dying moments with the remembrance of having aided his mother to imitate my father's signature to a document by which an income of five hundred a-year was wrested from me to his own use. I had no witness to this important attestation, nor could I prevail on the seaman to repeat it; so my little patrimony is now enjoyed by a lad of sixteen, who promises already to outshine his father in daring profligacy."

"Your step-mother is dead, too—and the Merton property in Kent sold to pay her debts and your father's."

"Yes, and thus I have found myself cut off from every expectation which my birth entitled me to form. But I perhaps ought not to complain. Necessity has goaded me to professional exertions, while else I might have wasted my days in comparative idleness."

"Well observed!" said the old gentleman, with the look of an approving schoolmaster, who applauds himself for his pupil's proficiency. "I see you have not forgotten the lessons I used to give you when your vacations were spent with me. 'Charley,' I used to say to you, 'whatever you do, shun idleness, otherwise you can never be half a man.'"

"I do indeed remember you took great pains to eradicate that vice in me," said Merton, "and I know no service of all you have rendered me for which I ought to be more grateful."

Salscroft was well pleased by this, and introducing his chair between Amy and Merton, and addressing the former, gave her an account of the thrifty habits by which his fortune had been acquired.

"I had all Franklin's maxims by heart," he said; "never slept after five, winter or summer—never forgot that a penny saved is a penny got—took care of interest as well as principal—and minded my own concerns."

Here rapping on the floor with his cane for the host, who was ready to obey the slightest signal, the old gentleman ordered a supper of the best that the neighbourhood could supply, with covers for three, for he insisted that Merton should relax his sick diet on this evening.

Bowing full low, the innkeeper joyfully bustled away to consult with his wife how best to do honour to so liberal a guest. Kitchen and pantry were presently in a steam, and the savoury scents that issued therefrom, and found their way to the olfactory organs of Salscroft, appeared to render him considerably impatient for the coming repast. In the interval he required to know the nature of the affront that had led to Merton's duel.

"I must learn the truth," he said, positively. "I like the thing which is right between man and man; and I promise thee, if I thought Charley Merton capable of a mean action, I would discard him with as little remorse as a counterfeit guinea."

The interesting paleness which loss of blood had spread over the mild features of Merton, was at this moment exchanged for a deep crimson suffusion.

"Trust me, Mr. Salscroft," he said, "the loss of your favour would bring a cloud over the rest of my life, and at present it is sufficiently dark. You shall, however, know the truth and

judge of me as you see fit. Of my French marriage I apprised you."

"You adverted to it in one of your letters, I believe, but so slightly that my poor wife and I hardly knew whether you were jesting or in earnest."

"In sad and sober earnest," Merton rejoined; and with some ill-repressed agitation, he related his intimacy with Charlotte Monckton, and their separation.

Salscroft listened rather restlessly until Merton came to Charlotte's sordid desertion of him, when, rising energetically the old gentleman exclaimed—

"Let her go, then! and I heartily hope you were not such a fool as to grieve after the vixen?"

"I am afraid I was that fool," said Merton, not able to restrain a sigh to the memory of departed feelings, which had exercised over him no inconsiderable power.

"Then, my dear boy, though you have my compassion, I really don't think you are entitled to it. What! grieve for a wife who could throw you aside as easily as her glove?—and for what? Because your circumstances happened to be more cramped than she expected!"

He broke off, for the clatter of plates and dishes, and the tinkling of glasses, announced the supper. The table was occupied with more delicacies than might have been expected on so short a notice and in so retired a place; four candles illuminated the smoking repast, the blind was let down, and the attendants were dismissed. The old gentleman rubbed his hands, surveyed the viands with the eye of a gourmand, grumbled a little at the barbarous cookery of the English, and at the absence of certain Asiatic condiments, and then, in the heariest good humour, after handing Amy to the table, took his seat, and made an abundant meal.

Merton, to gratify him, and to support the spirits of Amy, which were in a state of painful confusion at the position in which she felt herself to be placed, managed to support himself upright in an easy chair at the table, and to essay a slender portion of the good things provided. Momentarily his eye watched with tender solicitude the fluctuations of Amy's countenance, and perplexed thought occasionally contracted his otherwise smooth and expansive forehead.

When the cloth was removed, the landlord brought a couple of bottles of old port wine.

"Can't you find any claret or champagne down in your cellar, landlord?" inquired the Indian merchant.

The landlord smiled from ear to ear, for to his heart he loved a liberal guest.

" I wish I could oblige you in either particular," he said, " but they are articles there is little demand for this way. If I kept such, they would stick by me like a murder. Nevertheless, I will undertake to have any wine or dish your worship pleases next time you honour the Wellington."

" And that shall not be far distant," said the hearty old gentleman, " for you have really given us a capital supper, and I am very well pleased."

The landlord was no less so, when Salscroft announced his intention of remaining at the Wellington until his young friend was sufficiently recovered to accompany him.

" You seem to have proved his best doctor, sir," said the landlord; " only this morning he seemed too ill to live over the day. I am glad to see such a speedy change."

" Now I am ready for the rest of your story, Charley," said Salscroft, when the host had withdrawn.

" You will readily understand, my dear sir," said Merton, slowly and hesitatingly, " that what remains to be said has a relation to the dear and excellent being now beside me. Mr. Salscroft, I know of old, has a heart which Franklin's worldly maxims could not spoil, nor the pursuit of wealth harden. He will be your friend as well as mine. Mr. Salscroft, allow me to preface my statement by entreating your most indulgent consideration. Miss Clifton, at least, is worthy of it in the highest degree, and fervently do I rejoice in the opportunity that your unexpected arrival affords me of engaging your sympathy and assistance to relieve her from the distressing perplexities in which I have been the means of involving her. In a word, if you adopt me as a son, you must adopt this lady as a daughter."

" Hum! ha! I suspected as much," said Salscroft, taking in at a glance the marks of superior rank and breeding which Miss Clifton's every look and movement betrayed; " well, I don't know I shall make any objection, if friends are willing, and all things agreeable."

The face of Merton brightened with joy.

" Then you esteem my divorce from Charlotte a valid one ?"

Certainly, it was a Catholic rite, and might be dissolved by Catholic power. Had it taken place in England, the Romish Church could not have dissolved it. But it was a French affair, which is a very different thing. For my part, I hold you as truly free from that vixen's shackles as if you had never put them on.

"AHA! CHARLEY MORTON," EXCLAIMED THE TRAVELLER, THROWING OPEN THE DOOR, "I HAVE FOUND YOU AT LAST THEN."

THE COTTAGE GIRL.

SHE WAS WEEPING ON HER BROTHER'S NECK.

"YOU hear, Miss Clifton," said Merton. "There are few who will not think with Mr. Salscroft."

"I cannot," said Amy; "to me it is not the rite so much as the oath of the mind. You were no Catholic, and had no idea of the holy ceremony being dissolved by human means at the time when you engaged in it."

"Nay, my dearest Amy," said Merton, with earnestness, "do not, I beseech you, sacrifice me to a mere scruple of fastidious delicacy! If Charlotte herself—if Mr. Salscroft—consider me disengaged and free to offer my hand where the choice of my heart has fallen, and if the general opinion of the world inclines on my side, must not your objections be a little strained? Surely you cannot entertain the shadow of a fear that one pulse of my heart can ever again beat for the woman who has so abused and betrayed it?"

"On my word, young lady," said Salscroft, "I think there is not a freer man in Christendom than Charley Merton."

"I am bold to acknowledge, sir," said Amy, blushing, "that I should be very glad to think with you, but—it is impossible."

Merton deeply sighed, and sank suddenly back on his seat.

Much alarmed, Salscroft arose and knocked loudly for assistance. Amy sprang to her lover, and perceiving his countenance assume the complexion and sensibility of death, her own instantly took the same appearance, and gasping, "He is gone!—he is gone!" she fell back, and was caught by Salscroft, who strove to revive and comfort her with almost paternal kindness.

"Charley has only fainted," he said; "I have fatigued him something too much; they are gone off for the surgeon, and all will be right presently. Come, cheer up—I will befriend you both to the utmost of my ability."

Merton's recovery was, howewer, slower than had been anticipated, and Amy's agony was wrought up to a pitch that fully revealed the extent of her interest in him to Salscroft, who, instigated partly by native kindness, and partly by a propensity to busy himself in other people's affairs, resolved to take the whole management of the young people's love matters on his own hands.

"For the deuce is in it," thought he, "if with love on their sides, and gold on mine, something may not be done to make them happy. Yet I see not clearly what. Let me think. How if I were to get up a treaty of matrimony between this Charlotte Monckton and the old sugar-planter of Yakbur Yakoof? She would be out of their way then. Or bribe a churchwarden to insinuate her name in his register of deaths? No, hang it, no, I can't hit upon it. But I am resolute to do something."

Salscroft's good intentions were put in train on Merton's

reviving, when after being fully let into the confidence of the lovers, he undertook to reconcile Squire Clifton to his sister; and for the relief of their minds whom he was desirous to serve, as well as because he was a mortal foe to procrastination, ordered his carriage to be got ready by five in the morning, and careful directions given to his postilions how to find the place whither the innkeeper of the Wellington transmitted his bulletins to the squire of the progress of Tracy's disorder, at which place no doubt was entertained of Salscroft being able to obtain an interview with Clifton.

It seemed very delightful to the vivacious old merchant to be employed on this delicate and important commission, and strong in the sense of his own self-importance, and the omnipotence of wealth, he was quite sanguine as to the result.

"Good night, my boy! I shall not see you in the morning," he said to Merton, at separating, after pulling carefully about his ears an embroidered silk night-cap that he drew from his pocket, "and when I return, you shall see your brother-in-law with me, (I ask your pardon, Miss Clifton,) and we will be all merry together. Take care of yourself while I am absent. Mend fast, and depend on me. Miss Clifton," (she was then retiring,) "I wish you a very good night. Stay, on second thoughts I should have asked if you have any personal message to entrust me with."

"No, sir," said Amy, a modest pride struggling with her anxiety for his success. "I hope my brother may be propitiated by your kind appeal for me, but I cannot in my own person or language submit to sue him. And if you should prevail," she added, "his own heart must assure him of my gratitude."

"One thing more before I go," said Salscroft to Merton, after Amy, with a respectful curtsey to the old gentleman, and a brief and embarrassed parting salutation to her lover, had withdrawn, lighted to her chamber by the hostess. "I don't rightly understand what you meant to have done with you assumed name."

"To have avowed that it was assumed would have ruined my plan as effectually as my premature meeting with her brother has done."

"Granted; but of course you know that the ceremony which you tell me was to have made you one before commencing your voyage out would not have been worth a farthing in point of law if it took place in that false name? and this poor lady

would have been liable at any hour to be flung aside for a new favourite."

"On my honour, Salscroft," Merton with energy exclaimed, "it was my steadfast purpose to have the ceremony repeated in my proper name as soon as we had joined you and your lamented wife on the Ganges."

"There is no security for that beyond your own word, you know," said Salscroft, making a side nod of dubious import and propping his nose on the gold head of his cane, his habit in any perplexity.

"In all my life previous did you ever hear of one unworthy action of mine?" Merton proudly asked.

"Can't say I have. But after imposing so cleverly on this young lady, may you not be fancying it necessary to impose on me?"

"I am sorry you construe me so unfavourably," said Merton, coldly.

"Unfavourably! not at all. I am willing to think the best of you, and do the best for you, as you shall find."

Merton, as Salscroft was retiring, called him back to remind him that the sole object of the interview he was about to seek with Clifton was that Amy might be received again with kindness by her brother.

"I shall see what is to be done," said the old merchant, conceitedly.

Merton then anxiously refreshed his memory respecting circumstances calculated to remove whatever shade appeared to hover over the pure name of Amy. A respectable widow niece to Merton's deceased father, had met the fugitives from Rosedale by appointment at Liverpool, and remained the companion of Amy in the hotel and on the vessel, while Merton was mostly absent settling affairs having connexion with his deceased step brother, the smuggler captain. A young woman, her daughter, as Amy's attendant, designed to share with the lovers the perils of the sea and their fortunes in India. Mother and daughter, when the duel took place, were with Amy in the merchant-vessel, which was then taking in exports at a harbour, a short distance from Liverpool, and there Amy expected Merton to rejoin her, and there she was to have spent her last day in England on shore, and to have parted for ever with the name that had hitherto been identified with her existence.

Instead of the bridegroom, came the harrowing news of the duel and its results; and the road-side inn where Merton lay

being only three miles distant, Amy instantly landed, and walked thither with her new attendant, while the widow returned to her home.

These and other details, which had been entrusted to Salscroft for the satisfaction of the mind of Clifton, the former promised to deliver in the most advantageous manner.

Merton spent a perturbed wakeful night. He was conscious that he had greatly deceived himself respecting his conduct to Amy. It would not bear reflection. And the thought that she was now placed in dubious and painful circumstances by her generous affection, and high-mingled trustingness, was beyond measure grievous to him.

Amy no less passed a wretched night; and when the wheels of Salscroft's carriage rolled away from beneath her window, she felt an eager impulse to follow it, and cast herself at her brother's feet, and pray that her offence might be obliterated from his memory, and that she might be received again to his confidence and his love. But with amended experience, she had acquired some of the pride inherent in her famly blood, and until she could feel assured that her brother confined his displeasure to her imprudence in respect to appearances, she resolved not to approach him. After a sorry breakfast in the little closet the hostess of the Wellington had allotted to her, and which the confined accommodations of the house compelled her to share with her maid, (a country girl, whose awkwardness and ignorance often by contrast reminded her of the graceful and intelligent Ruth,) Amy remained weeping and musing in sad perplexity of mind, until a respectful message from Merton induced her to join him.

Notwithstanding his vigils, he was better, and strove to conceal his own depression by his exertions to support her spirits. The attempt had failed, however, and both were sunk in a silent reverie of dejection and suspense when the returning wheels of Salscroft's vehicle rattled up to the inn door.

"It is impossible that he can have seen your brother in this short interval!" exclaimed Merton.

"He has!—he has!" cried Amy. "I hear the voice of Percy!"

Hardly were the words pronounced, ere she was weeping on her brother's neck.

"I told you, Charley, I would manage it all for you!" exclaimed Salscroft, rubbing his hands with great glee. "I met Mr. Clifton nearer than I expected—knew him by his resemblance to the young lady—accosted him, introducing myself as

Tracy's friend—invited him into my carriage to talk over matters—turned the horses about, and brought him here."

"Mr. Merton," said Clifton, distantly and haughtily, " be under no mistake; the explanations and apologies afforded by this gentleman have convinced me that you are less culpable than I had supposed, but sufficient dishonour remains to keep us lasting enemies. I am here to rescue my sister, not to form any hollow reconciliation with one who has occasioned Miss Clifton so much humiliation, and myself so much peril and distress. Prepare instantly," he said, addressing his sister, " to accompany me to London."

" From *you*, Mr. Clifton," said Merton, with keen sarcasm in his look and tones, "this high talk of dishonour sounds strangely, considering what your own actions have been—what they at present are."

" Ha !" fiercely exclaimed Clifton, " that retort again !"

" Again and always," said Merton, " when you presume to taunt me with dishonour."

" For pity's sake, dear Merton," exclaimed Amy, " enrage him not. Provoke no more hostility, I entreat. My dear Percy, you do not, indeed you do not make sufficient allowance."

" Allowance !" exclaimed Clifton; " what think you must be my present feelings to find you here together—to know that an insuperable bar exists to the only means by which my sister's character could be redeemed from popular scandal—to know that she can never again take her proper place in society—to know that in her native home and neighbourhood she is eternally disgraced ?"

" If the evils arise that you speak of in terms so exaggerated," said Merton, " they will pierce a thousand times deeper to my heart than yours. But be just at least, and acknowledge that such a dilemma as the present never entered my calculations, nor could have occurred, but for your own hot ire."

Without replying to this, Percy again urged his sister to prepare.

" I stay here no longer than a post-chaise can be got ready," he said.

" Farewell, Miss Clifton," said Merton, with a melancholy firmness, as she turned her sorrowful glance on him, when re-entering the room after obeying the decisive orders of her brother. " Be happy, and forget me."

Amy smiled sadly, but her voice was mute. Salscroft, vexed

by so hopeless a termination of the affair, in which both his good-nature and vanity were warmly interested, now interposed.

"Squire Clifton," he said, with a preliminary cough, to give solemnity to his address, "I really think, if you will permit me to say so, that your method of curing this sore is none of the best. Though until this day a stranger to you, I will venture, by your leave, to point out a better."

Clifton turned an impatient ear, and Salscroft went on.

"That foolish French connection is thought on the continent legally dissolved; let it be so considered by you, and I will make a round settlement on these young folks, for a handsome establishment, the first instalment payable on the marriage-day."

"You are liberal, sir," said Clifton; "but it seems to me to augur unsoundness, either of judgment or morality, to imagine I would consent to Miss Clifton's marriage with Merton, after what has been told me respecting Charlotte Monckton."

"But, squire," persisted Salscroft, still unwilling to disbelieve the omnipotence of his wealth, "I can write four ciphers after the number of my thousands, and they shall be heirs to all. I am getting an old man, and cannot, in the nature of things, live many years longer."

"If you had all the riches of the East to bestow on them," Clifton rejoined, "my sister should not give her hand to Merton during Charlotte's lifetime; although, I confess, it affords me some relief to see this disposition manifested."

Hurrying his sister away, the two were soon travelling rapidly on the high road to the metropolis. During the first few miles they spoke not to each other. The heart of Amy was depressed to the lowest ebb by the parting from Merton. His profound, though gentle affections, and his elevated taste in the works of nature and of art, furnished her with a variety of endearing reminiscences never to be blotted from her memory, and mingling with all her thoughts.

It was a consolation to know he was not left without a friend able and willing to contribute to his comfort, and she had good hopes that his recovery was secure. But oh! to know that the hope of their union was utterly extinguished—that they must meet no more, or meet only to sorrow and part—this was suffering indeed!

Fortunately one misery counteracts another. Despair deadened all apprehension of the reception she was to receive from those to whom she had been known. She was indifferent to their opinions now, for she had no longer aught to hope or to fear.

Her loss of credit, however, or the apprehension of it, rankled fearfully in her brother's breast. He perfectly understood the pure and even superior motives which had betrayed her into imprudence, and wished to be kind and indulgent to her, remembering she had been so to him, but his voice refused to address her except in harsh abrupt tones, and when he looked on her, a quick, resentful fire was in his eye. The retorts of Merton had penetrated also to the quick, and assisted to throw him into a violent commotion. These unpleasant thoughts were at length partly diverted by their arrival amongst the endless squares and streets whose ranks of palaces accommodate the favoured children of rank and fortune in our mighty Babylon.

The lodgings Percy had previously occupied in town, to which he now introduced his sister, were situate in one of the most retired and stately of streets. The house was one of fifty, all of striking loftiness—constructed with a pleasing dash of the antique—fronted by stone balconies running along the first and third stories, by noble doorways opening into halls, and windows which afforded tantalising glimpses of splendour to the poor passer by.

Here Amy found her life very little different from what it had been at Rosedale. She was perfectly retired; strolled occasionally into the neighbouring parks, at more rare intervals joined on horseback the brilliant cavalcades of the ring; read, mused, painted, did everything as formerly—excepting that the soul of gaiety and enthusiasm, which once made her so charming, was gone, and had left in its place only a forced mirth, like sunshine playing over clouds which they can neither dissipate nor gild. Reading was only pleasing as it touched the chords of love and woe—painting as it recalled Tracy (for by that name she loved him best)—and musing as it enabled her to indulge her sorrow. Such was the habitual tone of her mind, though often striving for the mastery, and at times exerting a spirited fortitude. Ruth was not forgotten by her. She felt the most anxious interest in the Cottage Girl, of whom she could only hear that, after returning to her parents, she had again disappeared, no one knew whither.

This information almost incapacitated Clifton from prosecuting his ambitious political views. Night and day he was perturbed, restless, gloomy. The lightest contradiction, or impediment to his wishes, drove him to frenzy, and every moment not dedicated to severe employment, or necessary refreshment, was spent in stalking to and fro the room, his eyes on the ground, his features convulsively agitated. In these moods, in which it was easy to detect the workings of remorse, he could endure no observation, not even that of his sister.

CHAPTER XVI.

" Whither, 'midst falling dew,
  While glows the heaven with the last steps of day
Far through its rosy depths, dost thou pursue
  Thy solitary way ?"—BRYANT.

LEAVING those whose troubles had their source chiefly in imagination or error, we resume our narrative of Ruth, who, blessed with the purest and soundest of minds, was yet doomed to be a mark for misfortune's keenest darts—who, though sinned against, not sinning, was yet abandoned to shame, penury, and despair.

Her astonishment and distraction, when the narcotic that had been administered to her gradually lost its stupifying influence, and she found herself again a captive in Clifton's villa, and became sensible of the extent of her wrongs, was expressed in language and gestures so much more violent than her betrayer had looked for, that he exchanged his persuasive soothings for fierce and passionate intimidation, ere he could silence her loud complaints. And when this was done, it was only because nature was exhausted, or because the desperate will was retiring within itself to muster its forces for a new resistance. Sometimes she shrieked for her father, sometimes for Maynard, apparently unmindful that she was cut off from the assistance of either. Clifton suffered neither of the women-servants to approach her, lest her piteous entreaties might win them to assist her to escape ; but her cries were often heard by them, and the younger, after Ruth had been a week in the villa, declared to her companion, " No heart of flint could bear it, much less one of flesh and blood," and forthwith took an opportunity to set the poor prisoner free.

This time Clifton gave himself no unnecessary alarm respecting Ruth's personal safety ; and doubting not that she had returned to her parents, he turned his active thoughts in new channels, of which sufficient has already been said. It must however be observed, that at this time the idea of offering pecuniary compensation to the victim of his unbridled passions, and her injured family, had not polluted his conceptions. His mind was wavering as it had ever done from the first hour of his meeting Ruth, whether or not he should humble himself to a marriage with her

The stern voice of conscience, whose tones in his breast were ever clear and powerful, said yea—but while he hesitated, his evil genius, in the shape of some accidental circumstance, or association of ideas, provocative of worldly ambition, pronounced a more decisive negative. To vary the words of the Hebrew historian, "There was long war between his love and his ambition, but his ambition waxed stronger and stronger, and his love weaker and weaker." So he added to his crying sins against Ruth, that of forsaking her.

We have now to trace her wanderings after her second escape from the villa.

It was ten o'clock at night; there was a full moon contending with drifting clouds; a shrill wind which now and then hurled rain in the face of the shivering girl; and around was spread a wide and varied prospect, intersected with cross-roads, and thinly scattered with farms and the small cottages of agricultural labourers. Whither should she betake herself? It was a perilous question! Home she dared not go. Yet where else could she find a refuge?

Mechanically she struck into the first track that presented itself ead whither it would, crossed a broad and shallow stream by means of stepping stones. In the centre she paused; the scene had an air of soft serenity which found its way to her heart. She looked upwards, clasped her hands, and her lips moved without a sound as in one who dreams. The events of the last ten days seemed unreal—the desolation that had fallen on her incredible.

"By this time I should have been Maynard's wife," she presently murmured. "Poor—poor man! His heart will ache for me as well as for himself. God send him comfort! And my father!—Oh! I must never see his face again. He would kill me. And my mother—she would upbraid me; and the neighbours—they would scorn me! Yet I am not to blame—God knows I am not!"

She bent down to the water to moisten her lips and brow, and a few burning tears mingled with the rippling current. Few they were, for her's was a harsh reality of suffering which could not evaporate in the melting mood. In a few minutes a distant halloo aroused her to a bewildered terror, and fearing pursuit, and remembering the lateness of the hour and the solitude of the country, she hurriedly pressed toward the nearest house she could see, traversing meadows, lanes, and pastures, until at last coming to a large farm, she sank wearily down in an outhouse, which offered a temporary shelter, and a heap of fragrant hay for a bed

Ruth was not given to imaginary or superstitious alarms, though at times susceptible, as are the strongest minds, to the passion of fear. Alone in this strange shed, with night and solitude around, she felt little of the vagaries of fancy which might be supposed to assail her in such a situation. Perhaps the "tempest in her mind," now that she felt safe from Clifton's pursuit, obliterated all other sensations. As night advanced and she lay on the loose hay between sleeping and waking, she fancied herself still in the villa, and starting up with a shriek, called on her father for assistance. Then she dreamed that Maynard's housekeeper was making horrible grimaces at her—then that she was sitting beside the squire in his sporting room, happy and undeceived—and anon, that her father, with a terrible countenance, stood by her, menacing her for the disgrace she had brought on him.

"It was all treachery!" escaped incoherently from the sleeper's lips. "Their drugs took away my senses."

"Lord help the poor young castaway!" exclaimed, in feeling tones, a grey-headed farming man, who, with his master, entered the outhouse at dawn of day, and discovered, with surprise, the beautiful young creature extended there. "Thou'st been used, I warrant me, to a better bed and a seemlier homestead."

The farmer—not one of the plain practical sort, but of that modern species, the gentleman farmer—gazed on the sleeping beauty, with exclamations of admiration. He was a thin smart figure, near six feet high, in white top-boots, a coat of Newmarket cut, with silver buttons, and a drab hat. His countenance was remarkably ugly, and his long lean hands garnished with nails like birds' claws. He had the appearance of one "sicklied o'er," and rendered a mere wreck by animal indulgence.

"Tim," he said. speaking short and quick, "dost know anything of her?"

"No, truly, poor thing!" replied Tim.

Their voices broke the sleep of Ruth, who sprang wildly up, her hair loose and disordered, her cloak closed with a nervous grasp over her bosom, her bonnet dangling by the ribbon from one hand.

"You have made free with my tenement, young woman," said the farmer, looking hard at her, "and I must know who you are and whence you come."

"I am sorry!—Oh! sir, have pity!" Ruth exclaimed in accents indistinct and broken.

"Take her to the kitchen, and let her have a basin of porridge or some bread and cheese," said the farmer, "and then send her into Mrs. Morrison and me"

Ruth was conducted by the farming-man to the spacious kitchen, where she presently was seated at a substantial country breakfast among half-a-dozen clownish-looking men, and as many rosy maids, having previously bound up her hair and refreshed her her hands and face, so that she had no longer the wild appearance which had first distinguished her when seen by the farm inmates. Her deep sighs and wandering looks still, however, excited curious attention as well as compassion, especially from Mrs. Morrison, into whose presence she was ushered in a room adjoining the kitchen, filled with handsome furniture, plants, pictures, and more than one instrument of music.

The lady—for a lady she appeared—was seated by a large fire, burning in a bright steel grate, a favourite dog at her feet. She was hardly forty, and had been tall, but now was bent—had once been eminently beautiful, but now looked care-worn, and faded, Her eyes were hollow, her cheeks sunken, her hair strewed with untimely snow. Mrs. Morrison had been of poor, her husband of rich, extraction. Her marriage with him had been one of necessity, almost of compulsion, and the relation had been embittered not only by Morrison's detestable conduct, but by remembrance of one whom she had loved, whose premature death her marriage had occasioned. They had no offspring to inherit their vast estate, the profits of which the one scattered without care, in company and the turf, the other in acts of beneficence.

Mrs. Morrison's sympathies for her distressed fellow-creatures, especially the poorer sort of her own sex, were unbounded; it was therefore with compassionate interest she regarded a girl so fair and so young as our heroine, apparently homeless and broken-hearted. Finding that she could gather nothing from her as to her misfortunes or connexions, the lady inquired—

"If any thing could be done to alleviate the distress under which she appeared to suffer?"

Ruth sought for employment—any employment—and she would be thankful.

"What can you do?" asked the lady.

Ruth answered she had been lady's maid, but could perform household or dairy-work.

Mrs. Morrison agreed to prove her abilities and conduct in the former capacity, "regretting," she said, "to see so pleasing a girl lost to society."

Here, then, Ruth found an asylum for some weeks, until the too obvious admiration of the farmer, and the sudden demise of his wife, induced her, after much irresolution, to return to her parents.

Mrs. Morrison, compelled always to appear gay, and to mingle in a round of company, at whatever expense to her true feelings, had long had recourse to the stimulus of ardent spirits, which ultimately destroyed her. She had been doing the honours to a considerable party, having previously wrought up her spirits by unusual draughts of brandy, when, cards being introduced, she arose, excusing herself from play, and moving across the room with her accustomed grace and dignity, enclosed herself in her room until the inebriation of which she was conscious, though it had escaped others' observation, might be more completely under her controul. Her absence being at length remarked by the guests, Morrison, in one of his black humours, proceeded to recall her. He found her sitting dead in her chair.

Soon after this catastrophe, on the sabbath-day, having a month's hire in her pocket, which she had received from Mrs Morrison, Ruth turned her face homewards, not without dire mis givings.

She approached the cottage in the evening, her limbs trembling, her heart palpitating, and looking through the window, beheld the family gathered about a small round table, on which rested the " big Bible," out of which, in a voice of solemn expression, her father was reading.

Whether fear of his sternness, or reverence for his high moral qualities, most prevailed at that moment in Ruth's mind as she gazed on his countenance, across which a candle threw its feeble light, we cannot determine. Her sensations were mixed, but filial love was stronger under all. She fancied he looked altered for the worse, that his grizzled hair had retreated farther back from his brow, and become more mingled with white, that the lines of his face were plowed deeper, and that its contour was more severe—an unfavourable omen.

The chapter was finished—the family kneeled before their chairs, and her father, in a low deep voice, commenced his supplications to the Most High. Ruth who had beheld no such scene since she left home, shrank within herself as one too much abased to mingle in it.

" Yet why should this be?" she inquired of herself. " My mind acquits me. I will go in; and if my father will not receive me, I can but leave again.

She softly lifted the latch of the door, and joining the devotional group, unheard except by Sally, to whom she signed to be silent, slid into the same posture as the rest, just as her father, with emotion, besought "the Lord to take compassion on the stray sheep, and to lead her back to the fold."

At these words Mrs. Summerfield sobbed hysterically, and her

husband abruptly closed his petition. Both had risen ere they perceived that the stray sheep had been brought back—that she was before them! At the sight of her Summerfield started back as from an adder—his face assumed its most withering aspect, and his figure seemed stiffened to iron. Mrs. Summerfield, too, snatching Sally from her sister's embrace, assailed her with a volley of reproaches; and both husband and wife forgot, in their hatred of her imaginary guilt, the pity and tenderness due always, to the repentant—forgot that it is not the part of true wisdom to break the bruised reed,

"What has brought you back here, my fine madam?" cried the mother. "Has your gay lover wearied of you? And after revelling in wantonness and in finery as long as you could, have you come back to plague and trouble us in the poor home you have disgraced? Woe worth you, Ruth!—but you are mistaken if you think to do that. I will have no great man's mistress darkening my fireside? You may go back where you have been."

"Ah! Ruth, Ruth," exclaimed Summerfield, "thou hast destroyed thyself and us!"

Ruth, who had not yet risen from her knees, was unable to articulate a word of explanation, and this, joined to the humiliation of her attitude, confirmed the parents in their injurious impressions. Summerfield took his hat and left the cottage, which was the signal for the mother to pour out her lamentations and reproaches without stint or measure on the quaking culprit.

"Get off your knees," she began—"I want no such mockery here! You have proved yourself a deceitful, wicked girl, and all your father's good lessons, and all my example, have been thrown away upon you. But we have quite done with you; and if you you cannot persuade your gentleman to marry you, you must shift for yourself as well as you can. It will be grievous enough for us to think of you, and to have you here always before our eyes, a monument of shame, like Lot's wife, we will not."

"Mother," said Ruth, rising, and recovering her voice, for her love of Mrs. Summerfield was totally unmixed with the awe she experienced in the presence of her father, "mother, you are cruel and unjust."

"Ah! child," exclaimed Mrs. Summerfield, uplifting her voice to a still higher pitch, "it is you who have been cruel;—cruel to your good father, who neither eats nor sleeps, so burdened is he with grief and disappointment—cruel to me who have nursed you, loved you, toiled for you—cruel to your sister, whom you have given an example of infamy which may I never live to see her follow!—cruel to your brother. who, if he should prosper in the world, will always have to think of your shame as a foul blot on his family—cruel to us altogether, for when we were looking to you to be the wife of an honest and respectable man, and to receive that assistance from you which we were led to expect, you left us all in debt, and sadly off for food and clothing, to shift as well as we could—cruel to Maynard, who—"

"If you will hear me," interjected Ruth—but her mother sharply interrupted her.

"I will not hear anything from you! If you were to swear that it was not of your own free will you have been living with the squire, I would not believe you! I tell you, Ruth, I have been in as much peril from this young Clifton's father, as ever you could be from the son; but was my conduct like yours? No, Ruth—a lesson was read to the fiend that he will remember to the day of doom!"

Her delicately moulded features kindled and flushed into triumph, as her disordered imagination began to exert itself on this fatal theme, her deep blue eye expanded, and her gestures became animated even to extravagance.

"Oh! yes," she cried, "I shall see him crouching and quaking then, as high as he thought himself. And Roger and I can face him without fear; for if he accuses us of hurrying him out of the world before his time, we can so answer him that what we did to keep ourselves from being defiled by his wickedness will turn to his own condemnation."

Ruth was struck with mute dismay at this indirect admission on a subject that had only ceased to agitate her mind when superseded by other distracting causes of inquietude.

"You have made a dreadful acknowledgment, mother!" she said, "and I understand from it that the missing Squire Clifton is DEAD, and—Oh, gracious heavens! that my parents took his life.!"

NOTICE.—With this Number is Given Away a Coloured Picture for binding with the Work. Another will be given with the next Number. Order early.

"HAS YOUR GAY LOVER DESERTED YOU?"

THE COTTAGE GIRL.

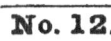

"IF YOU REMAIN HERE ANOTHER MOMENT, I WILL DRAW THE TRIGGER."

"SILENCE, for mercy!" Mrs. Summerfield in a wild whisper
articulated, glancing toward the door. "You would not
bring your father and mother to the gallows?"

"She has done as bad as that in bringing us to this," said
Summerfield, re-entering the cottage, his eyes reddened with
emotion that he had been out to indulge alone.

"But what now, Hannah," regarding her piercingly, "have you been speaking to this unhappy girl of what you should not?"

"I hardly know what I have been saying," replied Mrs. Summerfield, sinking on a chair.

"You can tell me," said the cottager to his daughter.

"I never can forget it," Ruth rejoined. "It concerned one who—who I suspect—that is whom my mother confesses—"

"I confess nothing!—I confess nothing!" Mrs. Summerfield gasped.

"My dear, be yourself," said the cottager, with steady composure—"all is well thus far. Let Ruth repeat to me what you have said."

"It was that the squire had been hurried out of this world by your means."

Summerfield's firm look hardly moved a muscle.

"I thought you knew what value to place on your mother's sayings when she is excited," he said. "You have distracted her mind."

Ruth's natural sense was strong and keen, and she was much older in the world than when first introduced to the reader. Convinced she was, therefore, despite her father's cool disclamation, that a fatal truth lurked in her mother's words; and yet was not her confidence in the integrity of her parents unabated. She wished to express these convictions, but while casting about for the most suitable and impressive words she was left alone. Her mother retired, supported by her father's arm, and no word of kindness fell from either.

"If I were as guilty as they think me," Ruth said to herself, her feelings rebelling against this treatment, "would not their harshness drive me back to evil? At least, ought they not to fear it? But my soul is innocent; and though I must again turn me to the cold world, I will starve sooner than it shall cease to be so."

She lay down on her old bed, but only intending to rest until the break of light should enable her again to go forth in search of a habitation.

"How many quiet hours I have slept away, how many pleasant dreams I have dreamed, here," she thought, as she counted the wakeful moments, whose slow unvarying progress was marked by the pendulum of a Dutch clock fastened on the wall opposite to her. "Such sleep—such dreams—I cannot now enjoy—I never may again!"

She had taken no notice of her favourite bullfinch, her own petted bird, which she had instructed in so many curious ways,

especially improving its capacity of imitating tunes, so as to render it the admiration of many. But her attention was now drawn to the intelligent little creature, for the cage door having been accidentally left open, it fluttered in freedom about the house, and on her calling to it in a tone of endearment, darted to her with shrill notes peculiarly expressive of delight. When she had fondled it some time, she let it go, and it hovered above its unhappy mistress, tuning its throat to a portion of the melody of "Roy's Wife," which were the last of several that she had taught it. The associations suddenly awakened were too much for Ruth, and remembering how he had betrayed her by whom that melody had first been sung in her hearing, she turned sick, and, springing up, rushed to the casement for air. But still the bird pursued its imitative lay, happy in its ignorance of human griefs, until the first blue gleam of opening morn was hailed by a more natural, buoyant, and varied strain. Ruth then found a partial vent for her anguish in tears, and returning to her bed slept feverishly an hour. She was awakened by her sister, who had come to talk with and to comfort her.

From her Ruth learnt many particulars respecting Maynard and her parents since her abduction, and to her she confided the true story of her wrongs. The affectionate talk of the sisters gradually sunk into silence, and the younger slept. Ruth then arose, and kissing the slumberer's sun-burned brow, whence some mirthful fancies of Queen Mab had already dispelled the brief sadness that their conference had shed on it, tied on her bonnet and cloak, took up the bundle and bandbox which enclosed all she was worth, and with fervent good wishes for those she was leaving, crossed the threshold, and was moving down the lane, but a thought struck her, and returning, she placed on the Bible one of the two half-sovereigns which she had earned under the Morrisons.

When Sally awoke she saw her father dressed and standing beside her. He had reflected much, repented his stern reception of his favourite though as he imagined erring child, grieved for the language his wife had used to her, and was resolved that his pride should stoop to pardon the poor penitent, and to hear her story.

He had to hear, it, however, not from Ruth but Sally, while his heart was rent by the result of his inconsiderate austerity, joined to his wife's bitter reproaches.

The impress of truth was on the recital Sally imparted for her sister, and the distressed father resolved instantly to seek out young Clifton and to demand redress for his poor child. Maynard being sent for, and made acquainted with what had occurred, resolved to accompany Summerfield to London, where Clifton then was, after they had endeavoured to trace the lost one.

The letter of Clifton offering " pecuniary compensation," which had been consigned to the flames before half the contents had been read, had given the address of a solicitor in town at whose chambers Clifton might be communicated with, and this address Summerfield fortunately remembered. To support the family during the absence of the cottager, Maynard gave Mrs Summerfield a sovereign.

" And if our return should be hindered," he said, " and you want more, send to my man at the mill."

" My true friend," said Summerfield, " you have already laid me under obligations larger than I see any hope of repaying."

" I think you are in your dotage, man," Maynard roughly returned; " what use have I for money, and Ruth lost to me !"

As they were taking leave of Mrs. Summerfield the small present Ruth had left on the Bible was found by Sally.

" She had two half-sovereigns earned at the farm where she has been living," cried the latter, " this must be one of them, and it is left for us. See, here is a bit of paper with some writing on it."

The writing ran thus :——

" Half a month's hire given me by Mrs. Morrison of Oakenford —I hope my dear parents will not refuse it from their unhappy and injured, but innocent and dutiful child. God bless you all ! If I can get engaged in a comfortable family you shall know."

To this Ruth, though no poetess, had in the intensity of her feeling added the following effusion :——

> " From my dear home forlorn I go,
>   No hopes, no joys, my steps attend,
> Without a solace to my woe,
>   But thoughts of death, the mourner's friend."

" Oh ! my dear, dear girl !" exclaimed Mrs. Summerfield, wringing her hands, " it is I who have driven thee to this ! Oh ! wretched, wretched mother !—I shall see her no more !—I shall see my Ruth no more !"

" Peace, Hannah," said her husband authoritatively. " We have each been to blame, but lamenting avails not. For my part I am thankful to find in this extremity that though my daughter has been a sufferer, she is not a guilty one. This revives me under all."

" You hardly deserve that I should." said Maynard, " for having

so wronged her in your thoughts. Which of us was right now about that Mounseer Frenchman's story?"

" You, I confess."

" To be sure I was; but let me only get hold of Mounseer, and if I do not lay on his calico jacket some other stripes than it now bears my name is not Harry of the Mill. By all the corn that ever was grinded he shall dance like another St. Anthony."

" His assertion was a quibble," observed Summerfield. " At leaving Rosedale House with Clifton the fellow declared " she neither spoke nor cried out;—why no, it is evident now that she could not, being stupified by their infernal drugs !"

I'll quibbble the rascal !" cried Maynard, making an emphatic flourish as if wielding a horsewhip. " He shall find that I can quibble too in a way he won't like. Slash! slash !—aye, by my father's soul he shall smart, and no mistake! But let us be moving."

CHAPTER XVII.

" The clouds are black'ning, the storms threat'ning,
　The cavern doth mutter, the greenwood moan ;
Billows are breaking, the damsel's heart aching,
　Thus in the dark night she singeth alone,
　　Her eye upward roving :
The world is empty, the heart is dead surely
　In this world plainly all seemeth amiss ;
To thy heaven, Holy one, take home the little one,
　I have partaken of all earth's bliss,
　　Both living and loving."—COLERIDGE.

RUTH walked three miles at a quick pace, when a London waggon turning into the road, the thought occurred to her whether she had not best take a place in it, as she had heard that country girls, honest and active, were much prized as servants in the metropolis, and Mr. Morrison, of Oakenford, could be applied to for a recommendation.

She was ignorant of Clifton's being in London, or the idea would not have found an instant's place in her mind, for, though residents of the great town know they might dwell there twenty years without meeting any person they know, Ruth would certainly have calculated on falling again into his hands.

To London then she went; the old waggoner moved by her pathetic voice and gentle manners, reducing his fare to her means, and leaving her a half-crown to pay for a lodging at her journey's end. At every place where he stopped to bait he offered her something to eat or drink, with a blunt and awkward courtesy, but of the right genuine sort.

The world is not so bad as represented; evil and good walk hand in hand, and the unnatural union can only be divorced by the angel which shall proclaim " Time to be no longer." To look only on the fair or the foul side is to take a partial and incorrect view of human nature.

When the lumbering vehicle in which Ruth had travelled stopped at its appointed place of destination, the waggoner going into the inn returned with a direction written on a bit of dirty paper.

" Thou'lt find a cheap and decent lodgin'-house here," he said : " and there be a register-officer hard by where thou may'st for a shilling get any place thou loikest best."

From her heart Ruth thanked him, and, encouraged in her plans, proceeded to find the house whose directions she had received. Ere she had gone far the waggoner sent a boy after her to conduct her to the place, a civility most desirable for on emerging from a narrow street, hemmed in by houses, whose extreme height was to her eye almost fearful, the throng, the noise, the bustle of Cheapside, made her feel the solitude of her condition, and the vastness of the vortex on which she was launched, to a degree that bewildered her senses. Under happier circumstances, the brilliance of the lights in the great thoroughfares through which she with difficulty kept the boy in sight, the splendour of the shops, and the variety that greeted her eye and ear on every side, would have filled her with ecstasy, but now she experienced a relief when turning from these animated scenes to the stillness of the narrow lanes and alleys, through which the boy, merrily uplifting on his thin treble voice the last popular comic ditty with a running accompaniment on the area railings performed by his stick, conducted her to a court in which the houses looked old and grim, and projected their smoky upper stories so closely toward each other that the sky was barely visible between them. One beaming star however was seen above those dingy masses of brick and mortar, and their dingier inhabitants, on whom a philanthropist might imagine it was

shedding its fair rays to encourage them amid their hardships to remember that an eye of love was on them.

The court had altogether an air of antiquity, but not the antiquity which we meet in some hoary ecclesiastical pile, or the edifices of feudal grandeur, for here there was no beauty, nothing to stir the lofty associations of history, or to gratify the taste for the ideal—but all was sombrous, oppressive, murky. It sat on the little misshapen church in the corner like one of its own carved monsters vivified—it hovered like a spectre over the churchyard crammed to the surface with bodies that had once felt the tide of life rioting through their veins, with sculls that had once harboured souls capable perhaps of lofty things, with hearts that had thorbbed in passion and melted in joy and sorrow. And for the spirit of the past haunting the dark dens called houses in this court, where could we find a more complete personation than in the little old antiquary, who, in the very darkest, oldest, and complicated of them, was seen plying a few tools of odd construction, to what purpose was a favourite riddle with the children who gazed through the shop window on his indefatigable labours, Rap —rap—rap. The same eternal sound of the hammer, in the same thick twilight, never relieved even in July. He had a beard like a jew—his skin was begrimed—his coat of grey woollen, and being much too loose for his shrunk dimensions, gave him the air of a magician.

What added to the curiosity he inspired was a tradition that many years before he had found a great sum in an old cabinet he had purchased at a sale. It was supposed that he had much riches hidden in odd corners about his house, and that he slept each night with a blunderbuss under his pillow, and other weapons within reach. His house was his own too, and he had valuable property in old furniture, plate, pictures, and jewels.

As this old original's domicile was the oldest and gloomiest in the court so that in which Ruth was lodged was the newest and brightest. Half a dozen families—who managed to exist God only knows how—occupied the upper stories; in the lower the Mistress kept furnished lodgings, namely a kitchen and two chambers. One of the latter Ruth occupied with a mother and daughter, half-starved creatures, who made up linen for the shops which sell ready-made apparel.

She had the liberty of preparing her food in the kitchen, when the fire and utensils were not wanted for others, in which case her duty was to wait her turn, since she was only to pay eighteen pence per week.

The first payment was made in advance, and this, with a shilling to the register-office, which guaranteed her a situation either as housemaid or lady's-maid in some respectable family, left her all but destitute. The register-office, like many other institution. which hold out fair promises, proved tardy and unsatisfactory.

"Never mind, thought Ruth, " I have lived hard at home, and know how to make a penny go far— if I can only keep away downright hunger I shall do well enough."

The first day a few pence she had supplied her; but the second saw her without breakfast, without dinner, sitting at the window, looking across at the old antiquary rapping with his small hammer as usual among fragments of old carving, strange ghastly pictures in filligree frames, mutilated statues, black oaken presses, and a hundred other dusty worm-eaten curiosities. She had a spirit not easily conquered by impediments. She could endure too with a fortitude and good-temper uncommon at her years. But when, after a longer fasting than she had known even in the worst days of her parents, she flew to the register-office, and found no situation forthcoming at all likely to suit her, her courage failed and she fainted. There was a great bustle by the people of " the register" to recover her, and then they gathered from her broken expressions something of the nature of her distress.

"Bless me !" cried the mistress of the tobacconist's shop where the office was held, " what a simple young creature to think of coming to London with only a half-crown ! Did you fancy places were as plentiful as the stones in the street ? They may be so of some sort, but my register don't find any but such as are respectable. If you wanted any low-lived situation, you should have told me."

"Your shop bills deceived me, ma'am," said Ruth, faintly, " but you will please to let me know how soon you can get me something."

"There's the addresses of two places of all-work." They were tossed disdainfully over the counter, and eagerly received. " But," said the lady, " I should have thought you might have managed to live a week or two by pledging some of your clothes, for I suppose you did not think of a London situation without being well stocked."

Amid all the extremities of a life of poverty with which Ruth had been acquainted, she had never known her parents resort to the pawnbroker, therefore that resource had not till now occurred to her. She instantly availed herself of it to appease the cravings of hunger, and then, without loss of an hour, pressed to make application to the persons whose addresses had been given her.

One of them, to her discomfort, was the old antiquary opposite and not liking the look of the house or the old man, she found out the other, which was by no means eligible, nor, she was fain to believe, reputable. A number of young women, tawdrily dressed, were laughing and romping about the place, and so many compliments to her beauty were paid, and such an unnecessary anxiety expressed to engage her, that Ruth felt herself relieved when she was on the outside of the door, and resolved never again to be on the inside.

So she presented herself in the den of the old antiquary, not without difficulty for the shop was sunk three steps below the level of the court paving, and those steps where impeded by curious rubbish. The gloom of the place was more perceptible within than without; and before Scipio Robinson, as the bearded hermit of modern antiquity was named, could be roused from his monotonous hammerings to attend to her, she repented of her application.

The shrill and snappish "Eh?" with which he suspended his task, after her thrice-repeated announcement that "she had heard Mr. Robinson wanted a servant," did not tend to reassure her. Nor had he patience to attend to the explanation of her errand, however brief, but called for "Becky," who emerged on the summons from the shades at the back of the shop.

The appearance of Becky Robinson was not more propitious than that of Scipio. Bating a trifling allowance for the difference of sex, they were the counterpart of each other. Equally grim—equally crabbed—equally aged; they had lived together all their lives in this strange abode; and until Miss Becky began to feel the infirmities of age, had kept no servant, owned no relation, nor suffered any individual, except on business, to cross the door stone.

It would be impossible to describe the unpleasant sensations with which our heroine followed the priestess of these murky regions through a very chaos of musty furniture to the only room which was permitted to see the light of a fire or exhibit any attempt at arrangement. It was spacious, but so low as to affect one who had not been used to it, very unpleasantly. Everything bore tokens of neglect : but notwithstanding, the very beautiful and massive, though incongruous furniture made a striking appearance. Some articles in that obscure room had graced a palace of the sixteenth century—others were of even earlier date—but nothing was modern. Miss Becky was a woman of very eccentric manners, but gold was hid in the rough ore. Ruth at first found some difficulty in comprehending her. She surveyed our heroine from head to foot, shrugged her shoulders, shook her head.

"You think yourself pretty, I suppose?" she said.

The question was point blank, and Ruth answered with humorous sincerity, and the utmost naivete—

"If you please, ma'am."

The grim spinsters thin lips relaxed.

"You are not ashamed to be vain then?" she said.

"I hope so," rejoined Ruth.

The spinster relaxed still more.

"Sit down," she said, and Ruth obeyed.

"Where do you come from?"

"From the country."

"Where?"

"I have been living at Mr. Morrison's farm, Oakenford, in the north. I was lady's-maid to his wife."

"But I want no lady's-maid."

"I shall be happy to serve you in any way, ma'am," said Ruth, anxiously; "for, indeed," she burst into tears, "I am destitute, except by disposing of my few clothes, and I detest going to the pawnbroker."

"Very right—they live by ruin," said Miss Becky, with emphasis—"they are like the worms in the churchyard, that fatten on decay. Take off your bonnet."

Ere Ruth was engaged, she had to wait the arrival of Morrison's letter, for Scipio Robinson and his sister required to be thoroughly satisfied of the honesty of any stranger whom necessity compelled them to introduce to their habitation. When that answer did arrive it was directed to our heroine, and contained an offer of his hand, and urgent entreaties that she would return to Oakenford.

"And his wife has not been dead three weeks! I would not have him," Ruth exclaimed, "if his acres were sown with diamonds!"

Morrison's declaration, and her contempt of it, raised her considerably in the estimation of those she was desirous to serve, and the vacant situation became hers, but on different emolument, to which light duties might to some have served as a counterpoise, Ruth, however, made these duties heavier from choice, by exercising the habits or nice cleanliness, which had become to her a second nature, in rooms and among utensils that had until then been a stranger to them; and she was besides more indefatigable in her attentions to her master and mistress, and more anxious to be useful to them in ways not included under the precise terms of her engagement, than more venal and sophisticated characters would have dreamt of in her place.

Miss Becky very soon gave up the direction of the internal econ-

ony to Ruth, who brought so many new and costless comforts about the dull place, and at the same time so pleased her and the old man by her frugality, and the plastic accomodatingness of her disposition, that before she had spent a month with them they ceased to regard her as a servant. The old antiquary often relaxed into jocoseness as she sat with them at meals, and his sister unbent her hard features to smile on the amiable and clever girl.

But when Ruth was alone in her chamber, whence all her exertions had not been able to banish a dreariness and a closeness —when instead of the music of her cottage bullfinch, she heard the grating monotony of some Italian boy's hand organ—when the loveliest moonlight could find no entrance into her room except perhaps a few weak and scattered rays, for the height of the opposite houses, the narrowness of the court, and the blocking up of her window by time-worn furniture—and when thoughts of her parents and their mystery, Maynard and his blighted hopes, Percy and his inconsistent and cruel conduct pressed on her mind —it was then she indulged herself in fits of anguish, of tenderness, of regret, which by day she controlled with uncommon steadiness and fortitude.

One night after several hours of these sad reflections, Ruth was alarmed by a smell of fire, and rising to ascertain the cause she hurried to the room of her mistress, who was standing in the middle of the floor, a rushlight in her hand, and her features exaggerated with extreme terror.

"Oh! Mrs. Rebecca," exclaimed Ruth, "the house I am sure is on fire!"

"Worse than that—worse than that," returned the old lady, "I have heard steps moving about the rooms below. Hark!— did you not hear a whispering!"

"I will go call my master," said Ruth.

"Aye, do—do—do—and I will reward to-morrow, if it please God we be not murdered! There is a loaded pistol in that drawer, take it with you, and fire if you see but a mouse stir."

Ruth took the weapon and the light, left Mrs. Rebecca locked in her room, and moved with a hasty but courageous step across a wide landing, and ascended a flight of stairs at whose top lay the chamber of the old antiquary. Here her blood was frozen by the sight of a ruffian apparently standing sentinel at the door, while a scuffling within gave dreadful token of what was going on. Without a moment's hesitation she fired, and the housebreaker dropped. Stepping over his body, she sprang into the chamber, and beheld the old man prostrate by the iron-bound

trunk, which he was franticly endeavouring to defend against a stout desperado, whose murderous ferocity had just been arrested by the unexpected report of the pistol.

With a presence of mind almost unparalleled, Ruth levelled the weapon, (whose contents were already discharged) at the breast of this second ruffian.

" You may escape if you will," she said, " but if you remain here another moment I will draw the trigger, as I did on the wretch outside."

Ruffians are generally cowards, and the present case was no exception to the rule. The fellow dashed out at the door, stumbling over the body of his comrade, and leaving behind the booty that had tempted them, as well as their instruments of housebreaking. Having forgot the wax-light usually carried by such depredators, they had supplied its place by flaming combustibles, which had occasioned the smell of fire that first alarmed Ruth.

The gratitude of the old antiquary, thus narrowly saved from a dreadful death by the intrepidity of Ruth, promised to be generously displayed. He gave her on the spot a turquoise ring, and made her a thousand professions of what he would do for her in future. Mrs. Rebecca was not less thankful, and pressed a five-pound note on Ruth.

She was now on an increased footing of favour and consequence with the Robinsons, but before she could enjoy it long her altered health led to a discovery which at once destroyed the balance of her mind. Darkness and horror enveloped her thoughts; she was depressed to the last degree, and was often heard muttering to herself, and weeping and moaning. Mrs. Rebecca was concerned about her, and strove earnestly to penetrate the reason of this change, which she at last set down to the death which Ruth had been the innocent means of inflicting on the robber. In this conviction her brother Scipio agreed with her, and as it saved the unhappy girl much trouble in her replies, she tacitly acquiesced, and listened over and over to their arguments against the foolishness of grieving for an act which had only saved the gallows a burden, and without which Robinson could not have been rescued.

At length the time came when they must either be undeceived or Ruth quit them. She chose the latter, and while the old maid was taking her afternoon sleep, and the antiquary hammering away as usual, she stole out, leaving all she was worth behind her, except the apparel she had on. A glimmering of some desperate project of self-destruction was in her mind. Religion—her parents—all was for the moment centred in herself

and her sad situation. She pressed through the crowded and brilliant streets, loathing their sprightliness, and wishing that heaven would send down on her head one of its consuming bolts, or that the earth would gape and swallow her. The bells rung out loudly and joyfully, she knew not wherefore, but their sound was unearthly in her ears, and seemed to triumph in her misery: At the end of the Strand she paused, uncertain what way to pursue.

"But it is no matter," she said internally, "whither I go—this night shall be my last!"

Crossing over to Whitehall, Ruth strayed slowly through St. James's Park, and reached Hyde Park just at its gayest period. Incessant was the roll of carriages, intermingled with hundreds of noble equestrians on their docile and highly-trained steeds; and mechanically, as she saw others stop to gaze. Ruth stopped also.

Among the groups that passed her mounted on horseback, one, as it approached, rivetted her gaze. It consisted of two ladies and two gentlemen, laughing and chatting apparently in the highest spirits, and followed by two mounted grooms. The first lady and gentleman were unknown to her, so was the other lady, who was young and beautiful, but in her companion, whose fine face was radiant with pleasure, she recognised Clifton! On swept the gay party—and SHE, the poor victim, was left behind to weep and suffer as she might.

"He is happy, and forgets me," she said, tottering to a friendly seat which happened to be near her. "This—this is worse than all!"

Hitherto, unknown to herself, a secret belief in the reality of Clifton's love for her had greatly assisted to sustain her spirits; but they now broke down to the last degree on beholding him apparently so devoid of care—devoting himself to another while she was forgotten and forsaken.

While Ruth continued to sit abandoned to despondency the darkness closed in, and the park became gradually cleared. She hardly noticed the change, until two equestrians, nearly the last on the circle, and in earnest conversation, walked their horses slowly past her. They were Clifton and his fair companion, at the sight of whom a jealous madness seized on Ruth; she felt a sensation to shriek forth on her betrayer the direst invectives that ever tongue gave utterance to; but the sounds died hollowly away, and she fell senseless to the earth.

Long was it before life and its miseries opened again on Ruth, and then they appeared in erroneous colours. Her impression was strong that she had drowned herself as she had meditated on quitting the house of the old antiquary, and that the world of spirits was around her, while she still lay fettered in the chilling bands of death. Some strange wild words escaped her, to which her nurse (for she had been conveyed to a hospital), replied in soothing terms.

"Pray can you tell me," asked the poor patient, "whether my father and mother know that I am dead?"

"Not a word of it," replied the nurse.

"I am glad of that," sighed Ruth, "I have grieved them enough."

And with an expression of satisfaction she reclosed her eyes, and slept. At awaking, her senses were clearer, and she arose on her elbow, and gazed around the hospital ward in wonder. The nurse had on her knee an infant in the coarse habiliments which charity supplies, and Ruth understood what had happened.

"Let me not see it!" she exclaimed, covering her pale face with her paler hands as she sank back on the pillow.

"It's a fine babby, though it come afore its time," said the nurse; "and please the Lord you'll both do well now, though we did not expect it an hour ago."

The nurse proceeded to question her poor patient respecting the names, means, and place of residence of her parents, and seducer, but to all such interrogations, in whatever shape they were put, as long as Ruth remained in the hospital, she was inflexibly silent. To the matron, to the doctors, as well as to the nurse, she expressed her gratitude for their attentions to her, and for the kindnes she had received, as well of sympathy for her desolate and sorrowful condition as of professional assistance, but she was unmoved by their expostulations to suffer application on her behalf to be made to her friends.

After a protracted illness she was dismissed from the hospital with her fatherless babe. A shilling had been given her, and she had been earnestly advised to make her way to her home.

"But I will never do that! I will not carry there more trouble and shame," Ruth said, as, pressing the helpless little one instinctively to her breast, she wandered on heedless of the direction she was taking, and only anxious to reach some place of solitude. The day was unusually resplendent. Spring had arrived to cheer these northern climes, and in a hundred nooks in the metropolitan suburbs were seen budding trees and bushes; sweet-smelling wall-flowers, crocuses, and other early productions of Flora, were selling in posies about the streets; and the sunshine lay on the stones in golden floods, streaming down the

atmosphere so unalloyed that it would not have disgraced Italy. The anxious sombre countenances of the busy folks in the throughfares seemed to brighten with the weather, and sickly nerves felt braced, and languid spirits revived.

But there is a point of misery when the joyous influences of the blooming year cease to be left, or only excite remembrances of former joys that aggravate present pains. Ruth's mind was on the sunshine of sweet Rosedale, on the birds that sang there, and on the flowers that grew there.

But Rosedale she no more must see, nor any one who dwelt in it. The reproaches of her mother were written on her memory with a pen of fire. Her father's start of abhorrence when he saw her before him, and his stern accusing look, she would not encounter again for worlds. After resting in different places to wile away the time, the unfortunate girl, about six in the evening, turning from the City Road, pursued a tranquil walk by the new River, where on one bank foliage overhangs the stream, in no unpleasing imitation of romantic nature, while on the other, a walk within palings level to the water's-edge, invites the meditative or the melancholy to loiter away the sweet hours of evening, when the distant hum of the great city is but just audible, and the music of harp and flute, or the voice of some sweet singer, comes by fits on the still air from the open windows of pleasant homes, where twilight and love are met.

Here walked Ruth, stopping often to fix a longing eye on the darkening water. It looked so cool, so quiet, that she felt powerfully tempted to seek within it the peace denied her in life. The birth of her child, and the means and period of their departing out of existence, would then remain for ever hidden from those whom she regarded, and this was what she earnestly wished. But the most potent inducement was the strong impression she had received, from the sight of Clifton and the young lady mounted by his side in the park, that he had ceased to love his Cottage Girl, and that hope from him there was none. Of all agonies, as before said, this she found the worst. Before her maternity she had hardly known the force of her attachment to him; now it displayed itself in all its length and breadth. A number of wild projects entered her mind for discovering where he lived in the metropolis, and how far he was engaged to the companion of his ride. But London was a wilderness to which she had no clue.

" And while you and I, my boy, rove houseless here, he," she vehemently exclaimed, " may be happy with his richer love, casting no thought on me, nor caring whether I starve, beg, or perish. Yes, yes, I can fancy him at his costly table, the hand-

somest and the falsest there, if a thousand sat round it! I can see him smile on her as he has smiled on me—I can hear him whisper to her as he has whispered to me. And she, poor lady! will listen to him perhaps as gladly as I did. But she will not be so deceived—no, no, no—she is rich, I am poor!"

Proceeding at a swifter pace, for each moment saw her more excited in mind, Ruth regarded not the shadows of night that were falling fast around, nor the dew that began to descend in a soft shower. Her way grew more deserted, lying over wide waste fields, smelling not disagreeably of burning bricks, and exhibiting here and there broad red lights from growing kilns. Ruth slackened not her steps, until, leaving these open fields, she had traversed a couple of miles along a beautiful road, bordered chiefly with the decorated villas and mansions of London citizens. Her strength then failed her, and she rested on a bank, hushing the clamorous wailings of her babe, which, refreshed with nutriment, soon slumbered on her knee, happily ignorant of the peril to which its little life was exposed. The young mother's head drooped over it, and was not lifted again for upwards of an hour. Whether she slept or swooned, or brooded over her despair, we know not, but at last she raised her face heavenwards, and the moon, breaking through inky clouds, seemed to greet her with hope.

" There is One left who will not forsake me!" she ejaculated. " Have I not read ' when thy father and mother forsake thee, then the Lord will take thee up?' We are not quite comfortless, my poor boy, and though now we are wandering like guilty outcasts, there is One who reads the heart and will recompense us."

This softer mood was but momentary. The deadly gripe of jealousy tugged fearfully at her heart-strings, and she could not banish the idea of Clifton and his new love gay and happy while she was wandering in darkness and destitution. This brought on again the fascinating thought of suicide. A moment's pain, and she and her child would have passed from all the agonies of the present, and all the anticipated horrors of the future, to rest, or—happiness.

In this faith she sought again a place where her resolution might be carried into effect. None such for some time appeared; but just at midnight, when the moon, gliding over the heavens in solemn and majestic beauty, now occupied their centre, Ruth stood by the brink of another branch of the New River.

TWO EQUESTRIANS IN EARNEST CONVERSATION PASSED HER.

THE COTTAGE GIRL.

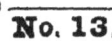

"I AM POOR AND SORROWFUL."

THE unhappy girl cast her eyes around; no individual, no dwelling, met her view.

"I am alone," she said. "None see me but my eternal Judge. Have mercy on me!" she prayed, kneeling on the grass. "Reproach hath broken my heart! Those who should have taken pity on me had none. I am cast off by lover and parents—I am the scorn of my acquaintances—I am poor and sorrowful! In Thee and eternity are all my hopes. Take me, then, O Heavenly Father, to Thy mercy! Farewell, my parents!—my kind sister! —dear little Billy!—Maynard!—and the lanes and fields of

Rosedale! I shall never be with you again. Be happy, Percy, if your conscience will let you, for you will hear no more of her you have destroyed. Smile, flatter, drink, and laugh, I shall not hear you—I shall not see you. Marry who you will—I shall be insensible to the scene. My heart will have ceased to beat, and neither your bride or you will be able to give one pang more."

With the last words, straining her child to her bosom, and her eyes still turned above, she inclined her body forward, and dropped gently into the water, which, parting for a second, closed above her!

CHAPTER XVIII

" Make no more offers, use no further means,
But with all brief and plain conveniency
Let me have judgment."—SHAKSPEARE.

LOOKING back a few months, we return to Maynard and Summerfield, who arrived in London, and presenting themselves at the chambers of Clifton's London solicitor, a staid grave man, the latter arose from his desk as their names were whispered by his clerk; and when the door was closed, and they were alone, spoke at once to the purpose in these words :—

" Mr. Clifton, if I mistake not, sent you, a short time ago, a proposal of compensation for injuries resulting to you for some unfortunate transaction in which he had been involved. You have only to state the amount of your wishes, and, if within reasonable compass, I am instructed to say that they shall be attended to."

" No compensation such as he has proposed will suit me," said the indignant father. " My expectations from the squire are very different. But they must be stated to himself, not to any third party, and I am here to learn where I may find him."

" That I have no authority to impart. Whatever you have to say must be communicated through me."

" I will not submit to that," said Summerfield, firmly. " If Mr.

Clifton will not see me I shall appeal to a magistrate. The means he took for depriving me of my daughter are punishable by law; and though the exposure will be as painful to me as himself, I will not spare him on that account."

"I am but imperfectly informed of the cause of your complaint," said the solicitor; "but it is apparent that, succeed you ever so well, you can only obtain what Mr. Clifton is already willing to surrender."

"By giving me damages, the law will speak its sense of my injuries," said Summerfield; "but if I take hush-money for my child's infamy, I shall be unfit to breathe the same air with honest men. I had rather starve in a ditch!—I had rather see my poor wife and the dear children I have left with her, gasping their last in famine and nakedness! The bread would choke us that was purchased by Clifton's bounty. No, sir—tell him that, with all the scorn a man is capable of feeling, I refuse his compensation!—that, much as I abhor his conduct to my daughter, this base offer is still more detestable to me!—and that these grey hairs of mine, which he has helped to whiten, shall not go down to a grave fouled with the reputation of my having profited by my daughter's shame!',

"You are excited, sir, composed yourself," said the solicitor; his official indifference giving way under sympathy and respect.

"It is easy to talk of composure, when one is not feeling the sharp spur of affliction," returned Summerfield, impatiently and bitterly. "I have prated of it myself, the Lord forgive me, but now—now composure is a sound of empty mockery! There is no composure for me until Mr. Clifton takes my wronged daughter by the hand, and names her wife!"

"Surely an improbable hope," said the solicitor, gently, "if I am rightly informed of the disparity between your daughter's rank and his."

"And why improbable, sir?" Summerfield rejoined. "It was not so long since he was willing to overlook that disparity, and made liberal promises if my friend here would yield her up to him. My daughter preferred the miller to the squire—and I was proud of her choice, as proving she loved goodness better than rank; but just before the marriuge day the squire lured her from her home on lying pretexts, deadened her senses by some sort of opiate, and carried her to a house provided on purpose, trusting that persuasion and despair would make her the poor passive wretch he wished. But she had been taught better though; a spirit was within her which no force could bend. Her reputation was gone, and she left him."

"You may be proud of such a daughter," said the solicitor.

"And so he is!" exclaimed Maynard in a choked voice; "for though she was the prettiest lass in Rosedale, her beauty was nothing to her merits. Clifton tried all means to mislead her, but nothing, save downright villainy, could prevail. She can never be mine now. But while I have a penny it shall not be spared when it can serve her. So comfortable as we should have been in the mill! But what use grieving, it is all over."

"As a husband and father myself I can feel for you—as a solicitor of Mr. Clifton I can only beg you to reconsider the offer made to you, or should you wish to transmit any other proposal I am quite willing to be the medium."

"You still refuse, then, to say where Mr. Clifton lives?" said Summerfield.

"When I have consulted with him respecting your wishes he may meet you here," said the solicitor, evasively.

The friends spoke together apart. Summerfield then turned again to the solicitor.

"Report to the squire what we have spoken, and to-morrow we will be here again to know his answer."

"Not to-morrow, but on Wednesday, or the subsequent day, if you please."

"Delay is serious to us," said Summerfield. "For me I am a very poor man, as you seem to know; and while I am waiting on the leisure of the squire, my family and myself are supported almost entirely by the kindness of my friend. I am no petitioner in this case either, but come rather to demand a right, and I consider Squire Clifton ought not to keep me from my work or my home an unnecessary hour."

"On Wednesday, at the present hour, I shall be ready with Mr. Clifton's reply," said the solicitor, in the decisive manner with which one concludes an interview. "But you have not informed me where your daughter at present is, Mr. Summerfield."

"I wish to heaven I knew!" exclaimed the cottager. "She returned home, but receiving not so patient a reception as she ought to have had, left us again the same night, and I can hear nothing of her."

"If it will be any satisfaction I can assure you this intelligence will disquiet my client. He has expressed to me considerable anxiety about the young woman's fate, but I believe comforted himself with the hope that she was safe in her home."

"I would give all my thousand pounds that I have in Rosedale Bank if she was," groaned Maynard. "But I am deceived if she is ever there again. To speak my misgivings, I doubt our

errand to the squire is lost labour, and that she has made herself away."

Summerfield, though in reality a load of apprehension pressed on his spirit, refused to admit such a suggestion.

"His daughter," he said, "possessed more courage of mind than to fly from affliction to suicide. She knew how to bear distress. From his knowledge of her character, he was sure that she would struggle bravely with the sorrows and difficulties it had pleased Heaven, through the guilt of others, to cast in her way."

"I hope you may be right," said Maynard, despondingly, "but for my part I have small hope."

"Think you, that in her necessitous condition, she may not have resorted to an evil of a different kind from that of suicide?" suggested the solicitor.

"No, I do not think so, sir," Summerfield forcibly rejoined.

"I beg your pardon, I had no intention of increasing the pain you must feel at present. Yet, if I might advise, all your exertions should at present be employed to discover where and in what way the young woman is existing."

Summerfield and his friend then consulted with the speaker on the best means of pursuing their inquiries, and departed to put them into immediate practice, arranging to return as soon as they had heard of her, while the solicitor promised to state to Mr. Clifton the precise nature of their demands, and the painful business with which they were occupied.

We have already seen the uneasiness and remorse with which Clifton received the latter part of this communication. He bade his solicitor, when they next called, offer them a ten or twenty-pound note, not as going any way toward making amends for what had happened, but simply to defray the expense of the search after Ruth.

Summerfield's determined rejection of his former proposal of compensation brought the blush to Clifton's cheek.

"A man so poor," he said, with affected indifference, "one would not expect to refuse a couple of hundred pounds—nor would he, but that he thinks to make a better bargain. He would have me marry the girl, but he must remember I was once denied the hand he wishes to force on me. Had he then spoken one word of consent to my suit, all that has since come to pass of a painful nature would have been spared."

The solicitor, in whose private office these words had been spoken, left his chair, and, after rubbing his hands by the fire, assuming a particularly grave expression of face, said—

" I should be presuming very much to interfere, but as a father myself, Mr. Clifton, I must say I pity that poor man from my soul."

" Doubtless, and you might make something worth while if you carried his action successfully through for breach of promise," insinuated Clifton, with a bitter play of sarcasm on his features.

Wounded feeling tinged the parchment cheek of the lawyer slightly, and his voice trembled with irritation as he rejoined—

" Mr. Clifton, you wrong me in your thought. I would not be the means of putting you to annoyance for the best fee that ever was paid to lawyer. I was the town agent and the sincere and humble friend of that unhappy man your father. I was the adviser, if I may take it on me to say so, of his widowed lady, until you came of age to take the head of the estate. And if I have ever failed in my duty or regard to you—"

" You have been highly serviceable to me, and I respect no man more," interrupted Clifton ; " but you will best serve me now by reserving your sympathies and opinions for matters on which I require your advice. Trueman, I want money—five hundred at least—by eleven o'clock to-morrow. You must raise it, for this electioneering business has cleared me."

" It will not be difficult to get that accommodation."

" On my own security alone, and moderate discount ? "

" I think so."

" Well, oblige me by immediate attention to the business."

" I will ; but before you go, Mr. Clifton, I should be glad if you would look over your Rosedale agent's accounts for the quarter."

" Not to-day," exclaimed Clifton, after making an ineffectual effort to fix his attention on the details of pounds and shillings, which Trueman hastily began to recapitulate. " I am not able to follow you with any acuracy. I drank too much wine yesterday, and it has left me a wretched headache. Come to my lodgings to-morrow at luncheon, and bring the money and books with you."

" He is going in the wrong path, following his father's steps," said the solicitor, with concern, when the door had swung behind the young squire. " Yet I cannot altogether give him up in my mind. Assuredly there is in him a frank and kind nature—and I persuade myself that he must before long reform his ways, and live as becomes one of his understanding. If he were once married I should not fear him ; and if this poor girl has only kept herself above the gulf which the world spreads for the desolate young female, I should rejoice to see her made his partner, as she has an unquestionable right to be."

A forntight of suspense and remorse, which he was too proud to acknowledge, passed heavily along with Percy Clifton, before Summerfield and Maynard called again on the solicitor to communicate the failure of their exertions to discover the lost girl.

Maynard now was the chief spokesman, and his grief seemed to find a salutary vent in detailing the methods they had employed in searching for Ruth, in proclaiming her merits, and lamenting her loss; while it was often curious how habitual respect for the squire mingled with and modified his keen resentment. With Summerfield it was far otherwise. No softening or healing influences accompanied his sorrow; the harsher passions to which his nature was prone were all called into full play, and the virtues by which they were in general counterbalanced were thrown into the shade. Hate, wrath, and desire of revenge, against his child's betrayer, blazed in his eye, brooded in his breast, and gave to his speech a startling effect.

"Mr. Clifton wishes to be at the expense of the search for your daughter," said the solicitor to him, after some conversation with Maynard, "and, independently of any idea of compounding for your grievances, I am empowered to present you with this twenty-pound note.

"My hand," exclaimed Summerfield, bursting into vehemence, "shall rot from my body sooner than I will touch aught of Cliftons, until he does justice to my child's memory, supposing her dead, or is willing to marry her if she be living!"

The office-door at this moment opening, Clifton entered, and the sight of him filled both Maynard and Summerfield with unspeakable emotions of rage and indignation. He himself for the moment was embarrassed at the unexpected presence of the poor field-labourer and the miller, whom he had so deeply injured. Recovering himself, with a slight inclination of the head to each he inquired of the solicitor if a letter had arrived from his Rosedale agent, and being answered in the negative, would have retired again, but Summerfield, by a sudden movement, placed himself in front of the door.

"Squire Clifton," he said, "I and my friend have been wasting much precious time in the hope of seeing you, but you have denied yourself to us, and now we will not lose this chance of letting you hear from our own lips what we intend to do, unless you find some way of dispossessing people's minds in Rosedale of the idea which has got footing among them, that it was by her own free will my Ruth left us for you—and unless also you bind yourself to marry my child if she should be found alive."

While he spoke, the solicitor, feeling that his presence must

tend to check those admissions and concessions which he considered his young client ought, and hoped he would make, passed out of the office; and Clifton, replying to Summerfield with less embarrassment, demanded—

"What it was he and his friend intended to do in case their dictation should fail to influence his actions?"

"Publish your conduct to your constituents of the borough—carry the case to some good lawyer, and commence a prosecution," said Maynard, catching the words from Summerfield.

"And I suppose you will bear the expenses?" said Clifton, drily.

"No, you shall do that," returned Maynard; "the damages will cover all, and leave something to the good."

"Well, I am always glad to hear my friends prospering," said Clifton, sarcastically, "though sometimes it is by strange ways. Proceed in your undertaking, I will by no means hinder it."

"And this is all your answer!" ejaculated Maynard. "I would have called that man a liar who should have told me this—I would not have believed it had it come from other lips than your own. When I look back and remember our merry hours at the mill, and at the Three Crowns; and when I call to mind the generous actions I have seen you perform and the good things I heard you say;—I am fairly astonished and bewildered! and ask myself if the Squire Clifton I knew two years ago can be the villain who stands before me?"

"Villain!" echoed Clifton, fiercely. "But you are a vulgar, fellow, and these coarse phrases are comparatively meaningless with you—they belong to your common language, and deserve no notice from a gentleman."

"A gentleman!" said Summerfield, sternly. "If you are a gentleman, I thank God that made me vulgar. But once again to the point, do you refuse all justice to my child?"

"When she is found." Clifton answered, I will give you my decision."

"And if she is not found will you clear her memory in Rosedale?"

"I will do nothing in the matter until her fate be ascertained."

Clifton, saying this, passed Summerfield, and went out into a sort of ante-room, where a clerk sat transcribing. The solicitor was there, and accompanied the young squire to the door, where the latter, appearing visibly agitated, said—

"Advise them to go back to Rosedale, it is folly their staying

here. I think it possible Ruth may be found in some of the villages or scattered farms around, w' ere their advertisements have not penetrated. Tell them if nothing else remains to be done to inquire in person at every house within twenty miles of the borough. I would to God she were found.

"Summerfield will accept no assistance from you for his expences."

"I do not respect him the less," said Clifton. "But his high-mindedness does not wholly proceed from principle, as he would have us believe. From some cause, which I cannot comprehend, this man and his wife have always had an aversion to me. I see he is thirsting to set my constituents at war with me, and to involve me in the trouble and expense of a law-suit. If he does so, I shall leave him no inch of ground

CHAPTER XIX.

"The proudest heart that ever beat
Hath been subdued in me."—*Anon.*

CLIFTON returned to his lodgings, where his sister waited dinner for him. As soon as she heard his knock, Amy met him at the door.

"You are behind your hour" she said, in a tone of pleasant rebuke.

"I know it," he replied, entering the dining-room with her;

"and now I bring no appetite with me, so that your meal must be solitary."

"I have taken too many solitary meals of late," said Amy, looking anxiously in his face.

"Perhaps you have; but had you been inclined you might have entertained company daily, for my political start has carried me into circles such as I once could scarcely have aspired to."

"Lady Vernon's to wit," Amy quickly responded. "But as to company, Percy, you know well it is a sacrifice to me to see

any one but yourself. My spirits are not what they were. The vapid smartness, the pert scandal, the prim monotony of ordinary society, I can no longer away with. My soul loathes it."

"I hope I am impressed with a due sense of your reservation in my favour," said Percy, forcing a smile.

"I know not whether you are or no," Amy returned, her bosom trembling with a sigh, "for you have grown very reserved and cold with me. Perhaps you think I merit it. And yet you should be tender with me, remembering your promise to our mother, and that I have no near relation left but you."

"My dear sister," said Percy, rising and affectionately embracing her, "if I have been unkind and neglectful, forgive me. In heart, believe me, I have not changed. I love you tenderly, and you deserve my love. At the same time, think not my opinions are in the least changed as to the imprudence of your conduct in respect to Tracy."

"I desire not that they should be," said Amy, faintly. "You cannot judge me in that affair more harshly than I do myself."

"But there is no need for tears—enough have been shed already on that score," said Percy, tenderly. "Come, banish all thoughts of the disagreeable subject; the dinner cools while we talk."

They sat down together at the table, but the dishes were sent away scarcely touched. As the wine appeared, Amy, observing the tokens of an uneasy mind on the face and in the movements of her brother, ventured to ask if "Ruth had yet been heard of?"

He answered briefly in the negative, adding—

"Her father and the miller seem inclined to despair."

"How despair? What do they suppose has become of her?"

"Something fatal," replied Percy with external calmness.

"Heavens!—that beautiful and amiable girl!"

Percy went on cracking nuts for a minute, and then speaking of the Lady Vernon, to whom his sister had shortly before alluded, began to tell some laughable anecdotes which he had heard from her witty ladyship some days before. But no smile from Amy rewarded his efforts. An unusual gravity sat on her features which her brother was determined not to notice.

"You have not told me how you liked Lady Vernon," he said.

"Not at all," replied Amy.

"She is an excellent horsewoman!"

"And a vain flirt."

"Accomplished!"

"In all things that require neither heart nor soul."

"A wit!"

" If a plentiful stock of ill-nature, and a few standard bon-mots can make her so."

" I never heard you so severe in my life."

" If you will cease to talk of her, I shall cease to be severe on her."

" An alliance with Lady Vernon would at once place me in a most promising connection with the government. Her uncle is a member of the cabinet—her father a leading man of peers—her mother a lady nearly related to no less than five noble houses. So splendid a match can never again be proposed for my acceptance."

" Proposed for your acceptance!" Amy slowly repeated.

" Proposed for my acceptance. Her father, yesterday, when I called in Belgrave square, drew me into conversation, in the course of which he told me he had observed my attentions to Lady Vernon, and they had met his approbation, since so talented a volunteer as myself in the cause of the government only wanted, he was sure, the patronage he could procure me in order to rise to the very summit of political eminence."

" And your answer?"

" I was quite at a loss how to extricate myself becomingly from the dilemma in which my folly and Lady Vernon's forwardness had entangled me. However, his lordship could not conceive the possibility of the untitled descendant of a decayed family declining the hand of his daughter, and therefore, I believe, he attributed my hesitating answers to excessive humility. I was obliged to leave him with this impression on his mind."

" This is what flirting comes to, Percy. I hope you will have done with it henceforth."

" The flirting was chiefly on Lady Vernon's side," said Percy. " She flattered me out of all reason; and in the presence of the great, distinguished me in a manner sufficient to set an inflammable brain on fire."

" With all this, think you Lady Vernon entertains for you one touch of real affection such as poor Ruth Summerfield felt? Think you if she should see you no more she would be less witty—less gay—less coquettish—than at present? Would there be one smile the less upon her cheek? Would she lose one ball or soiree for your sake? Would she voluntarily resign the homage of her numerous admirers for one hour to grieve for you?"

" Why should I too curiously inquire? It is enough that Lady Vernon is willing to be mine, and her dashing kindred are ready and able to assist me up the ladder of preferment at is a brilliant chance!"

Clifton crossed the room, repeating with much energy the last exclamation.

"But you will not avail yourself of it?" said Amy.

"I am srongly tempted to do so," he rejoined. "All that I have been longing for, writing for, striving for, will then be mine. With such supporters as Lady Vernon's friends, who knows to what I may attain! There is comparatively little rising talent for statesmanship in the country. I feel powers within me yet unfolded, and in the fitting sphere they may perform great things. Now, if I yield this opportunity, my present powerful allies will fall from me, the father and uncle of Lady Vernon will have as much disposition to injure as now they have to serve me, and farewell ideas of greatness!"

"And let them go, if they must be bought at the expense of honour and peace of mind," said Amy, with animation. "But it is not necessary they should. It was the exertion of your talents first procured you notice, depend on the same for your progress. Patronage is at best a humiliating resource."

Clifton hardly heard her; he was walking to and fro wrapt in the intoxicating visions which the proposed match opened to him. His figure seemed amplified as he moved, his step was elastic, his head erect, and his eye danced in the light. Amy became silent and thoughtful, wholly unable to reconcile the contrarieties of her brother's character. At length she rose to retire, but he detained her, and she saw that his countenance was changed.

"It is over," he said, drawing a long and deep breath—"the dazzling temptation is conquered! and I will write before I sleep to Lady Vernon and her father, stating that I have a pre-engagement, and am compelled in honour, however reluctantly, to resign the bright hope held out to me."

Amy remained leaning over her brother while he rapidly, yet with great care and delicacy, composed these letters, and, the important business concluded, she exchanged a slight pressure of the hand with him, and they parted for the night.

Next morning Clifton was much out of health, and complained of having had a wretched night.

"I believe I shall be no better," he said, until that girl is found."

"Then you have not quite forgot Ruth?" said Amy.

"I could sooner forget myself," he answered, with hasty emotion.

"You have always been reluctant to speak to me about her, Percy."

"I have—I am. It can be no pleasant thing to confound my

own damned treachery toward her; and to dwell on her matchless virtue would only make my guilt appear more hideous."

"And if she is found—"

"If!" interrupted Clifton—"she must, she shall be found! I were lost beyond redemption else."

"And when she is, what are your intentions?"

Clifton made no immediate answer, but subsequently, as Amy sat embroidering lace by the light of a parlour lamp, he placed himself on a sofa opposite her, and said—

"You asked me this morning what I purposed in regard to Ruth. It is a question I have never been able satisfactorily to answer to myself until last night."

"Then you have made up your mind?"

"I have. Cost what it may I am resolved."

"And that resolve?"

"First let me tell you what has led to it. When the news of your elopement with Tracy reached me, my feelings were such as I shall ever remember with horror. They taught me, however, a practical lesson, which is burnt in on my conscience never to be erased. I understood then, the miseries inflicted by a seducer on his victim's relations. I beheld my own guilt reflected in that of Tracy, and abhorred the image! The just retorts with which he rebutted my angry charges, brought home still more to my breast the wrong that I had committed. Remorse worked terribly with me, and lo! I am determined to trample on pride and ambition, and marry Ruth."

"I scarcely expected this, though I may have hoped it," said Amy, a generous tear for Ruth's brightening prospects glistening in her eye.

"And you are quite insensible to the attractions of the wealth and fashion by which your brother has been courted? You are quite ready to renounce all the advantages which his union with a high-born lady would procure you? You can even be gratified by the anticipation of his returning to his rustic borough to doze away the best years of his life as an obscure country squire, wedded to a cottager's daughter? I should be glad of a little of your apathy."

"There has been a time when I should have resigned all you speak of with more regret," said Amy. "At present, I am dead to the fashions and the splendours of the world, and retirement and peace is all I wish."

Her voice was tremulous, and her brother instantly reproached himself for the ungentle manner in which he had spoken.

"I am eternally giving pain to those I best love," he said.

"But you shall accompany me on your harp in a song, as a token of forgiveness—and I will not go out this evening, if that will be any gratification to you."

"Indeed it will; and you have already gratified me more than you will believe, by putting an end to your painful reserve. I appreciate your confidence—I enter with sympathy into the struggle you have experienced—and I glory in your present resolution."

CHAPTER XX.

Brightly beam the starry lights,
Softly trip the graceful throng,
Mirth performs her jocund rights,
Sweetly mingle laugh and song;
Eyes of beauty—arms of snow,
Jewelled tresses—bosoms fair—
Fairer than the pearls they show,
—Who would guess sad throbs are there?

MARY BENNET.

A GREAT moral change, whose full extent was not understood even by himself, had indeed taken place in Percy Clifton. It is said, and, we believe, proved, that every few years the whole framework of our corporeal nature undergoes a complete renewal. Something analagous to this takes place in the invisible part of the human being, especially in the earlier years of existence. The soul may be almost felt to grow during the intermediate stage between youth and manhood. Thought expands—the will strengthens—volatility subsides—and the main features of the character mould themselves into the shape they are permanently to wear.

Through this intermediate stage Clifton was now passing. His overflowing ardour was pouring itself into the channels of honourable ambition.

"And who will lightly say that fame
Is nothing but an empty name?
While in that sound there is a charm
The nerves to brace, the heart to warm;
As, thinking on the mighty dead,
The young from slothful couch will start,
And vow, with lifted hands outspread,
Like them to act a noble part."

The consequence was, he no longer found any temptations in the irregularities to which he had been formerly addicted; and had it not been for the stings of regret left by actions which could not by repentance be undone, he would have experienced in the path he had struck out for his indefatigable energies and fine powers, a solid satisfaction to which in his riotous days he had been a stranger. The terrible scourge of remorse could scarce fall more hardly on any man, for he wore no mail of casuistry to defend himself from its strokes. He deceived himself in no respect as to the turpitude of his conduct to Ruth, but, contemplating it in all its naked deformity, abhorred himself for it. Indeed at all times he was remarkably free from self-deception, which spreads its mists over more metaphysical and delicate minds. He was also, strange as it may sound after what has previously been said of him, very tender of conscience; and though his perception of right and wrong was more accurate than refined, he did not suffer the less on that account. His fever-fit of passion being over, and all his temptations running in the way of ambition, there was really some merit in his resolution to do justice to Ruth, to which he would probably never have been brought by any means less retributive than his sister's elopement, however great his remorse might be. Nevertheless, his anxiety to withhold a knowledge of his intention from her parents and friends denoted that he had rather compromised with his pride than overcome it.

Amy was distinctly charged to guard the secret within her own breast, and her brother chose rather to subject himself to misconstruction than have it thought he had been influenced for a moment by the treats of Summerfield and the miller. Not even to avert an annoying prosecution, would he deign to enter into any explanation with them, though he received early intimation of its commencement. He now amply returned the aversion with which Summerfield regarded him, and talked of Maynard with angry contempt, as a good-natured, disappointed old fool.

He suffered dearly, however, for this unreal dignity. The case got noised abroad, and excited much talk; and as Clifton was no stoic under an injured reputation, he often returned half mad with

irritation from scenes where he had experienced an altered reception, or been the mark of unpleasant observation.

Yet he was bent on shunning none of the places to which he
had previously resorted; and on one particular occasion, when a
ball was given at the house of an elderly dowager who had much
distinguished him with her notice prior to the affair, he determined to appear there with his sister, though he knew that Lady
Vernon was to be present, with a large circle of her friends—all
now estranged as he had expected.

The dresses were to be fancy costumes; and after he had prevailed against Amy's reluctance to go, her imagination seemed
to revive anew in the consultation as to the equipment of herself
and her brother, and the characters they should sustain.

Her memory was employed for days in recalling all the most
dazzling personages of romance which had ever interested her,
and, as likings generally go by opposites, she was most pleased
with those that least described her own yielding and variable
character.

Her brother was at once amused, gratified, and vexed, at the
almost childish enthusiasm with which she entered into this
trivial matter, while he looked on with no other interest in it
than as he should give the lie to a report he had heard that he
would not venture to appear there.

"I have it!—I have it!" exclaimed Amy—"You shall be a
Grecian captain! Theirs is the finest costume in the world, and
will set off your peerless figure to a marvel, as the French say."

"You forget I cannot speak the modern Greek tongue."

"Nor can anyone else who will be there."

"That is as far as we know. No, I will none of your Grecian
fripperies."

"Well then—a Magician—you can carry it off something
sublimely if you will. Your eyes are fiery enough for a dealer in
diablerie—you have height for the dark robe—and a face fine
enough to harmonise with the majesty of a flowing beard. Will
you be a magician?"

"A monkey, so that you will bore me no more. How you
can take such pleasure in these things I cannot understand. I
have not seen you look so cheerful since—"

He stopped, for the cheerfulness abruptly vanished, and left
paleness and anguish in its place.

CHARLOTTE, FLINGING BACK THE VEIL, STOOD UP.

PERCY endeavoured to lure Amy back to the costumes and characters, but found this scarcely easy; the charm was gone.

"You have not told me in what you intend to appear," he said, gaily.

"I had intended to thrum my lute as a French glee-maiden of the thirteenth century."

Percy had some objections to this guise, but it was finally adopted, and with her brother as the magician, she arrived at the splendid entertainment, quite unapprehensive of the severe trials to which she was there to be exposed.

Clifton believed that her elopement was unknown; but as they entered the long suite of gorgeous rooms, through which groups of figures in the costumes of various ages and nations were gliding, he heard sundry whisperings—"How did they obtain cards ?"—"One does not wonder at him, but really her boldness is beyond everything !"—"Though masks are forbidden, she certainly should have put one on before appearing here !"—"Lady Vernon told the whole story last night at the marchioness's soiree —she had it from Miss Monckton."

"Miss Monckton, who is she ?"

The answer escaped Percy, who drew his sister rapidly forward into the thickest of the crowd, where they escaped particular observation. After a short interval, in which neither thought of the imaginary characters they had assumed, they passed into a room comparatively deserted by the masqueraders, along each side of which refreshments were laid out, attended by footmen. Beyond this there was a spacious conservatory, whose twilight hues and cool fountain were refreshing after the glare and tumult of the scene they had just left. They entered, and occupying unseen one of the seats by the fountain, found themselves unintentionally listeners to an extraordinary conversation between Lady Vernon and a bevy of fair dames and squires, who were divided from them by a screen of plants and a glass partition. Her ladyship occupied a low divan, around which her satellites stood or lounged. She was an exceedingly diminutive figure, about twenty-eight or thirty years of age, with long light hair, completely strewn, like that of a Grecian bride, with flowers and gems. She wore a rich cymar, a tunic and trousers embroidered in gold, a pair of loose exquisitely-worked slippers, and a veil of fine tissue of gold. Those around wore dresses of various devices. There was one figure, however, which by far outshone Lady Vernon's, both in splendour and in beauty. This was no other than Charlotte Monckton, in the attire of a Barbaric Empress, wearing a turban and a robe of gorgeous colours. Her majestic and voluptuous figure, and her strongly-defined features, so expressive of dark and deep passions and a relentless will, admirably accorded with the imposing garb she had chosen. She was distantly related to the Vernons, on her father's side, who, it will be remembered, had been an East India officer. When he was but a dependent cadet, he married a portionless damsel, and was thenceforth, to the hour of his death, estranged from all his noble friends.

On his daughter's returning from France to England with her aunt, her hopes had rested on reviving an intercourse with them, and she wrote to them in a manner best calculated, as she hoped, to accomplish the desirable object. As no notice, however, was taken of her application, she had been obliged to linger in the obscure shades of Rosedale, sighing for the paradise of fashion, which she could not enter.

Not long before the evening of the dress-ball, her aunt received in a letter from a London friend, the casual tidings that it was thought in certain circles young Clifton was to be promoted to the high distinction of an alliance with Lady Vernon. It at once occurred to Charlotte that Lady Vernon must be unacquainted with Clifton's seduction of the Cottage Girl; and she thought by a little clever finessing, it would be easy to make this tale a means of opening the door which barred her entrance into high life.

She left in dreary solitude her good but fanatical aunt, (who loved her as people love the last link which holds them to the earth), and hastening to London, left at the house of Lady Vernon her card, and a brief and humble, but impressive note, requesting a private interview on a matter of the highest importance to her ladyship.

On the following day she found admittance to the high-born lady, to whose particular turn of humour she contrived to adapt herself with so much address, telling the whole story of Ruth Summerfield as far as she had been able to glean the truth, and something further, and bringing forward her relationship to the Vernons so carefully, and yet so prominently, that she at once attained her hopes, and was entertained as a guest, though on rather a dubious footing.

Lady Vernon had the more readily grasped at the story of Ruth, because she had but that day received the letter in which Clifton, though with the utmost nicety of expression, declined her hand, an act of independence which the fair coquet could by no means brook with patience, and she rejoiced in an opportunity of being able in her graceful malice to give out in the place of the true cause of the disappearance of Clifton from the ranks of her adorers, that "if she could have entertained a serious thought of Mr. Clifton, which of course was quite impossible, his conduct to a certain poor girl made it perfectly out of the question."

Charlotte was too acute not so see very soon through her shallow ladyship's artifice. She had indeed a little malice of her own to gratify, as having herself had hopes of Clifton; but this was a feeling requiring only casual mention, as she was occupied with far deeper passions at present, having made two extraordinary discoveries, namely, that the Tracy with whom Amy Clifton had eloped was in reality her own husband under an assumed name—and that he was the adopted heir to an immense fortune.

Vainly would one attempt to show the tumult of mind into which these tidings plunged the selfish and aspiring Charlotte. She bitterly regretted her separation from Merton—she even called to mind his gentle virtues, and the fondness which he had lavished

on her during the brief period of their intimacy, with a sort of
regretful kindness, and began to study how to wind anew the
broken fibres of affection around the heart whence she had so
mercilessly rent them away.

Salscroft having taken a house in the western suburbs for him-
and Merton (who was recovered from the effects of the duel),
was indulging his restless habits of activity in filling it with
furniture, which being partly brought from India, and partly
bought from the stores of curious brokers, proved heterogeneous
enough ! the reputation of his wealth, and the eccentrcities of his
taste, made him a sort of lion among that numerous class of London society who, like the Athenians, had little to do but to watch
for "some new thing."   Nor will it be supposed that the young
and gifted artist, who was to inherit Salscroft's fortune, failed,
with his expectations, his fascinating melancholy, and his genius,
to attract attention.   He was welcome everywhere ; the productions of his pencil—productions which perhaps till now had slept
unnoticed—were lauded by young and old, and filled up many a
spare niche in drawing-room and boudoir.   Internally he smiled
at the insipid, indiscriminating, and often designing flattery, which
he received.

"I should hold myself in contempt," he said, internally, "if
one throb of elation could be produced in me by such worthless
praise.   One genuine look of a silent appreciation of my work—
one sentiment of hearty interest in the thoughts I have embodied—
would be worth all these hollow plaudits.   They please Salscroft,
however, and therefore I must submit to them."

His sensitive modesty, and habitual sadness, which the painful
termination of his acquaintance with Miss Clifton had increased,
would have induced him to prefer a life remote from the society
of his fellow-men, devoted wholly to his profession, which to him
was his own exceeding great reward, and his only relief from
mournful thought.   But he submitted his own inclinations to those
of Salscroft, not from a truckling spirit of interest, but to gratify
in his declining years one to whom he felt he owed a degree of
reverence, duty, and affection, scarcely inferior to that of a son for
a parent.   Some of the whims of his benefactor proved however
almost too hard to be borne.   Amongst them was that of attending
the fancy-ball in question, both in Indian costumes, covered with
a rich display of jewels. In vain Merton entreated to be excused,
Salscroft would take no denial.

"If I must go," said the former, "I will not compete with the
splendour of your attire, but serve as a foil to you."

Accordingly, there appeared in the brilliant assemblage to which

we have already conducted Clifton and his sister, the corpulent old merchant, and ex-functionary of the British government at Calcutta, clothed in a white and blue joobah, or rich striped satin Damascene robe, girded around his bulky waist by a girdle studded with blazoning diamonds, his head encircled by a twisted shawl of splendid hues, the ends of which drooped to his shoulder with gold fringe, while over the centre of the old man's tawny and wrinkled forehead glowed an immense carbuncle, which flashed back every ray of light that darted on it with tentold brilliance.

Merton made, as he had intended, a strong set-off to this effulgence, being in a plain black domino. He early contrived to separate himself from his companion, and hovering about the entrance to watch for Clifton and his sister, whom he had found were by some expected to be present, he became an anxious listener to the taunting whispers by which she was received.

"And I am the cause of this!" he muttered, as he sedulously kept them in view until they entered the conservatory. He then drew near the group gathered round Lady Vernon, but so as to be unnoticed, and beheld standing among them, in all the pride of her commanding beauty, she who had once being his Charlotte, but who could be so no more—she who had reaped the first harvest of his affections, and wantonly destroyed them.

For an instant his thoughts rolled back on former days; their enchantment was renewed, he forgot all except that before him stood the wife of his bosom, the love of his youth. Her cold satirical voice broke the spell; the rising tear was checked; the rising sigh suppressed. The charm passed from her beauty, and he regarded it with as much indifference as if it had been painted on canvass.

"What said you was the name of the individual with whom Miss Clifton eloped?" Lady Vernon asked, addressing Miss Monckton.

"She dare not take my name upon her lips!" murmured Merton, aside.

Charlotte replied that it was Tracy.

" He was a poor drawing-master or something of that sort, was he no ?"

" A poor artist, madam."

"Not so poor as when you were his wife," muttered Merton, " for then he was poorest where he thought himself most rich, but in winning the affection of Miss Clifton he acquired an incomparable treasure."

" How came she first to love Tracy ?" Lady Vernon asked.

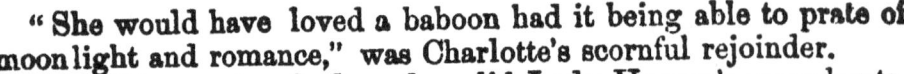

"She would have loved a baboon had it being able to prate of moonlight and romance," was Charlotte's scornful rejoinder.

Lady Vernon laughed, and so did Lady Vernon's sycophants.

"And this was the woman that Amy dignified with the name of friend!" thought Merton.

"What is that story of young Clifton your ladyship was telling last night?" inquired a whiskered fop who had just joined the group.

"Ask Miss Monckton there, she is my informant," replied her ladyship, languidly.

"The squire," said Charlotte, in a subdued tone, " is the proprietor, as you all know, of a very sweet little valley called Rosedale, where a cottager named Summerfield has, or had, a pretty daughter, whom Miss Clifton was so imprudent as take into her service, knowing that her brother professed attachment for her, and thinking it delightfully romantic that he should fall in love with a simple young—"

"Miss Monckton may spare the rest," said Clifton, coming forward, with suppressed rage, "unless she can confine herself to the truth more strictly than she seems inclined."

"In what have I violated truth, Mr. Clifton?" asked Charlotte, haughtily, her cheek taking a deeper tinge of crimson.

"In more instances than I will offend you by enumerating," he replied, " but especially in the aspersions you have been pleased to put forth against my sister."

"Excuse me for interfering, but really," observed Lady Vernon, drily, " when you introduced your sister here this evening, she ought to have been accompanied by her husband."

" And by whom ought Charlotte Monckton to be accompanied?" returned Clifton, forcibly. " Is there no one whose proper place is by her side? under whose protection she ought to be living? whose happiness ought to be her chief care?"

"There is not," said Charlotte, firmly.

" Base woman!" ejaculated Merton, aloud, and, unable to bridle his resentful feelings, he hurried away.

Charlotte started, and as her eye glanced round in search of the speaker, the deep crimson hue deserted her cheek.

"Who was that?" inquired Lady Vernon.

"One who may know more of Miss Monckton's past life than we," said Clifton, meaningly.

" If there be an offensive implication in your words," said Charlotte, haughtily, recalled to her self-possession. " I can assure you that my life may defy the scrutiny of the world."

Clifton bowed ironically.

"Yet I," he said, "have found it prone to see very far into a millstone—very inventive, too, where there is nothing to be seen."

"Did you not know who that impertinent domino was, Charlotte?" Lady Vernon asked, rising from the ottoman, and taking the arm of her cousin.

"Possibly I might, had he not been in haste to slink away."

"Or had the recognition been more welcome," Clifton could not refrain from saying, though inaudibly.

One of the group said it was Mr. Merton the painter. who had such high expectations.

"Impossible!" exclaimed Lady Vernon, and the exclamation was echoed by other voices. "He is such a delightful young man; mamma is patronising his pictures. I am quite sure he could not think of insulting a companion of mine. However, I will seek him out and ask him."

The whole group moved away.

"There they go," exclaimed Clifton to himself,—"folly and malignity, coquetry and craft! But what am I to be thus severe on them? The worst that their envenomed tongues could speak of me would fall short, infinitely short, of my deserts. But my poor Amy!" he said, altering his tone, on perceiving his sister by his side, stricken with humiliation and sorrow, "your punishment has been too severe. Your beloved Charlotte has had small mercy on you."

"I will not blame her," Amy rejoined, "she never understood me or my motives."

Amy then reminded her brother that it was by his wish she had consented to visit this gay scene, and begged he would remove her quickly from it.

"Or," she added with a tremulous smile, "I may have to make a sensation here, as Charlotte would scoffingly say, for I feel a kind of oppression indicative of a hysterical outbreak."

Her brother felt deeply for her, but exhorted her to remain until the company should break up.

"The slanderers must not have it in their power to say they drove us hence," he said.

"Why should we heed them, dear Percy? Oh! let us go."

"You heard Merton?"

"I did," Amy falteringly rejoined, "and saw him."

"Had I known he would have been here, you should have visited the North Pole rather than this place. But you must not seem to avoid him—or any one else. Come, take heart; try the strings of your guitar, and let us to the dancing-room. Make the effort for my sake."

"To please you I will; but should I fail in the attempt keep your temper."

"You must not fail, my gentle sister, even though you avenge yourself, for an hour's constraint on your feelings, by a fortnight's indulgence of them afterwards."

"It is to gratify you—if that prove not a firm pillar for my fortitude, nothing can."

They mixed with the general melée of masqueraders, and Amy, exchanging a look with her brother that made his heart bleed for her, resumed in appearance her forgotten gaiety, danced with spirit, and when the orchestra was hushed, attracted delighted listeners to her sweet lays, and the soft tinkling of the lute.

Merton kept at a distance from her, sensible that the sight of him would only give pain, and wandering about, without feigning a gladness he did not feel, had placed himself against a light rose-wreathed pillar at one extremity of the ball-room, "chewing the cud of sweet and bitter fancies," when he beheld amid the dancers the elephant-like person of Salscroft, with Charlotte Monckton for his partner. The dance concluded, Salscroft led Charlotte very gallantly to the refreshment room, and after remaining some time in earnest conversation with her, found his way to Merton, his face charged with joyful matter.

"Come this way, Charley," he said, drawing him a little apart, "your wife has been appealing to me to persuade you to forgive her."

"I cannot be jested with on this topic," said Merton, sharply and angrily.

"I am not jesting."

"Not jesting!"

"I am serious as ever I was in my life!"

"Charlotte seeks my forgiveness!"

"Aye! And I must say I think it would be as wise to let the past be forgotten on both sides, and take each other by the hand once more. You are both older, and should be wiser, than when you are separated. She is a fair-spoken and handsome young lady, 'and promises well. I said I would use my influence with you."

"And she wishes a re-union?"

"She does."

"Then I can divine her motive. She beholds me standing in a higher worldly position than that I occupied formerly, and would share it with me. Her penitence has been excited by the talk of your munificent intentions towards me, not by any due sense of her conduct, or any revival of her love. Were it others

wise, indeed !"——Merton paused, and then added— " were it otherwise, I might forgive the countless miseries she has occasioned me, but never—never—receive her to my heart again."

" Well, you know best, Charley—all I wish is to see you happy."

" Happy with Charlotte I can never be more. I have accustomed myself too long to hate her. Her scorn of all my early tastes—her selfish, cold, and worldly mind—and her cruel separation from me merely because she found me poorer than she thought, have divided us for ever. I cannot respect her. I have ceased to love her. And as she dissolved our marriage, dissolved it shall remain."

" It is an unhappy business, that is certain," said Salscroft, shrugging his shoulders, " and I wash my hands of it altogether."

The old merchant and his heir were the first to quit the rooms, an example soon followed by Clifton and his sister.

Charlotte, who marked closely the movements of the former, knew not whether to augur favourably to herself or unfavourably from their hasty departure; but having broken ground, determined, if possible, to carry her point by a coup-de-main on the morrow. She in the meantime made a confidant and ally of Lady Vernon, whose carriage next forenoon halted before the house of Salscroft; and her ladyship requesting to see Mr. Merton about a picture she designed to purchase, was ushered into his studio, followed closely by Charlotte in a large loose cloak and black veil, by which her person and features were half concealed.

Totally unprepared for the suddenness and boldness of this step, Merton did not at first recognise Charlotte, and was displaying the picture which had been made the pretext for the visit, when his eyes all at once becoming rivetted on Lady Vernon's companion, his face turned ghastly with extreme emotion, and Charlotte, flinging back the veil, stood up.

" I have come, Charles," she said, " seeking for a pardon, and hoping for a welcome."

It was with difficulty Merton commanded himself to reply that as far as she felt worthy of forgiveness she might be assured of it from him.

Lady Vernon hastened to say that Charlotte was her second cousin, and she was extremely desirous of seeing her reconciled to her husband.

" Pardon me, madam," said Merton, " I no longer acknowledge that title. Without any adequate cause it was rent from me, and it cannot again be renewed."

"By Amy Clifton it may, if not by me," said Charlotte, scornfully.

The pale expansive forehead of Merton partook of the flush of indignation which covered his face, but after a moment's reflection he answered—

"That as an allusion had been hazarded to that pure name with which detraction was at present so busy, he felt it incumbent on him to state to Lady Vernon that it was true, after a long period of hopeless and solitary sorrow, chance had conducted him to the dwelling of Miss Clifton, in whom he had found the kindred mind, and the feminine virtues, which he had once hoped to meet in her who stood before him—that it was true Miss Clifton, ignorant of any impediment, graced him with her regard, and that he loved the excellence in her—that it was true he had prevailed on her, she being still unacquainted with his previous marriage, to accompany him as his wife to Calcutta—and, unfortunately, as he believed for all parties, the precipitance of her brother had brought on a premature explanation, and Miss Clifton withdrew her consent.

"These," he added, "are the true particulars; and I trust to Lady Vernon's candour for substituting them in the place of the purely imaginary ones. which have been circulated within the sphere of her influence."

"My present business," said Lady Vernon, drawing up her swan-like neck with a haughty air, "is not to talk or to hear of Miss Clifton, but to see Charlotte, in whom mamma and I take much interest, reconciled to—"

"Permit me to interrupt your ladyship, and to say that the matter in which you take so lively a concern is too exquisitely painful and delicate for friendly interference."

"O very well, I take my leave. Charlotte I shall detain the carriage ten minutes, if then you do not appear I shall conclude—"

"Conclude nothing, madam, that has reference to a re-union of myself and your cousin—that is impossible," said Merton, with all the emphasis he could employ.

"And why impossible?" Charlotte asked, when they were alone.

"Because," he replied, "I am in no respect improved since you left me, and if I was abhorred then, I cannot expect to be agreeable now."

"You were not abhorred. I left you only because you were too misanthropical, and we had no means to live respectably."

"Misanthropical!—there never breathed a man who better loved his fellows than I. Misanthropical!—was I not the happiest of the happy when you appeared at all content? Did I not

enjoy the simple pleasures of my domestic fireside? Had you ever to reproach me with an ill word until I learnt your consent to the divorce?"

"I had not."

"And I deny that we were too poor to live respectably. A retired and quiet respectability was in my power, my profession insured that, besides promising something more for the future. But you were ambitious for splendour, for adulation, for a gay and public life, which my resources—and, you supposed, my taste—denied you. Yet as I prospered, think you I could have restrained your wishes where they might be innocently gratified? No—the probability is I should have immolated my own in a great measure to yours."

Charlotte answered she should understand him better for the future, and she was willing to say or promise anything which might tend to soften his resolution.

Merton, however, though far from proud, had a strong pertinacity of disposition, which in some cases might be termed obstinacy, and never relinquished a resolve he had once deliberately formed.

Charlotte grew fiery as the certainty of failure became apparent; her large black eye darted forth menacing gleams, and her language grew every minute more bitter and unguarded.

"I have condescended too far," she said; "but do not plume yourself on the confessions and concessions I have made, they were only feigned for the occasion; and could the former days be revived, I should just act as I have done."

"I do not doubt it."

"And think not to marry Amy Clifton—I shall prevent that—and find means beside to plague you both."

"Likely enough; I know you capable of mean revenge."

Charlotte departed in great heat, leaving Merton disturbed, but gratulating himself that he had not been imposed on by her hypocrisy.

She was now the professed enemy of himself and Amy, but instead of busying herself with injuring and distressing them, Charlotte found a more satisfactory mode of employing her thoughts. Believing Merton firm as the rooted rock in the resolution he had expressed to her, she at once accepted the hand of an old nobleman, whom she had attracted on the night of the masquerade, Count Borgio by name, highly connected, the proprietor of a palace and extensive vineyards in the papal states, who was quite willing to acquiesce in the decision of the church of his country on her former marriage.

The doting fondness of this grey-haired count could deny her nothing; under his auspices she launched her vessel on the fluctuating waves of fashion, with all sails spread, devoting every feeling, every talent, every energy she possessed, to the dissipation of gay life. After the celebration of the nuptials by a Catholic bishop, in the presence of the Vernons and many distinguished foreigners, a month was given to the most brilliant gaieties of London, and then the count and countess, with their retinue, passed to that gayest of capitals, Paris, where Charlotte anticipated a season of unclouded eclat, and whence it was intended to proceed to Venice.

Her aunt she had neglected, or forgotten, and when she apprised her of the change in her condition, it was in a manner betraying that the callousness of her feelings had been increased if possible by her elevation. The venerable lady, then on the extreme verge of existence, and cleaving fondly to her convent habits of rigid seclusion, was yet so moved by the unkindness of the niece to whom for twenty years she had supplied the place of father and mother, that she travelled with much pain of body and mind to the metropolis, where arriving too late to give the last blessing she had meditated to the thankless child of her love, she at once sank under the stroke of death in a private house at Chelsea, belonging to a few Benedictine recluses among whom she had found a loving and pious reception. She had barely time to send, through the medium of the Vernons, to entreat the presence of the former friend and husband of her niece, who arrived nearly at the same moment, and just as her spirit was taking wing.

She lay in an easy attitude in bed, her hands closed as if in the act of prayer, a crucifix before her on the coarse but neat counterpane, her looks serene and benignant. She was a fine-looking old lady, and inspired reverence in all who beheld her. Amy particularly had been partial to her, and as she found herself received by an apostolic benediction at once affectionate and fervent from those dying lips, and as she remembered the happy hours of trusting friendship she had spent in the Hermitage of Rosedale, it was no wonder that the tears gushed from her eyes while bending beside her.

"Thy heart hath been pierced as well as mine, by the unkindness of my niece," said the venerable sufferer. "Well, the light of eternal glory be revealed to thee, for thy comfort! Requiescat in pace, my child, is the conclusion of all tribulation to those who have the hope which can never can deceive."

She turned her eyes on Merton, who approached, conducted by a priest who was in attendance.

"I wished to see you, sir," she said, " because there has been

enmity between us on account—on account of events that took place in Switzerland. I do assure you, had my niece desired to remain with you I should not have interfered; but the case being otherwise, my duty to my church prompted me to divorce her from one whom I thought likely to lead her from the true faith."

Your motives need no explanation—I fully appreciate them," said Merton cordially.

" I die in charity, then, with you and all the world. My property I have bequeathed to the use of the destitute and the faithful. It shall not go to swell my niece's train of vanities. A legacy within this hour I have added for you each. And now give me your hand, Mr. Merton—Miss Clifton, give me yours. I have heard of your engagement, I know the worthy qualities of both, and it is my dying prayer that you may be blessed in each other, and in the enjoyment of the one, infallible, and everlasting faith."

She then in a voice of hope and faith, repeated part of a hymn to the Virgin—

> " Hail! thou good and gracious mother,
> Virgin brighter than the sun,
> Crowned with glory which no other
> Eyes but thine could look upon."

In the midst of this, her voice and her life failed together.

CHAPTER XXI.

> " For ever do you say? Oh! not for ever.
> I will not think but there is some bright star
> That yet will shine upon us,
> Though now the clouds lour on our path."
>
> OLD PLAY.

AMY, after the scene related at the close of the last chapter, accepting the attendance of Merton to the lodgings occupied by herself and her brother, he ventured to hint, that " some obstacles to their union had been removed since last he saw Miss Clifton,

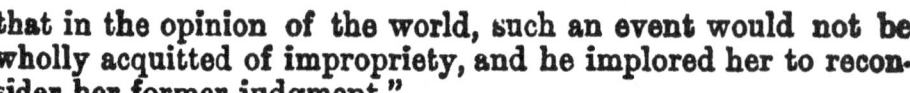

that in the opinion of the world, such an event would not be wholly acquitted of impropriety, and he implored her to reconsider her former judgment."

"You will think, perhaps, Mr. Merton, that I have given you this opportunity purposely—and so indeed I have. Since the marriage of Charlotte, I have heard it rumoured that ours would follow, and I have gladly availed myself of a chance of coming to a final understanding with you. It is useless, and worse than useless, for either of us to be deceiving ourselves with hopes that can never be realised. Had I only listened to you when you told me at first on the Rosedale hills, that it was necessary we should part, how much trouble and disappointment might have been spared! It was my fault, and mine only, Merton, that I was misled. You wished to leave me, and would have done so, had I not displayed my weakness to you, and melted away the resolution which duty and honour induced you to form. I have since seen, and bitterly repented of, my error. We can never be more to each other than we are at this moment."

"Then so it must be," said Merton,—"and why should I grieve? After life's fitful fever I shall sleep well, I doubt not. My past days have been heaped with sorrow—disappointed hopes —a cheerless, loveless home—unsatisfied affections—what of that? in a few, very few years, all will be forgotten. My future presents only a dreary waste, unblest by the sweet domestic ties which gladden other men; but I will not shrink from it. Let fortune's bleakest winds blow round me, I have still one comfort left me—my profession· —and that must be my solace."

"I hope you may find it so," said Amy, suppressing her own emotion; "and amid the pleasures and toils it brings you, forget not, that though we may never marry, and must not meet, I shall be to the last hour of existence, yours and yours only. No other, my dear Merton, shall ever fill the place which you have occupied in the affections of Amy Clifton."

She was too calm in her decision for Merton to hope to change it, and in reality it met with his secret approbation, however painful it proved. Her character rose in his estimation, and appeared in a new light, for, in dooming him to so hopeless a banishment from her presence, she was imposing a restraint on her own feelings, of which previously he had hardly conceived her capable. And this was done, not from any of the ordinary motives which arouse the female breast to self-government, as fear of the censures, or deference for the authority, of others, but solely from a sense of what was purely right and fitting in the cruel and difficult position in which she was placed. With heightened admiration, and consequently regret, he therefore reluctantly acquiesced in a permanent separation. Yet as he left her, he could not refrain from distantly observing, that, in the uncertainties of human life, there was an event might happen which would remove the last shadow of an impediment.

Amy understood that he alluded to the possibility of Charlotte's premature decease, but shocked at the temptation of connecting a hope with such a possibility, she made no direct reply.

After this conversation, the distress of mind under which Amy secretly laboured, was for some days very great; there were periods when she questioned the necessity for the decision she had made, when she wished it revoked, when she fainted under the burden she had imposed on herself.

"Have not my notions been too narrow?" she asked of herself. "How could the existence of one who legally has no claim on Merton, and who is now the acknowledged wife of another, affect our peace? My objection is fine-spun of her once having had a claim on him. Surely I have acted quixotically, and the sacrifice was not required of me."

Yet despite these doubtings and questionings, she intuitively revolted from the idea of calling Merton husband while Charlotte existed; and supported by this just feminine feeling, she on the whole felt the satisfaction of self-approval tempering the pain with which she contemplated the desolation of all her hopes.

No such satisfaction ameliorated the pangs of her brother's more turbulent and guilty soul.

He, at this time, was anxious to return to Rosedale, for though every means that had been employed for finding Ruth had failed hitherto, he still persuaded himself that she must have found a refuge somewhere around her native place, and his anxiety could not trust wholly to the inquiries even of her father and Maynard. Amy determined to return with him to the old house in which all her life, save the last few months, had been spent. Every stone of its battered walls—every leaf that trembled to the passing wind about its ancient battlements—every article of furniture it contained, was dear to her. She had a thousand fascinating visions of the marvellous stored within its wide oak chambers, and her foot could not tread on a spot in or about them which her youthful sensibility had not peopled with affectionate associations.

By Clifton and herself it had previously been intended she should go back no more, at least for some years, for though he had taken care to give his agent and housekeeper, and, through them, the neighbourhood, the best vindication of his sister's equivocal departure thence that the fact admitted, yet it would be

unpleasant for her to mingle again in the society to which she had been accustomed.

She was now, however, bent on avoiding all society, and on returning—not to make the old halls ring as they had been used to do with merriment, but to lead a strictly secluded life in their shade, and to employ the legacy of a thousand pounds left her by Charlotte's aunt in promoting the comforts of the poor on her brother's estate.

It was late on a warm cloudy night when the carriage in which Amy left London with her brother entered the well-known valley. The road, with its high-banked hedges overhung with unpruned trees, ran by the back garden of Summerfield's cottage, and the glimmering light of a candle issued from the shed there. In his impatience to know if any thing had been heard of Ruth, Clifton, judging by the light that the cottagers were not at yet rest, bade the coachman stop, and dismounting, leaped the lower garden fence, and proceeded toward the shed. The padlock of the door was hanging loosely on its staple, and supposing one of the family within, he knocked and called aloud. He was answered by a frightful shriek, and dashing open the door to discover the cause, he beheld Mrs. Summerfield standing in a white night-dress on the littered ground, and the candle whose beams had attracted him, flaring aslant in her hand.

It was impossible to conceive any thing more ghastly than the wild terror of her death-like countenance, combined with the strangeness of her appearance in such a dress, in an out-house detached from the dwelling, as she gasped forth—

"Clifton!—My God, defend me!"

"Pardon my abrupt appearance, Mrs. Summerfield, Clifton said, half withdrawing in astonishment, " I have but just arrived from town, and seeing a light here, stopped the carriage to inquire whether Ruth has been heard of yet."

Mrs. Summerfield gazed at him bewildered, and then passing one hand over her brow, faltered—

"I—I—thought you had been the spectre of your father."

"The spectre of my father, Mrs. Summerfield—a singular thought!"

"Ruth—did not some one mention Ruth?" she exclaimed, casting her eyes wildly around.

"I wished to know if Ruth has been found?"

"Found!—no, nor ever will be," was the half frantic reply. "Your family bring a curse on all they are connected with."

"HAVE MERCY ON ME, REPROACH HAS BROKEN MY HEART."

THE COTTAGE GIRL.

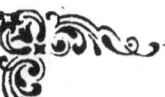

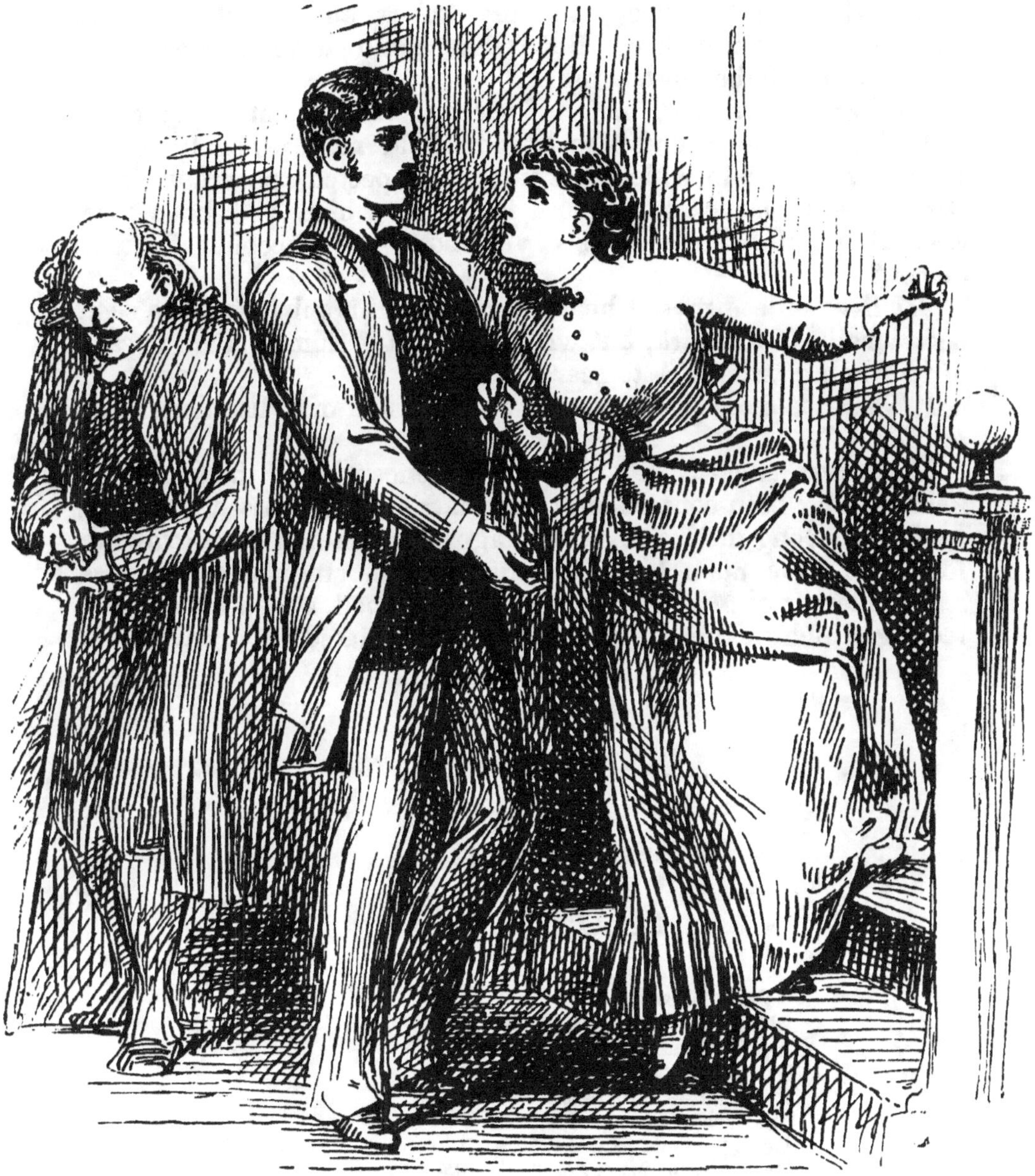

CLIFTON CAUGHT HER TO HIS HEART.

VERY unpleasantly impressed with this strange incident, Clifton returned to the carriage.

"I always thought her half mad," said Clifton, as he described to his sister, who had heard her shriek, the remarkable gestures, appearance, and expression of Mrs. Summerfield.

"It is extraordinary what she could be doing in that place at this midnight hour in such a guise! It seems to me as if she had

been walking in her sleep, and my knock and call at the shed door had awakened her. But what could have brought the spectre of my father in her mind?"

"I have heard that many of our ignorant tenants believe he walks," said Amy, " and Mrs Summerfield most probably shares the superstition; in which case your unexpected appearance, and strong resemblance to our lost father, of which you have been assured by all who ever saw you both, may account for her alarm."

"I have indeed myself heard it said that his spirit is to be seen occasionally in the park, but why should Mrs. Summerfield dream of its coming two miles to scare her."

"There is no accounting for the delusion of a disordered imagination."

Percy was silent; and, though no conception of the Summerfields having been concerned in his father's death crossed his mind, he felt a strong dislike of the cottagers, which had been growing for some time upon him, and to which the singular appearance and the terror of Mrs. Summerfield in the shed, added an unquiet feeling, which was not suspicion, but approximated very nearly to it.

CHAPTER XXII.

"Pale, pale she stands
A fluctuating joy is on her face;
And ever and anon there comes a look
Of wonder, as of one aroused
From some unquiet dream.
She weeps and smiles, and trembles as she views
Dear faces so long loved and lost
Gathered around her."—THOMAS.

IT was with a thrill of mixed emotion that Amy found herself once more within her ancestral halls, where, with a flood of tears, she threw herself into the arms of the attached and faithful housekeeper, by whom she was welcomed, and to whom from infancy she had been endeared.

"You have the same warm and condescending temper that ever

you had, my dear lady," said Mrs. Wilson, wiping her spectacles. ".But dear-a-me! you are sadly changed in looks."

"Something thinner I believe," said Amy, "but my own country air will soon restore me."

Percy had paused at the gate to give some directions to his valet concerning his horses, and now followed his sister into the elegant room where Mrs. Wilson had prepared a fire and supper. A full length portrait of his father hung over the mantel, and his glance immediately recurred to it with a deep and painful interest. Amy too turned her gaze on the same object, and was powerfully struck by the increasing resemblance of her brother to the figure there pourtrayed. The same thought was expressed by Mrs. Wilson in a lively exclamation, as she held up the candle that they might the better view the features which seemed to frown down upon them from the canvas. The figure appeared moulded with equal symmetry and strength; the face was aristocratic, bold, and perfectly well shaped; but about the vivid eyes there seemed to lurk the cloudy remembrances of acts unblest, and the lower features were more coarse, and the forehead less broad, than that of the living resemblance, who now surveyed this portrait of the parent over whose fate there hung so deep a mystery.

Before retiring to rest, Amy looked in on her deserted boudoir All stood as when she had left it. The table was strewn with sketches from the pencil of Tracy, and as she took them up she was painfully reminded of the changes she had since seen, of the sad experience she had gained, and of the blank which was left in her affections.

"Unreflective impulse—unenlightened confidence—rash generosity—into what danger, pain, and mortification, have they not betrayed me!" she thought. "Alas! were the besetting infirmities of character but early discovered and guarded, how many tragic occurences would be averted, how many hearts saved from breaking, how many deaths prevented! An absence of ill intention is not sufficient to prevent unhappiness in ourselves, or occasion it to others. I, heaven knows, had no ill intention, and yet have I placed myself in circumstances, subjected myself to insolent insinuations, which to think of scorches my cheek with shame—and narrowly missed being the cause of a premature death to an only brother, and to one no less dear."

The sleeping closet communicating with Amy's dressing-room, which had accommodated Ruth when the latter acted as personal attendant to her, was also entered by Amy ere she slept.

"Ah! poor girl," she exclaimed, "would to God you were here to welcome me little did I think I should ever see you

here more! But I fear—I fear. It must be near ten months since she left the cottage of her parents according to their account; surely, if she had been living, she must in that time have seen some of the many advertisements which have been sent forth to induce her to return to her friends; and if she had seen those advertise- she would not—she could not—have stubbornly refrained from relieving the minds of her father and mother from their dreadful apprehensions. She had too unselfish a concern for the feelings of others. There is certainly another conclusion we might arrive at beside that of her having destroyed herself, and it is that which is to Percy, if I guess aright, the most poignant of all. She may have been driven to a degradation too great for her ever to present herself more among those who have loved her, or even to com- municate with them. She might have found herself in circum- stances so extreme as to control the natural purity of her mind. Her dread of her father is very great, and in such a case she would not dare, I am sure, to let him know her mode of life."

It was this very thought, as Amy conjectured, that distracted in the most intense degree the mind of her brother, while yet the fate of the Cottage Girl was involved in uncertainty. But it was not confined to him, Summerfield felt it like a serpent gnawing at his heart; and there were times when Maynard feared also, and anxiously pushed forward the prosecution against the squire, that at least they might have the gratification of revenge on him, as far as the law would afford it them.

As much delay occurred before the decision of the bench was announced, the miller exerted with the electors of the borough against Clifton, who, on a re-election occurring during the recess of which he had availed himself to return to Rosedale, was thrown from his parliamentary seat.

"Aye, aye," boasted Maynard, after this triumph, which seemed to give him the highest possible pleasure, "aye, aye, I have taught him what it is to play the villain; and I have other corn on the grindstone yet. Every penny of my hard-earned thousand pounds, that I have kept safe and fast till lately in Rosedale Bank, shall go if need be to teach him what is what."

Summerfield's thirst of revenge against Clifton was less openly manifested, though far more steady and intense.

"Does it not give you some relief, my old friend, that the squire has lost his election?" Maynard asked, as they sat together by the cottage fire.

"Very little, Harry," replied Summerfield, "he will suffer too little from it for me to feel relieved. A drop of water cast on that blazing fire would make no difference to its heat. Nor does

this what you tell me make any difference in my hate to the villain who has robbed me of my child. Nothing can relieve me but to see him stripped of all he now boasts. I would not have him die, for then his pains would be over, but I should like to see him enduring all the miseries that poverty can bestow, writhing in sickness without a friend to comfort him, and despised by all whose opinion he cared for."

"Why, I can't say but he would deserve all that," said Maynard, "and I should not care to see him brought to such a pass. But there is small likelihood of it, and as we can't punish him as much as we would, let us do it as much as we can."

"The people hissed the squire when he came on the hustings," said Sally. "I wish you had heard them, father. He was so pale, and frowned so on them. Some that were near shouted my sister's name, and a stone flung at him hit his face. They cried —'Off!—off!'—but he would not stir until he had made his speech, though nobody could hear a word he said, there was such an uproar."

"There is some one at the door, Sally," cried her mother, in a voice of eagerness and fear, dropping the knitting on which she had been engaged.

It was Mrs. Wilson from the great house, and every one arose to receive her except Summerfield.

"Don't disturb yourselves," she said. "Thank you my dear," to Sally, who hastily dusted and placed a chair. "And how are you, Mr. Maynard? I have not seen you this many a day. Mrs. Summerfield, you are looking sickly—I will send you down a little wine, it will give you strength and spirits."

"She must be excused from accepting your kindness, Mrs. Wilson," said the cottager—"no gift from Rosedale House shall enter here."

"Why now that is foolish pride, for what can the wine be worse for having stood in the squire's cellar? Besides, it is not his gift, but his sister's. She has had a legacy left her by the old lady of the Hermitage, and intends to spend it on the poor of her native place. I have had directions to examine into the wants of all the cottagers round, and especially I was to come here, and desire you to think nothing of the rent which is just falling due, and if you need any other assistance you are only to mention it."

"Tell Miss Clifton that I want justice!" exclaimed Summerfield, "let that be granted by her brother to the memory of Ruth, and I will trouble neither of them for more."

"Well, Mr. Summerfield, justice I think you will have. Some whispers have reached me, I will not say how, that Squire Clifton means better than he says."

"Hark! there is some one coming up the lane," cried Mrs. Summerfield, whose sense of hearing had become unnaturally acute by the secret fear she for years cherished, and by the more recent anxiety for the recovery of her daughter.

It was the postman, with a letter for Summerfield, containing the result of the prosecution.

He and Maynard together ran their eyes over it—and both at the same moment exclaimed—

"Failed! Is it possible?"

"What has failed?" inquired Mrs. Summerfield, quickly, "The prosecution?"

"Aye, the villain has triumphed!"

But how?—but how?"

"Read for yourself," said the cottager, with a brow of livid darkness.

"Read it aloud," said Maynard, "it is short enough to tell such a story."

Before she had time to do so, the rapid galloping of a horse was heard. It came close to the cottage, halted, and a moment after the squire himself appeared. He was dressed as for a journey, and his face was flushed with a joy that pride could not restrain.

"You have lost your suit," he said to Summerfield; "and you," nodding to Maynard, "have narrowly escaped the burden of the expenses of it. They have saddled me with them, however, and I shall not grudge them under all the circumstances. Had your daughter been found, Summerfield, I do not scruple to confess that her testimony might have prevented me from gaining the day—for that I did her wrong I do not any longer attempt to conceal, any more than I wish to justify myself. To all the world I am now willing to vindicate her."

Of course this voluntary declaration from one so high of spirit struck the cottagers with surprise.

"This is well said, as far as it goes, squire!" cried Maynard, "but the worst of it is it comes too late to do any good to our poor Ruth."

"I have reason to think otherwise," said Clifton, "or you would not have seen me here."

"She is found, then?" cried Mrs. Summerfield, his look and tone both inspiring her with this happy assurance.

"Is it so, squire?" asked Maynard, while the cottager, less easily moved to hope, as he had been less slow to despair than his wife or his friend, waited in silence the answer which Clifton was slow to give.

"I received this morning a dirty and almost illegible epistle," he said, 'signed Scipio Robinson, and dated from London. This person tells me that he is a dealer in antiquarian curiosities, that he has prospered in his vocation, and has lived with an unmarried sister sixty years in his present residence. But I see you are impatient to know what this old worthy can have to do with Ruth."

"Does she live?" asked Maynard,—"tell us but that!"

Clifton, however, went on.

"After Mr. Scipio Robinson has given all the particular account of himself and his sister, he proceeds to say, that he has had six months in his service—"

"Our Ruth?" interposed Billy, who, sharing the excitement of the moment, had drawn himself close to the side of the squire, and was watching every word that fell from his lips.

"Yes, my man, our Ruth."

"The Lord be praised!" exclaimed Summerfield, in a loud and solemn voice. "I knew my child could never act unworthily!"

"Mr. Scipio Robinson," continued Clifton, in a graver manner, "informs me, that five weeks ago Ruth left his house without any previous notice;"—he paused, and the looks of the anxious listeners fell. "She was during that time the inmate of a hospital—and when discharged from thence attempted self-destruction."

Summerfield placed his hand over his eyes.

"It was only an attempt though—she was saved, was she not?" said Maynard.

"She was," Clifton replied, his voice and countenance becoming animated, "but, as I gather, almost by miracle. Under a bank near the spot she had chosen for her death, a poor Irish brickmaker, who had been toiling all the previous day in a field hard by, and was without the shelter of a roof, had lain himself down to sleep on the grass, the night being clear and warm. About midnight he awakened, and seeing something unusual on the surface of the water, approached the bank, and beheld Ruth as she rose the third time to the surface. He brought assistance, but before she was taken out she had apparently ceased to exist. Conveyed to the nearest public-house, however, she was restored, and returned to the Robinsons, having escaped by many entreaties the ordeal of an appearance before a magistrate. In the house of the Robinsons she was attacked by brain fever, and in her delirium often mentioned my name, coupled with that of Rosedale House. This circumstance, my correspondent says, induced him to communicate with me, in the hope that I might know her parents, of whom she often talks, and inform them of what had befallen her.

I should add, that they found in her box, a card of my country address, which they copied on the letter sent me."

" Maynard," said Summerfield, drawing him aside, "you must help me to go up to London to fetch my daughter and that shall be the very last assistance I will ever ask from you."

" The last !—pho, pho, I hope not," said Maynard, thrusting four sovereigns in his hand—"it is yours as willingly as ever it was mine."

" Well, Henry, you shall never lose by me," said Summerfield, emphatically. "I would have suffered anything rather than have submitted to owe to any other man the obligations which I owe to you. If I dont pay you to the uttermost farthing, I shall not be able to sleep in my coffin."

" I will never deny that I love my money," said Maynard, " or that I should be willing to receive back the little I have lent to you if you were doing well—a time that I heartily wish were come ! but chiefly for your own sake, and that you know, without making many words about it."

" I do, indeed, know, Henry, that you are a friend of a million," said Summerfield, wringing his hand; " and be sure, that men like me, who would rather a thousand times give than receive a favour, value true kindness more than those who care not how many obligations they load themselves with. I say again, if I have strength spared me the next few years, I will pay you to the last farthing." " Hannah,"—turning to his wife—"have me ready a clean shirt and stockings directly. I will go by the seven o'clock coach, squire—you will let me know where to find the house of this Mr. Robinson."

" It will be needless, Mr. Summerfield, I intend myself to bring her back, as I was the occasion of her going. As your suit has failed, you will know I do this from no compulsion—and my temper I think with all who know me will be proof sufficient that I could never have been brought to this submission by the clamours of friend or foe. My wishes are these, and I beg them to be distinctly observed;—Next Saturday week, if Ruth be able to support herself at all, I intend to marry her openly, in the little church of St. Thomas, in Highwood. Her father and mother may attend us there, and I hope will spend the after part of the day with my sister, who will be alone to receive them. I desire the presence of no others. You may make this intention of mine as public as you please. My wish is to render the fullest justice in my power to Ruth. To you, Maynard, I have a few words to say in private, if you will favour me."

The miller hesitated, and tried to imitate the sullen dignity of

his friend, but a certain old feeling of good fellowship for the squire, and the easiness of his nature prevailed. The two withdrew to the lane, by which, as the reader knows, the cottage was approached.

"I hardly know how to address you, Maynard," said Clifton,—"and yet why should pride interpose to prevent me from making to you the apology, and expressing to you the deep compunction, which I really feel for the dishonourable usage you have received from me? By all that man can swear by, I would do anything in the world, submit to anything, to make you amends. This is impossible, however, I have deprived you of a lovely wife, who, if she had not an ardent passion for you, yet entertained a respect for the worthy friend of her father, which might have proved no indifferent substitute. I will not palliate my bad actions, not in the least degree. Mad passion drove me on—and there is all my excuse."

Maynard's voice was hardly articulate as he rejoined—

"We are told, squire, to forgive the sins of others against us if we would hope for forgiveness. I must try I suppose, however hard it be, to forgive the bad part you have acted by me."

"You shall be no loser by doing so. When you go back to your mill, look round on it—it is your own! Of the sum you offered me for it, I cancel one half as a partial reparation."

"I can't say," replied Maynard, as the tear strayed down his open face, "but that it will be some comfort to me to call the old mill my own, for I have a sort of fondness for it. But yet it will be only a dreary place to me, without the dear girl whose lightsome voice and step I thought to have within it. But what can't be cured must be endured. I will not play the part of the dog in the manger; as I can't have her, why—I wish you happy with her, and hope she will be happy with you."

Clifton cordially shook hands with him.

"I will not forget this," he said; "and as long as I live, my house shall always receive you with a hearty welcome, and I shall feel personally gratified whenever I can see the miller at my table, whoever else happen to be my guests."

"And the sharp treatment you met on the hustings—"

"I value it not. I am all but elected for a more important place, and so, unintentionally, you have done me good service. Had it been otherwise, the injury you have received from me would have withheld me from resenting a thousand such affronts."

He sprang on his horse, and rode rapidly away.

"I can't tell how it is," Maynard meditated, "but it is im-

possible for me to resist his cajolery. Here am I, with so many reasons for hatred, talking about forgiveness like an old woman, and
accepting five hundred pounds indemnity from him for the loss of
a sweet wife, like a pitiful sneaking scoundrel. Yet when all is
said and done, I can't but feel a spice of liking for him, and that
is the truth."

Meantime a joy, lively but not unalloyed, had taken possession
of each breast within the cottage, not excepting that of Mrs. Wilson, who had been almost an unnoticed observer of this sudden
and happy reverse.

" There was not a breath of this stirring in Rosedale House
when I came out," she said. " Quite sure I am Miss Clifton
knew nothing of the squire having heard of Ruth, or of the wedding being to take place so soon. But I congratulate you, Mr. and
Mrs. Summerfield, and of course I expect to see you in a much
better house, and in a more thriving way of living, than at present.
The squire is not a man to do any thing by halves. In good or
evil he has a large spirit, and of course his lady's father and mother
will not be neglected by him."

" I should be sorry to owe any thing to his bounty," said
Summerfield.

" You have had great reasons to dislike him, to be sure," returned the housekeeper; " but one must make excuses for young
blood. Many a bad youth turns out a good man; and I remember
my mother used to say a reformed rake makes the best of husbands."

" I think your young squire's mother did not find it so," said
Summerfield, with unguarded haste.

" No, poor lady," and Mrs. Wilson shook her head mournfully.
" I recollect as if it was but yesterday when she was married to
Mr. Clifton. It was on a midsummer day, three and twenty years
ago. I was just thirty years old, my birthday had been on a
Thursday previous. Ah! I was then a young widow, and well I
remember how it made the tears trickle down my cheeks to see
the wedding party, and to hear the service in which I had taken
part only a short time before. Mrs. Clifton was a saving, conscien-
tious woman, but a little too strict, perhaps, in her way of thinking,
and it drove her well nigh mad to see her husband's rioting and
extravagance. He loved nothing better than to fret her, and I
believe in my heart that much of his wickedness was feigned to
irritate her. There was a time when she was jealous of you, Mrs.
Summerfield, and used to watch him in his walks disguised in one
of my dresses, to see if he visited your cottage. But there, now,
I am getting on my old stories again, when it behoves me rather
to be moving home."

"You will stay and drink tea," said Summerfield. "Here Sally, bustle, and get the table spread."

"Thank you, but I think I must be moving," said Mrs. Wilson, rising, yet evidently desirous of more gossip, and only requiring pressing to honour the cottagers with her presence for the rest of the evening.

Summerfield was really desirous that she should be gone, partly because the mental malady of his wife, which had been sensibly increased under the distress which the misfortunes and the uncertain fate of Ruth had occasioned her, kept him in secret fear whenever she was in the presence of strangers, and partly because the discovery of his daughter, and the speedy prospect of her marriage, had agitated him exceedingly, and he longed to be free from the presence of this good gossip that he might give vent to his feelings, and converse unrestrained with his family and his friend. Finding herself not urged to remain, the stately housekeeper looked out at the cottage door, observed that it seemed likely to rain, and returning again to her chair, asked Sally if she would not like to see her sister's wedding with the squire.

"And I will," replied Sally; "my brother and me will go up one of the aisles where no one will notice us."

"And shall you not be very proud to see your sister married to a gentleman like Mr. Clifton?"

"No," replied Sally, with spirit, "my sister is as good as him."

"Indeed! How so, pray?"

"You talk too fast, my dear," said her father. "Your sister in respect of money and rank is not as good as the squire, but in every other she is far better."

"They call her the Rosedale Beauty in the town, father," said Billy.

Mrs. Wilson found it necessary to take up the cudgels on her young master's behalf, not being able to digest the independent expressions of the cottager.

"I am sorry," she said, interrupting herself with a cough, "that you should be so very bitter, Mr. Summerfield, against the squire; he has done wrong, no one can dispute, but surely since he is willing to make amends—"

"He cannot make amends," interrupted Summerfield, almost rudely.

"Cannot?"

"No, Mrs. Wilson, that is beyond his ability," said Summerfield, with a groan.

"Really to understand you, sir, is very difficult. Mr. Clifton, of course you must know, might bring to Rosedale House a bride

equal or superior to him in rank and fortune; and, although I would be the last to say a syllable against your daughter, who has an unquestionable right to be his wife, yet I must say, that there are not many young gentlemen, with his rising talents and his high birth, who would act as he is about to do. It is greatly to his credit, and gives me much pleasure,—but I always thought he had a good heart, and used to tell his mother so, but she poor thing would not listen to me, so much she disliked him for his resemblance to his father."

"And that is why I dislike him," muttered Summerfield; and aloud he rejoined—

"The squire's condescension is very great, to be sure, and I ought to be thankful for his ever having deigned to take notice of my daughter, but, strange as you may think it, I do not; nor am I flattered by his raising her to this unexpected honour. I should have been much better pleased had he left her where he first saw her, she would then have been the wife of the miller—a man worth twenty Squire Cliftons—and I should have felt as confident of her future happiness as I now do of her future misery."

"Very well, sir," said Mrs. Wilson, rising stiffly, with displeasure in her look and mien, "I see you are out of humour, and I shall take my leave—good evening, sir."

"Stay, Mrs. Wilson," said the cottager—"I am a blunt, straightforward, unpolished man, and am more apt to speak my mind than to study the feelings of those I talk with. But I meant no offence to you, personally, quite the contrary, for I respect you much."

"I cannot stay to hear you speak disrespectfully of the squire," said Mrs. Wilson. "He has been kind to his dependants, and I have eaten his bread, and that of his mother before him, for nigh thirty years."

"I had no intention to offend you," repeated Summerfield, "and I thank you sincerely for the trouble you have taken in bringing Miss Clifton's kind message, and feel as grateful to the young lady herself as any one can do who may feel the benefit of her charities. At the same time I decline to receive her aid, and from this reason, that it is unnecessary. The farmer I have laboured for, professing to have found my knowledge of field business more than commonly useful to him, and having a thorough dependence on my honesty and soberness of life, offered me some months ago, a more responsible place in his estate, which, now that my daughter is found, I shall gladly accept. It is a situation which will give me two pounds a week, and with this

I shall soon, if strength of limb be spared to me, clear all I owe, for my wife and I can live on a quarter of that, and Billy and Sally must provide for themselves."

"You never told me this!" exclaimed his wife, a ray of gladness—unwonted visitor to her disconsolate features—lighting up lip and eye.

"I have not, my mind has been quite occupied with my daughter, and while she was missing I felt unequal to the charge which I should have had to undertake. But lightened of that heavy load, I shall turn heartily to my business, and be able soon to do all I wish in the way of discharging arrears and creating comforts around me. Maynard is ignorant of this as well as you. It is a joy to come for him, for a joy I know it will be to his honest heart to see me in the way of prosperity at last. I have been many years at a low ebb, not from want of perseverance or energy, (if a man may say as much of himself without pride), but the stream always seemed to run against me, and I could never make any way."

Here Maynard re-entered, after his conversation in the lane with Clifton.

"Where is the squire, Henry?" asked Summerfield.

"Gone," replied Maynard, in a hoarse and depressed voice.

"And I have not learnt where to find the house of that Robinson, or what conveyance he is going by. Here, Billy, my boy, on with your cap, and run your hardest to the great house, ask to see the squire, if he be there, and tell him I shall start from the Three Crowns at seven o'clock, and if he is not going by the coach, he is to send me word where I am to find your sister in London. D'ye understand?"

"Yes, father," replied the sharp little fellow, and away he flew like an arrow from a bow.

A hasty tea was partaken, and then Mrs. Wilson departed, discovering that her presence was not altogether agreeable, and failing to extract anything like friendly talk from Mrs. Summerfield, while there was small harmony between her and the cottager, she attaching undue importance to the nice distinctions which divide rank from rank, he despising them—she as jealous of her own dignity from those she considered as inferiors, as she was punctilious in upholding the dignity of the Cliftons, and he caring neither for the one or the other. Internally, Mrs. Wilson declared that if he was the squire himself he could not carry a higher head.

"He treats me with no more respect" she said, "than if I was one of his poor neighbours! though he ought to remem-

ber that he is not my equal at present, whatever he may be hereafter."

Clifton and Summerfield ultimately set forth together the same evening in the chaise of the former, and, travelling all night, entered London the following morning, and soon found their way to the close and dingy precincts of the court where the old antiquary's house was situate. A yellow fog had increased the sombre aspect of the place, and the little bearded man, in his grey wizard-like gown, was hammering mechanically, as usual, in the midst of his worm-eaten stores. A lamp burning dimly on the counter exhibited this singular original to the young squire and Summerfield, and excited no small surprise in each.

" What do you please to want, gentlemen ?" asked the old man, rising with haste, as his practised glance surveyed the gentility of the squire's appearance, while he was not sure, being partially deaf, that they had not asked for some article which he had for sale. " I have all sorts of commodities, gentlemen, for every country in Europe, and of all dates that you can mention. Will it please you look over my collections ? Rare articles, gentlemen ! very curious, very curious indeed ! No broker in London has such valuable collections ! Old furniture—old armour—old carving—old pictures—old plate—old tapestry—old medals—old statues—old—"

"Our business," said Clifton, cutting short the catalogue, " is to reply to a letter which you addressed to Squire Clifton, of Rosedale House, in the north."

" Clifton—Clifton," mused the old man, putting his finger to his forehead, and looking down, " I don't recollect that name."

" You wrote about my daughter, Ruth Summerfield." the cottager impatiently interposed.

" Oh, aye—aye—to be sure I did. And are you her father ?"

" I am."

" And this gentleman ?"

' I am a friend of Ruth," said Clifton.

The old man seemed pleased at their arrival, and desired them to walk up stairs, but Clifton remained below until Ruth had been prepared to meet him.

She was sitting on one side of the cheerless fire in the low-roofed spacious sitting-room, when she heard a heavy step following that of Robinson on the stairs. Her eye was fixed on the door with keen expectation, and as it unclosed, she rushed into her father's open arms !

As soon as Summerfield was somewhat composed, Ruth, weeping on his breast, and her arms clinging around his neck, as if she

feared he would again discard her, he told her that he had not come alone.

"My dear mother is with you, then?" she eagerly exclaimed. "But I do not see her—have you left her down in the shop?"

And not waiting for an answer, she ran, weak as she was from recent illness, down the stairs, at the foot of which she found herself caught to the heart, not of her mother, but of Clifton!

It was a great shock, and followed by extreme nervous agitation, which lasted more than an hour, during which she trembled violently, was incapable of speech, and suffered spasms in the throat, so as to excite a lively alarm for her life.

Robinson and his sister, uncivilised as they appeared in person and manners, were kindly concerned for her, and Mrs. Becky readily exerted herself for her recovery.

Ruth was much changed since Clifton and her father had last seen her. The lovely tints of the rose, which the pure country air and a life of healthful exercise had spread on her cheek, had quite deserted it, and her slight figure was so much slighter, and her fair complexion so much fairer, and marbled as it were by the fine azure veins appearing through the white skin, that, as Mrs. Becky whispered to Summerfield, she seemed "not long for this world."

"We had two doctors to her only a week ago," said the old lady, "and I was up three nights with her. She saved my brother and I from being murdered when our house was entered by burglars about four months ago, and we thought she was not herself properly after that night."

So spoke Mrs. Rebecca Robinson, who, however, from unconscious expressions which had escaped Ruth during her delirium, had become acquainted with the real cause of the unhappy girl's flight from her service, and her desperate attempt at suicide. With agonising entreaties, Ruth, in her first lucid interval, had prevailed on her mistress to keep her secret, and it was kept, for the old maid, whose disposition was exceedingly crabbed and morose, had imbibed such an affection for the poor supplicant on account of her sweetness and docility of temper, and felt so grateful for the courage she had shown at the time of the burglary, that to refuse her request was impossible Ruth had subsequently told all her sad story to Mrs. Rebecca, who wanted not the gentler feelings which are the grace of her sex, though they were hid beneath much that was disagreeable. Ruth received compassion from her, and Mrs. Rebecca briefly, but with genuine sincerity, promised that she would both keep her secret and befriend her.

Clifton, as Ruth slowly recovered from the melancholy state into which his arrival with her father had thrown her, held one of her slender hands in his, and, heedless of the presence of the Robinsons, spoke to her in the language of earnest fondness, assuring her that he was come to take her back to Rosedale, where preparations were going on for their marriage.

Ruth shrunk from him, and hid her face on the breast of her father, who kissed her snowy brow again and again, while his arm supported her on a chair beside one on which he himself was seated.

"Have you not one word for me?" Clifton asked. "Your father knows I speak the truth, and that next Sunday week is fixed for our union. Miss Clifton is waiting to receive you with the love of a sister. Forgive then, dearest Ruth, the unhappiness I have caused you, and place confidence in me once more. My future life shall be devoted to your happiness."

Still Ruth spoke not to him, and seemed unable to endure even to look on his face, dear as it had been to her.

"You have learnt to hate me, I fear," he said, in a proud and passionate tone. "I can hardly wonder, and yet I was hardly prepared to find it so. Speak; and tell me if I am hated."

"Don't talk to her yet, squire," said Summerfield, "she has not recovered herself, and I dare say has recollections of you which are anything but soothing."

"She does not hate you," said Mrs. Becky, beckoning Clifton a little apart, "I know better than that. Bless you, she wears next her heart some withered rose leaves that she says you gave her when first she knew you. While she was ill, I was curious to open the bit of silk that they were wrapped in, and afterwards I asked her about them."

The countenance of Clifton was again irradiated with pleasure, and he and the old lady continued in close talk about Ruth for a quarter of an hour, in the recess of one of the windows formed by two tall black cabinets. Mrs. Rebecca then hastened to get ready a dinner, of which she insisted the strangers should partake before they set out on their return, and Clifton remained standing alone in deep meditation, gazing out through the window on vacancy.

THE COTTAGE GIRL.

SHE STARTED FROM HER CHAIR.

THE dinner consisted of boiled salt beef and carrots, flanked by a jug of water for Robinson and his sister, and a pint of porter for their guests.

Clifton's politeness induced him to seem to relish the meal, though not only were the viands distasteful to him, but the soiled cloth, and the rudeness of the arrangements altogether, disgusted his nice appetite, bred as it had been to luxurious refinement. Summerfield had no such qualms, and ate with tolerable appetite what was set before him.

Ruth the while, with Mrs. Rebecca's assistance, prepared to accompany them back to her dear native place. Her box was placed on the chaise, and leaning on her father's arm, she left the house, and took her seat in the chaise.

Old Robinson and his sister shook hands with her, and wished her all happiness, to which the former added a few significant words, of which Ruth took no notice at the time, though long afterwards they recurred to her memory.

"You will hear from me one day," were the words he spoke.

During the journey silence prevailed—each seemed in reverie. Clifton was, however, solicitously attentive to Ruth; at every stage he procured her some slight delicate refreshment, inquiring with a tenderness that gave a value to each trivial inquiry, whether she was sufficiently warm?—if she would wish to alight?—and how she felt herself?

At length the rich fields, and romantic green lanes of Rosedale, opened to the view of Ruth, who, highly excited, was hardly able to see them for fast flowing tears.

"We are near the cottage!—we are near my dear home!" she exclaimed. "I see the corner of the thatched roof, and the tree that grows beside the porch. And there is my mother, and Sally, and Billy!"

In her impetuosity she turned the handle of the chaise door, and springing out at a bound before the wheel stood still, was in an instant clasped in her mother's fond embrace. Summerfield followed, and withdrew them within the cottage.

"I was very cruel to you," sobbed Mrs. Summerfield—"it was through me, my dear, you went away. Oh! you must have suffered much since."

"I have indeed, mother," said Ruth; "but it is over—and I see you again—and dearest Sally—and my brother too!"—kissing them as she spoke.

"But you shall suffer no more," said Sally. "We will keep you with us if you think you will not be happy with the squire. We shall all do very well now, for father is to be Farmer Williams' chief managing man, and you can keep to weaving pillow lace. I am sure you can do enough of that to support you if you are not taken from it by other work."

"Ruth shall just do as she feels inclined," said Summerfield, "but bestir yourself, Sally—take this box in your mother's room, and carry away your sister's bonnet and cloak. You, Billy, run to the mill, and tell Maynard to step here."

"No, no," said Ruth, "I cannot see him. He has been too much wronged, and I too much disgraced."

"Maynard has gone on a journey," said Mrs. Summerfield, "and will not return until after the wedding is over."

Summerfield sighed as he received this intelligence, and said in an under tone—"Ah! poor Henry!—it was perhaps best."

CHAPTER XXIII.

"I see a hand you cannot see
Which beckons me away;
I hear a voice you cannot hear
Forbids my longer stay."

LEAVING Ruth in the cottage, Clifton rode on to his mansion, and bursting into a room whence the tones of his sister's harp proceeded, he exclaimed—

"Give me joy, Amy, give me joy! Ruth is fairly restored to me!—brought back in life and safety!—and though not in perfect health, only needing a few days' careful nursing, and a few visits from Doctor Walcot, to whom I will send in the morning. Give me joy, my dearest sister!—my long anxiety is at an end—my conscience is eased of an Atlas load. She is safe!—she is safe!"

"It affords me unspeakable pleasure to hear you say so," said Amy, rising with animation, and pushing the harp from her.

"I knew it would!" exclaimed Percy, "and my satisfaction is all the more exquisite for having you to share it. But you must go and see her at once—I have left her with her parents."

"I have not a moment's hesitation in complying with your wish," said Amy, hastening to put on her scarf and bonnet.

Percy strode rapidly to and fro the room the few minutes she was absent, and the instant she reappeared, hurried with her to the chaise, which rolled rapidly back to the cottage.

"This attention from you," he said, "will gratify Ruth, and impress her, I hope, with the reality of my intention to make her happy."

"I hope it will impress her also with the reality of my own personal affection for her," Amy rejoined.

"Yet pause a moment," Clifton said, as the humble dwelling appeared. "Remember, this act of condescension on your part is a tribute to my intended wife, not to her family. And, indeed, I do not approve of Mrs. Wilson's making familiar visits to the Summerfields."

"I am ignorant if she has done so," Amy returned.

"I sent her to them to offer a temporary assistance if they needed it, but it was declined, and not, I believe, in very humble terms,"

"There is something very, very strange, about the characters of those people," said Percy, "and I detest any connexion with them. But I must now only think of Ruth—she is not answerable for their insolence."

"I did not exactly say they were insolent."

"I have no doubt they were so; I know so well the stubborn pride of the man, and the insane bitterns of his wife, against all that emanates from us," said Clifton.

"I should be sorry if I have increased your dislike to them."

"That were hardly possible."

As Percy uttered these words, the vehicle stopped under the branches of an immense chesnut tree, which extended its hard roots about the pebbled threshold of the cottage porch, where a cock was strutting and crowing, and a pet guinea pig of Ruth's young brother peeped out from under the thick leaves of the scarlet-runners and eglantine clustering on the sides. The bullfinch fluttered in its cage outside the latticed window on the whitewashed wall, and sang cheerily, as if to hail the return of its lovely mistress. Clifton's attention was drawn to it by a snatch of the tune of " Roy's Wife," which the bird piped with energy, not a little to his surprise and pleasure, for he rightly guessed from what association in the mind of Ruth that melody must have been taught to the gifted little creature. He well recollected the day when he had sung it in her presence in the mill, on the first rise of his passion, and involuntarily he repeated the two lines which on that occasion he had sung with so much emotion and pointed emphasis—

> " How happy I if she were mine,
>   Or I were Roy of Aldivalloch."

The chaise was dismissed, Clifton and his sister intending to walk home. The former did not enter with Amy, but remained pacing the lane for some time, reflecting with complicated feelings on the event to which he had irrevocably pledged himself.

" It is done," he said—" there is no retracing my steps—marry her now I must and will. Must!—it is a word hateful to me; rather let me say I am privileged to take this step. Her beauty would grace a coronet; and she has virtues to match it—sweet inartificial virtues—such as seem rather to emanate spontaneously from her nature than to be the result of laboured cultivation. If

she were unconnected, I would choose her, though the present necessity did not exist, before all the rank and fashion in the world. I love her!—and yet not as formerly. My feelings flow more tranquilly, and I fancy in a deeper channel. But her relations—her relations! To connect myself with them is a thought abhorrent to me! I detest them, and distrust them. They have an antipathy to me and I to them. Ruth, when she is my wife, must separate herself from them. She shall reside as much as posible at a distance from this place. The villa shall be her country residence, and while the Parliament is sitting she will be with me in town."

At length he entered the rustic dwelling, and, as he did so, he encountered the same look of terror from Mrs. Summerfield which had struck him so much when he surprised her at midnight in the shed. She had been sitting with her eye gazing on vacancy, while her eldest daughter was conversing with Miss Clifton, and her husband and little boy were absent in the garden gathering potatoes for the supper. Starting from her chair, some inarticulate words trembled on her tongue, and she sank back in a fit.

Clifton was startled, and experienced a very unpleasent sensation, which hovered over his mind like a shadow of something hideous, but impalpable and indistinct.

Summerfield was called, and with calmness he begged Mr. and Miss Clifton to take no notice of the occurrence, for his Hannah was subject to fits, and had long been in a very low state of health.

"She seems to have an odd delusion about the spectre of my father," said Clifton.

"And many other delusions as odd," returned the cottager, with perfect equanimity.

"Her mind, then, you think, is unsound?"

"Aye, poor thing, trouble has made it so."

Summerfield withdrew the invalid, as she began to recover into her chamber, the door of which he locked, while Ruth, whose wounded heart had just began to re-awaken to a hope of happiness with Clifton, was now fearfully damped by the revival of the mystery which had given her formerly so much disturbance of mind. A warning look from her father, seen only by herself, placed her on her guard, but the reader may imagine with what feelings she could look forward to a union with one whose parent had in some way, she dare not imagine how, met his death through the instrumentality of those nearest to her blood and affection. She was certain, however it happened, there must have

been tremendous provocation.   She could have staked her salvation on the certain assurance that the deed had not amounted to murder—that plunder had made no part of the motive which led to it—and that if not absolutely justifiable, it had been excusable, perhaps, indeed, as she had sometimes suspected, necessary, to save the honour of her mother.   Revenge was the only vice which, in her conception, could by any possibility have betrayed her father into wilful homicide; and with his enlightened conscience, and power of will, she could not believe that even this, his most besetting sin, could have overcome him so far.

From this dreadful and mysterious topic, her thoughts were detached with some difficulty by Clifton, who, taking a chair beside her, which his sister vacated for him, entreated her to say that she was reconciled to him, that she forgave the past, and would consent to become the partner of his life.

"I thought you would have married that lady I saw you riding with in the park," she said, faintly.

"You saw me with!   When did you see me there?"

"O, just before—"   She stopped, and shuddered.

He bent his head close to her, and whispered in very low accents.

She replied as softly, the tears bursting in a torrent from her eyes.

Clifton passed his arm fondly round her waist, pressed her closer to his side, and endeavoured to animate her to hope for the future.

"The future cannot give me back the dear boy I left in the river," she murmured, with suffocating sobs.   "I was saved, but he perished!"

"The river!" he echoed, in unmitigated astonishment.   "Was it not in the hospital the child died?"

Ruth shook her head.

"Great God!" he exclaimed, detaching his arm from her, "I understood Mrs. Robinson wrongly, then."

"She knew all, but feared to tell you," said Ruth.

"Let me know the truth," he said, after a pause of considerable agitation.

"It is like a frightful dream to look back upon," she said.   "I can remember nothing clearly, all is confused, dim, and horrible. The sickening feeling that you had forgotten and forsaken me— the dread of exposure to the scorn of those who had known me —the frenzied feeling that it would be better to give my child a moment's pang to spare it from the misery of years—its last sob —my clutching it tighter to my breast in the agony of drowning that our bodies might not be divided—the terrible moment when I opened my eyes again on the world and found it had been left in the cold and watery bed to which I—I had consigned it—Oh! my God!—"

" Speak softer—and be calm,' said Clifton, in a tremulous but soothing voice. " What followed ?"

" My brain was so confused by the distress I had endured, that I hardly know what I said or did. The place I found myself in was a bedroom in a tavern, which stood alone at the corner of a wood. No one was with me just then but an old servant of the house, stone deaf, who, when I asked for my child, hastened to call in the other persons who had been endeavouring to recover me, and were busy preparing a bath, and heating blankets. These were the landlady and her daughter, who had been directed by a medical student lodging in the house. I inquired if nothing had been found with me, and when they told me ' nothing,' and that I had lain so long in the water, and remained so long insensible, as to make my ever coming to myself again a wonder, I felt that all was over for the poor infant, and I remembered nothing more for I know not what length of time."

Her face drooped on Clifton's shoulder—his arm again embraced her, and he felt deep contrition for the guilty passion which had left him, the only offender, comparatively free and unscathed, while it had burdened his guiltless companion with such intolerable suffering. He felt the visitings of natural affection for his child too, and pressed her to reveal all concerning it that remained untold, which she did in disjointed sentences, and with great mental distress.

" Those about her had not understood the expressions in which she alluded to the child—they consented to her supplication, that she might be spared the degradation of appearing in open court before a magistrate, to answer for the attempt on her life, on condition she gave up her name, enabled them to replace her in the custody of her friends, and promised not to repeat her effort at self-destruction. She sent them to Robinson—he accounted plausibly for her temporary alienation of mind, as they called it. She returned to his house, and brain-fever ensued."

All these particulars Ruth with trepidation hurried over.

" And the offspring of my blood is left to decay like some worthless animal, without baptism or burial!" Clifton exclaimed, in a low tone of dismay.

" I hope—I hope not!" Ruth hastily replied. "Alas! I have but hope. And yet Mrs. Robinson loves me, I know, and would spend much, and take a great deal of trouble, to do me service

She promised to undertake the finding, and the decent interment, of the poor child. ‘ Leave it to me,’ she said, ‘ I owe my life to you, and my brother's life, and the safety of more property than you know of : and I think it no more than a fair return on my part to help you, as far as I can, in this unfortunate business.’ ”

“ But she cannot accomplish her kind intention without assistants, and if she has assistants, how can we depend on the secresy which, for so many reasons, is important ?”

“ One only—the poor brickmaker, to whom, chiefly, I owe my preservation—is all she thinks of, I believe. Being a man without hearth or home, he is glad to do anything for a trifle of money, and is truly Irish in warmth of heart, as well as extreme poverty.”

“ And when is the result to reach us ?”

“ As soon as any success is met with—to-morrow, I hope and pray. I shall not sleep until I hear.”

Clifton was very unsatisfied with the confused and imperfect accounts he had been able to extract from Ruth, relative to her child ; but seeing how it distracted her to dwell upon the theme, and fearing the consequences of her doing so in the present weak state of her health, he forbore to question further, and felt it incumbent on him to support her spirits under the melancholy reflections they had to sustain, while he felt no small apprehension for her ultimate peace of mind, under the agonising thought that she had been the means of her child's death, not inadvertently, but wilfully, and he could only hope, that her recollection of the despair and agony of her mind at the time, would exculpate her to her own satisfaction.

“ Now, is it all settled, good folks ?” Amy asked, rejoining them, after having engaged herself as long as possible in talking apart with the young boy and girl of the cottage, concerning their sports and employments. “ Have your arguments succeeded in obtaining pardon and consent from Ruth ?”

“ I persuade myself so,” said Clifton.

“ Then she has proved generous indeed ?”

“ I shall endeavour to pay her for all,” said he, emphatically.

“ O, don't promise too much,” his sister returned. “ I can assure Ruth she will find you a sad scapegrace at the best—bringing in your pointers over the best carpets—sitting till near midnight at the wine—and spending I know not how much in racing and betting.”

“ Stay, stay, my dear sister, you are judging of my future by the past—that is not fair. I am setting up for a reformed character, you know—in all except the pointers ; there I own I am incorrigible.”

"I shall believe the reformation when I see it, and just as far as I see it."

"Cannot you trust me something further than this, Ruth?" Clifton asked.

The question was unfortunate, reminding Ruth too powerfully how fully she had once trusted him, and how cruelly she had been deceived. Her lip quivered, and she was silent. He observed this, and whispered earnestly—

"Do not, I entreat you, allow your mind to dwell on what cannot be recalled or restored. Look only on the prospect which is before you. See in me your husband, and in Amy your sister. We will both cherish you as the dearest to us on earth. Be cheerful, then! bright days are in store for you, brighter than any you have known."

Clifton and his sister were gone when Summerfield came out of the chamber where he had been busy in attending on his wife. Despite the firm stoicism of his natural temper and the command he had learned to exercise over his external appearance, he looked now disordered and alarmed.

"My dearest father!" exclaimed Ruth, "tell me how my mother is, and let me assist her."

"No no, child," said Summerfield, "you must not come near her at present; let her have a night's rest, and then she will be all right again."

"But I will not distress her by talking of any thing painful; only let me see her, and help her."

"Not to-night, not to-night. Go to bed, my dear child, you require rest yourself after your journey, weak as you are. Let Sally make you some mulled ale, and then sleep quietly, and God bless you."

He hastily retired again. As he opened the chamber door, Ruth caught a glimpse of her mother stretched stiff and pale as a corpse on the bed, and a few minutes after she heard her exclaim,

"Persuade me as you will, Roger, I have seen him!"

"I tell you it was all a mistake, a gross deception of your fancy," said Summerfield warmly.

"Will you tell me so?" cried his wife, angrily, "why there—there—it is in the room with us while you speak!"

"You will drive me mad if you persist in this superstitious folly!" exclaimed the cottager. "The dead cannot arise."

"You will not convince me," returned his wife. "The Witch of Endor raised Samuel, and I know I have seen—"

"Silence, foolish, obstinate woman," cried Summerfield, peremptorily, "you forget who is in the next room."

Their voices dropped to a pitch at which the words became no longer distinguishable to Ruth, but what she had heard was enough to deprive her of sleep for the most part of the night. In the morning her mother did not rise, but Ruth was permitted to see her, though with much caution. While she stood by the bedside, Mrs. Summerfield, watching an opportunity when her husband was out of hearing, caught the hand of Ruth, and whispered plaintively—

" My dear, you will soon lose me."

" What can induce you to think so?" Ruth tenderly asked.

" I have had warnings, my dear, awful warnings—the dead have risen to tell me that my day is on the wane."

" Oh! mother, how can you believe such impossibilities?"

" Can that be impossible which I have seen and heard? But you are as unbelieving as your father. I tell you a spirit has passed before my eyes in the shape of one, whose memory I have reason to curse, and at this moment it whispers in my ear—'Hannah, Hannah! prepare—prepare.'"

Ruth threw a fearful glance round, as if she half expected to see the shape her mother's imagination had evoked, and was relieved by the hasty entrance of her father, which checked Mrs. Summerfield's communicativeness concerning the tokens of fate she had received.

It was under these ominous circumstances the Marriage Day drew nigh. Never came a day under more ominous ones.

On the one hand was the mystery of old Clifton's death, and the growing insanity of her mother—on the other was the remembrance of her child, which must ever be a source of melancholy with her, if not of fear. It seemed as if some ruthless destiny had wound up her innocent life with shameful and ensanguined events, like a lily floating on a dark and turgid stream. Often, alone, she attempted to review the only action of any consequence for which she could blame herself. Little had she foreseen the colours in which that action appeared to her when she found herself saved, and her infant irrevocably lost! With agony for the loss, with bitter self-reproach, had mingled the wild dread of being called to a public account for its death. With a heart bursting under a mother's anguish, she durst not mention its name aloud, nor pray to have its remains sought for, until the severity of the conflict brought on the brain-fever, from whose ravings Mrs. Robinson learnt the painful truth, not without alarm for her, since the latter was aware, that though Ruth had been pure in intention, and only erred in yielding to the dictates of despair, yet, that were it to be known the unfortunate girl had become a mother, and deprived her child of life, she would be placed in a dangerous dilemma.

While the marriage of Ruth and Clifton was in preparation, the kind old maid did for the ill-fated little being what circumstances permitted, though at some risk to herself, as she very strongly set forth in the letter which announced its quiet interment in the corner of an unfrequented churchyard near the scene of its death. She had been obliged to involve in the doubtful matter a friend who she had been staying with, while fulfilling her promise to Ruth, but there need be no fear of her. Mrs. Rebecca grumbled a good deal in the midst of her kindness. It had cost her much, she said, though she did not grudge the money, considering who it was for. She had given ten pounds in all to the brickmaker, who had managed better than she had expected. He had borrowed drags openly, but took care they should find nothing until night had dispersed the two or three persons whom curiosity had detained while passing the lonely spot. The child was then found, and carried, wrapped in a large shawl, to the cottage where Mrs. Robinson was waiting to receive it. There it was placed in a neat little coffin the brickmaker had himself manufactured the day before, and ere the morning it was safely and secretly deposited in its final resting-place.

Mrs. Robinson described accurately the place where it lay, and ended with the information that the brickmaker was returning to Ireland, and that he declared " he was as proud to do the young woman (meaning Ruth) a kind turn as to take the gould which ud carry him back to the sight of his mother's cabin in Killarney. Sure he knew it was the heart-break made her do what she did, and let them who wanted to cast the stone at her feet, feel what that was first. She meant no more harm to the bairn than to herself, and it was not her fault that she had outlived it. He wished the tongue might rot from his mouth, if ever he said a word to bring her into trouble."

The parents of Ruth were as yet ignorant of the principal of their daughter's sufferings during her absence from them ; and though to her mother's ear she would have been glad to unburden her spirit, she was prevented by the unhealthy state of mind of the latter, and by the command of Clifton, that the birth or death of the child should not be mentioned to anyone in Rosedale. His sister, he said, was as ignorant as her parents of these circumstances, and should remain so.

Thus, with a spirit perfectly guileless, Ruth was doomed all her life to be the depositor of gloomy secrets ; and thus the veil

of oblivion was abruptly dropped over the brief mortal existence of the infant son of Clifton and the Cottage Girl.

> "On him the eyes of mortal men
> 　Shall never, never light again.
> 　Memory alone might steal a glance,
> 　　Like some wild glimpse in sleep we're taking
> Of a long perished countenance,
> 　That is forgotten on awaking."

But enough of the dark side. In this chequered world there can be few situations imagined which have not their bright aspects. How much less when an union is in prospect between hearts that love.

The daily attentions of Clifton and his sister, with whom Ruth now, for the first time, found herself on a familiar level—the unintermitting anxiety of the former to repair the evils he had committed, by every means that his circumstances and his affection could supply—joined with frequent walks and short excursions in their company, and the gentle stimulus afforded by talking over Clifton's future plans for advancing his name and improving his estates, in all which, Ruth began to take the interest proper in one who was to be the partner of his future days —all this, despite every unfavourable influence, restored her to partial health and serenity ; and though a dark midnight was in reality closing around her, the fitful moonlight radiance of hopeful love tinged the gloom with its delicious rays.

CHAPTER XXIV.

The marriage bells ring joyously,
    O'er field and down the chime is heard ;
And villagers trudge merrily,
    With many a pleasant look and word,
To the old church, which, reverently,
    The old and shadowy woodlands gird.

                                        MARY BENNETT.

THE morning of the Marriage Day rose cold and clear. By five all the inmates of the humble cottage of the Summerfields were astir, and at seven they took their breakfast together. An air of touching solemnity pervaded the group. Perhaps the most cheerful was Mrs. Summerfield, who was entertaining the idea, however delusive, that her husband and herself would be safer when Ruth was the wife of Clifton. Summerfield was particularly grave, and ever and anon drew a long sigh, for the marriage was hateful to him, and he trembled for the future tranquillity of his child, his prejudice scarcely permitting him to see any good quality in the squire, such as a father might rest his confidence upon. He feared that the poverty of her origin would be a source of bitterness, and that the libertine caprices of her husband would induce him to neglect her.

With these forebodings full upon him, he opened the Book of God, and performed the devotional service for the morning. As they knelt down to prayer, the depth of his paternal anxieties infused into his language an affecting eloquence. He besought the Deity that " an especial providence might watch over Ruth ; that she might be endowed with heavenly wisdom to bear meekly the honours of the high station to which she was now called ; that in her prosperity her heart might not be lifted up or become hardened, and that she might not forget the insubstantiality of all temporal things ; and that, if it should please High Heaven to try her in the furnace of affliction, she might come out from it purified as fine gold : and that, at the last great day, when the heavens and earth should be dissolved, she might be found among those of whom it might be said, ' These are they that came out of great tribulation, and have washed their robes and made them white in the blood of the lamb.' "

He arose with glistening eyes, and as Ruth twined her arms around his neck, and relieved her full heart in tears, he murmured a hasty "God bless you! God bless you! You have been a good daughter, and I have no doubt you will make a good wife. But don't expect too much—you will most likely require patience and fortitude."

"Clifton loves me, father."

"I hope he may always do so."

"He will—he shall!" exclaimed Ruth. "I will never offend him. And he shall be so happy that he shall not have a wish away from his wife."

"Far be it for me to sadden your hopes," said her father, "but in the course of a married life, my child, differences may arise of which you can now form no notion. The more you love your husband the more intensely will you feel any unkindness from him, and the tenderness of your feelings will perhaps induce you to construe into unkindness that which is not meant so. I again say, do not expect too much. You marry, not a demi-god, but a man—a changeful, irritable, proud, impetuous man, imperfect in all respects."

"Yes, perfect in one, surely, father—in love for me."

"Not even in that respect. There will be times when it will burn low, and seem about to be extinguished."

"But I will revive it again."

"On your skill in doing so depend all my hopes for you, for there can be nothing much the matter while your husband loves you. Look jealously to his regard; when the flame sinks, feed it with anxiety. Keep him yours by the bonds of affection, and trust not to any other. Now prepare for church; at ten he comes."

It was with unusual pride that Mrs. Summerfield assisted to array her lovely daughter in garments suitable to her new condition. They had been sent by Miss Clifton, and consisted of a dress of white satin, with a pelerine of rich foreign lace, a veil of Brussels lace, a bonnet of fine Tuscan straw, and gloves of white embroidered kid. To this was added a complete set of pearl ornaments—the gift of the bridegroom.

Just as the dressing was completed, and the bracelets and the necklace being clasped on, a merry chime of bells broke on the ear, borne from a distance on the swell of the wind, and in the same moment Billy, in a new suit of corduroy, ran breathlessly in with the shout—

"The coach is coming!—the coach is coming!"

"Here, Sally, clear the table—put those chairs in their places —call your father!" cried Mrs. Summerfield, and her flurried

directions being obeyed, she received with her husband, at the cottage door, the distinguished bridegroom of her child.

He was in the highest spirits, and looked eminently handsome. His fine person was attired to the fullest advantage ; his dress-coat was a superfine blue, his waistcoat of an exquisite white foreign velvet, and a massive chain of gold crossed the breast. He seemed disposed to be in good humour with every one, and said pleasantly to Sally, as she dropped him a curtsey—

"You are an old friend of mine, you know, Sarah. Do you remember the letter you carried for me to your sister when she was so angry with me that she would not read it?"

"O yes, sir."

"I must keep your services in mind. What sort of a husband would you like? Perhaps I may be able to find you one among my acquaintances."

"I should like one," replied Sally, with all her accustomed quickness, "who would be good to my father and mother."

Clifton bit his lip; it was a shrewd hint, he thought; and, passing on, he greeted his bride with graceful tenderness.

"This day is the commencement of a new life to each of us," he said, "and I trust we may never have occasion to look back upon it with any sentiments but those of satisfaction."

"Amen!" exclaimed Summerfield.

The cottager then withdrew with his wife, the latter to don her best gown and bonnet for accompanying the young pair to church, the former to endeavour to persuade her to remain at home, as he had at times observed in her, during the last few days, aggravated symptoms of mental derangement, and he became now hastily in alarm lest she should suddenly break out in the presence of others and utter something concerning the last Squire Clifton which might kindle the suspicions of his son or his friends, if not actually disclose the fatal secret.

The carriage, meanwhile, was drawn into the road at the foot of the lane, and waited there about half an hour, watched with great interest by some half-score of the tenants of the poor dwellings near, who were all talking with great wonder of the good fortune Ruth Summerfield had met with after all.

She, notwithstanding the happy nature of the present meeting, was oppressed with melancholy, for which another reason was superadded to those with which the reader is familiar. She had hoped, nay, expected, that Clifton would have proposed some substantial assistance for her father, which might raise him above the casualties of a life dependent upon daily labour for others, or, which was what she most desired, that he would have been will-

ing to assist them with money to pitch their tents in another land.

But Clifton had heard, from his housekeeper, that Summerfield had disdainfully declared he would be sorry to receive any favour from his wealthy son-in-law at any time, and he was resolved that the stiff temper of the man should bend before he made any proposal. Nevertheless, he had taken care they should be provided for the occasions of the present time, through Ruth, who now told him she feared their appearance would hardly please him, as she had been unable to prevail on her father to accept anything.

" I shall be sufficiently pleased," Clifton rejoined, " appear as they will, if their presence gratifies you ; I would else willingly have dispensed with it."

" I could have wished my father to be with us," Ruth said, " but my mother's uncertain health—"

She stopped—

" Would render her remaining at home desirable, you think," Clifton said.

Ruth uttered a faint affirmative ; she could not breathe to him the apprehensions which, equally with her father, she entertained from the progress of her mother's mental disorder.

" My sister," said Clifton, " is angry with me for having deterred her from making one of the ceremony. . But her presence would have given more pretension to the affair than I desired. It is already too public. The bells have been rung against my express wishes : and though I selected the little church of Highwood, on account of its privacy, I hear the villagers around are quite on the tiptoe of expectation."

Mrs. Summerfield had manifested a positive intention to be present at church, and now maintained it, both against the wishes of her daughter and husband, which had been frequently expressed during the last fortnight.

" You had better not go, I tell you," said Summerfield to her apart, as they were preparing to set out. " You know there is no depending on your health for one hour I shall be miserable until you are safely back again."

" It is no use talking, go I will," said Mrs. Summerfield, tying on her bonnet. " The church of Highwood was that I was married in, and I have not stood under its roof since that hour. This will be my second visit—my third will be in a coffin."

" Take your own course ; we have now escaped suspicion many years, and may escape it still, if you can only be mistress of yourself. But if not—we are lost ! "

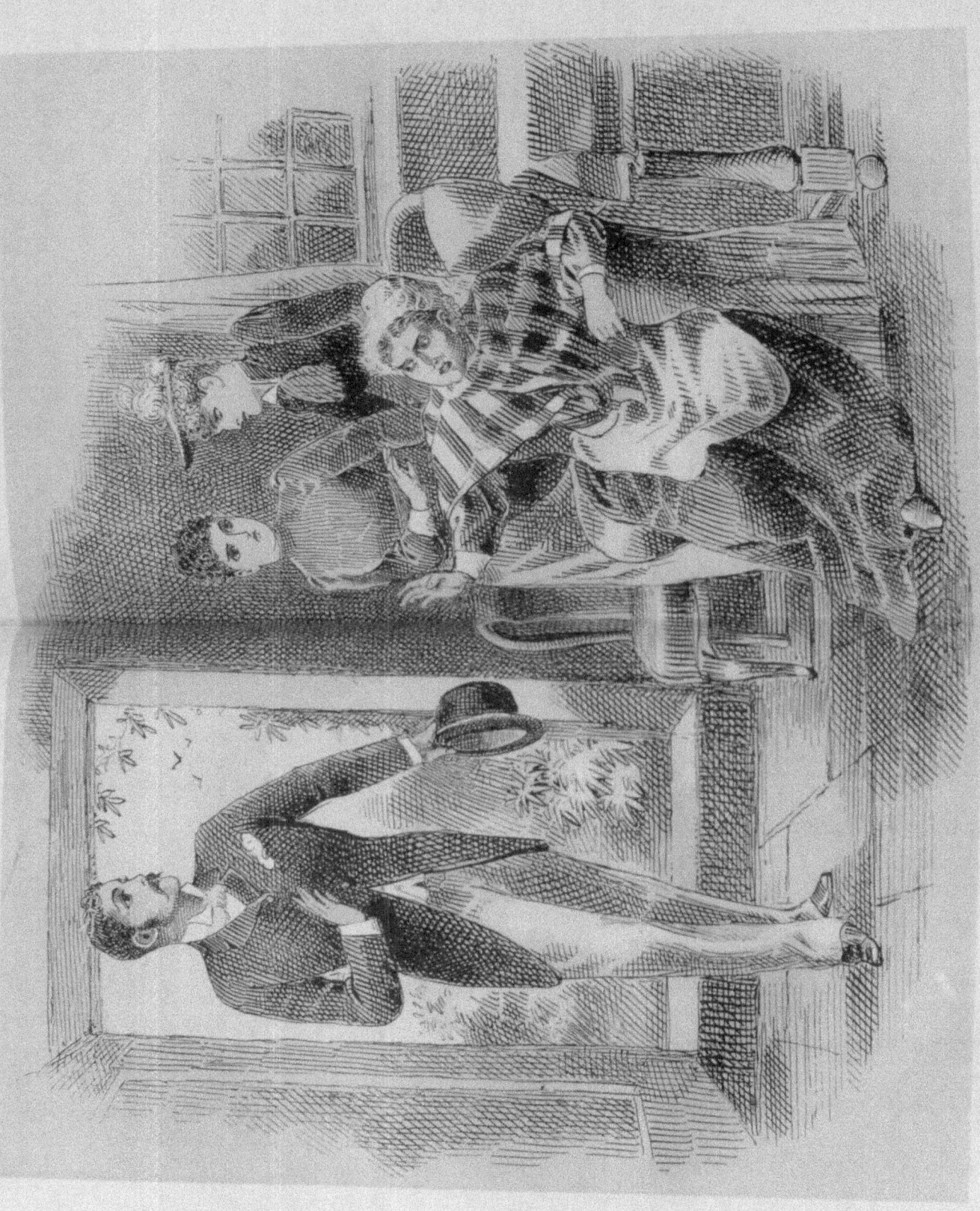

"CLIFTON ENCOUNTERED THE LOOK OF TERROR FROM MRS. SUMMERFIELD."

"VILLAIN! I WILL MAKE YOU SAY SOMETHING ABOUT HIM!"

"WHEN Clifton spoke to me about your fancy of his father's spectre," went on Summerfield, "I thought I felt the drop of the gallows falling from under my feet—I seemed to choke—and how I answered him so calmly I cannot tell. Now, you don't seem to see the mighty danger you have escaped. He had all but taken alarm; and though the thunder-cloud has passed over without an explosion, the slightest thing will rouse him to a conjecture of the truth—therefore, beware!"

"I know you think me out of my senses at times, Roger, but I know what I am about as well as you or any one. It is lost labour cautioning me. I will never bring you into any danger; depend on it; I can guide myself quite well enough to avoid that."

"Was there no fear of your bringing me into danger, when you crept half-dressed at midnight to that place of horror, as if you wanted to make yourself stark mad? What could you go there for?"

"I knew the old Squire's ghost rose at twelve o'clock, and I was determined to ask him why he troubled me, who never meant to injure him. It was through his own wickedness he perished."

"Certainly, and should not that fact make you more at ease than you are? You start at every strange step you hear, and if you happen to see young Clifton, unexpectedly fall into fits. Your restless fears make me as restless as yourself, and we are both as unhappy as if the deed had been a crime instead of an accident."

"It is foolish, to be sure, but I am weak as water under this horrible secret; and I think the trouble I have had about Ruth so long has made me worse, for I never had these fancies—if they are fancies—about the old squire's spectre until lately. I must try to be stronger, from this day—my mind being easy about my daughter will help me."

"But you WILL go to the church this morning?"

"Why not? I feel better than I have done these dozen years. I shall like to see the old church, and the ceremony which makes my daughter a lady."

"Woman's vanity!" ejaculated Summerfield.

"I have as little as most people of that," said his wife; "but one can't help being a little proud to see one's child, after being poor and despised, look so like an angel, so beautifully dressed, and the bride of the squire of the manor. Ah! if I could only forget where the old gentleman is lying, and where he died, I should be this day a happy woman."

"What! and Harry Maynard miserable! For my part it will not pass from my thoughts that Ruth ought to have been his wife, that she was stolen from him by detestable treachery, and that he, poor fellow, is now neglecting his business because he cannot bear to be in Rosedale while this wedding is afoot. I could, with goodwill, spend this day in mourning for his sake. Come, since go you will; it is full time we were off; we must walk sharp not to keep the squire waiting at the church, and take the short cut over the fields."

When they had been gone a short time, Ruth affectionately bade adieu to her sister and brother.

Clifton's carriage then drew up to the cottage, and as it departed Ruth cast a fond look back on the dwelling of her youth, whose small lattices flamed with the beams of the morning sun, about whose humble thatch the swallows were twittering, while the chesnut tree before the door seemed alive with happy-hearted warblers. Her brother and sister stood under the porch waving their hands to her till she was out of sight.

In the road all the neighbours stood to catch a glimpse of the bride and bridegroom. Clifton scattered among them a handful of silver, which was received with joyful exclamations.

The distance from the cottage to the church was four miles, and the road lay over a landscape of uncommon attractions. Lowland and upland were rich in wheat fields and pasturages, intersected by groves of lofty trees. Gradually these groves extended themselves, and the green meadows became narrowed between their lofty ranks. The road then began to ascend a gentle eminence, from the brow of which the church was visible in a hollow, surrounded by a few scattered dwellings, almost lost among trees, and constituting a village.

The leaden roof of the sacred building seemed in the glowing sunlight transmuted to gold. The single square tower, heavy and low, was the resort of a congregation of large birds, which kept up an incessant cawing and chattering, and careered in flocks round and round the time-honoured edifice. Occasionally one of these familiar birds, detaching itself from its fellows, would light on the back of a sheep nibbling the grass among the graves of the pleasant churchyard, or perch with a lively cry on a tombstone, as if bidding good morrow to the dead who lay below. All the concomitants of the scene were those of innocence and quiet sanctity, blended here and there with relics of feudal days. There were some very curious tombs both in the yard and the building, and in the former they were agreeably chequered with light and shade transmitted from overarching trees. A few very ancient yews formed a sort of irregular avenue to the church entrance, which was semicircularly arched, the work of forefathers who had been six centuries mouldering in dust. The least of the works of man is more durable than he. He cometh up as a flower, and is cut down, and the place thereof knoweth it no more.

A number of neatly-dressed rustics, carrying bouquets of flowers, were waiting in the avenue to see the bridal party enter the church. As Clifton gave his hand to Ruth to descend the carriage steps, she lowered her veil from her bonnet, for there was much eagerness to obtain a glimpse of her face among the beholders, and the expressions of admiration were so audible as to call the red into her cheeks. Here, too, Clifton scattered silver, and entered the church amid thanks and hearty wishes.

Beautiful and solemn was the interior of the church, in which young Squire Clifton and his bride now stood before the rails of the area occupied by the communion-table, where the aged vicar was ready with his clerk to perform the holy service. The windows were of antique gothic, filled with heraldic painting, and representing among other arms, those of the renowned Arthur Clifton of the days of the Commonwealth. The pavement of beautiful marble was lined with receptacles of noble dust, and the walls were covered with scutcheons, monumental effigies, and recording tablets. Near the altar stood a tomb, the most conspicuous in the building, both for beauty of workmanship and for size. Its inscription set forth in Latin that it enshrined the mortal relics of ARTHUR CLIFTON, who was beheaded by the cavaliers in arms for Charles the Second, and of his lady, who, unable to survive him, cast herself from the tower, at the moment when the axe was uplifted in her sight which drank the blood of her husband, and having faithfully partaken of his earthly fortunes, she shared his grave, and was made partaker of his everlasting bliss.

The rite which was about to be performed in this small but exquisite gothic fane, ought, according to the vulgar superstition of the country, to have proved happier in its results, for the sun, whose beams shining on a hymeneal altar, are supposed to give good augury, streamed in rich belts of glorious effulgence through each storied window across the aisles, imparting warmth and life to the monumental effigies, steeping the marble pavement in surpassing colours of crimson and of purple, and shedding over the white garments and pale face of the bride a saint-like glory. And as if to aid the happy influences of the sun, no sooner had the opening words of the irrevocable service commenced, in the slow and impressive utterance of the reverend clergyman, than a robin, which had flown into the church, fluttered around the bridal group, singing as if its little heart were ready to burst with joy.

CHAPTER XXV.

"Through Bertram's dizzy brain, career
A thousand thoughts, and all of fear."—SCOTT.

As soon as Mrs. Summerfield had entered the church, and cast her eye on the name of Arthur Clifton, inscribed on the tomb mentioned at the close of the last chapter, her husband observed that she became excited, and there flickered over her pale and pinched, but still beautiful features, the insane expression which he had observed too often on it of late. With an oppressed heart he kept his eye upon her, and his anxiety rapidly increased during the progress of the ceremony, which seemed to him of intolerable length, for he observed her frequently turn her head toward the tomb, shudder, and murmur to herself. Her singular bearing, and total inattention to what was going forward, was soon noticed by Clifton and the clergyman, and the latter casting on her a glance of rebuke, paused as he was about to pronounce the concluding benediction on the new married couple, for instead of kneeling with the rest, she stood still, regarding the tomb with a terrified stare.

It afterwards occurred to Summerfield, when recalling these dreadful moments, that, although she knew perfectly well that the tomb had been erected to the renowned Clifton of Cromwell's time, yet she imagined it had been raised to the memory of the bridegroom's father, whose name had been Arthur, a delusion which assisted to recal the spectre of her thoughts.

As the clergyman paused, and added to his displeased glance a sign that she would take the posture of humble reverence, her husband whispered to her sternly and emphatically; and accustomed by long habit to yield implicitly to his guidance, she bent beside him. But, although her knees were on the steps of the communion altar, her gaze was still on the tomb, and the prayers of the clergyman fell without any meaning on her ear. The iron firmness of Summerfield gave way at that critical moment; he lost his presence of mind, and command over her. His strong features, in which care had indented many a hollow and premature wrinkle, were now overspread

with a dark hue, and his voice was tremulous, as, the service being over, he endeavoured to recall her to a sense of where she was, and in whose presence she stood.

But it was in vain; she only arose to stare more intensely on the tomb, until her eyes seemed ready to crack with the intensity of her gaze, while every limb was contracted and stiffened in extremity of terror.

" What is the matter, Mrs. Summerfield?" Clifton inquired, his mind again hesitating on the verge of suspicion, and his attention sharpened to the most acute degree.

The unfortunate woman made no reply; she seemed carried out of herself; and though her bloodless lips moved rapidly, no sound issued from them for some seconds. Each present naturally looked in the direction of her gaze, but they saw nothing to account for the state into which she was thrown.

" This is another of the fits she has become so subject to of late," said Ruth; " it was wrong of her to come, and unwise of us to permit her."

" Hannah!" exclaimed Summerfield, shaking her by the arm— " Hannah !—do you hear me ?—recover yourself." But his words failed of effect, and the irresolution of his voice and altered complexion, fanned the smothered fire of distrust in the mind of Clifton.

" Have you ever consulted Dr. Wolcot on this mental disorder of your wife, Summerfield?" he asked.

" I have not," replied the cottager.

" I am rather surprised at that. He would willingly have given you a gratuitous opinion of her case. But hark !—she speaks."

" In the very dress—the very same we buried him in. And the blood and foam on his lip—but no mark of the blow."

Such were the hollow accents that escaped Mrs. Summerfield, which the manner of utterance gave a double import.

" This is most extraordinary!" said Clifton, starting. " To whom, Summerfield, does she allude?"

" To a mere phantom of her imagination," was the embarrassed reply. " But do not disturb yourself about her. Ruth, my dear, I must bid you good bye here, since it will be impossible for your mother and I to spend the day at Rosedale House, as Mr. Clifton and his sister had kindly planned. I must get Hannah home as well as I can, and call in the doctor to her."

Then in a lower tone, Summerfield adjured his daughter to hurry her husband away as fast as possible; and Ruth, taking Clifton's arm, observed, that her mother was worse when any one except her father was a witness to these attacks.

"He alone knows how to deal with them," she said, "and the best we can do for her is, to leave her to his care. I wish the clergyman and his clerk would not linger, they only increase her disorder by seeming to notice it."

Percy Clifton had meditated profoundly while she spoke.

"There is something in all this which I must better understand before I leave this place," he said. "Mrs. Summerfield, what is it that so much affrights you?—whom do you see?"

"Whom do I see?" she exclaimed, turning her face sharply round,—"Why, don't you recollect your own father?"

"Oh! do not listen to her," said Ruth, pressing his arm with imploring earnestness,—"she knows not what she says—she is not in her right mind."

"That I believe," said Clifton, shaking off with little gentleness the hand of his bride. "But, notwithstanding, there is matter in her madness which I have been dullness itself not to have suspected before. Clerk, close and lock the church door—let none pass in or out. Summerfield, you must explain these mysterious expressions of your wife."

"Who can explain the wanderings of insanity?" said Summerfield.

"I will have no subterfuge!" exclaimed Clifton. "Disguise will not serve you. You know something of my father's death."

"You have no reasonable grounds for such an assertion, squire; and I can't but say, I should have expected the peace of your wife to be too dear to you for you to risk it by attempting, before her bridal is an hour old, to ruin the character of her father."

"Talk not to me of your daughter," said Clifton, his furious passions now all awake, "I ask you of my father."

"I have nothing to say about him," said Summerfield.

"Villain!" thundered Clifton, "I will make you say something about him."

"By what means?" coolly returned Summerfield, who had now fully recovered his self-command.

Clifton answered by rushing on him, and collaring him.

"Vile breaker of clods! Confess!—confess!" he exclaimed. "Confess that your seeming integrity and independence of character have been mere masks to cover guilt the most horrid that thought can conceive! Declare where, and in what manner, my father perished! Confess the monstrous guilt your wife has unconsciously betrayed!"

Summerfield was a man of considerable muscular strength; in a moment, by a strenuous effort, he had shaken himself free of Clifton, and seizing a form on which some poor old women were

accustomed to sit to hear the Sabbath services, he elevated it in a most determined attitude of defiance.

"I have suffered too much from you and your father," he said, "to bear hand of yours on me. Keep back! if you would not have this pavement dyed with your blood. But this is foolish," he said, replacing the form, yet standing firmly on his guard, "my elder years should have taught me better than to be provoked by the hasty suspicions, or the rash actions of an unthinking boy."

Clifton turned with foaming lips to the reverend gentleman who had performed the rite.

"You are a magistrate as well as a clergyman," he said—"to you I commit the safe custody of this man, whom I charge with the murder of my father."

"A dreadful charge!" exclaimed the clergyman, turning a glance of commiseration on the poor young bride, who thus again saw the chalice of happiness dashed from her lips, and stood mute and aghast.

"I expect you to act promptly and efficiently, sir," said Clifton, perceiving him exhibit symptoms of irresolution. "Secure the person of this man and his wife, and send proper persons immediately to examine their cottage. I shall myself oversee the search."

"However unpleasant be my duty, I have no choice but to fulfil it," said the clergyman; and he gave some whispered directions to his clerk, who hastily quitted the church.

"Fifty circumstances now rush to my recollection!" said Clifton, striding to and fro the area before the communion-table, with clenched hands, and a countenance of such intolerable fierceness, that Ruth felt her heart die within her as her timid glance encountered it. "Fifty circumstances," he repeated, stamping his foot, and glaring askance on Summerfield, "all of which confirm me in my suspicions. And I think I have been infatuated—spell-bound —blind as any mole, not to have seen their drift before! Oh! cursed chance, that the discovery should have taken place now instead of a month—a fortnight—or even an hour ago, before I had connected myself with one who doubtless has assisted to disguise the truth from me!"

"Percy Clifton," said Summerfield, in a commanding tone, "if you have the spark of the spirit of a man in you, attempt not to involve my innocent daughter in the suspicion you attach to me. Remember, you are now bound by oath to protect and cherish her under all possible circumstances."

"Villain!" exclaimed Clifton, "do you dare to tell me of what I am bound to do? I suspect you all!—aye, ALL!—father, mo-

ther, and children! And I will unravel the mystery, and then ascertain what part Ruth has acted in it. If I find she has connived to shield you from punishment by concealing any thing which has directly or indirectly affected my father's life—if I find she has played a double game with me, pretended love while she was hiding from my knowledge a matter every way so momentous to me—if I find she has suffered me to make propitiatory advances, and to stoop my dignity to the destroyers of the author of my life—if I discern this, (and my mind misgives me strangely), I swear I will never acknowledge her, but hold her utterly and eternally alienated from my fortune and affections!"

"It is a sinful vow," said the clergyman, "made without due consideration, and I hope hereafter to be recalled."

"Never," said Clifton, "never!"

"I hope it will."

"No—I swear!"

The vicar saw that his young friend had lost the power of rational judgment, being wholly possessed by the violent passions which had been aroused by the sudden suspicion of his father having been murdered by Summerfield, acting upon a haughty spirit, previously but half contented with the part it had stooped to play.

The reverend gentleman then spoke to Summerfield.

"You have borne an irreproachable name hitherto," he said. "and it gives me a pain and a disappointment which I hardly can express, to see you suffering under imputations so awful. You will, of course, remember, that whatever you may be disposed to say, it will be my duty to record; and, perhaps, as to-morrow I must examine you in public, I ought not, in strict duty, to address you as I am now doing. But I have thought well of you, and I would recommend you to speak the truth at once, and explain to Mr. Clifton the mysterious expressions of your wife.'

Here Percy Clifton showed signs of extreme impatience.

"I give you thanks, reverend sir," said Summerfield, "but I don't see why I should be called to explain the ravings of a maniac, though she may be my wife."

"This is certainly evading the matter, and must rather tend to aggravate than to allay the doubts already excited. Here we have a gentleman of fortune mysteriously missed, and no clue whatever found to elucidate the mystery of his fate for fifteen years; then we hear a female, to whom I recollect perfectly well he at the time of his disappearance paid attentions more particular than became a husband, a father, and a gentleman—we hear this female, I say, Mr. Summerfield, conjuring up the semblance of the missing

gentleman with an appearance of agony and terror which none who has witnessed it can forget, imagining she sees blood upon his lip—that he wears the very dress she and some one or more persons buried him in—and remarking that she sees no marks of the blow. These are not ordinary ravings, Mr. Summerfield, but seem to point to a foregone conclusion."

"Oh! speak—speak, father!" Ruth implored. "Explain, I beseech you!"

"To tell the story here would avail me nothing," said Summerfield. "After what has passed, I must go before a public jury, and there—God defend the right!"

The clerk now returning with the parish constable and four assistants, Clifton was about to hurry away to search the cottage, but Summerfield, in the energy of his anxiety for his daughter, which superseded all personal considerations, appealed to him strongly not to desert her, after having inflicted on her so many prior wrongs, and so much sorrow; but Clifton, whose propensity at all times was to act first, and think afterwards, was only the more obstinate and enraged, and having agreed with the clergyman that his carriage should be employed to convey the prisoners to the gaol in the small town of Rosedale, where they were to be lodged until set free, or committed to take their trial at the county castle, he left the church abruptly.

CHAPTER XXVI.

"Why should we faint and fear to live alone,
    Since all alone, so Heaven has willed, we die,
Not even the tenderest heart, and next our own,
    Knows half the reasons why we smile and sigh?

SUMMERFIELD was handcuffed without opposition, while his eye wandered from his daughter to his wife, and from his wife to his daughter, as if his only concern was for them. Perhaps but for the consequences to them it might be doubtful whether he would have wished to recall the discovery that had taken place. The dread of it had long embittered and distracted his existence, and it had given him such an incalculable amount of anxiety to watch, govern,

and conceal, the aberrations of his wife's mind, that he actually felt relieved by the certainty that the mystery must be dissolved and his fate be brought to a final issue. Whatever his doom might be, he resolved to bear it alone, and hence prepared his mind to make, on the following day of his examination, a complete statement of the manner in which the deceased squire had fallen by his hand, and by taking the whole burden of the guilt—if guilt it should be construed—on himself, exonerate his wife.

With this honourable purpose he persuaded himself she could only be subjected to a light and temporary punishment as an accessory, let the sentence on himself be ever so severe ; and he was disinterested enough to find in such a belief the highest earthly satisfaction his case would admit of. Yet, there was enough to make the heart of the husband quail for her sake, since he knew that as her life was more dear to him than his own, so his was to her the most precious of the two ; and when she should become sensible of the jeopardy in which she had placed him, he dared not contemplate what her state of feeling would be.

There was however, a hope—a hope—a sad hope—that the insanity which hitherto had darkened over her mind only in occasional clouds, might now remain stationary, and that the light of reason, which could only serve to reveal the catastrophe she had occasioned, might either permanently or for a considerable time be excluded. But this hope was dashed to the ground in the moment that it arose, for Mrs. Summerfield suddenly quitted the seat on which she had been placed, and passing her eye with wonder from her husband to the constables who had the charge of him, and from them to the clergyman, who was presenting with a countenance of compassion a goblet of water to the pallid bride, she inquired—

" If anything had occurred to interrupt the ceremony ?—and where the squire was ?—and what was the matter with Ruth ?—and why," she added, " why are those irons on your arms, Roger ?"

Each present was thrilled and silent.

"Speak, some one !" she cried, "what has happened ?"

" You had better not ask, Hannah," said Summerfield, in a voice at once affectionate and grave. " Had you submitted to the wishes of myself and your daughter, and not come here this morning, the present trouble would have been spared. But your intentions were good, and we do not blame you. though we may suffer."

"Suffer ! How can you suffer through my having come here this morning ? What have I done amiss ? Speak, Ruth, if your father will not, and tell me what I have done ! It is impossible I can have—" She stopped, and looked keenly on the constables

and her husband—"And yet it may—it must be so. My thoughts are in confusion. I feel as if I were walking on the waves of the sea. You all look ghastly to me, as if I saw you through a horrid mist. Let me remember—the tomb—the spectre—yes, yes, I see it now. But why are you ironed, Roger? Ruth is the squire's wedded wife, and for her sake he will protect us."

No, my dear mother," said Ruth, with as much meekness as grief, "Mr. Clifton has left me—he will not acknowledge me. We are all ruined together."

"Ha!—is it so?" cried the wretched mother, "then the only consolation left me is to die—here!"

She ran, and threw her arms round the neck of Summerfield, who was stirred with an agony that showed itself in the large drops of moisture with which his forehead was bedewed, and in his hoarse breathing.

"I hope, sir," he said to the clergyman, who intimated to him that he must now enter the vehicle which was at the church door, "I hope my wife and I may be allowed to be together in the gaol, at least for the present."

"I will speak to the constable," said the reverend man, whose disposition, in truth, inclined more to the gentle benignity of the Christian, than the inflexible firmness of the dispenser of public justice.

"And my daughter—my poor Ruth," said Summerfield, his eye glistening as he looked on her, "where is she to go?"

"My lady," said the reverend gentleman, in some hesitation, "would willingly receive the squire's young bride at the vicarage —but my magisterial duties might furnish objections. However, as it will be necessary for her to be present to-morrow at the examination, I think until then she may—"

"Excuse me, but if you please," interrupted Ruth, "I will go with my parents to the prison. My mother's state of health needs my attention, and I must not be divided from her."

"So let it be," said Summerfield, "let us all go together. Come, my Ruth! be not down-hearted, I have a clear breast respecting this that I am accused of, that you may depend upon. And your husband must see the injustice of his conduct, sooner or later."

"Too late, perhaps," said Ruth, and with these words she rallied herself to assist the tottering steps of her mother to the chaise, in which the parish constable seated himself by Summerfield.

A harrowing humiliation consequent on this new turn of affairs was the passage to the coach through the graveyard, amid the eager gazers who but an hour before had seen them entering the sacred edifice under such different circumstances.

Perhaps there had not occurred—could not occur—in the life of Summerfield, a minute of more blasting horror. He moved with a rapid step, a downcast eye, and a cheek of burning red, and stumbling on the carriage step, an oath burst from his lips, for the first time in Ruth's recollection.

To render this scene more excruciating, the rustics thought it incumbent on them to groan, and hiss; not that they had any clear knowledge of the charge on which Summerfield and his wife and daughter were to be conveyed to prison, though they knew it was something about the old Squire Clifton's death, but that they were secretly pleased at the humiliation of a family of their own class which had promised to rise above them, and also because they fancied it behoved them to show their sympathy in the squire's grievances, even though they had learnt the nature of them afterwards.

Mrs. Summerfield felt no pain from the gaze or the insults of those by whom she was surrounded; all was indifferent to her after the consciousness of the wreck she had made. In a sort of waking dream she saw the church and village of Highwood receding in the distance, and in half an hour heard the wheels of the vehicle rattling over the flinty pebbles of the town of Rosedale. The people stood at their doors, but if the rumour of the arrest of the Summerfields had reached them they made no noise or stir, until the carriage driving down a hilly street, passed under an embattled gateway covered with grotesque heads and figures, and containing in its upper part a room, or long hall, in which the municipal authorities of the township were wont to hold their meetings. Here there was a crowd collected before a prison of a grim aspect, whose low-grated windows descended to within a foot of the ground, and enabled the curious to mark the immense width of the wall, as exhibited in the side stones of these horrid apertures.

This was a prison of the olden time, and remained in its pristine darkness and filthiness, filled with bad air, and noisome damps.

Summerfield entered the unprepossessing building amid groans and yells, which so affected Ruth, that she had to be supported out of the carriage by the constable. The rude clamours were hushed at the sight of the fainting girl, whose lovely features were hardly less white than her bridal garments; and humanity also prevailed, when Mrs. Summerfield, with a bewildered and death-like aspect, stepped out, apparently unconscious whither she was being led.

The prisoners were taken into a stone room, where there was no fire, and very little light. Ruth shivered with cold, with grief, and with dread. Her father tried to raise her courage and her

hopes'; in the former he succeeded, for Ruth inherited much of his own stoicism, though without the intolerant harshness which in him had blended with it, but hope was dead within her.

"You must not think of me," she said, with a sad smile, "I shall support my burden well enough. Cheer my mother, and let us think what can be done for Sally and Billy."

Summerfield's orders having prohibited the children from leaving home while their sister's marriage was taking place, their plan for seeing it by stealing up one of the aisles was frustrated; but as Ruth now pronounced their names, their voices were heard, and the poor boy and girl, sobbing and affrighted, sprang in, and flew to the bosoms of their parents.

"O mother, mother!" cried Billy, his blue eyes distended and his heart beating, "the squire has come back to the cottage with a lot of strange men, and turned out your boxes, and emptied the cupboards, and broke my ship to pieces that I finished last week with the sails and rigging."

"And they have pulled down half the roof, father!" said Sally, "and ripped up the beds, and were tearing the planks from the chamber floor when we came away."

Summerfield looked at his wife, she did not understand what the children were saying, but spoke to Billy of a school he should go to when his father was in the new situation.

"And then I shall expect you to be a scholar," she said.

Billy looked dubious in her face, and, slinking from her, approached Ruth.

"And how came you to seek us here?" the latter asked.

"One of the strange men told us you were all carried to the gaol, for murdering Squire Clifton's father. But he tells a lie!" said the little fellow, clenching his fist, and almost choking with the excitment of his feelings, "he tells a lie!—and so I said outright to him."

"I only wish Mr. Maynard had been there," said Sally.

"So do I!" echoed Billy, he'd have laid his stick thick over the backs of some of them before they should have touched what they had no business with."

The mention of Maynard brought another anxious cloud over the face of Summerfield.

"Would that good and generous friend believe the story he had to tell?—or must their friendship, which had weathered so many storms, give way at last? Must their vessels, after sailing so long in company, drift apart before this hurricane? It was but too likely. And though I shall feel it sorely," said Summerfield, "I shall be nerved for the shock."

Ruth wished to ask her brother and sister if those who were searching the cottage had been in the shed, but restrained herself, though her suspense was dreadful. Yet the worst she apprehended from an examination of the tenement in the garden was a discovery of the gold watch she had seen hidden there; how much, then, was she shocked when the turnkey informed them that the body of the deceased squire had been found buried beneath the earthen floor of the shed, under a quantity of litter.

"An inquest is to sit to-morrow," said the man, "and your examination will not take place until after the verdict has been given."

Summerfield hardly changed countenance at the tidings, and his wife was unconscious of its import.

"What!" he said to Ruth, whose looks expressed all she thought, "do you now flinch from me? Are you willing to be cheated by appearances, and distrust my word?"

She was silent.

"You, too, think me a murderer!" he said. "Well, a few days, and all shall be told. I only wait my examination. But look to your mother!"

Mrs. Summerfield slipped from her chair, and lay motionless on her face on the floor. She was raised, and the prison doctor being called in, pronounced her in a dying state. The shock she had received in the consciousness of the secret she had unintentionally betrayed, had struck at the root of life.

"Take off those handcuffs!" she murmured, "my daughter is the squire's lady, and he will not allow her father to be so degraded."

They placed her on a temporary bed, hastily made up on two benches tied together. It was evident she thought herself still in the church; and during the melancholy hours that succeeded, while her lamp of life was barely glimmering, she continued by turns to address the spectre of the deceased squire—to inquire what disclosures she had made to place her husband under arrest—and to reiterate, "My daughter is Clifton's wedded wife, he will defend us!"—or words to that effect.

The night wore away in this disconsolate manner. Summerfield sat by his wife in one immovable attitude, rarely so much as turning his head; and keeping his eye fixed on her lethargic countenance. He could not wish her to survive the discoveries which had been made, to endure the horrors of the examination and the trial, and to hear his doom of death.

"No," he said, internally, "she had better die now, insensible to the terrors which stalk before me, and unconscious of the desolate condition of her children."

But though reason spoke thus in him, and though with external calmness he watched her gradual dissolution, his grief was not the less intense. She was passing away who had been the bride of his youth—his twenty years' companion—the affectionate, and as far as reason would serve, safe depositor of all his most secret thoughts—the mother of his children—the sharer of all the pleasures and the cares with which his life from boyhood had been chequered. And he could not forget that it was her faithfulness to her marriage vows that had entailed on her after-days such an overwhelming burden of misery.

"The truest and most affectionate wife that ever man had, she has been to me," he said to Ruth; "and I hope that when she is gone, both her children and the public will do her justice. In her poverty she spurned the overtures of a wealthy villain, and, though beautiful and flattered, clung to her mean cottage home, and to her obscure and despised husband. She merited the highest happiness that earth could give, but it was the mysterious will of God that she should reap nothing but sorrow."

At four o'clock in the morning, the intellects of Mrs. Summerfield collected themselves in one expiring effort. An iron lamp resting on a table near her, that blended its uncertain rays with the faint morning light that found its way through the cobwebbed iron-bars of the windows, showed to her failing sight her family gathered around her. She recognized each with marks of tenderness; and, addressing the doctor who stood beside her—

"Sir," she said, "I wish, while I have time, to unburden my mind concerning Arthur Clifton's death. Though no witnesses can verify what I have to tell, the statement of one who is on the edge of the grave may have some weight with the jury who must decide my husband's doom."

The governor of the prison was summoned, and in his presence, and that of the doctor and the turnkey, Mrs. Summerfield made a startling statement on oath.

THE COTTAGE GIRL.

CLIFTON DEMANDS AN ANSWER FROM RUTH.

"MY husband, Roger Summerfield," said the dying woman, "was the only son of a farmer, who died in debt. Roger was then twenty-two years old. Mr. Arthur Clifton offered him the farm, provided he would make himself responsible for his father's debts. He worked early and late on the farm for two years, when one day Mr. Clifton rode up to a gate, and beckoning him, said, 'Roger, I have something of consequence to say to you. You are thinking of the widow Forester's daughter, for a wife, I hear.'

"'Why, yes, I am. We have been long acquainted, and only wait till I am out of debt, and nearly established here.'

"'You must think of her no more,' said the squire.

"'Why not?" he asked.

"'The squire laughed, and clapped him on the shoulder.

"'No, my good Roger,' he said, 'you must not marry Hannah. I am thinking of her myself. She is pretty, and I shall take her up to town. But you shall have a wife notwithstanding, a fine woman too, only something on the decline—splendid accomplishments, dashing manners. You will be the envy of all the country side; and hark in your ear—what I have lent you shall be cancelled on your wedding-day.

"Roger's blood boiled, but he governed himself, and reminded the gentleman that he had a wife already. Mr. Arthur Clifton only laughed more loudly than before, and said that should be no obstacle.

"Roger then assured the squire he had mistaken his character, and that of the girl he had to deal with.

"'I shall put Hannah on her guard,' he said, 'and depend on it I shall protect her from you, though I lose all I have been striving for.'

"There was a diabolical sneer on Mr. Clifton's face, as he cautioned Roger to consider before he opposed him.

"'I want no consideration,' Roger replied, 'and if I could help it I would never after this exchange a word with such a villain.'

"'Then,' said the squire, 'render up this farm, and see your accounts with me are even to a penny, or, if there is a prison in the county, you shall rot and starve in it.'

"All this Roger told me the same day—and in a month, he was in prison for the money the squire had lent him, with the view as we both afterwards firmly believed, of working him to his will While he lingered in confinement I was daily persecuted by the wretch who had so grievously misled him. Once the squire visited his prisoner, and urged again his abominable proposals, but they were rejected with scorn and rage. The squire left him, vowing revenge, both against him and me. About this time, my mother's death placing me in possession of her little hoard of savings, (she had been a hard-working, thrifty woman,) I was able to release Roger, and we were married on the same day that he was set at liberty. We took the cottage in which my husband and I have lived together since then. At this time it was not the property of Mr. Clifton, but came into his possession afterwards. Roger engaged himself as a day-labourer, and I by lace-weaving brought in enough for clothing, and incidental expenses. For four years we saw little of Mr. Arthur Clifton—for four years we were happy, if ever mortals were. Though poor, we lived comfortably and contentedly. The faith and affection of each had been tried and found perfect. We were grateful to each other, envied no one, and were envied by few. But one day I received an order from Mrs. Clifton for lace for a ball-dress, which, after sitting up two nights to finish, I took to Rosedale House. My work had been approved, and I was returning through the park at dusk, when all at once I saw the squire by my side. That was the beginning of a new system of persecution, to which I was exposed during several weeks. Whenever my husband was absent from my side, the squire was sure to be near. I knew not what to do. A foreboding was in my mind that to tell Roger would be to cause some fatal catastrophe. But this hesitation the villain so far mistook for success, that I durst no longer maintain silence. I told my husband all—his passions, though slow to rise, were ever terrible when aroused, and of this I had forewarned Mr. Arthur Clifton. His brutal laugh I cannot forget. One fatal night—it was the last of his existence in this world—learning by some means, unknown to me, that my husband would be threshing at a distant farm until a late hour, he abruptly entered the cottage, where I sat by the fire, hushing to sleep with a hymn the infant which I was rocking in the cradle beside me. He had been dining with some of his loose companions at the Three Crowns, and was half intoxicated, or feigned to be so. With all the audacity in the world he locked the door, put the key in his pocket, and placed himself on a chair close by my side. I asked him the meaning of such conduct; he replied in the fulsome language of flattery, declaring he could not support existence any longer without me, and that, in short, I was in his power, and must submit to the infamy he designed me. I told him I would rather die, but this, as usual, only provoked his ridicule.

" ' My husband,' he said, ' would not return for several hours—the cottage stood alone, and no outcry of mine could be heard beyond its walls. It could therefore be no sin of mine to yield to necessity. He would settle upon me an ample income, and I should want nothing my heart could desire.'

" ' Yes, Mr. Clifton,' I replied, ' I should want everything if I wanted peace of conscience. What good would your money do me if I knew that my children had to blush for their mother's infamy?—if my husband had to curse the hour when he gave his home and heart to me? Your profligate splendour does not dazzle me in the least—there is nothing in it to desire. My present happiness is perfect, but for one drawback—your disgusting attentions. Leave me then, Mr. Clifton—you could not seduce Hannah Forester, nor can you Hannah Summerfield.'

" ' As you defy me,' he said, ' I will be d—d if you triumph.

You have given me a pretty long chase of it, and now I have you at bay.'

"I eluded his grasp, sprang to the window, and shrieked for help. My husband then rushed in the backway; he knew the desperate character of the squire well enough to be uneasy while I was alone, and had left his work, and hurried home, in consequence of a fellow labourer having seen the squire crossing the 'Barley Close,' near his cottage, and appearing to be going in that direction. At his entrance he rushed on the squire, and struck him with his arm on one side the head. Mr. Clifton fell;—there was a gurgling in his throat—blood and foam on his lips—a rapid movement of the eyelids—and, with a half-breathed curse, he died! So suddenly the deed had been done, that we could not entirely persuade ourselves he had ceased to live, until the warmth had left his body.

"We then consulted what was best to be done. My husband was for attempting no concealment, but my terror was so great, that, unfortunately perhaps, he determined to bury the ghastly remains in the shed, and keep the transaction a secret.

"When he had dug a grave about a foot deep, I assisted to place the body on his shoulder, and it was covered up. We put out the lights immediately after, and went to bed, but our agitation was too great to allow us to rest. The next day my husband did not go to work, but employed himself in covering the floor of the shed with straw and litter, which has not since been removed until the finding of the body. All the cottages in the neighbourhood of the Barley Close, where Mr. Clifton was last met, were visited, and ours was among the rest, and inquiries made concerning him. Being then ill of a nervous fever, I escaped this questioning, or certainly the secret must have been suspected, for I could not have disguised my agitation. My husband was as strong as I was weak. He rightly said to me we were no way answerable for the shocking event that had happened; the squire fell by his own wickedness, the hand of heaven must have guided the fatal blow, or it could not have taken such instant and deadly effect.

"Roger did no more than any other man under such provocation would have done—he struck him, but with no more intention of taking life than at this moment they have who hear me."

"Such being your feelings," said the governor, "I still wonder you did not make a voluntary disclosure of the matter to Mr. Clifton's wife and friends. His reputation for gallantry, and his attentions to you, were sufficiently well known to have furnished a partial corroboration of your story, and the appearance of the

body would have supplied the rest. Now, the state of the corpse does not admit of satisfactory examination, and the length of time you have suffered this secret to lie dormant seems to argue against your account of the manner in which the death was occasioned."

"I am sensible, sir," said Mrs. Summerfield, "that it would have been best not to have concealed what had occurred—my husband at the time told me so—but my fears kept me from being convinced, and he was over-ruled by me. There was no mark of the blow on the body, but by the blood on the lips I fancied it must have caused internal injury, and that our destruction must follow a discovery."

"And you avouch that the death-blow was made with no weapon or instrument whatever?"

"With his arm, or clenched hand, the blow alone was made."

"And it was a single blow—it was not repeated?"

"He struck but once."

"You have said," remarked the doctor, "that some time passed after Mr. Clifton fell before you were persuaded he was really dead. What measures did you take in that interval for his recovery?"

"All such as were within our reach without calling in other persons. We took off his neckcloth, unbuttoned his shirt-collar, tried hartshorn, and many other things. But death has a look of its own which can hardly be counterfeited, and the squire's was that look. His pulse and heart had stopped beating, his jaw had dropped, his eye was glazed, and his skin was of a ghastly yellow."

The doctor walked aside with the governor.

"You knew Mr. Arthur Clifton," he said, "and can tell me what was his habit of body, his mode of living, and his age?"

"His age," replied the governor, "was, I should suppose, about forty—I cannot say exactly. He was a gluttonous epicurean in his table, and the hardest drinker it was ever my lot to encounter, even in those times, when the bottle was apt to be circulated more freely than now. He was bloated and had frequently been cupped by the advice of his physicians."

The doctor meditated.

"Then taking all these circumstances into view, and granting this woman's story to be correct that he was inebriated when his decease took place, I venture at once to pronounce that Mr. Clifton died of apoplexy, or some analogous disorder. There have been instances where a blow on the temple has been instantly fatal to a person of plethoric habit."

"If you are right," replied the governor, "there are few who will not say that he merited his death, and that this family are greatly to be pitied."

"Greatly indeed!" responded the doctor. "Their history is a most remarkable domestic tragedy. The singular coincidence of a mother and a daughter equally famed in their turn for personal beauty, and in their turn inspiring a passion in the squire of the neighbourhood, the one the father, the other the son—the unhappy consequences resulting in each case—the length of time the body of the elder squire lay concealed—the individual by whom it was found, his own son, and that son the same morning married to the daughter of the woman for whom the guilty passion was entertained that had shortened his father's days;—all this gives an uncommon interest to the present melancholy scene."

The governor retired, the doctor returned to Mrs. Summerfield, felt her hand, counted her pulse, which was failing fast, and giving some whispered directions to a female of the prison establishment, who now came to assist the sufferers, also departed.

Mrs. Summerfield did not survive the declaration we have given above an hour. As she could swallow none of the medicaments presented to her, and begged to be left alone with her family, it was in their prescence alone that she expired.

A deep and awful silence reigned around, only broken by the hard breathing of the dying woman, the sobs of her children, and the melancholy tones of the town church-clock chiming the third hour of the morning. She signed to Summerfield to pray for her, and standing erect, in a sonorous voice, he commended to Him who gives and takes away, the departing spirit, imploring that he might be reunited to her in the land where partings are unknown, and that their dear children might find an everlasting friend in the Father of the fatherless.

He was unable to finish his petition. His voice faltered, ceased; and after standing for a moment wrestling with his agony he turned away and gave himself up to a paroxysm of the wildest grief. Ruth passed round the bed, and pressed his hand to her heart.

"Dear—dear father!" was all she could articulate, but the intensity of her sympathy, the force of her own grief, were sufficiently apparent in her tone and in her look.

Summerfield pressed her to his breast—strongly, but in silence. He then relinquished her, stooped over his wife, who now lay in a stupor, breathing only at long intevals, kissed her attenuated features, and again relapsed into uncontrolable agony. Mrs. Summerfield revived.

"I have been a long trouble to you, Roger," she said.

"Oh peace, peace, my love!" he exclaimed, "your faithfulness and affection have outweighed all."

"I have fretted you with my repining—my wretched temper has made your cares double what else they would have been."

"Think not of it. It was your disordered mind, and not your will."

"No, I cannot satisfy myself so. I need mercy, and not vindication. Oh! they have much to repent of who yield to a gloomy and irritable temper."

She turned her eye on her eldest daughter.

"My Ruth," she said, "my unhappy Ruth!"

The accents were expressive enough. Ruth shivered and sighed. But she begged her mother not to feel anything on her account. She hoped she should have patience as regarded herself, it was only for her parents she grieved.

"You acquit us of premeditated crime, I hope?" said Mrs. Summerfield.

"I do," Ruth emphatically replied.

"And you will endeavour to supply my place to your brother and sister?"

"Nothing I can do for them shall be wanting—they are all I have to live for."

"Farewell then!—I am going," said Mrs. Summerfield. "If the dead can benefit the living I will be near you, Roger, in the sore warfare you have to go through. The Lord in His mercy send you an honourable acquittal!"

She ceased, and spoke no more!

CHAPTER XXVII.

"No ill report shall move my constant heart
From thee, my wronged and ancient friend to part;
Thy planet still, though doomed to swift decline,
Shall to the last companioned be by mine,
My aid, my trust, as ever still shall be,
Thine and thy children's, freely, cordially."—ANON.

It was on the second day after these events Maynard returned to Rosedale, expecting to see his old friends rejoicing in the happiness of their daughter, and themselves fairly·launched on the tide of prosperity. As his way to the mill lay past the cottage, he made up.his mind after some hesitation to call, and learn how the wedding had gone off. The day was lowering, and the heaviness of his spirits corresponded with the gloom of the atmosphere. Still there was in the miller's sadness a secret satisfaction arising from a peaceful conscience, a disinterested disposition, and a cheerful temper.

"There is not an individual breathes who wishes Ruth joy of her marriage more sincerely than I!" he said, as he proceeded slowly down the road near the cottage. "But what now?—why is that crowd gathered in the lane? I hope the wedding is over, I was told so, or I would not have come here this day for fifty pounds."

He stopped in considerable emotion, but there was something in the gestures of the throng which did not harmonise with the idea of a bridal. He approached nearer, and perceived that constables were endeavouring to keep back the people who were eagerly pressing forward, in which attempt they were far from successful.

Astonishment filled his mind, and with accelerated pace he reached the scene of tumult.

"Here's the miller come back," cried one.

"And knows nothing of what has happened," said another

"Why what is it?" demanded Maynard, with irritation. "What has happened beside the wedding that was expected when I left the dale?"

"The wedding! There never was such a wedding since Rose-

dale stood where it does! The ghost of old Squire Clifton appeared in the church and forbade the ceremony, and Hannah Summerfield fell on her knees and confessed to young Percy that she and her husband had murdered his father."

" This is some trumpery invention," said Maynard, impatiently.

" 'Tis a true one, however. The young squire parted from the bride in the church with high words, and she is now in prison with her father and the children."

" And what is more," interposed another, eager like all vulgar persons to communicate ill tidings, " the inquest have brought in a verdict of wilful murder against Roger and Hannah Summerfield, and Roger has been examined, and is to take his trial at the next county assizes."

" And his wife," said the previous speaker, " will be buried to-morrow night in the ground adjoining the goal."

" Buried !" echoed Maynard, aghast—" BURIED ! Is Hannah Summerfield dead ?"

And as clamorous affirmatives and explanations thickened around him, he pressed to the cottage through the throng, which gave way that he might pass. The dwelling was in the possession of the town authorities, from whom, with various excited feelings, he received a correct account of the marvellous discovery that had transpired at the bridal, and the exculpatory statement made in her dying hour by the cottagers wife. He beheld the cavity whence the half-dcoemposed remains of the missing squire had been a few hours before removed, for interment in the family vault. He was shown the places in the thatch where the cottagers had concealed the gold watch, and other property, that had been on the person of the deceased.

He then hastened immediately to the gaol, and obtained an interview with Summerfield. The latter was seated at a small table, perusiug a Bible, but at the entrance of Maynard, he arose, and stood silent, as if desirous before speaking, to ascertain the sentiments of his friend. Maynard waited until the gaoler had retired to the outside of the door, and then sinking on a chair, he spread his hand over his eyes, and shook with a convulsive tremor.

' You did not expect to see me here, Henry ?" said the prisoner, at length breaking silence.

Maynard made no reply, and Summerfield again seating himself, a silence of two minutes ensued. It was broken again by the latter.

" You will not wonder that I am anxious to know if I have still a friend in Henry Maynard ?"

" To the last gasp," said the miller.

"I am not left wholly comfortless then," said the prisoner.
Another pause ensued.

"You have heard all?" Summerfield asked.

"All," rejoined Maynard.

"And you believe Hannah's story of the event which has wrought so fatally in my family?"

"As I believe the gospels. And so must every one who knew old Clifton."

"But have you no fear that my affectionate wife misstated the catastrophe to screen me from the extreme punishment of the law?"

"No, not even to save you would she have taken a falsehood on her lips. Truth has been the glory of her life, and was not likely to be forfeited in death."

"I thank you from my soul!—a thousand thousand, times I thank you!" exclaimed Summerfield, walking to him, and shaking him by the hand. "Next to the acquital of my own conscience is the support of my friends. With these united I shall meet my trial with fortitude and hope. I am guiltless, excepting of the concealment of the body. And if the day goes against me, I shall meet my fate as becomes a man."

"No judge in his senses would convict you of the capital offence," said Maynard. "If you had striken down the wretch with the first weapon you could have laid hold upon, it would have been but justifiable homicide."

"I don't quite despair—nor dare I hope," said Summerfield.

"Who is going to plead for you?" Maynard asked.

Summerfield replied "Whomsoever the court pleased. He was indifferent; his case required not the gloss of oratory, and he would be better pleased to have it stand on its own undefended merits."

"Leave all that to me," said his friend. "I will engage counsel for you, the best I can find, and pay them in proportion to their zeal. And now, your children, how are they disposed of?"

"For the present in this building, where they are kindly treated by the governor. But with whom they are to be lodged when they leave it, is to me unknown. My Ruth is abandoned by her husband, on the unfounded notion that she has been privy to my secret. But I was always too fearful of involving her in my danger; and though her mother's singular manners and expressions at times excited her wonder, she was always too dutiful to press for a confidence she saw I was unwilling to give."

Maynard wished to see Ruth, and a message from him to the

governor through the turnkey procured her re-admission to the cell, where she had passed most of the previous day with her unfortunate father. She entered in the same dress in which she had been married, though it was now soiled, and stripped of its ornaments; and her hair, instead of being neatly braided and curled as formerly, drooped loosely in tangled yet rich masses on her neck behind, and was drawn plainly and irregularly back from her fair forehead, leaving every feature unshadowed in the repose of settled melancholy.

Maynard could not look upon her without tears. She was altered, oh! how much, since he first cherished the vain hope of creating an interest in her affections; but she was still most beautiful! perhaps more so than in her happier days, for the uncommon sorrows she had had to sustain had touched her with an almost ethereal grace, soft, sweet, and sad. Patience was in all her lineaments, in all her words and gestures, but it was the patience of despair, a flower growing on a sepulchre. In three days she had seen all her bright expectations extinguished—she had been renounced by her husband in the very hour of marriage, and abandoned to anguish. But she bore these distresses with a gentle fortitude that won the admiration of all who witnesssed it, accompanied as it was by many little touching traits of the fineness of her sensibility, while the depth of her love for Clifton was not doubted by any. She seemed to forget herself in her concern for the awful situation of her father, and the forlorn condition of the two young children left homeless and motherless. Even her grief for her mother's death was a subordinate feeling. All her thoughts were how to comfort and to serve those who had been bequeathed to her tenderness. In her conferences with her father she seemed no longer young; all that could bear on his cause, either favourably or unfavourably, she discussed with a precision of thought, a force of intellect, and affectionate zeal, that almost made Summerfield doubt whether this keen-minded, strong-hearted woman, could be the same daughter who two years before sported in his cottage a simple, uneducated, unthinking girl. Her very language had since her unfortunate Marriage Day, become elevated both in matter and in manner, leaving on the hearers impressions not easily effaced of respect and compassion.

Of all who perceived those effects of accumulated trouble on Ruth, none, we may be sure could be more deeply affected by them, than her old admirer, the miller, whom she had not met since the period when the machinations of Percy Clifton prevented their union, and betrayed her, though wholly innocent, to misery and shame. During the twelve months that had elapsed since then, she had undergone griefs, whose minute history would have filled volumes; griefs, which, if spread over the longest life, must have entitled her to complain, that she had received more than the ordinary allotment of acid in the cup of existence, how then was she to reflect on the bitterness which had been compressed into that one year!

Ruth had prepared herself to meet the miller with calmness, but as soon as she found herself in his presence, such a crowd of dismal recollections assailed her, that as she extended her hand to him, and inquired after his health, the tears gushed in torrents from her eyes. Maynard scarcely touched, and in a moment resigned, her hand; and respectfully addressing her by the name of Mrs. Clifton, stammered something of the pain he felt for Mrs. Summerfield's death, and the circumstances in which he found his friend Roger.

Ruth made an effort to collect herself.

"We know not," she said, "whether to hope or to dread. And my father," she added, "has suffered something on your account, fearing his enemies might have persuaded you to think with them."

"Not so," rejoined Maynard, "I have met with no one who has made an attempt to prejudice me; if I had they would have failed. What I have heard has quite satisfied me, though you may believe I was dreadfully shocked at first."

"No doubt you were," said Ruth, shuddering.

"But as I said, I am quite satisfied of Roger's innocence," resumed Maynard, warmly. "He has been infamously used."

"He has!" exclaimed Ruth, emphatically; "but reflections on the past are only useful so far as they serve the purposes of the future. A trial is decided upon, and we must meet it full armed. I could wish some good lawyer to undertake the defence."

"I have been speaking of the same thing," said Maynard, "and have promised to take that matter on my own shoulders. And while it is going on, and until Mr. Clifton bethinks himself in respect of his treatment of you, I hope you will not take it amiss if I offer my mill as a home for you, and your brother and sister. It is but a humble place for Mr. Clifton's lady, and he ought to be ashamed of himself that you are in a predicament to need such a refuge. But while things are as they are, I hope for old acquaintance sake you will not refuse to make the best of it. I wish you to look on me as an elder brother, or, as a father, Ruth, and it it is in such a light that I make this offer. Mr. Clifton cannot object, since he has provided you with no better place. Besides, he knows me well enough, and will be sure I could not look on Mrs. Clifton with any eyes but those of pure respect."

"Henry," said Summerfield, "one who is more jealous for the good of Ruth than Mr. Clifton—I mean her father—will be surety for your motives, and he accepts your kindness. My children shall go to the mill."

Maynard seemed as pleased as if their doing so was not to benefit themselves but him; and, in truth, one who finds his own good in that of others, must of course be benefitted by each kindly action of which he is the author.

Ruth remarked that ere the week closed, her father would be removed to the county castle, which was ten miles distant from Rosedale, and that she should wish to be near him.

"And that you shall be," said Maynard. "A customer of mine, a decent widow woman, well known to your father, keeps a tobacco-shop not a stone's cast from the castle, and you shall be lodged with her. But now I will run home and see all ready for you. I left my trusty man, Dick Wyatt, and his wife, in possession, while I was absent. I hope nothing is amiss; but your troubles have made me nervous, I think, and I dread to cross my threshold, for fear I should see the machinery broken, or hear that I have lost my best customers, or that some of my debtors are bankrupt, or that my furniture is burnt, or some other misfortune happened."

None of these apprehensions were realized. The miller found affairs as well as he could expect, considering that when a master is absent from his business it has a propensity to retrogade. After a hasty review of what had been done in his absence, he called the woman he had left in his premises into the sitting-room.

"Mrs. Clifton, and her brother and sister, will be lodged here until their father is taken to the castle. I wish them to be entertained as well as my place will admit of. My room is the best of the two chambers, let it be made as neat as possible for the use of the bride and her sister; you and Wyatt can still occupy the other, and Billy sleep with the lad in the loft."

"And how will you manage, Mr. Maynard?"

"I have provided for myself at the Three Crowns. Now look about you, and if anything be wanting that you can get quickly to make things look better I will give you the money. Don't forget the carpets—they have never yet been down. I bought them," he subjoined to himself, with a suppressed sigh, "for a very different occasion. But what must be, must be."

When he had seen all in the precise order he wished—and he was much of a formalist, like most old bachelors—he ordered tea to be made ready, and a good fire to be kept burning in the sitting-room grate, and then hastened to bring his sorrow-stricken young

guests to his hospitable hearth. He took with him a cloak he had been at the pains to borrow to shield Ruth from the cold evening air, not knowing how she might be provided.

This little mark of consideration particularly affected her, coming from one whom it had been her misfortune to disappoint so bitterly, while he, who ought to have been the guardian of her health, cared not how, or where, she was accommodated. Sally had her pelisse, Maynard tied a worsted comforter round Billy's neck, and thus the three left the gaol with their kind friend just as it grew dark enough for them to be unnoticed. The lively and sometimes pert repartees of a quick natural wit in which Ruth's young sister had formerly indulged, were now repressed by the remembrance of the afflicting scenes of the last three days, and the child was sunk in dejection, which stupefied all her faculties. The boy was excited, talked much and vehemently of his mother's death, and the search of the cottage, which two scenes were indelibly engraved on his memory.

"I wish you had seen Ruth's bullfinch," he said to Maynard, "it looked as frightened as me and Sally. I had let it out of the cage just before, and it flew all about so that I could not catch it again, and it is lost now."

A gate admitted them into a wide irregular field beyond the town, and half a mile in advance appeared the mill, rendered conspicuous above all the surrounding country by the rising ground on which it stood, and its own picturesque elevation. The body of the building, with its massive round walls, and narrow windows, might have reminded those who now behold it of the strong towers of the border barons of former ages, had they not been ignorant that there had ever existed such barons or such towers. The stream which surrounded the mill like a moat would have favoured the comparison. But without the aid of fancy Maynard's mill, and the scenery around it, were sufficiently interesting. It was seen in a pale atmosphere, although in the west, opposite the traces of the sun's decline, were visible in a sea of blood. Here and there some object caught the crimson reflection, which grew less and less vivid, until all was pervaded by the mild genius of twilight, and then darkness succeeded.

Midway in the field Ruth stopped short; she heard issuing from a hedge near them the voice of the stray bullfinch which had been the favourite plaything of her happy hours. The boy also recognised its sweet tones, and ran to try to capture it, but the bird eluded him, flew past its former fond mistress, whose familiar call it disregarded, and was lost in a neighbouring thicket.

"Whom we love most forsake us, or are taken from us," said Ruth, mournfully. "It is unwise to place our affections on the changeful creatures of earth."

"Not wholly so, surely," Maynard rejoined.

"Perhaps not wholly; and yet sooner or later every affection must bring us sorrow, for either those we love must be taken from us, or we must be taken from them."

"As to that," said Maynard, "it is my opinion that we should not look too curiously into the future. To be miserable to-day because what we value may be taken from us to-morrow, is rank folly, and impiety too. When the stroke falls we should bear it patiently, and make the most of every blessing that remains."

"You speak justly, Mr. Maynard," said Ruth, in a tremulous tone.

"You see, Ruth," he resumed, "we should be careful what notions we form, while smarting under calamity; they are as likely to be too gloomy as those of prosperity are to be too bright."

"You are right," said Ruth, again, but the melancholy sigh she breathed with the words seemed to contradict them.

They were now following the banks of the mill-stream which conducted them past a beautiful grove of alders, in which Ruth had often held interviews with Percy Clifton, and where the same moon now rising above the spot had heard his professions of eternal love, professions how grossly violated since.

"Oh! Clifton," she internally ejaculated, "perjured! doubly perjured! False and cruel!—treacherous and base! Oh! retribution must be hanging over thy head, if in this life the wicked meet punishment. If not—dread the next!"

As these bitter thoughts arose in her mind, voices were heard, and two men emerged from the grove. The foremost had the mien and dress of a gentleman, and was in deep mourning, while the other, though respectably attired, and also in black, had that in his appearance which denoted a lacquey, though perhaps a favoured one.

"Sacre! my thoughts are my own, sir; and begging your pardon, my own they shall remain, for if I should speak my mind of her you would not thank me."

Ruth required not to hear these words of Jean Andre, which were audibly spoken, to recognise him and his master. She stood still, and involuntarily withdrew her hand from the arm of Maynard. Clifton was passing without perceiving who they were near him in the gloom, when Andre, in a tone which the devil surely must have prompted, exclaimed—"My young mistress!— and with the miller!"

Clifton halted as if electrified. The uneasiness resulting from secret misgivings as to the justice of his conduct to Ruth, made him unconsciously eager to seize at the first additional excuse which might present itself for his unreasonable passion. Had there been no malignant prompter at his ear, he would have disdained the meanness of connecting a thought of jealousy with a man so far above all moral taint as he knew Maynard to be. But he was suddenly heated by the infernal suggestion of Andre, who hated the miller on account of a chastisement which the latter had most deservedly inflicted on him, as a reward for the equivoque by which he had made it believed in Rosedale that Ruth had been a willing victim to his master.

"How now, madam!" exclaimed Clifton, addressing Ruth, with a sarcastic fierceness that sent the blood curdling to her heart. "Whither are you going? I thought you the dutiful companion of your worthy father, the solace of his hours of solitude in his prison cell; but I find you are not quite so much of a martyr to filial duty as you have been thought."

"Mr. Clifton," said Maynard, indignantly, "you make the blood boil in my veins. What has Ruth done to be so treated by you? A Turk could not be guilty of more execrable tyranny. I can hardly express myself—hardly speak—so much am I astonished! After all the wrongs she has experienced at your hands—without a fault that can be reasonably laid to her charge!"

"Permit me to ask, madam," said Clifton, abruptly, "whither you were going?"

"I will answer that," said Maynard. "As you had deserted her, I—"

"Excuse me, Maynard," interrupted Clifton, "I demand an answer from Ruth. Unfortunately she bears my name, and my honour is concerned in what she does. I ask you once more, madam, whither you were going when I so abruptly met you?"

"To Mr. Maynard's mill," replied Ruth, distinctly.

"Indeed," exclaimed Clifton, and the word fell with withering emphasis on her ear. "You were considerate!—I thank you. A delicate step. And how long was it your intention to remain in Mr. Maynard's mill?"

"Until you removed her to a more suitable place," said Maynard, "or until—"

"Sir," said Clifton, waving his hand impatiently, "I am not presuming to question you—if my wife chooses to throw herself into your arms you are not to be blamed. Very good, madam, you intended to recompense me for the crimes of your father by residing under the protection of your former lover. Now, please to listen to what I have to say to you."

"HOW NOW, MADAME!" EXCLAIMED CLIFTON, ADDRESSING RUTH.

HE TURNED ON HIS HEEL, AND RUTH FELL, INSENSIBLE.

"I AM under the protection of my father's friend, of my friend," said Ruth, with spirit.

"Do you dare to tell me so?" exclaimed Clifton, transported with passion.

"And why should she not dare?" asked Maynard. "You cannot be foul-minded enough to doubt my motives?"

"I do not doubt your motives," said Clifton, with bitter irony. "But I will not baulk your plans. Proceed—the path is clear. There stands the mill, and the fair woman of whom you are enamoured is nothing loth. Proceed, I say."

"Are you a man or a monster!" exclaimed Maynard. "I despise your suspicions, and none but a profligate could have conceived them."

"Why are you angry?" said Clifton, in the same biting tones of mockery in which he had last spoken. "I have told you that I will not prevent your plans—that you may proceed with your prize. I give my wife to you—she is yours. Why stand you hesitating?"

"For pity, if not for shame, consider what you are saying."

"I say my wife is yours."

"I wish to God she were!" exclaimed Maynard, with a vehement outburst of feeling. "And so she would have been but for your damned villany, and that of the French jackanapes who now stands mouthing behind there. Master and man deserved to go before judge and jury for that job, much more than my friend Roger deserves to go before them."

Clifton coolly returned—

"I have no more to say—there lies your path."

He was turning away, when Ruth, with unutterable agony, pronounced his name.

"Your pleasure, madam?" he asked, with freezing sternness.

"Mr. Clifton!—Percy!" she implored, "do not leave me in this manner! I have intended nothing—done nothing—which merits your anger. Mr. Maynard has inconvenienced himself to give my brother and sister, and myself, a shelter. He is generous, kind, and good."

"Very!" exclaimed Clifton, "especially to the beautiful Ruth. Who doubts Mr. Maynard's goodness?—Not I. Even his thousand pounds that are in the Rosedale Bank would not be spared, I daresay, if they could minister to her pleasure, or assist the murderer, her father, to escape the due punishment of his crimes. But there lies your path!"

He turned on his heel, and, as he walked rapidly away, Ruth fell insensible to the earth, whence she was lifted by Maynard, and borne to the mill.

CHAPTER XXVIII.

This is man's vengeance! hear it not ye stars!
And thou, pale moon! turn paler at the sound;
Man is to man the sorest, surest ill.
A previous blast foretells the rising storm;
O'erwhelming turrets threaten ere they fall;
Volcanoes bellow ere they disembogue;
Earth trembles ere her yawning jaws devour;
And smoke betrays the wide consuming fire;
Ruin from man is most concealed when near,
And sends the dreadful tidings in the blow.

YOUNG.

When Clifton had walked a hundred yards, he turned to his valet.

"Andre," he said, "leave me. And, do you mark, when you return to the house, bring me all the information you can."

Andre did not ask what information it was his master desired, he understood that, and, turning back, dogged the steps of the miller, and those under his care.

Clifton crossed a stile into the narrow road which led to his park, and with rapid strides approached the house, whence issued the mingled tones of his sister's voice and guitar. He paused under the window at which she was seated, and distinguished a few mournful stanzas:—

All things fair how fast they fleet!
The rose soon ceases to be sweet;
And o'er its dry and withered leaves
The chilling blast of autumn grieves.

The brightest day must soon decline;
The loveliest form its charms resign:
The longest life must have an end;
The proudest heart to fate must bend.

Time swiftly speeds, and bears away
All that we love to dark decay;
And ere our tears of grief are dry,
Their fount is shivered—and we die!

He found her sitting without light, except what was afforded by the last lingering beams of evening.

"I have been listening here to the rustling of the ivy," she said, "and thinking of him who was this morning laid in the vault of our ancestors, until I was so oppressed with melancholy that there was no relief for me but to vent myself in song."

"You are fortunate that you can find relief in anything," said her brother—"more fortunate than I."

"Will you allow me to tell you the cause of that difference?"

"Certainly."

"You are troubled by prejudice, pride, and passion, and these I have discovered are deadly foes to tranquillity. They will neither let us be innocently happy, nor patiently sorrowful."

"How am I prejudiced?" demanded Clifton quickly.

"You will be irritated if I tell you. I cannot see your face in this darkness, but your voice informs me that you are already inflamed in temper, and before we talk more together you had better take time to cool."

"In what respect am I prejudiced?"

"If you will be yourself, and sit down by me, and listen without these starts of violence, I will tell you."

"I am in no mood for fooling, Amy!" exclaimed Percy, fiercely. "I cannot forget, if you can, that the murdered remains of my father have been but a few hours entombed, and that it is my cursed hap to be the husband of his murderer's child! Plagues and death! when I think of the humiliation—I may say the infamy— of the matrimonial connection I have formed, I could tear the hair from my head with rage! It will hang round my neck like a millstone—impede all my plans for political success—disgrace and sink me!"

"Percy," said his sister, laying aside her instrument, and approaching him with affection, "you are distressing yourself by exaggeration, believe me, you are. I am equally interested with you in the fearful discovery that has been made; and at first I was inclined to share in your resentment against Ruth, on the supposition that she must have known or suspected the secret which her parents had successfully guarded from all others. I have not advocated her cause with you, I have not blamed you, for abandoning her to contumely, but——"

"The pith of your argument, what is it?" demanded Clifton, with extreme impatience. "I cannot listen to wordy speeches to-night. I am not well."

"It is just upon the hour of dinner," said Amy looking to her watch, "we will talk no more until that meal is over."

" Nor then, unless I can hear something more agreeable from you than false imputations. How am I prejudiced ? Proud I may be, and for aught I know passionate too. But I wish to know in what I have exhibited prejudice ?"

" I am on tender ground here," said Amy, " and it may seem extraordinary that I should endeavour to lessen the guilt of a man charged with the murder of my father, or take the part of one who is supposed to be an accessory though, of course, after the fact. I will, however, be true to my own convictions, even though they should clash with yours. The result of the examination with respect to Summerfield has not pleased me—nor am I easy when I reflect on the painful—most painful—situation in which Ruth is left. Suppose the marriage ever so disgraceful to you, it has taken place."

" Wondrous information ! " exclaimed Percy, sarcastically, " Think you I do not know it."

" You do not act as if you did. Look here." Lights being brought in, Amy took a Prayer Book from a shelf, and opened it at the Marriage-service, pointed to the words—" for better, for worse."

Clifton gnawed his lip as his eye rested on them.

" For worse indeed ! " he muttered ; and then thrusting the book aside, leant his arm on the back of a chair in unquiet meditation. Suddenly starting from this, he asked on what grounds his sister presumed to question the decision of the magistrates by whom Summerfield had been examined.

" On several," she replied; " the declaration of his dying wife—"

" Which was invented to save her husband," interrupted Clifton. " But go on."

" On the testimony of the doctors, that no appearances of a violent death could be discovered on the body of our unfortunate father—"

" Because decomposition had proceeded so far that they were unable to make a complete investigation. But proceed. Remember, however, before you go farther, that the medical testimony was merely negative—they could not affirm dissolution had taken place by natural means."

" Then, thirdly," said Amy, " the property found in the thatch, exactly amounting to what we have always heard our father had about him when he disappeared, incontestibly proves the honesty of Summerfield, since none knew better than we how much he has suffered from poverty, while a costly watch and bank notes have lain untouched within the reach of his hand."

" It may prove his honesty—or it may not—for there might

have been risk in availing himself of the property. In either case it is no proof that he did not destroy life wilfully and designedly in jealous revenge."

"Even then, considering the provocation—"

"Regarding which, we have no information to be relied on, and that the deed was not premeditated—"

"It might have been so, though there is no evidence."

"And remembering how my father's character verifies Mrs. Summerfield's declaration, I feel inclined to wish, were it but for Ruth's sake, the cottager had been committed to take his trial for something short of wilful murder."

"A kindly wish, but one hardly to be expected from my father's daughter," said Percy in great displeasure.

"There now, I see you are angry with me—but I cannot help it. I speak what I feel, and what I believe."

"I beg, however, that you will reserve your sentiments on this subject, for privacy," said Percy.

"Certainly I shall: but I have not done. I must recur again to Ruth—to your wife—"

"To my plague!"

He spoke with a vehemence that at once told his sister something had occurred, of which she was yet ignorant.

"Have you seen Ruth since you went out?" she asked.

"I have—and where do you suppose I met her?"

"You yourself, told me she was in the gaol with her father—you cannot have been there?"

"No, but I was on my way thither, like a fool, intending to send Andre in with a note I had written, to procure an interview with her."

"I rejoice to hear it!"

"When I met her with Maynard!—her old lover!" going to take up her residence in his mill! Would you credit it? Would you think her capable of so far forgetting the relationship between us? Maynard loves her now as much as ever he did; he had even the insolence to confess as much to my face, and that he wished she were his wife." At that instant Andre made his appearance.

"Well?" said his master, "speak out; what have you learnt?"

"My mistress has gone with Mr. Maynard to the mill."

"She has!" ejaculated Clifton, his face glowing with colour, and then turning pale.

"Yes, sir, I was close to them, though they did not see me. The miller was uncommonly kind to her, and she went with all the readiness in the world."

"She did!" exclaimed Clifton, crossing the room with clenched hands, in violent agitation. "After what had passed between us, she could go! I was not prepared for this."

"You may retire, Andre," said Miss Clifton, perceiving that her brother grew more and more excited.

"No, let him stay," said Percy, "I will write to her; Andre shall take the note immediately, and I will tell her—" •

"To come here," said Amy. "This is Ruth's proper home. And I entreat you, my dearest brother, for the sake of all your future life, send for her, and let her be received with kindness and consideration."

"Clifton gazed on his sister a moment, with a countenance in which hesitation blended with rage.

"Here!—come here!" he repeated. "No, not while I call these walls mine shall she come here."

'She must, Percy, and immediately too!"

"She shall not!"

"She shall, or I depart. Your wife has more right to this place than your sister. It is no matter how poor she has been, or what her relations are. You have, before the altar of our holy church, endowed her with all your worldly goods; she shall, therefore, either immediately enter into possession of her own, or this very night—this very hour—I leave your house."

Clifton abruptly left the room. In a few moments he returned with an open note in his hand, which he handed to Amy to read.

It was couched in a style she had not expected; addressed Ruth as "his beloved wife—beloved, notwithstanding all that had passed—adjured her to hasten immediately to Rosedale-house, where, if he had been harsh or unjust, he would make every acknowledgment," and added an invitation to Maynard to sup with him.

Amy threw an eloquent look of rejoicing on her brother, and the note was sealed and despatched, with directions to Andre to wait for an answer.

"I can taste nothing till they arrive," said Percy, "therefore, if agreeable to you, postpone the covering of the table; and perhaps you had better make some addition to what is provided."

Amy gave the necessary orders, and set about such other preparations as occurred to her, for the reception of her sister-in-law. These occupied the time of Andre's absence, during which she perceived that Percy was expecting his return with eagerness. As he stayed long, the brother and sister had little doubt that he would return accompanied by Ruth and Maynard, and therefore,

when at length his voice was heard in the entrance-hall, hastened to meet them.

Perceiving Andre alone however, the countenance of Clifton fell.

"Whom did you see?" he asked.

"The miller, sir," replied Andre.

"And did you wait as I bade you for a reply?"

"I did—on the steps outside the mill, for Mr. Maynard had not the civility to ask me inside."

"Why, I believe he is not very partial to you, Jean, and I daresay you are not at a loss to know the reason of that."

"No, faith! sir," replied Andre, with a shrug and grimace. "He gives me credit for helping to deprive him of the beautiful wife he coveted. But I only obeyed my master."

"No more of that," said Clifton angrily. "Deliver the message you have brought."

"I have none to deliver sir."

"How!—no message!"

"No, sir. When Mr. Maynard thought I had cooled myself sufficiently on the steps, he gave me to understand that neither he nor Mrs. Clifton had any answer to send."

"And this was all?"

"Yes, sir."

"There can be no doubt they will be here directly," interposed Amy. "What say to our meeting them?"

"No," said Percy, after a moment of angry thought—"no, that will be too much concession. By the degree of haste which Ruth makes to join me I shall prove the extent of her wishes for a reconciliation. By the readiness of Maynard to replace her in her husband's protection, I shall judge how far my jealousy was unjust. Look out for their approach, Andre, and give us notice the moment you see them. To-morrow," he said to his sister, as they re-entered the dining-room, "if she does not come, I shall start for London, and thence I shall not return in haste."

An hour of suspense passed, and Clifton seemed suffering too intensely for the display of passion. Frequently he arose and walked into the open air, then again returning, paced the room from side to side. In this manner eleven o'clock arrived.

"How self-deceived was I!" Clifton bitterly exclaimed. "I fondly imagined she would be overjoyed when she read my note —that she would fly to me fraught with joy and affection."

"It might have been better if you had gone yourself to the mill instead of sending Andre," observed his sister.

"It might have been better if I had not sent at all," Clifton sharply replied.

"I cannot think so," she returned.

"You do not think then that I have been mortified enough? You defend the present conduct of Ruth towards me?"

"No indeed, I neither defend, nor can I understand it; I should not have supposed her of a disposition to resent wrong by wrong, much less to turn a deaf ear to overtures of kindness from the husband she loves. I say there is something I cannot understand. Can Andre have delivered the note?"

"What a question! How would he dare do otherwise?"

"Few would dare, certainly; but if there lives a man who would dare any thing on my conscience, that man is Jean Andre. I wonder you retain him."

"I wonder myself; but the fellow has good parts notwithstanding his faculty for lying, and has a sort of attachment for me, and studies all my humours, and that is no slight recommendation. There is nothing clownish about him! he has tact, and is amusing in his way. Then though he has a knack at falsehood, it is not with me he would venture to exercise it—he has too much judgment. And I do not think where it is played off there is malice in it, but it springs out of a spirit on the qui vive for fun and mischief."

"You ought to know him best," said Amy dubiously; "but when to-night he described the reception the miller had given him, his tone seemed the very quintessence of malice."

"You are wronging him; but we will question him again," said Percy; "not that I for a moment doubt his delivery of the note, but to satisfy you."

Andre repeated his former answers without any seeming prevarication, and Amy at once abandoning her doubts, acknowledged to her brother that Ruth had now given him real cause of complaint.

"But be not rash," she added; "by no means leave Rosedale until after another interview with her. She has suffered much from you, and you ought not to be nice in measuring the advances you make. Go down to the mill."

"That assuredly I shall not."

"Do, I beseech you. I know what you will suffer, if you depart in this unsatisfactory state of mind; and the misery of Ruth must be extreme."

"Then, why did she not embrace the opportunity of terminating it? As far as regards her connexion with me, she might this evening have done so. Why is she now lingering under the roof of my rival? Rival! the word blisters my tongue! To have a rival in an inferior for the affections of my wife, and she to grace him thus, is insufferable! But I shall only become in-

furiated if I suffer my thoughts to dwell upon it.   It is now close on midnight, and we hear nothing of them.   You will bear me witness that I am not answerable for what may follow; that I have in the kindest terms invited Ruth to her legal home, and declared my regret for any error she might have to charge against me, since the moment which united us."

"Yet make one effort more."

"Not one, by heaven."

"Or permit me to go to Ruth.   Never mind the lateness of the hour, my maid and your servant shall attend me.   You will thank your sister when you see her returning with your wife, and an incalculable amount of future unhappiness to all parties will be spared."

"It is useless urging me," said Clifton.   "Neither I, nor my sister, shall take one step more, until Ruth manifests a corresponding advance to those we have already made.   If while I am absent, she should claim to be received here, or make application for pecuniary funds, follow the dictates of your own mind.   I leave you carte blanche for such cases.   But let her forget that she has a husband in Percy Clifton, for her conduct this night has confirmed all my suspicions of her double dealing with me in the matter of my father's murder, it has shaken to the foundation the strong trust which I had in her love, and leaves me doubtful whether, after all, her father's friend is not preferred before me."

"That I will never give credence to," said Amy.   "On my life Ruth loves you."

"I must have better assurance of the fact before I again flatter myself with the belief of it.   However, I know the full import of what I have said, and intend to abide by it."

He was interrupted by Andre, who inquired at what hour he would set forth for town on the morrow.

"As soon as it is light," replied his master.

"I hope not," exclaimed Miss Clifton; "wait at least the day over, it may bring an elucidation of what now disturbs you."

Clifton however persisted in his determination, stating that he should breakfast at the house of a nobleman on the road.

"And now my dear sister," he said, "we will part at once that in the morning I may not disturb you.   A week ago I had anticipated happier days than I am now likely to see, but though they may not be happy, I have a hope they may be distinguished, and herein lies my consolation.   The vanguard of the great battle now waging in the state, shall see me in the midst of it.   The glittering prizes held out for adventurous ambition, shall find in me a competitor for them who will not easily be outrun.

"Ah! my dear brother," said Amy, earnestly, "take care these prizes are not bought too dearly. Rank and power too often harden the heart, make it selfish, unfeeling, and worldly. What the exercise of your talents can contribute to your own real welfare, or that of the nation, I shall rejoice to hear of, but it must not be at the expense of the domestic affections, which you ought now to be assiduously cultivating. Again I say, wait the issue of another interview with your wife."

But her words fell on regardless ears.

Clifton had entrenched himself once more behind a bulwark of resentful pride where the shafts of remonstrance could not touch him; when Amy reflected on the uncomplying obstinacy Ruth had manifested in the contemptuous silence with which she had treated his affectionate request in his note that she would at once leave the mill for her husband's abode, where he waited with open arms to receive her, it rather seemed surprising that he had not been more aroused by passion than that he should be deeply affronted.

Amy supposed Ruth's object was to avenge herself on Percy for the three days unfeeling neglect she had experienced from him, but this harmonised ill with her preconceived ideas of the Cottage Girl's amiable disposition. She considered too that Ruth should make some allowance for his anger in consequence of the extraordinary discovery out of which it had sprang; and she thought it unwise when the flag of truce was held out by the belligerent party, for the other, and the weakest, to refuse it. Thus herself in a measure offended with Ruth, Miss Clifton suffered herself to be bound by a promise not to see or write to her without Percy's sanction.

Thus was the iron that had entered into the soul of Ruth rivetted there more firmly than ever—thus link after link was added to the fetters with which affliction had loaded her.

We hardly need say she had not received the note Percy had sent her, or, that if she had, both herself and Maynard would joyfully have hastened to comply with the requests it contained.

The next returning sun saw Percy Clifton's hurried departure, and in the excitement of political warfare, the throbbings of ambition, the applause of assemblies, and the intoxicating notice of the laurelled or diademed demi-gods of the high places of the earth, he soon lost, except at passing intervals, the pains of grief and of remorse.

CHAPTER XXIX.

Few and short were the prayers that we said,
  And we spoke not a word of sorrow,
But we steadfastly gazed on the face of the dead,
  And we bitterly thought of the morrow.

WOLFE.

NOTHING could exceed the kindness and respect Ruth meantime received from Maynard. He was anxious in the extreme to place her at ease in his abode, to support her hopes for the impending trial of her father, and to excuse the impetuosity of Clifton, which had inflicted on her such unmerited pain.

"He was badly bred up," said his generous advocate. "The unnatural dislike of his mother, drove him to ill company, whose example taught him to indulge his hot brain in every whim, fancy, or passion, it could create, good or bad. By starts he could be everything his best friend could wish him, and something more, And though there has been no more steadiness in him, hitherto, than in a wave of the sea, he may in time mend in that respect, as he has in some others. He is fond of you, and when this lamentable trial has passed over, if not before, I sincerely think you may be happy with him."

Such arguments Maynard often used, and Ruth listened to them, mostly in patient silence. Occasionally a tear would be visible on her cheek of lustrous paleness, and a sigh would struggle from her bosom, but she never complained, nor willingly introduced nor prolonged conversation having any more than the most distant reference to her own griefs.

After her distressing interview with Clifton by the alder grove, she had remained alarmingly ill throughout the night, and part of the following day, attended chiefly by the respectable woman who was for the present acting as housekeeper to Maynard, Sall being unable to do little more than weep and wail, as she hung on the neck, or watched by the side of her suffering sister. At length, Ruth was partially tranquillised, and insisted on returning to the

gaol, that she might see the face of her mother once more ere the coffin was closed.

"She went thither with Maynard, whose arm was needful to support her trembling steps. As they passed the alder grove, she cast a terrified glance towards it, and Maynard answering her thought, inconsiderately remarked, that Clifton had left home for London. The effect of this news was for the moment such as to fill him with inexpressible alarm. Her look grew fixed and wild, and she gasped for breath.

"I was beside myself to tell you that," he said, vexed beyond measure; it escaped me unawares. But don't despair. He will come to himself by and bye, and post back again to you as fast as he went."

"Have patience with me, Mr. Maynard," she said, tremulously. "I am exceedingly troublesome to you—to you who have been so good, who have had so much to complain of."

"Think of yourself, my dear, not of me," said Maynard, and the "my dear" came with a touchingly paternal sound. "If I could see you happy, or likely to be so, I should not want comfort, I promise you. but as I have told you one half my news, 'tis little use withholding the other. Last night, when you were so ill, that whether you would live or die seemed equal odds, who should come to the mill, while I was red-hot with the insults of the squire, but his French lacquey, with a challenge for me, as he said. I told the rascal I could neither shoot nor fence, and was too good a judge to stand as a mark for the squire to try his skill upon. And so I tore up the note without reading it, and left the fellow, but afterwards coming out of the mill, I saw him still standing on the steps, 'waiting,' he said, with abominable grimaces, 'my answer about the duel.' I sent him packing with a stroke of my cudgel, for which he promised before long to thank me in a way of his own. There was a wicked meaning in his tone, and I own I am not sorry he is out of Rosedale."

"I know not," said Ruth, "why you should encounter these unpleasant scenes for me. Perhaps some persons whom Mr. Clifton could not object to, might be found in Rosedale, who would be willing, during a few days, to give me and my poor brother and sister a refuge, for a trifling consideration. I cannot, I must not, expose you an hour longer to the inconvenience, the misconception, and the injurious treatment which your kindness to me has drawn upon you."

"Ruth," said the miller, stopping short, and striking his stick violently on the ground, "if you leave me now I shall think it the unkindest action that ever I received in my life. I care no-

thing for the squire's violent language now it is over, he will repent of that, and be glad to make me amends. He knows what I am, if he would but let his heart speak, and speak it must before long, and then he will be ashamed of his foolish jealousy, as well as of sending a challenge to an old miller who never handled any other weapon than his cudgel. I confess I did think him wiser than that, notwithstanding his hair-brained folly."

"It shall be as you will, Mr. Maynard," said Ruth. "Mr. Clifton has evidently abandoned me, and I will not grieve the only true and constant friend left to my father and myself."

Her voice failed her for a moment, but after a slight pause she proceeded—

"If you are willing to prolong your trouble, I will remain under your care until the trial, as my father directed."

"By so doing you will give me uncommon satisfaction," said Maynard; "and for one reason in particular, if you will let me name it, and that is, if you were to leave my mill now, uncandid people might choose to say there had been cause for the squire's freak of jealousy, supposing it to have got abroad."

"Say no more about it, I entreat you!" faltered Ruth.

"I will not, I will not," returned the miller. "And now about your poor mother; your father wished me, in the name of her family and friends, to petition the vicar, that her remains might not be laid in the gaol ground, but interred in the yard of the church were the unfortunate discovery took place. The good man, who looks upon her as I do, in the light of a martyr rather than an offender, has taken on himself to consent, but the funeral must be quite private; and in order that it may be so, it will take place at two to-morrow morning, and the grave will not be made until after sunset."

"Alas! my mother!" ejaculated Ruth, "what a life, what an end, has yours been! But I will not lament for her; she has been the means of giving a fearful warning to the wicked, and she is now in the land where her abundant sorrows will be more abundantly recompensed."

They were now at the goal, whose black-arched portal, like that to Dante's infernal regions, had silently warned many a captive of former days whom its gaping aperture had enclosed to "Leave all hope behind."

Ruth whispered to Maynard as they trod together the chilling stone passages of the interior, not to distress her father with the mention of their meeting with Clifton.

Summerfield was permitted to be near the coffin of his wife during the few last hours of her remaining above ground, and

they found him sitting at the head, his forehead bowed on the closed lid, and resting on his clasped hands. He did not alter his position at their entrance, but seemed abstracted from all outward things.

It was the first time Maynard had seen the corpse—when last he parted from her whose likeness it bore, she was in her customary health, and more than her ordinary spirits. Taking his hat reverently from his head, he approached with timid steps.

The coffin was a common parish one, of deal wood slightly daubed over with black paint, and bearing neither name or date.

It rested on a rude bench; no pall was spread over; nor was there around any of the accompaniments of mourning. Yet in the apartment there was something not wholly out of keeping with the solemn mystery of death. Like all the rest of the prison it was built of stone, blackened by time, and shaped into a number of gloomy arches of early gothic, crossing and intersecting each other, and stooping their extremities to short bulky columns. The light of the waning day admitted through the grated windows was insufficient to diffuse more than a twilight gloom, which in the hollow arches remote from the windows was converted into a midnight intensity of sombre shade. Rembrandt might have chosen the scene for his powerful colouring, but even his sublime conceptions could scarcely have dived into, or his wondrous skill embodied, the interior workings of the agitated spirits of those grouped around the dead prisoner, at the moment when the bereaved and captive husband in silence raising his head drew aside the lid, so as to enable his daughter and his friend to view the inanimate relics of what had once been beautiful and glad, loving and beloved.

"Oh! my mother—my mother!" faltered Ruth, overcome by the sight. "Silent!—cold!—pale! Not a word!—not a look! Gone!—for ever gone!"

"Forbear, my dearest child, forbear," said her father, in a low, solemn voice. "She is not dead, but sleepeth. She lives as truly as you do or I. What say I, as truly?—yea, far more so! she enjoys a completeness of being beyond our present capacities. Without this confidence I could not survive this sight."

Fast down the broad cheeks of Maynard rolled the tears. He had not the high faith of Summerfield, though he had attended church regularly, and held its ministers and its ordinance in high veneration. He could not fix his mental eye with any clearness upon an existence beyond the grave. He believed in it because the church asserted it; sometimes he meditated on it, but after all Maynard could not rid himself of certain sceptical doubts. His

spiritual faculties were not expanded, and immortality was the
hardest of all truths to him, because it can only be comprehended
by those faculties. Whatever came immediately under the cog-
nisance of his senses, or accorded with the state of things amid
which he had spent his life, he could understand, but his per-
ceptions of all else were dim. He could not livingly realise what
was remote or obscure; he could not understand without difficulty
that the star glimmering on us from a distance too amazing to be
computed, could be a world as substantial, as large, and as varied
as this he inhabited; or that there could be any power in the
universe capable of revivifying the dead, or that there could be
any mode of intellectual existence different from the human.
Herein lay the chief distinction between Maynard and his friend.

Summerfield had a large capacity for large truths, and this had
imparted to him a superiority felt by all who approached him.
But it was under adversity his dignity of mind was most conspicuous, and he seemed fortified with a philosophy which some
of the world's most famed and favoured men might have envied.
Yet he had enjoyed no more opportunities of improvement than
are within the reach of all his class. Milton, Burns, and the
Sacred Writers, formed his whole library.

While we have been making these remarks, the reader will be
pleased to suppose that midnight has arrived—that affection's
last look has been taken of the countenance never to be seen more
—that the last pressure has been given to the icy hand and marble lip—and that on the cottager's virtuous though unhappy wife,
the last ray of earthly light has shone. The wheels of a poor
country hearse was then heard at the gaol portal; the nameless
coffin is brought forth, and the grating sound produced by sliding
it into the hearse jars on the nerves of Ruth and Maynard.

Then the scene shifts to the benighted churchyard.

Unbroken solitude pervades the mournful scene. The white-
horned owl in the chancel window of the old church uplifts its
dissonant shriek to hail the spirits that flit past its perch. The
decaying yew that has spread its branches so many ages over yon
remote corner shudders in the night gale, for beneath their shade
an empty grave yawns for its prey, and is satisfied.

THE COTTAGE GIRL.

"IT IS IMPOSSIBLE THERE CAN BE A VERDICT AGAINST YOU!"

THE earth rattles on the coffin lid—the ceremony is despatched by the curate, unwillingly detained from his comfortable rest—the spades are busy—the dread aperture is filled—and there is another mould added to the hundreds scattered near ; and so ends another human history.

O life! O death! mysteries of mysteries, who can fathom?

CHAPTER XXX.

Who stands here as my accuser?
Ah! wilt THOU be he?"

SHELLEY.

IN a few days after her mother's interment, Ruth removed with her sister and her brother to the lodgings Maynard had engaged for her near the county castle in which her father's earthly destiny was to be decided. The affecting declaration and sudden death of Mrs. Summerfield, had augmented the general interest this extraordinary case excited, and the popular current now set as strongly in favour of the accused as it had done against him, when first the body of the missing squire was discovered. In every house were held conversations, in which the matter was keenly discussed, and conjectures and opinions framed, as to what ought to be the verdict of the jury, and the sentence of the judge. That Summerfield would die was not expected, a positive horror was manifested whenever such a result was named as likely to occur, and petitions were resolved upon on his behalf before the session opened.

His children were objects of much compassion, and some unknown person, conceiving they might be ill-provided for, sent to the vicar for their use twenty pounds. The clergyman himself conveyed this money to Ruth, and something in the expressions which fell from him induced her to think he knew the donor, whom in her own mind she believed to be Miss Clifton. The money, however, came from Maynard, who hit on this delicate mode of furnishing Ruth with necessary comforts during the two months which he saw must pass before the trial came on. This assistance came to Ruth at a most welcome time. She was entirely penniless, and accepted it with a tear of unaffected thankfulness to her anonymous friend. And Maynard

had the gratification to see, that the unexpected relief thus afforded her was the means of preventing much that would else have been unpleasant to her feelings.

Every alternate day he superintended his trade at the mill, which it has been previously said was ten miles distant from the castle; the intervening ones he spent with Summerfield and Ruth, generally quitting Rosedale in time to breakfast with the latter by taking advantage of the stage coach which passed the Three Crowns early in the morning. He always found her in her sitting-room dressed in a superior manner, sitting beside a window, which commanded a view of the castle, and closely engaged in making mourning apparel for her sister and herself.

"I find my needle tranquillise me more than anything else," she said, when Maynard remonstrated with her on her close application to the duties she imposed on herself. "Besides, I must perform the part of a mother to Sally and Billy, as I promised her who is gone."

"But you must think of what you may yet have to undergo, and take care of your health."

"I am prepared for all; she who would have suffered so much under this dreadful hazard is at rest, and that soothes me."

Several weeks had glided away—the dreadful day was near— and Ruth had heard not a word of Clifton. Maynard never mentioned him, a sure sign that he had nothing to communicate likely to give her comfort.

At length, as Maynard and herself were leaving the castle, after spending some hours with her father, she asked, in a hesitating voice, if he had nothing to tell her of what was passing in Rosedale.

"I wish I had," he rejoined, "that is, anything you would care to hear."

"If you have any news let me know it."

"Why," said Maynard, "Mr. Clifton's speech in the House of Commons is making some noise, and there is a talk of his getting a baronetcy." To this was added, with hesitation—"He will come down as a witness at the trial."

Ruth, after hearing this, appeared sunk in thought. They had reached her lodgings, but Maynard led her past the door, and into a retired walk leading to green heights of solitary beauty, from whence the ancient city to which the castle belonged appeared scattered over the opposite hill in wild disorder like the broken ranks of an army. The evening star was already lighting its incomparable lamp in the west, and a soft vermilion glow tinged the calm river which flowed in the hollow between the hills. The

distant hum of the streets was distinguishable to the ear, and had no unpleasing effect.   The cattle lowed in the pastures; the birds retiring to their nests twittered a few parting notes; the evening primrose unfolded its shortlived beauties; the pale bell-flowers, whose tendrils trailed along the hedges, closed and drooped lifeless; and a few red lights began by degrees to twinkle through the haze which rested on the gabled dwellings of the city, and their intermingling foliage.

The miller and his companion stood a moment to contemplate the scene on one of those round elevations of earth, called barrows, which are the repositories of the dust of our early British ancestors.   Simultaneously their gaze turned on the castle.   It occupied the highest point of the city, and its towering battlements looked down on a precipitous rock.   No more imposing object could be found in modern England.   The keep that kept guard over one of its walls seemed a strong fortress in itself, and the appearance of vegetation which here and there presented itself to close the antiquity of the pile, added in grace what it took away in sternness.   That keep could not but excite in Ruth sickening sensations, for on the roof of that commanding tower, whence thirty miles of uninterrupted prospect were visible—on that keep felons underwent the extreme vigour of the law—on that keep the condemned, after having just stepped from the confinement of a dungeon, breathed all at once the sweet pure air, beheld a sight calculated above all others, to call up regrets for the beautiful world they were quitting, and the next instant were pushed into the horrid abyss of an infamous death.

"Oh! was it possible, that notwithstanding the hopes which had been held out her father might perish there?"

The question made her senses reel, and she hastily left the spot.

Presently she adverted to Clifton, and learned from Maynard that he was still in London.

After this, he was not named between them, and the near approach of the trial absorbed the minds of both.

The evening previous to the momentous day, after Summerfield had held a long interview with the talented counsel whom Maynard had engaged for him at the cost of a hundred guineas, he was visited by his three children and his friend.   The latter was determined to anticipate no peril in the ordeal of the succeeding day; he had worked himself up to a thorough conviction that Summerfield must be acquitted, and he would allow no arguments to shake his trust.

"It is impossible," he said, "there can be a verdict against you.   The counsel says so—everybody says so."

"Everybody may be wrong," said Summerfield, gravely, "Let us be prepared for evil or for good. You have done all on my behalf that could be done, and to the last every pulse of my heart will throb with gratitude such as human language could not utter."

"I wish," said Billy, "they would try me instead of you, father."

"And suppose they should condemn you, my boy?"

"I should not mind much, if you might live to take care of my sisters, for Mr. Clifton has quite left Ruth, and I don't know what they will do without you, father."

"My gallant little hero!" muttered Summerfield, putting him from his knee with glistening eyes. "One has in such children a fair excuse for wishing to live."

It could not escape her father's notice that the abrupt mention of Clifton had deepened the distress which filled the eye of Ruth.

"My dear child," he said, with overflowing emotion, "your lot is more to be lamented than mine. The afflictions of your parents have fallen on you with a crushing weight, and if I should have to leave you——"

"Which, please heaven, you will not this many a year!" interrupted Maynard.

"If I should," Summerfield proceeded, "it will be a vast addition to the pain of my ignominious end to know that I leave my excellent and tender daughter forsaken by him she has loved only too well. For your maintenance, and that of Sally and my boy, I am less troubled. You have been bred to industry and to frugality, and I know that while Maynard lives you will neither of you want."

"That you may rely upon," said the miller, brushing away the tears from his eyes. "But I can't allow any more of this dismal discourse. As sure as the sun is in the heavens, Roger, you will be acquitted, and then we shall see Ruth occupying her rightful place in Rosedale House, and at peace with her husband."

"May your prophesy prove true!" ejaculated Summerfield, and with these words he affectionately dismissed them. "I shall not sleep this night," he said. "To be exposed as a public criminal to the gaze of the multitude who will throng to see me tried, will tax all my firmness, and I must prepare for it."

More than Summerfield were wakeful that night. Ruth watched the lingering moments until the sky above the garden on which the window of her lodging looked was dappled with the

approaching sunrise. She then hastily arose, performed her devotions, and attired herself for the court. The dead black of her dress strongly set off her delicate complexion, and a Madonna cast was given to her lovely features by the simple braiding of her auburn hair, and the meek tenderness which slumbered on her drooping ivory lids. But when these lids were fully raised, the tranquillity of the Madonna was not visible in the gazelle-like eyes they veiled. A restlessness was there, subdued but still apparent—a fearful expectation—and ever and anon a resolved fortitude—all calculated at once to inspire pity, anxiety, and admiration.

When she had prepared her mind and her person for the dread business of the day, she called up her sister and her brother.

"Awake!" she said, in tones which roused them in a moment, "the day has come when we shall either see the end to a long trouble, or be orphans indeed! Dress quickly; and forget not your father in your prayers; when next you see him his freedom or his death will be decided."

When the three descended to the sitting-room, Maynard, in a new suit of black, was there, and Ruth asked if his hopeful expectations remained still firm.

"As the castle rock," he replied, cheerfully. "But I wish the day was over."

"I dare not echo your wish," she said, in a shuddering tone. "I would rather wish it had never dawned."

The landlady had prepared an unusually excellent breakfast, of which she did the honours, but the coffee was for the most part left untouched in the cups, and neither her eggs nor her ham could find any to do it justice.

"Did you not tell me," said Ruth to Maynard, "that the judge is apt to incline to severity against the criminals brought before him?"

"It was the counsel who said so," rejoined Maynard.

There was then a long pause, and after that some trivial remarks on the weather and other common-place topics, interrupted by Ruth, who, pushing back her chair in hurried excitement, exclaimed—

"It is time to go—I hear the bell chiming half-past eight."

The landlady wept as she assisted the trembling girl to draw on her shawl.

"God bless ye, poor things!" she ejaculated, as the children began to sob and weep in the excitement of their feelings; "if your father does not have a happy deliverance. it will not be for want of good wishes."

" Take us with you, Ruth—take us with you," entreated Sally.

" The scene will be too much for you to bear," affectionately answered the sister.

" If you can bear it so can we," they remonstrated.

" If I can bear it ?" repeated Ruth, wildly; " alas! I know not that I can bear it."

" Then do you stay with us."

" Sensibly said, Sally," interrupted Maynard. " Mrs. Clifton had better not go; I have argued with her against it to no purpose. I don't believe she will be able to get through half the trial before she is dreadfully ill."

" I hope otherwise," said Ruth; " at least I will venture the experiment, and exert all the strength that woman may."

" Then take us with you, again urged Sally; and unable to withstand the children's importunity, Ruth consented.

As they were about to go the landlady pressed upon the young people and Maynard " a little brandy to warm their hearts. You'll need something, I doubt," she said, " before this weary day is over."

" Well thought of mistress," said the miller, and placed in his pocket a small bottle full, in case a cordial should be needed. To this he added a paper of biscuits, and took care to see that Ruth was provided with smelling salts.

Ten minutes after, she was entering the castle gate with him and her brother and sister.

Murmurs of sympathy were audible among the concourse of persons assembled in the area within; and on their admission into the part of the castle appropriated to the administration of public justice every eye in the crowded assembly was fixed on them.

Many a heart felt its pulses quickened at the sight of the impenetrable crape veil which concealed the bewitching countenance of Ruth. Some who were there had sighed among the train of rustic admirers of the Beauty of Rosedale; some still nursed the wounds which she unconsciously had inflicted; and some who had envied her triumphs, felt, perhaps, a secret satisfaction mingle with the natural feeling excited by her present distressing situation.

It might have been a question whether the father or daughter awakened the profoundest interest.

Maynard chose a place as little conspicuous as possible, but commanding a full view of the bench and the bar.

The judge shortly took his seat. His countenance was one of

iron inflexibility, and so far agreed with what Ruth had been told of his disposition to severity.

As the prisoner was brought in Maynard observed Ruth's hands were tightly clasped together on her knee, and that she was wrought up to an excruciating pitch of suspense. Her lips were parted, and the breath issued from them laboriously.

Summerfield entered the dock with a bearing of fearless calm; he trod firmly, and bowed respectfully to the bench. His eye took in at a glance the whole assemblage, resting only for a moment on his children and Maynard.

The clerk then read the indictments, which charged him with having on the 10th of March 18—, in the parish of Rosedale, feloniously and with malice caused the death of Arthur Clifton, Esquire, and concealed his body and certain property.

To the usual question of Guilty or Not Guilty, Summerfield answered with the emphasis of sincerity—

"Guilty of concealment of the body and property, but not guilty of the murder!"

"He speaks the truth!" said a loud voice at the extremity of the court.

"Remove that disorderly person," said the judge.

The constables would have done so but could not discover the speaker. When silence was obtained, Summerfield was required to say whether Guilty or Not Guilty.

"Not guilty of the Murder, my lord!" he exclaimed.

The chief witness called by the crown counsel were the son of the deceased, and the surgeons who had examined the exhumed body.

At the appearance of Percy Clifton a fainting flush of scarlet passed across the cheek of Ruth, her hands were more tightly compressed, and her breath more stifled in its passage.

In the act of recognition Clifton glanced with fiery haughtiness on the prisoner, whose firmness almost forsook him as he thought of his daughter exposed to the double agony of hearing her father accused by her husband. He wished she had not been there, and expected every moment to see her carried senseless from the court.

There was nothing in Clifton's evidence new to the reader. It embraced what previous to his marriage he had been able to learn from his mother and connections of his father's disappearance, and the singular dislike the Summerfields had at different times displayed to him; the reasons he had for believing that dislike had its source in his personal resemblance to his father, and a sense of conscious guilt in the cottagers. In a

vivid description of what had taken place in the church at his marriage, he so critically emphasised the delirious words which had fallen from Mrs. Summerfield, that the conviction of the populace as to the absence of an intention of murder in the fatal blow to which those unconscious words alluded were for the moment shaken. The rest of what he said referred to the place and condition in which his father's remains had been found. The first part of his evidence was corroborated by the housekeeper of his deceased mother—that relating to the important words spoken by Mrs. Summerfield in the church, by the vicar and his clerk—and the latter part by the constables who had assisted in disinterring the body.

Looking round the court as he was retiring, the eyes of Ruth suddenly encountered his. Both recoiled before the mutual shock —darkness gathered on the brow of one, overwhelming anguish on the other—and Clifton passed out.

" You are ill," said Maynard to Ruth, anxiously.

" Mr. Maynard," she said, unconsciously laying her cold damp hand on his, and pressing it hard, " I am not so strong as I imagined—I fear I shall be obliged to go out."

" Take a little of the brandy—try the salts," said Maynard, hastily. " Billy, my boy, ask the folks behind to open the windows."

A current of air assisted Ruth to quell the rising faintness, and again she gathered all her faculties to listen, to mark, and to endure.

The witnesses now being examined were the surgeons, who both alike avouched their incapacity to pronouce how the death of the deceased had been produced in consequence of the progress which decomposition had made in the body. From one of these gentlemen Summerfield's counsel elicited that no marks of injury were perceptible, but this was neutralised by the crown counsel extracting an admission from the other that a blow might have been maliciously and fatally given without producing any marks but such as the state of the corpse prevented them from detecting.

This closed the case for the prosecution.

The defence was then ably and energetically gone through. Mrs. Summerfield's last declaration furnished the foundation, and witnesses were called in its support.

The vicar of Rosedale gave evidence that both before and after Mrs. Summerfield's marriage the deceased had paid peculiar attentions to her.

Maynard had not told Ruth that he was to appear in evidence,

but she now heard his name called, and he made his way to the witness box. He was called there to speak to the respective characters of the deceased and the prisoner. His answer was characteristic.

"My lord and gentlemen, if you desire to know the character of the old Squire Clifton, you have only to think of all that is most mean and monstrous; if you wish to learn what that of the prisoner is, you have only to think of what is most honest and praiseworthy. I knew the old squire as well as I know Summerfield, and should be puzzled to name a single good quality he had, while in my friend Roger I swear I know no ill one, except perhaps that when his blood is up he is apt like many of his betters to let passion master him."

The counsellor for the defence bit his lip at this last admission.

"Bravely spoken, miller!" cried the same loud voice from the throng which had before disturbed the proceedings. Peremptory orders were issued that the intruder should be excluded, but again the constables were at fault. Nobody would point out the offender against decorum, for he had given voice to the impulsive fervour of many who were panting for the prisoner's acquittal.

Maynard was harshly ordered by the judge to stand down; and after several other witnesses had been questioned, the farmer on whose lands Summerfield had worked many years spoke in high praise of the prisoner's general conduct; and with this the evidence for the defence being closed, the proceedings were suspended half an hour, the spectators for the most part retaining their seats.

CHAPTER XXXI.

"One thing more, my child,
For thine own sake be constant to the love
Thou bearest us; and to the faith that I,
Though wrapt in a strange cloud of crime and shame,
Lived ever holy and unstained. And though
Ill tongues shall wound me, and our common name
Be as a mark stamped on thine innocent brow
For men to point at as they pass, do thou
Forbear, and never think a thought unkind
Of those who perhaps love thee in their graves."

SHELLEY.

RUTH suffered herself to be withdrawn by Maynard and her sister into the open air of the castle court, and to avoid the gazers there ascended the bulwarks of the walls. This castle had been one of the strongholds built at the Norman Conquest in the twelfth century, but of the original fortress little more remained than the exterior walls, the towers, and the keep. Within the vast square inclosure a goal and court-house, with the governor's residence, supplied the place of the warlike garrison of former days. The walls, whose gigantic elevation was half concealed by the bold bulwarks of earth thrown up against them, seemed nevertheless of everlasting strength. Ruth could remember when the sight of them had filled her childish thoughts with wonder, and many a wild story of the marvellous invented by the cottage evening fire for the amusement of her brother and sister owed its origin to awful impressions of the "castle." But now those hours of simplicity and peace were no more. In the long line of majestic ramparts stretching before her, she beheld only the dread barriers which for three months had held her father in bondage. The delicious plants which the taste of the governor had caused to be trained over their inner surface, and cultivated on the sloping banks of the bulwarks at their feet, affected her as if they flourished around the scaffold of her parent. · To her they had the odour of death—to her they were like flowers smiling on the edge of an abyss which had whelmed all she loved.

·" Cast it away," she said shudderingly to Sally, who plucked a rose from the wall as they passed by it—" touch nothing which grows around this horrible place! Cast it away !—if you had my feelings you would as soon touch a serpent."

"Nay, the flower is innocent enough," said Maynard, " and this place will show in another light to you, when you hear it ringing with the shouts of your father's acquittal."

"I do not anticipate that," said Ruth, despondingly.

"Then you ought, and so I tell you plainly. Do you think any one person of all the crowd sitting within that court-house yonder, anticipate anything else ?"

"I think many of them are persuaded there will be an unfavourable sentence.'

"The more fool they. Why have I paid a hundred guineas to your father's counsel, if not to get him off?'

"I am afraid your money will be useless.

"Now really, Mrs. Clifton, you make me quite out of temper," said Maynard. " What evidence has there been to convict him upon ?"

"Too much. That declaration of my mother's may be used against as well as for him. It confess-es the blow—the appearance of blood—the instantaneous death—the hasty burial. I heard persons near me conversing as it was produced in court, and the burden of what they said answered to my own thoughts, that it was impossible my father could be acquitted."

Maynard here ejaculated a peevish "pish !"

" All now turns on one single point," continued Ruth—" malice or no malice—this is what the jury has to decide, and I have little hope in their verdict."

"And I have no fear," said Maynard. " But it is now time to return."

As they descended the bulwarks, the eye of Ruth was raised to the keep, and to the sky, with awful forebodings. Approaching the court-house, she beheld Clifton conversing with two gentlemen of the long-robe at one of the entrances. His face had much unhappiness depicted on it, and his gestures and rapid utterance betrayed mental irritation.

Ruth and her companions passed him unseen, and with throbbing hearts resumed their places in the court. The bench were

already collected; intense stillness prevailed; and expectation sat on every brow.

> "With still and earnest face
> Pallid with feelings which intensely glowed
> Within.

Ruth attended to the brief but powerful address of the crown counsel, who, as she had foreseen, made use of the declaration of her mother, representing Summerfield as a man disposed to dangerous fits of passion, to obstinate revengeful animosities, and as having deprived the deceased of life in the madness of revengeful jealousy.

"The precise manner in which the murder was committed," said the learned gentleman, "cannot at this distance of time be ascertained with any certainty; for who that considers the natural anxiety of the prisoner's wife to save her husband from the penalties attached by law to his crime, could place entire dependence on her account of the transaction?"

The sympathies of the populace swayed like a reed shaken by the wind, as he pressed home the charge against the prisoner, and a faint murmur of approbation as he sat down rang like a knell on the heart of Ruth.

"Don't be downcast!" whispered Maynard to her; "you shall hear my counsel crush in two minutes all this fellow has been vamping up. My life for your father's? He is as safe as any mortal man now living. Softly! the defence begins. Now courage, courage! a few minutes more and all will be well."

The harangue of Maynard's counsel was lengthy, and of a different order of oratory from that of his opponent who had just sat down. Its flowery imagery and flowing periods were well calculated to make an impression on the general audience, though less adapted to send conviction into the minds of calm-judging men like those who were the arbiters of Summerfield's fate. The closing peroration was on the wrongs and sufferings the prisoner had experienced; and he called on the court "not to add to this unfortunate man's life of undeserved misery a death of dishonor—not to brand the children of a woman whose incomparable virtue had alone occasioned all these miseries with the obloquy which necessarily attached to the offspring of condemned felons—not to forget in their capacity of judges that they were husbands, fathers, and men, who under the gross provocation the prisoner had endured, must have been more than human not to have lost sight of strict self-command."

During this address, Maynard's excitement threatened to overleap all bounds: he groaned, clenched his hand applauded as audibly as he durst, and gazed into the countenances of those about him, to see how they were affected with eager eyes, whence tear after tear rolled rapidly down.

In the ear of Ruth the pleadings of the advocate of her father sounded tame; she could have wished him a tongue of fire in such a cause. The tricks of oratory were sickening at such a moment. He should have sent forth his remonstrance as the voice of a mountain torrent, his persuasions should have swept over the hard cold hearts of men like a warm gale loosening the frost-bounds of winter. She longed to take the place of that "ice-hearted counsellor," to cast herself at the feet of those stern judges, and pray their mercy. But this could not be. The tedious formalities of the law might not be broken. Their end however now drew nigh. The judge addressed the jury.

Alas! it is evident to all but Maynard that his opinion leans against the prisoner. Ruth perceives it; unutterable darkness falls on her spirit, deep, dense, and horrid; how the interval passes while the jury are absent, she knows not; some kind words are addressed to her by Maynard and her sister, but she catches not their import; the roaring of a thousand waves is in her ears,— while judge, counsellors, and audience, float before her in one undistinguishable chaos.

As the foreman of the jury appeared, she breathlessly arose, grasping the hand of her sister in her right hand, that of her brother in her left, and drawing them close to her side; but when the fatal word " Guilty," was pronounced, she sank down again as if struck by some invisible hand.

Maynard seemed no less electrified, but caught tenaciously the next moment at a recommendation to mercy, which accompanied the verdict, in consideration of the prisoner's excellent character, and the provocation he had received.

This merciful clause Ruth heard not, being carried hastily out of the court in convulsions to a room in the governor's house, where every assistance was humanely rendered. During the brief confusion caused by her removal, Summerfield was so much agitated that a chair and a glass of water was brought to him. When he had recovered himself, he was asked if he wished to say anything before sentence of death was passed upon him.

Immediately he resumed his standing posture, and with extreme animation exclaimed—

" My lord, the death of Arthur Clifton was the vengeance of God, not mine. As I hope for heaven I never intended to take his life. No man in this presence who has the spirit of a man, would have done less than I did. I cannot repent the blow; and

if I must die for it, my case is hard. The concealment of the body is the only matter that lies on my conscience, and for that I have suffered long and bitterly. I have had fifteen years of broken peace, of restless nights, and fearful days—I have seen the wreck of my wife's reason, and stood by her death-bed,"—(here his voice was broken)—"I have witnessed the destruction of my children's prospects, and endured nearly a quarter of a year's imprisonment. I am aware all this can now do me little good, at the same time I think it right to declare my wrongs and my innocence to your lordship in the most solemn manner before your lordship condemns me. In the face of heaven and earth I swear no thought of murder ever entered my mind!"

He ceased—the judge drew on the black cap.

"Prisoner at the bar," he commenced, "you have been found guilty by an impartial jury of the crime of wilful murder, which it has been attempted to defend on the plea provocation received. But the laws under which you live do not permit assassination to be justified on any such grounds. No man is at liberty to avenge himself for injuries done him, but through the medium of public authority. Again, it has been attempted to attribute to natural causes the death of the gentleman whose remains after so many years have been by the hand of Providence brought so remarkably to light; but while there is no testimony of this beyond your bare assertions and those of your late wife, there are, in the long concealment of the body, in the jealousy and hatred you entertained against the deceased, and in the delirious expression which have fallen from your deceased wife, ample grounds for the verdict returned by the jury. And however reluctant I may be, considering the excellent character you have borne in your native place, I feel bound to warn you against founding any hopes whatever, on the recommendation which the jury have thought fit to append to their verdict. In this world hope is cut off from you, and you must immediately prepare to undergo the sentence of the court, which is—that you be taken to the place whence you came, and from thence to the place of execution, and there be hanged by the neck until you be dead, and may the Lord have mercy on your guilty soul!"

"Amen!" exclaimed the prisoner, uplifting his eyes fervently

"You shall not die, Summerfield!" exclaimed the same loud voice which interrupted the early part of the trial, and by the connivance of the persons in the part whence it issued, and in the bustle of the breaking up of the court, the offender finally escaped.

Summerfield's first anxiety when he returned to his cell was to know the state of his daughter's health, and he was not long in suspense.

She came with his younger children, and a scene ensued to which no words are adequate. Their tears, their despair, quite unmanned him at first, but by degrees he recovered himself sufficiently to receive Maynard with composed mournfulness.

"Suspense is now over," he said, "and in a few days I shall tread the path of immortality with my beloved and martyred wife. Last night I either saw or dreamed she stood before me in all the beauty of her youth. The bloom was on her cheeks, and her eye was smiling and bright. 'Roger,' she said, 'be strong in faith and in hope! we shall meet soon.' There was a meaning in this vision which we should lay to heart. There be times when God speaks to us through dreams, and this was one of them. Yes, my children, my friend, we should be wise, and grieve not as persons without hope. Were my life prolonged our parting must come at last; and seeing that it is written in the Book that cannot err 'that the day of one's death is better than the day of one's birth, we ought not to lament more than the manner of my departing. But enough of myself. You, my children, will remain near me during the little while I have to live. And you Maynard—"

"Will try if nothing more is to be done for you. Though the judge chose to throw contempt on the recommendation of the jury, it may be the secretary of state will not. Our good vicar of Rosedale intends to address him to-morrow, and other petitions will accompany the vicar's. I don't despair yet."

"My dear friend," said Summerfield, earnestly, "the worst that can now happen to us would be the nourishing of false hopes. Oh! let us beware of them. Rather let us strive by religion and reflection to reconcile ourselves to what must be.

"I reconcile myself to your death!" exclaimed Maynard, with impatient and passionate feeling, "never—never! I say if you do suffer this sentence you are a murdered man; and I hope the jury and the judge who condemned you may be able to sleep quietly in their beds, that's all. Religion and reflection! they are very well in their place, I respect them as much as any man, but they will not persuade me to be reconciled to any thing so barbarous, so cruel, so unjust, as this sentence of yours. All that will reconcile me is to hear that it is cancelled, and that you are forgiven."

THE COTTAGE GIRL.

"WHAT HAVE I BEEN SAYING, RUTH?"

"WHAT says my daughter? Does she hope with you?" Summerfield asked.

"Oh, no—would that I did! but I dare not, I dare not!" Ruth in broken accents replied.

"It will be a blot on this country, a lasting disgrace which nothing can wipe away, if Roger is allowed to die!" cried Maynard. "He must not—he shall not! We will move heaven and earth rather! We will petition the king!—we will petition his prime minister!—and will petition everybody whose influence can be of any service!"

"But, Harry," said Roger Summerfield in a tone at once argumentative and persuasive, "don't you know that all this and more has been done by others without success?"

"I am not sure that it has—at all events our attempts are very unlikely to fail when we have such men engaged in them as the vicar of Rosedale, and some others that 1 know."

"Why, Henry, you are so much in earnest, and so confident, that in spite of my reason you arouse the love of life in me. You positively think that the petitions will prove successful?"

"Certainly I do."

"Then I also will trust in them."

"Ah! if that trust should be deceptive," Ruth faltered.

"It cannot—it shall not! exclaimed Maynard.

"You spoke thus before the trial," Ruth faintly said.

"And I spoke right, for if the jury had been composed of sensible men they must have acquitted Roger. But I know most of them, and they are as dull fools as are to be found within a hundred miles. Hang them! I would have them whipped from here to Dover. And as for the judge—but I will say nothing of him."

"You had better not," said Summerfield, "for here come those who if they hear you speaking to his disparagement may forbid you to visit me again. They come to remove me to the condemned cell, therefore we now must part."

"Oh! my dear father!" said Ruth, in a low but fervent voice as he embraced her, "when you are alone in that terrible cell, and dark thoughts gather around you, remember my mother's words that you repeated to us just now, and be strong. You have a home of blessedness in view to which the scaffold will be but a threshhold for you. One moment on the drop, the next in heaven! Think of this father, and fear not the pains of death, which are quickly over. Be resigned, and don't trouble yourself about those you are leaving. There is a Father of the fatherless whose eye will watch over us, whose arm will shield us, and who will lead us through quiet paths until we arrive at the bright mansions of joy where you and my mother will receive us."

Her concluding words were half inaudible, and for a minute she hung sobbing on her father's breast.

Maynard then lent her the support of his arm to her lodgings, where for their reception, and that of the children with them, the landlady had prepared the comforts of an excellent fire and warm supper in the little parlour looking on the garden.

"Though the days are warm, the evenings are chilly," she said—"and I knew Mrs. Clifton liked a good fire."

"You are very good, Mrs. Lister," said Ruth, sinking into the easy chair with a long drawn sigh.

"And so your father, poor man, has been condemned? Well-a-day' God's above all, that's one comfort, as I said when my good man died. But you have no need to despond, for I am told there was a recommendation from the jury, which is rare to be heard of, and it is not to be thought after that your father will die."

Mrs. Lister was a good-looking woman of sixty, of comfortable circumstances, and rather superior habits, retaining after six years of mourning her widow's garb, not for idle show, but out of the real respect in which she held her husband's memory The front of her house presented to the view, a shop stocked with tobacco and cigars; the back looked on a tolerably large garden, in which the widow took much pride. Several fine trees of different species were scattered about it, throwing their shade on beds of flowers edged with an outer row of prim box, and an inner one of the daisy-like thrift flower. These beds were watched by an assiduous gardener, who suffered no intruding weed, let its form be ever so graceful to insinuate itself in these cultivated spots, nor any of the stray leaves of autumn to wither on the smooth paths.

Maynard was leaving the house by the garden after he had partaken supper with Mrs. Lister and her young lodgers, when the former came hurrying after him to speak a few words out of their hearing.

"What do you think, Mr. Maynard," she said, "will Mr. Summerfield get off after all? Some say he will, and some say he will not. I talk hopefully to the poor things inside to help them to bear up, but what do you think?"

"Think! Mrs. Lister—why that he is as safe as you or I."

"It does me good to hear you say so. But what of Mr. Clifton? He was at the trial, so I hear. Did he not speak to his sorrowful young wife? Does he mean to forsake her entirely?"

"It seems like it, Mrs. Lister," replied Maynard, bitterly.

"He must be a hard-hearted young gentleman to punish her for her father's deeds," said Mrs. Lister.

"Aye truly; but hard-heartedness is the fashion, Mrs. Lister. However, I must wish you good night. You will attend well to Mrs. Clifton, poor girl, and don't let her be much alone, for then she is apt to mope."

"She is a sweet, angelic-looking creature," said Mrs. Lister; "if my Sarah had lived she would have been just such another. But do you know, Mr. Maynard, I was talking with some one to-day who had told me all about the preparations you had made for your marriage with her, when the squire carried her off. I never heard so much of that disappointment of yours before, and I assure you I felt—"

"Good night, Mrs. Lister," said Maynard, quitting her abruptly, and a moment after, the small white gate, which terminated the path they were upon, swung loudly after him.

"He cannot bear that subject at all," said Mrs. Lister to herself, as she sauntered back to the house under the dark boughs of the trees. "It must have gone to his heart, and a great pity it is, for he is a thriving, careful, good-natured man, and an easier life she would have had with him, I'll warrant, than with this wild, random squire. Yet they say Mr. Clifton is a great man, up among the Londoners, and makes grand speeches in the Parliament House, and he is to be a baronet too. But what comfort is all this to his poor desolate wife, if she must be an outcast from his prosperity, and be treated with neglect and contempt?"

Maynard vented more than one suppressed groan, whose source he cared not to acknowledge to himself, as he took his way to the city tavern, where for a week past he had been accommodated, the deep interest he had taken in the trial of Summerfield having detained him for that period from his mill. He wished to forget that he had ever connected a dream of domestic joy with Ruth—and though such forgetfulness was difficult, the pure principle which prompted it well rewarded the attempt.

CHAPTER XXXII.

"Abhorred slave
Which any print of goodness will not take,
Being capable of all ill!"

SHAKESPEARE.

NEXT day, Maynard was recalled to some consideration of his own concerns, which recently he had entirely neglected.

As neither he nor the children of Summerfield could find admittance at the castle this day, he spent the chief part in considering and promoting what was necessary for the application to be made to the secretary of state, on the behalf of the condemned, being materially assisted by Ruth, who exerted as much quickness of thought, and energy, as if she had no sorrow preying at her heart—or rather we should say, more, much more, for when the mind is free, not only is the body delicate, but the strength of the superior faculties is apt to slumber. Adversity creates powers of its own; the same Divine Hand which strikes the blow, provides the shield to meet it.

As evening drew on, Maynard announced to her his intention of walking to Rosedale by the light of the moon, which was now at the full. Ten miles was a trifling distance in his estimation, and aided by his stout cudgel, he hoped to reach the old mill by ten o'clock. Beside his own business, he had it in view to obtain on the following morning some influential signatures for Summerfield, from responsible householders about the dale. Ere setting out, he had tea with the widow Lister and Ruth, in the trellised arbour in the widow's garden. Beside the children, there was added to this little party the meek vicar of Rosedale, who, with the miller and two gentlemen of independent means, resident in the city formed the deputation, which had volun-

teered to wait on the secretary of state, and sue for the life and
pardon of Summerfield. Though with a strong hand Ruth restrained the hope which ever and anon struggled in her heart,
yet its presence was betrayed by the kindling of her eye, and
the animation of her tones, as this journey of benevolence was
talked of. Unconsciously she adopted the confident views of
Maynard, and though the vicar was less sanguine, he was too
tender-hearted to check anticipations, which afforded so much
relief to an affectionate daughter and friend.

The first four miles of the ten which Maynard walked that
evening, lay over wide waste fields, covered with wild grass,
cheating the eye with a semblance of cultivation where none but
nature's hand had been at work. Wider and wider opened the
prospect, and still the same coarse waving grass, and tall undu-
lating weeds, overspread the face of the country, which had been
but of recent years rescued from the overflowings of the sea by
the process of draining. In this monotonous region, scarce a tree
or dwelling was to be seen; stunted hedges alone broke the unvarying sameness of the view, no birds were on the wing, and
the solitary cuckoo was out of sight, whose occasional plaintive
and eternally-repeated notes came now and then on the stilly
air; no cattle were grazing, no sheep dotted the level sward, and
a single husbandman returning from his day's toil to his poor
cot was the only human being Maynard had met, when he began
to approach the heights, at whose feet the fair Rosedale displayed her pastoral loveliness.

Maynard had walked sharply, as well to dissipate the sombrous reflections excited by the unmerited afflictions of Summerfield and his family, as to escape from scenery so wearisome to
the eye and depressing to the spirit. The traditions of robbery
and murder, with which it was sullied, perhaps, had some effect
in speeding him onwards more rapidly, stout-hearted though he
was.

Day had now wholly withdrawn its light—that all-penetrating
and cheerful light from which knavery shrinks—and nature was
pervaded by the obscurity congenial to unhallowed pursuits. The
miller quickened his pace still more, and took a bye way, which,
though it led over the hills, was considered nearer than the level
one he had been pursuing. He soon, however, repented his
choice, for besides that the way was rendered fatiguing by its
lying up hill, the spring rains had swollen every pretty rivulet
which he had to cross (and their name was legion), and in some
places the soil proved so treacherous, that at every step his feet
sank to the ankles. With these obstructions, he made but small

progress and was glad when the full moon, suddenly bursting from its vapoury shroud, enabled him to see whereabouts hs was, and to clear himself of the mire. As the road was manifestly impracticable, he endeavoured to force his way in the direction of his home through huge blocks of grey marble, which bestrewed the hill he was upon. Sometimes he climbed a moss-covered heap, sometimes groped his way in utter darkness with a horrible feeling of uncertainty whether his next step might not be in some one of the many deep chasms with which the side of the hill was seamed. At length, to his great joy, he heard the deep baying of his own watch-dog, a sound his ear could not mistake, and while he was asking himself with delighted surprise whether he could really be so near the mill, as that sound indicated, the baying was repeated nearer, and as it seemed to Maynard more fiercely than he could imagine any necessity for. Presently the deep-mouthed bark was renewed within a still shorter distance, and succeeded by a owl so dismal and protracted, that it startled the raven from its eyrie, whose hoarse croak, heard in that craggy solitude of almost impenetrable gloom, seemed, no less than the howl of Maynard's sagacious English mastiff, to presage impending calamity. The miller was not more free from a belief in omens, than the illiterate dwellers in country places are. He perspired extremely, and his hair stiffened on his head.

"My God !" he muttered, "what new misfortune is to happen now ? I think I have had enough, and seen enough, for one lifetime."

Just then he turned the brow of the hill, and beheld, spread out at its foot, his native dale, sleeping half in moonlight, half in shade. There was its translucent waters—its nightingale-haunted groves—its ancient park and mansion—its sm   town, half buried in ivy and orchards—its fields richly laden with the plant whence man derives his most necessary aliment ;—but where was the mill ?

" Maynard rubbed his eyes, and gazed in much wonder on the conspicuous spot scarce a quarter of a mile off, where he had expected to see its sails reposing on the bosom of the air, the merry lights twinkling in its narrow windows, and reflected in the stream which surrounded the building. Those lights were extinguished, and the substantial building was as entirely effaced from the landscape, as if the genii of the Arabian lamp had after their long oblivion revived to play their pranks in merry England, and in obedience to some son of mischief, whirled it from the place where it had flourished so long.

"I must be mistaken," said the bewildered Maynard, starting from his momentary traces of amazment, "the mill MUST be there, though I cannot see it. Surely yonder is where it should be? It is impossible in a week's absence I should have forgotten the place where most of my life has been spent! There is a mist over the spot, but I see the three elms, and the white-washed farm chimney. No! I am not deceived in the place—and my mill is gone!"

"It is gone," echoed a malicious voice, whose abrupt tones curdled Maynard's very heart-blood, as they issued from under a sort of rude gigantic archway, formed in one of the blocks of granite scattered around.

"Who are you that speak?" demanded Maynard, after a moment of thrilling silence.

"One who owed you a debt, and has now paid it."

"Ha! I know that voice. Dog! come forth—come forth! or I will drag thee."

And without hesitation Maynard rushed into the cavernous archway, and dragged by the collar into the moonlight—Jean Andre!

The meagre sallow visage of the Frenchman was distorted with a grimace of wicked exultation, blended with pussillanimity, for it was no woman's hand which grasped his throat, no common fury which animated the worthy miller.

"Grinning ape! tell me what thou hast done!" exclaimed Maynard, hoarsely.

"What you cannot undo," replied Andre.

"I will shake the life out of thy worthless body if thou dost not answer plainly. What has become of my mill?"

"Sacre! is it not where you left it," cried Andre, mockingly. "Are you sure you did not carry it in your pocket to the trial? Ha!—hold!" he entreated, as the miller shook him furiously, "you throttle me!"

"I will," Maynard rejoined, in accents almost unintelligible with passion, "wretch! I will, if you venture any more of your cursed ridicule! Tell me, is my mill burnt?"

"Aye, Sacre! the rats have had a roasting."

"And you have set it on fire?"

"You will find it as hard to prove that as you did to get a wife. Sacre! take your hand from my throat!"

The hollow and fierce barking of the dog, and the outcries of a tumultuous crowd of men and boys straining up the difficult acclivity of the hill or mount, now reverberated wildly among the rocks.

"Sacre!" exclaimed Andre, changing his mocking tones to one

of abject terror, "let me go, miller! For God's sake let me go, or I shall be torn in pieces by that mastiff of yours!"

A burst of confused exclamations arose as Maynard was recognised.

"Who have you there with you?" asked Wyatt.

"Jean Andre," replied Maynard.

There was another clamour of tongues, exhorting the miller to—

"Hold the villain fast! for he had set the mill on fire, and all was destroyed but part of the walls!"

"If he does it will be because I cannot help it," said Andre, and suddenly slipping his head under the out stretched arm of Maynard, he broke from his grasp, and fled like a hunted tiger-cat, now climbing, now diving, now on the top of a mass of granite, now scrambling up the face of a precipice, now creeping on hands and knees along tracks where none dare follow him except the bold mastiff, who hunted him as the stag-hounds hunts the deer. The animal's very nature seemed changed, and its fleetness and agility was such that it was difficult to imagine it had not been born for the wilderness and the chase.

Unfortunately for Andre the moon shone in unclouded splendour during this singular pursuit, revealing his motions distinctly. Those who followed the dog cheered it lustily onwards, and so keenly absorbed it was in the tracking the flight of the destroyer of the property which it had vainly endeavoured to protect, that even its beloved master was unregarded. Cliff and gully, crag and cavern, rung with the echoing shouts of the men, and the menacing bark of fearful warning which announced impending death to the fleeing wretch. At last Andre sunk exhausted on the top of an immense pile of marble granite that he had attained almost by miracle, and at whose base lay a pool of great depth, stagnant, and mantled with green slimy vegetation. Neither dog nor man could ascend where he had ascended, and they were debating on what was to be done, when a frightful shriek from Andre announced to them that he was falling! The place on which he sat was slippery and sloping, and he had no hold by which to secure himself but the patches of moss which grew in the crevices. To these one after another he clung—one after another broke away — and the wretch saw himself within an inch of inevitable destruction. The moon exhibited to Maynard his dilated eyeballs, and the frightful contortion of his features, as with another shriek that rent the air he slipped from the edge, and turning over in his descent, and catching at the void air, dropped heavily into the black pool! The mass of corrupt weed with which the water was encumbered prevented him from rising to the. surface.   The dog ran round and round the edge, barking with rage and disappointment—the men and boys stood gazing on the rock, the pool, and each other.

Maynard first spoke.

" How came he at Rosedale?—his master is not there."

Wyatt replied—

" Last night he came in a distressed plight to the mill, saying Mr. Clifton had discharged him a month ago for some trifling fault, he had parted with his last penny, and was not able to obtain another situation at present, nor had any friends who could assist him.   He begged me as we had been companions formerly to let him stay that night in the mill."

" You should have given him a shilling to get a bed elsewhere," said Maynard.

" What after he had behaved so ill to you!" exclaimed one who stood by.

" When a person needs my charity, I make it a rule to forget any ill they may havedone me," said the magnanimous miller.

" But go on, Wyatt. You say he begged to stay in the mill —you did not allow that, I hope?"

" I was over persuaded, master, seeing him so disconsolate, and little thinking that any harm would come of it.   It will be a grief to me as long as I live for your sake, and a caution for my own."

" Well, well, you have shown yourself not so trustworthy as I thought, but I think you had no ill design."

" Indeed, master, I had not."

" And how was the mill fired?"

" I cannot tell exactly.   My wife and I were awakened early this morning by the barking of the dog that we had left near the settle on which Andre had stretched himself.   We found every place full of smoke, the dog terribly excited, Andre gone, and fire bursting out on all sides.   Directly we opened the door the dog darted away, and we saw nothing of it more until half an hour ago, when the fire was over, and the mill in ruins."

" The building is quite down then?"

" Only part of the bare stone walls is left."

" The old mill!" ejaculated Maynard, with almost affectionate regret—" my own mill! as I had just begun to call it. But what use grieving?   'Tis gone—and there's an end!   Where did you find the dog?"

" Beating about the hill, smelling with its nose to the ground, and every now and then howling with might."

"I never saw a cleverer brute!" cried one of those who stood by, "it was as plainly searching for Andre as we were."

"Aye, that was it!" exclaimed Wyatt. "It must have had a struggle with him in the night by the state it was in; but we are quite in the dark how Andre got away from it, as we are how the animal came to be roused by his setting fire to the place, for one can hardly think there was sense enough in the creature to understand the nature of what he was about."

"There is more sense and more soul in that dog than in many a human being," said Maynard.

"More sense, master, I grant you," said Wyatt, "but the soul is another thing entirely."

"A very treacherous thing sometimes, Dick, as you have dearly proved, for you and your wife had like to have been burned to death by the infernal plottings of a man boasting of a soul, and been saved by a dog without one. After this, mind you hold dogs in reverence, and be cautious of men. But we may as well be moving. There is nothing to be done for this unhappy fellow, I suppose?"

"I should think not," said Wyatt; "he has escaped the gallows, and here he may lie till doomsday for me."

"And for me!" cried several voices.

"To save his life would be impossible," said Maynard; "it would take an hour to get the implements for dragging him out, if after all it could be done."

"That it would—so let him stay where he is," rejoined Wyatt.

"Aye to be sure," exclaimed the crowd, "let him stay where he is! such a villain can find no fitter grave; he is not worth the trouble we must have in removing him."

And so Andre was left under the stagnant and corrupt water, a prey to the noisome reptiles that infest such places. The rock from which he had fallen enveloped this pool of death and horror in a perpetual sullen shade, that never reflected the sweet beams of moon or star, or the rising or the setting sun, impervious to the light of heaven, and so far emblematic of the dark spirit just driven from the human form that had perished in its depths.

Some of the vices of Andre we are sorry to say had received encouragement from the example of his late master, from whence let us learn how important is the conduct of employers in its influences on those who serve them; for is it reasonable to expect goodness in the uninstructed and the laborious while those endowed with the blessings of education and comfortable circum-

stances give the rein to sensuality, and uncharitableness? It is not. Let the well-informed set the task of improvement to those within their sphere not by cold precept, but by their own exertions in that golden cause. Unfortunately, vices are sooner imitated than their opposites, and while Andre could laughingly pass from one descent of wickedness to another, stimulated by Percy Clifton's dashing profligacies, and ill-judged resentments, he was totally insensible to the nobler movements of feeling, the brilliant generosities, and the forceful energy, which relieved the darker traits of that most unequal of characters. A sort of blind liking he had for his young master, and had exerted much ingenuity to promote his unworthy pleasures, but when Clifton deserted the paths of dissoluteness for those of ambition, Andre was no longer a desirable servant, his habits being frequently found discreditable, espescially his growing love of strong drinks, hence his discharge, without a character, a home, or a friend, and in a state of mind prepared for the most desperate atrocities.

Maynard turned with grave thoughts, in which self formed a small portion, from the dread spot which held all that could decay, of this one of the many infatuated worshippers of evil, who abound, and ever have abounded, in the world.

"I forgive him," he said, casting back a glance on the black and weed-burdened pool. "He has paid the full penalty of the injury done me, and who cannot be satisfied with life for compensation, can be satisfied with nothing. I hope where he is gone there will be the same forgiveness for him that I feel, the horrors of such an end have been punishment enough."

The sight of the smouldering ruins of his mill as he approached the scene of desolation affected Maynard acutely. Now and then a bright flame shot up anew, and was with haste extinguished by the jets of water which the mill stream supplied. By one of these expiring remnants of fire, after the moon had set, the miller beheld in the darkness of early morning the displaced rafters, the disabled machinery, the half-consumed furniture, the unroofed and besmirched walls, of the place he had left a week ago so neat, comfortable, and thriving. The outer stone steps were left standing, and the tears rushed to his eyes as he beheld on them a large oil picture which had been precipitated there on the falling in of the building.

It had been executed by a village artist, and represented, at the age of sixteen, Hannah Forester, afterwards the wife of Summerfield. Though a sorry daub, he held it in high regard, as well for its likeness to Ruth, as a relic of a long-renounced attachment, and the semblance of one never to be seen more by

mortal eyes. He had bought this treasure many years ago of the tyro who had sketched it for the ornament of his window as the likeness of one whom everybody in the dale knew as the loveliest damsel of the vicinage. Carefully the precious possession had been hidden from sight in a dark closet adjoining his own room, and he wondered how much it had escaped being consumed. So eager he was now to rescue it from its perilous position that he was not nice in avoiding hazard while making the attempt. The broad plank which had sufficed for a bridge over the mill stream still remained, though damaged, and he was strongly advised not to attempt to cross it; but in the midst of their dissuasions the picture was preserved, the plank giving way immediately after Maynard had withdrawn his foot from it.

The safety of this picture (which artistically speaking was not worth ten shillings), and of those persons who were in the mill when the fire broke out, seemed partially to reconcile Maynard to the loss of his property, of which, saving his thousand pounds in the Rosedale Bank, nothing remained but the smoking fragments before him. Yet such a loss was calculated to make a bitter and lasting impression on his mind, for he was a man who cherished no light attachment for the home and objects to which he had been familiarised. A change of residence was to him like a change of country, and filled him with uneasiness in the anticipation. To create anew the concomitants necessary for his domestic comfort and his trade, apart from the cost, (for the mill had been uninsured,) occasioned sensations of discomfort that perhaps can only be understood in the after part of life by those whose habits, like his, "plant," as Charles Lamb said of his own, "a terribly fixed foot."

However, the mill was gone, and the only alternatives left were to rebuild another in its place with the money he had saved, or quit the dale. Either was harsh enough to him, and many moments occurred when he was tempted to curse the memory of the malicious destroyer, had not his wrath been appeased by a recollection of the despairing shrieks and distorted countenance of the wretch falling from the rock. In a strait what to do Maynard delayed fixing his plans until he knew the final fate of Summerfield. The loss of his trade meantime, and consequently of many pounds, was inevitable, and though he was not quite patient under the knowledge that his customers were taking their orders elsewhere, he did not allow his vexation to prevent him from doing all that previous to his misfortune he had intended in furtherance of a reprieve for his friend. The deputation of which he formed a member met however but a freezing reception from the minister of state in London to whom they applied, and who were compelled to return to await in suspense the reply which they were assured should be forwarded as soon as the necessary enquiries had been instituted.

CHAPTER XXXIIL

"The small birds rejoice in the green leaves returning,
  The murmuring streamlet winds clear through the vale,
The hawthorn trees blow in the dews of the morning,
  And wild scattered cowslips bedeck the green dale.

But what can give pleasure, or what can seem fair,
While the lingering moments are numbered by care?
No flowers gaily springing, nor birds sweetly singing,
Can soothe the sad bosom of joyless despair."

                                        ANON.

THE fever of the spirit produced by deferred hope, was now felt in its highest intensity by the children of Summerfield. His youngest girl had from the first shock of his arrest, sank into stupified despondency, and Ruth now saw her sister's illness added to the long list of their distresses. Still she bore up with unexampled fortitude, and only found in each new stroke, a new necessity for the control of her own griefs, and the exertion of her powers.

How little do we know of the heroic force of mind, with which some of the gentlest of the frailer sex are endowed. At little more than eighteen years old, this fragile girl—this evanescent flower of humanity—sustained thrice the number of sorrows, plerplexities, apprehensions, and disappointmeuts, than have bowed like reeds men, who had seemed to stand firm as mountains. The true greatness of woman operates in the paths of affection and duty, unobtrusively, silently, perhaps, unobserved, as in the steady devotion of Ruth to her calumniated father—in the exertions she made to relieve her mind from anxieties, on account of his children—to animate his trust in a heavenly life, which could alone enable him to bear up under the awful uncertainty of his situation—and in her exemplary attention to the sick bed of her young sister, when her own frame was drooping to the very earth, under the load which her spirit had to sustain. Her time was divided between fatiguing ministratious to the fear striken child. and agitating interviews with her unfortunate father.

Sally's disorder increasing, Ruth relinquished her nightly repose—such as it was—to watch by her side. Hour after hour she sat in the darkened chamber, listening to no voice but that which gave feeble and mournful utterance to the wanderings of delirium, ready, at the slightest movement of the recumbent sufferer, to present the cooling drink to the darkly-crimsoned lips, parched with the fever in the blood, to smooth the pillow, calm the irritability of disease, cheer the languishing mind, and assist the skill of the medical gentleman whose aid she had engaged. Sally had the quick sensibility and impatient temper of her mother, which often taxed severely the gentleness and self-devotion of her sister. She frequently asked if her father's reprieve had arrived, and being answered by a sad negative, wept with distraction so ungovernable, that it left her as weak as a new-born infant.

After one of these paroxysms, the chamber being hushed as death, and the excited sufferer, locked in a sleep of exhaustion on the bed, Ruth took up the pillow and bobbings, with which she had begun a piece of lace, that she hoped would remunerate the doctor attending on her sister, and employed herself sedulously until an advanced hour of the night. The plerplexity and loss her father's unfaltering friend had met with, from the destruction of his mill, engaged her thoughts some time, and she could not avoid fancying, what a blank there must be left in the familiar landscape from which that interesting old building had been blotted.

"The dale would hardly seem itself to me," she thought; "the mill was the most prominent object within it and many a time have I looked on its broad sails dancing in the wind, or sleeping in the moonlight."

Her brother had offered up his brief prayer at her knee, and was laid to rest in a small crib near the fireplace by which she sat. Ruth particularly loved this promising little fellow, who the day preceding had numbered eight years, and as she plyed her bobbins she often upraised her head to gaze with sad affection on his bright sleeping countenance. The fair crisp hair, disordered by contact with the pillow, formed itself into many a sunny ring about his boldly arched brows, where already with some exaggeration, but more truth, it might be said that " every god did seem to set his seal." His large blue eyes, which reflected thought beyond his years, were now closed in slumber, and on their lovely lids hung two crystal tears.

"Dear child!" murmured Ruth, as she wiped these away, and kissed his rosy cheek, "you are an early sorrower. May the rest of your life after these fearful days be passed in happier scenes!"

He moved at the sound of her voice, and in his dream pronounced the name which above all others thrilled her to hear. His limbs slightly quivered with agitation, and the hand resting on the variegated patch-worked quilt folded itself tightly up.

"Mr. Maynard would not have left my sister so!" exclaimed the sleeper, energetically and distinctly.

"Ah! no, he would not, my Billy," Ruth articulated, tears bursting from her eyes as she drooped her brow on his pillow.

"What have I been saying, Ruth?" asked the boy, starting awake, and winding his arms about her neck. "I was dreaming that I went to Rosedale House to ask the squire what he meant by leaving you in this way?"

"And what said he?" asked Ruth, forcing a smile, which was sadly at variance with the melancholy tears streaming from her eyes—tears such as slighted love alone can weep.

"If I had not waked so soon I should have been able to tell you," replied Billy, in accents of disappointment. "But when I grow older I will make the squire answer, and in right waking earnest, for his treatment of you, But you shall never live with him again, Ruth, for I will maintain you myself."

NOTICE.—A Beautiful Presentation Plate is issued with this Number of "The Cottage Girl."

"OH, MY DEAR FATHER!" SAID RUTH, AS HE EMBRACED HER.

THE COTTAGE GIRL.

"RUTH," DEAREST GIRL, COMPOSE YOURSELF."

"THERE is nothing you can do for me, dearest boy," said Ruth.

"I will stay by Sally while you lie down."

"And how will you keep awake?"

"Oh, by reading the Arabian Nights Mrs. Lister lent me. I have not finished the fisherman's story yet."

He cheerfully roused himself, and with injunctions to call her if Sally was restless, Ruth cast herself on the crib, where extreme fatigue speedily induced repose.

Ere she had slept long, the phantasma of the world of dreams gathered about her. She saw the surging crowds collecting — tumultuous unpitying crowds — to behold her father's execution, and the picturings of fancy occasioned her little less agony than the reality could have done. The castle keep exhibited on its roof the fatal crossbeam, and beneath stood her father. Aloft in the heavens appeared a small golden cloud, which suddenly began to descend, and the people on the ground, the walls, and other elevations near uplifted their fearful eyes toward it. As it touched the platform an angel stepped forth from its centre, bearing the likeness of her mother, with garments so glorious that they seemed to scatter stars as she moved. Momentarily, the dazzling vision appeared and faded, and the dreamer found herself in a very different scene, though still in the midst of thronging multitudes.

> " Ah ! then and there was hurrying too and fro,
>   And gathering tears, and tremblings of distress."

The place was a glen she had once seen, and only once, among the barren hills skirting her native dale. By the side of a dark cataract, nearly hidden from view by hanging roots and shrubs that grew in their clefts, she saw Percy Clifton and his valet, with whose dreadful end Maynard had acquainted her. She approached them, and perceived that Clifton was ghastly pale. and that his dress and hair were stained with clotted gore. Still, without speaking of this, she with frenzy reproached Clifton with cruelty and falsehood toward her, and Andre with having acted perfidiously in first assisting to betray his fellow-servant to his master, and then speaking evil of her to her husband.

"Be silent, Ruth," Clifton replied, in dreadful tones, "be silent. You have been deeply injured, but now you are more than avenged!"

The bands of sleep were broken abruptly, but these words were livingly grafted on her memory for ever after, and as she resumed her watch by her sister, an impression of evil about to happen to Clifton was powerfully on her mind.

"Can it be," she mused, "that retribution is at work for me! Ah! if so, spare him, Eternal Judge—spare him whom I have loved! Let not his offences to me be reckoned against him!

But the doom of Clifton was already registered above in the unalterable Book of Fate, and the angel of wrath had sealed the page.

The solitary candle in the chamber was burning low in the socket, the fire was dying away in the grate, when to dispel, if possible, the mists which were gathering gloomily over her thoughts, Ruth drew aside the window curtain, and looked forth on the widow Lister's garden, where the flowers were sleeping in shadow and perfume. The lamps of heaven seemed almost to have exhausted their light, but as yet, there were no other signs of approaching day, except the cheering cock-crow, at whose

sound the spirits of darkness are said to take flight. To Ruth it suggested only the distracting question whether the day it heralded would bring her father's reprieve, or whether it would see the issuing of the warrant for his execution. It was dreadful to think of his standing thus between two worlds, upheld only by one forlorn hope, which the next hour might be dashed away.

The sombre flow of her meditations was relieved by a feathered warbler of the night, which, ere it fled the landscape for its downy nest, sang a parting strain from the laurel bushes under her chamber window. Its mellifluous tones at that still season, sounded so sweetly, and were so pensively delightful, that they stirred in her mournful heart responses of intense feeling, which, though forlorn enough, possessed a luxurious charm. Reproachfully to the sweet melodist she spoke in the language of Scotia's peasant bard—

> " Thou mindst me o' departed joys,
> Departed never to return."

They also reminded her—as what did not that had the tone of truthful tenderness?—of Maynard's disinterested and noble friendship, which at present was the balm of her existence, the staff of her trust. When she compared the unaffected goodness of his life, his benevolence, his unselfishness, his constancy, and his truth, with the reckless self-indulgence, the ungovernable passions, and unstable purposes, of Clifton, she sighed at the contrast! the captivating person and the manners of the latter sank into insignificance before the moral superiority of the unpretending miller, and she deeply regretted the early bias her affections had taken. The admirable behaviour of Maynard to her under the peculiarly embarrassing circumstances in which she had been involved since her marriage, especially elevated him in her estimation, hovering as it did with exquisite propriety between the distant respect suitable for Squire Clifton's wife, and the kindness of a familiar friend. Such behaviour gave her higher impresssons of his intellect than anything she had ever known of him previously. Yet she was uninformed of the brightest action of his whole life. She did not suspect that the twenty pounds sent her anonymously as she imagined by Miss Clifton, emanated from this great-hearted man. Though done in privacy, this certainly was one of the few meritorious deeds that deserve to be proclaimed from the house-tops. It was a deed of liberality contrived with the express object of sparing her the burden of obligation, which he was aware no right-minded woman would wish to incur from an admirer whose devotion she was unable to reward. So that, though an ill-used and

disappointed lover, far from abusing in the remotest degree the confidence her cruel necessities compelled her to repose in him, he had studied by every means how to banish the shades of uneasiness which he foresaw their present intimacy might bring on her delicate mind, suppressing the yearning fondness which he felt for her, and inducing her to believe that the passion was extinct which could only perish with the heart that enshrined it.

Yes, Maynard still loved her, still worshipped the very ground that bore her footprints, the very air she breathed. In the presence of her beauty he could have gazed away his soul, a magical charm lured him to her society, and made every moment precious that he spent near her. Taintless however was his love; she was sacred in his eyes. To him her peace was infinitely dearer than any gratification of his own—nor was his love that of the sentimental philosopher who raves to the world of eternal and exalted passion when his most fitting task would be to crush or smother it. There was a pith and savour of manhood in Maynard's mind which led him to the right, as by instinct. Yet though controled with power—hardly giving breathing room, hardly acknowledged even to his secret thought—his love was still most fervent, most changeless, most imperishable.

During the second week after Summerfield's condemnation, while the reprieve was still delayed, and the sister of Ruth prostrated in sickness of mind and body, he seldom had a glimpse of the latter, but rarely a trait of excellence in her conduct escaped him, for the widow Lister described what an excellent nurse Mrs. Clifton made to the young patient, and how sweetly mild she always looked and spoke, and what good things she had taught that fine boy her brother, and how she employed every spare moment with her lace weaving as if she had nothing else to think of.

"Aye, Mrs. Lister," said Maynard, "few girls would bear trouble like her—and what trouble!"

"I have known some who could bear a good deal though, Mr. Maynard."

"Because they did not feel it, Mrs. Lister—because they were insensible."

"Very like—very like. But with your feelings, Mr. Maynard, I must say you have borne the loss of your mill better than I should have thought."

"I have borne worse losses better though."

"Indeed! I never heard you had any great loss before this."

"One the world could not supply, Mrs. Lister."

"Oh, now I understand,"—said the widow, in a confidential and sympathetic voice, "you mean the loss of your intended wife. Yes, I daresay that was worse, for there is nothing so grievous as disappointed love. But fill your pipe, Mr. Maynard, and I will send for a glass of ale to moisten it."

"When I return, I am going once more to see if my friend's reprieve has arrived."

Maynard went to the residence of the governor of the castle within the walls. He was ushered into a room filled with the rich fragrance of costly exotic plants, and covered at the sides with rare pictures. The governor received him with a gravity that dismayed his visitant.

"I regret to have to tell you," he said, "that your hopes are disappointed, the goverment have not thought fit to comply with your petition, and Summerfield is ordered for execution the third day from this."

"Then the boasted laws of this country are cruel, and its administrators partial and unjust!" exclaimed Maynard, violently. "I will forswear England, and rather live under the barbarism of heathens than her fair-seeming justice, which is but hypocrisy. May I see the secretary's reply?"

"There has none arrived from him in a direct form. My communication is this."—placing the order for Summerfield's death in the miller's hand.

"Then there is still a hope," exclaimed Maynard. "I wish you good day, Governor; I shall go to London again, and see the secretary to-morrow."

Maynard returned to the widow Lister's dwelling, and required to see Ruth immediately.

She came down stairs into the small back parlour, the wanness of her complexion, and the hollowness of her eye, telling of her late harrassing vigils by her sister's feverish couch, and of the sickness of the heart.

Maynard's heavy look at once infused into the mind of Ruth the dread confirmation of her worst apprehensions.

"Strengthen me, heaven, to bear what is to come!" she internally ejaculated. "Mr. Maynard," she then said, with white and quivering lips, "do not fear me—let your tidings be spoken, I will not shrink to hear them. You cannot?—then let me anticipate you—my father dies?"

"No, no," Maynard rejoined, though distressing embarrassment marked his manner, "the deputation was promised a direct reply from the secretary, and that has not arrived. I should like to consult the vicar, but he is at his vicarage in Rosedale, and every

moment now is worth an age. The governor of the castle here is as stern and formal as one of his own prisons. Only this morning I was saying to one of the gentlemen who went with the vicar and myself to town, that it might be as well to apply a second time to know why the promised answer was not sent to us, and now I am determined to set off directly, even if I have to go alone. The word of a minister of state is surely worth as much as another man's, and the deputation have a right to expect and demand his reply."

"But Mr. Maynard, you have not told me what tidings you have."

"They should come from someother tongue than mine, Ruth. It stabs me to the soul to have to speak them, for though the firm conviction is with me still that your father will be reprieved, I may not be able to impart that trust to you."

"Ah! I perceive what it is you would spare me the knowledge of—but why? If I cannot endure to hear that my father's death-hour is fixed, how shall I bear to lose him? Tell me, tell me the worst!"

"Thursday at ten—"

"Thursday!" exclaimed Ruth distractedly. "And to-day is Monday! So soon! Less than three days. Must Thursday see my father in his coffin—must Thursday's sun go down upon his grave! Must I never look upon his honoured face after Thursday! Must his reverend head never be seen by his children again! Must we never hear his voice more!'

'Ruth, dearest girl, compose yourself. There is hope I tell you yet."

"I will hope no more! No hope of mine but has deceived."

"Yet listen to me."

"Not if you talk of hope—I am not to be consoled that way any more."

"But you that have been so patient hitherto, will you sink now?"

"No, I will be patient still. But in this world all hope, all joy, is over for me. Death and wretchedness envelope my path —there is no ray of light in the thick darkness but such as shines to immortality. Thank God, I do see that."

"Then with that to comfort you, bear up as hardily as you can until you see me again, for I must bid you a hasty farewell."

"God bless you, Mr. Maynard! I was wrong to say my path was wholly dark. Every cloud that has lowered on it has been gilded by your kindness—though kindness is a cold and common

word for actions like yours. Without your support I could not have acquitted myself as I have under these mighty trials."

"Do you say so? Then I am repaid for all. The disappointments and the losses I have had are all outweighed by the pleasure of hearing you say that I have been of service to you."

"I should be colder than December's snow could I forget the benefits you have heaped on me—insensible and base not to feel a lifelong gratitude. What you have done to relieve the distresses of my parents I regard as benefits to myself. The money you have lavished—"

"Oh, perish the money! never think of that now, Ruth. It has done better than I ever hoped from it if it has won me any regard from you."

And unable to trust himself longer on so agitating a topic, Maynard hastily took leave.

We pass lightly over the two succeeding days. They were marked by the utmost extremity of human woe for Summerfield and his children. The approaching end of the former was chiefly embittered by the unhappy situation in which he was leaving Ruth—deserted by Clifton, unprovided with the means of life for herself or those under her charge.

On the eve of the day appointed for his death, in taking his solemn leave of them, he gave them his parting advice and counsel.

In compliance with the ardent wishes of her sister, Ruth had conveyed her in a hackney coach to the castle, where an officer of the prison carried the enfeebled child in his arms to those of her doomed parent. Thrice during the farewell interview Sally fainted, yet would not be removed. The strength of her feelings at such an age, for she was not yet fourteen, surprised some as much as her elder sister's fortitude. But strength was the prominent characteristic of the Summerfields. The young boy was firm in his trust on Maynard. He could not be persuaded that his father would die, for Maynard had said otherwise. Summerfield regretted the absence of his friend on an errand he judged fruitless; and thinking he should never see him more, wrote a letter of gratitude for the past, and bidding him an eternal farewell. This was not the only proof of the fullness of his heart toward Maynard—he bound a vow on the consciences of his children to the effect, that if ever fortune shone on them, they should recompense the good their father had in his misfortunes received from the miller.

That dismal night the children of Summerfield took no rest.

The widow Lister remained with them most of the time, after a visit of kind condolence from the vicar of Rosedale, who, by his benign air, and a felicitous application of pious argument, in some measure softened the anguish of the orphans. He assured them that he had conversed with their father at some length, and found him perfectly fit to die, nay, stretching all his soul with ardent longing heavenward.

When the vicar and Mrs. Lister were both withdrawn, the orphans crept close to the fire and each other, Sally reclining on an easy chair, her features burning with fever heat and excitement, the pallid and deep-thoughted Ruth seated by her, and Billy at their feet.

"Another hour gone!" Ruth suddenly exclaimed, in tones scarcely above her breath, as the cathedral clock boomed slowly and mournfully on the silent night.

"Only nine hours left!" said Billy, after reckoning a moment.

"See how precious is time now," observed Ruth, impressively, "and yet how much have we wasted."

A Bible lay on her knee, out of which she read a few of the glowing sentences of the Apostle Paul triumphing over death.

Mournfully after that passed away another hour, and the deep-toned steeple clock again knelled slowly on the hearing of the forlorn watchers. The voice of their mourning then went forth on the breeze of the night, and pitying angels wept at the sound.

The bell tolled three!

"In seven hours," said Billy.

"Cease—cease to reckon!" exclaimed Ruth. "Let us remember only how my father bade us spend this time. Come, kneel with me."

While her voice, broken by lamentations, ascended to the pitying Father of the human race, the footsteps of remorseless time steadily advanced, and with its mighty voice the cathedral bell proclaimed the hour of four.

"Not our will but Thine be done!" exclaimed Ruth, her streaming eyes uplifted.

Soon after, in low and tremulous tones, the orphans sang together a funeral hymn. Day broke the while.

"It is our father's last!" said Ruth—but here we draw the veil.

CHAPTER XXXIV.

"As sweet as sunshine after wintry rain,
Or after famine as the golden grain,
Or as the pleasant morning fair and bright
To travellers 'wildered in the gloom of night;
Or calm, after the tempest's raging flow—
So welcome and so sweet is gladness after woe."

On what various and dissimilar scenes of this tumultuous state of existence are the sunbeams shed that gild the opening day! They fall on bridal circles, where the tear and the smile blend together on the countenance of beauty, and young hearts are panting with happiness the highest that mortality is permitted to enjoy; they glance upon the cold faces of the dead who can rejoice in them no more; they penetrate the narrow cell where the prisoner awaits with sensations that never yet have been adequately described, the summons to execution; they mock with their brightness the children of affliction; they waste their beauty on the heartless rabble who press to exult and to make merry in the expiring agonies of a fellow being.

All nature seemed glad on the fatal morning when the guiltless Cottager of Rosedale was to suffer the sentence of the law. The atmosphere was fraught with healthful influences, and rich with golden sunlight; the great tower in the south castle wall

seemed to smileamid its strenness, and rustled its dark ivy on the breeze that sweptaround it; eventhe horrid cord suspended from the gibbet on its lofty roof seemed in mirthful motion; and the gilded clouds diversifying the blue heaven momently varied their form and positionas if controlled by the caprice of some "tricksy" spirit, some delicate Ariel.

· And the same morning that rose so bright on the miseries of Summerfield and his children rose as brightly on the fashionable hotel in London where Clifton was endeavouring, not unsuccessfully, to stifle in dreams of self-aggrandizement the accusings of conscience   Absent from his lowly bride, the charm of her beauty was no longer felt; the remembrance of her virtues he discarded, for it was only productive of remorseful uneasiness; and his obstinate resentment against her was continually fed not only by jealousy of Maynard, and her supposed contempt of the olive branch he had held out, but also by recurring to the indignities he had received, or supposed himself to have received, from Summerfield, while he wilfully closed his eyes to all the mitigating circumstances attending what he called the murder of his father, and persisted in his belief that Ruth had been in her parents' confidence in that matter.   The high-born lady whose hand he had rejected for that of Ruth was still unmarried, and beholding her frequently in all the splendour of wealth, rank, and fashion, commanding the influence for want of which he found his ambitious schemes barred by insurmountable impediments, he cursed the precipitant resolve which had made him the husband of the Cottage Girl.

The exertions that had been made for a remssion of Summerfield's sentence he had heard of, but spurned at the idea of their proving successful.   With stern satisfaction he had seen the Thursday approach on which Summerfield was to die, and at the hour of ten he congratulated himself that his father was avenged.   But as he left the hotel he encountered one of his old jovial companions, the son of a peer, though a giddy and needy profligate.

"Clifton," he said, "I was coming in search of you.   I have news, such as may hardly please you."

"I cannot attend to you at present," said Clifton, unceremoniously, for he was anxious to shake off this early acquaintance, and was indifferent as to the mode.

"May I never shuffle a card more if you escape me so." muttered the young debauchee.   "Hark you, Clifton, you had better hear my news.   Come let us have a bottle of champagne at the next tavern and I will open my budget 'tis a weighty one, as I live by betting."

"I am engaged," said Clifton, walking more rapidly.

"So am I," returned the other, inserting his hand under the elbow of the squire. "But you will pay for a bottle, Percy, if only for the sake of the merry days and nights we have had together. I am without a shilling now, poor devil that I am, or I would not tax your purse. The wheel of old dame fortune may turn round in my favour yet however, and then call me a pitiful knave if I deny my old friend Percy a bottle of whatever he likes."

Clifton could not resist this appeal, and they were presently seated in the private room of a genteel tavern, with decanters and glasses before them.

"I'll give you a toast," said Clifton's companion, slowly filling his glass.—"Here's to your speedy freedom from the shackles of matrimony!"

"Hold, Jack," said Clifton, frowning, setting down the glass he had raised to his lips—"who authorised you to venture such a toast?"

"My love for you. Percy, nothing else. It is the best wish a friend like me can offer."

"Perhaps a friend like you could indeed wish me no better" said Clifton, with a satirical expression playing on his lip. "But your news?'

"Your father-in-law is reprieved. Nay, never start, nor look angry, it was not I reprieved him—he might have hung to eternity for me."

"On what pretence is he reprieved?'

"How should I tell? All I know is, his life is spared, and what is more he is transported only for five years."

"Who told you this fiction?" demanded Clifton.

"It was talked of openly at the Sporting Club last night, and many wondered how you would take it. For my part, were I you I should be glad the poor fellow was spared for his death cannot reanimate the old squire, or advantage you, and considering the affair occurred so long ago, and that the old gentleman was compounded of such unprofitable elements—"

"Jack," interrupted Clifton, "be so good to make your allusions to my father, if they are necessary, with respect.

"Did I do otherwise?—then I ask your pardon. But you are terribly proud, Percy, and think vastly too much of your family. But what say you to dinner?—I have eaten nothing to day."

"Have what you will, but I dine elsewhere," and he arose to go.

"Stay a moment,"said the other,—"your baronetcy will turn out mere smoke."

"You can know much about that," said Clifton," with assumed indifference and contempt, though his clear pale complexion showed the kindling of angry pride, and his voice betrayed an interest too deep to escape observation.

"I know you will not get it."

"How do you know?"

"That is my business; but if you do, may I lose my next quarter's allowance that I stand in so much need of."

"Where can you have gathered information on such a subject?"

"Why, there's the rub! This you may be certain of, the relatives of a certain young lady of rank who was proposed to you in marriage would have made Percy Clifton a baronet before this had he not been fool enough to refuse."

"I believe it," said Clifton, his eyes glancing fire. "A fool I was indeed!"

"And further, Percy Clifton may thank them that he must continue plain Mr."

"Of that," said Clifton, "your report by no means convinces me, for it is not to them I look. Dinner comes, however, so I leave you."

With a levity adopted to disguise many miserable feelings springing out of the degradation to which he was reduced, the other allowed Clifton to discharge the reckoning, and then borrowed from him five pounds. Clifton hurried from the abandoned spendthrift, who had been the associate of his early days, with mingled pity and disgust. On his own account he was highly irritated, suspecting from what he had heard that in society where he had been familiarly known his aspirations after a baronetcy were ridiculed, and that not to gain it after all would inflict a wound upon his dignity which could never be healed. Goaded by these thoughts, he lost no time in ascertaining more explicitly how his views prospered in the quarter whence he had hoped the coveted honour would have emanated. He found that Lady Vernon's friends had contrived to prevent him from obtaining it.

In proud natures of quick susceptibility, a failure in anything which has engaged their mental energies, or staked any part of their reputation, often induces despondency, and paralyses the exertions, by which alone the disappointment could be retrieved. Though this is a weakness to be lamented, it is not always to be subdued. The highest natures are not more distinguished by the earnestness of their undertakings, than by their magnanimity; he could achieve much, but could not endure. His self-

possession was wholly overthrown by the slightest failure in anything on which his mind was set. Even the bright parts of his character turned to darkness, and irritation next to madness ensued, if his non-attainment could be supposed to diminish his consequence.

After the title, which in imagination he had already clutched, had melted from him, a gnawing restless discontent took possession of his soul. He was jealous of all with whom he conversed, lest they should see how deeply the denial of the boon had mortified him; and while he affected to be unmoved, he inwardly writhed under the fancied comments made on his chastised ambition. And all this insufferable humiliation he ascsibed to his marriage with the poor Cottage Girl.

"Had I only guessed the wrong she was doing me, in withholding the secret of her father's crime," he thought, "I should have spared myself that costly sacrifice.

The commutation of her father's punishment tended also to perpetuate the breach between Ruth and her husband. Had Summerfield been executed, Clifton's vengeance for his father's death, now but half appeased, would have been finally at rest; but the existence of the man whom he considered to have murdered his father, he, in writing to his sister declared, must be ever a barrier to a reconciliation with Ruth.

Amy on her part rejoiced that Summerfield had been spared, and frankly remonstrated with her brother on the harshness of his dealings with his wife, telling him, that she retracted her promise of not communicating with Ruth, and intended to see her and bring her back to Rosedale.

To this Percy answered in heat, forbidding Amy to converse with Ruth, unless she wished to give lasting offence to her brother.

"What then is to be done?" Amy wrote in return. "Are you and this estimable girl, who have pledged yourselves to each other till death, to live always separate? And is your wife to be left without home or provision?"

"No," replied Percy, in answer, "she shall sign a deed of separation that shall divide us permanently, but provide liberally for her maintenance."

While he is preparing to carry out this purpose, we return to Maynard, who being informed at the office of the secretary of state that his friend's reprieve was about to be sent off, returned to the castle by twelve o'clock on Wednesday night, when the sound of the hammer on the roof of the keep, told him that the apparatus of death was preparing It was not until the hour

fixed for the execution was near, that the reprieve reached the
governor of the castle.   The sensations of Summerfield, saved
nearly at the last moment from a death so undeserved and terrible
to soul and sense, were unutterably profound, and the lofty composure which had marked his demeanour since his trial was lost
in emotion, when he beheld again the children from whom he had
believed himself to be divided to the end of time, and the friend
who had taken so active a part for his redemption from the dread
fate, which just before had appeared inevitable.   There was shaking of hands, and plentiful weeping, and rapturous exclamations.
The five years Summerfield was to spend in fetters and bondage
in an alien land, was thought little of during the first gush of joy,
excepting by himself, and he forbore to damp their overflowing
happiness by pointing out the sharp thorns that bestrewed the
path which yet he had to tread.   When, however, the effervescence of feeling caused by his deliverance, had subsided, those
years he was to spend in captivity, darkened and lengthened on
their view, and as day succeeding to day brought more near the
inevitable separation it expanded into greater importance, and
was anticipated with increased dread.

"Oh, father," sobbed Sally, when she heard the day was fixed
for his removal to the sea-coast, whence an appointed vessel would
convey him to his far distant place of exile, "I am afraid you
will be as much lost to us, as if there had been no reprieve.   I
am afraid we shall not see you any more."

"My dear," rejoined her father, "the same providential hand
which has been stretched out to rescue me from an unmerited
death, will, I hope, conduct me back to you."

He spoke in the tone of confident augury, but Ruth could not
contemplate the changes which trouble and gathering years had
wrought in his health without melancholy misgivings.   Could
his shattered frame sustain the slavish labours, hardships, and
miseries, which his sentence entailed?   Was it not too likely that
he would die under them?   In fancy she beheld him expiring,
amid cold-hearted strangers—in fancy she viewed him interred
in foreign soil.

"My father!" she exclaimed, " gladly if it were possible would
I lighten by my own participation, the sufferings you must undergo, and though this cannot be, I shall feel in idea all you endure in reality.   I shall see you driven as a slave to your daily
toil, the companion of depraved wretches, without a kind voice to
speak to you, or a kind face which you can look upon.   Oh! I
shall imagine it all, and with a bursting heart shall often wish
you had joined my mother in the realm of the dead."

"How truly do I wish I had!" Summerfield rejoined; "her present rest seems to me enviable indeed. But we must not shrink from the burdens imposed on us, our proper part is to bear them with cheerful resignation, so they will be found profitable in the end for the correction of what is evil in us, and the increase of what is good. I do not say that I can look forward to five years of slavery, distant from my family and my native land, with a quiet mind. God knows how I shrink under the cross given me to bear, but He has said 'I will never leave nor forsake thee,' and I know that He is as present at New South Wales as here."

"Could we not take a passage to the same place, and be near you still, father?" Billy asked.

"You might had you the means, and were Ruth unmarried."

"Mr. Clifton will make no objection, he will be glad if she is where he can never see her again, and then he will marry some grand lady."

"That was thoughtless spoken, my boy. See, you have made your sister weep."

"I am sorry, Ruth," said the frank-hearted child, tears of repentance and sensibility filling his fine blue eyes. "I am very sorry."

"It is very likely you are right, Billy," said Ruth, with irrepressible anguish. "Mr. Clifton I feel persuaded, would make no obstacle to my departing anywhere out of his way. I have heard that he regrets now the splendid alliance which he gave up for me, and that if he could he would divorce me."

"No doubt," said Summerfield, in a tone that sounded like an execration,—"he is deeply dyed in wickedness and capable of anything. I have prayed and striven in vain to keep in check the hatred I feel toward him. To hear his name carries me out of myself From the first to the last his conduct to you, my dear and amiable daughter, has been most perfidious and cruel. Some grievous punishment will light on him for it either in this world or the next."

In perfect sincerity Ruth hoped not. She had no malice against him; and though he had abandoned her she ardently desired his good. Not that there was any apathy in her feelings, but she clung to the belief that he had once loved her, and that covered many sins. She reminded her father too that though Clifton now scorned his humble bride, his marriage with her had been a voluntary reparation of former wrong, and that his renouncing the hand of a titled lady for her sake was an undeniable proof that he was not wholly vicious.

"Where is the man that is so?" Summerfield rejoined. "The guiltiest on earth must sometimes hear and obey the voice of conscience. But it is no father's part to stir the mind of his daughter against her husband, and I forbear."

Before the cottager was removed from the castle to commence his dreary voyage he heard with inexpressible pain a new misfortune threatening Maynard, far greater than the burning of the mill, this was the stoppage of the Rosedale Bank, and the consequent loss of the most part of his savings laid up therein. For some days it was doubtful whether the stoppage would not be merely temporary, and Maynard was willing to hope the best. Nevertheless, his anxiety was extreme, and it was while he was in this perturbed state of mind that he took a farewell of his friend, which, though more brief, was not less kind than if his attention had not been distracted by personal distress.

"If you lose your money," said Summerfield, "I shall feel, when the intelligence reaches me, more pain than even my wretched captivity can afford. I shall wish your liberality to me and mine had been spared, and bitterly grieve that in your need we cannot return what you lent for ours."

Maynard wrung the hand of Summerfield, and his eye glistened, and his voice was broken.

"I shall never regret that I have assisted you," he said; "and if I must lose my thousand pounds that I have thought so much of, the loss will be sharply felt, but it must be borne. I am but forty years old, and, thank God, I feel no falling off of strength, so it will be strange if I cannot contrive to keep the wolf from the door, seeing that I have none depending on me."

He broke off and groaned, for at that moment there was more on his mind than the apprehended loss of his money. After a brief pause he observed that Summerfield must leave his children in sadly precarious circumstances, and assured him that happen what might while he had a shilling they should not be destitute.

At the same time that Summerfield took leave of his friend, he parted also from his children. Each he embraced with overflowing eyes, and bade the two younger remember his previous counsels, and be kind and obedient to Ruth, who would guide them in all that was right. She that night left them in the house of widow Lister, and when at eleven o'clock the prison van conveyed away her father from the castle, Ruth followed him, accompanied after much persuasion by her good landlady, in the vehicle they had hired. The part of the coast where the prison ship was lying in which he was to be received was fifteen miles distant, and the sun was just rising out of the stormy billows when a boat with a single rower came gliding over the surf to receive the convict.

IN PREPARATION.—Another Beautiful Presentation Plate for
"The Cottage Girl."

THE COTTAGE GIRL.

RUTH CAUGHT ONE OF HIS HANDS AND KISSED IT.

IN the custody of an armed constable, Summerfield crossed the beach to meet the boat. It was a tempestuous morning, gloomy and cold. The sea rolled in waves of midnight darkness, and the surf flew over the tallest rocks. The heart of the unfortunate prisoner was heavy as lead as his eye traversed the agitated expanse before him, while his thoughts turned yearningly back on the children and the land he was quitting. What was his emotion when Ruth, rushing past the constable, threw herself on his neck?

"My darling girl," he faltered, "why have you done this?"

"Forgive me; I wished to see you once more, and to say to you much that I had forgotten; though indeed," she added, weeping violently, "it has passed from my mind again."

"You may remember it when you write to me," he said, gently disengaging himself to depart.

"Oh, father! father!" she exclaimed, "shall we ever meet again?"

"Doubt not we shall."

"And must you go then? Oh, dear father! may patience and comfort go with you! and may God incline their hearts in your favour, in whose charge you will be placed!"

"And may comfort be with you, who need it more than I," he returned.

The constable looking impatient, Summerfield was turning to step into the boat, when Ruth caught one of his hands, and kissed it with reverence and love. He blessed her, and elevating one fettered arm toward heaven, asserted solemnly his entire innocence of the crime of which he had been found guilty.

Once again Ruth delayed him, to ask if he had no message to leave with her, and if there was nothing she might do for him?

"It would gratify me," he replied, in a whisper, "if you would see your mother's grave, and write to me its exact situation, and you may enclose some token from it, if but a blade of grass."

The last moment of parting had arrived, and the boat bore him away.

She followed his lessening figure with streaming eyes, sending after him a hundred affectionate farewells. When he was no longer visible, she sat down a few moments on a point of rock, to gaze on the distant vessel which held her only and beloved parent, heedless of the furious wind that raged around, and of the tide that dashed over the beach, sprinkling her with spray. In this short interval, a young fisher lad, abroad thus early in search of shell fish, wading with bare feet and legs among the wet sands, pools, and rocky caves of the beach, came near enough for Ruth to hear the subjoined verses, as he sang them with forcible expression :—

THE CONVICT'S DEPARTURE.

He stepped into the boat, which was waiting to convey
The poor heart-broken Convict from his cherished land away;
He stepped into the boat 'mid the jeerings of the rest,
Who laughed to see his wild despair, and the anguish of his breast.

But his heart a blasted tree had felt the lightning's power,
And unheeded on it beat the petty passing shower;
His heart was lone and withered, that thought was flashing by,
As wildly from the cliffs he turned his hopeless eye.

The boat was pushed away, it quickly near'd the ship,
He stood upon the deck with ashy cheek and lip ;
His hands pressed hard his temples as though to give relief,
As he struggled to repress the volcano of his grief.

He thought upon the friends—and rigid grew his face,
Who lured him to his ruin, then fled from his disgrace ;
But the ship was swiftly cleaving the glassy waters blue,
And wrestling with his agony he murmured an adieu !

The words for the most past were so applicable to her father as to create in the listener a momentary impression of surprise, but the singer broke the spell by commencing a rude nautical ballad, and quitting the beach Ruth joined Mrs. Lister, who had waited till her patience was exhausted behind some crags a short way off in the vehicle which had conveyed them to the sea-side.

After they had returned to the neat and shining little home of the widow, Ruth suffered her lace-cushion and ivory pins to rest unemployed to the end of the day, notwithstanding she felt such pressing need of exertion, for her nerves were quite over-worn by the variety of distressing sensations she had experienced and her mind was busy with harrowing imaginings of the life or which her father had just entered. Mrs. Lister was extremely kind, but her kindness was evinced in a manner rather trouble-some to the object of her compassion. Agreeable to Maynard's hint she took care Ruth was not left alone, and the latter was glad when the hour of rest came that could alone free her from the irksome necessity of attending to Mrs. Lister's exhaustless talk.

"How little can this good woman understand me," Ruth ob-served to herself. "My spirits are not to be raised by such trifling means as those she thinks of. I have within me the only sources of consolation, and it is not by flying from myself that I can make use of their healing balm. My heart alone knoweth its own bitterness and its own peace, and to converse with it in solitude is that which at present is best for me."

Next morning Ruth was so far victorious over her own de-spondence as to renew her application to her lacemaking with resolved diligence, and the employment tranquillised her, and gave her a feeling of superiority to affliction, and added to the stability of her mind. She finished after ten hours unremitting industry the piece of lace whose profits were to remunerate the medical attendants of her sister, and at the close of the evening she took it to the intended purchaser, the lady of the governor of the castle from whom she received five guineas. The beauty of the work at the same time induced a friend of the lady to request that a similar piece might be prepared for her. Gratified that her skill in this pleasing art would enable her to maintain herself and those dependent on her until the health of Sally should be sufficiently restored for entering on some decided occupation, Ruth proceeded the same hour to the house of the doctor, who appeared surprised and affected when she placed before him what he knew from Mrs. Lister to be the earnings of her hours of dejection and loneliness, thanking him in modest terms for his successful attentions to her sister. He appeared to hesitate, as if about to return the money, but, changing his mind, wrote the receipt, and with a bow of profound respect. saw her retire.

There was a glow of virtuous satisfaction in the mind of Ruth as she returned to the widow's fireside, and after they had partaken of a frugal supper she paid Mrs. Lister for her lodgings, which left her but a few shillings of the twenty pounds she had anonymously received. This did not dispirit her, however, and she prepared to commence work anew the following morning, which she did by daylight.

Shortly she received a letter from her father, which informed her that when she received it he would have commenced his compulsory voyage.

Many an ejaculatory prayer she breathed for his safety on the perilous ocean, and fearfully she listened to the wind that shook the casement or thundered in the chimney, fancying that its voice spoke of shipwreck and death. While filial anxieties occupied a great part of her thoughts, others connected with her husband also pressed heavily upon her. She had a sort of quiet self-respect—a gentle pride—which forbade her to stoop before the high and haughty passions of Clifton, while there could be any danger of her submission being misunderstood as applying to his circumstances instead of himself. As she had suffered the ills of poverty, she of course knew how to value the advantages of fortune, but there was nothing mercenary in her mind, and while Clifton withheld from her his love and his esteem, the rest he had to bestow was dross in her estimation. She had no expensive habits to provide for, a plain subsistence was all she sought, and as her own industry could supply that, and as she had been accustomed to self-reliance, she was able to preserve an independence of feeling rare in females of her age.

When, therefore, the agent of Clifton sought her out to obtain her signature to the deed allotting her a separate maintenance. she mildly refused.

"It is wholly unnecessary," she said, "while any degree of health is permitted to me my own hands will supply my wants, which are few and simple, for I have been used to a life of many harpships. You may tell Mr. Clifton, sir, that I thank him for having wasted a moment's consideration on my necessities, and when they become too arduous for me, which at present they are not, I will make bold to solicit his aid. With regard to the separation to which he wishes me to subscribe. his wlll must be obeyed. I will never trouble him with my society while it is hateful to him; and if by signing this paper I could make him free to wed where his fancy is now wandering, I would do it cost what it might, but as no earthly power can annul his marriage with me I see no use in this formal document."

"The purpose of it, Mrs. Clifton, give me leave to say, is mainly to provide for you."

"Then, sir, I may the more boldly refuse to sign it."

"What good end can be answered by your doing so?"

"The satisfaction of my own feelings, and no more."

"But, madam, I entreat you to consider—will you leave yourself dependent on a precarious mode of livelihood, which may be interrupted by many unforseen events, and which at the best must be laborious to you, when by a stroke of your pen you may possess yourself of a certain provision, without care, or without toil?"

"What I have spoken has been well considered," rejoined Ruth, "I refuse to sign this deed."

"Most reluctantly shall I bear this answer to the squire," said the agent. "But I have performed my commission and can do no more."

When he had gone Ruth sat down and covered her face. Her lacerated heart bled unseen. An hour had fled ere she had stirred from her melancholy posture, and the shadows of night entered the window from the garden and stole over the apartment unobserved. The troops of humming house flies had left their sporting in the sunbeams to settle mute and motionless upon the darkened wainscoat or ceiling. The pleasant voices of children at their gambols came no longer from the green by the widow's dwelling; and the butterfly fled to its stately couch in the crimson tulip. A blissful repose had settled on all but the breast where grief had made its lodgement. A small fire was in the grate, without flame, but of an intense and beautiful glow, which barred the darkness of the floor and wall with a still, fervent, contemplative light, illuminating the lovely drooping head of the

forsaken mourner, while the hand that supported it was in deep shadow.

The door opened without arousing her, and Maynard was admitted by Mrs. Lister. She arose, and he perceived that her face was covered with tears.

"Has anything happened more than I know?" he inquired, with his accustomed kindness.

She told him of the visit of Mrs. Clifton's agent and its object.

Maynard muttered something to himself, but said aloud—

"I wish you had not refused to sign the deed. What he proposed was no more than your right, and it is disgraceful you should be toiling as you are while your husband is rioting in plenty."

"That is what Mrs. Lister will tell me," said Ruth, "but I had hoped you would enter deeper into my feelings."

"I wish to see you free from anxiety."

"How can that be?"

"I mean for your subsistence,"

"I am free from anxiety for that. But what has brought you here so late?—some misfortune I fear! What of the bank?"

"It is gone."

"No, surely not!"

"It is."

"And you are ruined!"

"Just so?"

"Oh, Mr. Maynard, this is a blow indeed! You are ruined!"

"Absolutely ruined. I have not twenty pounds to call my own."

"Yet you have paid a hundred to my father's counsel! And how much for his relief in other ways! Oh! this is insupportable."

"Trouble not yourself about me, Ruth—I have got over the first shock—and now I am come to take leave of you for a little while. I have to begin life anew, and go to see what can be done among those who profited by me in my prosperous years. No one will lose a penny by me that is one comfort."

"A substantial one to you I know it will be, Mr. Maynard. But sit with me half an hour before you take leave, you look very wretched."

"Why it is hard to lose at a single stroke all one has been priding themselves upon, and all they have been getting together with so much pains."

"It is hard."

"Not that I would thrust my troubles on you, your own are heavy enough."

"Not so heavy as to prevent me from sharing yours. But why do you not sit? I will prepare you a little supper; I have made ready many a one for you and my father in the cottage, Mr. Maynard. You recollect those happy evenings, I daresay?"

"Do I not! But I will not stay now, I am hardly collected enough; I must busy myself with something or other, or I shall go distracted. For the present you will stay with Mrs. Lister, I suppose, so that I shall run no hazard of not being able to find you when I return."

Ruth replied that she would remain there, and they parted with mutual kindness, Ruth feeling afterwards more lonely than ever.

But the trial of her patience had reached its acme, and brighter moments began to dawn.

The doctor, whose bill she had paid with the produce of her industry, waited on her with the unexpected and agreeable news that a subscription had been set on foot by the vicar of Rosedale, himself, and some other gentlemen who compassioned the forlorn condition of the orphans of Summerfield, and believed in his innocence, and eighty pounds had been collected for them. On the application of this sum they wished to know the mind of Mrs. Clifton. It was ultimately settled that Sally should be placed in some house of business, and that with the rest of the money a small house should be furnished for Ruth, in whose charge Billy should remain. Before, however, this last arrangement had been carried into operation, Ruth received a still more startling communication of a joyful nature, from the executors of the eccentric couple whom she had served in London, who, after living together all their lives, had departed out of existence nearly in the same hour, and shared the same grave. A will had been left, executed by them conjointly, and bearing the crooked sign-manual of each, bequeathing to Ruth the whole of the extensive property they had accumulated, excepting legacies to the persons they had chosen for executors. These were not private friends, but individuals of puplic trust, and unimpeachable reputation. By their advice Ruth immediately repaired to London, accompanied by Mrs. Lister, leaving Sally in the millinery establishment where public subscription had placed her, and Billy with a sister of the widow, who took charge of the shop and house.

Into the details of the busy fortnight Ruth passed in the metropolis, we shall not enter, it is enough to say at the expiration of that time, she found herself treading the streets, where once she had roved in misery and destitution, the undisputed possessor of

nearly fifty thousand pounds. But she was as sensible and as firm in prosperity as she had been in adversity. She did not alter the simplicity of her mode of life, or make any boast of this sudden and extraordinary turn of fortune; her whole thoughts were employed how to turn her riches to the alleviation of her father's misery, and the recompence of Maynard's generosity. The former she had heard had arrived at the penal settlement in moderate health, and thither she wrote to communicate the wondrous news, and to enquire if any money transmitted to him would be allowed to add to the increase of his comforts. A cheering answer was returned, that her father was allowed many indulgences; that there were hopes, as his conduct continued to inspire his governors with confidence, that those indulgences would be extended to wider limits—at the same time, he could make no use of money at present.

CHAPTER XXXV.

"Couldst thou look as dear, as when
    First I sighed for thee,
Couldst thou make me feel again
Every wish I breathed the then,
    Oh how blissful life would be!
Hopes that now beguiling leave me,
    Joys that lie in slumber cold;
All would wake, couldst thou but give me
    One dear smile like those of old."

MOORE.

IT was a great change this, which had happened to our young heroine, great in itself and its consequences. She had been poor, but was now rich; she had served others, now thousands would have been willing and eager to serve her; she had fared hardly, and arrayed herself on a scale of the nicest frugality, now it was in her power to cover her table with every luxury the world produced, and to strike with admiration by her resplendent attire, those who had beheld her in her obscurity. All that a worldly heart could covet might now be here. If she loved to tread in gorgeous balls, to revel in luxurious entertainments, to fly like a bird of passage from one bright realm to another, to gather around her the galaxies of fashion, to hear her beauty lauded, to see her courted by the distinguished and the titled—if this could afford her gratification, this in its

fullest extent was in her power. But none of these enjoyments had fascination for Ruth, while her father was an exile, her husband estranged from her, the generous Maynard unhappy, and her broken-hearted mother lying in the churchyard.

The first use she made of her wealth was to restore the amount of their contributions to those humane persons, who had subscribed for the maint-nance of herself, and her sister, and her brother. She took pains to collect their names, accompanying the money with a few lines to each. expressive of the high sense she entertained of the liberality which had prompted the donation that it was in her power gratefully to return. In composing these letters she was aided by the meek vicar of her native place, who was now her chief adviser; and if it was accounted a proof of wisdom in Queen Elizabeth that she selected wise councillors, such a selection was no less a proof of wisdom in our heroine, suddenly placed in circumstances of trial the most hazardous, perhaps, that youth and beauty could have to encounter.

"And you will return for me to Miss Clifton, the twenty pounds she was good enough to send me before my father had his trial," said Ruth, to the reverend gentleman.

"I think," he observed anxiously, "that I did not name Miss Clifton as the donor."

"You did not, but I felt secretly assured that relief came from her."

"You are mistaken," said the vicar, "Miss Clifton never entrusted me with money for you, though her own inclination I must believe would have directed her to supply your necessities."

"And if Miss Clifton was not my friend in that emergency tell me, reverend sir, who was?" exclaimed Ruth, in much surprise, which was of an unpleasant nature, for on this supposed proof that Miss Clifton was well-disposed toward her, she had based some comforting thoughts that now fleeted to empty air. "It was not Miss Clifton!" she repeated—"it was not Percy's sister! She could refrain from giving herself concern, as to whether I was provided or unprovided with the means of life!—she could leave me to the charity of strangers! Oh! I little thought her so cold-hearted."

"I cannot think Miss Clifton cold-hearted, though she is apt to err on the side of thoughtlessness," said the vicar. Some reason in particular must exist for her neglect of you were we but acquainted with it. I have not seen her for some time, she rarely visits church—mine at least—the flowery fields of fancy have in general more charms for Miss Clifton than the house of prayer. Yet, God forbid I should say or think there is no religion in her.

I hope, and believe, her thoughts are good, and Christian, though she forsakes the assemblies of the saints."

The warmth with which the reverend man delivered these words showed that he took much to heart the disrespect shown by the young lady of Rosedale House, to the outward ordinances of religion, and though he abounded in charity, he could not refrain from a remark, to the effect, that had Amy attended the ministry more regularly, she would not have fallen into the lamentable error which had associated her name on the tongue of scandal, with that of a wandering artist of whom she knew nothing.

"I baptised her, and confirmed her," said the good man, "and her fine qualities are well known to me, therefore I grieve, that by her heedlessness she has innocently given occasion to the evil tongues of such as glory in the backslidings of their fellow mortals ; and, therefore do I regret, that she should withdraw herself from the place where she might learn to know herself, and the requirements of the church of which she has been called to be a member."

While he spoke, Ruth was bitterly canvassing in her thoughts the complete desertion she had experienced from her husband and his sister. No doubt existed in h r mind that Miss Clifton shared the resentful conviction of her brother, that Ruth had been a participator in the dreadful secret of their father's death, and though to herself, Ruth was sufficiently justified, she was conscious that were Miss Clifton to tax her with the fact in direct terms, she could not deny that a suspicion she had not communicated had existed in her breast some time befor the discovery. At once, and before she had learnt to whom she had been indebted for the gift she had attributed to the sister of Percy, Ruth unburdened her mind to her reverend adviser, respecting all she had heard and seen, bearing on the fatal secret prior to her marriage, and by his advice, she determined frankly to state the truth to Clifton and his sister, in the hope that they might construe her conduct more favourably, and if forgiveness was required, extend it. The vicar himself undertook the delicate responsibility of becoming the medium through which this explanation and submission was to be made, and the issue was anticipated by Ruth with unspeakable anxiety. She could not—she would not—think it could be other than a reconcilliation; there had been nothing in her conduct to justify a contrary result; if Percy retained any love for her, if Amy retained any friendship, there could be nothing to fear.

"Tell them the whole truth without disguise as I have told it

you," she said to the vicar, who, as gently as he could, strove to keep down her high-raised hopes. "Tell them whatever you think may dispose them to be at peace with me. Say that I am miserable at present—that I must ever be miserable while alienated from them. They cannot impute my submission to sordid views now; therefore, dear reverend sir, be not anxious to consult my pride, only if you can restore peace!"

"I am the minister of the Prince of Peace, and this mission pleases me well, and shall be zealously performed," replied the good man. "But you have not inquired from whom came that assistance which you laid to the credit of Miss Clifton. What think you if the giver was he who is now brought low, I mean our worthy Rosedale Miller?"

"Mr. Maynard!" said Ruth, with a start. "How came he to add to that catalogue of his benefits?—and why conceal that it came from him? But I see," she added, tears bursting from her eyes, "he was not content to serve me merely, he wished to do so without my feeling the burden of obligation—and this was while my husband and his sister cast no thought upon me!"

The knowledge of this delicate act of generosity penetrated deep to the heart of Ruth, deeper than anything she had known of Maynard previously, and from that hour, a new feeling sprang up in her bosom for him, a sacred tenderness, an undying attachment, which was not love, and yet was more than ordinary friendship. To recompence his goodness to her and her father, became the dearest object of her thoughts, next to the hope she cherished of a re-union with her husband. That hope was speedily dashed away. The vicar waiting on Miss Clifton, found that Percy had just arrived from London, and to him, instead of his sister, opened the mission of peace, but he was interrupted with formal politeness by Percy.

"Mrs. Clifton has chosen her own course," said the latter, "she must now abide by it. Had she been at present in destitute circumstances I might have entertained your mission with more favour, but as she is mistres of a large fortune there can no longer exist the slightest inducement for my intruding on her intention, or being intruded upon."

"What, Mr. Clifton!" remonstrated the vicar, "is the love you vowed to your wife in my presence no inducemnt for your reconciliation with her?"

"That love exists no longer," replied Clifton—"she has extinguished it."

"This is dreadful to hear!" said the venerable man, much distressed. "To report this to the amiable young lady, whose society you are rejecting, would be her death."

"Oh, you are mistaken," said Clifton, with haughty derision. "she is not so easily destroyed as you imagine. She can bear much from me I do assure you."

"She has borne much, squire," said the vicar, his meek spirit rising into indignant warmth.

"Perhaps she has," said Clifton, carelessly; however, she has fairly equalised our accounts, the balance hardly preponerates on either side."

"And you refuse to hear her explanation of the cause of offence between you?"

"I do. No explanations can remove from my mind the strong impressions I have received to her disadvantage. Nothing can revive the love which her perfidy has crushed."

"This is obstinacy, blind, headlong obstinacy, Mr. Clifton. I must tell you so, whatever be the consequence."

"Sir," rejoined Clifton, with increasing hateur, "neither your good or ill opinion, though I respect you as much as any man, can move me a jot. My wife has rejected my advances, placed herself under obligations to my rival, besides comforting and aiding the murderer her father. But it is not to my purpose to enter into the causes that have provoked my indignation against her. Enough—we are separated—and separated shall remain. I congratulate her on her recent good fortune, you may tell her, and feel that it has released me from every remaining obligation which could bind me to her. Being wealthy as myself her means of life will give me no more concern; as to its mode I am indifferent also, for as far as my dignity could suffer through her it has done so."

With these high and angry words Clifton bowed to his reverend visitant, whose looks expressed how much he was grieved, and retired from the room.

The vicar would fain have seen Miss Clifton, but as she did not make her appearance he reluctantly quitted the house. He returned to the vicarage, where Ruth waited in the society of the clergyman's lady. His sad looks foreboded ill, and her colour changed rapidly as she sat in silence to hear what he had to impart. On a signal from her husband the vicar's wife left the room, and then the reverend gentleman in a hesitating voice, and softening as much as he could consistent with truth the harsh words of Clifton, revealed the reception he had met with.

Ruth drooped her head on her breast as she listened, and all at once fell fainting from her chair. She remained some days in the vicarage suffering acutely in mind, but her affliction did not prevent her from caring for those who looked to her for guidance and support. She placed her brother and sister at an excellent board-

ing academy, withdrawing Sally from the millinery establishment in which she had just been received.

The Vicar was penetrated with sympathy for her forlorn condition, and he was aroused to something like a feeling of indignation at the contumelious behaviour of the squire at their late interview, insomuch that he felt doubly disposed to advocate the cause of the forsaken wife, whom he began to look upon as a much injured woman, although his habitual fearfulness of giving offence rendering him exceedingly sparing in the expression of his sentiments   a point so nice.   However, he invited Ruth to take up her abode in his vicarage until she should be able to provide herself with some residence suited to her changed fortunes.   The deserted girl gladly availed herself of this offer, for a lingering fondness led her to haunt the scenes where she had been happy in the love of Clifton, and where she perhaps secretly hoped she might one day meet him, and try if his stubborn resentment could not be softened by the sight of those charms he had once extolled.

While at the vicarage she in one of her lonely rambles found a small uninhabited tenement, whose appearance as well as the scene around induced her to select it for her habitation.   Rose Cottage had been framed evidently with an eye to the picturesque, and the attempt had been more successful than in many instances.   It was surrounded on every side by green slopes, on which grew trees of every height and form.   A brook went darkling under the shadow of their branches, whose existence would not have been suspected but for its tuneful murmur.

It was pleasant morning and evening to see the shadows of the trees lengthening or declining on the rich emerald turf, or in the deep summer moon to catch glimpses through the intermediate foliage of the cattle cooling themselves in the limpid brook, or to penetrate the many fascinating recesses formed by the knotted and indivisible branches which to the birds frequenting them made but one labyrinth of mossy twigs and tremulous leaves.   It was pleasant to see the moonbeams descending through those mazy elevations of interwoven branches in scattered patches of light on the dark sward.   It was pleasant to hear on the hushed air the tender bleat of the sheep, (indispensable accompaniments to a pastoral landscape).   It was pleasant too in autumn to hear the wind filling the woodlands with its mighty voice, scattering the leaves which summer had called into being; and impressing all nature with a solemn sadness, a foreboding of the wintry desolation coming on, and striking to the unthinking heart of man a warning of his own decay.   And in winter it was pleasant also to see the

bare skeleton forms of the giants of the dale clothed in a silver drapery of hoar frost, and decorated with gem-like icicles; to see the weeds fringing the brook crisped with glittering particles, and the snow-like finely sifted powder strewing the romantic cottage lawn.

And when no beauties were beheld without doors—and how seldom is that in the country, when the eye of observation is aided by a quiet, thankful, pious, loving mind—the interior of Ruth's lone dwelling afforded much calm delight, though of a pensive character. She had taken under her roof for her protection, Wyatt and his wife, whom the burning of Maynard's mill had placed in difficult circumstances. As he knew she regarded them, she hoped this would gratify him in some slight degree when he came to hear of it.

Wyatt was at present unemployed, except in the laying out of a flower-garden Ruth was planning; his wife, a taciturn, unassuming body, was of no particular service in a domestic point of view, and her spirits were too monotonously dull to render her an agreeable companion; but she was very humble, placid and willing, therefore Ruth overlooked her deficiencies.

The building had no upper stories; a sitting-room and drawing-room were in the front, two bed-rooms in a kind of wing on either side, and culinary offices behind. A lawn below the cottage had a sun-dial in its centre, and was wildly overgrown with bushes that had not been pruned for many years. The windows were oriels, or what is commonly termed bow-windows, in the finest style of the gothic, delicately and elaborately carved in stone, and filled with small panes of coloured glass. The doorway, and other points of prominence about the building, exhibited chisselled heads and wreaths of foliage, and the walls were trellised and perfumed with rose trees of uncommon beauty, whence the name of this elegant little retreat. The chimney—that unsightly part of most modern buildings—was so contrived as to be an ornament instead of an excresence. A dove-cote was elevated on a tall pole a few yards off from the cottage, at the back, where Ruth designed an English flower-garden. Very near were several beehives, and both the bees and the doves became favourites of their youthful mistress.

She had found several profitable modes of occupying her time. The vicarage was near, and the vicar's wife and two daughters—plain, well-informed, good women—were intimate with her, whose singular fortunes had engaged their pity and interest, She took part in their charitable labours for the instruction and domestic

prosperity of the poor of the dale, contributing in money more largely than they, as her means were greater.

Amongst others, many of the cottagers near the deserted dwelling of her parents, whom she had known familiarly in former days, had reason to bless her elevation.

With all this, Ruth's time wore heavily away, until the vicar's wife took an opportunity when they were conversing familiarly together, to point out her deficiences in the acquirements desirable for one who was taking a superior position in society, advising her as she was yet so young to commence with vigour the task of mental cultivation. Ruth was grateful to her frank adviser, but scarcely would have followed her counsel had there not been a quickening impulse in the hope. that she would be pre paring herself for ultimately filling her rightful place with credit in the house and social circle of her husband. This was an incentive, powerful indeed, and under its influence she daily devoted many hours to assiduous study, under the tuition of the ladies of the vicarage.

It was surprising to herself how cheerfully many days thus spent passed away, and at length she began to find herself possessed as it were of new senses, and new worlds of enjoyment, in music, in refined literature, in drawing, and in stores of information which seemed exhaustless. The sound of the piano was heard in her sitting apartment, and the tasteful periodicals of the day, and prints calculated to elevate the imagination and refine the soul, appeared on her drawing-room table. A substantial character was added to her acquirements by the vicar himself, who was a man as learned as amiable, and as communicative as learned. With maps and globes before him. he lectured her on the weightier matters of geography, history, philosophy, and subjects connected with a knowledge of the Scriptures. Nor ever had pupil a more patient teacher, nor a teacher a more docile, pupil· Only occasionally her attention would wander when a thought revived of her father's exile, of Maynard's adversity, of her mother's mournful end.

Where Maynard at present was, or whether he had yet heard of her changed circumstance, she could not tell, nor did it appear to her in what manner she could effectually serve him, as she ardently desired to do. Her father's parting commission respecting the grave of her mother she had accurately fulfilled, and had formed a plan for erecting a monument to that mother's honour which she did not as yet communicate to him.

Months flew by after the vicar's profitless interview with Clifton on Ruth's behalf, and the squire had returned to town.

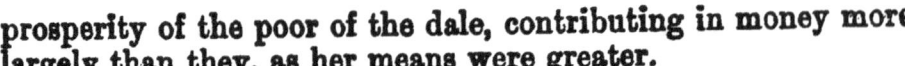
IMPORTANT!—Another Beautiful Presentation Plate will accompany No. 25 of "The Cottage Girl."

THE COTTAGE GIRL.

"HE COMES! HE MAY HAVE REPENTED!"

VARIOUS reports reached Rosedale, prejudicial to Clifton's reputation. Disappointed ambition had destroyed his quick sense of honour; he was reckless and unprincipled, it was said, and his temper was obstinate, fierce, and turbulent. At length he was again on his return with an eager and infatuated resolution to oppose, in one of the close boroughs afterwards disfranchised by the Reform Act, the election of a member of the family of the Vernons, by whom he had been humiliated in the matter of the baronetcy.

"He shall not get in whatever cost I am at to prevent it!" said the exasperated assailant; but though Percy spent much, and wrought himself up to a pitch of mad animosity against young Vernon, the latter won at the poll, and Clifton turned his horse's head after the election was over, toward his own estate, which he had considerably impoverished, with feelings of baffled and mortified emnity.

In this state of mind, he, for the first time during so long a period, encountered his wife, taking her evening walk, leaning on the arm of the vicar's eldest daughter. Whatever were his internal sensations he merely lifted his hat to the companion of Ruth, and with no word or sign to her whose heart leaped fondly toward him, dashed onwards with a speed that raised a cloud of dust in the white hedge-bound road; but when he had gone some distance, he halted in stern reflection, then wheeled his horse impetuously round to retrace its steps, muttering between his clenched teeth—

"She or I shall leave the dale for ever!—I will have no more such shocks as this! rather will I resort to means my calm moments must abhor."

CHAPTER XXXVI.

"O nothing rash.   By all that's good
Let me invoke thee—no precipitation."

COLERIDGE.

"HE disdained to cast a glance on me," said Ruth, in agonised accents.   "Now I am sure he hates me !   O Clifton !   Clifton !— But I will endure—I will not complain.   Nor will I," she added, warmly, "seek more to merit his obduracy.   I have stooped enough—too much—if, as I suspect, he rejects me for another."

"Let us return to your cottage," said her companion, "the unexpected sight of the squire has disturbed you too much for us to attempt the walk we had proposed."

"Hark !" ejaculated Ruth, a gleam of joy irradiating her face, "do you not hear his horse's hoofs returning ?"

The other listened, but distinguished only the tranquil sounds which the close of day calls forth in a rural landscape.

"It is his horse ! I can distinguish its buoyant pace almost as well as his own footstep.   It was the favourite bay on which he leaped the gate when—but those recollections must cease, or they will destroy me.   He comes ! O ! Louisa, perhaps there is hope still !   He may have repented, and—"

" Be firm, dear Mrs. Clifton."

" I will—I am," and she in a moment became externally so as Clifton re-appeared over a broad knoll which the road crossed.

Throwing himself from the saddle, he secured his horse's rein to a tree.   Ruth stood still, for she neither wished to shun or to seem to meet him.   The pulsations of her heart were audible when he approached with a step and mien of haughty resolution. She felt as if life or death hung on the interview which must now take place, and love contented with woman's pride, and hope with fear, on her exquisite features, in the momentary interval which brought him to her side under the shade of a mutilated granite cross, reared by Catholic devotees before the Reformation.   That cross was at a junction of two bye-roads, and close by it was the beautiful church in which the unfortunate marriage had been solemnised between those two, who since the hour which united them had been estranged.   There was the churchyard, in which ' the rude forefathers of the hamlet slept,' and within it was the dark yew, beneath which Maynard had seen Mrs. Summerfield laid to rest.   Down one of the bye roads a lad was driving cattle from a pasture, to shelter for the night in a farm a little way past the cross, and along the other were approaching some blithe milkers—merry maids accompanied by their peasant swains— therefore Clifton, perceiving the small gate of the churchyard ajar, requested the young ladies would enter the enclosure while he spoke with Ruth.

" I will remain here if you please," said the clergyman's daughter, who naturally thought it better for the two to converse unrestrained by the presence of a third party, and being timid of disposition, was averse to entering a spot so melancholy, when darkness was gathering over it.

" I would rather you heard what I have to say, Miss Henderson," said Clifton,

" You must excuse me sir," she rejoined.

" But you and your friends accuse me of injustice, Miss Henderson, said Clifton, passionately, " therefore you ought to listen to whatever I can urge in my own defence."

" Certainly, sir, and we are willing to do so, but at present Mrs. Clifton has a demand upon your sole attention.   I shall stroll round the Bramble Glen, and meet you and Mrs. Clifton before it is quite dark, either here, or on the way to Rose Cottage."

Clifton and his bride were left alone.

He held open the churchyard gate for her to pass through, and without hazarding a look into his face she followed his steps over

the mossy and sunken gravestones, whose inscriptions age had nearly obliterated. He paused within a few feet of her mother's grave, on a disused footway, in whose crevices the grass grew, and whose disjointed flag-stones were broidered with variegated autumn moss.

Ruth only became aware of the dark passions which possessed him when, harshly griping her wrist, he fixed on her his stormy looks, almost ferociously ejaculating—

"Torment of my life! is there to be no end to this? Are we to be jostling each other at every turn? And am I to be compelled to throw up the estate on which I was born, or suffer the perpetual annoyance of meeting, or striving to shun, one I have so much reason to hate?"

As she stood tremblingly silent, he more fiercely demanded—

"If every brief interval he could pass at his home was to be poisoned by anxiety to avoid her? If, in short, she was bent on remaining on his lands?"

"I cannot tell," rejoined poor Ruth, blanched with terror, and scarcely knowing what she uttered.

"Cannot!" exclaimed Clifton, with wrathful scarcasm. "Cannot! And why cannot you? Have you to consult the miller?"

Ruth threw a wild glance on the melancholy objects by which she was surrounded, and turned deadly pale.

"You have occasioned me the most insufferable mortifications that ever a man in my station sustained!" he cried, "and where they will end I know not."

His voice was hollow and broken, and so unlike his own that Ruth would not have recognised it had the speaker been unseen. Dreadful suggestions occurred to her, and distractedly she wished that Miss Henderson had not left her, or that she could see any person within call. But all was solitary and sad, and the breeze crept with a low murmur like the wail of the dying through the old yew tree. When she attempted to answer him her voice was unequal to the effort; and Clifton, disregarding her terrors, flung her arm from him, and strode with swift irregular strides too and fro the footpath. Presently, however, gathering courage she observed, though in a faint voice—

"Had you been true when first I trusted you, those mortifications would never have existed."

"Dare you taunt me now with that!" exclaimed Clifton. "Do you think I forget that while you seemed so innocent, so candid, and so fond, you were possessed of a deadly secret most nearly affecting myself and my sister?"

"You wrong me," said Ruth; "I had only a vague suspicion

that came not near the truth. Some mystery I certainly perceived between my parents, and an accidental discovery led me to connect it with the missing squire. But I was never entrusted with the secret of his death, much less did I suspect where his body was hidden."

"And if you understood there existed a mystery which had reference to my father, why was I not informed of it?"

"I had heard that the safety of my parents depended on my silence."

"How could that be, unless guilt ware involved in the mystery?"

"Alas! alas! I knew not. I only knew that they were incapable of crime, and that they enjoined my silence."

Clifton laughed ironically.

"Simple fool!" he exclaimed, "and were you capable of a confidence so childish? Incapable of crime! The hypocrites!—the murderers!"

"Oh! hush, Mr. Clifton," said Ruth; "think where we stand! Yon grave, where the grass is just beginning to spring, and the daisy to bloom, encloses one of those you are defaming."

Clifton drew back, slightly startled.

"My dear, traduced, broken-hearted mother, lies there!" Ruth continued, her voice interrupted by sobs. "Not the murderess, but—it will be spoken—the murdered!"

"By whom?"

"By Arthur Clifton, who tenants yon proud vault in which his son interred him. Oh! she was more than murdered; her sufferings far exceeded the brief pangs which an ordinary murderer inflicts!"

"Your mother's story I never credited; how these sentiments sound therefore in my ear from one bearing my name you may imagine. But they give me no surprise, and having eternally resigned my claims upon you as a wife, I will not quarrel with your partiality as a daughter."

"Eternally, Clifton!"

"As surely as we stand in the presence of the buried remains of my father and your mother—as surely as we see before us the hoary walls of the building where our mutual troth was plighted, —so surely we are eternally divided."

"Oh! not eternally!"

"Can you wish it otherwise after having placed so many barriers between us?"

"I intended none."

"No you intended to hoodwink me—to keep close the veil

which your parents had spread over their deadly secret. You did not mean to throw barriers between us, you only purposed to deceive my confidence. A chance discovery enlightened me, your duplicity was made plain, and our parting inevitable."

Here the tears of Ruth began to flow freely, and Clifton spoke in a milder tone.

"To what am I to attribute those tears?" he asked, "not to affection—had you loved me you could not have passed days and nights beneath the roof of Maynard."

"He was a father or brother to me," replied Ruth.

"He was a lover!" exclaimed Clifton, again raising his voice, "Did I not prove you both? My sister's arguments, and my own yielding feelings, induced me to write to you, soliciting a reunion, and inviting Maynard to a friendly meeting at my house, where former grievances might have been forgiven—why was that letter disregarded, and my messenger treated with insult?"

"A letter soliciting a reunion!—a letter! None reached me, and I am quite sure Mr. Maynard saw nothing from you to the effect you speak of. Who was the bearer, and when was the letter sent?"

"By Andre, that night when I met you with Maynard going to the mill."

"I recollect hearing afterwards that your valet brought a letter, while I was too ill to know anything that was going on, but it contained a challenge for a duel Andre said, and you will hardly wonder that the miller refused to read it, and tore it up."

Clifton was astonished; the look and accent of Ruth expressed perfect sincerity, and the deception was so in harmony with the mischievous character of Andre, whose revengeful hatred to the miller had since been too clearly evidenced, that as Clifton called to mind the fluctuating doubts regarding the delivery he felt irresistibly convinced, after some further explanation, that he had done Ruth and Maynard much wrong in his thoughts, and only to blame the worthless fellow he had employed for the silence which had covered an epistle that had cost him so many struggles with obstinate pride to write, and that had been reflected on with so much irritation.

This stumbling-block removed, Clifton softened considerably, and his jealousy of Maynard became lessened. There was, however, one point on which he was immutably resolved, and which Ruth was as loth to concede; this was that she should never see or correspond more with her father, unless she continued to dwell apart from her husband.

"My house was my father's before me," he said, "and no one shall dwell beneath it who holds intercourse of any kind with his slayer."

"Were I to promise you what you wish," said Ruth, "it would be impossible to prevent my father from writing to me, or, if he survives the term of his sentence, from attempting to see me."

"He must know on what conditions you share your husband's home, and if he desires your peace he will give you no temptation to break them,"

"But think what he will feel when denied all access to me. Poor old man! he will totter to the grave with a sad, sad heart! No tender wife, such as mother was, to cheer his life's decline; and I, on whom next to her he leaned, placed at a distance from him as great and more dreadful than that between life and death. Ask some lesser sacrifice, dear Clifton! Do not insist on this, it is beyond my strength—I cannot, cannot do it!"

"Ruth," said Clifton, sternly, "according to my estimation of your father's guilt he ought now to be lying as low as your mother there, incapable of giving you or me farther trouble. Never was a reprieve more ill-judged, more undeserved than his. And you must not expect me ever to hear or think of his existence with patience. A murderer's punishment, and a murderer's grave, was his proper doom!"

A deep sigh, and renewed tears, was Ruth's reply.

How could she hope for peace in the arms of him whose rancour against her beloved parent was so unappeaseable?

"I must never be happy," she said; "I cannot consent to your wish. Let us part in kindness, and—and for ever!"

"Your father is preferred before me," said Clifton, proudly and sadly—"be it so. Once more, however, I will give you an opportunity of making a different decision, Return to your cottage —reflect deeply—and to-morrow at sunset meet me alone at this place."

"Not here—oh! not here," said Ruth, with a shudder.

"At the Cross, then, and we can walk up the bye paths to converse."

It was just dark as they came to the gate of the churchyard, by which a figure they supposed to be Miss Henderson stood close under a hazel bush. Clifton addressed her by name, but moving forward without reply the shape whether mortal or immortal disappeared in a most unaccountable manner, and at one and the same moment Clifton and Ruth exclaimed—

"How like the figure of Andre!"

"It was his very gait, stealthy, slouching, and ungainly," said Clifton.

"And the very turn of his head which he seemed to carry on one side," said Ruth.

Clifton walked by the side of Ruth until they were near her dwelling; there was a war within him of tenderness and obstinacy, the latter after having been beaten from so many points adhering with hopeless tenacity to its last stronghold.

"I shall look with impatience for to-morrow evening," he said, "and if you decree our prolonged separation, I shall take measures or a foreign pilgrimage, then instead of never seeing your father more, you will see me no more, which may be easier for you to bear."

"Say what you will I cannot upbraid you," Ruth rejoined.

She was then turning from him, but he called her back, and snatched her to his embrace.

"I cannot bate an iota of my resolution," he said, "but if you love me you will yield."

"No—no," Ruth articulated, and in another minute she was in her own beautiful little home. The drawing-room was in darkness, but some one was playing on the piano, and not doubting it was Miss Henderson, Ruth was about to enter, but a feeling of electrical surprise arrested her foot on the threshold, and her hand on the lock, as the impassioned voice of Miss Clifton, after a minor prelude of mournful expression, gave tuneful utterance to

A DIRGE.

The winds loud are blowing, the white snow is strewing
The freshly-heap'd mould in the place of the dead,
The gaunt trees are quaking, the mourners' hearts aching,
As they turn from mortality's last chilly bed;
   And fervent their blessings are breathed on the slumber
   Of her whose worn spirit nought more shall encumber,
                The loved!—the lost!

Oh, smiling thou lieth, while moaneth and sigheth
The hoarse breath of January, dismal and frore,
Nor earth that hath made thee, nor all it brings round thee,
Can make thy hush'd bosom feel one tremor more.
   Fare-thee-well, fare-thee-well, and blest be thy slumber,
   Thou hast done with all terrors and fears we can number,
                Sleep, gently sleep!

Poor Pilgrim! thy travel, what thought could unravel,
O'er steep rugged paths and bleak wastes thou hast toil'd,
Where if ever a flower shed its fragrance one hour
Too surely the next it was rifled and soil'd.

Fare-thee-well, fare-thee-well, all calm be thy slumber,
Thy toils are all ended, and nought shall encumber
                                        Thy last deep sleep

Still we, the sad hearted, deplore thee, departed,
And while memory holdeth her seat in the mind,
With tenderness swelling, our hearts will be dwelling,
On thee and the past, by affection enshrined.
    Fare-thee-well, fare-thee-well, and blest be thy slumber,
    Undisturbed by the pain which our spirits encumber,
                                        Sleep, sweetly sleep !

Reluctant we sever, but not—not for ever,
Full soon we must lie down in darkness as thou,
Till time, earth, and heaven, to ruin are given,
And HE comes, at whose feet dead and living must bow.
    Then the graves will be rent, and broken death's slumber
    And new born creation no ills shall encumber,
                                        And joy fade not !

As the voice of Miss Clifton ceased, and she was running over the keys in various plaintive minor improvisations, Ruth stepped quickly to her.

"Miss Clifton !" she exclaimed, "is it you at last !"

"My dearest Ruth !—my sister I should say."

And rising with haste, Amy clasped and kissed her.

"And what have you thought of me all this sad time? But I guess—I guess. Percy's bad temper has so restricted me that I have been compelled to appear to you all my disposition most hates. And I daresay the vicar has been no great friend of mine, for wherever he has seen one merit in me he has been sure to find two faults."

"He is your true friend," said Ruth.

Mrs. Wyatt then having brought in the lights and retired the sisters-in-law gazed affectionately on each other, and observing that each looked older, and paler, and sadder, than they had anticipated, vented in mutual caresses, and mutual expressions of kindness, the fulness of their hearts.

"You, like myself, have been unhappy, Miss Clifton," said Ruth.

"I find it difficult to bring my feelings into subservience to reason," Amy rejoined, and her serious voice and blushing cheek conveyed more than the words in themselves implied. "I have not seen you since that dreadful day—your Marriage Day," she added, and as Ruth shuddered, she continued with much feeling —"You have been a sad sufferer amidst all the doing since then, and nobly have you acted, as I have had frequent occasion to hear.

Your unhappy father has found you a comforter in his dreadful hazards."

"Dear Miss Clifton, can you name my father thus mildly?" exclaimed Ruth, with animated and grateful surprise.

"If," said Amy, "I should tell you that I pardon him the death of my parent, or that I could endure his presence with calmness, I should deceive you or myself, but I believe most part of your mother's last attestation, and I grant their was provocation enough to take from your father's crime the blacker hues. I am therefore content with his reprieve, and mingle, perhaps, some little pity for him in my indignation, But you, Ruth—you—had no part in the deed which had like to have been so fearfully punished?"

"Nor knew I anything of it, Miss Clifton, beyond dim surmises," said Ruth, immediately entering on an unreserved disclosure of all she had observed in the humble home of her childhood relative to the mystery which was now finally ended.

"I am satisfied—quite satisfied," said Miss Clifton. "Had I been placed as you were, I should have acted as you did, only most likely with less prudence. Unfortunately my self-willed brother has other impressions, The progress of time has in some respects improved, in others deteriorated him. His dissipation and flightiness are gone, but with them are gone also much that I loved in him. We have had many contentions, and he is grown so irritable and harsh that it is no easy matter to please him. Whether or not, however, I was resolved to vindicate myself to you, and with that intention came here this evening. Finding you absent I waited, and the piano standing invitingly open I was tempted to try its tones, a boldness you will pardon."

"If I have anything which can give you a moment's delight, Miss Clifton, it will be doubly valuable to me. The good ladies of the vicarage have taken some pains to polish me for my new station. I am afraid I have wearied them at times when thoughts I would fain keep at distance returned to harass me."

"When with me you were eager to learn," said Miss Clifton.

"And now, the efforts I make are delightful in themselves."

When Ruth had said this she told Amy of her meeting that evening with Percy, subjoining—

"I have just parted from him when I entered here. We have conversed together, and there remains but one obstacle to our agreement."

"You communicate joyful news, Ruth?"

"Do not rejoice too soon, dear Miss Clifton—that one obstacle is likely to be fatal. To-morrow evening the decision that rests with me is to be made. I have to meet him at the cross by the church, and if you will be with me—"

"Better not! Percy and I have not of late accorded in our views of you or your friends. Alone you may have more power over him than were I with you. The result I shall anxiously wait to learn. Meantime may I know this obstacle?"

"I am required to reward my father's care and kindness in my early days, and his painful exertions for his family, by striking to the old man's heart another venomed arrow, which will rankle there as long as any that pierced him before—I am to think of him as if he were in his grave, as if eternal darkness and disgrace had covered his grey head—I am never more to see him, to write to him, or hear of him—he is to be an outcast from my heart, from my thoughts, and my home! He may return from exile, but he must not return to me—he may be drinking the bitter dregs of misery, but I am not to sweeten the draught!"—Distressing emotion interrupted her utterance.

"My brother cannot demand impossibilities," said Amy; "your affections and thoughts you cannot control; but it is his misfortune, perhaps, as well as yours, if they must run in channels he dislikes."

"I admit it, Miss Clifton."

"And if you are cut off from personal or epistolary communication with your father, the prohibition does not extend to your sister or your brother—through them you may hear of him, and influence his welfare."

"The conditions your brother prescribes will not allow my doing so."

"There will be no necessity for telling him."

"Then I should have to resort to clandestine conferences, and the conference necessary to tranquility of husband and wife could not take root under such influences. We had better remain apart than live together discordantly. Clifton has kept me at a distance too long not to be able to pass his time without me; considering for him, therefore, would be better to continue as we are, unless a better understanding can be come to than promises at present."

"What understanding would you wish?"

"As far as the distraction of my thoughts will permit me to reflect it seems to me," Ruth said, "that if, out of reverence to my marriage agreement, I submit to Percy's will, and

exclude my father to the end of his days from my habitation, and abstain from all open communication with him, I should be freely permitted to provide for him out of my own fortune, and there should be conceded to me an occasional correspondence, and permission to see him, when this could be done without infringing on my promise, and without attracting the notice of my husband or his friends. I wish, in a few words, that my father and I may now and then correspond and meet, strictly in secret, but under the indirect sanction at least of Clifton."

"This is fair enough," said Miss Clifton.

"I think it is," said Ruth; "much will then be yielded by me, as I shall feel a thousand times, in days to come, if my father's life be prolonged, which I can hardly wish."

"If my advocacy could serve you," said Amy, "you should have it. But, alas! sisters have in general little power over the haughty and intractible lords of creation, and my character has not been gifted with strength superior enough for an ascendency so rare. Still it may be helping your cause to speak my conviction, and that I shall do."

"And at the same time perhaps you will say for me, dear Miss Clifton, both to yourself and him, that it is but natural I should believe in my poor mother's last testimony, (which when I doubt I shall doubt all truth) and believing this it follows unavoidably that my father appears to my eye not as a guilty man to whom the law has been merciful, but as one deeply, deeply injured—as one suffering unmerited punishment—as one whom his children are religiously bound to venerate the more for his misfortunes."

"I grant these views may be perfectly natural, if not quite correct," said Miss Clifton, gravely.

"I must ever think them correct," said Ruth, unable to restrain her emotion, "I must ever think him utterly free from the stain of intentional homicide—I must ever think that God wrought a judgment by him on the wicked libertine, and that my father's hands are clean. But I have excited your displeasure; forgive me, dear Miss Clifton, this topic is fraught with so much that is harrowing and tumultous I lose myself in it." And she broke into a passion of tears.

"Oh! my dear mother," she exclaimed, wringing her hands, and seeming to apostrophise the empty air, "I will not grieve for thee—thou hast been taken from the sight and knowledge of evils that would have inflicted on thee a daily death. Thou hast not seen the husband who was dear to thee branded as a

murderer by the public sentence, or enduring the rigours of a penal settlement, or formerly banished from the hearth and presence of the daughter he prized, only too dearly."

"I cannot bear this, Ruth," said Miss Clifton, overpowered by the sight of her affliction; "if anything could make me think your parents clear of the odious charge, it would be the respect and love they have inspired in you."

"I have lost in one the kindest of mothers, in the other the wisest of friends," sighed Ruth. "Enough of this—your forbearance, Miss Clifton, shall be no more taxed in this way by me. Henceforth, the merits and wrongs of those who gave me being shall be buried in my own breast, providing Clifton only grants me what I have said."

"He will deserve to lose you else."

Diverting the conversation to other channels, and speaking of Maynard, Amy was told that Ruth, after many endeavours to discover where he was, had that day succeeded, and dispatched Wyatt to him with a brief and pointed note informing him that in return for the twenty pounds he had sent her by the vicar, during her father's imprisonment, she had replaced the thousand pounds lost in the Rosedale Bank, which was now in firm hands. Ruth had not a moment's hesitation in entrusting this to Amy, for she had no idea any one could attribute this liberality to other than the true motives of requital for benefits to her family. She was also far from supposing that Maynard still cherished for her a hopeless passion, though if she had, the thousand pounds would still have been his, so deeply she felt her obligations to him, and so firmly she rested on her own rectitude, and his unpresuming disposition.

The same evening Wyatt returned, and was called into the drawing-room, while Amy was still there.

"I never but once before saw Maynard so flustered," said the messenger, "and that was when the wedding he was looking forward to with Mrs. Clifton that is now, was cut short off by——"

"Wyatt," interrupted Ruth sharply, "if you have anything to say to me from Mr. Maynard I will hear it."

"Beg pardon, ma'am, hope no offence," said the disconcerted Wyatt, who was humble and anxious to please, but had an unfortunate tendency for saying or doing the very things a prudent person would have avoided.

Perceiving he had blundered again on something wrong, though he hardly knew what, his ideas became confused, and it was only after stammering a second or two, trying to recollect himself, that he produced a letter which, as Ruth glanced her eyes over it, called the colour to her cheek, and the involuntary sigh to her lips. She placed in the hand of Miss Clifton, not without inward reluctance.

"On my word," said Amy, "there is truth in Percy's conjecture that Maynard is still your lover—no blame to you, nor to him perhaps."

"Indeed you are mistaken," said Ruth, but her tone was not very confident."

"Am I mistaken?—then I will never trust writing more. Here in the first place he says, 'having heard of your prosperity months ago. and having no more opportunities of serving you, he had made up his mind not to see you again, though it was a resolution he found difficult to keep.' If love is not in this love is in nothing. Then—'he will not refuse the money, which, however, welcome for its own sake, is a hundred times more so for yours.' He hopes you will yet be re-united to my brother, and speaks better of him than Percy deserves, though it is plain he would give the world to be in his place."

"It grieves me that you should thus construe a warmth of language, rather unguarded perhaps, but proceeding from exuberance of friendliness only," said Ruth, painfully confused.

"My dear girl," Amy rejoined, pressing her hand, "you have no reason to feel hurt, Mr. Maynard does his best in these tell-tale lines to disguise the love he unquestionably feels for you, but it evaporates in spite of him. The specious mask of friendship once imposed on me. let it not on you. It is well for his own sake that he purposes to remain at a distance from you, and if you will take my advice this letter of his will never meet my brothers jealous eyes."

"I shall take no pains to conceal it from him," said Ruth, firmly.

"Then you will be wanting in prudence, so I tell you, who have been deemed the most inconsiderate of mortals."

"No correspondence as or shall take place between Mr. Maynard and myself, but such as at any given moment I am able to produce."

"Nonsense, you had better bid me destroy it,"—and Amy held the letter close to the taper flame.

"No, no," said Ruth, rescuing the perilled sheet, and securing it in a draw.

The advancing night warned Miss Clifton to hasten back to Rosedale House, whither she was attended by her own servant, who had waited in the cottage kitchen. Her steps were quickened at one moment by affectionate eagerness to meet the brother by whom she had been left solitary for two months, and retarded at another by dread of his undisciplined temper. The description Ruth had given her of his dark looks, intemperate language, and vehement gestures, when he commenced the conference in the churchyard, suggested to Amy the apprehension lest he had been foiled in his electioneering conflict with young Vernon, which the tone of his previous letters assured her would sting him to frenzy. On the other hand, the comparative calmness with which he had parted from Ruth, gave her hopes that she should find him in a tranquil mood. Then again she feared that he might be irritated by finding her from home at an unusual hour, for since her elopement with Tracy he had been extremely jealous of her movements. There was also a doubt in what light he might view her visit to Rose Cottage.

"But I only repent it was not made before," she said to herself.

Her interview with Ruth had been deeply interesting to her. Nigh four years had passed since delighted by the inartificial graces of her mind and person Amy had taken the Cottage Girl beneath her roof. The age of the young mistress then was that of Ruth now, whence it followed that Amy having numbered twenty-four summers, Ruth was just turning the angle as it were at which youth and maturity meet—in other words the age of twenty. Mentally comparing her humble acquaintance of sixteen with the young wealthy lady of Rose Cottage, Amy missed with regret some of the charms that had formerly delighted her, —the naive simplicity—the overflowing sensibility—the utter inexperience of evil—the hormonious temper, at peace with itself and all things, gliding on like an unsullied stream, tranquilly but not sluggishly, and in its lovely flow transmuting all the neighbouring objects reflected in it to images of delight;—these traits had wholly or partially given place to others superior but not so captivating. Her brown eye still floated in the light of vivid feeling, but the depressed eyebrow seemed to hold that feeling in powerful check; her fair feminine forehead was now more expressive of intelligence, but it had lost the celestial radiance which a cloudless spirit had enkindled; the roundness of her cheek had melted with its roseated hue; her lips had lost their fresh vermilion, and the enchanting smile that witched so many hearts. The whole countenance had changed its aspects. Melancholy and anxicty marked its repose—sad proof how familiar she had become with those enemies to youthful beauty.

IMPORTANT!—Another Beautiful Presentation Plate will be issued with the next Number (25) of "The Cottage Girl."

THE COTTAGE GIRL.

"OH, PERCY!" EXCLAIMED HIS SISTER.

HER appearance had impressed Amy with a profound sense of the pressure of her sufferings, and the force of her mind. In her step and mien she was not now the lightsome fairy that had been seen tripping over the meadows in harvest time years ago to bear her father's frugal meal, or in the summer evenings fetching the milk from the farm, or carrying from Maynard's mill the weekly bag of meal, watched or attended by the devoted Maynard. Her present firm slow walk, and sad, sober, almost dignified bearing, suited perhaps better with her new position, but the magic of the other position Amy dwelt upon with all the fanciful enthusiasm of her nature. Ruth's voice had partaken the general change. It had been passing sweet, and as glad as sweet, and as variously modulated as glad; now it chiefly rested on one grave thoughtful level, had a mournful cadence caught at passing intervals, was sometimes so low as hardly to be audible, and never rose above a very subdued pitch. All this had Amy noted and reflected on, when she found herself in her brother's presence.

He was standing at a window looking out on the giant oaks which on the north side of the house expanded their iron arms to the very walls. Ere he could speak she advanced and kissed him, welcoming him home. He had meditated receiving her with anger, but relented, and with a brother's warmest love returned her caress. Directly after the dark mood returned.

"Have you not been schooled sufficiently," he asked, "that you wander abroad at hours like these? Have you not been enough the theme of village scandal?"

"Nay, Percy, that is not kind," said his sister, reproachfully,— "you touch too nearly the wound that is yet but indifferently healed. I have been to Rose Cottage."

She spoke boldly, and without seeming to deprecate his displeasure, though she expected it. At first indeed, he looked thunderstruck, then a stormy cloud settled on his brow, but checking himself with a strong effort he walked over the room, muttering —"But it is no matter. A crisis is come. One way or other this hell shall cease!" Then stopping short, he said—"Well, I suppose she told you what had passed between us? You learnt how much I had yielded to her, and in what I am resolved?"

"I have learnt," said Amy, perceiving with what intensity of expectation he hung upon her answer, "that Ruth will consent to banish her father from the home she may share with you."

"She will!" exclaimed Percy, with sudden transport, but instantaneously resuming his previous manner, he said—"She has bethought herself in time."

"The sacrifice will be a mighty one to such a daughter," said Amy.

"The sacrifice is mine," said Percy, "who am compelled to see in my wife the daughter of the wretch by whom my father was hurled unrepentant into a fearful eternity."

"In this painful difficulty you must think a little for Ruth. Summerfield was a kind parent to her."

"He was a revengeful, remorseless homicide!" exclaimed Clifton, striking the table with violence, "and if his name be spoken again in my hearing by my sister or any other person, I shall not forgive the insult."

"If you can command yourself a few moments, Percy, I have more to say, if not, I really must entreat you not to speak to me except on topics that cannot inflame you."

"What more?" he asked, with hasty alarm.

"There are reservations to Ruth's submission."

"Oh indeed,"—and Clifton laughed fiercely,—"reservations are there? And what are these reservations?"

"She wishes it to be understood that she is to provide for her father—"

"Blasts on him!"

"Out of her own independent fortune."

"I have nothing to do with her fortune—wish to have nothing to do with it—let her dispose of it as she will—pension off all the convicts in his majesty's gaols if she chooses. Any other reservation?"

"She will refrain from all open correspondence obnoxious to you."

"She is most kind."

"But entreats you not absolutely to interdict her from occasional private interchange of letters, or more rare meetings."

"I see her drift, and here is my answer—Ruth shall never come beneath my roof unless she forswears wholly and for ever her homicidal parent. She shall not by all that is holy."

"Then I fear she will never come beneath it."

"And if not, I am content."

"I never thought to hear you say so—your affection has wonderfully cooled, Percy, in three or four years."

"What know you of my affection? I wish it had cooled, I have striven hard to make it so, and hate myself for every throb of love I feel for her."

"I see not why."

"You are purblind then, as you always were, to my honour and interest."

At these words Amy turned from him irritated and hurt.

"I speak I know not what," he said, "but you must bear with me. Ring for supper, and then I will give you an opportunity for contradicting most effectually, the charge I have laid on you of unconcern for my interest."

She rang accordingly, and during supper he gave an account of the borough election, and its (to him) mortifying result. He then entered into his late rash expenditure, which filled her with painful astonishment.

"To clear the debts I have contracted," he said, "the old oaks, the most precious part of my patrimony, must kiss the dust."

"Our fine oaks! that our ancestors have sat and fought under! —that will be a deprivation indeed!"

"There is one way to preserve them," said Clifton, with a peculiar intonation of voice, "and not only them, but the rest of our estate, which else I am afraid before long will find its way, large as it is, to the auction-room."

"And what way is that?"

"Marriage," replied Percy, emphatically.

Amy changed colour.

"You are married," she faintly said,

"But you are not," he returned.

"And never shall be," she said firmly.

"You will, and speedily too, if you have any regard for me, or if you desire the redemption of your own reputation. I have a proposal for your hand from Willoughby, my old sporting associate, a peer's son you remember, who is now, by his father's decease, Lord John Willoughby, immensely rich, and surrounded by influential connexions. Your marriage with him will at once set me on a level with the Vernons, and if I do not then make them bitterly feel whom they have warred against, I will forswear the name I have inherited from the stout old Puritan of the Commonwealth as one unworthy of it!"

Amy was aghast at this proposal, and reminded her brother of the profligate character of the proposed bridegroom.

"He has powerful motives to restrain him now," replied Clifton, "and his promises are fair. To-morrow he will be here."

"But you know my mind, Percy, and that I am averse to marriage."

"So are all women in theory, but they contrive to get rid of their scruples when offers arrive."

"So shall not I, Percy. My heart, if I must speak to you of what you already know, is pledged to one, and never will I change."

"Rank folly! or worse! Will you allow your heart to remain in the keeping of the husband of another?"

"We will close this unpleasant debate," said Amy, rising from her chair in indignant wrath.

"I expect you to receive Lord Willoughby as your suitor," said Percy.

"I most certainly shall not."

"Then there will be a fatal breach between us."

"If there must—there must," said Amy, and coldly wishing him good night, left the room

CHAPTER XXXVII.

"Oh hard art thou, tyrannic king!
Ruthless as savage bird of prey;
But furies rend that hell black wing,
That sees me thy foul hest obey."

LOVE'S MARTYR.

THE apartment in which the incensed Clifton was left alone formed part of the modern wing appended by his father to the more ancient structure. Thus the poetic tone, so to speak, pervading this relic of bygone days, might not be marred by the additions made, the new wing had been constructed on the side where the park trees grew close to the house, and a close-set avenue added to intercept the view. Percy had disliked this arrangement on account of the sombreness it gave to the interior, and he now strove to reconcile himself to the sacrifice of the venerable leafy denizens of his park by the reflection that at least he would be able to sleep without disturbance from the dismal creaking of the old boughs, or the roaring of the wind through their myriad leaves, sounds so congenial to the romantic spirit of his sister. His repugnance to the destruction of these trees, was however too strong and real to be eluded, and furnished one

of the motives urging him to press the suit of Lord Willoughby to his sister.

Suddenly it occurred to him that were Ruth and he reconciled, she could at once relieve his embarrassment; but if ambitious he was not sordid, and this consideration relaxed not in the least his arbitary resolve, that wholly and eternally she should renounce her father. Perhaps the convers happened, and feeling that he had a powerful inducement in his own interest to accede to her propositions, he relentlessly hardened himself against them, actuated by a highmindedness for which he gave himself much credit.

But his accustomed inconsistence prevailed, and while trampling down mercenary motives, he could contemplate confiding his sister's happiness to a man of whose depravity he had had ample experience. His notion that Lord Willoughby's moral character had suddenly become transformed was only an instance how easily that which is wished is accredited, and for this wish his reasons were many and powerful. Willoughby would be in his hands easy of management, and able to further largely the political schemes of his brother-in law. Willoughby could confer a title of many generations on his sister, which would enable her to re-appear with eclat in the brilliant circles where she had heretofore been merely tolerated, and where Percy longed to see her upholding her brother's dignity and her own, (her husband's was not thought of.)

Clifton also desired an honourable match for her as a remedial measure for restoring her fair fame abroad, and, "bating a few trivial objections," he thought "there can hardly be a more desirable one hoped for. Willoughby is still young, well made, has aristocratic features, cultivated manners, and received a college education. Perhaps there is too much of the horse-jockey and gambler in his speech, and too many traces of his dissolute life on his face, but those blemishes time and he must remove."

The prior attachment of Amy was an obstacle likely to have greater weight, but he overcame it by reviving his indignation against the artist, and vehemently insisted that it was disgraceful for her to cherish a thought of tenderness for so dishonourable a person. He was very bitter against the romantic folly, as he termed it, which induced her to controvert his plans for her prosperous settlement; and becoming more obstinate the more he reflected, came to the unjust and precipitate determination that he would press the affair forward by whatsoever means presented themselves undeterred by her weak sentimental fancies.

"If she is ignorant of her own welfare," he said, "I must take it into my own hands. She shall be the wife of Lord Willoughby, or cease to be my sister!"

No opposition to his arbitary will could Clifton endure, and Amy foresaw with unspeakable dismay the new unhappiness likely to spring out of a difference between them so momentous.

"My plastic easiness of disposition has misled him," she thought; "he erroneously imagines that he can erase at pleasure the impressions of my mind, and affix instead those of his own framing. He does not treat me as a rational woman, whose destiny is in her own hands, who is responsible for her own actions, and endowed with a distinct nature, having sweet and bitter fountains peculiar to itself, but he treats me as a child whose guidance and control lies solely with himself. This despotic dealing must not last, it has hitherto tended to keep me the feeble being I am deemed by some."

Thus internally resisting the encroachments of fraternal usurpation—though dearly loving her brother—Amy anticipated next morning meeting with her unwelcome suitor, who had arrived to breakfast. Her brother led her to his presence.

As they descended the staircase he frowningly remarked she was attired to disadvantage, and that her face was stained with tears.

Amy made no reply.

She was not, the reader knows, handsome, but her face and figure were of that kind which dress and animation might make appear so, and Percy was irritated that she had not her best looks on to receive the peer. Before their mother's decease, Willoughby being the favourite companion of Percy, was often at Rosedale House, where their carousals in Percy's sporting parlour had occasioned the elder lady so much vexation as to give rise to bitter quarrels betwixt her and her son. Amy had been a frequent meditator, and the aristocratic rake had often expressed his admiration for her, until checked by Percy in a manner that led to the breaking off their unprofitable intimacy. The needy profligate seldom came in Percy's way after this, when he did it was to borrow money, or to endeavour to lure the latter back to realms of folly. Percy never could refuse him aid in his necessities, and Willoughby, who amid all his worthlessness was capable of gratitude, no sooner found himself in possession of his father's title, with the domains, and other desirables thereunto pertaining, than he bethought him of Percy Clifton, and sending for him to a luxurious dinner, repaid what he owed, "the only

debt," he slily observed, "he had any memory for," and over the wine reminding Percy of his old liking for his sister, declared he knew no woman he had rather make Lady Willoughby.

Clifton caught at the bait, yet not so eagerly as to compromise his own dignity.

"You are welcome to visit her," he said,—"she is disengaged."

Thus originated this dilemma in which Amy found herself placed.

She met Lord Willoughby with embarrassment, which he shared, though from different causes.

"It is five years since I saw you, Miss Clifton," he observed, seating himself by her side.

"I think so, my lord," she laconically rejoined, and after a few ordinary compliments a frost seemed to creep over the conversation. An allusion to the races set it flowing again, and Willoughby entered into an important question relative to the respective m rits of two horses, which was rather suited to the turf than a lady's ears. Clifton touched the elbow of the sportsman in vain; dinner only checked the volubility of the suitor on his favourite theme. After the dessert Amy hastened to withdraw, but she was soon followed to the drawing-room by Lord Willoughby, Clifton purposely remaining behind.

" I have never forgot you, Miss Clifton," said the peer, plunging at once into the subject occupying his thoughts. "May the next fox-chase be my last, if I ever saw any lady I liked so well!"

"Your lordship does me unmerited honour," said Amy, not in the tone of diffidence or humility, but such as she hoped would check the rising declaration.

Willoughby, however, had never been easily abashed even in situations less to his credit.

"Your brother and I have pledged hands and glasses that we will stand by each other," he said. "My name and family interest will help him much, and his influence with you, he acquaints me, has already been employed on my behalf."

Amy could not be insensible to the amiable trait his attachment to her brother indicated, and she assured him she should be indebted to his friendship, any nearer bond of intimacy she must decline.

As he proceeded to press his suit more warmly, she felt herself called on for more explicitness.

"You distress me, my lord," she said—"I cannot accept your offer, much as I am flattered by it. My affections are lodged elsewhere.

In half an hour Willoughby rejoined Clifton with sullen brow. "I am rejected," he said.

"For the present only, I hope," said Clifton, endeavouring to soothe him.

The peer only replied by ordering the horses to be put to his carriage.

"You will not leave us yet," said Clifton, with disappointment and concern.

I shall go on to Downing, the hunt meets there to-morrow," said Willoughby, sulkily.

Clifton's cheek inflamed.

"Pshaw! be not so faint-hearted," he said, earnestly. "You must stay and woo her—you must stay and woo her. Her sex are proverbially capricious in their humours, and she is more fanciful than most. A few days will give her time for the advantages of this alliance to present themselves to her convictions, at present she is bewildered—taken by surprise—alarmed—confused. You must stay and woo her."

"I shall never succeed," said Willoughby, in the same sulky mood. "She confessed she preferred another."

"Ha! durst she do so!" ejaculated Clifton, walking hastily over the floor, and drawing a deep breath. "But heed not that," he said, earnestly, drawing Willoughby by the arm from beside the door. "She spoke in haste and folly. We must avoid precipitation. Let her have time to reconsider, while you remain here. Attention—persuasion—opportunity—and above all, perseverance, will not fail to break down the icy barriers she has reared—or I know nothing of the female heart."

Willoughby allowed himself to be detained, and made no objection when Clifton countermanded his directions for the preparations of his carriage. But it was sometime before the soothings of Clifton could restore him to good humour. His heart had become too much corrupted amid scenes of vice to be now capable of enthusiastic attachment for man or woman; but he had gleams of good feeling, and having been persuaded by an anxious mother to marry, as a preservative against a recurrence of his former disorderly habits, he had fixed his thoughts on Miss Clifton, but meeting a refusal was just in that state of mind when people marry out of pique those for whom they have no inclination, in the vengeful hope that those who have rejected their love will regret on finding they are lost to them.

It was Clifton's discernment of this tendency in Lord Willoughby that made him so extremely anxious to avert his departure from Rosedale, for he was sensible the offer would not be

renewed, and that the peer would very soon transfer his suit and patronage where they might prove equally acceptable. And when Lord Willoughby consented to remain, Clifton found other difficulties proposed. The former had scarcely heard of Merton, not at all of Amy's elopement, which had occurred while he was immured in a debtor's prison by his extravagance, and on his release the thrilling discovery connected with Clifton's marriage had wholly superseded that scandal in the clubs and other places in town, frequented by acquaintances of Clifton and Willoughby. Percy had rejoiced in his companion's ignorance of a matter so humiliating to Amy and himself, and though he knew it would be dishonourable not to remove this ignorance, he was tempted to silence by the keen desire he felt for the match. Amy's confession to her suitor of a prior attachment, filled him with smothered frenzy, for it stirred in Willoughby the very spirit of inquiry he was most anxious to keep dormant. He slurred as hastily as possible over the introduction of Tracy to his house, and represented him in an odious light as one who was seeking the affections of an unsuspecting young lady, knowing himself at the time the husband of another. Willoughby was not so well satisfied with all this as to remove Clifton's fears of his giving up his suit, and on the latter proposing an evening stroll in the park, Percy withdrew to command his sister's attendance, who had retired to her dressing-room agitated by her interview with her suitor and its dreadful consequences.

He knocked at the door, and in a voice which betokened distress he was bade to enter. With trepidation as he entered Amy arose from the couch on which she had been prostrated, and by a hasty motion effaced the traces of sorrow from her cheek. Her brother appeared calmer than she had expected, but there was that in his look not less to be feared. He came forward slowly, and folding his arms on his breast, stood at least a minute before the open window, apparently absent in mind. Even in that minute of expectation Amy, who at all times keenly appreciated whatever was beautiful either in itself or by association, could not refrain from an admiring glance at his fine figure, over which the shades of twilight were gathering. The form—combining energy and boldness of movement with graceful proportion, and dignified height—the eye to threaten and command—the forehead masculine, firm, and intellectual—the aquiline nose, and the clear brown complexion, every instant varying its hue as the swift blood mantled beneath—all these made an ensemble highly prepossessing. But the moment of fond admiration passed, and Amy sighed to think this noble form held a spirit so ungovernable.

Clifton turned to address her, and every word was measured.

"Amy," he said, "I have been some years your protector, your adviser—why is it you now reject my counsel?"

"I have not rejected it," she replied.

"How! have you not refused Lord Willoughby? But I will not speak of that now, happily the error may be retrieved, he remains here until you have reflected more wisely, and I have pledged myself to his ultimate success. See that you treat him well, I shall not brook trifling with—your former imprudence must be wiped away, though at some cost."

"O, Percy!" exclaimed his sister, suddenly flinging herself at his feet, and clasping his hand, which he strove to detach from her, "do not for the sake of the dead urge me beyond my patience. I implore you to spare me! I will never trouble you with my affections, only let them rest! Do them no violence! Let me live as I have lived, without feigning a regard that I shall never feel."

"Rise, and hear me quietly."

She arose, but it was only to sink upon the couch, and bury her face in her hands.

"Calm yourself!" he said, sternly, and she made an effort to do so.

"This match must go forward," he said, emphatically,—"it is inevitable. If you ask what has made it so I answer—your own imprudence. Aye, droop your head lower and lower yet —hide it in the dust for your shame! There is a blot on your name which nothing but this can remove. Reconcile yourself therefore to your lot. Consider, if you will, that you consent to a sacrifice, it is at least your duty, and must be encountered. Lord Willoughby waits you to accompany him in a walk round the park, 1 go meanwhile to Ruth. Look that you weigh well your words, that you school well your looks; and mark me, touch no more of your own accord on the forbidden theme; and beware if he mentions Merton that you throw over that man's conduct to you no delusive gloss; and," added Percy, retiring with the words, "take care that you manifest no reluctance to speak of Merton—conceal all that you can under a vizard of frankness. The magnitude of the occasion justifies policy. Any violation of my directions will cost you dear. I leave his lordship to you."

Amy having heard Lord Willoughby order his carriage, had hoped he was gone, but this scene with her brother undeceiving her she was in a tumult of mind that altogether confused her understanding. The stinging reproaches of Percy, and his

threat, (though what it meant she could not conjecture) agitated every part of her being, and the attachment which had wound itself so intimately around her heart and imagination made her loth intensely the image of the suitor whom her brother sought to force upon her.   Clifton indeed in this instance had miscalculated his sister's character.   He might have recollected that though easy, indolent, and yielding, she could, under wounded feeling, exhibit more resemblance to himself.   Her temperament was enthusiastic, her nerves highly excitable, and the suggestions or fancy to which she was prone readily enlisted themselves on the side of any strong emotion that assailed her—circumstances making a situation like the present more perilous to her than it would have been to many others.

In her distraction the cruel unkindness of Percy was uppermost.

"The brother that I have idolised!" such broken ejaculations escaped her as she began with rapid movement to throw on her mantilla and bonnet, not however with the purpose of obeying the command imposed on her by Percy to attend Lord Willoughby,—"The brother that I loved so dearly!—My only protector! Is this the way he fulfils his promise to the dead! A sacrifice!—yes, one he shall not find me submit to.   I deny it to be a duty.   It is for his own ends, and not my good that the sacrifice is demanded.   My reputation he says must be healed by this means.   O God!—my reputation! Must he reproach me with that, after the years that have passed ?   Cannot time with its boasted waters of oblivion drown the remembrance of an hour's rashness that was unmixed with guilt ?"

Lord Willoughby waited below in vain for her appearance, and after amusing himself sometime by thundering a bacchanalian air on one of the musical instruments in the drawing-room, and turning the leaves of Miss Clifton's album, he addressed himself to his own attendant, from whom he learned that she had left the house in haste immediately after the squire half an hour ago.

The astonishment of the peer was unbounded.

"This is strange usage," he said, in loud and angry tones, for he conceived himself a person of too much distinction to be thus slighted with impunity.   "Mr. Clifton leaves me on pretence of an appointment of vast importance, and Miss Clifton does not choose to appear.   Order the carriage round."

With a face of scarlet he was drawing on his gloves to hasten away, and through the window was seen the sable equipage in which he had made a show of mourning for his father's death, when Mrs. Wilson the housekeeper entered in great perturbation, her grey hairs escaping from under her neat cap, and the tears flowing down her cheeks, "to entreat his lordship to await the return of Mr. Clifton, who, if he found his lordship gone would be so aggravated against Miss Amy that she knew not what would come of it."

"Miss Clifton should have considered that, ma'am," said Willoughby, with mixed bitterness and malice, and bowing to her with the respect good-breeding taught him to pay to her sex however humble, he hurried to the front portico of the house. and leaping into his carriage, the dismayed housekeeper beheld it winding rapidly through the park and disappear.

CHAPTER XXXVIII.

"Thou know'st that I have not yet learnt to live
Without thee!   I go forth into a desert,
Leaving my all behind me.   O do not turn
Thine eyes away from me!   O once more show me
Thy ever dear and honour'd countenance."

WALLENSTEIN.

WHEN Percy excused himself to the peer for leaving him a short time while he kept his engagement with Ruth the hour appointed had not arrived, and instead of directly proceeding to the spot he had named for that evening's important interview, he on quitting his park diverged into a rambling track winding round the border of a wood, where the underforest of evergreens was interspersed with bright patches of green sward, over which the straggling tree-roots wandered, like twisted serpents, in search of nourishment, while the withered leaves that had dropped profusely from the branches strewed the clustering moss that clothed them.   Every step showed some sweet woodland picture opening on his sight, while sank in a hollow on his left appeared the old-fashioned church in which his marriage had taken place, and the pretty village beside it.   The thin

blue filmy smoke went up without a curve from the white chimneys of the cottages until it melted into placid air. The scent of the orchards was on every zephyr's wing. But Clifton felt no delight in that rural walk, and with an unrelaxed brow, an absent mind, he had approached the boundary of the wood, where a gate opened into a natural avenue. At this spot he paused to look at his watch, and finding that he was still too early for his appointment, turned aside half unconsciously to cross an irregular tract of pasture land, and came, without intending it, to the cottage of Ruth. A minute he seemed to hesitate, then approached the newly-dug garden, in which Wyatt was busied planting shrubs. Shading his eyes from the sloping sun-rays, the man looked up at the approach of a footstep, and seeing who it was, appeared for the moment struck dumb with surprise.

"Are you turned gardener, Wyatt?" Clinton asked, vexed at the impulse that had brought him thither after so long and pertinaciously avoiding the place; but he concealed his embarrassment under an air feigned cordiality to the plodding and well-intentioned fellow whom he had often seen at the mill.

"Yes, sir, and thankful am I for the opportunity—thankful to Providence, and thankful to the kind young lady who allows me to earn my bread this way. Though I am no gardener, only picked up a little from my father, who was a gardener under your father, Squire Arthur—there again now," seeing Clinton's look change, "I am always a blundering. I should not have mentioned him to your honour."

"Where is Maynard now?" Clinton abruptly asked.

"By this time I guess he is at his brother-in-law's, the miller, in Kent, but yesterday I saw him at Stoke Ferrers."

"I suppose the money he threw away in support of a villain and his family has been returned to him?" said Clifton.

"I believe you may say that, squire," replied Wyatt, with spirit; "Mrs. Clifton, saving your presence, was not the person to let such kindness as he did her father pass unnoticed. No, no—he has got his thousand pounds in the bank again sure and fast."

Clifton repeated the words—

"A thousand pounds!"

"Every penny of it, your honour, I carried the news to him myself, and should have done so before if Mrs. Clifton could have got to know where he was. He has been keeping out of the way on purpose, I guess."

"On purpose! How so?"

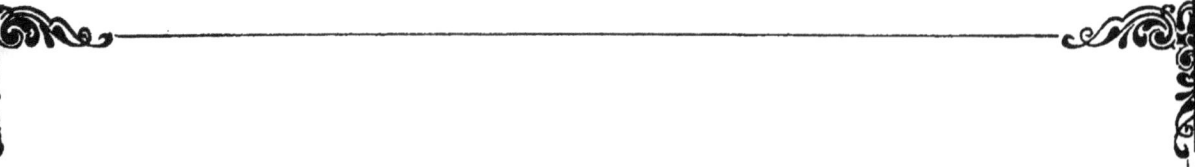
"That was a slip of the tongue.   It is a very odd thing I am always saying or doing what I should not."

"You meant something which I must known," said Clifton, half persuasively, half commandingly.   "What has Maynard been keeping out of the way on purpose for!"

"How should I know your honour.   If I was to tell you he would never forgive me, and I should be sorry to injure him or Mrs. Clifton with your honour.   I had rather tear the tongue from my mouth."

"You will injure neither.   Speak then, and freely, why does Maynard keep out of the way?"

"I can only tell you what I heard him say yesterday.   'Where have you hid yourself, miller?' I asked; 'Mrs. Clifton has been inquiring in all directions for you, and nobody knew where to find you.'   'They who wish to be lost are not easily found, Wyatt,' said he.   'That's true sometimes,' says I; 'but why did you wish to be lost, Mr. Maynard, when good luck is seeking you?'   With that he fetched a long sigh.   'There is no good luck more for me,' he says.   And when I told him he was mistaken, and gave him Mrs. Clifton's letter—"

"A letter!—what! she wrote to him!"

"She did, and he walked by the mill-wheel out of sight to read it.   I never saw any man look as he did when he came to me directly after."

"Why how did he look?"

"I cannot just remember exactly," said Wyatt, his dullness enlightened by the fierce and rapid emphasis of Clifton's interrogatory.

"Wyatt," said Clifton, slipping a sovereign into the man's hand, which he pressed hard, "tell me all that passed, forget nothing; and Wyatt, my good friend, let me know if you can what she wrote to him, and everything that may concern me."

"Nay, nay, squire," said Wyatt, presenting back the tempting gold with outstretched hand while he turned his eyes from it, "nay, nay, it shall never be said I took a bribe to bear false witness against my old master that I have been so much indebted to, or my present mistress, who is as bountiful, and more, than the vicar himself, God bless her! and reconcile you to her, sir, in His good time.   When she was Ruth Summerfield she was the bonniest and the blithest lass in all the dale! and now she is the gentlest, kindest, most charitable lady, that can be found within its borders.   No, no, I'll take no bribe to injure her or Mr. Maynard."

"I IMPLORE YOU TO SPARE ME!" SHE CRIED.

THE COTTAGE GIRL.

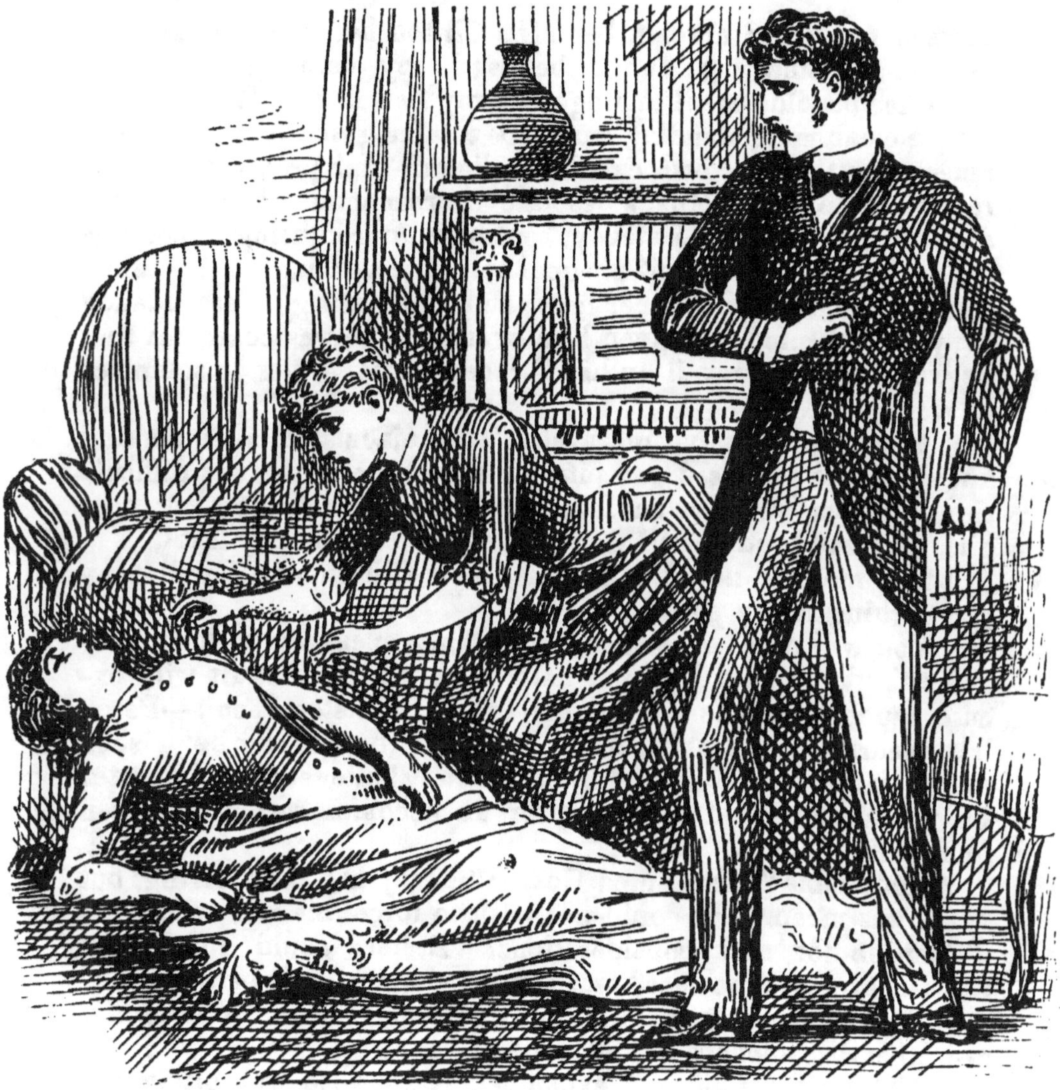

HE SEIZED HIS SISTER BY THE SHOULDER, AND HURLED HER FROM HIM.

"I ONLY required the truth from you," said Clifton. "As yet you have not told me why Maynard kept out of the way."

"Because he would avoid the sight of one he loves too well, and who can never be his, that is the pith of the matter," said Wyatt, hastily, allowing the sovereign to glide into his pocket, and recommencing his planting.

Starting from a momentary reverie, into which he was thrown by these words, and turning his eye on one of the cottage oriel lattices, what was Clifton's surprise to see there the face of his sister.

In a voice trembling with ill-disguised rage, he asked Wyatt if Mrs. Clifton was at home. Wyatt replied that he had seen her dressed for going abroad, but Miss Clifton had come to the cottage and detained her, and he believed they were together.

In her bewilderment and agony Amy had fled to Ruth, as one whose clear understanding would be a safer guide for her present emergency than her own excited feelings. Her prompt and bold resistance to her brother's despotic encroachments had been indignant impulses, but a steady, continued, unremitting opposition she rightly judged herself unequal to. By working on her affection for him, by arousing her fears, and by exerting the ascendancy his powerful mind had given him over her, she was conscious that he would either prevail in his purpose, or impel her to some act of frenzy.

"You must preserve me, Ruth!" she ejaculated, after making known to the surprised and pitying ear of the latter, the difficulties by which she was environed, "you must preserve me, dear girl, from my brother, and from myself, or I am utterly lost!"

"Tell me only how I can do it, Miss Clifton, and I will deny you nothing in my power."

"You will deem me selfish," said Amy, speaking with rapidity and agitation, "but I cannot help it—my present strait will excuse much with one so tolerant as you. Listen then :—Percy has incurred terrible expenses, and one reason why he wished me to marry Lord Willoughby is, I firmly believe, that the latter has promised to lend his name for an accommodation of fifteen hundred pounds."

"Impossible!" exclaimed Ruth; "Percy has been erring, but never was mean. He could not wish to force his only sister on a libertine for such considerations. Besides could not I have assisted him? What need was there for appealing to strangers?"

"It is not the money alone Percy considers; Lord Willoughby can otherwise advance his interests."

"Ah! foolish Clifton," exclaimed Ruth, with sad bitterness. "His ambition was a noble passion, and had he been less impatient of obstruction, had he remembered that all the schemes of man are as straws which the breath of Providence may disperse in a moment, had he ruled his own spirit, in short, he might by this time have been independent of such a man as Lord Willoughby."

"Too true," responded Amy. "His haughty and resentful spirit has procured him many powerful enemies, whom he equally dreads and scorns. He is intensely eager to make reprisals on these and anticipates being able to do so through my marriage— but rather than that I would do—I dare not think what."

"Beware the promptings of desperation," said Ruth, impres-

sively, smit by the compunctious rememberance of her own attempt at suicide, and the death of her child, "give them no place for a moment in your thoughts, Miss Clifton. You would repent them bitterly hereafter. Patience, on the contrary, can never give you uneasiness in the reflection, or require expiation when your final account is rendered."

"But my patience might degenerate into meek submission, Ruth. I assure you seriously I fear it."

"In your case submission cannot be right. There is no law divine or human, which empowers a brother to meddle with his sister's free disposal of her own hand and heart."

Amy sighed heavily, then abruptly said—

"Ruth, if you consent unconditionally to Percy's terms of reconciliation, you will relieve me effectually, if not, you must keep me with you here—for I will not return to Rosedale House."

"How can my consent relieve you?" Ruth asked.

"Most that Lord Willoughby's interest could do for Percy might be accomplished then by your means, provided you felt disposed, as I am sure you would, to devote two thousand pounds to his service."

"And does not Percy know—do not you know," said Ruth, reproachfully, "that whatever I have is his also? Our reunion was not necessary, any more than your marriage with Lord Willoughby, for him to obtain two, or twenty, thousand pounds. My next happiness to being with him, would be to serve him."

"But unless you were together he would not avail himself of your generosity," said Amy, "nor even to save myself from this dreaded match would I desire he should."

"And who but himself prevents our being together?" said Ruth—"is it I?"

"The question wholly rests with you now; he is inflexible in the unqualified demand he made on you, excepting that you are at liberty to provide for your father as you will, he seeks no control over your money."

Ruth heard with a bleeding heart, but she named her unfortunate father no more, and placed in Miss Clifton's hands a letter previously composed, announcing that she had settled on him a life-annuity, sufficient to maintain him in comfort in the rank of life to which he had been accustomed. The letter concluded in this strain :—

"And now, my dear, much-wronged father, I have that to tell you which will try all your fortitude as it has mine. We must meet no more in this world—my husband requires this of me; and however oppressive, considering all that has happened, I bend

to his will.   Nor is this all—you must write to me no more.   It breaks my heart to tell you this, but I should be indifferent to the pain of my own feelings could I spare yours.   Oh, my dear father! if you would send your poor Ruth consolation in this bitter trial, let her know through Sarah or my brother that you bear it better than I have anticipated, and that you transmit to me your forgiveness and blessing!   The only comfort I at present have is the knowledge that your age will be emancipated from toil and care.   May you have peace in your decline, my dearest father! and may your sun go down in brightness to rise on a more glorious hemisphere!   William and Sarah are improving rapidly at their separate studies, and will live, I trust and believe, to comfort you for the absence of her, who in weal and woe, in life and death, will be ever your affectionate daughter."

Amy for the moment forgot the emergency of her own situation in compassion for the sorrows of her youthful sister-in-law. She sat silent and thoughtful, while Ruth breathed no sigh, and shed no tear, but having decided upon her course, after hours of dreadful vacillation, found her mind braced anew, and filled with the placid heroism of one who looks above the world for the motives and reward of her actions.

"I think I have determined rightly," she said to Amy, " and if not, God knows my heart, I wished to do so."

"They were hard conditions," said Amy, warmly, " and it was most unfeeling of my brother to press them."

"They lie at his door for good or evil," said Ruth, gravely, " and with them all the previous anguish he has cost me—a fearful moment!   But I must not speak of him in this way," she said, hastily changing her tone, " he is my husband, and as such I am bound to honour and obey him—he is Percy Clifton, and therefore dear to my heart notwithstanding all the pangs he has inflicted on me."

"May you be happier with him than you now expect, dear and excellent girl!" exclaimed Amy, doubly revived by the hope that she had escaped the hateful marriage her brother advocated, and by the prospect of enjoying the home-companionship of a sensible, feeling girl like Ruth, for whose admirable qualities she entertained affectionate esteem.   The mutual confidence of the gentle sisters had reached this point, and Ruth had half betrayed a lurking hope (for when is hope extinguished?) that Percy might at a future time relent for his adamantine commandments concerning her father, and she was on the point of hastening to meet him at the Cross as she promised, when the door of the drawing-room was thrown open abruptly, and Wyatt announced him in a

tone fully showing the importance the latter attached to his appearance there.

It was on his sister Clifton turned his first gaze, and he addressed her first, in an inquiry where she had left Lord Willoughby.

Immediately closing the door (beside which Wyatt's curiosity would have induced him to linger), Ruth, seeing Amy durst not venture to reply, stepped promptly to her relief.

"Do not be angry with your sister," she said, entreatingly, "distress of mind has led her to disobey your wishes; but if I whom you once loved, can, with all I have, and all I am, make you atonement for her offence, I devote myself to your will."

Clifton had not removed his fixed gaze from his sister, which grew every moment more threatening, and the conciliating words of his lovely wife had glanced from off his heated temper like water-drops from burning steel.

"Amy," he a second time demanded, "where is Lord Willoughby ?"

Scarcely could the terrible objuration "Cain, where is thy brother ?" have sounded more awfully than did these simple words to the sinking heart of Amy. Half mechanically she answered—

"I have not seen him since you left me."

"You have not !" exclaimed Clifton, "you have not seen him ! What brought you here ?"

"Distraction of mind," replied Ruth, answering for her.

The passion of Clifton now swelled to a fearful height. He saw at once that every hope he had built on an alliance with Willoughby was dashed to earth, and his fears suggested what had actually occurred, namely, that his lordship had taken sudden umbrage and departed sans ceremonie. Forgetting where he was, forgetting the unmanly cowardice of personal violence against a creature incapable of resistance and dependant on him, utterly abandoned to the fury of the moment, he seized his sister by the shoulder, and hurled her from him with such violence that she fell extended on the floor. The noise of the fall and the shriek of Ruth, drew Wyatt and his wife to the spot, by whom Amy was raised insensible to a sofa.

"Monster !" Ruth exclaimed, now in her turn fired with passion, "who is now a murderer? You have killed her !"

Clifton, who had stood transfixed with dismay at the result of his own headlong violence, started at these words, and with livid look, clenched hands, and staring eyeballs, rushed like a madman

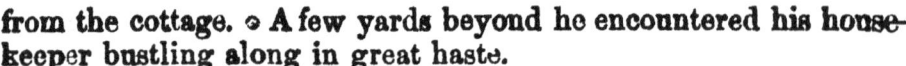

from the cottage. A few yards beyond he encountered his house-keeper bustling along in great haste.

"She was in search of him," she said, with trepidation, "to tell him that Lord Willoughby was gone."

Clifton did not manifest the surprise she had expected, but asked if she had seen his sister leave the house.

Attempting anxiously to excuse Amy, Mrs. Wilson replied in the affirmative, and while she was still speaking Clifton strode forward, but returning, said—

"Mrs. Wilson, go yonder,"—pointing to the cottage—"learn whether my sister be living or dead, and let me know—I shall wait about the house until I see you."

He turned away, and the venerable housekeeper hastened to obey him, ejaculating—

"Bless us! what in the world can he mean? They have met I see. I hope he has not laid violent hands on her, though what a man will do when passion masters him there is no saying. A violent person is as dangerous as a lunatic. I tremble all over. So haggard as he looked too!"

Amy recovered her consciousness, but was for some time giddy and ill. At the appearance of the housekeeper, she said, with emotion—

"I must not return to you again, Mrs. Wilson, my brother will slay me else."

"God forbid, my dear miss," said the old lady, in affectionate horror.

"He has used me barbarously!" exclaimed Amy, with floods of tears.

"Well, all will be mended I hope shortly," said Mrs. Wilson.

Amy looked up with curiosity, for the intonation of her voice conveyed a peculiar meaning, and Ruth, who stood by, perceiving in the look of the housekeeper that there was something to communicate of a private nature, seized the opportunity to retire. Entering her small bed chamber, then enveloped in darkness, she sank down on her knees by the white-draperied couch. Hope after hope had faded from her, and now that she had made up her mind to yield implicity to the arbitrary will of her husband, he slighted her painful submission, and once more abandoned her. It was with infinite difficulty that she was able to preserve herself from the horrid waves of despair that threatened to engulf her. But communion with her Maker infused new strength. She arose from her supplicant posture with a becalmed countenance and sitting down on her chair a few minutes endeavoured to ar-

range her tangled thoughts. She was interrupted by Amy, whom she had no sooner let in, than the latter threw herself ecstatically on her neck.

"Rejoice!—rejoice with me;" she exclaimed. "My misery is turned into joy! Mrs. Wilson has seen Merton!—he is in Rosedale!—he is close by! waiting an opportunity to speak with me. Charlotte died a year and a half ago in Vienna—the old nabob is also gathered to his fathers. And the conclusion is, dearest girl, that you must give me leave to see Merton in this abode before I sleep. I have sent to tell him he may come."

"Then my hesitation would be useless," said Ruth. "But have you considered—"

"I consider nothing at present!" exclaimed Amy, vehemently, "nothing, but that Merton is free, and loves me still!—nothing, but that my brother has misused me, and shall never see me more!"

With these passionate words she turned to listen at the door, tossing her disordered hair back from her face, which was all alight with love and eager expectation, and as soon as she caught the mild and mellow tones of Merton's voice speaking to the housekeeper, she clasped her hands wildly together, and darted from the chamber. As Ruth stood still in the darkness she heard their passionate meeting, and when the door of the apartment to which he had been conducted closed on them, the sobbings of Amy, and the fond murmurs of their voices occasionally reached her, striking her own desolation more forcibly on her aching sense. She had also to contend with the uncomfortable reflection that by permitting Merton and Miss Clifton to renew their acquaintance beneath her roof she was most probably offending Clifton on a very tender point, and so lending him another excuse for alienating himself from her. Their happy voices therefore sounded as her own knell, and she now found how much more difficult it is to rejoice with them that rejoice, than to weep with them that weep.

Yet she did rejoice with them, and heartily hoped their present meeting might be the precursor of a life-long union.

And so it proved.

Merton had been fortunate in finding access to Amy at a juncture so favourable for his object, when she was irritated by her brother's tyranny, and compelled to fly her home. Had he sought her a week before, his reception might have been different. All lighter scruples now vanished from her view, and he easily extorted a consent to their immediate marriage. It was performed in the cottage the next evening by special license in the presence

of Ruth and Miss Clifton's housekeeper. The vicar was loath to officiate on such a short notice, but his gentleness was not proof against the solicitations and arguments showered upon him. He saw that dissuasion would be useless, and regarded Miss Clifton as responsible only to heaven for the choice she had made. The ceremony was got up with so much haste that each party wore their ordinary dresses, and the ring was bought by Merton in the town of Rosedale scarce an hour before.

Little suspicion had Percy of this sudden change in his sister's lot. As soon as he had been told by the housekeeper that she was better, he had ridden off after Lord Willoughby, not with the hope of procuring a renewal of his addresses to Amy, but to smooth over the affront he had received. The tumult of Clifton's spirits found relief in rapid motion, and he cleared mile after mile with unabated speed, indifferent to the progress of night. He felt as if flying from his own fierce passions, which pursued like famished wolves gaping to devour him. The glowworm's little lamp burnt in the dark hedges, a few scattered stars relieved the gloom that hung upon the air, and unseen roses diffused their faint perfume about him. The country shortly grew more open, high hills revealed their craggy heights, and at their base he alighted before a detached hunting-box on the brink of a lovely lake. The inmates were not yet at rest, late as it was; lights streamed from the windows on the darkened water, and boisterous laughter and other sounds of revelry issued forth.

Percy knocked loudly, and his name procured him instant admittance. Giving his foaming horse in charge to a servant, he entered a brilliantly-lighted apartment, filled with gentlemen mostly in hunting suits of scarlet and white. They were congregated at a table where the bottle had circulated far too freely. Shivered glasses bestrewed the floor, which attending footmen watched for opportunities to clear away. A deluge of the ruby vinous juice overflowed the polished surface of the convivial board.

"Clifton, my fine fellow, ten thousand welcomes!" shouted one, grasping his hand and striking it violently.

"I thought you had turned craven, and forsworn the turf and the bottle!" cried another.

"Sit down, Clifton! egad, we will make a gay night of it!" said the host of the feast, a short, corpulent gentleman, the very reverse of a beau ideal of a fox-hunter in appearance, but in reality a celebrated Nimrod. The clamours of gratulation were stunning, and universal, if we except Lord Willoughby, who sat fixedly upright in his chair, with an imperturbable expression of offended dignity.

Clifton took the first opportunity, occasioned by a cessation of the tumult, to apologise to the peer for the slight he had received, but in such slight terms as the situation demanded.

"I perfectly understand all you would say," Lord Willoughby replied, in a tone intended to cut short further explanation. "The lady had her reasons, doubtless."

"She has been indulged until she has become as varied as the wind," said Percy.

"I find no fault with her," said Willoughby, "but against you I bear a resentment that will not be easily satisfied. Had you dealt sincerely with me before I came down, you would have spared me a useless journey, and your sister some pain."

"I do not understand this language, Lord Willoughby," said Clifton, haughtily.

"Possibly not," said Willoughby, "but there are those here who may assist you to do so. Trelawney," addressing himself to a gentleman on the opposite side of the table, "what were you telling me of Merton and Miss Clifton?"

"Only that they eloped together," hiccuped Trelawney.

"The knowledge of that fact was rather important to me, I think," said Willoughby, "and I am happy I have learned it under circumstances different from those I this morning anticipated."

A sneer was on his lip, and Clifton was completely confused. He writhed under the mortifying consciousness of a dishonourable concealment, to which he had been tempted by his eagerness to see Willoughby wedded to his sister. His distress was enjoyed by the disappointed suitor, who in triumph of heart added—

"Personal motives marred your candour, I suspect."

Clifton demanded he should retract these disparaging insinuations, and Willoughly refusing, a vehement quarrel ensued.

Willoughby taunted him with his unnatural conduct to his wife, and the whole room was thrown into disorder. Twenty voices were shouting together, and a division was made into two parties, of which Willoughby and Clifton formed each the centre. All but Clifton were more or less intoxicated, and he was equally incapable of rational self-government. Willoughby called for pistols, declaring he would have the quarrel settled on the spot.

Clifton was as ready for the murderous encounter as himself. Many opposed it, but the majority, under the influence of mad excitement, supported the terrible proposal.

Pistols were brought and charged, and Willoughby seizing one, Clifton more deliberately, but not less firmly, grasped the other. They gazed steadily in each other's faces, and retreated

some yards, having the table between them. The clamourers for fair play adjusted the distance, and gave the signal. Each pistol was discharged at the same moment, and the new-made peer received his death wound. He staggered a moment before he fell, and said, with a ghastly expression of countenance—

"You have taken my life, but you will not long survive me!"

This was noted and remembered. The catastrophe effectually sobered the whole party, who began each to regard his own safety, and to disappear. The host was terribly alarmed, sent for a surgeon, and had the body raised to the table. The cold drops stood on Clifton's brow, and a horror fell on his spirit beyond mortal skill to paint. What he had done in the heat of a moment was irretrievable—blood was upon his hands which all the waters of the ocean could not wash away. His unhallowed deed had stilled the beatings of a heart which had often throbbed in kindness for him. He cast one look on the yet quivering features which had so often caught animation from his own, and rushing past those who would have advised him respecting his flight, tottered to the open air.

Morning was upon the lake, but night and morning must henceforward be joyless to Clifton. The renovating breeze he eagerly drank in, for his breath was almost choked by the dreadful sensations under which he was suffering. His horse was brought to his call, he reeled into the saddle, and with a brain on fire left the fatal place. His present impulse was to abide the issue of what had occurred in his own house, or rather this was the foremost of many contradictory impulses.

Between five and six o'clock he entered the precincts of his park at racing speed, taking the nearest way across it, leaping a hedge, a patch of brambles, and a ditch, in a style that would have excited the admiration of the lovers of bold horsemanship. At every step the animal's hoofs scattered the dew from the long grass. Not expecting his return the domestics were wrapt in slumber. The housekeeper herself came down to give him admittance, but on the first sight of his face uttered a faint scream of affright.

"Bless and keep us!" she ejaculated, "the squire at this time in the morning! and blood on his brow!"

"I had a trifling hurt," said Clifton, in as careless a tone as he could assume to allay her alarm, "it is nothing of any consequence. Call up my servant, and let him look to the horse." Then as she was about to obey him, he called after her in a cautious tone, "Say nothing of the trivial accident I have had, nor of the marks you perceived on my brow."

He hastened to perform his ablutions in his dressing-room, and to change his apparel, that he had worn the preceding night bearing in different parts the fatal tokens of the recent calamitous event. His valet, who also performed the office of groom, having attended to the wearied horse, knocked to inquire if his master required his attendance. Clifton replied in the negative, and the successor of Jean Andre, a spruce, sleek, conceited cockney, stole to the housekeeper's comfortable parlour to ask her what she thought of the present aspect of affairs between their master and Miss Clifton, for his curiosity was moved by the prolonged absence of the latter, and the unwonted hour at which the squire had come back, as well as by the condition of the fine animal he had ridden.

"The creature was ready to drop, Mrs. Wilson," he said, "and covered with perspiration."

"It is not your place," said the housekeeper, assuming a stately gesture, "to pry into the private concerns of the squire or those belonging to him. You have your own business to mind, and don't concern yourself with anything else."

"You are always a taking one off," said the humbled valet. "When I lived at my Lord Trevernon's in Belgrave Square, the housekeeper and I used to have many a pleasant chat about the family. I learnt a great deal while I was there."

"You will learn nothing from me about this family," said Mrs. Wilson. "I have not learnt my duty in a day. My hair has grown white, young man, in the service of the Cliftons, and no one can say I ever made bold to talk of their private concerns to the servants under me. I like no undue familiarity either, Mr. Jobson, but let every one keep the station they are born to, and not stoop under it, nor seek to meddle with what is above."

She dismissed the rebuked valet with a dignified wave of her hand. She was a woman who had old-fashioned notions of discipline, and the distinctions of caste. No Brahmin could have entertained greater horror of overpassing the nice barriers that divide rank from rank. She religiously avoided encroaching on the privileges of those above her, and from those beneath her she was punctilious in exacting the precise amount of difference which she estimated as her due.

As she sat in solitary dignity at her breakfast, a fine tortoiseshell cat enjoying at her feet the luxurious hearth rug and the heat of the fire, and the polished kettle singing cheerily on the hob, the affairs she could not condescend to discuss with the valet pressed urgently on the worthy woman's mind. The blood on the squire's face that morning, and the excuse he had made for it, were pondered unsatisfactorily again and again. The condition of his horse, and his rejecting the assistance of his valet at his toilet, were both circumstances that set her conjecture to work. Had he been really hurt?—where had he passed the night?—what had been the occasion of his spurring home in such haste? Had he heard Merton was in the dale? On this last important point she hastened to satisfy herself. Clifton had not rung for breakfast, and she went to inquire where he would have it served.

"Anywhere!—nowhere!" he answered hastily, without admitting her.

Mrs. Wilson had been all her life used to his moody tempers, and flattered herself she knew exactly how to deal with them.

"You must have your breakfast somewhere, Mr. Clifton," she said positively, yet deferentially—"I shall bring it here."

"Where you will," he answered, "only trouble me not."

"I am afraid he has heard Mr. Merton is about," said Mrs. Wilson to herself, as she turned away—"but it behoves me to know that I may forewarn Miss Amy."

When she arrived with the breakfast-tray, Clifton took it from her, as an intimation that she was to retire immediately, but Mrs. Wilson inquired if she should not bring a little plaister for the hurt he had received.

"No, no," he answered hastily, "it is nothing worth a thought."

"To be sure I cannot see the mark of it," she said, "but you are looking dreadfully ill."

This was spoken with unaffected concern, and Clifton endeavoured to quiet her apprehensions on his account by assuring her it was nothing but fatigue.

"I am afraid you have not slept to-night," she said.

"Indeed I have not," he replied unguardedly, "I would to God I had! though I had never wakened more."

"I hope nothing unfortunate has happened, sir," said the good woman.

Clifton made a confused answer.

"Oh! Mr. Percy," cried the old lady, in accents of entreaty, "I hope you will not think me impertinently curious if I beg of you to tell me what has happened this night to disturb you, for plainly I see something has. I am no tattler or busybody, nor do I ever forget what is due to those I am proud to serve. But my soul is laden with trouble, Mr. Percy, on account of the children of my departed lady, who is in a better world. - I would lay down my life for yourself or your sister!"

"Your faithful attachment is not questioned, Mrs. Wilson;

I am sensible of it, and grateful for it, equally with my sister, who loves you well. With respect to last night, I believe I may as well trust you. A misfortune has indeed happened—one which"—he shook violently, and was deadly pale—" is irreparable! I have slain Lord Willoughby in a murderous duel—it was his blood you saw upon my brow! In a short time the officers of justice will demand my person, and I, who was made of flint when Summerfield was tried—I, who have been as adamant against his beauteous daughter—I, with all my stubborn pride, shall have to taste the bitter dregs which the felon's law administers."

His venerable auditor could hardly support herself; she looked shocked in the extreme. Against Willoughby she had always entertained a dislike, conceiving he had assisted to mislead Percy from the straight path of virtue : nor had his elevation to the peerage redeemed him in her estimation, but she " declared it was fearful to think of his having been sent so suddenly where he must reckon for all his doings."

She ventured to ask if the squire would not wish his sister and his wife made aware of the peril he stood in, and he rejoined—

" They have both small reason to be anxious for my preservation. And yet, women like, they will most probably forget all I have made them suffer when they find me in need of their comfort."

Mrs. Wilson observed she was sure they would.

" Well," he said, after meditating awhile, " I will throw myself on their forgiveness shortly—not yet, however—and until I bid you otherwise, be silent, Mrs. Wilson."

She promised to observe his commands.

" But, dear Mr. Percy," she asked, with solicitude, " will you not take some steps to save yourself? For the sake of those who regard you, if not for your own !"

" Those who regard me !" he echoed, with a groan, " where are they? I have alienated and injured all !"

" Talk not so," said Mrs. Wilson, wiping the mist from her eyes.

" Distress not yourself on my account," said Clifton, kindly. " They that sow the wind, must reap the whirlwind; I am now reaping the whirlwind in all its terrors."

" Ah ! Mr. Percy, if you had but followed your mother's counsel !"

" My mother's! No, Mrs. Wilson," he sternly rejoined, " counsel was required for, not from, my mother. It was her causeless dislike, her neglect of the duties she owed me, which first made me licentious, wilful stubborn, and rash. Her son can breathe no regrets, no blessings, on her memory. She was my earliest, worst enemy."

"It is awful to hear a dead parent spoken of in this fashion, Mr. Clifton."

"She merits neither more or less at my hands," said Clifton, forcibly. "With my foot on her ashes I could say the same."

"God forgive you !—God forgive you !" cried the housekeeper. "Not that I am saying," she added, in a softer key, "that Mrs. Clifton behaved altogether motherly to you—truth to say, she did not, and at times I have made bold to tell her so, for my lady condescended to converse with me frequently."

Clifton here intimated his wish to be undisturbed the remainder of the day.

"He had to set his house in order, and to perform much that should have been accomplished before," he said, and there was a solemnity in his manner which struck home upon the good woman's heart the danger that environed him.

"Dear Mr. Percy," she implored, "save yourself! O save yourself! and whatever you wish may be done through your sister, or," she added, hesitatingly, "through Mr. Clifton. You can write your wishes, and if I discharge any I will not fail to attend dutifully to them. Pray think of preserving yourself! My son-in-law, who keeps the ferry just beyond West Hill, would row you in one of his boats to the island opposite, and there secure you a vessel for what place you pleased."

"It is indifferent to me where I go," said Clifton ; "if you think such a plan feasible you may arrange it as you will. My thoughts for some hours to come will be employed on other matters than my own safety."

"I will manage it all," said Mrs. Wilson, and she hastened to send a servant for her son-in-law, who to oblige his wife's mother, and in consideration of a reward, gladly undertook to manage the squire's safe and secret passage to the island, and his transmission from thence to some foreign place which Clifton might in the intermediate time make choice of.

The forenoon passed in quiet. Clifton was to be at the ferry as soon as daylight had set, and before the moon rose. Mrs. Wilson twice approached his room, and conjectured by the frequent rustling of paper that he was engaged in writing, and ever and anon he walked about, groaned, sighed, and struck the floor with his heavy boot. At these signs of mental anguish she shook her head.

"Sad work!—sad work!" she ejaculated, then busied herself in packing for Amy's departure with her husband, according to directions she had received. It pleased her that Clifton had not suspected Merton's being in the dale, and she was resolved not to say anything, that might convey to Miss Amy a suspicion of what had happened to Lord Willoughby, lest her concern for her brother's peril might induce her to postpone the bridal. To be sure there was a likelihood of the news reaching Amy by other means, but Mrs. Wilson hoped this would not be the case. Merton had always been a favorite with her, his benignity, tenderness, and melancholy, had engaged her pity and admiration. He had been the only person with whom Amy had been able to indulge herself in speaking of the beloved of her heart, and the good lady in return for her confidence had taken a sympathetic interest in her ardent feelings, and now rejoiced in her felicitous prospects. She certainly lamented that he had never known Charlotte Monckton, whose heartless, selfish vanity, she had seen through from her first introduction to Rosedale House, and blamed him, not for having loved Miss Clifton, but for not having been candid with her respecting his unfortunate marriage. She had no patience with Charlotte's usage of him, it stirred all her angry blood. It would be requited on her yet, she had always been sure.

Some idea that Mrs. Wilson was his friend, had led Merton to her parlor window the preceding evening, when watching for an opportunity to meet with Amy, that he had vainly sought for days. There was an old-fashioned garden, with clipt hedges, formal statues, and an encircling terrace, to which he made his way. He knew Mrs. Wilson's window looked upon it, and ascertaining by the light within that she was there and alone, he tapped on the glass. The old lady immediately came forth to identify the impertinent intruder, but as a servant was attending her with a light he hid himself. Presently, she began to close the shutters, and he addressed her in a soft urgent voice, which she recognised with surprise, and at first with displeasure, but his pleadings soon found way to her heart, and admitting him with caution, she described the present trouble of her young lady on account of her refusal of Lord Willoughby.

Merton was transported by this proof that his image yet lived in the affections of Miss Clifton. He was agitated by tenderness, and by hope. He implored her to hasten to Rose Cottage, whither Amy had fled from her brother's tyranny, to announce his arrival, to entreat her to concede him a few minutes private conversation, and to acquaint her that Charlotte and Salcroft had both paid the debt of nature.

An account of the debt of the former may point a moral for some of the daughters of vanity. As the Countess Borgia she had, on the Continent, revelled in all that was splendid and gay, and agreeably to the detestable Italian custom a male cecisbeo was permitted to escort her in public, and visit her on terms more intimate than in England would be permitted to any but an affianced lover.

This insinuating, accomplished nobleman, a kind of Don Giovanni, made the ill-favoured, time-stricken Count Borgia, appear in disadvantageous contrast in the eyes of Charlotte, who admired the former as much as she abhorred the latter. In an evil moment she betrayed to her doting lord the real bent of her mind, confessed that she had only bestowed herself on him for the sake of his title and possessions, and vowed she should be heartily glad when it pleased heaven to rid her of the incumbrance attached to them.

The count was a genuine Italian, in whom the passion of jealousy is proverbially dangerous; he perceived that an intrigue was on foot between the countess and her cavalier, and under pretence of exhibiting to her one of the ancient seats of his family, confined her in a wretched edifice, crumbling on a wave-worn rock, amid the waters of the Mediterranean. Here this gay, audacious woman was abandoned to solitude—here, her bold, haughty, worldly heart, severed from all it delighted in, chafed and fretted, and literally wasted away. Her movements were sedulously watched; her farthest walks extended to the ramparts, whence only a dreary waste of sea and sky were beheld. In vain she framed devices for escaping her detested prison-house, and its no less detested lord. He anticipated them all. In vain she tampered with her servants—they loved her not, and the count had secured their interests. A desperate will fertilised her invention; day and night she busied herself with new projects. At last a man who supplied the castle board with fish, was prevailed on to bear to the nobleman, whose criminal passion had caused her well-deserved sufferings, a letter, informing him of her retreat, and imploring him to hasten immediately to her relief.

An answer was returned, ardent indeed in its tone, but advising her "to be patient under her insufferable hardships until the writer was able to comply with his adorable friend's wishes. He could never enough lament that at present it was impossible for him to do so, as imperative concerns called him that very day to Vienna.

THE COTTAGE GIRL.

RUTH SIGHED, AND FELL INSENSIBLE.

CHARLOTTE was too confident in the power of her own attractions to allow a suspicion to enter her mind that the ardour of his passion for her had been cooled by absence; she forgot that the profligate are never constant to one object; and burning to free herself from thraldom, formed a sudden resolve to follow to Vienna the man whom she imagined herself to love.

Aided by the fisherman, who was richly bribed, she left the lone ocean rock at night, having secreted about her person a box of valuable jewels.

Landed on the shore, her first anxiety was to turn these gems into current coin, which being accomplished at the nearest town, she crossed the Tyrol, and availing herself of such vehicles as the road afforded, made no pause in her journey until the beautiful palaces and gardens of Vienna were in view. She passed into a public promenade planted with rows of trees, and thronged with the equipages of the great.

After engaging the first suitable accommodations she could find, she spent some days in vain attempts to discover the abode of the Marquis Montserrat. The public walks and carriage-drives she visited daily in the hope of meeting him. And one evening this hope was realised. His chariot wheeled passed her. But the jealousy of Charlotte was kindled by the sight of an elegant girl who sat by him, and whose sweet face was turned to his with a look confiding, bashful, and affectionate, while his deep olive features, and full black eye, responded to hers with a serious, chastened fondness, that rebuked the vices of his forgotten mistress more effectually than tongues of angels could have done. He loved another, and that other, Charlotte felt instantaneously assured, was—what she could never be. Pangs of envy, jealousy, rage, and grief, rent her soul, as keeping the chariot in view through several spacious streets, she beheld him alight at the gate of a hotel of the first rank, and placing his arms on the waist of his elegant companion, lift her with the tenderest care to the pavement, where drawing her arm through his own, they entered together.

Charlotte also dismissed her carriage, and entering the hotel engaged two handsome apartments, and ordered dinner. As the obsequious maitre d'hotel, a Frenchman, was leaving her, she said to him—

"You have the Marquis Montserrat in this house, have the goodness to let him know that a relation craves a few words with him."

In a few minutes the Marquis appeared, and starting at the sight of Charlotte, looked at once annoyed and disturbed.

"Well, my lord," said Charlotte, "I was not much indebted to your haste; but I freed myself from the doting old tyrant without your assistance, and since you would not come to me, I have travelled to you."

"My dear soul," said Montserrat, greatly embarrassed, "I grieve you should have taken a step so precipitate. Count Borgia I am assured loves you profoundly; he was, we must confess, justly incensed, but your forbearance for a time might have propitiated him."

"And is this all your welcome, after I have taken a solitary journey of this length to meet you?" demanded Charlotte, fixing her keen eye on his.

"Countess," said Montserrat, after a moment's perturbed reflection, "let me speak candidly to you, for it is necessary. I have I confess erred grievously with respect to you, and to your noble husband, but truth compels me to say that error was of your own seeking. Had you repelled me, had you treated me with the disdain and disgust I merited, all would have been well for you. Let what is past therefore rest in silence. As to the present, I did not invite you to this unpleasant meeting, it was not through my representations you were induced to take this journey, I cannot therefore be held responsible for the unpleasant position in which you have placed yourself, and the best I can advise is, that you return to your husband, and by your duty and submission endeavour to make amends for those lapses from rectitude of which you must accuse yourself."

"Is this my reception?" again demanded Charlotte.

"It is utterly impossible I can give you any other," he replied, "for the truth is—I have been but a few days married."

Charlotte left the hotel the same day for other lodgings, where she grew rapidly ill. While stretched powerless on her bed of pain, her jewels and money were stolen by some unknown individual, and as soon as it was ascertained that she was destitute of means to meet the exorbitant demands of her landlady for board and attendance, the forlorn and dying stranger was conveyed to a debtor's prison, and there, in a room of miserable aspect, on a straw mattrass, her soul, a prey to horrors the most fearful imagination can contemplate, with none to pity, none to soothe, the once resplendent Charlotte Monckton drew her last breath. And the form that had been decorated in life with all that was gorgeous, and which she had so much delighted to display, were flung as it were into the earth, without respect, in the coarse habiliments of a common prison.

A priest had been introduced to her in her expiring moments, to whom she confessed the humiliating story of her life, expressing an earnest desire that he would send to Merton an account of her last days, and the papers that would be found on her person.

These Amy saw after her happy marriage, and their tenor affected her deeply. They had been penned under the immediate anticipation of death, under fear and despair, and they recurred with piercing regret to the ingratitude of the writer to Merton, whom they declared Charlotte could not upbraid with one fault of any moment. She had dissolved her marriage with him solely because he was not able to support her in the style she desired.

" He had since been fearfully avenged," the writings said.

In her dying hour Charlotte had felt regrets also for the manner in which she had requited the unworldly friendship of Miss Clifton.

"Oh! what would I give to have her near me now?" was one of the expressive sentences which met the eye of Amy, and drew forth tears of pity and forgiveness.

A first friendship in some natures resembles a first love, and though the object be valueless, leaves a sweet odour on the memory which can only be dissipated in the grave.

Salscroft had died of apoplexy, and some confusion in his affairs compelled his heir to visit Calcutta. It was when on the eve of this voyage Merton had returned to Rosedale to solicit anew the hand of Amy, and on obtaining it she consented to visit India with him. An order was despatched to a clothing establishment in London for everything necessary for the outfit, and directly after the ceremony the bride and bridegroom set out for Liverpool in the carriage of Merton, accompanied by Ruth, whom Amy, pitying her lonely and unhappy situation, and desirous of her society, had persuaded to accompany them thither. All the day previous she had hoped that Clifton would have sought her, and as hour followed hour only to renew her disappointment, she suffered inexpressible tortures. When the nuptials had taken place, she left Rosedale with eagerness, too surely convinced that by befriending Amy she had once more alienated her husband, and anxious to escape from a place where intense hope and fear threatened to overwhelm her reason.

She had been powerfully solicited by Amy, and hardly less by Merton, to go out with them to India, but though more than half inclined, she ultimately decided on remaining. Though at present she only saw her sister and brother at the vacations, she intended shortly having the former beneath her roof to finish her education under the superintendence of an able governess, and she could not reconcile her mind to relinquish this idea, or to place so wide a distance between herself and the dear objects bequeathed to her care.

She spent a fortnight with Merton and Amy in an agreeable lodging-house on a bold cliff bordering the sea, and often, stealing from their sight, found a melancholy pleasure in loitering on the sands, sunk in dejection, listening to the sullen dash of the waves, and the screams of the sea-gulls dipping their wing in the surf. Often she strained her view outward to look for the growing mast of some homeward-bound vessel, while fancy anticipated the longed-for period of her father's return from exile. And if

she should be prohibited from meeting him, she well knew there was one, who, if his life were spared would not fail to be there.

This remembrance of Maynard was not her only one while she remained by the sea-side. The letter Miss Clifton wished her to destroy was often in her thoughts, and she could no longer deceive herself as to the true nature of his feelings toward her. Wyatt had told her he was looking ill and unhappy, and it grieved her that one so abounding in goodness to others should be without the domestic comforts that he prized so dearly, and destitute of the affectionate attentions that are so sweet in periods of ill-health and depression.

The commodious vessel in which Merton proposed embarking with his wife for Calcutta uplifted its white masts, and fluttered its gay pennon, in the harbour opposite their apartments. The accommodations it contained for the voyage were most complete, and in addition, the considerate love of Merton provided whatever he thought would be agreeable to the peculiar tastes of his companion, and assist to beguile the tedium of the voyage. He purchased an exquisite pearl-inlaid cabinet, furnished with writing and drawing materials, a guitar and harp, and a selection of books, in rich garnitures, chiefly imaginative and poetical.

"I wonder if he will be always as studious of what is agreeable to me," exclaimed the smiling Amy to Ruth, when first Merton exhibited to her the arrangements he had made for her reception.

"My love," he responded with earnestness, "when I cease to be studious of what is agreeable to you, you or I must be greatly changed, and have ceased to be worthy of each other. May such a time never arrive!"

Their eloquent eyes sought each other's gaze, and reflected there a fulness of bliss which could only be exceeded in a perfect state of existence.

To poor Ruth such bliss formed a cruel contrast to her humiliating, neglected, half-widowed condition, and poignantly she felt it, but involuntarily her thoughts turned to Maynard, as one who, had she been his wife, would have left nothing to envy in the affectionate consideration enjoyed by others, while it was not forgotten by her that a stratagem most cruel, base, and wicked had alone prevented her from bearing that relation to him.

Nigh two days passed before they heard of the death of Lord Willoughby, and then Mrs. Wilson herself came on the mail to bring the tidings.

"Mr. Percy is by this time over at the Isle of Man," she said, "and I believe he will go from thence across the Irish Channel.

One of the gentleman who had a hand in the duel has a place called the Hermit's Hut, at Sea Grove, on the Irish shore, and Mr. Clifton and he intended to hide there. 'Tis a wild and dismal spot I am told, but if he be safe in it he may be thankful. I have not slept a wink since he told me of the matter, and shall not until I know he is quite clear of those who are searching for him. He had hardly left the house before they came, and I was strictly questioned I assure you, but they could not gather from me where he was to be found."

The consternation of her listeners was inexpressible.

Ruth could hardly persuade herself she was not listening to a dreadful fiction, so strange it seemed that Clifton, after sternly refusing to admit the slightest extenuation of the crime imputed to her father, could be shrinking into a solitude which she knew he must detest, in order to escape the avengers of blood that he had shed under circumstances far less justifiable than those her father had been supposed to have yielded to. In the best natures a questionable satisfaction will steal into the mind when those who have oppressed them by intolerant judgments are themselves thrown on the unmerciful constructions of the world, and Ruth was not free from this feeling, though she was too right-minded to encourage it, and if she had not been so on principle, her native kindliness, and the deeper sentiment that still pervaded her soul, would have as effectually counteracted it, and she must no less have commiserated Clifton, plunged by one precipitate act into a gulf so fearful. The question was then agitated in her mind "Could he in his trouble have still hardened himself against her?" and the inward response was that if she had been near him he could not. And why had she not been near him? She would have flown to him, even at the risk of a repulse, had Mrs. Wilson, before Clifton left his house, given her the least intimation of what had happened, which if she had been her friend she would have contrived to do notwithstanding the prohibition she spoke of, that at such a time ought hardly to have been observed. But she knew Mrs. Wilson was not her friend, but was prejudiced against her on account of her low birth, and the ignominy resting on her father. Such a prejudice was in exact conformity with that person's characteristic respect for caste, which induced her to look with no favorable eyes on a young woman raised from a cottage to Mr. Clifton's level; and although she compassionated as much as any one the sorrows of Ruth, and admired the sweet mixture of heroism, good sense, and firm affection, that all her actions displayed, yet it happened that the good woman never heard or spoke her praises without at the same time endeavouring to detract from her merit; and although every opportunity had been afforded her, no word on his forsaken wife's behalf had she ever breathed to Clifton; nor, though unrestricted by any command, had she ever found her way to the cottage of Ruth, until her young lady went there, and she had an express errand; nor, though in point of conscience she had felt bound to name her when Clifton was on the eve of flying perhaps for ever the seat of his forefathers, had she any real wish for their reunion. Perhaps she feared Ruth would not prove quite so passive a mistress as Amy Clifton, at all events she had a rooted repugnance to the idea of Summerfield's daughter ruling over Rosedale House, and of her upstart friends gaining a superior footing where once they would have considered themselves honoured by a seat in the kitchen.

"But if it comes to that," she thought to herself, "I must quit, loath as I may be. It is quite out of the question that I should treat as my betters those poor mushrooms, who, as I may say, have sprung from a dunghill, and who are the relations of the man who murdered the gentleman I served. It will be as much as I can do if I persuade myself to obey the orders of one of that set, and I shall not do that with great goodwill."

Even in communicating the exciting intelligence with which she was charged, there was a marked difference in the manners of Mrs. Wilson to Amy and Ruth, being to the latter frigid and stiff, according exactly to the degree of respect that was her due, neither more nor less, but to the former expressive in every glance and tone of heartfelt, spontaneous devotion, to her service.

"My friends are destined to be few,' thought Ruth, as with a painful sensation she marked this difference. "And those few are one by one sundered from me. I have done nothing in all my life to merit any one's dislike, yet I am hated and despised."

Her heart swelled to her throat, and she would have rushed from the room, but Amy caught her hand.

"My dear girl, whither are you going in such haste?' she asked.

The disengaged hand of Ruth was pressed to her heart and to her throat, and with wild unconsciousness she strove to free herself from the hold of her friend.

"You are overcome with this sad news of Percy's danger," said Amy, terror-struck by her appearance.

"With that, and with his entire forgetfulness of me," Ruth rejoined, in a proud, half-suffocated tone—"with that, and the injustice that pursues me."

Her eyes sparkled indignantly, but their keen fire was only

momentary, and with a long-drawn sigh she threw herself on the neck of her friend, who, by the sudden increase of her weight, and the powerlessness of her limbs, found that she was insensible. While restoratives were applied, Amy's tears dropped fast on the alabaster features which she continued to rest on her kind bosom.

"Dear unhappy girl!" she cried, "she must go with us, Merton, I cannot think of leaving her thus forlorn, thus brokenhearted."

"It is a question with me whether she would survive the voyage," rejoined Merton, observing the extreme delicacy which long suffering had imparted to her naturally slender shape and features.

"I had no conception Mrs. Clifton was so altered for the worse, as I now see she is," observed the housekeeper.

"She may be altered for the worse in health," said Merton, "but I think it was scarcely possible for her ever to have been more lovely."

"Not more, certainly," said Amy, warmly, incapable of any mean jealousy of the beauty her husband thus praised, though at another time she might have been tempted to wish she had possessed an equal share.

"If it is an idea that Mr. Percy did not think of his lady when he left the dale that has caused this sudden illness," said Mrs. Wilson, "I can relieve Mrs. Clifton's mind. He did think of her, and of his sister too, as this packet I daresay will testify."

Ruth was instantly restored to energy, and starting up, she waited with eager expectancy while Amy examined the contents of this packet. When the outer envelope was removed, two separate letters appeared superscribed to Miss and Mrs. Clifton, beside other papers.

Ruth hurried with her own to her chamber, and oh! who can imagine the complicated sensations with which she slowly unfolded a missive so momentous to the peace of her future life?—who can conceive the rapid transitions of intense emotion expressed on her countenance on reading as follows?—

"When this reaches you, the husband who has given you so much distress will be a fugitive and a wanderer, stained with more than your father's guilt, a curse to himself, and burdened with the intolerable reflection of the years of wretchedness he has entailed on you! Yet you may rejoice now, for your oppressor can never enjoy a moment's tranquility more, and every sigh he has drawn from you, will be expiated by a thousand groans wrung from him by tortures such as your gentle nature could not com-

prehend. Willoughby is dead, and I am his murderer. Though I had often behaved to him with scorn, he loved me, and would have served me, but his blood is on my hand!—his ghastly image haunts me!—his voice and your tears plead together to high heaven against me. I have given orders to my agent for the bulk of my estate to be sold, the rest I have settled permanently on my sister, and whatever I may be possessed of when my debts are paid will revert to you after my decease. Whether we shall ever meet again I am in doubt, most probably not, and if not, 'why then this parting was well made.' Endeavour then to think of me as I required you should of your father, that is, as though I were already in the earth, as if I had never existed. Make yourself happy; let my sister reside with you; see company; visit the gay places in which ladies usually delight—the theatre, the concert-room, the ball-room, and every other scene that purity such as yours may visit unstained, in order that you may lose the remembrance of him who, while he admires you, inconceivably more than he did four years ago, more than he did in that hour when he gave his name to you at the altar, who, while he entreats your forgiveness and forgetfulness of the past, feels himself hopelessly separated from you chiefly by his own unutterable unworthiness. And so a hasty yet eternal farewell to you, my fair and injured love! Attempt no correspondence with me. To you, to my country, to my sister, to myself, I am irrevocably lost!"

Fearful of the effect of renewed agitation on her enfeebled frame, Amy did not leave her long alone. Entering, she beheld Ruth stretched colourless on the bed, like a lovely image placed by some gifted sculptor above the tomb of a youthful saint.

"And such is to be the end of a love like mine!" ejaculated Ruth, as she gave Amy the foregoing letter to read.

"Your lot is indeed most melancholy," Amy observed, after laying it down. "You must, indeed you must, consent to be my companion over the ocean. It will be better for you."

Ruth shook her head.

"As you entered," she said, "I was considering how I might best save your brother's estate from passing into other hands. I believe I had best purchase it, and with that view I shall write to the agent without delay. Thus in point of fact, it will, of course still remain his own, while the money I shall give for it will answer all his ends without his pride, suffering from a thought of touching my fortune, since ours he is not willing for it to be."

"You are most thoughtful and generous," said Amy, "and I must thank you both for him and myself, since, although the sacrifice of the old house to strangers would disquiet me less than if I were there to see the wreck, it would do so more than I should like to experience."

"It shall not be sacrificed while I possess the means to save it," said Ruth.

"Then when I write to you from the land of fevers and mosquitoes I presume I must address to my deserted home? O changeful world! See the altered aspect of affairs! Ruth Summerfield the solitary mistress of my proud brother's domain—I, his sister, married, save the mark! and lounging in fine muslin on couches kept cool by artificial air, and wetted blinds, attended by a score of tawny slaves—and Percy,—but I am light and trifling; heigho! happiness makes one selfish as well as misery, let me tell you, Ruth. Were you ever selfish?"

"What a question!—am I human?"

"I should like to detect just a little selfishness in you, if only to bring you down to the ordinary level of mortals, for now you are so much above, in all virtue, that the more I know you, the more I wonder how such a flower sprung up in such a lowly soil."

"It was a favourable soil, Amy, favourable to moral health and vigour, though the winds were sometimes rough, and the atmosphere keen. But let us talk of more pressing concerns."

"Of nothing more now," said Amy, "you look as white as the window curtains, and must sleep awhile, then I will bring your tea here, and we will pass the evening together, while Merton and Mrs. Wilson entertain each other."

She drew the blind accordingly, and Ruth gladly availed herself of an hour's repose.

CHAPTER XXXIX.

"O, my offence is rank, it smells to heaven;
It hath the primal eldest curse upon't,
A brother's murder!—Pray can I not,
Though inclination be as sharp as will;
My stronger guilt defeats my strong intent;
And, like a man to double business bound,
I stand in pause where I shall first begin,
And both neglect.
O wretched state! O bosom, black as death!
O limed soul; that struggling to be free,
Art more engaged!"

SHAKESPEARE.

LET us shift the scene for a brief interval. An abrupt curvature in the shore of our sister island, in the Irish Channel, slopes in black jagged precipices to the edge of the sea ; these, shooting out their rocky roots, so to speak, far into the surf, form treacherous reefs, covered by perpetual foam, extremely perilous to the mariners who sail nigh them without skilful pilotage. Around this bend, or point, of land, sometimes designated Ballicary, sometimes Sea Grove, the waves in stormy weather rage with appalling fury, and the tempestuous blast is terrific there beyond human imagination. A briny atmosphere, when rough winds prevail, greatly oppresses the lungs of those who inhale it, and adds to the horrors of the place. The precipices are in the under part perforated with caverns, many of them exceedingly curious, some calculated to excite awful, others delightful sensations of wonder in the minds of beholders, and some yet unexplored.

Toward the principal of these caverns, at twilight, when the winds and waves of Ballicary Point were comparatively lulled, a boat rowed by two lusty sailors belonging to a small vessel moored in a creek at a convenient distance with difficulty made its way, and on withdrawing, left among the broken ledges of rock Clifton, and the gentleman to whose unprepossessing retreat he was being conducted.

Miles Lawrey was about fifty years old, with rough hearty manners, a person of rather clumsy make, and genuine Irish physiognomy. He had some pride of ancestry, not devoid of a reasonable ground, for they had been great in their day.

"But they have left me only a sorry portion," he said, looking round on barren rocks with a half rueful, half comical expression, after Clifton and he had clambered to the upper cliff by means of steps cut in the rock. "If, however, I welcome you to all I have, I can do no more you know."

"I assure you again it is very indifferent to me where or how I am lodged, or whether I am lodged at all or not," said Clifton, in a voice so hollow it might have issued from a tomb.

If the other had had any pride to consult it might have proved fortunate Clifton was thus indifferent, for the Hut, which in a preceding century, during the decline of the Lawrey family, had been transformed from a solitary hermit's abode into an inferior sort of mansion, was now in so neglected a condition as hardly to be habitable. An old man had been allowed to avail himself of such shelter as it afforded, free of rent, and the feeble twinkling of a light in one of the shattered windows seemed to intimate that he was within. If so, the knocks and shouts of Lawrey were alike without effect on him, and the patience of the gentlemen was exhausted, when Lawrey forced his way through a low vaulted window, and opening the front door proceeded to conduct his guest along a passage smelling of rats and damps to a low spacious room, on whose walls fragments of mouldering tapestry hung suspended, and whose only furniture consisted of a few crazy stools and chairs, and a black oak table.

"By St. Patrick, and all the other saints in and out of the Irish calender!" shouted Lawrey, "I would like to know, Darby Harty, what this is all about, man! Why did you not let us in?"

The old man, who was shivering over a low fire, was totally unmoved by this, and instead of answering the angry query of the master of the Sea Grove, muttered to himself in a feeble, querulous voice.

"He must be deaf," said Clifton, "deaf as the hearth he sits on."

"When I last was here he heard well enough—but that was long ago," said Lawrey, moving close to Darby Harty, who raising his head upon being touched, started, and appeared paralysed with fear, Lawrey took his hand, and spoke kindly to him, and though the words fell on sealed ears, their meaning was interpreted to the old man in the face of the speaker. When he had composed himself Lawrey made him understand they wished for a better fire and something to eat, and with a gold piece in his hand, Darby Harty set off to purchase what he could at the hamlet close by.

"I must look to this poor fellow," said Lawrey. "He had a daughter who allowed him a trifle sufficient for his support. I fear her help is withdrawn, he looks so woe-begone."

The mild features of the old man brightened with as much gladness as desolate age could feel, when Lawrey, on his reappearance with a basket of fish, bread, and other eatables, and a bottle of whiskey, after drawing from him the sad intelligence that his daughter had emigrated, and left him in want, managed to let him understand he should be provided for in the future.

Darby Harty cooked the fish over the embers, and spread the supper things on the table as neatly as the means at his command admitted.

"Now, squire," said Lawrey, as the fire began to blaze, and redden, while he compounded a tumbler of whiskey-punch, "now I think we may manage to put on here until you arrange your future plans."

"No place can be better," Clifton listlessly rejoined.

"It will never be suspected, if your housekeeper keeps her own counsel."

"She will do that," said Clifton, in the same languid key.

"Well then, draw your stool nigh the blaze, and eat and drink of what there is. 'Tis not such fare as you have been used to, but what then?" a man is not a man if he is not prepared for privation as well as plenty. Drink! and let the vapours pass—we were all as much to blame for poor Willoughby's fall as you."

"Let his name rest in silence," said Clifton, with a look of agony.

"Why I know you take the affair very much to heart, and I am sorry for it, for you see what is done is past remedy."

"Past remedy, indeed!" exclaimed Clifton, shifting his seat, with a gloomy wildness of the eye that struck his thoughtless entertainer mute. "You are quite right, Lawrey, quite right, the evil is quite remediless, and the curse of it must cling for ever to his slayer."

"Come, come," said Lawrey, "never take on this way about it. Why I have talked with professed duellists——"

"Professed murderers!" interrupted Clifton.

"Who have killed their half-dozen men, and never slept a wink less sound."

"I pity them their callousness," said Clifton, and rising abruptly, he expressed a wish for rest.

The old man, who had been busy airing the bedding of the only tenantable chamber, lighted him and Lawrey thither, they being under the necessity of sharing the same couch. In a little ante-room adjoining, a candle was left burning on a slab, and by its light, Lawrey, waking shortly after midnight beheld him there, half-dressed, sitting in a fixed posture, his elbow on his right hand, his left on the lower part of his face, while his eyes seemed to have receded far back into their sockets, and were strained on vacancy. Some time he remained thus; then folding his arms on his breast with a thrilling groan, arose, and without noise paced the narrow limits of the apartment, until observing the door half open which separated him from the chamber where Lawrey lay, he closed it softly, after listening whether his companion still slept, which Lawrey, by breathing regularly, induced him to believe.

The latter was not endowed with any remarkable delicacy of feeling on the subject of duelling. For the fall of Willoughby he attached no blame to any party; but regarded the lamentable event a mere matter of chance, a misfortune, certainly rashly hazarded, but according to the laws of honour, and therefore the broodings of remorse which he had remarked in his young companion were inexplicable to him, except in the view that they were excited by other circumstances.

"That poor young creature, his wife, has been harshly used,"

thought Lawrey, " he must be thinking of her—I will try to draw him out to-morrow."

Clifton was still pacing the little ante-room when Lawrey resumed his repose ; and waking late next morning he found his young guest's toilet was made, and that he was below.

" You rested but ill, I fear, last night," said the host, hastening to join him.

" Why the wind was boisterous, and your couch none of the softest," rejoined Clifton, a slight tinge of colour on his cheek.

" And what have you contrived for our breakfast, Darby ?" asked Lawrey.

" Bedad ! your honour," said the old man, with a smile of infine satisfaction, " only a quart jug full of the primest coffee that was to be bought in Sea Grove, and a dozen new-laid eggs, and a cake, and butter, and a piece of Farmer O'Donoghue's home-cured bacon."

" O then we shall do well enongh," said Lawrey, rubbing his hands by the fire, inviting Clifton to a seat at the breakfast-table, and placing himself opposite in an immense worm-eaten oak chair.

" I thonght I heard you up in the night," said Lawrey, addressing Clifton as the meal proceeded.

" I was cold and restless," was the embarrassed rejoinder.

Lawrey thought this hardly sufficient to account for the ghastly complexion, rigid attitude, and hollow mournful eye, of the previous night; but he did not utter his thoughts, for the manners of Clifton by no means admitted of confidential conversation; indeed, though Lawrey had passed the heyday of youth, there was too much frivolity in his bearing for so proud a heart as his companion's to choose him for its counsellor.

A point of no small importance it was, after breakfast, to devise means for speeding forwards agreeably the languid hours, there being no employment to give them interest, and apparently no amusement which could lend them more than a momentary charm, without risking personal detection and apprehension in the pursuits.

" We must not break cover, or we shall be hunted down," said Lawrey. " Having come hither by the sea way, we have escaped the vision of those who live in the neighbourhood, and Darby in making his purchases for our use, gives out we are friends of his own come to regale him with their bounty."

" Let the hazard be what it may, it is impossible I should remain long cooped up here," said Clifton—" I should go mad."

" I'll tell you," said Lawrey, " what we must do to make the long days seem short—we must turn to the cards, there is nothing else will serve our turn."

"I believe you are right," Clifton rejoined, and Darby being dispatched to buy or borrow a pack, returned with one that had been thumbed over some twelve months in a tap-room. Repugnantly Clifton took them into his white and well-formed hand, but his refined habits quickly gave place to the ardour of play, and there was no flagging of the pinions on which the subsequent hours sped along. It will readily be supposed that the game did not of itself afford the desired stimulus, but that this was derived from certain hazards connected with it, and in the present state of Clifton's mind it was necessary these hazards should be considerable, to arouse his attention thoroughly. He played deep then, but winning and losing alternately, ended the first day nearly with the same finances that he had when he began. The second saw him a winner of two hundred pounds, the third of double this; and Lawrey, who bagan to get irritated and unpleasant in his manners, insisted on doubling the stakes.

" That would be unwise," said Clifton, " you have already lost as much as you can bear."

" Had any one else said so, I would have called them impertinent," returned his host, turning red in the face, and looking disposed to be quarrelsome, for he was sensitive touching his poverty, and had besides drank the most part of more glasses of whiskey-punch than old Darby had ever seen emptied before by two persons at a sitting.

Clifton perceived he was excited, and throwing down the cards, said emphatically—

" We must beware what we are about, Lawrey; you and I have seen something too much of the effects of quarrelling over alcohol." A horrible pang shot across his brow, and he left the house abruptly.

THE COTTAGE GIRL.

"WHAT WOULD YOU DO, SQUIRE?" EXCLAIMED MAYNARD.

CLIFTON'S heedless steps wandered on, and gradually descending the precipice on which the hut stood, he about half way down turned aside to a spot of ill-repute on the coast, where a horrid aperture in the rock permitted a dim insight to a cavern. The brilliant moonlight stealing in through the aperture by which he stood, and through the entrance that fronted the sea, barely enabled him to distinguish two disconnected pools of inky blackness; one many yards below the level of the other, the lowest sending off a stream which hurled itself down a gulf whose far-off echoes were melancholy to hear, and strangely impressive to the imagination.

Awful thoughts were gathering on Clifton's mind as he lingered—thoughts on the world's mysteries, of the mysteries of human nature, of his own vices, of the grave, and of futurity.

He had never been in the habit of indulging or delighting in these bewildering speculations, but he was now unable to repel them.

Slowly he left the spot, with the hue of death upon his cheek, and his soul wrapt in more than funeral darkness. He remembered the shape resembling Andre which he had seen by the churchyard in Rosedale, and it imbued him with a vague forefeeling of some ' consequence yet hanging in the stars,' by which his destiny was to be controlled. All men are at some time or other of their lives, disposed to superstition, and Clifton at present was so ; he believed he had seen the spectre of the valet, to whom he had given so ill an example, whose wickedness had been exerted for his illicit gratifications, and whom he had left unprovided to the strong temptations engendered by necessity. It was most rational to conclude that the supposed spectre was an individual whose form had a resemblance to that of Andre when seen in the twilight, and Clifton, had he spoken on the subject, would have ridiculed any other idea ; yet, in reality, he was as firmly convinced of the immateriality of the vision, as of his own corporeal substance. Supernatural visitations are almost invariably connected in the minds of those who behold them in the shadowy realms to which all that live are hastening, and most frequently accounted forewarnings to some particular individual of the great change. In this light Clifton was disposed to view the reappearance of his valet, and the black fear of death knocked terribly loud at his heart and conscience.

When he returned to the roof to which he was at present indebted for shelter, Lawrey, who was eager to retrieve his losses, urged him to resume the cards, but Clifton rejected them with disgust, and retired moodily to bed. Next day he perceived a change in the demeanour of his host, which resolved him to abridge his stay. He determined first, however, to let Lawrey win back the money he had lost, and as much as would repay him for his hospitality. But before the cards were taken up again, tidings arrived of a nature to drive all lesser matters from Clifton's mind.

He was apprised of his sister's marriage from her own hand, and though pardoning his violence toward her, she assured him he must attribute the indecorous haste of this alteration in her condition entirely to it, as well as her having reconciled herself to the perils of a long voyage, and a burning climate, without taking any more affectionate leave of him than was comprised in the announcement of her intention.

The consideration that Amy had been driven by his selfish tyranny into an inconsiderate marriage, aggravated almost to insanity the disquietude Clifton was enduring, nor was it without painful throbbings of the heart that he contemplated such a parting—a final parting most likely—from the endeared associate of his gentler hours, his early playfellow, the girl on whose indulgent sympathy he had so habitually relied for all occasions of trouble or sickness, that its full value had hardly been appreciated until it was now withdrawn. He remembered his unkindness to her with self-abhorrence—he dwelt with tormenting accuracy on every amiable trait of her disposition—and amid such reflections, the last gleam of light, the last touch of verdure, seemed to wither and fade from his heart. He had no longer a sister! It was a blighting thought. The last and dearest of the ties of kindred was snapped asunder! The golden links of early association, of home fellowship, were rent away. He had no longer a sister!

"And I have been the means of banishing her!" he cried. "However, my joy go with her! I think Merton's temper is better suited than mine to render a woman happy, it has milder attributes."

"Or they must be harsh enough," said Lawrey, who had stolen on him unawares. "And who is this Merton you are raving to the winds about?"

"A person whom it was my misfortune to become acquainted with some time ago," Clifton replied, resuming the manner with which he knew so well how to ward off unpleasing familiarities.

That evening they were sitting over a supper of oysters, in the dullest spirits possible, while old Darby was enjoying his portion in the chimney-corner, and vainly endeavouring by his rich brogue, and quaint humour, to excite a smile on the leaden visages of the gentlemen, when a knocking was heard, and the son-in law of Clifton's housekeeper, a thorough-bred son of Neptune, made his appearance. He had been entrusted by her with a parcel for the squire, which he delivered with a backward scrape of one foot, accompanied by an application of his hand to the fore-locks surmounting his weather-tanned but well-shaped features. Clifton desired him to sit down, and a jug of beer and a slice of boiled ham was set before him, while what he had brought underwent examination.

As Clifton anticipated, the house at Rosedale was sold; but Ruth having stipulated with the agent that her husband should not know the real purchaser at present, Percy supposed that a stranger possessed it, and was irritated that information was not sent respecting the name, rank, and connexions of that individual. Such an omission appeared inexplicable.

A surprise of a different nature was excited by the high price paid for the estate—considerably more than he had calculated upon—and he felt assured whoever had it must have been eager for the bargain.

The messenger was rewarded liberally, and dismissed with replies to the agent and the housekeeper, and Clifton was left to brood over his shattered fortunes. His liabilities were all provided for, and he was still in possession of comparative affluence. But sufficiency is relative, it is the little more, or little less, than is possessed by others of our station which renders most of us satisfied or dissatisfied. The estate which had been his glory, and on which he had been born and nurtured, could not pass from him without calling forth stinging regrets, and he could see no prospect of ever being enabled to re-purchase it, or to possess himself of one of anything like the value. It was, therefore, beyond a doubt that he must sink some degrees below the station he had hitherto occupied, and this certainty was in itself fearfully exasperating to a spirit so impetuous and proud.

After learning the disposal of his beautiful domain, Clifton, with the aid of books and newspapers, cards and chess, wore out a dreary month longer in the bleak Hut of Ballicary Point, having reason to believe himself safer there than in any other place, from the pursuit which his agent and housekeeper wrote was in active operation.

His Irish host had recovered his losses with interest, and one serene twilight was engaged in smoking, reclined at ease on two chairs, while Clifton took his solitary walk among the crags and unfrequented paths abounding in the vicinity. Keeping an upward direction, the latter came before it was dark to the verge of the highest precipice of Ballicary Point, where sitting down on a parapet of stone he surveyed the extended prospect. All was grand to awfulness! but at the same time rugged, bare, and unprepossessing. The channel heaved under countless restless waves, which the north-west blast was lashing into fury; the opposite shores were rendered indefinite by the lurid vapours which obscured them; and the cliffs stretching on either side the giant precipice Clifton was upon, were singularly savage and inhospitable of aspect, though it was impossible not to feel the fancy stirred most powerfully by their darkling caves, and piled up masses, around which, hosts of the wildest sea-fowl perpetually hovered, blending their shrill and dissonant cries with the sublime voices of winds and waves.

While he sat absorbed in reverie, a voice shouted his name, and looking round he beheld with unpleasant surprise, no less a person than Maynard.

CHAPTER XL.

"From his tongue
The unfinished period falls, while, borne away
On swelling thought, his wafted spirit flies
To the lorn bosom of the dying fair."

THOMSON.

CLIFTON's looks were dark, and his mien haughty, as Maynard approached, but instantly recollecting that he had no proper cause of anger against the miller, and assailed by an irresistible consciousness of his superior worth, he corrected his first impulse, and advanced a few steps to meet him.

Maynard, before speaking, fixed a long, earnest, melancholy gaze on Clifton, in which there seemed to lurk a meaning more profound than he had power to tell.

The voice was tremulous and grave in which he then said—

"You will wonder for what purpose I am come hither squire; it is not to upbraid you for your unfriendly behaviour to me, or for anything relating to my friend Summerfield, or even for your long cruelty to his daughter. I know you well enough to be sure that your own reflections will upbraid you more than all I could say. But my errand is—"

Breaking off, he gazed again stedfastly and solemnly on Clifton, whose frame was pervaded by an universal tremor.

"For God's sake, Maynard, what can you have to say that needs all this preparation?" he exclaimed, "and how were you able to find me?"

"Your housekeeper directed me."

"Indeed! and what could be the occasion justifying her violation of my command to communicate the place of my retreat to none?"

"Never disturb yourself about it, squire! it was an occasion important enough."

"The nature of it?"

Maynard did not immediately answer, and when he made the attempt, he was interrupted by the violence of his grief.

"What can those tears mean?" exclaimed Clifton, shocked in the extreme. "You are neither child nor woman, Maynard, to find a pleasure in such soft droppings. You are extraordinarily affected; tell me—tell me the cause!"

"Your ill-used wife is—"

"Hah!—my wife! I might have known nothing could have moved you thus powerfully, but what had reference to her.'

"You would not have erred in that idea."

"And what of my wife, sir?" demanded Clifton, haughtily.

"She is on her death-bed, squire."

Clifton staggered backwards as if a bullet had struck him.

"Yes!" exclaimed Maynard, his voice half-drowned in emotion, "she is on her way to join her blessed mother—even by this time they may have met."

"You freeze my blood! ejaculated Clifton. "What—what has been the cause?"

Maynard was silent, but his grief-fraught eye rested on Clifton with a still, mournful, accusing glance, which the latter was unable to bear, and turned his own wretched look on the ground. They walked a few yards down the precipice in silence; Clifton then suddenly stopped, and burst forth with wild vehemence—

"Powers of the grave! if ye have not yet glutted yourselves with the fairest creatures of the universe, oh! spare her, and take instead the villain who has oppressed her!"

Again they moved downward, and Maynard next spoke.

"Ruth had been long wearing away," he said, "so Doctor Walcot told Mrs. Wilson; and the parting with Miss Clifton it was supposed gave the finishing stroke."

"Amy is gone then!" muttered Clifton.

"She is," said Maynard.

"And you and Doctor Walcot, and all the world I presume, are agreed that I have been the destroyer of my wife?"

"The opinion of all the world should be indifferent to you, squire, if you feel your own conscience free."

"Yes, IF," echoes Clifton, fiercely, "but if not, how then?"

"Then for all the wealth of England I would not be Squire Clifton."

"Well might you say so, if you knew all the fires that hell has lighted in this single breast!" exclaimed Clifton, wildly, striking his chest with his clenched hand, and closing his teeth so that the air hissed through them—"well might you say so, if you knew but the half of my untold agonies!"

"I have no doubt you suffer, squire."

"And you thank God I do so!" said Clifton, laughing bitterly. "You thank God that vengeance has found me at last! You glory in my horror of soul, and think of your once bright hopes I crushed—of Summerfield, and of the seduction, desertion, and sufferings of his daughter!"

"I think of them, certainly," replied Maynard, "but not the less would I relieve you if it lay in my ability."

"What! that you might heap coals of fire on my head?—So runs the worthy motives of you Christian pardoners, I believe."

"I don't claim to be thought more a christian than my neighbours, squire; but I know that what our good vicar of Rosedale preaches about the unlawfulness of revenge, and the duty of wishing well to one's enemies, is all right and true, and I can't for my life help trying to forgive when I see my injurer in trouble, and recollect the social hours we have passed together, and the good qualities he once seemed to possess."

"Seemed, indeed!" groaned Clifton. "Oh! Maynard, my good fellow, I am steeped in crime! I am black as hell! I can never undo what I have done! A man-slayer!—the blood of my friend on my hand! And soon the ashes of a broken-hearted wife will be crying from the earth against me! Oh! cursed,

cursed precipitancy! Would to God I had been strangled in the hour of my birth! O fool!—fool!—fool! Sister, wife, and friend—all gone! Amy driven to an ill-advised marriage, and an unhealthy clime!—Ruth broken in heart by my infatuated cruelty!—Willoughby bolstered in blood for an eternity! But what is to compel me to endure all the horrors of these reflections? This—this shall end them!"—and to Maynard's alarm he with an air of desperation plucked a pistol from his bosom.

"What would you do, squire?" exclaimed Maynard, grasping his arm, and endeavouring to wrest the deadly weapon from him.

"What would I do?" echoed Clifton,—"I would remove a cumberer of the ground—an excrescence of humanity—who is hateful to himself, and pestilential to all within his influence!"

"At least you shall not harm yourself while I am near you," said Maynard, positively, "Give me the pistol!"

The weapon exploded as he strove to seize it, but no injury was done, and after a wild and furious stare on Maynard, Clifton thrust the empty implement of death into his pocket, and leaning against an upright rock complained in a subdued tone of faintness. Maynard saw a brook near at hand, and a relic of a broken pitcher, in which he brought a little water, and sprinkled on the face of his companion.

"If before committing error the miseries it entails were clearly foreseen, surely," thought Maynard, "it would be avoided."

But the consequences are often foreseen, and yet braved, such is the fool-hardiness of man, such his incurable tendency to self-deceit, such the powerful suggestions of his passions.

As soon as Clifton was better he learned the express nature of the mission Maynard had undertaken, and how it came to be entrusted to him. In the first place Clifton perceived, though Maynard would have gladly concealed the fact, that the latter had, though at a distance, contrived always to be informed of the state of Ruth's health and fortunes, and hearing that after returning from seeing Amy and Merton embark for Calcutta, she had been seized with a dangerous illness, he came with haste to Rosedale, and continued to hover about her dwelling, until he learnt that Ruth had a desire to see him, her impression being at the time that she had but a short time to live. At the sight of her faded charms, that had so long been precious to his soul, he

was overcome by a thousand piercing thoughts; when she spoke, the soft, melodious, sympathising tone, only aggravated his pain, for he believed it sounded in his ear for the last time; when he contemplated her face to imprint the delicate features with their chastened mournfulness of expression more dearly on his memory, the anguish was unspeakable with which, glancing mentally into the future, he foresaw them in a few weeks or days bereft of the lustre of life, unanswering to the invocations of friendship, cold and insensible; the radiant eye radiant no more, veiled in dull film; the lovely lip unfanned by the odoriferous breath that now played over them; all, all changed, and resting in the shadow of the grave, where none might behold her more. After endeavouring to console him with the argument of religion and necessity (to which Maynard appeared to listen, remembering how incumbent it was on a judicious friend to support her fainting spirit, instead of assisting to depress it), she addressed him very seriously.

"She knew it would be a consolation to him after she was gone, if he had been the means of rendering her the last important service she should require from anyone, and she was assured whatever his sentiments were regarding the conduct of her husband to her, he had some respect to Clifton, and had not forgotten that he had acted nobly in some instances. Now Clifton she earnestly desired to see before she closed her eyes for ever, and to whom could she so safely as to Maynard entrust the secret of his retreat? on whom else could she so well depend for expedition, and care for Clifton's preservation from those who sought to arrest him?"

"I would walk the world over could my doing so bring an hour's additional peace to your mind," said Maynard, with a gush of the purest tenderness.

"I believe you," said Ruth, emphatically, "and my last breath shall thank you."

She urged him to speed, for her eagerness was great to see Clifton once more. Some bitter sensations the mention of him had called forth in Maynard, and the latter sighed to perceive how, even on the threshold of eternity her spirit clung to him. But his happily-constituted nature was readily wrought to self-forgetfulness, especially in whatever could administer to her comfort whom he had loved with such unwearied constancy, such matchless disinterestedness.

He left Rosedale, for the greater speed, on Clifton's favourite horse, which the latter had directed his agent to sell at the same time with the estate, and which Ruth had preserved with it. In the stable of an inn by the waterside, Champion (so the steed was named) found accommodation while Maynard crossed the channel in a steamer, and following the minute directions Ruth had given him made his way after landing to Ballicary Point.

Clifton instantly prepared to obey the awful summons he had received, reckless of the danger he might incur, and absolutely refusing to adopt any disguise by which to shelter his person from recognition. Many precautions had been suggested by Ruth, and would have been zealously aided by Maynard, but Clifton rejected them all with an obstinacy admitting of no dispute. Accordingly, after Darby Harty had received a handsome present, and Miles Lawrey many thanks for his hospitable attentions, Clifton left Ballicary Point to attend the death-bed of his suffering wife.

When Maynard and he had reached the opposite side of the channel, the former pointed out the inn where his horse was lodged.

"Was it not sold with my estate?" exclaimed Clifton, in surprise.

"Yes," replied Maynard, "but your wife purchased both, therefore both are still yours."

A flash of joy illuminated the gloomy countenance of Clifton.

"Is it possible! That was the reason then why my agent reserved the name of the buyer. I perceive it all. The meaning of the unexpected liberality of terms strikes home upon me. Excellent girl! I would requite thee had not a just Providence put it beyond my power. It is now too late. I am a despairing fugitive, to whom nothing can bring peace—and thou—But why talk? My horse, Maynard! since mine in some senses it still is."

It was quickly brought forth, and he vaulted into the saddle.

"Here we separate, squire," said Maynard, "but I will come after you to Rosedale in case I may be able to assist you to leave it again, for you must not stay there. I will keep my promise to Mrs. Clifton of befriending you in all that I can, and you will find me a safe adviser so far as you please to make use of my services."

"I am obliged to you," returned Clifton; "but if I keep my present mind I shall not attempt sequestering myself any more. If Ruth dies, a prison will be as agreeable a place as any other to me; and if she does not," he added, "it will be the same, for I can never enjoy her society with the brand of Cain upon my brow. All places will be alike horrible to me, and if I endured the present existence at all it will only be because I dare not ad-

venture any other. Gracious God! what do they forfeit who forfeit peace of conscience! There is nothing in the universe left that can delight! The present is intolerable—the past sickening—the future a dreary vacuum, a region of frightful shadows.''

Maynard's kind heart was penetrated by his language.

"You have been misled by the violence of your passions," he said; " but your past experience is not without its bright spots—your present may be softened by the assurance that Ruth heartily forgives you and loves you—and your future need not be so hopeless if you are truly contrite."

The overflowings of Clifton's remorse had betrayed themselves inadvertently, but his pride could not bear the voice of reproving truth, or even of consoling kindness.

"I am glad," he said haughtily, "that those bright spots to which you allude are not entirely overlooked. I am glad some recollection is preserved of the spontaneous principle of honour which induced me to marry, and to make a considerable pecuniary sacrifice to compensate you for the disappointment I had been the means of inflicting."

"Compensation to me was out of the question—nothing could compensate me," said Maynard, with force; " and as to Ruth, poor girl, she did not seek to be your wife. Had you not grossly injured her, no friend of hers would have desired such a marriage for her, and the wrong done to her fame not even marriage could wholly atone for. You should not therefore, take too much credit to yourself for your honourable intentions; crimes like those you committed were too monstrous, too cruel, to be wiped away by any after act. You robbed me of a dearly-beloved wife, just when we were on the eve of our bridal. You by treachery unprecedented, plunged an innocent girl into suffering and humiliations the most distressing that could be conceived; and since she called herself your wife you have visited on her rigorously evils she had no part in."

Clifton thought of her drowned babe, and of her secret agonies that she had so toughingly unfolded to him when their union had been in agitation after he and her father had brought her from the Robinson's in London. He shuddered, and with a hasty parting word to Maynard rode of.

" Wretched as he is, and deservedly so, I envy him, for he will receive her last breath, but I maynot—I must watch at a distance for the blackest moment of my life," said Maynard, with a sigh, as, entering the inn, he drew near the fire of a small, neat, unoccupied parlour, with a tankard of ale beside him. The ale

stood unregarded long, and though the fire was bright and the weather moderately warm, he was cold to heart while a sickness, the result of preying grief, and neglected meals assailed him. At length his face was sunk in his hands, and he gave vent to gushing tears.

Appropriate is the familiar term aching for that pain of the heart he felt. It was a lamentable spectacle in a world so abounding in the thoughtless, the selfish, the vicious, and the intemperate, to see a man so richly endowed with the opposite moral qualities thus borne down by hopeless grief, and might have tempted some to presumptuous questionings of the Providence which had thus left an amiable spirit desolate, a benevolent heart uncheered, perfect integrity unrewarded.

> "The blossoms opening to the day,
> The dews of heaven refined,
> Could nought of purity display
> To emulate his mind."

But the ways of heaven are not as our ways. There is an indescribable peace springing from virtuous conduct, and noble feeling, which is in itself a rich reward; moreover, there is a life where all wrongs shall be redressed, all goodness abundantly recompensed; and besides, there was prepared for Maynard a happy return for his goodness over and above all this. The peace of self-approbation he at present enjoyed, and therefore his grief was not of that gloomy character which marked Clifton's; it chiefly fed itself on the memories of her he loved, whose dissolution he was expecting, memories which, while they heightened his sorrow, were sweet withal, and about even the most trivial of which hung a fascination readily to be conceived by those who lament the dying or the dead.

He slept at the inn that night, or rather occupied a chamber, for he could not close his eyelids while uncertain whether Ruth yet lived or not. He spent each hour in mourning. Sometimes he would cast himself on the bed, and call audibly on her name, and address her in terms of fondness and anguish. Then he would arise and pace the floor and weep, wishing he had the eloquence and holiness of a saint to plead with heaven that her dismissal from the body might be without pain, and with a quiet mind.

Early in the morning the blast of a horn under his window called him forth, and having paid the landlord the preceding evening, he at once mounted the stage-coach in which he had purposed to return to Rosedale. Ere he arrived there an

event had occurred that had been wholly unanticipated, which we hasten to relate in the next chapter.

CHAPTER XLI.

"Who knows what the coming hour,
Veiled in thick darkness, brings ?"

WALLENSTEIN.

ABOUT four o'clock in the afternoon Clifton began to approach Rosedale over the hills. The cloudy front of heaven was of a dull leaden hue, affording hardly a glimpse of the fair blue ether beyond, and wholly veiling the sun. Around were vast quarries of stone and marble, cheerless and bare, where the clink of some solitary labourer's hammer, a sound not wholly unmusical in the solitude, issued as he rode by.

He passed near the spot where his valet Andre had met his end, and could not forbear slackening his pace to cast a glance in the direction. As he did so he beheld a pedestrian, whose figure he fancied familiar to him, by the side of the road, advancing slowly in the same direction that he was going. A single glance enabled him to perceive that the stranger was of the middle height, walked erect and firm, was clad in a coarse rough great coat, clouted shoes and gaiters, and assisted his pace by a stout cudgel. Of his face Clifton could hardly obtain a glimpse, for the hat which shaded it was broad in the brim, and pulled quite down to the eyebrows, while a folded shawl was tied round the throat muffling the lower features. Besides this the stranger kept his head averted, as if purposely—at least so Clifton imagined—to avoid recognition. There was something startling to the latter in this rencontre, and as he rode forward he turned round in his saddle to take another view of the individual who had excited his curiosity.

"It cannot be Summerfield!" he said to himself. "Yet the figure, movements, and size, exactly resemble his! There wants some months to the period assigned in his sentence for his return. Can he have stolen back clandestinely?"

Clifton spurred forward in doubt; and the pedestrian advanced on the same road, which had on its right a lofty range of imposing quarries, while its left sank sheer down into a frightful gorge, called by the country people 'Thieves Gully,' extending half a mile in length, and overrun at the bottom with heather and weeds.

The stranger had not walked far beyond the place where Clifton had partially recognised him ere he turned aside to address a man sitting at work among the dispersed masses of stone and marble at a quarry foot.

"Good day to you, Rory," he said.

The man peered wonderingly in his face, with hesitation, doubt, and surprise.

"Don't you know me, Rory?" he asked.

"Arrah then, I don't know that I do," replied the man, in manifest perplexity.

"Yet we were near neighbours but a few years ago," said Summerfield, for it was indeed him.

"Holy Mary, defend me! is it yer livin' silf entirely that my blessed eyes see this day?" exclaimed the labourer, springing up from the ground and shaking hands with his old respected neighbour. "The saints look down on us, but I could dance a jig this moment. Whoop!—lara-la!" He cut a caper, and shook again and again the hand of Summerfield, whose emotions were as heretofore controlled by a powerful mind or he would have wept at this first unsophisticated welcome back to his native place. "But faix, Roger Summerfield," said the man, assuming

an expression of friendly mystery, " it's French leave you must have taken of the folk over the water, for your time's not out I'm thinking."

"You are mistaken, Rory," said Summerfield, quietly, " I had a year cut away from my captivity and exile, thanks to Him who watches over the faithful people of his adoption, and overrules all their wanderings in this desert-howling wilderness."

" But how was that ?" inquired the other. Sure it's in luck you've been, Roger."

The mercies and the blessing of the Lord have been showered as manna on my path—the very clouds have dropped fatness," said Summerfield; " and though disgraced among men, and driven from my own people and my own land, my integrity was known to the Most High, and He has made it manifest."

" But I would like to know all about it," said Rory, eagerly.

" Your curiosity may be satisfied in a few words, Rory. My walk and conversation pleased those who were set over me, and they were converted into friends, and believed my story of the persecution that my dear sainted wife had endured from Arthur Clifton, and admired the perfectness of her conjugal virtue under temptations so strong, and I was soon placed in a responsible situation as under-turnkey, in which capacity it pleased God to make manifest my uprightness by uncommon means, for a pocket-book filled with gold and bank-notes supposed to have been lost elsewhere was found by me in one of the dark passages of the convicts' prison, and if I had retained it none could have suspected me; but I remembered there was One who seeth in secret, and restored the treasure as I found it to its owner. This was in the second year of my bondage, and at the end of the third I was sent for to the house of the British governor of the island, to whose son the money had belonged, and he informed me that at the end of the next twelve months he would be answerable for my freedom, and if I would stay on the island he would have a responsible situation to offer me on one of his sheep farms, or if I returned to England he would pay the expenses of the voyage. My heart was laden with thankfulness, but I preferred to return to my children and my own native dale. He kept his word to me in regard to paying my passage, and gave me twenty pounds when I left the island. So you see, Roger, though I went out in disgrace, I have come back with honour—by such ways does the Lord lead his chosen,"

" And I'm for ye to the very core of my heart ! But och ! dismal is the hour of your coming, Roger, for I doubt you'll never see your daughter Ruth, that's Mrs. Clifton, alive, poor

sowl! She's dying of nervous decline over at the big house that she bought only so lately. Grate need have I to be sorry, God help me! and all the childer and the poor of the dale into the bargain, for many were the helps she dishthributed in times of need to them she had known in her humble days."

The strong-minded cottager staggered beneath this stunning blow.

"This is a cross I was not prepared for!" broke in faint and faltering accents from his lips. Gracious Father! must I meet my long-suffering and endeared girl only when she is incapable of receiving pleasure from my return?"

"I'm just going home," said the labourer, drawing on his jacket, and gathering up his tools, "so I'll walk along wid you, and tell you all about the news. There's the squire is under hiding for killing a lord in a duel, that's to say he was, for I saw him ride by just now."

"I thought it was he," said Summerfield. "Think you he is going to his wife?"

"Maybe he is, for sure the hardest heart that ever man had must bend when death's in the way."

"Hitherto then he has hardened himself against her?"— (Summerfield had not received Ruth's last letter, and he knew not what might have taken place during the recent months.)

"That quarry stone there might have been softened as asily," said Rory. "He has been in her house but once, and then only for a few minutes, and never a step did she take inside his before she bought it with her own money."

"Bought it!"

"Surely; pretty nigh all the estate is her own now. She paid six thousand pounds to the squire's agent for it, so I heard —some say a great deal more. 'Tis all the talk in the dale."

"And she is dying you say in Rosedale House?—dying alone, though mistress of all this wealth?"

"Sure as Ireland is Ireland, Mrs. Clifton, poor sowl, is in Rosedale House, and it is her own, she came there in her carriage with Mrs. Wilson from Liverpool, where Miss Clifton that was went on board for Calcutta wid the gintleman she is wedded to. 'Twas a sore parting, 'tis said, between the young ladies."

"My daughter dying!" cried the unfortunate cottager, casting his swimming eyes upwards. "Rory, I must leave you now, I will see you again soon, I am going to Ruth."

THE COTTAGE GIRL.

OH! NEVER COULD THEY FORGET THE LONG, LOUD SHRIEK SHE GAVE.

"I MUST recover myself alone before I go to Rosedale House," added Summerfield. "Tell me but one thing more. Is Maynard in health? Does he prosper? Has Ruth recompensed to him her father's obligations?"

"Faix! if you don't call a thousand pounds recompense enough, I don't know what else would be."

"She has given him that sum?"

"Every penny, he has it in Rosedale New Bank, and I heard she saw him yesterday."

"And his health?"

"Faix! bad enough; to look at him he's quite another man intirely from what he was. Cheeks all hollow—floridness all gone—and as thin round the body as can be."

"Where may he be found?"

"Most likely at the Three Crowns."

"Thanks to you, and for the present good-bye, Rory; as I said, I will see you again, if strength to sustain this heaviest of all my afflictions is vouchsafed to me."

He pulled his hat lower over his brow and walked hastily forward.

While this colloquy had been taking place between Summerfield and his old neighbour, Clifton's progress had been interrupted by the restiveness of his horse. Without any apparent cause it swerved suddenly to the right, so as nearly to throw its rider from the saddle, in which case he would have been hurled headlong into the "Thieves Gully." Clifton was, however, too good a horseman to be easily dislodged, and though in his efforts to govern the capricious movements of the animal he encountered considerable difficulty and danger, he succeeded in inducing it to proceed, but only a few paces. Again it started aside, snorting, sweating, and trembling, nor could Clifton at all account for the violent agitation it exhibited. He threw himself off—sought to soothe it by caresses, and to lead it gently forward, but for several minutes it refused to stir except in a sidelong or backward direction; at last it went, and Clifton resumed his seat. But a third time it seemed struck with terror, and came to a dead halt, as if something stood in its path invisible to other ken than its own.

"This is unaccountable!" exclaimed Clifton, in vain employing whip and spur.

He dismounted a second time, but the animal was not to be enticed forward; it stood as if carved in effigy, with fore feet advanced, and body drawn back, and eyes glaring red and wide. The patience of its master now gave way; he resumed the saddle, and applied the whip with so much energy that the poor creature was perforce roused to action. It reared and plunged in the attempt to free itself of its harsh rider, and failing, shook its mane wildly, expanded its nostrils, and effectually resisting all further control, plunged down the steep bank on the right.

At that moment Summerfield came within view of the fearful scene. He beheld with horror the frantic rush of the horse into the deep and dangerous gorge; he saw it roll over in the descent; start again to its feet at the bottom, but Clifton was not in the saddle! he had been flung off, and with his foot entangled in the stirrup was dragged over the broken rocks among the prickly furze and heather, and into a stream formed by nature which led down from the heights.

Summerfield looked behind him for the quarry labourer that he might have his assistance in an effort to save Clifton, and shouting the name of Rory, plunged down the side of the gorge at the imminent peril of his own life, lowering himself from stone to stone, and bush to bush, as best he might.

Rory ran up to the spot where he had descended, but durst not attempt to follow him in the same way, and flew along the road looking for a safer place of descent, while Summerfield reached the stream in which the horse and rider were just on the point of sinking.

He managed to catch the bridle of the horse, and drawing it to firm ground, disengaged the foot of Clifton from the stirrup; the animal then pursued its frenzied flight, and the Squire of Rosedale lay a bleeding and disfigured corpse at the feet of his injured wife's father!

CHAPTER XLII.

"Then quick his lovely May, her form upon his cold corse flung,
  And o'er his pallid face her long dark locks like cypress hung."

"A beacon light—a warning light—shall shine his memory,
  While summer burns, or winter blights, the blossom and the tree."

MOORISH BALLAD.

AFTER some delay the quarry labourer reached the bottom of Thieves Gully, and joined Summerfield, whom he found kneeling on the ground, supporting the head and shoulders of the ill-fated squire, and endeavouring in vain to restore animation by sprinkling his face with water from the brook that flowed beside him.

"This is a dreadful accident, Rory," said Summerfied. "I am afraid he is gone."

"Sure it's no wonder, dragged over the stones as he was!" cried the man. "Och! och! 'twas a piteous sight!"

"We must have help," said Summerfield; "send the first person you can see, with a board to bear him to his house. Let Doctor Walcot know what has happened. Fly! every moment

may decide his life or death. And, Rory, take care the news does not reach my daughter, if she yet exists."

Away ran the man, leaping over stones and briars, and scaling the high bank in the most practical part. The situation was thrillingly impressive in which he left Summerfield. The cause of all his daughter's sorrow—her guilty seducer—her unrelenting husband—had perished fearfully in his sight, and lay weltering in blood in his arms. She was avenged at last—oh! how awfully. But did the sight of that bruised corpse give her father sensation of triumph? Could he look with exultation on those fine features marred?—on that eye, so often lighted by the wild fires of passion, and the bright glow of genius, now quenched for ever?—on those everlastingly-silenced lips, whose eloquence had oft called forth plaudits from the proudest senate of the world? No! it was not exultation Summerfield felt, though his best and fairest child had been brought, as he was led to believe, to an untimely deathbed by Clifton's impetuosity, pride, and obstinacy. Yet his mind reverted with mixed sensations to the inextinguishable thirst of vengeance, and the haughty disdain, which Clifton's look had betrayed when last he saw him in the court hall where the trial for the murder of his father had taken place.

"Then it was I and mine who were in extremity," thought Summerfield, "but his time is now come, and his glory is brought low; while I, though mists still gather about me, am rising out of the valley of humiliation. Yet let me not triumph over my stricken adversary—God forbid! From his sterner vices I have not been exempt. My antipathy to him because he was his father's son was sinful and unjust—fear of a discovery of his father's death gave it force, and since that fear has been removed I have ofttimes repented it. Pride and hate and malice steal disguised into the Christian's heart. Mayst both thou and I, Percy Clifton, find mercy in the place whither thou hast been so awfully and suddenly despatched!"

In a quarter of an hour a mournful procession was seen gliding slowly along the peaceful fields of Rosedale towards the secluded park which had called him owner who now lay pale and gory on his rude bier. It was borne by quarry labourers, and Summerfield walked close before it.

His return from exile, and the pleasing circumstances that had led to it had been breathlessly communicated by Rory at the same time as the squire's fatal accident to all the villagers whom he met, and the exertions Summerfield had made to save Clifton had been circulated with equal rapidity, so that among the crowd of rustics who gathered about the procession, and attended its solemn

progress, Summerfield found many friendly greetings, especially from the members of the household of the farmer whom he had formerly so long and faithfully served. The congratulations would indeed have been clamorous but they were restrained by the decencies of the present melancholy occasion.

Just as their feet had begun to tread the green turf of downy softness which clothed the park,

> "With anemone and violet
> Like Mosaic paven,"

the horse whose unaccounted fright had caused its master's death galloped past, and stopped quaking in every limb at the stable-door, which it struck with its hoof, snorting loudly. Mr. Jobson, the late squire's valet and groom, easily secured it amid a crowd of eager gazers, who failed not to note that it was flecked with foam and blood, that the saddle from which Mr. Clifton had been thrown was turned round the animal's body, and that the fatal stirrup trailed on the ground. While this incident was passing, the procession was met from the house by a lean ghastly-looking personage with a very consequential air. It was the learned doctor of the dale—for learned he assuredly was, and skilful too.

"What, Mr. Summerfield, is that you?" he said, shaking him by the hand. "I am glad to see you returned! This is a terrible business! the account of it has reached the house, but we have not yet told your daughter, who is extremely ill."

The assurance that his daughter still lived was some comfort to Summerfield.

"Is there any hope of her recovery, sir?" he said.

"I fear not. However, she is fortunate in her doctor, if I may have leave to say so. If Anthony Walcot cannot save her no one can. I have not my diploma without desert. Mr. Summerfield, of that if time served I could give you curious ex-emplification. But let us see this unfortunate gentleman. I have restored some who you would have thought had drawn their last breath, sir. My practice in surgery is well known. I hardly know whether I excel most in dealing with the phar-macœpia, or with the knife and lancet. Let me see—ah! no pulse—no breath—dreadful injuries! This case is beyond me. Life is quite extinct—quite."

The bier had halted to give the doctor an opportunity for a momentary observation of him who was thus borne uncon-sciously along; the sheet which had covered the shattered body was immediately afterwards replaced over the face, and again the

sad group advanced. When near the front doorway of the house (which was ornamented by a raised portico, whose scrolled entablature and cornice rested on four columns of marble of the neighbouring hills, and whose steps were decorated with plants in porcelain vases and jars), the well-dressed housekeeper, with her venerable silver hair smoothly parted and shaded by her lace cap, hurried toward the bier, her wonted stateliness of deportment forgot, but as soon as she caught a glimpse of the outline of the figure of her master beneath the linen covering, and the crimson stains which had been produced by contact with his injuries, she hurried back again as quickly, unable to bear the sight, and, sinking on the entrance steps, was obliged to be supported into the house. One or two of the other servants who thronged the doorway also appeared much moved; and Mr. Jobson, the valet and groom, coming from the stable with the other man-servant of the establishment, whispered to him—

"That it was a precious bad job for him, for the squire had given him good wages and perquisites, and now he would have to hire himself somewhere else, though he should have been more sorry by half if the housekeeper had not been so starched and uncompanionable-like. The housekeeper of the last place he lived in was as free and friendly as could be, but Mrs. Wilson might be the lady of the house herself."

While the body of Percy Clifton is placed in the entrance-hall, whose antiquated windows throw purple and crimson rays upon the sheet which envelopes it, let us pass up the finely-carved staircase of oak, step from niched landing to landing, and enter the north chamber looking on the quaint garden with its formal yew hedges, clipped bushes, and central dial plate. It is a chamber how unlike any our humble heroine had in her early youth ever dreamed of occupying! Walls of a soft blue that might be atmospherical, where the birds almost seemed to flutter their wings, and the bees to sip honey from the exquisitely-imitated roses; thick carpets of eastern manufacture; bed and window drapery of sky blue velvet, with white silver fringe; chairs of ebony and pictures whose sunny landscapes, and graceful figures, filled the soul with beauty. In this enchanting room, decorated with a hundred curious articles of vertu, Ruth sat with the vicar and his daughters. She was sunk back in a large commodious chair (for that position was easier to her than entire recumbency), her fairy feet in loose satin slippers resting on a footstool of curious worsted work; a white quilted dressing-robe loosely encircled her small but beautiful proportions, and her bright hair was hardly visible from beneath the soft rows of lace of a close-fitting cap which shadowed but could not disguise the loveliness of her countenance. An open Bible was on her knee, and she listened with rapt attention to the pious exhortations of the vicar. His daughters, two exceedingly plain-featured but excellent girls, sat one on each side of her, and their meeting glances of awe and affright, unseen by Ruth, showed they had been made aware of what was passing below. By an admonitory glance their father warned them to be careful not to betray the disturbed state of their minds, yet his own voice was unsteady as he continued the conversation in which he was engaged.

"I hear a strange commotion in the house," said Ruth presently, turning her eager eye towards the door. "Excuse me, reverend sir, but I must know what occasions such unusual sounds. I fear—"

She paused, and her breath was drawn quick and hard.

"What do you fear, my dear Mrs. Clifton?" asked the reverend man, taking her hand with respectful sympathy.

"That the officers have arrested my husband," she replied, breathlessly. "I sent for him—selfish, inconsiderate that I was—and now I am afraid he is come, and they have been on the watch, and he is fallen into their hands!"

"Be at ease, Mrs. Clifton," said the vicar, "the squire has nothing now to dread from the officers you speak of."

"Where is Mrs. Wilson?—where is the housekeeper?—I must see her directly!" exclaimed Ruth. "Be good enough, Louisa, to ring for her."

Mrs. Wilson came, and as her anxiety to spare the sick girl the dreadful news of Clifton's death was not so great as to conquer the outward appearance of the grief which agitated her, Ruth's quick eye at once detected it. She sat upright, and fixed an earnest gaze on her.

"Oh! Mrs. Wilson," she said, "your master is in the house, and arrested!"

Mrs. Wilson only answered by sobs and tears.

"This is my doing!" exclaimed Ruth distractedly. "If I had not sent for him all would have been well. But he shall not be taken away until I have seen him."

And though she had been reduced to extreme feebleness by her disorder, she arose and moved to the door, but was stopped by the vicar.

"Do not attempt to detain me, I must and will see my husband. He is my husband, and they shall not take him hence until I have seen him."

"I assure you there are no officers in the house."

"Then what is the meaning of Mrs. Wilson's distress?"

"I wish I could have concealed it, but it is impossible," sobbed the housekeeper, losing all self-command, and throwing up her clasped hands distractedly. "Oh my master!—my dear young master!"

"Mrs. Wilson," said Ruth, with energy, "I demand to know the meaning of these outcries? What has occurred?"

"You had better retire until you can control your feelings," said the vicar, addressing the housekeeper. "I will acquaint Mrs. Clifton with the distressing occurrence."

"What occurrence, sir? Oh! speak quickly. You torture me more by suspense than you could by the worst intelligence. Where is Mr. Clifton? Has he arrived?"

"He has," replied the vicar, with an expression in his tone and look profoundly sympathetic—"he has returned, but an accident has happened—"

"Let me go, sir!—Louisa, let me go!" cried Ruth, breaking from them; and slipping out at the door she glided in her white apparel like a pale spirit along the gallery and down the stairs. The lowest flight of the latter led into the hall, and as she stepped on them she looked down, and beheld the sheeted body on a low table, and a crowd of persons around.

Oh! never could they forget the long, the loud, the heart-rending shriek she gave; never could they forget the sight of the lovely being who in all the delirium of love and horror rushed through the throng, and, casting back the sheet, shrank a moment in unutterable dismay at the sight of the blackened and gory wounds, and then throwing herself forward, with arms extended, fell senseless across the body of Percy Clifton.

CHAPTER XLIII.

"Where now is gone my morning star?
Where now my sun? its beams are fled."

GERMAN MINNESINGER.

RUTH knew not that it was in the arms of her father she was borne back to her room. Delirium succeeded to a long and deathlike swoon, and when the delirium passed away she tasted no food, took no sleep, and was reduced to such an extreme of nervous weakness, that Dr. Walcot judged it unsafe to permit her to see her father, or to be made aware of his arrival, lest any additional agitation might prove instantaneously fatal.

An opportunity being watched for, the carefully-toned inquiry was put to her whether she had any wish respecting the interment of Mr. Clifton, to which she replied mournfully in the negative.

"She entrusted the arrangements solely to Mrs. Wilson, who

she was confident, knew the mind of her late master perfectly, and would do all that befitted the occasion. The housekeeper was also to write to Amy the distressing tidings of her brother's death."

An early day was fixed for the obsequies, and it dawned in gloom and tempest. As the hearse with all its nodding plumes received it sad burden, the red lightning gleamed in the faces of the bearers, and a crash of thunder seemed to threaten the extinction of the universe. A blast of wind followed, that shook many a strong bough from the park groves, and then the windows of heaven seemed opened, and a deluge of rain descended.

As soon as the impetuosity of this thunder-shower had partially subsided, the cavalcade was set in order, and began to wind its slow length over the park, while in her chamber, raised on her bed by the supporting arms of the vicar's daughters, Ruth beheld it through a low window, from which the plants and curtains that obstructed her view had been removed at her request. The only sound that escaped her quivering lips was the name of him whom she beheld passing to his sepulchre.

"Clifton!—Percy!" She repeated it in tones of plaintive anguish, and when the imposing train had passed from view—carriages, horsemen, spectators, and all—she pressed her hands on her bosom with a long tremulous sigh, and fell back fainting on the pillow.

Yet she lived on!

Mrs. Wyatt and Jobson, at her desire, had been sent with the chaise for her sister and her brother, who arrived on the day of Clifton's interment. Hardly had they alighted ere with tears of transport they found themselves clasped to the bosom of their surviving parent. With gratification he quickly observed the improvement that had taken place in their deportment, pronunciation, and language, while their blooming looks bespoke perfect health, and that buoyancy of spirit which is the result of health, combined with easy circumstances, youthful vigour, and an unsullied conscience. William had grown tall, and was of a noble well-proportioned figure, his sunny countenance revealing uncommon feeling and intelligence. Sarah, now in her seventeenth year, was short of stature like her sister, and hardly so finely moulded, while her features were less regular, and her complexion less delicately beautiful.

After they had been left a little time with their father in a room retired from observation, the housekeeper rather coldly announced—

"That young master and miss might see their sister, but were not to speak to her more than a few words, and to say nothing of Mr. Summerfield being in the house."

Their presence was soothing to Ruth, and she retained them near her until they retired to rest. The housekeeper came to light them to the chambers she had selected for them.

"You will see they are made comfortable, if you please, Mrs. Wilson," said Ruth, in gentle accents.

"Assuredly, madam," replied the stiff old lady, with a manner of infinite ceremony. "I do not forget that Rosedale House belongs to you, and it shall be my study, madam, while I remain in your employ, to pay every attention to yourself and friends that my duty enjoins; but as soon as you are restored to health, madam, I shall feel obliged to you to look out for some person to take my place."

Ruth made no reply, but her sister and herself exchanged expressive glances, as Sarah bent to kiss her at parting for the night.

On the following evening her sister and brother again sat with her, when all the bustle of the costly funeral had ceased, and throughout the house silence mournful and deep prevailed.

"And so Mr. Maynard was in the churchyard?" said Ruth, after a long silence.

"He was in Doctor Walcot's gig, that followed next after the mourning carriages," said Sarah. "I should have thought he would have been included in the list of regular invitations—he is not so vastly inferior to some of the gentlemen who were present, and had been all his life a tenant of the estate, and a near and intimate neighbour of Mr. Clifton. No one could doubt that the squire had a great respect for him, though they were latterly at feud."

"Peace, Sarah," said Ruth, "there were reasons for the omission of Mr. Maynard from the funeral guests, such as I cannot now explain.'

"I am well assured," said Sarah, "that no one were present who lamented Mr. Clifton more than he, though one might doubt it who considers their past history."

This last clause was in an under tone.

"Sister," said William, who appeared to have been admiring an antique bureau of carved oak, but whose attention was suddenly aroused by the mention of his father's friend, "sister, if Mr. Maynard had died I should have lamented him more than I can Mr. Clifton. Mr. Maynard lives to do good to others, Mr. Clifton lived for himself."

He perceived that he was wounding Ruth, and paused.

subjoining in an altered tone, regardless of Sarah's becks and signs :

"I would say something that would please you if I durst, but the doctor insists you will be worse for hearing it, though the vicar does not think so."

"The doctor of course must know best," said Sarah, sharply. "I wonder at you, William."

"He has done nothing wrong," said her sister. "Let me know what you are striving to conceal. Fear not but I shall be firm; neither joy nor sorrow can henceforth affect me much. What I have borne has deadened me to both."

"On the faith of that assertion I bring," began Dr. Walcot, entering the door, but Summerfield, unable to contain himself, rushed past him, and an interview inexpressibly touching took place between the cottager and his widowed daughter.

With melancholy joy Ruth scanned her father's features o'er and o'er, remarking in melting tones that his long slavery had wrought fewer furrows there than she had expected to see.

"Only your hair is thinner and whiter, dearest father," she said.

"I see changes in you more important than that, my child," said Summerfield, sadly, contemplating her wan and wasted features.

She sighed deeply, and her speaking eyes told the story of her sufferings.

"When did you arrive?" she asked (for she was ignorant that her father had witnessed the catastrophe which proved fatal to Clifton, it having been merely stated to her that her husband had fallen from his horse). Summerfield answered a week, which greatly surprised her.

"It was mistaken kindness to keep me in ignorance of your arrival," she said. "Your presence, and that of my dear sister and brother, has already given me new life. I think I shall not die so soon as I expected, though there is little left me to desire on earth. I should be glad—glad to die!"

"Now I see it is time for me to interfere," said Dr. Walcot. "To-morrow, if you are as well as to-day, you shall see your father again. At present I insist you are left perfectly quiet."

Summerfield saw the necessity of complying; he took a tender leave of her, and was followed by her eyes to the door. Her sister sat up with her that night—Clifton's first night in the earth—and despite the doctor's interdiction of speech they conversed much, unfolding to each other the inner workings of their hearts, recalling scattered reminiscences of former joys and griefs, reviving the image of their mother in their thoughts, and heaping recollection on recollection of him so recently committed to the earth.

A new-born happiness was experienced by Ruth in the discovery that her sister—thought of till recently as a child—possessed a soul capable of answering the deepest echoes of her own and that, in educating Sarah, she had been polishing a jewel which was to enrich herself. An invaluable bosom friend Sarah proved to her, bound to her by the mingled ties of gratitude, admiration and love.

The confidence of her sister elevated her in her own estimation, and she studied to repay it by all the attention in her power. She would suffer no one to give medicine or food to Ruth but herself, and wore herself out with night-watching by her side. Remonstrances had no effect upon her.

"Ruth relinquished her rest for me when I was ill at widow Lister's," she said, " and now I will yield up mine for her. She worked night and day then to support me and my brother, and to pay the expenses of my illness, I have not the same opportunity of proving my love for her, but all I can do I will."

Her devoted ministrations contributed more than anything else to the recovery of Ruth, who by slow and almost imperceptible gradations approached to a state of convalescence.

The first time she left her chamber was on a splendid summer day. the windows of the house were all open to admit the air, and the gay butterfly flew at will in and out of the handsome apartments.

"Not yet," she said, as Sarah, on whose arms she leaned, was turning to descend the stairs to the drawing-room, "not yet;" and opening a door she entered a long, narrow, dusty gallery, dimly lighted by small painted windows, whose dull rays exhibited to view a number of faded family portraits. "Here I have often stolen along to meet him," sighed Ruth. "Ah! how well I recollect that first evening when he drew from me a confession of my love. Andre entrapped me hither by a falsehood, and in that room, Percy's sporting parlour—"

They entered it ere she finished her sentence. She gazed around with swimming eyes. No one had entered the room before since Clifton had left it. The ashes were in the grate, a half-burned candle, and a half-filled wine glass, stood on the

table, surrounded by electioneering papers and torn letters, and his favourite pointer had stolen in after the sisters, and stretched itself whining on the littered hearth-rug. Ruth stooped to pat the faithful animal, and by its mournful solemnity of aspect it seemed to comprehend the nature of the grief with which it was called to sympathise.

Slowly, and with floods of tears, Ruth suffered herself to be withdrawn from that place of agitating recollections, but as they passed the chamber in which he had been used to sleep, she suddenly withdrew her arm from that of her sister, and turning the key which was in the lock entered with a faltering step. The room had been dressed in black, for here the body had lain preparatory to its interment. The ordinary hangings of the bed had been exchanged for black velvet, which were partially looped up to display the rich pall that had covered the coffin, and still trailed its heavy border on the black cloth that spread the floor. Ruth drew near, fell upon her knees, and buried her face in that sable drapery. Sarah delicately retired to the outside of the door, and in a few mintues her sister rejoined her in a more composed frame.

Descending the stairs, Summerfield met them. Ruth smiled as he beheld him, bade him good-morning in a cheerful tone, and to his anxious enquiry how she felt, replied considerably better. Placing his arm around her, he supported her weak steps to the drawing-room, where William eagerly flew to greet her, placed the cushions on the sofa, and drew it near the fire. Their attentive kindness was balm to Ruth, the more exquisite because she felt it was deserved. The holiest, the liveliest affection was reciprocated in that reunited family, and as they gathered round the fireside, and listened to each other's voices, and poured out the best feelings of their soul in unrestrained confidence, and marked it mantling on each other's countenances the flush of vivid thought, or melancholy moonlight hues, each, even the new-made widow, and the returned exile, found a peace, the dearest on earth, still the unquiet throbbings of their breasts, and tinge the vale of sorrow with rays of heavenly beauty.

After an early tea and dinner, of which Ruth partook a little, silence settled on the group, and the shades of evening began to be diffused through the apartment. One of the window-sashes was closed down, in the other was placed an Eolian, which not beginning to sound very quickly, Ruth requested her sister to give them a specimen of her musical capabilities, and selected the Dead March in Saul, which Sarah executed very tolerably at the

grand piano.   Among Summerfield's superior natural tastes was a love of music, provided it were of a solemn and elevated kind, and the devotional strains of Handel so riveted his attention that Sarah proceeded to play for his gratification piece after piece of the inspired composer with increasing precision and expressiveness.   In "I know that my Redeemer liveth" she added her voice, which was full and of good compass.   Summerfield's eyes suddenly filled with tears; his lofty faith was quenched in irrepressible agony, and he started up.

To Ruth's inquiry whither he was going, he replied to the churchyard to see the grave of her mother.   He had not been there yet, his firmness had failed him every time he had thought of it, but he could delay no longer.

"Did you not go when—"

Summerfield understood her unfinished sentence, and replied in the negative.

"Then you have not seen the grave-stone I have placed above my mother?"

"If you have shown her that respect unasked, unprompted," said Summerfield, fervently, "you have laid on your father another obligation of gratitude which he will feel to his dying day."

THE COTTAGE GIRL.

ON A STILE NEAR THEY PERCEIVED MAYNARD.

RUTH keenly enjoyed the luxury of the surprise she had prepared for her father, but contented herself with prompting her brother to be his companion. The two went accordingly one evening to the churchyard.

Summerfield found that it was not a simple gravestone Ruth had placed over her mother, but one singularly beautiful of design, and equally so in workmanship. A low fluted canopy of the shell form ; beneath the canopy, which was supported by four winged angels, the mound itself was arched in with fluted stones so as to preserve the shape, as seen in some antique sepulchral monuments of gothic times. One of the angelic bearers held a scroll, on which was inscribed——

This tomb was erected
By a mourning and admiring Daughter
To the memory of HANNAH SUMMERFIELD,
Who, under circumstances of Severe Trial,
Held fast to Holy Virtue ;
And amid Adversity and Temptation
Was a Faithful and Devoted Wife.
After long years of gloom,
Unable to survive the unmerited
Disgraces of those she loved,
Her Spotless Soul, denied rest on Earth,
Sought it in Heaven.

Tear chased tear on the furrowed cheek of Summerfield. It was long ere he could tear himself from the spot. He then beheld his son surveying the more pompous but infinitely less beautiful vaulted tomb which had been recently opened to receive the young squire of the dale. Beside his son stood Maynard. This was not the first meeting of the long-parted friends, but it might have been, so energetic was the grasp of the hand, so fraught with unstudied kindliness were their mutual glances.

"This is your first visit here since your return, is it not ?" said Maynard.

"It is," replied Summerfield.

"And what think you of yon tomb, and its inscription ? "

"What think I of it !" exclaimed Summerfield, with a burst of emotion, "I think that if there be one thing above another which renders her who sleep there dear to this heart it is that she has given me such a daughter as Ruth ! God bless the dear girl, and restore her sick soul to peace ! How long has that tomb been erected ? "

"But recently, though I heard it was prepared twelve months ago."

"Do you know who made it ? "

"A young sculptor just rising into notice, introduced to Mrs. Clifton by the vicar."

"It is a beautiful work ! " ejaculated Summerfield.

"I think so," said Maynard ; " often do I come here about this hour or later to look at it. I love to see the moon shining on it —I have frequently read the inscription by its light. What is it I wonder makes us love to linger about the last home of our friends ? when one encourages the inclination it grows to a kind of passion. I know nothing delights me so much now as to sit

on that grass opposite your Hannah's tomb, and watch the moon and stars shine down on it, and listen to the wind creeping in and out the old yew tree. Sometimes a bat whistles by with its imp-like wings, and sometimes a white owl whizzes over my head, and shrieks until I fancy all the little birds in their nests shrink to hear it; and sometimes the old sexton comes with his bald head and spade and mattock to dig a grave, and he and I have some gossip about the folk of the dale, dead and living. But whether he does or not I am pleased to be here."

Summerfield and his son walked almost in silence with Maynard to the park gate, where Maynard left them, after making an appointment for the ensuing day.

Ruth had retired to bed ere her father's return, having sat up almost longer than her strength could bear. The Eolian's ethereal notes continued to swell and sink upon the air most part of the night, and she lay awake listening to them, and pondering former scenes she had passed through with Clifton, of which those ecstatic notes reminded her. Near dawn she slept, and awoke refreshed. This day was as gorgeous as the proceeding, and with a mourning mantle thrown over her shoulders, and a crape veil loosely over her head, she ventured out of doors sustained by her father's arm. After slowly traversing the garden alleys, beneath a sky of incomparable blue, the west wind sporting on their path, they seated themselves in a cool grotto at the farther end, where they found Sarah and William.

"And so," said Summerfield, addressing the latter, after a slight reverie, "you call yourselves a young gentleman and lady now, I suppose, and think you have done with poverty and all its ills."

"I hope so, sir," said Sarah, smartly.

"Sir," echoed Summerfield, with good-tempered sarcasm. "And why sir?—why not father? I think polite education in modern days has taken a mortal antipathy to that good old English word. William called me 'papa' yesterday, and to-day Sarah calls me 'sir.' Is sir or papa more musical than father? or why is this unnecessary and foolish popular refinement adopted?"

"I suppose because the great people like to be distinguished from the small," said William.

"It is a pity they are reduced to such frivolous modes," said his father. But to return to what I was saying. I suppose you think you have done with vulgar labour? though your father has all his life been content to live by it."

"I know we must do something for our livelihood," said Sarah, "and sister intends to give my brother a learned profession after he has been at college, if he attends properly to his studies."

"Yes, yes, fine schemes you are entertaining I doubt not," interrupted Summerfield, half smiling; "but do you know that to prepare a young gentleman for a profession, and to support a young lady in such a life as you are anticipating, requires much money?—and do you know that you have nothing, and I have nothing? Your sister's fortune is her own. She has already done to the utmost of what I could desire from her, and there is no reason why she should encounter such heavy expense for you, but an important one why she should not, and that is you have nothing to support the character of a lady and gentleman should you be unable to get forward in the world, and should anything happen to deprive you of her assistance."

"Nay now, dear father, you are conjuring up imaginary impediments that cannot really exist," said Ruth. "While I live they shall have nothing to complain of on my part, and if I die my property will be theirs equally, subject only to the annuity I have settled on you."

This was the first Summerfield had heard of the provision she had secured to him, and while he expressed his thankfulness, and the pleasure this affectionate consideration gave him, he was too high-minded to be induced to accept it.

"He should return to his old employment on the farm where he had worked so many years," he said; "and it was very hard if his labour could not suffice to supply him with enough for his own wants, which he rejoiced to think were few and simple. The bread of independence was sweet to him, sweeter than any with which his table could be supplied."

"My dear father," said Ruth, "you wound me by this language. Can you be less independent for accepting a trifle from the superfluity of your daughter?"

"Say no more about it," said Summerfield decisively. "I may be peculiar in my disposition, but while these hands of mine can work, and while I have my ordinary strength, I will not hang a dead weight on you, my Ruth. When I am infirm and old, I may accept your kindness, until then you will have enough to do for your sister and brother, who, I give up to your direction."

These words relieved the two latter, who had begun to fear from the tenor of his language, that he would withdraw them from their refined learning and sparkling anticipations, and com-pcl them to share his humble labours. But Summerfield designed no such folly; and it was his desire to see their education perfected, and their well-trimmed barks scudding on the sea of life before the mild gales of favouring fortune, that strengthened him in his resolution not himself to tax the liberality of his daughter, until he was absolutely incapacitated from labour. He did, however, consent that she should stock him a farm, and that he should expend his strength and skill for himself—not for others. In this undertaking ultimately he was joined by his friend Maynard, who also possessed considerable knowledge of agriculture, and was still without a settled home. After many consultations it was resolved that Rose Cottage should be transformed to a farm house; or rather, that a farm should be appended to it, the present five rooms being kept nearly in their present state, the walls left covered with roses, the stained oriel windows unremoved. The flower garden Wyatt had begun to lay out was prettily enclosed, and a large yard and orchard, planned, with a dairy and cattle shed, and all the other appurtenances of a superior farm. Wyatt and his wife still occupied the place, and were permanently engaged. Ruth took the greatest interest in the progress of the building, which her father reported to her daily, for he still slept at her house. She entreated him to spare nothing that would render it commodious and comfortable, and Summerfield frequently wanted urging to this, for he was extremely chary of expense, and always solaced himself with ideas of future repayment.

At length the farm was finished, but not before nigh a year had rolled away since Percy Clifton's death. When Ruth had paid all the bills of those who had been employed on the work, she presented the whole a free, unconditional gift to her father, including a hundred sheep, ten cows, pigs and poultry, and interior fittings up.

All this time, though her father had been in daily intercourse with Maynard, she had not seen the latter. She had never invited him to Rosedale House, but had occasionally sent civil messages when she knew her father was about meeting him, and these, though apparently slight, had a perfume of kindness about them which Maynard felt but too sensibly.

The farm was opened with a house-warming feast on a liberal scale. All the old acquaintances of Summerfield and Maynard were invited—nearly all the neighbourhood indeed—and such potency has superior fortune to attract the notice of the world, and to induce it to forget humiliating events, that many of the gentry around came to this hospitable feast, given by a man who a short while before they would have disdained to honour by a familiar nod.

CHAPTER XLIV.

" Sometimes with secure delight,
  The upland hamlets will invite ;
  When the merry bells ring round,
  And the jocund rebecks sound,
  To many a youth and many a maid,
  Dancing in the chequered shade ;
  And young and old come forth to play,
  On a sunshine holiday ;
  Till the livelong daylight fail,
  Then to the spicy nut-brown ale,
  With stories told of many a feat,
  How fairy Mab the junkets eat,
  When done the tales to bed they creep,
  By whispering winds soon lulled asleep."

MILTON.

We have erred widely from our aim, if the reader has not some concern for the peace of mind of Henry Maynard—some anxiety for his happiness. And yet, so readily does the fancy resign itself captive to intellectual superiority, and an attractive exterior, and so slow is it to feel the full beauty and greatness of unadorned virtue, that we feel doubtful how far we have succeeded in creating the sympathy we desire for him in the refined reader. But though we acknowledge the mind of mighty powers to be a grand object, and a brilliant imagination a magnificent thing, and perfectness of shape and feature a priceless endowment, yet we dare uphold, and that most strenuously, that there is something in humanity vastly more grand, infinitely more magnificent and inestimable, and that is goodness. A sincere, just unselfish heart, oh! what can compare in value with it? A calm, unobtrusive, obliging, cheerful temper, is not this far more than the fleeting lustre of an eye? or the symmetry of features, which unruly passions are perpetually darkening? For want of these qualities how many households that might have been prosperous and happy have been wrecked!—for want of these qualities how many a dear-loved individual has deceived, and fretted, and destroyed, the heart that trusted him!

And if goodness of the heart be the finest thing in nature, then Henry Maynard, plain and homely as he was, was a fine fellow! and well worthy the reader's hearty concern. We have seen him capable of imperishable constancy, both in love and friendship—we have seen that his feelings are of a texture exceedingly fine, and wonderfully disinterested—we have seen him capable of immolating his own inclinations to promote the welfare of others, —a rare and difficult accomplishment!—and we have seen a refinement of generosity exercised by him toward Ruth, which words would poorly praise.

She, as time gradually subdued the first distraction of her grief for Clifton, often mused in her solitary hours on what Maynard had felt, and done, and suffered for her. We have before observed, that the delicacy of his kindness had at length inspired her with sentiments difficult to be defined—with a peculiar friendship, tender, holy, and unalloyed, whose influence, though unseen, was still operative. Whenever she looked back the most striking contrast was presented by his conduct and that of Clifton; and when it is remembered that she had been separated from the latter from the hour of her marriage to that of his death, and that from the first dawn of her intimacy with him to its close he had given her nothing but anguish, anxiety, and disappointment, while on the other hand Maynard had invariably been her comforter, her benefactor, and friend, it will hardly be wondered at, that the poignancy of her regret for Clifton lessened with each rolling month, and that the virtues and the love of Maynard, became more and more remembered. Let not the living deceive themselves. It is only worth that can preserve their memories long in the affections of surviving friends.

Something like hope had occasionally been revived with Maynard since her widowhood; the fears which are the shadows of love had revived also, since he had heard that no less than two overtures had already been made for her hand; one by Morrison of Oakenford, her former suitor, and the other by a baronet, a second cousin of the deceased Percy. Both had been unequivocally rejected, that was some comfort, but still Maynard trembled lest some other wooer should prove more successful. Could he have watched the hidden movements of her mind, he would have been convinced this was a fear wholly unfounded; love, in its undivided essence, she could feel no more; and if there was a sentiment at all approaching the nature of love, which by any possibility the future might recommend to her heart, such a sentiment was likely to be in favour of him to whom she owed so much, whose disparity of years she now regarded as a trivial circumstance, and whose person she beheld through the beautifying medium of friendship and gratitude.

When the feast at the farm was in preparation, Sarah one evening had been there, and was accompanied back to Rosedale House by her father. They were speaking of the happy changes that had taken place in their circumstances, and of the comfortable prospects before them, when Summerfield emphatically observed that one thing only troubled him now; could he see that altered he should be able to say with holy Simeon 'Now let me depart for mine eyes have seen thy salvation.'

"And what is that?" asked Sarah, curiously.

Her father seemed in no haste to reply.

"My life on it I can guess!" exclaimed Sarah. "You wish that Maynard—'

"Hush!" said her father cautiously. "You comprehend me, I see. But do not startle the ear of your sister with the matter."

As soon as Sarah reached home she watched for an opportunity to speak confidentially with Ruth, which did not occur until the hour of retiring to rest.

"This morning," she said, "I suppose you had made my father as happy as it was possible for him to be. But I find it otherwise. One thing is wanting—"

"Indeed—what can that be?" asked Ruth, in no small surprise.

"You would scold me, or at least be hurt, were I to tell you; but I will incur the hazard, for you cannot be implacable."

"This is an odd preface, my dear Sarah,"

"To an unwelcome subject I fear. My father then earnestly wishes that you were a little less rich, or sombody a littie more; that you were a degree plainer, and somebody a degree handsomer; that you were a little older, or somebody ten years younger."

"I will not affect to misunderstand him, Sarah, but it is my hope that his wishes are uncalled for, and that Mr. Maynard has found that peace restored of which it was my misfortune to deprive him."

"I can assure you he has not," rejoined Sarah, earnestly. "To be sure his love for you is not altogether such as younger men feel, but it is very fine for all that. If you were to marry him, Ruth, you never could repent it. He would worship you; you would have everything your own way; and as for his temper, you know it is incomparable."

"I have not now to learn Mr. Maynard's virtues," said Ruth, calmly, but forcibly. "I learnt to appreciate them in my adversity, though once I slighted them. But as for marriage with him, or any one, no, no, Sarah."

Sarah had tact enough to know that she had said enough, but having once set this stone rolling she was determined it should not stand still for want of additional impetus. She had a busy day on the morrow at the farm, decorating it with May-thorn and flowers for the feast. William was her assistant in this agreeable task, and when it was over tea was placed at the door which opened on Ruth's flower-garden, and the blooming and happy sister and brother conversed at the table with Maynard and their father. Mrs. Wyatt waited on them, and in the intervals when she was out of sight, a gay colloquy took place.

"I think I never saw you looking so well, Mr. Maynard," said Sarah, with animation.

"And I think I never saw him looking worse," said her father.

"He is pale enough," said William.

"That is the very thing," said Sarah; "I mean by looking well, he looks interesting."

Maynard laughed and blushed, for he was as modest as a girl under compliments.

"Are you turned flatterer?" asked Summerfield, good-humouredly, pinching his daughter's cheek.

"Yes," said Sarah, "because I have a purpose to serve by it."

"I hope you have no design on my friend's heart," said Summerfield, with assumed gravity.

"O that is sufficiently secured, I believe," said Sarah, slily, "is it not, Mr. Maynard?"

"Fie, Sarah, fie!" cried her father, sternly, for he perceived by Maynard's disordered look that his daughter was pressing too closely on the heart-wound of his friend.

"Indeed, father, I shall speak quite freely to Mr. Maynard, for he is, or may be, my elder brother."

"What reason have you for saying so, saucy girl?" asked Summerfield, with a flush of sudden delight.

"If Mr. Maynard will walk with me homewards I will tell him," said Sarah, quitting the table and tying on her bonnet.

The agitation of Maynard was beyond disguise. When they had gone a short distance Sarah assumed a serious tone.

"I hope you will not think me light or unfeeling," she said. " No one can wish you happy more truly than I; and as a proof, I will befriend you with all the interest I can command in a certain quarter, if you will tell me truly whether you are as wishful to succeed there as my father supposes."

Maynard looked on the ground, then at the sky, then straight-forward, and sighing, answered—

"That he was not so foolishly presumptuous as to imagine there was any chance for him."

"That is not answering my question," said Sarah. "Come, you will deal faithfully with me I know. Do you in truth love my sister still?"

"I will tell you no falsehood," replied Maynard, with great and evident embarrassment, "yet I am unwilling to say the truth."

"Why so?"

"For her sake, Miss Summerfield. I would not have her afraid to meet me—I would not have her on the rack lest I should trouble her with attentions that must be distressing to her —I would not for the value of my thousand pounds see her studying her looks and tones to me, and perhaps, speaking to me with coldness when she is friendly to all else. Not a single moments uneasiness would I give her if I knew it."

"But I am asking for my own satisfaction, not impertinently. I hope to serve you, or to suggest how you may serve yourself."

"I am not one capable of finding words to express my feelings," said Maynard, with emotion; "if I could, God knows you would soon be convinced how truly I still love your sister!"

"I was convinced of it before I asked," said Sarah, "but I

could not be too confident on such a point. Well now, Mr. Maynard, I feel a sort of presentment, a kind of pre-conviction, that if you renew your address with courage my sister will be yours."

Maynard crimsoned, and shook his head.

"Sarah was too sanguine on his behalf," he said. "It was quite impossible Ruth could stoop to him. He was poor, and had nothing at all to recommend him. When he had formerly ventured to lift his eyes to her they were both differently circumstanced. He would not attempt to woo her—he would never disturb her by a breath of what he felt, or of what he wished."

"And where will be the wisdom of that if I tell you that you will be likely to succeed?"

"It is impossible—it must be impossible."

"Not if you are courageous," said Sarah, and she sang—

> ' None but the brave,
> None but the brave deserve the fair."

"Tell me," said Maynard, catching her hand impetuously,' "tell me if Ruth has given you any reason to beli-ve—"

"You must not ask me any such question," interrupted Sarah. "What may or may not have passed between her and I in our familiar talk I am not at liberty to say; only observe, to-morrow you will see her, and if you do not renew your proposals to her in some shape or other you will greatly disappoint your well-wishers."

They were in the park, and not to mar the force of this speech by further discourse she at once left him.

When Sarah entered, the housekeeper was with Ruth, complaining of the conduct of a destitute girl she had hired.

"Ah! poor houseless creature!" exclaimed Ruth, in accents of pity, " be patient as you can with her, and with all the servants, good Mrs. Wilson. I have been poor as they, and know by sad experience how much they have to undergo in their struggles with a harsh and exacting world. God help the poor of the earth! their sufferings are immeasureable. They have to contend with all life's harshest vicissitudes. Though sick and weary they must toil on, and all they have to anticipate at the end of toilsome and thankless journey is the stinted bounty of a poor-house. Alas! those that are more favoured, Mrs. Wilson, should think much of them, exert much forbearance, and make it a sacred duty to endeavour to ameliorate their condition, and elevate their character. They are deplorably ignorant; before we judge their faults harshly we should instruct them."

"You have an uncommon feeling heart, madam," said Mrs. Wilson, warmly, "as I had good cause to know when I fell down stairs six months ago, and when you took my poor misguided grand-daughter into your service."

"I have been well rewarded by your ceasing to dislike me, Mrs. Wilson," said Ruth, smiling.

"O dear, I am distressed and ashamed, believe me, madam, when I think how my old fashioned notions misled me. But you have forgiven me ; and I have seen so much of your charitableness, propriety, good sense, and affability, madam, that I shall be proud to serve you as long as I am able."

"And I shall feel equally gratified in retaining you, Mrs. Wilson."

The housekeeper curtseyed and retired, and Sarah began to discourse of the glad morrow for which her young heart was bounding, when she anticipated the song, the dance, and the presence of gay beaux.

"Mrs. Wilson was there this morning, and arranged her pickles, confectionery and preserves," she said. "I don't think the old lady can quite reconcile herself to father yet. She has a peculiar manner for him, distinct from every other person—but he does not mind it. O I had nearly forgot to tell you that the barrel of strong ale you sent over is incomparable ! a thousand praises have been showered on it by all who have tasted it, not excepting Mr. Maynard. By the bye, he walked with me almost to the door."

"And why did you not invite him in ?" asked Ruth, hastily— "but I remember, I had given you injunctions to the contrary. Yet to-night was of little consequence since we meet to-morrow."

She walked to the window, and there remained sometime in fixed meditation.

Sarah practised her lessons at the piano, and though her attention was awake to every movement of her sister, her presence was soon forgotten. She perceived that Ruth was absorbed in perplexed communing with herself, and now and then sighed, and pressed her hand to her forehead. Sarah played on, and Ruth walked gently to and fro the apartment, her eyes bent downwards. At last stopping, and drawing her watch from her bosom, she expressed surprise that it was so late. The sisters

betook themselves to bed, where both lay several hours awake, the one conjuring up light visions of the entertainment of to-morrow, the other seeking to fortify herself by every variety of argument in an important and noble resolution, which will form the conclusion of our narrative.

"Are you awake, Sarah?" Ruth asked, when the former turned on her pillow. Her sister's arm affectionately encircled her waist, and they began to converse.

"And what did Mr. Maynard and you talk about when he escorted you?" asked Ruth.

Sarah withheld her own part of that conference except where it was absolutely necessary to elucidate his. Nevertheless, her sister found much room for chiding, though in so indulgent a key that Sarah could not think her very angry.

"Maynard was wise to wish to conceal from me information that can only be painful, and would be wiser did he conceal it from himself," said Ruth. "And you have done wrong, my dear Sarah, to force into the light the weakness of an excellent heart."

"Weakness! I don't call it weakness to love you," exclaimed Sarah, with vivacity. "In my estimation it is the greatest proof he could give of a superior nature."

"Trifler!" ejaculated Ruth.

"Say what you will, I was determined to have the truth from him, and I have had it. And I wish to my heart of hearts there were a couple more Robinsons within reach, and a set of housebreakers to give them a fright, then I would see if I could not creep into their favour by playing the heroic, as somebody did, and get their immense fortune bequeathed me, in order to be able to render that man your equal who fee'd with a hundred guineas my father's counsel, and who, when you were poor, and he comparatively rich, was ready to spend all he had for you, and those most dear to you."

Ruth bade the chatterer go to sleep, and feigned to do so herself.

The first thought of Sarah in the morning was to ascertain the state of the weather, which she pronounced admirable for dancing on the green.

A seriousness calm and deep was on the brow of Ruth. In the middle of the forenoon they went together to the scene of hospitality, which preserved amid abundance a rustic character peculiar animating. The icy fetters of false refinement were banished; persons spoke and looked naturally; the young and

happy laughed and sported; the elders gathered in knots to converse of "auld lang syne." The dinner was substantial, and spread in a large barn decorated with boughs and flowers. Rich and poor mixed indiscriminately, and there was hilarity throughout. Endless were the jokes—loud the laughs—and those who neither joked nor laughed seemed equally in their own way to enjoy the feast.

As for a long period Ruth had only been visible abroad in retired walks, or where benevolence claimed her presence, her appearance here had proved no mean attraction; and hardly had she arrived, ere she was overwhelmed by the greetings of a number of acquaintances, both high and low. He, however, whom she had prepared herself to meet was not there, and his absence left a void that was almost painful. Maynard was absent at dinner too, and Ruth was frequently on the point of asking for him but checked herself. When the barn was cleared of the viands and tables her father lent her his arm, and they walked on the open green slopes, and about the premises, while the numerous guests dispersed themselves in all directions. She never remembered to have seen her father so truly cheerful, though he occasionally sighed, and observed to her—

"How proud his Hannah would have been of this day!"

"There is one absent whom I had expected to see," Ruth at length observed, finding that Mr. Maynard did not present himself."

"Harry had promised to be elsewhere," said Summerfield, "at least that was his excuse. You may judge if was a true one."

"I, father! how can I judge?—how can I tell what promises Mr. Maynard makes?" said Ruth, colouring.

"There is the signal for the dance," said Summerfield, not choosing to dwell upon the theme. "Here come the fiddlers, and the company are placing themselves. Their go William and Sarah with their partners. I would have had no such light doings but for them. Well they foot it prettily, I confess, and look so happy, that I could not wish to deny them the enjoyment. You will not join them I suppose, my dear?"

Ruth replied in the negative.

As Summerfield withdrew from her to see if the elder people were comfortable, the vicar's daughter, Louisa, came up, and proposed while the dance was going forward, that they should take a quiet walk, as she believed neither Mrs. Clifton nor herself were fond of gaiety, though ever so innocent. The two stole away ac-

cordingly and took the meadow path which brought them in sight of Maynard's ruined mill.

The spot had been untouched since the fire, and began to have quite a venerable look, grass growing between the blackened heaps of rubbish. On a style near they perceived Maynard; and Ruth, disengaging her arm from her companion, walked quickly forward, and addressed him by name.

He sprang from his attitude of thoughtful repose, and turning round stood motionless, emotion the most intense disordering his whole aspect.

"My friend! my benefactor!" exclaimed Ruth, giving him her hand with frank cordiality.

He was disconcerted almost to tears.

"Why were you not at the dinner?" she asked.

He stammered an apology, and lending her and Miss Henderson his hand to cross the stile, walked forward with them.

Approaching a cottage, Miss Henderson suddenly recollected she had to make an inquiry after the health of one of the inmates, but assured Ruth she would overtake her presently.

The absence of Miss Henderson added to Maynard's confusion of mind; he paused, as if he would gladly have waited for her; but with the charming simplicity of her younger days, Ruth took his arm, and they ascended the side of a woody eminence, whence the ruined mill was beheld on one side, and the farm on the other. The green before the latter presented a most pleasing picture. Groups sat on chairs or banks under the trees, others strolled about or stood as spectators of the sylvan dance; and Ruth was able to distinguish her sister in her white dress, and head-wreath of natural flowers, exhibiting her fashionable steps in a quadrille.

"How happy they seem!" she exclaimed, "Why is it, Mr. Maynard, you are not with them? You must return with me, and take your place in the dance. There have been many inquiries after you."

"There may be inquiries," rejoined Maynard, "but excepting your father and sister, and perhaps poor Wyatt, no one there, or anywhere else, will care two straws for my presence or absence."

"How can you say so!" Ruth exclaimed, with an air of pleasantry. "I saw Nancy Dawson there, whose regard for you everybody knows. She would not dance till you came."

"Pshaw! the silly flirt."

"And there was Farmer Wilson's gay daughter looking very uncomfortable, and inquiring what could possibly have kept

Mr. Maynard away on that day above all others. And your old admirer Miss Deborah Pinfold, the dressmaker, was trumpeting forth your praises in abundance."

"Her trumpeting will not make me think her other than a ridiculous, lying old maid." said Maynard..

"I never heard you so harsh," cried Ruth. "Seriously, Mr. Maynard, I wonder you do not marry. There is hardly a girl in the dale who would not be proud of your hand—and the farm wants a mistress."

"It must want one for me," said Maynard, bitterly. "I never intend to marry."

"O, if you have taken a resolution there is no more to be said," Ruth rejoined.

Maynard thought there was something mischievous in her tone; and remembering his conversation with Sarah the preceding evening, his heart rose high, and abandoning himself to an eager impulse he seized her hand, and exclaimed in a voice half-drowned in emotion—

"Oh, Ruth! all women are indifferent to me but one, and that is you."

Ruth withdrew her hand in apparent anger, and began to descend the grassy eminence. Maynard stood still a moment, then hastily overtook her. His manner was now distant and respectful, and seemed to say—

"I will not again offend you."

He began to speak of past days, and of her mother.

"You alone saw her buried," said Ruth, expressively—"you alone. That recollection must be a lasting bond between you and her family, Mr. Maynard. And they have many others, equally imperishable—I, in especial."

Sighing, she broke off, and leaned affectionately on his arm. Entirely forgetful of Miss Henderson, they turned aside to an excavation in the hill, called the Fairies Parlour. Roots of old trees forming the ceiling, and in their interstices the wren built its small nest; the furze flower grew on the turf floor; ivy clothed the walls. Near the entrance was a stone so richly coated with moss, that it was soft as a seat of down. On this Ruth placed herself, and Maynard stood beside her.

THE COTTAGE GIRL.

A FIGURE SUDDENLY INTERCEPTED THE WANING LIGHT.

ALONG the nearest bye-road villagers were returning with their baskets, donkeys, and carts, from the town market, and in the field still nearer, a dairymaid sitting on a stool was milking, and singing in pure light-heartedness a favourite ballad that had found its way to the great metropolis.

CHAPTER XLV.

"And whilst thou livest, dear Kate, take a fellow of plain and uncoined constancy; for he perforce must do thee right, because he has not the gift to woo in other places; for these fellows of infinite tongue that can rhyme themselves into ladies' favours, they do always reason themselves out again. My comfort is that old age, that ill layer up of beauty, can do no more spoil upon my face: thou hast me, if thou hast me, at the worst, and thou shalt wear me, if thou wear me, better and better."

SHAKSPERE.

"THAT beautiful view reminds me of much I would give the world to forget," said Ruth, after silently surveying it a space. "Yonder I can just espy the thatch of our deserted cottage," —she shuddered—"yet the sight of it is not wholly terrible, for there I have seen happy days, there I was first sensible of Mr. Maynard's kindness, there he first stepped in to relieve my father in his need, there I anticipated a marriage that, had it taken place, would have given me lifelong peace."

"Do you say so!" ejaculated Maynard, sitting down beside her, with sudden transport.

"Yonder is the park gate where my ill-used friend warned me of the duplicity I afterwards experienced," continued Ruth, not caring to rebuke the emotions she was exciting, "and there is the coppice where he was insulted for his generous protection of one abandoned by her proper protector. The mill which was to have been my peaceful home lies yonder in ruins—like all the bright hopes I formerly cherished—but I have not forgotten what pains its kind owner took to assist an unhappy father to redeem a wanderer from destruction." Her voice failed her a moment, and Maynard passing his arm around her waist unreproved drew her tenderly to his bosom. She wept a few bitter tears, and growing calmer resumed with energy—

"No, I have not forgotten all that you have done for me, nor shall it ever be forgotten! and it never can be fully recompensed."

"One kind word from you, Ruth, recompenses all a hundred times over!" exclaimed Maynard.

"Deserted by Clifton—by all the world—I still had a friend in you," continued Ruth. "Nor does my memory retain one instance in which you pained me by an allusion, however remote, unbeseeming the wife of another. I know you loved me always, but you concealed your feelings, and was as a brother or a father to the forlorn orphan. And then that twenty pounds—oh! Mr. Maynard, when the vicar told me it was from you it came, and when the delicacy of your motives displayed themselves to my mind, my soul expanded towards you as it had never done before! Repayment for such actions is beyond human capability; but to show how deep and living is the impression they have made on me, and to show you also how I estimate the unspeakable benefits you rendered my father when the clouds hung heavy on his path, speak what it is you wish, and I will deny you nothing that a grateful and virtuous woman may grant."

"You know my heart, Ruth."

"I do, I do, perfectly—and you know mine. I cannot love you as I did Mr. Clifton, I should deceive you if I were to suffer you to think that possible. Oh! be careful you understand this fully. It is but a wreck of a heart I have to offer —still, if you covet it, it shall be yours; and wreck though it be, there is an energy of kindness for you still left within it, a kindness such as I can feel for none living beside."

"But you are a lady now, Ruth," said Maynard, "a wealthy lady, and have lovers of wealth and rank; I am but a poor fellow, with nothing to boast of but a love for you which all the ice at the poles could not chill, and plain probity, truth, and sincerity."

"That love and that probity are my dependence," said Ruth.

"I am afraid you are doing violence to your inclinations, and hurting your prospects, by condescending to me," said Maynard. "However, may heaven forsake me if I do not all my life study to make you happy!"

"I know you will," said Ruth, smiling. "But stay—before we proceed farther in our conference there is a dreadful secret you must know."

She spread her hands over her face, and the flush of shame and anguish stained her brow and neck.

Maynard looked startled. but the sight of her distress quickly annihilated his curiosity.

"Whatever it be let it rest in your own keeping," he said. "I am not anxious to fathom anything you would wish hidden."

"But this you must know," said Ruth, with a deadly tremor.

"Good God, what can it be!" exclaimed Maynard. "I thought we had done with dreadful disclosures."

"I am not sure this will surprise you," said Ruth, hesitating, "for you knew the abominable treachery I experienced."

She then, in low faltering accents, with sobs and gasps of agony, acquainted him with the birth and death of her child, a secret that hitherto she had not whispered even to her father, her sister, or Miss Clifton.

"Bless you, my dearest girl!" exclaimed Maynard as she finished, catching her with ardour to his breast, and wiping away the fast flowing tears, "could you think that would surprise me after all I know? It does not, I assure you; I am only saddened for you, to think how much more miserable you have been than even your nearest friends can conceive. But cheer you, dearest girl! a faithful friend you have in me, and one who will love you while a pulse of life is left to him!"

The words were on his lip when a figure suddenly intercepted the waning light, and raising their eyes, they beheld Summerfield, who had stolen on their privacy unaware, and heard Maynard's concluding sentence, and surprised them while the arm of Maynard was around the waist of his daughter, and her glowing cheek pressed to his rapturous heart.

The happiness of the lover could hardly be excelled by that of the father, who, advancing to them, took their hands, and as he joined them between his own, uplifted his eyes in devout thankfulness.

"This is to me the climax of earthly good!" he exclaimed. "Nothing more remains beneath the sun for me to wish beyond this. Here the most earnest longings of my earthly affections terminate. Omnipotent of earth and heaven, I give thee thanks for this hour, and I supplicate Thy best blessings temporal and eternal for these two. O bless Thou the friend of my adversity with long years of joy! and heal the breaches which grief and injury have made in the peace of this dearest child of my soul!"

CHAPTER XLVI.

"What was the world to them,
Its pomps, its pleasures, and its nonsense all?"

THOMPSON.

WE have brought our story to the concluding point, and have only now to add a few particulars.

The feast at the farm broke up early without leaving weariness or repentance behind. Summerfield having slipped out during the dancing to look for his friend had met Miss Henderson coming from the cot at which she had made her passing call of benevolence, and learning that his daughter was with Maynard, followed them in the direction she pointed out. The three went back together. Tea, coffee, and steaming home-baked cakes, composed the afternoon meal. A complaint of indisposition, which the langour of her looks confirmed, formed a pretext for Ruth's withdrawing early. Her young brother made a show of accompanying her, but was glad to be dismissed when Maynard overtook them and volunteered to supply his place.

By ten all the visitants were returning to their homes over moonlit fields and lanes, and by eleven the inmates of the farm were at rest. The engagement between Ruth and Maynard was suspected but not positively known in the dale until after the expiration of another year, when other overtures being made for her hand, the suitor was calmly informed that she had been two months the wife of Mr. Maynard. The news was rapidly dispersed, and of course variously construed. Both were greatly beloved, and dewy eyes were seen among the villagers, rejoicing in an union which ensured peace to two hearts so worthy of it. But those whom it had despoiled of their matrimonial hopes objected with their friends to the match as a ridiculous affair—dwelt upon the rank which had been offered to the acceptance of Ruth—feared she would repent her folly when it was too late—reproached Summerfield as the principal promoter of it—sneered at the disparity of age and fortune of the pair, &c. &c.

Little heeded they the unfavourable opinions of those whom they had been the innocent means of disappointing. In the calm enjoyment of social blessings their days flew lightly by. Maynard's whole concern was to requite by unceasing kindness, watchfulness, and consideration, the sacrifices of rank and fashion which she had made to render him happy. The slightest shade of uneasiness, the faintest trace of indisposition, could not manifest itself in the idol of his heart without exciting his vigilance, and his habitual tenderness was redoubled by anxiety until the cloud or the ailment was removed. If he had occasion to leave her for a day or two, every post brought the humble and unaffected, but fond outpourings of his love. He returned with eagerness, and each accent of his voice, each glance of his eye, told her how dear she was.

In her pecuniary affairs he would never intermeddle. Her fortune he cared not two straws for. She was the girl of his heart, and he should be just as happy with her in the old mill, were it standing, as in Rosedale House. He would never dispose of a penny of her money except to gratify herself.

He spent a portion of each working day assisting Summerfield to cultivate the ground about the farm, and to oversee the management of the dairy, the cattle, and orchard. This employment was enlivened by attending markets and fairs in the way of business, and as he liked to have plenty of work on his hands, he planned two large windmills, one at each extremity of the dale, which soon began to rear their bold brows above the soft woodland scenery, to the ineffable delight of Maynard, who declared that 'let fine gentlemen and ladies talk of their grand buildings, nothing could equal a mill; the country was not the country where there were no sails dancing merrily on the wind. He loved a mill to his heart—there was nothing of man's making like it.'

And to this opinion Maynard stoutly adhered to his dying day. Of all the noble paintings Rosedale House contained, one particularly delighted him—it was a ruined mill on the Rhine in Germany, sketched boldly, with all its romantic concomitants of castled height, and deep ravine, and waving woods, and placid water; and this suggested an idea which Maynard hastened to put into execution, namely, to obtain a painting of his own favourite mill in the act of burning, which, when finished to his satisfaction—the red flames grandly illuminating the midnight darkness enshrouding the landscape—

he hung over a chimney-piece in the farm, beside an improved version of that likeness of Hannah Forester, Ruth's mother, which he had so gallantly rescued from the fire. His watch-dog was superannuated in a noble kennel of the yard of Rosedale House, where its deep-mouthed bay may still be heard, stirring up the hollow echoes that sleep in the dingles of the ancient park.

Though a bridegroom, Maynard retained his knotted cudgel, and though master of Rosedale, never fails to spend two evenings a week at the Three Crowns, reading the news, and smoking with Summerfield, not refined cigars, but veritable tobacco, in a garb as plain as that of the miller of former days.

Happy the beggar who meets him on the road! half-pence are sure to be forthcoming, perhaps a sixpence, for Maynard is not to be persuaded that the cares of parish guardians render individual liberality a work of supererogation; he loves with his own hand to lighten the miseries of the indigent, nor deems it an excuse for witholding his bounty that he can only render a temporary benefit. Happy the unfriended labourer who solicits his aid! He takes delight in creating employment for those that have none, and this he has done to a considerable extent, with Ruth's co-operation, by planting waste lands, building small cottages, hedging, fencing, and other works. The estate has a busy thriving aspect, pleasant little homes and gardens are springing up about it, and hardly a sad countenance is seen in the dale.

Gaunt famine stalks round about it—but there all is plenty and content, sweet smiling hope and radiant joy laugh in the fields, and sport in every glade—there all is harmonious, all is fair!

Ruth, when she consented to become the wife of Maynard, was led by her good sense to forego the scenes of refined luxuriance to which her beauty and her wealth, had she chosen, might have admitted her, but where the plain virtues of her husband must have been cast into the shade. She the more readily renounced these dazzling scenes because her own tastes inclined to simplicity, and her mind to seriousness, and because she fancied herself deficient in that acquired politeness of manner which is the fruit of early training and long intercourse with polished society.

From the period of their marriage being made public, Maynard and herself twice attended church together each Sabbath, and it was noticed that her dress was invariably grave and plain, so that no incongruity was ever perceptible between her appearance and that of her husband. There was no affectation of superior gentility in her deportment, and her ordinary habits were restricted to housewifery and practical benevolence. Her accomplishments, that in the hope to please Clifton she had taken such pains to acquire, were rarely resorted to, or laid aside altogether, for the only music Maynard cared to hear was a simple ballad, the only dancing that pleased him was that which a light heart prompted, when accuracy of steps or of figure was no object; and as for drawing he did not mind whether she excelled in it or not— the thought it was an endless attainment, while she had money to pay an artist for what she wanted in the picture way,'—and though this remark excited a smile from Ruth, it was not a disdainful one; she prized his moral worth too highly to scorn mere deficiencies of taste. When he found that she was giving up all these things for him he endeavoured to lead her back to them, fancying she must regret their loss; but Ruth had by this time established daily duties of a more useful character, which interested her as much; therefore smiling, she assured him that she 'had no time to spare, and must leave to Sarah all the lady-like accomplishments it had formerly been her ambition to obtain.'

"I have no wish you should deny yourself anything under an idea of pleasing me," said Maynard; "make yourself happy, it is all I desire."

"I am happy," returned Ruth, "as happy as earth can make me, as happy as the memory of the past will let me be."

She sighed, sunk her face in her hand a moment, and let fall a tear.

"Never mind the past," said Maynard, cheerfully, as he wiped the tear from her lovely cheek, and kissed the eyelid whence it had emerged, "forget it—don't dwell upon it."

"If I did," ejaculated Ruth, with a strong shudder, "if I did, I should sink, heart and nerve! But I employ all my minutes closely, and that, and your kindness, dear Maynard, banishes disagreeable thoughts, though now and then they will start up anew. But you may depend on my not encouraging them," she said, rising, and resuming her cheerfulness. "I know they are enemies to be banished, not friends to be entertained—and that puts me in mind I have a lot of poor folk to entertain to-morrow, which is Christmas-day, and there is some clothing to be finished that I have to distribute. It is a good thing to have no time to be miserable."

To dignify small things by the manner of performance is peculiarly the wisdom of Ruth, who, untroubled by the vagaries of fancy, possessing a clear understanding, singleness of purpose, and a conciliating disposition, readily brings her actions, even the most minute, to the test of moral principle. All the virtues flourish in her daily life, but flourish like the flowers that shed their fragrance in some leaf-curtained woodland hollow, where few eyes behold them.

As maternal responsibilities open before her, she meets them nobly; her duties to her family are discharged with steadfast zeal, with glowing affection, with indefatigable industry.

The birth of two sweet children, equally healthy and beautiful, completed the bliss of Maynard and of Summerfield. It might almost be doubted which rejoiced the most in the soft nurselings. They early learned to hail the arrival of grandfather at the house—grandpapa was a forbidden word—to rival each other for the first kiss, and to clamber on his knees, where, bending his grey head over them, he blessed them, while his thoughts fled, as they were wont to do, to her, the tender wife, who was cut off by death from a participation in his joy.

The harsher prominences of the cottager's character, having been the creation of unprecedented difficulty and misfortune, became softened down when those adverse influences ceased, and a finer old man, or one more majestically amiable, never sat by a daughter's fireside.

In our concluding notices of the subordinate characters mentioned in this volume, we shall commence with Sarah, who until very recently was looking forward to the graceful and honourable employment of a tutoress to the children of her sister; but at an annual concert given in the music hall of the small town of Rosedale, she had the good fortune to attract the notice of a young gentleman of respectable fortune, and spotless character, to whom she was married, with prospects as fair as ever dawned on the gay vision of youth and inexperience. It was a blithe and sumptuous bridal; the youngest daughter of the vicar was bridesmaid, William Summerfield brideman, Summerfield gave his daughter away, and a déjeuner for a numerous company was provided in an apartment of grand dimensions in Rosedale House after the party returned from the church. The déjeuner concluded, an affectionate leave was taken of the bride preparatory to her setting out for Germany, her husband having procured the appointment of secretary of legation there. Ruth was the last who bade her adieu, and the sisters retired a little apart to indulge their feelings unrestrained. Sarah threw herself on the neck of Ruth, and they wept silently a few moments.

"Thank God I leave you happy!" exclaimed Sarah.

"At peace, you should say," said Ruth, significantly correcting her.

"At peace, then."

"Yet you might add that I am happy too, if to be happy is to be the worshipped wife of the best of men—if to be happy is to see my children bidding fair for life and health, to know their provision is sure—if to be happy is to have no earthly wish unsatisfied. Yes, happy I am—supremely so—when the deep and dark fountains of memory that my breast contains remains sealed—but this is not always the case. The bitter drops will ooze forth now and then, Sarah, and very, very bitter they are. This is said to you only, none other must know that I ever cast a glance on that spot where his mangled body lies in its crimsoned shroud. Clifton! it is a name I never speak to living ear, but in my dreams I often see him. He comes before me then in all the fascination of former days, and when I wake the tears are on my cheek. But I dash them away with abhorrence. My kind, my good Maynard, ought to have all my thoughts, and I detest the treacherous sleep which robbed him of any portion of them. We shall not be able to converse thus any more. I shall miss you—but to know that you are happy will reconcile me eventually to a parting that I now painfully feel. Farewell, then—your husband calls you—I hear the wheels of the carriage. Farewell—farewell!"

William Summerfield is now at the university, where his talents are vigorously putting forth their shoots, and promising a rich in-gathering of fruit when the season of prime arrives. A lad more handsome and frank-hearted, more affectionate and bold, never trod the green earth. He is the pride of Ruth's heart; her interest in the development of his mind and powers is intense, and she regards herself as the architect of his rising fortunes. What profession he may ultimately adopt is uncertain, but whichever it be he is sure, in her estimation, (and her judgment is generally accurate), to rise to its highest

honours. She sees in him a genius as radiant as that of Clifton, but combined with the firm principles of self-control, which that unhappy young man wanted.

The venerable housekeeper of the family of the Cliftons died in the house, after her prejudice against the low-born cottagers had spent its acid, and left her heart full of the balm of love. During her fatal illness Ruth directed that every respect should be paid to her, in consideration of her long and faithful services to the Cliftons. She took on herself the delicate task of ministering to the drooping mind of the sufferer, conversing with her frequently and cheerfully, and surrounding her with all that could enliven and at the same time spiritualise her thoughts.

"I am not worthy of so much goodness from you, madam," exclaimed Mrs. Wilson, shortly before she expired, as Ruth adjusted her pillows, and inquired if she felt composed. "It troubles me much to think that I did not do my duty to you when Mr. Clifton was living. I might have done something to lessen the unhappiness of your separation from him; perhaps, had I taken my opportunities, I might have done much toward bringing you to a reconciliation with him, for I had influence with him sometimes, dear gentleman! But I could not brook the idea of his having a poor girl for his lady, though I loved you notwithstanding; and besides, that dreadful discovery of my former master's body in the shed—"

"O forget all that now, dear Mrs. Wilson!" exclaimed Ruth. "I can quite excuse you. Tranquilize your mind. Is there any thing you wish for more that I can procure you?"

"Nothing—nothing," was the energetic reply. "I will only trouble you to read again that paragraph in your last letter from Mrs. Merton which spoke of me."

The dying woman closed her eyes while Ruth read the affectionate farewell of Amy. Mrs. Wilson shed a few tears, ejaculated a wish that she might have seen her dear young lady once more, and raising herself in the bed, strove, with Ruth's assistance, to trace a few words to her with a pencil, but sighing as she made the ineffectual effort sank back again on the pillow and expired.

The news of Mrs. Wilson's death reached Amy in India when the latter was in weak health, and the loss of the dear old lady following that of her brother and two infants, threw her into a state of nervous melancholy, which defied medical art. The enervating Indian climate also proved destructive to

her, preying equally on mind and body. The scorching heats infused their deadly fire into her veins, consuming the life-fluid, and wasting her fair proportions, while her pulse was so feeble as hardly to be perceptible, and her head drooped powerless, and her eyes were veiled in immoveable despondency. It became apparent to Merton that her reason was fast becoming alienated, and questioning her physicians closely they confessed his apprehensions were far from groundless. They advised an immediate return to her native air and native scenery, on which latter her imagination was for ever dwelling, and Merton hastened to unburden his anxieties to Ruth, whom he wished to receive her.

The latter promptly responded to the appeal of friendship. The voyage was made; and when the ship entered the harbour she was on the shore to receive the invalid. Wrapped in the voluminous folds of an Indian shawl, attended by a black woman as domestic, and leaning on the arm of Merton, Amy stepped once more on English soil, and such was her enthusiasm at the moment that she could have knelt to kiss it.

"Welcome back! welcome back!" exclaimed Ruth, meeting her with sisterly ardour. "Our sweet Rosedale will brighten into a second spring at the sight of you, and the old house will don a new coat of moss and ivy for joy. There is your guitar still on the seat of the north chamber window, just where you left it, and everything you loved about the place has been unmolested. Only I have beside a world of improvements to show you. You come to a home, my dear Amy," she added, cordially, "a home which shall be as truly yours as it is mine. You will find it more cheerful than it used to be, for my little ones sport about it without the least fear of the spectres there used to be so much talk about. I thought the power of exorcising demons was confined to Romish priests, but my merry youngsters have exorcised a whole troop of them. Not so much as the patter of a cloven foot is to be heard in the grey galleries; not a glimmer of a supernatural light will deign to appear; all is prosaically lightsome from the topmost turret to the donjon cellar."

"It will be less fascinating to me then, though probably more wholesome," Amy remarked, and Ruth observed that her voice was weak, exerted with effort, and quickly relapsed to silence. The latter felt deeply for Merton, whose mild and pensive countenance quivered with the saddest bodements whenever he turned his eyes on his beloved wife.

"I give her to your care," he said, addressing Ruth, all the anxiety of his soul trembling in his tone.

"But I shall be a peremptory nurse," said Ruth, purposely adopting a sprightly manner, while her glance was fraught with sympathy.

"You will be a wise one, and a gentle one, I am well convinced," returned Merton, forcibly.

"A willing one, at least," said Ruth, with equal emphasis.

"And I trust in God a successful one!" exclaimed Merton.

"Doubt it not," Ruth with animation responded, "doubt it not; I pride myself in unusual skill in dealing with all sorts of ailments—it is my grand accomplishment."

They entered her carriage, and her lively judicious conversation so entertained her companions during the ride, that already Amy looked better, and Merton hopeful. Maynard joined them on the slope of the hill descending to the dale.

Merton got out and walked with him. As they proceeded, beneath a changeful April sky, Maynard frequently paused to point out his various improvements, and turning aside from the direct path brought his companion in view of Summerfield's comfortable thatched farm, standing in the midst of its smiling corn and pasture land, and overlooked by the green brow of a hanging acclivity. Summerfield himself was directing the operations of a knot of labourers in a ploughed field. On Maynard's calling to him, he joined them. Merton inspected all the farm arrangements, and finally went over the house. Coming to the picture of Maynard's burning mill, he appeared considerably amused, and pleasantly jested with the latter concerning it."

"O, you are quite free to laugh!" cried Maynard, somewhat disconcerted; "it is not so good a picture perhaps as you could have painted, but it cost me twenty guineas, and I had it done under my own eye, and gave the artist his board all the time."

"The picture is a tolerable specimen of modern art," said Merton. "Pray did the painter sketch it at the time of the fire?"

"Not he, he never saw my mill or the fire either, but he drew both from my descriptions."

"And I presume this person in the foreground is intended for you? and this—"

"Is Jean Andre, the French jackanape incendiary! skulking behind the trees and stones."

"And that lion-like mastiff?"

"Is my watch-dog."

Merton accepted some refreshments, and then Summerfield and Maynard accompanied him to Rosedale House. Amy had gone to rest. Next day divers walking excursions were planned, but the natural indolence of Amy had been so fostered and confirmed by the habits of an Indian life, that she could scarce be induced to stir on foot; her old passion for riding on horseback, however, fortunately, revived, and this healthy exercise was of infinite service to her. The superior strength and clearness of Ruth's understanding gave her great ascendancy over the more unequal and imaginative character of her friend, and she resolutely exercised it in withdrawing her from the self-indulgent habits calculated to nourish her mental malady. She lured her into the open air while the morning dew was on the flowers; she gathered cheerful society about her; she engaged her in active works of benevolence; and in a few weeks fairly succeeded in dispelling from her mind the gloomy vapours of despondency.

Amy constantly ascribed her recovery to Ruth, whom she loves more than a sister's love.

"Mistress is a blessing to all that come near her!" exclaimed Wyatt to Maynard one day; "rich or poor, they find themselves obligated to her; she's the sensiblest and beautifullest young woman ever walked on English ground."

"So she is, Wyatt," exclaimed Maynard, "and I am the most fortunate man in the world to have such a wife!"

"But are you never afraid, master, that she thinks of the young squire? She was very fond of him—"

"Mind your work, Wyatt, and don't talk of what does not concern you," said Maynard, gruffly.

"Well now, to be sure! that's just like me," ejaculated Wyatt, as Maynard walked hastily away, "I'm always putting people in mind of what they most wish to forget—always treading on tender toes. I could find in my heart never to open my lips again."

Near the old park Merton and Amy having fixed their residence, engirt with a perfect arcadia of sylvan beauty, where trees of pendulous shoots display their graceful foliage on the banks of naiad-haunted brooks and mimic lakes, where summer alleys, green and cool, stretch into deepening woods, and the pleasure barque dips its oar into the sparkling stream, or lifts its snow-white sail to catch the western breeze. Often on the side of a green mound, rendered attractive to the romantic

fancy of Amy by the remains of a religious house of Knights Templars, may be seen a happy party, consisting of the Mertons, Maynard, Ruth, and Summerfield, and sometimes the brother of Ruth. They sit upon the grass, or sometimes loiter about; the little children pluck the flowers that grow amid the grass, or chase each other down the slope; Amy touches her guitar, and its wild and plaintive tones appeal irresistibly to the heart; Ruth sings her artless ballad, and Summerfield cannot withhold the favourite " Auld Lang Syne." There are no intruders on their careless mirth, except the birds which inhabit the venerable oaks that overshadow the spot. A rill of limpid water bubbles up within the shattered walls which the bold Knights of the Temple once tenanted, and pours itself down the side of the mound, swelling into a wide stream below. White chimneys and tufted tree-tops appear intermingled in one direction—in the other the eye glances over a distance of many miles to reach a boundary line of misty hills at the horizon—in a third the town of Rosedale is seen straggling irregularly up from a river's brink—and in a fourth the panoramic prospect extends over a varied scene of ample extent, and extremely fertile.

When the party leave the spot it is generally to sup at the farm in rural fashion.

Not always, however, can Amy content herself with these simple pleasures. She is as gay and enthusiastic as formerly; her by-gone intimacy with divers acquaintances of the beau monde has been revived, and she gives frequent entertainments of a showy kind. As Merton can well afford them, he sees no necessity for restraining her inclinations, her heart being neither corrupted nor hardened by them. Besides, they love each other well, and he knows that it is impossible to change the natural bent of the character.

Much he had found to forgive in Amy, but more to love and admire; and so wayward is man's heart, that he could not confidently affirm if she had fewer faults he would not have loved her less. But then her's were truly faults, not vices. Vices she had none; and the passionate tenderness with which she regarded him invested her with an attractiveness that he would have been sorry to exchange for perfection. And knowing that he rather tolerated than enjoyed the distinguished society she gathered around her, Amy eagerly at each interval strove to repay his indulgence of her inclinations by partaking of his love of Nature and of study. She could turn with

equal gusto from the crowded saloon to the still twilight retreat—from the frivolities of dress to the starry pages of phi-
losophic or poetic lore—from the light chit-chat of conceited
fools to the contemplation of the forms of nature and the immortal products of art. This versatility while it had its incon-
veniences, had also its charms; and Merton, while he wondered
and sighed over inconsistencies, adored her.

Experience proves it is not always the most esteemed who
are the most beloved.

We must not conclude without naming Mrs. Lister, the
respectable widow with whom Ruth was lodged while her
father was under sentence of death in the castle. Mrs. Lister
had imbibed a strong affection for the young person whom she
had seen enduring calamities so exquisitely painful and humiliating with so touching a meekness, so uncommon a fortitude,
and such high principled exertion. Moreover, it had given
her a world of satisfaction, she declared, when Ruth married
Mr. Maynard, for she never could abide that disdainful, hard-
hearted Squire Clifton, who, to make himself a great man, to
be sure, would have sacrificed both his wife and his sister.
She did not think in all her life she had ever heard anything
which gave her so much pleasure as the news that Mr. Maynard was married, though she declared it was very singular it
should be so, after such strange things as had happened since
he first courted Ruth Summerfield.

Ruth had made it a law to forget none who had befriended
her in adversity. Mrs. Lister she felt particularly bound to
remember for many little kindnesses which at the time had
been felt precious, and she sent for her soon after she became
the wife of Maynard, and entertaining her with liberality,
presented to her a handsome crape shawl as a token of remembrance. The worthy widow returned to her home quite happy.

In this manner did Ruth reconcile to her superior fortune
those with whom she had been intimate in her low estate.

With one scene more of pleasantness and peace, to be narrated
in our next number, we will quit her chequered history.

THE COTTAGE GIRL.

"WE HAD BETTER, BOTH OF US, FORGET THE PAST."

IT was autumn, and the hedgerows had parted with their sweet flowerets, but there were blackberries in plenty, and here and there a wild rose yet remained on the stalk; the frog croaked in the ditches, and the snail was on the path; the shadows of the trees sloped in prodigious magnitude athwart the bright sunlit grass, where the flocks of Summerfield were feeding without fear or care; the black crow winnowed the upper air, the throstle sang on the pencilled spray of the elegant beech tree, and the whistle of the hedger came cheerily over the mead.   The children ran hither and thither at will, and made wreaths of the fading convolvulus to decorate their brows.

The group went on leisurely, chatting and laughing in perfect ease and good humour, until Summerfield, who was in advance of the rest, placed his foot on the stile leading into the " Barley Close."   Beyond that stile Ruth had not been for many a day, and with a hasty accent she called on her father to return, but he passed over, and proceeded with a firm step.   Maynard perceived that she trembled, and added his own voice to induce Summerfield to return—but the latter was deaf.

"This is weakness which must be conquered," said Ruth, crossing the stile with hasty resolution.

A sadness came over the party.

> " One fatal remembrance, one shadow that throws
>   Its bleak shade o'er like their joys and their woes."

Summerfield advanced at an accelerated pace.

" Surely he is not leading us to the cottage !" exclaimed Ruth.

She pressed Amy's hand significantly, and observed they had better turn back, and leave the gentlemen to follow their pleasure.

The cheek of Amy flushed high, while that of her friend was deadly pale.   There was a momentary struggle on the part of the former ; she then said resolutely—

" I will go forward.   I have never yet seen the spot where my ill-fated father rested so long."

Merton was silent, but not pleased, and Maynard watched with anxiety the changing countenance of Ruth.   Amy had made up her mind, however, and to the cottage they went.

They found it not in the ruinous condition they had expected. The tree before the door was surrounded by a seat of turf, and a table covered with fruit and wine was before it ; the walls had been repaired and newly whitewashed ; the thatch relaid ; the swallow restored to its home in the eaves ; and, with a starting tear, Ruth beheld the vacant cage which her favourite bullfinch had occupied hung in its old place beside the polished lattice which the evening sun was gilding.   A tidy old body, who had been an old acquaintance of her mother, stood upon the porch and curtsied to the visitors.

" Why, Dame Allison !" exclaimed Ruth, " how long have you dwelt here ?"

" Only sin' last Lord's Day," replied the old woman. " Mester Summerfield put me into the place to order it, and see

till it, many thanks to him! and I am to be free of rent and firing, and grow my vegetables in the garden behind. Some folk say they wad be feared to stay here o' nights, but I put my trust in the Lord, and the darkness is as light till Him."

With various sensations the party entered the cottage. All the marks of the visitation of the constables had been effaced—planks of the floor were restored to their places, and white and clean they looked—the simple furniture that had been there during Mrs. Summerfield's lifetime stood in the same places in which Ruth remembered them formerly; and as she looked around she half expected to see her mother's attenuated but lovely figure filling the high-backed chair or emerging from the interior chamber. Filled with her remembrance, Ruth sank on her knees before that vacant chair, and, sinking her face on it, indulged in a fit of tears, which no one attempted to suppress. She wept also when she entered the chamber, and beheld her mother's bed, and drew aside the simple dimity curtain as if to look on her face on the pillow.

Next they proceeded into the fatal garden, and there stood Summerfield beside a peach tree which had been planted on the spot where the body of Arthur Clifton had been buried for fourteen years. The shed had been removed, and the garden enclosed with a tall holly hedge. Around the peach tree was a circle of blooming flowers, and the sides of the garden were planted neatly with sweet herbs, vegetables, and fruit.

"Draw near," said Summerfield, addressing Amy and his daughter with dignity. "This, Mrs. Merton, is the spot where these hands of mine stretched your father's body in the earth. Guiltless of his murder they were, I take my oath. The heaven above us knows it—his spirit knows it. If I had ever cherished a thought against his life, conscience would not suffer me to seek this place; but I do seek it, and that with an easy mind. Your father died by his own vices, and the decree of God. And you, Ruth, my dear child, and all who now stand around me, never more shun this place as though it were a spot of terror—an accursed place. Here is no harm. You see the peach tree and the flowers flourish as well here as in your costliest garden. It was but an ordinary grave that was made here; the tenant of it died but as thousands die. Be cheerful, then; the Spirit of God is in this place as well as in every other, and where His spirit is the guiltless mind ought to be at peace.

Before retiring homeward, the party partook of the repast before the door. A solemnity crept over all. Even the chil-

dren were silent and thoughtful. But as the manners of Amy were such as intimated her full belief in the cottager's innocence of intentional homicide, this hazardous visit passed over without irritation, and without the least discordancy of feeling. The walk to Rosedale House was pensive but calm. Maynard and Ruth hung a little back, conversing on touching reminiscences of her mother, and the vicissitudes they had personally experienced in love and fortune.

Somehow or another, the visit to the cottage and the solemn words which Roger Summerfield had spoken over the grave of Arthur Clifton, had cast a gloom over the heart of the miller. His mind became suddenly impressed by a sad foreboding, and he involuntarily pressed more closely to him the soft arm of his loved and loving wife.

Sorrowful though his thoughts were, however, he chattered to Ruth, and spoke lovingly of the past and hopefully of the future; chasing away from his brow as well as he was able, the heavy shade of woe, lest it might fall upon her innocent soul also. Glad was he when they reached home, and when, after dismissing his friends, he was enabled to excuse himself to Ruth and fly to the solitude of his own chamber.

"What can this feeling mean?" he said to himself, as he gazed out upon the broad lands of Rosedale. "Can it be that my poor Ruth, who has gone through an ordeal of sorrow, such as might well have crushed and blighted her heart for ever, is again to be made the plaything of fortune? No! I will not believe it. Providence, which I have ever found just and merciful, will forbid further suffering for her."

Then, after a moment, he started as a second thought burst in upon his honest mind.

"Perhaps," he exclaimed; "perhaps, after all these years, my old fault—my folly—is about to be punished, to return upon me in the midst of my hardly won joy. Oh! Ruth; would that I had told you all, long—long ago."

He had pressed his hand to his burning, aching brow, when the soft warm arm of Ruth Maynard stole around his neck.

"What ails you, dear husband," she said, tenderly; "you were well and happy but a moment since, and now you seem ill and feverish, and in sorrow?"

He pressed her tenderly to him, and kissed her warm lips.

"Yes, yes, Ruth," he said; "I am well, but—but—I have something to tell you, Ruth. Sit down here and listen to me. I have done wrong to you, Ruth, and you must forgive me."

"You, Henry—*you* done me wrong?" she said, smiling, while her large eyes opened wide with astonishment; "why, what on earth *can* it be? I will warrant it is something very terrible."

"Nay, then, Ruth," said the honest man, holding her hand in his; "you may not think it a matter of jest when I tell you; though, I know your kind heart will find excuses for me. What *I* blame myself most for is, that I should have told you first.

"When I was about one or two and twenty—it matters little which now—I fell into the company of a family named Lansdowne—a man, a son, and a daughter—a family which bore anything but a good name; but which had contrived so far to keep up against bad reputation as to remain undisturbed in a cottage near my father's mill.

"The daughter, Lucy, was a fine, handsome girl, rather too bold to please most people, and just the one I would avoid now. But then, I soon learned to admire her, and often found myself comparing her to the quiet country lasses round about, much to the detriment of the latter. I thought her false pride the result of natural dignity; her evil looks the gleamings of beauty. I forgot the stories I had heard in regard to her father and brother; I ignored all the sneers I heard levelled at her, and in an evil hour I married her. Ah! Ruth, you may well start, I should have told you all this before.

"Well, this marriage I resolved to keep secret, for my father was in failing health, and angry as he already was with me for speaking to the Lansdownes, I knew well how terrible would be his wrath at the knowledge that she was my wife.

"For two months, therefore, we met in secret; until one evening, when I had with difficulty succeeded in leaving home to come to her, I found the cottage in confusion, and the brother away, while the old man was cursing and raving like one bereft of his senses.

"A few words sufficed to explain all. An old lover of Lucy's had been prowling about the neighbourhood of the cottage for the last few days, and with him she had eloped, taking with her all the money, and trinkets, and clothes I had bought her, besides many things belonging to her father. My grief and anger you may imagine, Ruth; but the latter soon predominated. I saw myself duped and degraded in my own eyes; and I only thanked Heaven that I had not disclosed to my father the secret of my unlucky and disgraceful marriage.

"It was some two years after, that news came to me of her

death. She died in want, in some wretched hovel in London. The certificate of her death was sent me, and a few scrawled lines written in a man's hand, saying that she had hoped at the last moment for my forgiveness and pity.

"Poor thing!" murmured Ruth, leaning forward, and kissing her husband on the forehead. "And is this all you have to ask forgiveness for—for not telling me a story which might have pained me when I loved you less? Why, Henry dear, if you offended me a hundred times more than in this, do I not remember the cruel words I once spoke to you—the long, long, weary time of sorrow you had to suffer through me? Fear not, dear husband, that this will in any way alter my feelings towards you. We had better both of us forget the past."

He had just responded to her embrace, and was about to speak, when a knock was heard at the door.

"Come in." cried Henry, and a servant entered with a note —a hastily-scrawled epistle—which ran as follows:—

"Sir,—You are wanted at the 'Bull Inn' directly. Some one who knew Lucy Lansdowne is there."

Henry Maynard leaped up with an exclamation of astonishment and alarm, throwing, as he did so, the letter into Ruth's lap.

"There shall be no more secrets between us, Ruth," he said. "You see, my gloom was not for nothing. I, who have spoken so bitterly of others, am about to bring some sorrow upon you."

Ruth would not have been human had not a shade of anxiety entered her mind as her husband said these words.

To see Maynard, generally so calmly happy and contented, a prey to such strong emotions was so extraordinary as certainly to justify her experiencing some alarm; but true woman—good wife that she was—she tried her utmost to cast aside all evidences of her own fears in order to quiet and comfort him.

"Dear Henry, do not distress yourself unnecessarily," she said; "this man may merely wish to see you to give you some information in regard to Lucy's death. Shall I come with you?"

"No, no, dear Ruth; what would the people say to see the mistress of Rosedale visiting a stranger in a low inn?"

"Yes; but if I *am* mistress of Rosedale, I am your wife, and, as such, ready always to share your sorrows and your difficulties. Nevertheless, if you would rather go alone, do so, Henry. Take care of yourself, and be assured all is well."

He kissed her tenderly, promised to return soon, and quitted her.

Presently she heard the clatter of his horse's feet, and saw him bending over its head, as he urged it rapidly along the road.

There had been a time, not long ago, when the sight of his departing figure would have been a welcome spectacle to her; but now as she watched him she felt a yearning of the heart towards him, and from her inmost soul she sent up a prayer to Heaven that if any danger or grief menaced him, the hand of Mercy might be stretched forth to shield and protect him.

CHAPTER XLVII.

THE LAST CLOUD.

MEANWHILE, Maynard, on reaching the Hall, had demanded of the servant "Who brought the note?" and had learned that a little boy had given it hurriedly to the domestic, and ran off without waiting for an answer.

"There is some evil in this," he murmured, as his horse bore him swiftly towards the "Bull Inn;" "this man—no doubt the villain who inveigled her away—has heard of my good fortune, and has resolved, no doubt, to make money by working on my fears. But he shall not—he shall not. Oh! how glad I am that I told Ruth everything."

With these thoughts rushing through his troubled brain, he hurried on towards the inn, and on arriving there was ushered into a private room.

Here by a fire was seated an individual whom, he felt certain, he had never seen before.

He was about the same age as himself, with a dash of grey in his hair; a thin, sallow face, with a cunning, depraved look about it; a powerful figure, with a semi-military appearance in it, and dress which was positively in rags.

He was smoking a long pipe, and before him on a table was a pewter full of beer.

"Good evening, Mr. Maynard," he said, as the master of Rosedale entered; "glad you've come. Sit down by the fire, and make yourself at home. Drink, eh? No; not good

enough, I suppose; got particular since you walked so nicely into Rosedale; is that it?"

"Come, sir," said Maynard, somewhat testily, "I do not know you, and your manner is anything but prepossessing; be civil; keep your place, and tell me your business quickly."

The man laid his pipe down on the table, took a large draught of beer, and placed a hand on each knee.

"Oh! as for that, Miller Maynard," said he, "you needn't be so high and mighty. I've known the time when you weren't so grand, and I'm going to tell you something which will make you less grand than ever. My name is Luke Warner, if you must know."

"I remember it well. You are the villain who inveigled away my wife."

The man indulged in a low, chuckling laugh, as if he were enjoying vastly some joke in which he would not permit his companion to partake.

"Villain, or no villain, I am he," said Warner, "and I'm going to tell you something which is very important, and I expect before you go you'll offer me a lapfull of money not to tell it to any one else."

"It may be, or not," said Maynard, breathing thickly. "Be quick with your story."

"Well, then, in the first place," said Luke Warner, "you acknowledge that you did marry Lucy Lansdowne twenty years ago?"

"Yes, yes."

"And you acknowledge that a short time since you married Ruth Clifton, the widow of Percy Clifton of Rosedale?"

"Yes! what then?"

"Very good," pursued the man; "very good. Some eighteen years ago you received a letter, and a certificate purporting to be the certificate of the death of Lucy Maynard. That certificate was a false one. She was not dead."

"Not dead? What then?"

"She lives. She is there!"

As he spoke, he raised one hand, and pointed towards a door at the further end of the room, fixing his eyes meanwhile upon the face of Henry Maynard, as if enjoying his emotion.

Too evident, indeed, was this emotion. This woman, who had tarnished the brightness of his young days, had returned now, if this man's words were true, to ruin his happiness for ever; to step in between him and the dearly beloved one for

whom he had battled so long, and whom he had so dearly won; to cast a slur upon a reputation which he had strived so hard to save; to take from his Ruth the name of wife, from his children his name and his fortune.

"This cannot be," he murmured, pressing his hand to his brow.

"Nevertheless," said the ruffian, coolly, "it is so. Come with me and judge for yourself."

The man rose, took the lamp from the table, and, approaching the door, opened it.

"There," he said; "were not my words true?"

Seated in a chair by the fire was a woman of some forty years. Though she was younger than Maynard, the winters which had passed so lightly over the honest brow of the miller had silvered and thinned her hair, and dimmed her eyes, and hollowed her cheeks, and attenuated the form.

Where now was the firm, bold, elastic step; the bright gleamings of those daring orbs; the rich roses of those rounded cheeks; the glossy beauty of those auburn tresses; the glorious loveliness of that majestic form? Gone; gone with the light of the heart was the light of beauty; gone for ever, as hope had gone before it!

She gazed timidly at the pair as they entered, and remained silent.

Luke Warner thrust his hands deep into his pockets, and eyed Maynard triumphantly.

"Now isn't this a clever stroke of business?" he said. "I have come upon you just at the right moment."

"Yes, villain," murmured Maynard, "you have come upon me at the moment when all my hopes were fresh. Lucy, did you not wrong me enough that you should feel it necessary to bring this new sorrow on me? Why did you concoct the false news of your death that you might lead me into a crime such as I have committed?"

"You have committed no crime, Mr. Maynard," she said, faintly; but, catching Warner's eye fixed savagely upon her, she stopped suddenly.

"No crime!" cried Maynard, excitedly. "Will Ruth think it no crime when she finds that she is not my wife? Will she think it no crime when she and her children are found the one without a husband the others without a father, and both ruined and disgraced? Oh, Lucy Lansdowne, the curse of Heaven will light upon you for this!"

As he spoke the wretched man, overcome by the violence of his feelings, sank into a chair and sobbed aloud.

"Here, here," said Warner, "we needn't have all this. Just give me the cash—I want enough to take us comfortably to America, and we'll never return again. Come, let it be a bargain, and thus save yourself all this trouble you think so much of."

For an instant a glimmering of hope entered the miserable man's heart, and he looked up.

Should he close with this ruffian and buy his silence in order that Ruth might for ever be ignorant of her misfortune?

But after a moment his honest heart refused to accede to it; he would not even buy Ruth's happiness with an imposture— for had he not sworn never again to keep a secret from her? and this, the greatest secret of all—a secret which would weigh upon his life and sap its sweetest foundations—how could he keep that from her?

"No," he said, "I will make no bargain with you. I shall not buy your silence. I myself will break this secret to my wife —to Ruth, I mean—and bear my burden as I should, like a brave man. Lucy, you will of course remain here for to-night. In the morning I will make some arrrangements; but now you must let me go, for my heart is panting with emotion and my brain is on fire."

He rose as he spoke faintly, as if the news had taken from him all his strength, and made a movement as if to go.

"Stay," cried Luke, in a threatening tone, "stay! Am I to understand, then, that you refuse to give me any money?"

"Yes, I refuse."

"Very good. Then, I'll take good care to make you. There's not a man, woman, or child in Rosedale that shall not scoff at you and leer at you both; not a corner shall there be where you can show your heads."

"Your threats are idle, man," returned Maynard; "they fall upon one so crushed that he could laugh in the face of death!"

In another moment he had left them and passed out into the highroad.

Oh! how bitter the feelings of the honest man as he approached the house which had, of late, been the scene of so much happiness and joy.

All nature seemed changed; the air blew more chilly; the tress looked more spectral; the house, as he neared it, appeared prison-like, and the lights in the windows dull and unearthly.

There was the bright glare of a lamp in his room, seeming to him gloomy and sepulchral, like the candles that burn for the dead.

"Good Heaven!" he murmured, "she is waiting up for me. I shall be compelled to tell her all—this night."

With a staggering gait he ascended the stairs after passing the surprised servants, and, with pale face and horror-stricken eyes, passed into the room where his Ruth sat reading, looking beautiful and graceful in the simple attitude she had assumed.

"Oh! Henry, my husband!" she exclaimed, springing up when she saw him, and clasping him to her heart. "What ails you? What misfortune has overtaken us? Can your fatal presentiment be true?"

Maynard sat down by the chair she had occupied, and drew her hand towards him.

"Ruth," he said, in a voice choking with emotion, "Providence, in its wisdom, seems to have selected you as the object of unheard-of sorrows, and I, who, of all others, have endeavoured to shield you, am chosen as the one to bring the last crowning woe of all upon your dear head. Oh! Ruth, my girl, how shall I ever tell you? How can poor Harry Maynard, who has loved you so long and battled for you as for life, be the one to tell you you are a ruined woman?"

Then the strong man bowed down his head, and wept again in the bitterness of his deep, deep sorrow.

"Ruined! Henry," repeated Ruth, "you exaggerate. We have wealth in plenty, and health too, thank Heaven. If we lost our wealth, what then? we could work to live. Never fear, then, dear husband; if I have lost my property, we can labour as we both have done before."

"Oh! it is not that, not that, Ruth," said Maynard, "it is worse than that; worse, far worse."

"Oh! what can you mean?" exclaimed Ruth, clasping her hands in alarm.

"I mean that we are ruined; that you are not my wife; that you and my children are nameless; that the one I had thought dead, lives—lives to be again my curse, to blight my hopes, to bring destruction and shame upon you and my little ones. Oh! Heaven, it is hard—hard to bear."

Ruth was weeping now, but she drew his head down upon her bosom and whispered words of consolation.

Then by degrees he told her all—told her of the compact offered and refused, and begged her to forgive and aid him.

"Forgive you, I will not," she replied, "because there is nothing to forgive; aid you I will. Are you certain that this is your wife?"

"Certain—alas, too certain," replied the wretched Maynard; "time has changed her but in age and misery. Poor, ragged, and attenuated, she is still the Lucy Lansdowne of old. Oh! Ruth, my loved one, what is to become of you—of you and our poor little ones?"

Ruth saw plainly how deeply and terribly the wound had sunk into his heart; and overwhelmed as she felt by her new misfortune, which had converted her into the comforter of him who had so long comforted her in sorrow, she resolved to endeavour to persuade him to delay further speech on the subject till the morrow.

"Let us not speak of it more to-night. A night's rest and a few hours' thought will enable you to face the difficulty with greater courage and reason. Retire to rest now, and in the morning I will help you in doing things for the best."

He allowed her to dispose of him as she would, and without a word he led her to her room. At the door he raised her hand to his lips, and left her to return to his own chamber. She was no longer his wife.

Rest! Ruth had talked of rest, but what rest could come to him, whose heart was bursting with the intensity of its sorrow; whose whole being was throbbing, as it were, with pain; whose brain was on fire; whose mind was racked by a hundred bitter thoughts at once?

He turned up the lamp to its full extent that he might not be startled by the shadows and thoughts; and though the night was chilly, he flung open the casement, and listened to the voices of the night.

The wind was at its play—rushing hither and thither, dashing against the trees that opposed it, and rioting amid the branches, and running at headlong speed down the avenues where the old house stopped its course, and sent it shrieking back again towards the highway. It seemed as if it brought mocking voices with it from the burnt mill, telling the unhappy man to come back to it; laughing at him for his ambition; jeering at him for the sudden loss of his happiness, and whispering his sorrow in low tones to the night prowlers.

And all this time a leaden weight was upon his soul—a dreadful foreboding that some fresh exciting scene was yet to be gone through—that the cup of his sorrow had not yet been drained to the dregs.

At length he closed the window once more, and sat down by the fire—to listen! Something seemed to tell him to listen! All was still, save the voices of the night wind without—within everything was as quiet as the grave. Not a soul was stirring in the house; whether the household was asleep or not there was nothing to prove what thoughts—peaceful or terrible— were keeping their eyes unclosed.

Yet, through all this stillness there seemed to come a warning for him to listen, and he did so intently, sitting there by the fire quietly, in spite of the whirlwind which was coursing through his brain.

Presently he heard a tapping sound, whose meaning he could not understand, but which gradually grew louder and louder; then came a slight crash as of broken glass, and the fall of a heavy substance. After this, all was again still.

"There is robbery or murder meant here," thought Maynard; "it is well that my presentiment led me to remain up."

Lowering the light of the lamp, he took it in his hand, and opening the door as gently and noiselessly as he could, he glided along the passage towards the chamber where his money was kept stored away.

Entering, he concealed himself behind the heavy window-curtains, where he could see all, having first taken down the pair of loaded pistols which hung on the wall near the chest where his property, or rather, Ruth's property was concealed.

He had not long to wait; but to one who watched eagerly, as he did, the time passed but slowly. Presently, however, he heard the slight creaking of the stairs, as the stranger, whoever he was, ascended slowly, endeavouring to avoid all noise; and, in another moment, the door was pushed open and a man entered.

There was no attempt at concealment about him; it was Luke Warner, and behind him came Lucy Lansdowne.

"Now, then," said Luke, brutally; "since you've been fool enough to come, hold the light and keep quiet. If you make the slightest noise, I'll kill you."

The woman did not seem in the slightest degree alarmed or overawed by his threats.

"If you strike me," she said, in the same undertone which he had adopted, "I will cry out, rouse the house, and tell all."

"I'd take care of that, my lady," he said; "before they could come, you'd be a stiff 'un. Here's the lantern, take it, and hold it steady."

The woman took the lantern, and held it while the man knelt down and began with a small chisel to force open the box. Maynard, however, still waited; Lucy had said "she would tell all." What could it be that she had to tell? Perhaps she would speak again.

After a few moments she let something drop from her hand, and the sound re-echoed loudly through the still house.

The man sprang up with an oath, and struck her savagely on the shoulder.

"Keep quiet, will you?" he cried. "Do you want all the house here? Do you want to spend your life in gaol?"

"Better that than to ruin an innocent man, and bring disgrace on his helpless children. You had better leave me alone, or you'll find I'll tell everything, and spoil all your beautiful plans."

"Hang you; you're talking at the top of your voice," said Luke, threateningly; "will you keep still?"

"Hold! cried Maynard, stepping forward and turning up the light of the lamp, which, until now, he had kept shaded behind the heavy curtains. "Hold! or you are a dead man."

Luke Warner turned round, and, seeing the pistol which the Master of Rosedale held levelled at his head, he stopped short.

The different aspects of the three faces would have served a painter for a study.

Henry Maynard, stern, pale, implacable; the robber, green with the hue of fear, and distorted with anger; the woman, strangely moved, yet showing no symptoms of alarm.

"As for you, Luke Warner," said the miller, in a loud voice, "this nightly visit is nothing more than I might have expected from one who has spent his life in debauchery and crime, and has ever been too idle to live except by despoiling others of their hardly won earnings. But from you, Lucy, this was not to be anticipated. Have you not done me sufficient wrong? Have you not triumphed over me enough, that you should come hither to rob, not *me*, but the woman, who, through you, has been brought to ruin and to shame? This money which you seek to carry away with you belongs to Ruth, not to me, for, since you are here, I am no longer her husband, and this property is no longer mine."

"Oh! believe me, Mr. Maynard," said the woman, eagerly, "I have not injured you so much as you believe. You are not so ruined as you think. Keep Rosedale, and enjoy it with the one you love; for I——"

"Silence, mad woman, what would you say?" shouted Luke Warner, seizing her fiercely, while at the same time he drew a knife from his breast. "Silence, or I will bury this in your heart!"

"Touch her," said Maynard, firmly, feeling his heart elated by the hope of he knew not what, "touch her, and you are a dead man!"

"Save me from him," cried Lucy, "and I will tell you all. I fear not death. The torments I suffer, the misery I endure, is worse than the grave can be! No peace by day, no rest by night! Unhand me—Luke—I *will* tell him! Luke was——"

A savage blow stopped her; a blow which struck her backwards; a blow so fierce and strong that she gurgled out unintelligible words, and fell back senseless on the floor.

At the same moment Maynard fired his pistol, but missed his aim, and in another moment the ruffian was upon him.

They were both powerful men, about the same age; and it would have been difficult for any one to predict which would obtain the best of it.

The contest, however, only continued for a few moments, for the report of the pistol aroused the house, and a serving man rushed into the room just as the villain had freed his right arm, and raised the knife to strike. In a very short time he was overpowered, and was being held down with a pistol to his head, when Ruth and the servants came crowding in, half dressed, and in terrible alarm.

The man servant soon effectually bound the robber, while the wounded and still senseless woman was raised, and laid on the bed.

"Now, then, Luke Warner," said Maynard, "tell me what it was that Lucy wished to say when you interrupted her with your brutal blow. There is now no use in concealment; you are helpless in my hands and will soon be in prison."

"I refuse to tell it," returned the man, doggedly.

"If I give you your freedom and let you go, will you tell me?" asked Maynard.

"Yes," he said, while a cunning twinkle, which he could not repress, beamed in his eye, "yes, release me, and I will tell you."

Maynard saw at once that the man intended to deceive him.

"No," he said, "I will not trust you. Providence will yet defend the innocent and punish the guilty. Lucy will perhaps recover sufficiently to speak, and reveal this new mystery,

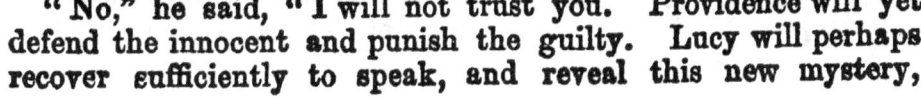

which, I feel certain, affects my happiness. John," he added to the serving man, "go and fetch the constable, and let this man be taken at once to prison."

Luke Warner's features were distorted now with a hideous grin of malice.

"Good," he said; "let it be so. My lips shall be closed, and her secret will die with her. See, she is still senseless; before morning she will be dead, and in her grave will be buried your happiness."

The man's words seemed true.

Lucy lay breathing heavily on the bed, her face pale as in death, the blood still welling from the wound in her shoulder.

"Oh! trust him—trust him!" said Ruth, imploringly. "Who knows, Maynard, what terrible secret is concealed from us? Who knows that his words may not bring joy back again to our hearts? Release him, for my sake, Henry, release him."

Maynard thought a moment.

"If we do," he said, "and he deceives us, we have no hold on him; but, for your sake, I will do so. John, unbind him."

The servant man did so, and Luke Warner stood once more free before them, while all stood anxiously waiting for his revelation; the servants, who knew nothing of the sorrow of their master and mistress, but who had learned to love and respect them, being as eager to hear as Ruth and Maynard.

But they were all doomed to disappointment.

The treacherous villain had observed that the window behind him was open, and he had resolved to make an effort not only to effect his escape but to carry with him untold the secret, upon which he depended for obtaining a large sum of money from the Master of Rosedale.

"Come," cried Maynard, impatiently, "speak. I have released you as you wished. When you have told us the truth you are free to go."

The man raised his hand as if to enjoin silence, while he addressed him, and then, when all were in a state of expectancy, he leaped suddenly backwards and dashed towards the window.

In an instant it flashed across the minds of Maynard and the man-servant, that the thief was, after all, resolved to deceive them, and they both rushed after him.

But they were too late.

With the energy so characteristic of a hardened criminal escaping from justice, Luke Warner had flung open the casement and dropped on the outside.

THE COTTAGE GIRL.

"Good Heavens! exclaimed Maynard, "he has spoken of the secret dying with Lucy Lansdowne. It will die with him too. That fall must have been his destruction."

Taking up the lantern which the robber had brought into the house, he directed its rays downwards, but could see nothing. Presently, however, a loud moaning was heard, which plainly showed that Luke Warner was still there and in deep agony.

"We will go down and bring him into the house," cried Maynard, excitedly; "perhaps in such a moment as this his heart will soften and he will reveal his secret as some kind of atonement for the past."

On reaching the rear of the house, they found that Luke Warner had fallen on a heap of sharp stones and was in a deplorable condition, quite insensible and seemingly crushed in every limb.

Maynard stooped down and glanced at him with an expression of agony.

Gently they bore him into the house—gently and tenderly—this rough, sinful man, with the cloud of crime so heavy on his brow.

But it was quite in vain—this gentleness—this tenderness.

Crushed in the midst of his wrong doing, taken home in the very act of perjury and deceit, destroyed with a load of hate and vengeance at his heart, the man of sin had gone to his account ere they laid him upon the soft bed within.

"He is dead," murmured Maynard; "my last hope seems truly gone now."

He stood for some minutes gazing at the body, a crowd of strange feelings pressing upon his heart and weighing down his soul.

So strange and wild and exciting had been the events that had been crowded into the last few hours, that he must be forgiven, if for the time he gave way to despair and looked upon his lot as an unjust one.

He was aroused from his sad reverie by the intelligence that the doctor had arrived.

Eagerly he darted up into the room.

"Well, Dr. Ashton," said Maynard, anxiously, "what make you of your patient?"

The doctor shook his head.

"I really don't know," he said; "she is in a very critical state. I can say *one* thing for certain—she cannot live! Whether she will ever recover her senses is very doubtful."

"That is what I earnestly hope for," said Maynard. "She has something to tell, which, left untold, will affect the happiness of my family for ever. You may think, then, how eager we are to hear her voice again."

"Well, well," said the doctor, "I will do my best, and you must help by kind and patient nursing, Mrs. Maynard. I will send her some medicine, and you must see that she is not moved."

When the doctor had gone, Ruth begged Maynard to retire to rest, while she and one of the female servants sat up with the stricken wanderer; and, at length, yielding to her entreaties, he left her with the one he had once called his wife.

How shall I describe the despair of Ruth and Maynard as day after day passed, and Lucy made no sign? How paint their joy when the dull eyes opened, and a faint voice whispered—

"Is he here? Can I speak?"

Tenderly Ruth had watched her; night and day she had sat by her side, and now, when the voice had come again, her strength gave way, and she yielded to her great sorrows in a passionate flood of tears.

"Weep not," said the dying woman, "weep not. I am going to bring joy into your heart, and give peace to Maynard and a name to his children. Oh! weep not that I may die unhappy and unforgiven. You are Maynard's wife—I never was."

Then, as they both leant over and listened eagerly to her hushed voice, she told them how the sinful man—so lately gone to his account—had been married to her a twelvemonth before her father and brother had frightened her into consenting to a union with Maynard; how she had begged and implored them not to force her to such a crime, and how, by cruel and bitter threats they had driven her to it.

"I never wished to deceive you as to my death," she said; "but Luke was always with me, and I couldn't write. I tried all I could to undeceive you; I did, as I hope to receive mercy. Oh! forgive me, Henry—forgive me, Mrs. Maynard—that I may die in peace, and know, at least, that your anger has not placed a barrier for ever between me and Heaven."

Ruth stooped down and kissed her on the forehead.

"I forgive you wholly—truly from my heart," she said, "as I hope to be forgiven."

"And I too, Lucy," said Maynard, with much emotion.

The erring woman did not last long after this.

She was just able to tell them where to obtain the certificate of her marriage, and to give them a few details which would

make their task easier, and she was gathered home to her Father.

And thus, with her spirit fled the last cloud from off the home of Ruth and Maynard.

Re-united, strengthened in love, in hope, in mutual confidence, they pass on their way in sunshine.

Bright their path; with the love of children, with the esteem of friends, with the respect of neighbours and dependents, who greet them gladly when they roam together in the vicinity.

The grey-headed woodman whom they pass at his work answers their kind salutation with a glow of pleasure on his sun-burned visage.

The cotter's child in the lane forgets its curtsey in a broad smile of joyful recognition, for to them its parents owe their neat home, and the employment by which it is supported.

Sweet Ruth! long—long may the husband and the father enjoy the happiness of thy presence! Long may the friend, the sister, and the brother, find in thee the secret and affectionate counsellor! Long may thy children enjoy the priceless benefit of thy monitions and instructions! Long may the artless damsels of thy vicinage look up to thy amiable example! Long may thy native meads bloom beneath thy tread—and the taintless air, perfumed with summer sweets, caress thy downy cheek —and the woodland choristers hail thee in their ecstatic warblings—and the ambient sun light up thy shining hair—and the willow-shaded stream reflect thy delicate symmetry!

And when these know thee no more—when thy form is no longer visible beneath the willows, or the meeting branches of thy sublime oak trees—when the majestic swan sees no more thy shadow in its own delightful element—when the winds wail for thee in vain in the familiar paths, and the timid deer forsakes its covert to look for the gentle mistress who is departed for ever —when the grey dawn rises, and the red sun sets on thy silent sepulchre—oh! then shall admiration and love thither make its frequent pilgrimages to shed the tear thy virtues merit.

Calm may it fall; calm as the dew of Heaven, soft as the flowers which youthful hands will scatter there—meet ornaments for the sainted grave of the COTTAGE GIRL.

"ELINOR CLARE" *will follow in* Weekly Numbers.

N.OTICE.

THE COTTAGE GIRL'S

EDITION OF

ELINOR CLARE

IS ONE OF THE

Most interesting Stories ever written, and will make a splendid Companion work in all respects with

THE COTTAGE GIRL.

ELINOR CLARE

Will be published every TUESDAY,

And Original Pictures, printed in Colours for binding with the work, will be given away.

ORDER OF YOUR BOOKSELLERS

ELINOR CLARE.

1d. Weekly.